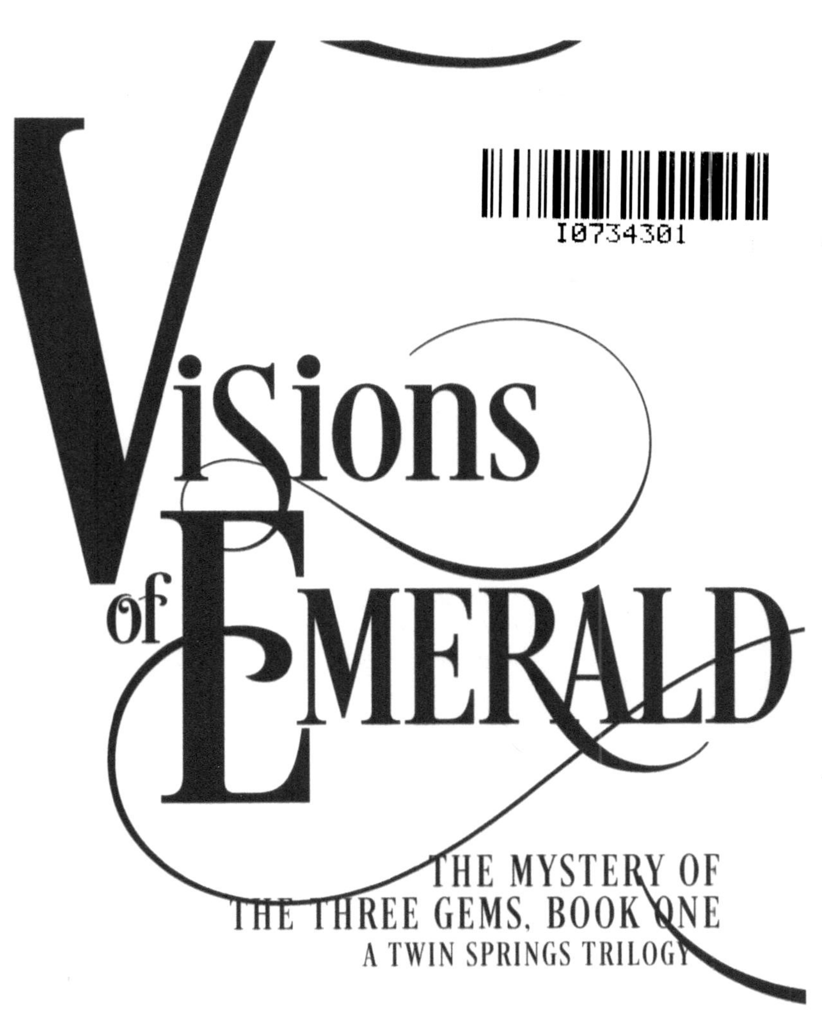

Visions of Emerald

The Mystery of the Three Gems, Book One

A Twin Springs Trilogy

DEE ARMSTRONG

VISIONS OF EMERALD
A Twin Springs Trilogy
The Mystery of the Three Gems

By Dee Armstrong

Published by: Big Dipper Publishing
Copyright © 2018 by Dee Armstrong, LLC
Cover design by Fiona Jayde Media
Author Photographs: Katie Lewis Photography
Print Edition ISBN-13: 978-1-949551-07-5

This work of fiction contains strong language, sexual content, PTSD episodes, possible triggers and some historical language from the 1920's that is considered to be offensive by today's standards. Age 18+ readers only.

This is a work of fiction. Names, characters, places, brands, media, and incidents are either the product of the author's imagination or are used fictitiously. The author acknowledges the trademarked status and trademark owners of various products referenced in this work of fiction, which have been used without permission. The publication/use of these trademarks is not authorized, associated with, or sponsored by the trademark owners.

ALSO BY DEE ARMSTRONG

The Mystery of the Three Gems,

A Twin Springs Trilogy

Visions of Emerald

Sleepwalking with Ruby

Haunted by Amethyst

The HAUNTED Series, A JD Wolfe Investigation

Haunted by A Broken Oath

To my loving family.
Your support made the difference.

Part One

CHAPTER ONE

1 May 1928

Why did I follow General Rockwell to these God-forsaken mountains? "Just to pay our respects", he said. Fool. But I saw the potential of Twin Springs and convinced the Private's widow to sell to the General. He should be grateful. Instead, he gives me a new mission—one without glory that reduces me to commanding servants, not men.

Even the mighty General doesn't know about the wealth that runs below Twin Springs. I knew the tide of war had turned in my favor when I caught the colored chef slipping through the secret passageway behind the bookcases. With a little ingenuity, plaster, wood and paint, I created a secret room. My Headquarters. From which I'll win this war. From the other side of the wall, everything appears to be on the up and up. My office is an ordinary room with a table, chairs and an insignificant desk raised on a platform. Only I would think to hide a lever within the desk's small drawers. A simple twist of the knob and I slip into my Headquarters to plan.

I am a man of caution. In case the perimeter of my Headquarters is breached, who'd think to look for another secret passage-way? No one. But with the push of a button, an ordinary bookcase reveals a stairway that leads down to my new creative endeavor. Running moonshine.

I'll have to dispose of the chef. After all, Flamme knows my secrets. But, I'll keep him around until the right opportunity presents itself. I might need a patsy to blame for the moonshine.

I will lay siege to the General's three daughters, his Gems, and vie for their trust and affections. I'll begin with Emerald. Plant my seed within her. Then, I'll belong, and I can address her as he does, Emma. His sweet Emma will be mine.

I'll dispose of the other two sisters, guaranteeing that any future descendants who inherit the hotel from this point forward will be from my seed. The hotel will belong to me, to my lineage, as it should be.

Lt.

CHAPTER TWO

*I*f Isabella Fairbanks had known that morning would change her life, she would've hidden better. But, at the tender age of eight, her friends called her Izzy, her father was larger than life, dreams were make believe, boys were gross, and ghosts lived only in books. Most of all, she'd be able to live within the safe walls of Twin Springs Hotel and Spa forever and ever. She couldn't have been more wrong.

Izzy paused before deciding which wing of Twin Springs' attic to hide in. She picked at the torn wallpaper with her fingernail and nibbled on her lip. Leaning forward, she snuck a glance further down the corridor. The thick mass of her blonde hair swung forward and blocked her vision. Annoyed, she crinkled her nose and shoved it out of her face.

The attic's hallway transformed into a playground and before her stretched a runway of possible hiding places. Decision made, she sped through the seemingly endless hallway. Exhilaration pulsed through her compact body and drowned out the soft thuds of her tennis shoes on the threadbare carpet.

Her sister's counting down bounced off the cracked plaster walls. "Ten, nine, eight—"

Excitement bubbled within Izzy and she skidded into a room, where an errant ray of early morning sunlight struggled through a window covered with decades of dust, narrowly lighting it. Mindlessly, she crawled over boxes that crunched under her weight and squeezed herself behind a tottering, half-dressed Christmas tree.

Something brushed against the back of her hand, almost like a soft breeze. Snatching her hand close to her chest, she sucked in a breath and swallowed a scream. She couldn't believe her eyes. Beside her, in a gauzy pink dress with a white apron tied over top, crouched a young woman not quite as tall as the Security Manager's son, Niles. She blinked hard, but the woman was really there. "Gosh, you aren't supposed to play in here," whispered Izzy. "It's off limits to guests."

Her sister's countdown sounded off in the distance. "Six, five—"

The woman's mouth curled up at the corners and her green eyes glittered in the dimly lit room. She pressed a slender finger to her lips and motioned for her to follow.

In the distance, Ava yelled out, "Ready or not, here I come."

Izzy squeezed her eyes closed, drew her knees in tight to her chest and scrunched down. Resting her forehead on her jean clad knees, she clenched her muscles to keep from moving. Every sound, no matter how small, rattled around in her head like nails in a cup.

Her sister thundered past the door where she hid.

Gradually, she opened her eyes. Tinsel had stuck to her face and she peeled it away. Peering out from behind the tree, she checked to see if the coast was clear. A relieved breath swooshed out of her and she plopped back down, wiped her dusty hands on her equally dirty white t-shirt and pushed her hair back to study the woman.

Her brow furrowed. How could she get her to leave and not give her away? After all, guests weren't supposed to be in her special place. But she just sat there, staring at her. Her father's phrase of "guests first" chanted in her head and the woman's smile grew as if she could hear her thoughts. "I'll help you find your way back to the Grand Lobby. But you can't tattle and tell my dad that I was playing in the attics. Deal?"

The woman nodded, and she could've sworn she whispered within her head, "Deal."

Izzy scrambled over the boxes and paused to check for Ava at the door. "We must make it quick. My sister will call me a cheater if she can't find me up here."

Allowing the woman to follow, she trotted down the hallway to the back stairs but the woman veered off through a door that she'd never explored.

In a mock whisper, Izzy called out, "That's the wrong way!" She chewed on her lip. "Oh man," she bellyached to herself, "I'm gonna get in trouble if you get lost." She flipped around and chased after her. "Wait!"

But the woman ignored her. Further down into the belly of the hotel they wandered. She strolled just ahead and paid no notice to her calls to wait.

Jogging to catch up, Izzy skidded to a stop at the end of a hall where double silver doors stood sentry. But the woman was gone. Suddenly uneasy, she pushed up onto tiptoe and stretched to see through one of the circular windows high in each of the doors. Unable to gain enough height, she cracked open a door and peeked inside.

With her legs crossed at the knee, the woman was perched on top of a shiny counter. Izzy's heart beat hard against her ribs. Getting caught in the hotel's main kitchen was way worse than playing in the attics. She pushed through the swinging doors, "We're not supposed play here."

The woman's head tipped to the side and she grinned. A loose strand of hair fell into her face and she twisted it up and around the knot of blonde hair piled high on her head. "Hungry?"

The woman's voice was super soft and Izzy leaned in, "What?"

Her face lit up with soundless laughter and she gestured for Izzy to help her gather a mixing bowl, spoon and ingredients.

Izzy broke eggs on the rim of the bowl and allowed the gold and white gooeyness to seep between her fingers. As she sifted, flour filled the air, floated softly down and covered the counters in a thin film of white. She added the rest of the ingredients and mixed the batter. Holding the bowl tight against her chest, she carefully folded in the blueberries. With the help of the woman, she turned on the big stove, seasoned her first pan and learned the sound the batter makes when it hits a pan heated just right. Together they made blueberry pancakes.

"What's your name?"

The woman's lips curled with pleasure and she nodded. She pressed her finger through the flour-covered counter and wrote her name.

"Emma," said Izzy. Her breath blew the flour and erased the letters. Hitting her chest with a flour-whitened hand, she proudly declared, "I'm Izzy." She bit into one of the pancakes and purred with happiness every time one of the blueberries popped their sweetness into her mouth.

"Are you a mom? Did you teach your own daughter how to cook?"

A shadow of sadness dimmed the woman's smile and she shook her head.

She stared into the woman's eyes and realized that she'd found not only a new favorite place to play, but also a friend. "You'd be a real good mom. My mom's one of God's angels."

"Izzy!" Her father's voice reverberated through the room. "What's going on in here?"

Jumping, Izzy dropped the warm pancake onto the counter.

Her father stood before her, filling the space of the kitchen with his presence. Niles smirked behind him. She felt there was judgment within the boy's deep brown eyes. Even though he was only a couple years older than Ava, his size belittled his age. Izzy envied his height but she'd never let him find out.

Standing beside Niles, Ava struck a dramatic pose with her hands propped on her hips. The crown of her sister's black hair shimmered within the spread of light and her gaze sparkled with annoyance. Izzy could've sworn that green sparks shot out of her sister's eyes. Right away, she wished her own green eyes could shoot sparks too. At the grand old age of ten, Ava could handle anything. She had a secret superpower that bent others to her will. Izzy nibbled on her lip and silently begged for Ava's help.

Their father stepped forward. "I'm waiting for an explanation."

Shifting her pose, Ava grabbed his hand. "Wow! She made breakfast." She winked at Izzy, slipped under their father's arm and hugged him, "Cool, huh Daddy?"

"I, I," stammered Izzy. "We made blueberry pancakes."

Her father surveyed the mess within the kitchen. "You're covered from head to toe with flour. Who helped you?"

"Emma." Izzy turned to introduce her new friend but she was gone. Her brow furrowed and she bit her lip. "Where did she go?"

Niles taunted her, "Dizzy Izzy has an imaginary friend."

Ava pushed him. "Don't call her that."

Her father loomed over her and she felt the joy of cooking leaking out of her. Unsure what else to do, she plucked a warm pancake from the top of the pile and handed it to her father.

He bit off a piece and chewed, his attention never deviating from her face, even though the kitchen staff had begun to file into the room for the next shift. His chewing slowed and his gaze glowed brighter. Glancing between her and the pancake, he broke into a smile so gigantic that it crinkled the skin at the corners of his eyes. "Melts in my mouth."

Pleasure coursed through her and warmed her heart. His approval shone over her and she knew that no boy could ever top her dad. She rushed forward, threw her arms around his waist and hugged him tight. "I'll never love anyone as much as you!"

He crouched down from his massive height and their green eyes met. He kissed her flour- powdered nose and sniffed her neck. "You smell like vanilla."

She giggled.

With a swipe of his finger, he wiped the tip of her nose clean and ordered, "Don't come in here by yourself again." His grin softened his words. "Make sure you help clean up the mess." He turned to address the Executive Chef, who stood tall at the pass, a beacon in his bright white jacket. "Put her to work." He winked down at her. "Let me know if she gives you any trouble."

Izzy's gaze followed her father. His shoulders pressed back and his stride strong and sure. Following in his footsteps, Niles stuck his tongue out and trailed behind.

Returning the insult by sticking out her own tongue, Izzy entwined her fingers with her sister's. "You know, Ava, I'm really going to yell at Emma when I see her again. She snuck out and left me to take all the blame."

Ava's gaze searched the room. "She must've found a really good place to hide."

Izzy ripped the last pancake in half and gave one piece to her sister. Her heart raced with a new found excitement. A craving that consumed her. She just had to make something else for her father to taste. She must feel the warmth of his approval again. "It's okay," she muttered, her mouth full of pancake. "Emma already showed me the best playground ever. Here."

Later that night, as she snuggled into her pillow, her thoughts returned to Emma and cooking. Bit by bit, a dream formed around her. One with an older version of herself.

. . . In the distance, the tower's clock began to strike its midnight tune. The air stilled and the fine blonde hairs on the back of her neck stood. She stiffened. A primal fear, that she didn't quite understand, seeped into her veins and pumped her heart. One word reverberated through her subconscious. Run!

But she had nowhere left to go. Before her rose an impregnable wall of fallen rubble blocking her escape. Her bare feet kicked up dust from the dirt floor as she turned and looked back towards where she had come. She'd trapped herself at the end of the tunnel, like a mouse in a maze, afraid to retrace her steps but unable to move forward.

A vibrating rush of air exploded through the tunnel and propelled her backwards. She lay, unconscious, unmindful of the rocks that fell around her, sealing her in and removing her last hope of escape.

Just an hour earlier, she'd laughed in delight as her long flowing party dress twirled between her and the man she loved. She'd tasted the sweetness of champagne from his kisses. Sensed her beauty reflected in his gaze. Never again. She'd failed. Failed herself and her love.

Her chiffon dress was bunched up around her legs, torn and covered with a fine mist of dirt from the blast. Her long hair was no longer in an intricate topknot but wild and loose around her shoulders. Escaped locks splayed across her face and covered the fresh bruises that bloomed high on her cheekbone.

Between the final bongs of the clock, a spider web of cracks silently formed in the tunnel walls. Leisurely, warm spring water seeped down the dirt walls and darkened them. Rising around her, the water enveloped her in warm loving arms and held her until the last breath left her body. Her once bright blonde hair, darkened and wet, reached out along the water's surface and she floated, encircled by the water's embrace, until time and love no longer held any meaning. . .

Izzy surged up in bed and sucked air into her deprived lungs. From that day forward, no matter how hard she tried, she was unable to hide from the dream.

CHAPTER THREE

*S*itting on a submerged bench, cold winter air swirled around Isabella, but she snuggled down into the warmth of the Hot Springs pool, ever mindful of her cardinal rule—*Never allow the water to cover your head.*

She glanced over at Theo Beaumont, a guest. They'd snuck into the Hot Springs after hours. But, being with him was worth any wrath that her father might bring.

Theo's eyes were like molten silver. His light ebony skin, toned and muscled. More than that, he listened. Cared about her dreams and aspirations. She was in love and it felt wonderful.

Stars and the submerged lights cast an ambient glow over the darkness that surrounded them. At the corners, water poured off large boulders creating tiny, personal waterfalls and smooth river rocks lined the edges. Across from them, a large, cascading waterfall muffled the sounds of the outside world. Maybe they should duck under the wall of water, snuggle on the moss-covered shelf, trail their toes through the power of the rushing water. No one would discover them there. It would be just the two of them. And their dreams.

She knew better than to fall for a guest but something about Theo made her heart pound within her chest and cast all caution aside. "Has it only been a week?" she questioned. "It feels like I've known you since, forever. When do you check out?"

Placing his arm around her shoulders, he pulled her close. "We're supposed to leave tomorrow, but I'm going to see if we can extend another week."

Heat radiated from his bare chest. Only her green string bikini and his trunks separated their skin. Her fingers stroked the muscled ridges of his chest, down to his abdomen. She sighed. "Then you're back to college to finish your Masters."

"And you're off to England for your apprenticeship with a three star Michelin Executive Chef." He kissed her on top of the head. "You'll be an awesome Chef one day."

She groaned, "Dad says, if I want to run the main kitchen at Twin Springs, then I need to start at the bottom and learn from the best. Someplace where they don't know I'm the owner's daughter."

Theo opened his mouth to reply but the pool's gate jiggled. "Quick, duck under the water." He moved to push her under.

Panic exploded within Isabella and she slapped at his hands, "No. I can't." She screamed, "No!"

But it was too late. He'd pulled her beneath the surface with him.

Water flooded into her mouth. She gaged and choked. Instantaneously, she struggled and ripped at everything around her. A light flickered back and forth above the water and the dream of her drowning pressed her down.

Strong arms pulled her to the surface. "Are you okay?" Enveloped in Theo's embrace, his concerned gaze was only inches away. "Sorry, Isabella." He squeezed her tight and she could feel his heart pounding against hers. "You scared the crap out of me."

Her chest heaving, she choked out between breaths, "Don't. Ever. Do. That again."

He smoothed her wet hair back and placed tiny kisses all over her face. "I'm sorry. I thought you could swim."

She felt like a fool. The old nickname Dizzy Izzy rattled in the back of her head and shame flowed through her. "I can swim." She steadied her breath and leaned her forehead against his chest. "It's just that I have this fear of drowning," she mumbled. "Since I was a little girl, I've had dreams about suffocating under the water."

He squeezed her tight. "Forgive me." He tilted her chin up and pressed his lips against hers.

Her heart thundering in her ears, she sunk into the kiss. Her hands slid up his muscled chest and around his neck.

A blinding light broke the two apart. "Dad!" she cried out and she shriveled inside at being caught. And with a guest. Lifting her hand, she attempted to block the light. "I'm sorry—.'

"Theo's in the pool, k-i-s-s-i-n-g," jeered a young girl's voice. "First comes love, then comes marriage, then comes a baby in a baby carriage."

Theo groaned. "My sister." Effortlessly, he lifted himself out of the water.

Outside of his embrace, the water cooled around her.

He snagged the flashlight from his sister and clicked it off. "What are you doing out of bed?"

"What are you doing in the pool?" challenged his sister.

Her vision blurred from the flashlight's beam, Isabella could barely distinguish the two forms in the darkness. She blinked. Theo had wrapped his tall form in a white robe. He grabbed his little sister by the hand, "I'll be right back." Stalking off, she heard him grumbling. "You're such a pain."

Isabella leaned her head back against the smooth edge of the pool. Her dreams were just that, dreams. Childish dreams. "I'm a strong swimmer," she reassured herself. "I'm safe."

Thinking about Theo and his sister, she grinned. At one time, she'd been the little sis, spoiling her older sibling's fun. She spread her arms and water flooded into the split she created on the surface. *How could something so soothing be so dangerous at the same time?*

Something brushed her foot. She frowned and pulled her feet in. "Theo?" she called out.

"Yes," his husky voice answered.

"You're back." She relaxed.

Something grazed her ankle.

Her brows knit together. "I hope you didn't give your sister too hard of a time."

A vice like grip encircled her ankle and dragged her under. Water flooded into her open mouth and she choked. Pressing her lips together, she attempted to preserve what little air she had. Her long hair swirling around her, she kicked at the hand but it held strong and dragged her further and further down, towards the deep end of the pool. To the bottom.

Pressure built up in her chest as she struggled to escape, but she was held firm. Stars twinkled above and lights played off the water's surface. No matter how hard she squirmed and kicked, she couldn't reach them. The last of her air escaped in tiny bubbles and floated up towards the top. She watched as they left her to die, the edges of her world darkening.

Then she was free.

She floated for milliseconds, until her brain kicked into gear and she clawed her way to the top. Choking, she broke the surface, sucked fresh air into her deprived lungs and swam to the pool's edge.

Manic laughter pelted her from the distance as she coughed up water and clung to the side of the pool. Exhausted, she laid her head upon her arms. "I can't believe you think that's funny," she whispered. "I hate you."

Arms trembling, she strained to lift herself out. Once free from the water, she collapsed on the hard tiles and pulled her knees up into her chest, wrapping her arms around her shaking legs. Tears rolled down her cheeks as she wept into her knees. Lifting her head, she shouted, "I hate you, Theo Beaumont!" Her shoulders racked with sobs, "I hate you."

CHAPTER FOUR

he next morning, trees flickered past Theo Beaumont's
sightless gaze and snow swirled around the car as his
family drove through the Blue Ridge Mountains and way from
Twin Springs.

All he could think about was Isabella. Her thick, sunny, yellow
hair, bubbly laugh, and those eyes. He smothered a groan. Her
eyes shimmered like emeralds.

"I think you should start right away," his father's voice carried
from the front seat, but didn't break through Theo's delicious
musings.

He drummed his fingers upon his knee. He hadn't been able to
convince his parents to stay longer. When he'd told Isabella and
bent to kiss her goodbye, she'd shoved him away and stormed off.
His heart felt like a boulder within his chest. *Was she upset that I
couldn't make it back to the pool? Did she think I didn't care?*

"Theo!" His father's stern voice pierced his thoughts. "Are you
listening?"

He sat up straight and glanced up at the rear view mirror.
Inwardly, he cringed at the disappointment that he saw in this
father's blue eyes. "Sorry."

His sister giggled next to him. "He's in looove."

"Shut up, Maddy," he griped, but lovingly tugged on one of her black curls. "You're lucky that you're only eleven. Otherwise . . ." He wiggled his eyebrows and she laughed.

"That's exactly what I'm talking about." His father pumped the brakes as he maneuvered a hair-pin turn. "You need to wet your feet in the family business. Do the next two years on the job with me."

"Huh?" Stunned, Theo's mind raced to catch up with his father's conversation. "What about college? I'm so close to my masters."

"College will be there. You need to learn how the real business world operates."

Theo's mother placed her hand on her husband's arm. "Maybe we should slow down."

Swiftly, the car decelerated. "I don't think we got the best directions from that young man at the Front Desk. I sure don't remember these turns."

Theo's brain hummed with possibilities. Maybe if he wasn't at college, he could see Isabella more. The idea appealed to him. His family owned a global properties and investment company. In England, they ran a chain of hotels and high-rise office buildings. "I could work at the branch in London."

"Is your girlfriend going there?" asked Maddy. "You should've seen them last night."

"You don't know what you're taking about," he shushed her. "Stay out of it."

The epitome of style and grace in her silk pant-suit, his mother turned in her seat and asked, "What girl?"

"That's exactly what I'm talking about," declared his father. "Girls and drinking. That's what college teaches our kids today."

"You were drinking?" his mother's silver gaze widened. "With a girl?"

Maddy wrapped her arms around her shoulders and pursed her lips into a pouty kiss, making smacking sounds. Her black curls bounced around her small face. "They were k-i-s-s-i-n-g," she chanted.

"N-no," stammered Theo. The possibility of any time with Isabella faded the further they drove.

"Don't tell me no!" Anger deepened his father's voice. "One day, you'll take over the family business. You need to experience the hard knocks of the real world. Turns boys into men. Work a sixty-hour week and you won't have enough energy left to waste your time with girls and drinking."

"I wasn't drinking!"

His father hit the brakes and they skidded around a corner. The car rocked.

"I don't feel good," his sister wailed and rolled down her window.

Snowflakes and cold air swirled around inside of the car. His father grabbed a napkin and scrubbed at the inside of the windshield. "Close the window, Maddy. It's fogging up the car. I can't see."

She leaned her head further out the window.

If he wasn't going to London with the possibility of seeing Isabella, then he wanted to finish college. He leaned forward. "I don't want to wait on finishing my degree. All my friends will be graduating. I don't want to be left behind."

"Left behind! You see working with me as being left behind?"

His mother un-clicked her seatbelt. She turned and knelt on her seat. "Calm down. If you want to finish college, I'm sure you and your father can come to an agreement."

She laid her hand on his father's forearm. "Let him follow his dreams."

"I don't know, Jacqueline." His father's gaze met hers and he sighed heavily. "Alright. I'll think about it."

She addressed his sister, "Madison Jacqueline Beaumont, close that window." Even mad his mother was beautiful. Her dark hair was smoothed back into a bun at her neck and her silver eyes glittered against her smoky ebony skin.

"I'm going to be sick," Maddy moaned and leaned her face further into the cool wind.

Theo squinted to see through the swishing windshield wipers and twirling snow. There was something in the distance, coming straight at them. "Dad."

"Don't worry about it we'll talk about it later."

A van. His heart beat hard in his chest. A white van was speeding straight towards them. "Look out!"

His dad swore and swerved.

Maddy screamed.

Theo heard his father's foot slamming against the brakes. Over and over. But the car spun and skidded sideways.

Clutching the seat in front of her, Maddy's screams pierced the air.

"Hold on!" shouted his father as the car shot over the cliff.

For an instant, the cold air was filled with silence. The world around them was bright with clouds. Beautiful. As they plummeted, Theo rose in his seat. Snow covered trees rushed past. Then the world exploded with the sounds of metal screeching against trees and Maddy's high pitch screams. The car plowed a path down the steep mountainside and came to a jarring stop. The sudden silence was deafening and the world around him faded to black.

Theo came to with snowflakes swirling in the cold air. He licked his lips and tasted blood's metallic flavor. The car had landed sideways, pinned between the mountain and the branches of an enormous oak tree. He hung from his seatbelt with his sister weeping below him.

"Maddy," he croaked. "It's going to be alright." He braced himself within his seat and un-clicked his belt. Carefully, he dropped down and stood on the doorframe. The car shuddered beneath his feet. "Look at me."

Maddy's eyes met his.

"We've got to get out of the car."

She nodded.

"Hold on to me." She wrapped her arms around his waist. "Get clear of the car. As fast as you can." He un-clicked her seat belt and lowered her down, through her window, to the ground below. "Now you, Mom."

He turned but her seat was empty. "Mom?" He ground his teeth together and held back the tears that blurred his gaze. The windshield was gone. The cold mountain breeze and snowflakes slapped his face. His world shattered, the gates flooded open and his body was racked with pain. "Mom!" he shouted.

His father moaned, dangling above him.

"Oh God, Dad."

Bracing his feet on the headrests, Theo climbed out of his window and knelt on the driver's door. Tiny pieces of glass littered the inside of the car and covered his father's still body. Blood soaked his blonde hair and dripped down his pale, white skin. "I'm going to pull you free."

He made a gurgling sound, his breath barely visible in the cold air. The steering wheel was jammed deep into his chest.

Straining, Theo attempted to pull his father out. He wouldn't budge. Wedged between the seat, the steering wheel and the tree.

Blood ran down from his father's nose and pooled in his mouth. Theo pulled his shirt over his head, used it wipe the blood away and pressed it against his father's nose. More blood trickled from his ear. "It's going to be alright. I'm going to get you out."

His father stared. His pupils were wide in a glassy sea of dark blue.

And Theo knew. His father didn't have much time. "No, don't leave me. Hold on Dad. Please don't leave me."

He embraced his father around the neck and held him close. "Please don't go."

"Take care," his father whispered in his ear. "Take care of the girls."

Choking on his tears, Theo whispered back, "I will. I promise."

"Beaumonts never break their promises," his dad choked out the words, and he was gone.

Stunned, Theo stared down at his father. "I caused this. I shouldn't have been arguing with you. Distracting you."

Grief overwhelmed him. "My fault," he chanted, crying on his father's shoulder. "I'm so sorry." Sobs racked his body. "All my fault."

Unsure how long he cried, he rubbed at his face and leaned back onto his heels. With the pad of his finger, he drew each of his father's eyes closed. "I promise. I'll take care of the girls."

His tears had soaked his father's white shirt. A drop of blood fell along with the tears and spread into a circle of crimson. Another drop fell and pooled. Sniffling, Theo rubbed his nose, thinking he had a bloody nose. But droplets continued to form, spreading across his father's shoulder.

Theo looked up and into the beautiful, unseeing, silver eyes of his mother. Her body was draped over a branch above his head.

"No!" Gut wrenching sobs permeated the air. He'd already failed. "I promise. I'll take care of Maddy. I promise."

CHAPTER FIVE

The sun peeked over the mountains and cast shadows off of the headstones of the dead and across the feet of the living, there to pay homage to a boss, friend or mentor. Mourners swarmed around Isabella and flooded the grassy area before the casket. Her father's casket.

Standing beside her sister, Ava, she shook the hands of her Twin Springs' family as they passed along their sorrow and condolences. Thanking them for coming, she gave each person a sprig of lavender from a large basket. They laid the flower on top of her father's casket and his favorite scent filled the air around them.

Her gaze flickered from their drawn faces to where her father lay. Her chest ached and she rubbed at it with the heel of her hand. The most important man in her life was now gone and she'd been chasing her own dreams so hard that she hadn't seen him for over a year.

Pressing a tissue to her nose, she sniffled and whispered, "We should've come for Christmas." Instead, she and Ava had met in

Munich and enjoyed the Christmas Market. "Can't get that time back."

Her beautiful head bent, Ava brushed away tears with her fingertips and croaked, "I know." Her glossy black hair fluttered in the wind. "You've been working in London. But I was only a quick flight away. I should've been checking on him."

Their childhood friend, Niles, came and stood at her side. His great height and grizzly bear width cast a shadow over her and darkened her already bleak world. "At least he's with your mother."

"Thank you. That is something," she murmured. Inside she screamed that she didn't care. She wanted him with her. With Ava.

"How will you girls run the hotel on your own?" He rubbed the shaggy brown beard that covered his face. "It's a heavy burden, Twin Springs."

Shock reverberated through her body. She and Ava now owned Twin Springs. They were responsible for the Grand Dame's future.

Her gaze flowed over the large crowd. Almost every soul before her was employed by the hotel. Whether or not they could put food on the table for their families depended upon her actions. Her judgment. Her decisions.

Ava's fingers entwined with hers and she glanced over to her sister's matching green eyes. Grief, sorrow, and something else dwelled within her sister's normally steady gaze. Was it fear?

But Ava would soon return to the stage where she belonged. Then, it would be up to her to carry on their family's legacy. She leaned in, pressed her forehead against her sister's and embraced her in a tight hug, sharing for a moment their sorrow and combining their strength.

With a deep sigh, she leaned back, and whispered. "I know." With the pad of her thumb, she wiped away the tear that had escaped from the corner of Ava's eye. "But it's all going to be okay."

She turned back to Niles. "You're right. It'll be tough." She responded with false bravado. "We'll figure it out."

"Don't worry," added Ava.

"Remember, I'm here to help." Niles kissed each sister on the cheek. "Benjamin Fairbanks was a father figure to me, too."

"Yes." She hugged him and handed him a flower. "We can always rely on you."

Niles moved on but the significance of his words weighed heavily upon her shoulders, as she turned to receive the next person.

"Oh, Izzy." Smothered in a massive hug, Isabella sunk into the soft body of the woman who'd nurtured her wounds, from a scraped knee to a broken heart, after her mom had passed.

"Maude," taking refuge in her soft brown gaze, she replied, "I'm so glad you're here."

"Psh, mi nina," she clutched Isabella's hands between her own. "Your father had the biggest heart of any man I've ever known." She crossed herself. "Rest his soul. How a stroke could have snuck up on him, I'll never understand."

Pushing back the tears clogging her throat, all she could do was nod. How would she ever fill his shoes? The weight of the responsibility compressed her chest. She could barely breathe.

"Mi querida, you come down to the kitchens." She patted her hand. "We'll cook up some blueberry pancakes and remember him. Si?"

Swallowing hard, she pulled her lips into a semblance of a smile. "Yes."

CHAPTER SIX

*S*team rose from the emerald green casket as the budding morning warmed the earth and Theo understood that even though his friend and mentor, Benjamin Fairbanks, had already joined his ancestors around him, the grief of the living had just begun.

Over the heads of the mourners, he glimpsed Isabella's corn silk hair, captured up high on her head. Her beautiful emerald eyes swept the crowd and his heart thundered within his chest. Feeling as if he'd been gut punched, his breath swooshed out of his chest and the past five years faded away. She was just as he remembered.

Emotions coursed through his tall frame. Yearning and loss. She'd traded her tomboy jeans and t-shirt for a black pantsuit, but he could still see the Isabella he'd fallen hard for. The woman he'd compared every woman to for the last five years, all of whom he found lacking.

He squinted and looked closer. Beside her tall, slender sister, Isabella appeared even more dainty and fragile. Her lips quivered as she spoke and her face was pale, drawn.

"Take care of the girls."

His father's words reverberated through his brain and he took an involuntary step forward, but the priest escorted the siblings to their seats. They settled into the front row and the priest's robes rustled in the breeze as he hunched over each sister, held her hands and murmured words to ease their sorrow.

Theo faded into the back of the crowd, to where the trees shadowed his height. His attention zeroed in on a flash of bright pink among the crowd. A woman in a silky pink pant-suit glowed in contrast to those shrouded in black around her. Heat inched up his neck. "Maddy."

He resisted the urge to grab up his little sister and yell at her, because that was an indulgence he no longer allowed himself since their parents' death. Now he must protect her feelings. Be her biggest supporter.

He swallowed a groan of embarrassment and his lips formed a thin, taunt line. He shook his head at her lack of respect. Purposefully, he eased the muscles in his face so that his disappointment wouldn't show. "She's only sixteen," he mumbled.

"Que?"

His attention swiveled towards the voice at his elbow. Maude, from the hotel's kitchen, stood beside him. Her brown hair was covered by black lace and a small black handbag was tucked under her arm. Even she'd swapped out her usually bold, vibrant clothes for the veil of black. "Nothing."

Her gaze searched the crowd where he'd been staring. Only the slight raise of her brows acknowledged the fact that she'd noticed Maddy's attire. "It's good of you and your sister to attend."

"Of course, we came."

Maude's teenage son stood beside her. His face was pale and taut with the pain of loss. Theo estimated the lanky boy was around the same age as his little sister. Even though Marc's suit was still creased from the bag, it was black and respectful.

"Ben was a friend of my parents." His gaze flickered to the twin headstones on the outskirts of the graveyard. "After their death, he became my friend. My mentor."

She nudged her son. "Sentarse con Maddy."

The teen nodded and moved up the aisle, threading his way along the knees and legs of the mourners, and sat in the empty seat beside Maddy. Ignoring the boy, his sister pulled out her cell phone and began texting.

Maude made a slight humming sound in the back of her throat. "It must be hard on your sister, not having another woman to guide her."

His mother's smiling face flashed before his eyes, an exact replica of his little sister's, and a wave of protectiveness crashed over him. "We make do."

Maddy wound a ringlet of her ebony hair around her finger and a flash of green winked at him. His mother's emerald ring. Right then he understood.

Maddy hid her pain beneath a shroud of pink. Otherwise she would've never worn such a coveted family heirloom.

"I understand my sister can be," he paused and searched for the best word or phrase. *Intrusive? Pain in the ass?* He chose a more appropriate word. "Challenging. But I give her whatever she wants."

Maddy continued to play on her phone instead of giving those around her the reverence they deserved. "If I have anything to say about it, she'll never want for anything. She's had more heartache than any little girl deserves."

Fellow mourners settled in to pay their respects and the wooden seats groaned as if unable to bear the weight of their sorrow. From personal experience, he understood that the world around them was gray even though the rising summer sun had already begun to shine. The priest's monotone voice lowered into an opening prayer and the crowd hushed.

With the priest's words, handkerchiefs were pulled out of pockets and the sleeves of the women to stem the flow of tears. Isabella's head dipped and she dabbed her eyes. He wished he could absorb her pain.

Once again Maude hummed beside him. "When did you last see her?"

Obviously, nothing was missed by the older woman. "A little over five years ago."

"A boyhood crush then?" More humming and her brow arched. "How old were you then?"

"Twenty-five." He gave a self-mocking chuckle. "I was a stupid boy. It wasn't until the day after I left her that I learned the responsibilities of a man."

She clutched the sleeve of his suit and whispered furiously, "Are you saying that you got Izzy pregnant?"

"No, no." He splayed his hands out before him. The minds of the fairer sex. Young or old, he'd never understand how women ticked. How they formed their conclusions. "It was the next day that my parents passed away. Then I gained the responsibility for my family's business. For my sister."

His gaze flowed over Isabella and her sister. They rose, placed flowers on their father's casket, then stood guard and gave their undivided attention to the people who continued to form a long line before them. "That was the day I put boyhood dreams and wishes aside for duty and responsibility."

He studied her dainty frame. Her lily white skin was almost transparent with grief. Her smile was genuine, though, as she greeted those who wanted to pay their respects. "How is she?" The words slipped from his mouth.

Maude pulled a rosary from her handbag. She rubbed the beads between her fingertips and worry creased her brow. "I'm not sure. She's tough. But rumor is that she's given up the idea of finishing her apprenticeship and becoming a chef."

He rolled his shoulders back and, as much as he hated to lose her again, he responded, "She shouldn't. She can go back and finish. I'll handle everything at the hotel. Just like I promised her father. Then she can return and be Twin Springs' Executive Chef. If she wants."

Maude hummed again and he was beginning to realize that meant he screwed up in the older woman's eyes. "No. Her father could've just handed it to her. She'll want to earn it herself. Comprehende?"

He was prevented from questioning the validity of Maude's comment when a man appeared beside him. The Security Manager name badge glinted gold against the breadth of the black suit that spanned his wide shoulders.

"You've met Niles?" asked Maude. "His family has worked at Twin Springs for generations. He grew up with Isabella and Ava."

"Of course." For such a giant man, he moved surprisingly quiet. "Benjamin spoke highly of you."

"Such a sad day." The man's deep voice reminded Theo of rocks tumbling down a mountainside. "Must remind you of your parents' funeral."

"What?" Pain stabbed his heart. "What did you say?"

"You're parents. I wasn't the Security Manager when they died, just worked in the lobby, but I remember their funeral. Just days after Isabella left for London. I'm sorry for your loss."

Clenching his teeth, Theo refused to return to the last funeral where not one but two caskets had laid in the place of honor. Where his sister had wept unbearably next to him. "Thank you."

"I always wondered why Benjamin allowed them to be buried in the family's private graveyard."

Theo swallowed hard. Reeling from the conversation, he murmured, "The plots were a generous gift from Ben. Allowed my parents to be buried in the mountains where we spent our last family vacation together."

Out of the corner of his eye, he could almost discern the two headstones where he'd just laid fresh flowers. Someone shifted within the shadow of the trees. A man, his cap pulled low, looking out of place in jeans and a grungy shirt.

"Who's that?"

"Who?" asked Maude.

He turned back, "The man in the trees."

"I don't see anyone," replied Niles.

Theo searched the edge of the forest, but the man had disappeared. "Never mind."

"How are you going to tell them?" asked Niles.

His brows furrowed. "Tell them what?"

"That you were with their father when he had the stroke. That you were the last person to speak with him before he died. And now you and your sister own Twin Springs."

Maude smacked Niles on the chest with a quick swat of the back of her hand. "It wasn't his fault that he happened to be with Ben both times."

Theo's blood boiled. "We don't own the hotel. We purchased half the hotel," he corrected, "to help Ben pay off old debts, renovate and keep the doors open." Five years ago, he would've punched the man. Not now.

Instead, he kept his hands busy by straightening his tie. His voice lowered to a tone he'd later recognize as his father's. "I'll tell them when I think it's best. Neither you nor anyone else who works for Twin Springs will breathe a word about either subject until I am ready."

The man snorted, "Good luck."

"Let me make myself crystal clear." Theo stepped closer. His voice was deadly soft. "If Isabella or Ava find out that my sister and I own part of the hotel or that I was the only one present when their father had a stroke, you'll be the first one fired. Then, who ever has the big mouth. Got it?"

Maude spoke up, "Isabella isn't stupid. She'll ask questions."

He studied Isabella and Ava. He knew that, like everyone else gathered here, these two people were loyal to the Fairbanks sisters. But he had a promise to keep to Ben. To take care of his girls.

He might not be allowed to coddle her like he did Maddy, but Isabella deserved one day to grieve before life's realities closed in on her. Before her world changed. "Give her today to be with her sister and say goodbye to their father. Everything else can wait. The hotel can wait." He could wait.

He tugged his gaze from Isabella. The sun had burned away

the mist and revealed the glory of Virginia's Blue Ridge Mountains that encircled them. Tucked into the spectacular setting behind the sisters was their legacy and his albatross, Twin Springs Hotel and Spa.

Theo scrutinized the archaic hotel with its grand staircase leading up to a columned veranda with a fountain sputtering in front, brick walkways, massive lawns and extensive gardens. Quickly, he calculated the immense amount of man-power and money required to maintain the opulence. And now, due to the death of the man before them, bringing that monstrosity of a red brick hotel back from the depths of bankruptcy was his Herculean task. He rolled his shoulders and the ramifications of a 'deathbed promise' soaked into him, became a part of him and melded with an older, more sacred vow. He'd take care of Benjamin's girls. No matter what.

He glanced over to the Fairbanks' sisters. He yearned to hold Isabella, to comfort her, but he understood that the sight of him would bring added pain once she discovered that he owned half of her inheritance. A part of him wanted to rush up to her, tell her, crumble to his knees and beg her to not hate him. But was that best for her?

It didn't matter. Whether he told her today or tomorrow, she'd think he was underhanded. She'd hate him either way. After all, a broken heart needs somewhere to place the pain.

CHAPTER SEVEN

The next day, Isabella sat on the edge of the Hot Springs pool, her legs dangling into the water. Heat rose from the pool and combatted the cool mountain air, causing a mist to roll across the surface. Unable to sleep, only the morning sun had beaten Isabella to the pool. By midday, it would be filled with splashing kids. But now, it was serene. Quiet.

"I knew I'd find you either here or in the kitchens," said Ava, gracefully settling down beside her. Even in exercise clothes, her sister looked as if she'd stepped out of the pages of a fashion magazine. "Did you have a restless night, too?"

She trailed her toe through the water. "Yeah, bad dreams."

Concern wrinkled Ava's elegant brow, "About Dad?"

She shook her head and tucked an errant strand of hair back up into the top-knot. "No, about drowning. Always about drowning."

Ava laced her fingers with hers. "Dad always thought it helped to talk about it."

"I guess." Isabella sighed heavily but it was moments before she could bring herself to share, even with her sister. "I could feel the hot springs' water rising. Inching a path up my face. The circle of air around my mouth became smaller. And smaller." She sucked in a deep breath, as if it was her last. "Until it was devoured and spring water poured into my lungs." Slowly, she released the air, remembering. She'd woken, gasping for air and drenched in sweat, the scent of vanilla floating around her and suffocating her within its sweet aroma.

"Oh, Izzy. That's awful." Her sister wrapped her arm around her. "How can you even stand being by a pool?"

"I have to." She drew her knees into her chest and wrapped her arms around them. "I can't let the dreams win. Let the water win."

Quiet, the girls stared out over the water.

Isabella asked, "What did you dream about?"

"I'm not sure," Ava shrugged. "I just remember these golden eyes." She sighed. "I woke up on a lounger in the Garden Room, snuggled up to a pillow."

"Me with nightmares, you sleepwalking again. It's got to be the stress of Dad's death."

"And of Twin Springs." Ava scrambled to her feet. "You conquer your fears. Get your laps in. We'll need to strategize later."

Isabella did as her sister suggested. Spent a good half an hour switching from stroke to stroke as she crossed the pool. Always with her head above the water.

Drying off, she slipped into the ladies' bathhouse and tugged on a pair of black skinny jeans and matching tank top. She twisted a bandana, then wrapped it around her head and tied it at the base of her neck, right behind her ear. Fully prepared to meet her sister, she grabbed her bag, crossed the lawn and entered through the side doors into Twin Springs. She passed through the wide hallways, papered in creams and draped with antique furniture. Taking the elevator up to her room, she dumped her bag on her bed, shut her door and turned to track down her sister.

Out of the corner of her eye, she glimpsed a woman wearing a pink dress with a white apron tied over top. Memories tingled in the back of her head. Something was familiar about her. "Wait," she called out.

But the woman slipped through a nondescript white door.

"Excuse me," called out Isabella as she followed her down the stairwell, just catching a glimpse of her dress, around each bend. "Ma'am."

As Isabella knew it would, the staircase opened up to a long hallway that ran towards the kitchens. "Where did she go?"

Rushing down the hall, she pushed open one of the tall, gray, swinging doors and entered the main kitchen. She searched for the woman but she was gone. "Darn."

The kitchen bustled around her. Drawing in a deep breath, she absorbed the aromas sizzling in the air. "Home. I'm finally home."

She trailed her fingertips lovingly along the cool, clean surface of a stainless steel countertop. The kitchen staff was hard at work. A portion prepped for the evening dinner service. Another portion churned out hot, buttery biscuits, hand cut hash browns and mounds of fluffy golden scrambled eggs. Wait staff in crisp white shirts and black pants hefted up huge silver trays and carried them into the Main Dining Room for the breakfast buffet. Here she could separate herself from reality. "No Pain. No sadness. No nightmares. Just hard work and my kitchen family." A wide smile spread across her face. "What would it hurt to spend an hour in the kitchen?"

Marc returned her welcoming grin. The tall, lanky boy was elbows deep in a sink of suds. His Yankee baseball cap faced backward and captured his coffee colored hair close to his scalp. A couple strands broke free from the confining brim and curled around his ears. She walked over and pinched his bulging bicep between her thumb and forefinger. "Nice guns for a thirteen year old."

He flicked suds at her and flexed. "Sixteen and ripped."

"Please." A giggle escaped and sounded foreign to her ears. She wiped bubbles off her nose. "Your mom can still whip your butt."

He shrugged, then glanced over his shoulder. "Nobody messes with mamacita."

Following his gaze, she couldn't miss Maude chopping away at her station. Her cook shirt exploded with neon colors. A pill box chef cap, in a nauseating lime green, was perched high on her head and attempted to trap her cocoa brown curls. "I'd better say good morning."

Laughter fled from his young face and his voice lowered. "The Chef doesn't like talking. I'd wait until after service."

Ignoring his advice, anticipation and joy soaked in and filled the hole in her heart. "It'll be good to cook with an old friend."

She tied a Twin Springs signature green apron around her waist, washed up in the hand sink, and dove in to help the older woman. She bumped Maude lightly with her shoulder. "Marc grew up."

Maude's shoulders stiffened. She leaned forward and scanned the kitchen before shuffling closer. In a low whisper she said, "Si, I caught mi Marcos texting three different girls last night."

An unladylike snort erupted from Isabella, followed by a chuckle. "Oh," she winked at her, "a player in the family." She dragged the word player out for emphasis. "He must get his moves from his mama. You were pretty saucy in your younger days. Led the boys in a good chase." Her laughter rang out.

A porcelain plate slammed down on the pass counter. Shards of shiny black dining ware and food shot through the kitchen. The two women jumped apart.

Isabella looked up. A large man, bursting the seams of his Executive Chef jacket, strutted at the kitchen's pass. His toque hat was shoved firmly down on his head and framed the growing redness of his pallid face.

A slender, teenage girl followed in his wake. Dressed in what appeared to be her mother's church clothes, she relaxed against the doorframe. With her fingertips, she smoothed imaginary creases from her gray silk blouse and her black designer slacks.

The chef's face ballooned with anger until his words surged forth. He addressed the kitchen. "You giggle! Like school children? While you pass off this swill as food to one of the owners!" He gestured towards the teenage girl. "Do you have cabbage for brains? Can't you prepare a special meal for our in house VIP's?"

In awe, Isabella glanced from the vein protruding on the chef's neck to the girl's long, black corkscrew curls that bobbed in agreement to every word. When she realized that her mouth hung open, she snapped it shut. She lowered her voice, "When did Dad hire him? I can't wait to tell Ava that the chef thinks this young girl is her." Incredulous, her voice rose. "Who is he, anyway?"

Maude's gaze slid away. Without responding, she hummed in the back of her throat, bowed her head and resumed chopping.

"Who am I?" he bellowed. "I'm Executive Chef Dubois. Who the hell are you? I didn't hire you." He gave a contemptuous smile. "Doesn't matter." His thick finger pointed towards the swinging silver doors. "Get the hell out of my kitchen!"

Deathly silence filled the room. None of the staff moved and the food sizzled unattended.

Heat scaled her cheeks. Obviously if she didn't know him, he didn't realize who she was. Hoping to spare everyone further embarrassment, she responded quietly, "I'm Isabella Fairbanks. My family owns Twin Springs."

The girl balled her fists on her hips and straightened from the doorframe. Anger pruned the light black skin on her face and formed premature lines around her full lips. "You don't own this ancient ruins of a hotel. My brother and I do. We purchased it from the lazy old man who ran it."

Rage surged through Isabella and blood pounded in her ears. *Had everyone lost their mind?* Her gaze narrowed. "Lazy old man? Ancient ruins?" Her voice sounded like chipped glass and the knife in her hand pointed at the teen, emphasizing each word with a sharp jab in the air. Her vision clouded with her fury. "No one, I repeat, no one speaks about my father that way."

"Are you threatening me?" The teenager threw her shoulders back. Looking down her nose, she hissed, "We'll see about that." Teetering on her four-inch heels, she exited through the Main Dining Room.

Maude's fingers encircled Isabella's shaking wrist and coaxed her hand down. "Carino, my sweetheart, they're owners of the hotel. Some say, your father began turning control over to them about six months ago."

Her stomach clenched. She shook her head and backed away. She searched the faces of the people she'd known all her life. "No..."

Executive Chef Dubois stood victorious at the pass. The kitchen crew kept their eyes down cast and were unable to meet her gaze.

"No. They don't own Twin Springs." Her arms dropped to her side. "My father would never sell. The hotel was a part of him." A part of all of them. Her breath caught in her throat and she struggled to push words through. "Do Ava and I even have a home anymore?"

She saw the sympathy in Maude's eyes. With care, she placed the knife down on the shiny kitchen counter and removed her apron. Methodically, she cleaned up her space. Sympathetic gazes pierced her heart with every move she made.

Maude grabbed her arm. "I'm sorry, Izzy. Sorry about your dad. About the hotel."

Her warm embrace engulfed Isabella.

"It can't be true. Why didn't someone tell me?" The smells of the kitchen combined with the fragrances of her childhood memories. She inhaled deeply and filled her lungs.

At the pass, Chef Dubois resumed bellowing commands. Marc once again sunk his arms elbow deep into the suds. This was her place. Her playground. Her safe place. *It's mine!*

She stepped out of her friend's embrace, pressed her shoulders back and lifted her chin. "Where will I find this new owner?"

"I'm not sure. Maybe in your dad's office." Maude splayed a hand over her ample bosom. "What will you do?"

Isabella ignored the pain crushing her heart. Her voice rang out across the kitchen, "Fight for my place."

CHAPTER EIGHT

eaving the back areas of the kitchen, Isabella exploded into the colored and vibrant world of Twin Springs. She strode down the wide walkway between the indoor promenade of boutiques. The arching, white paned windows of the different shops displayed a wide variety of goods ranging from children's toys, to unique gourmet kitchen tools, to luxurious candles, soaps and lotions and ending with specialty fishing and hunting gear. She weaved between the guests that milled about with green striped shopping bags in hand. Their excited chatter filled her ears.

Turning right, she executed a distracted wave to a maid polishing the antiques and glass tabletops sprinkled throughout the lobby. She marched between the lines of matching pillars that bordered the Grand Lobby and created intimate alcoves on each side of the expansive walkway. She drowned in a new nightmare and muttered under her breath, "Dad sold the hotel? Impossible. He lived and breathed for Twin Springs."

A gust of fresh air flowed through the open doors scattered along the outside wall. They led out to a wide, covered veranda, which stretched the length of the hotel's front. Lounge and rocking chairs, cushioned with yellow flowered and green leafed pillows, welcomed arriving guests. As a child, Isabella and her sister had woven their way in and out of those doors under the watchful eye of their father and the staff. Remembering those carefree times, she kneaded her bottom lip between her teeth. The more she thought about it, her father couldn't have sold Twin Springs without telling either herself or Ava.

She plastered a bright welcoming smile on her face and nodded at three bellhops buttoned up in black jackets, piped with dark green. One of the bellhops glanced away and pulled slightly with the crook of his finger at his short, stiff collar. He leaned away from the check-in counter and pretended that he wasn't just teasing the two young women working at the reception desk.

Everyone avoided her gaze. Yesterday, she'd assumed her father's funeral had caused the unusual treatment. But today, she understood that everything in her life would never be the same. *I won't allow strangers to take over.* Her hands clenched into fists and she rapped her knuckles on the counter, demanding their full attention. "Where's the new Hotel Manager?"

One of the Front Desk clerks stuttered, "I-In the back office."

Isabella nodded and rounded the desk. Outside her father's office door, she smoothed any loose strands of hair behind her ears.

Her fingers trembled on the knob of the office door that once belonged to her father and she gazed at her refection in the brass doorplate that proudly stated Hotel Manager. She stopped short. Her mind flooded with images of her father, of his office. She knew to the left, a nutmeg colored leather couch stretched beneath a great arched window. To the right, huddled two wingback chairs covered in a brocade of deep purple and creams. Her father's sturdy oak desk would anchor the room, and he wouldn't be sitting behind it.

His loss stole her breath. She sucked in a deep breath and squared her shoulders. "This office belonged to Dad. With him gone, I should be the new Hotel Manager of Twin Springs." Resolved, she entered the room, and the memories.

Conversation halted in mid-sentence. She sighed in relief. Her sister sat on the couch, leaning forward as if to press a point. She looked beautiful in a flowing dress with her gorgeous long legs crossed at the knee. She resembled a movie star, gracing the stage with her long black hair shimmering in the sunlight.

Niles was hunkered down next to her. His khaki pants and forest green Security Manager polo shirt hung in a frumpy mess from his massive, thick frame.

A toe tapping from across the room drew her attention. With her arms crossed, rage glowed in the young girl's eyes and turned them to molten silver. "She's the one who threatened me in the kitchen."

At the girl's words, she sucked in two deep breaths in a vain attempt to calm the anger that boiled in her gut. "I didn't threaten you."

The man behind her father's desk rose and Isabella's world closed in on her.

Overwhelmed her. Suffocated her. Pressure tightened her chest, and she struggled to catch her breath. In an expensive black suit and steel gray tie, Theo Beaumont resembled a man of the world that was in charge of his own destiny.

His lean frame had filled in. Hardened. His crisp, white collared shirt contrasted against his skin, the color a rich black coffee mixed with heavy cream. His ebony hair was cut short and tapered. A traitorous piece of her heart missed how his bangs had once swept across his forehead and shadowed his mischievous eyes. Her gaze drifted from his full lips, to his high cheekbones and up to the smoky gray of his gaze. She glanced between his eyes to the girl's identical pair and her mind rebelled. "He can't be your brother and the new owner." Not after what he had done to her. "No, he can't be."

She felt light headed, the room spun around her and her stomach revolted. She swayed on her feet. Desperate to keep her nose above the swirling waves of emotions rolling through her, she lifted her chin a notch. "You're back."

CHAPTER NINE

heo's long stride ate up the distance between them and
he gripped Isabella by the elbow before she toppled
over. Standing close, he breathed in. She still smelled of sweet
vanilla.

Clenching his teeth, he resisted the urge to bury his face in her
hair and nuzzle her neck. Instead, he maneuvered her to a chair.
"Move over, Maddy," he ordered.

"Don't call me that," she hissed back. "Use my middle name,
Jacqueline. Mom's name." But she moved and her glares promised
retribution.

He felt Isabella trying to tug her arm free but he firmly guided
her slight frame into a chair. She was so delicate, scraping five foot
in her bare feet.

He remembered the last time they'd been alone together. Their
bodies slick, wet. Her gorgeous curves clad, thankfully, in the
smallest bikini. Her green eyes had reflected the swirling waters of
the Hot Springs pool. Just the memory had hot blood rushing from
his pounding heart and heating his limbs.

Slapping his hands away, Isabella spit out, "I'm fine. What the
hell are you doing here?" She shook her head. "It doesn't matter.

Explain to your sister that the Fairbanks own Twin Springs. Have for generations. Then get out."

Jacqueline's eyes widened and she squeezed her hands into tight fists. "Shut up, shut up, shut up." She pivoted on her stilettos towards her brother. With an accusing finger, she pointed towards Isabella. "Tell her we own this rotten old hotel now. Not her. Not her stupid sister. Tell her she can't talk to you like that and kick her out!"

His sister's temper tantrum splashed cold water over him and he retreated to his place at the desk. Responsibility, duty and promises dulled his senses and tensed the muscles in his shoulders. He sunk into the Hotel Manager's chair, shifted his weight and attempted to adjust to his new situation. Biding his time, he picked up his silver pen and twirled it through his fingers.

Both women's outrage emanated towards him. His sister hoped that he'd rip into Isabella, while Isabella's pain was hidden behind her anger. How could he defend one without hurting the other? Carefully, he chose his words. "I'm sorry for your loss."

She glared at him.

He was right. She hated him because they owned part of the hotel. He cleared his throat and tried again. "You don't fully own Twin Springs."

"See!" the teen exclaimed. "You get out!"

Isabella's face paled. Turned almost ashen. "No," she whispered.

"Wait." He was screwing everything up. "You're also wrong, Maddy. We don't own the hotel. Only half. We are joint owners with the Fairbanks."

Isabella flinched as if he'd struck her. She paused and her gaze narrowed. "Dad wouldn't keep a secret of that magnitude from us." She shook her head in denial. "Not from us."

Annoyed with the cards lady luck had dealt, Theo juggled his duties to Maddy, the damn hotel and his desire for Isabella. How could he explain his family's involvement and ownership without increasing her hatred towards him and destroying his chances with her? *Keep your voice even, stick to business, lull her away from thinking of you as an adversary.*

He cinched his gray tie up, tight against his throat. "As per the agreement between your father and my parents, Ben maintained sole control of running the hotel. We decided to be, shall I say, silent partners."

Isabella bounded to her feet and stalked over to her father's desk. Her anger reached out towards him. "What changed?"

She leaned over the wooden surface and heated words tumbled from her beautiful mouth. Her words buzzed around him unheard as he focused in on her gorgeous face just inches from his.

"Did you find out that my father was ill and swooped in to take advantage of the situation? Did you try to persuade a dying man to sell you the rest of Twin Springs? Or did you and your sister bring on more stress to help him into the grave? Where you could then try to steal the hotel out from under my sister and me?"

Tears welled up in her eyes and his heart wrenched. *No, please don't cry. Anything but tears. Hit me, hate me. Just don't cry.* He itched to pull her close. Comfort her. Stroke her silky hair until her rage abated. Instead he squeezed the pen inside his fist.

She continued ranting. "You evil—"

In a blur of motion, Maddy slapped Isabella across the face and her head snapped to the side. "Shut up! My brother isn't hateful. Or evil. You are!" she screamed.

Shock vibrated through the room. He found himself standing, not sure how he got there, and realized everyone except Niles had also gained their feet. A hand-print of scarlet welts flamed against the side of Isabella's face. Horrified, he watched her raise her tiny hand and lightly touch her cheek with her fingertips. His breath came hot and heavy and his chest swelled with shame. The anger within his voice whiplashed through the room. "Maddy."

His sister threw herself against him. Instinctively, he wrapped his arms around her and she cried into his shoulder. He whispered into her hair, "What were you thinking?"

Her body shuddered with more sobs. "Jacqueline."

A low rumble rolled across the room, germinating from within Niles' gigantic body and growing in volume as he rose from the couch. His dark eyes narrowed into slits and his lips thinned out into a formidable line until they disappeared.

Theo didn't need to see the expression concealed behind the man's shaggy beard. One foolish teenage girl commanded his attention. His sister.

Theo stopped him with a steely look. "I'll handle this."

The mountain of a man's gaze pivoted between Isabella and Maddy. He hesitated. Another rumble sounded deep within his chest, but Isabella laid her palm on his hairy arm and whispered close to his ear. With a curt nod he settled back against the couch and drug a stunned Ava down beside him.

The situation had spiraled out of Theo's control. How could he protect Maddy's feelings and not offend Isabella? *Damn it, I'll lose either way.* He smoothed the long curls on his sister's head soothing her. "They're just words."

"Don't call me that." Her voice sounded muffled and faltering through her sobs.

He held her tenderly by the shoulders, looked down at her tear stained face and into the eyes that so closely resembled his mother's. His heart wrenched and stripped him of his anger. How would his father have handled his wild sister? "Apologize for hitting her."

He held his breath. Maybe, just maybe, she'd listen to him this one time and not embarrass them both further. "We don't resort to violence. They were just words." He tensed, ready to move and protect Isabella if needed.

She twirled around and gave a reluctant, "Sorry." before burrowing into one of the high backed chairs.

Disappointment settled into his gut. He'd hoped that one day his sister might demonstrate the poise of their mother. But obviously, she had years of growth left to go. His gaze bounced to Isabella, checking, taking measure of her pain. Surely, her face stung. Yearning to comfort her, he stepped forward, but stopped.

Isabella pinned her shoulders back and focused in on his sister. "No, I apologize." She touched Maddy's shoulder. "I understand the need to defend your family." She inhaled a deep breath and dazzled him with her kindness.

Immediately, he recognized the generous heart of the woman he used to know. *Amazing.*

"I shouldn't have said those things, um…Jacqueline?" Reluctantly, her gaze skidded to meet his and he attempted to capture her attention and read the thoughts hidden behind her soft, green eyes.

Unable to pierce her defenses, he shrugged. "Let's all sit down and figure this out."

Isabella perched on the edge of her chair.

World War III was averted but the muscles in his shoulders refused to release the pent up tension. He struggled with his conscious. For closure, she needed to know how her father died. But would she blame him, like Niles did? Imply that he was somehow responsible? Should he keep quiet until he had a chance to gain her trust?

Niles shifted his weight on the couch and he understood that if he didn't explain then the huge man would. Ignoring everyone else in the room, he spoke straight to her. "Your father called me about a year ago. He requested that I come out to visit Twin Springs and talk about possibilities. He told me that the hotel had a bad run of luck lately. Things had been breaking more than usual. He wanted to discuss with me about perhaps updating the hotel, turning things around and bringing it back to its former glory. He asked for a loan and I gave it to him. In return, he gave me half the shares of the hotel." He paused and searched her face for understanding. "Six months ago, he called and wanted me to see the changes he'd started. I couldn't make it right away. So, I sent my sister out first and started to tie up some lose ends with other family business projects. I arrived less than a week ago."

Leaning forward, Isabella's heart swelled in her eyes. "Was Dad sick? Why didn't you tell us to come? So we could be with him.

Help him." She swallowed hard and her gaze swiveled towards Niles and pinned him. "Why didn't you call us?"

Theo spoke up. "Your father seemed fine. Strong. Excited about his plans."

Niles stared at the ground and mumbled, "Even if your father was sick, he wouldn't have wanted to upset you girls. He wanted you to finish your apprenticeship and he didn't want to interrupt Ava's Broadway career."

With a slight movement of her hand, Ava waved Niles off. She directed her attention towards him. "Mr. Beaumont, please continue."

Hoping to win over Ava and soften Isabella, he countered, "Theo, please."

The beautiful woman assessed his every move, but she tipped her head in acknowledgement.

Theo handled millions of dollars in business deals each week. Boardrooms full of men shuddered when he entered, but the three women inside this room had reduced him to an unschooled little boy. "The day he had the stroke, we were walking the grounds of Twin Springs. He mentioned that the sun was a little too bright and that he must not be the man he used to be because the walk wore him out. We headed back."

He paused, not wanting to continue. To cause her pain. But she needed to know. "It was tea time in the Grand Lobby. He went to grab an ice water but his hand missed the glass and he stumbled against the table knocking over cups filled with tea. His face was redder than his hair. I just thought he was embarrassed and asked if he wanted to continue later when he wasn't tired."

Ava spoke up. "Dad would never have admitted a weakness."

Theo couldn't take his eyes off Isabella's averted face. Her eyes were pressed closed and he just knew she was holding back tears. She nodded in agreement with Ava's statement. "No. I guess not. So I brought two glasses of water with us to his office. He complained about a slight headache from the summer sun but wanted to finish going over the blueprints for his new tower. We were leaning over the plans on his desk when his words became jumbled and confused. He was thirsty but gagged on the water. He gave me a lopsided smile and joked that he couldn't even hold his drink anymore. But, looking into his eyes, I could tell he was concerned. I called out to the Front Desk as he dropped to the floor."

He couldn't continue to tell her that Ben's words were a muddled mess—Grand Dame, protect, daughters, future generations. But Theo understood. Ben wanted him to take care of his daughters and a sacred vow was given.

Niles added, "By the time I arrived, your father was unconscious."

Theo straightened his jacket and resumed. "My sister sat with him. Held his hand. Talked to him. Niles and I decided to call you both right away. But he slipped away too quickly for you to come."

Hands clenched on the arms of her chair, Isabella fought to control the emotions crashing against her defenses. Finally, she turned towards his sister. "Thank you for sitting with him. For not allowing him to die alone."

Jacqueline shrugged and mumbled, "I wanted you to be able to say good bye. I'm sorry you didn't get the chance. I didn't get to say goodbye to my parents either, before they died. It sucked." She looked away and tried to wipe her eyes without anyone noticing. She flicked her hair over her shoulder. "Whatever, it doesn't matter anyway."

"I can't believe he's gone." Ava rubbed her palms across the tops of her thighs and cleared her throat. "Where do we go from here?"

He captured Isabella's gaze with his and held his breath, waiting for her next move. In business, you never showed your cards. Never showed how badly you wanted something. And he wanted her. Even if being near her meant he must have this dying hotel rotting around his neck.

"Alright." She tilted her head to the side, the same way he

remembered. The edges of her lips tilted up into a fake smile that was overly bright on her pale face. "We'll buy you out."

"No!" Jacqueline shouted.

Damn it, Maddy. Theo ground his back teeth together. He frowned at his little sister and for once she quieted down. "What my sister means is, do you have the financial capital to purchase our portion?"

Isabella nibbled at her lip and locked gazes with her sister. Ava shook her head. "We can get a loan."

Lady luck purred and he suppressed a satisfied smile. He leaned forward and pressed his advantage. "Your father was already in the red because of the incidents. Or, you are, now. That is, until, or if, the insurance claim payments come through." He leaned back and played his last card. "Even if the claims are paid in full, you need Beaumont capital to continue to renovate. Otherwise, you're just prolonging the hotel's death. Bookings have declined by forty percent over the last couple years. Twin Springs is dying. And without me, you can't do anything to help it."

CHAPTER TEN

Isabella studied the man before her. Hard as steel, his gaze didn't waver and he bided his time. He remained cool, collected and in charge. If Twin Springs was dying, neither she nor her sister knew how to save her. Growing up, their father had handled the business end. Sure they'd helped out, but the back offices still remained a mystery. She hated feeling powerless.

She glanced at her sister, hoping for grand inspiration. Deep in thought, Ava twisted one of the many silver rings on her fingers. Isabella reflected upon their childhood; of Christmases in the Grand Lobby, and of the hum of the kitchen as she and her extended family worked together creating dishes for the guests.

Her gaze met Ava's. She breathed in deeply and enjoyed the mingling scents of vanilla, roses and lavender. The signature scent of Twin Springs. The fragrance of home. The strength of past generations filled her.

Throwing her shoulders back, she addressed Theo. "Nearly one hundred years ago, Twin Springs almost burned to the ground. But my family came back from the ashes of ruin and rebuilt her into this grand hotel. Royalty, presidents, diplomats, and movie stars have graced our halls, danced in our ballrooms and slept in our suites. Because of my family, the hotel survived the depression and

World War II. She'll survive this. We'll survive this. Twin Springs must have a Fairbanks at her helm. We're the backbone of the Grand Dame."

She and Ava stood, united. "We want one year. One year to turn the hotel around. If at the end of the year, we cannot buy your shares…" She paused. The possibility of failure stole the air from her lungs.

But Ava continued without missing a beat, blending her belief and confidence with her sister's. They became one voice and a united front. "Then we'll sell you our shares."

Isabella cast her a grateful smile, relieved she understood the need to maintain ownership. She stuck her hand out to Theo. "All or nothing."

He was entranced by her. She glowed with an inner flame that blazed bright. Drawn by her passion, he wanted to envelop his body within her light until he too burned. *Magnificent, she's magnificent. Her passion for her family and for her home.*

Triumph and satisfaction coursed through his veins. He'd have one year with her, one year to figure out his mistake from five years ago and fix it. One year to discover if she'd again share some of her passion with him until he once again felt whole. "Agreed. I'll have my lawyer pull an agreement together for you both to look over and sign." His strong hand clasped around her small one, engulfing it, and her flames stroked a path up his arm.

Isabella's breath caught and she snatched her hand back as if she'd just made a deal with the devil.

His heart ached when she rubbed his touch off against her black pants. He wasn't sure what he'd hoped for, but it wasn't that she'd be revolted by him.

"You can't make any agreement without me!" Jacqueline shouted. Hatred glowed in her young eyes. Hatred for Isabella.

"We'll talk about it later, Maddy," Theo said in a quiet, but firm, voice. Once again sitting, his gaze never left Isabella's face.

The teenager's body quivered with fury. "You don't listen to me. You never listen to me. My name is Jacqueline, and I own twenty-five percent of this hotel. Damn—" she hesitated, her bravado faltering. "Damn you!" Wondering if she went too far, she finished with a meek, "So, I get a say."

"Maddy," Theo drew out the word, his full attention now on his little sister. He tightened his grip on the silver pen. Against his will, some of the cool faded from his demeanor. She was going to screw up the deal. "We'll talk about this later," he replied sternly.

Isabella rubbed her temples but her hands shook, so she hid them in her pockets. "We'll leave you two alone to work out the details on your end. Sis, are you ready?"

Ava smoothly replied, "Of course."

Niles also stood. Holding his hand out, he signaled for the sisters to leave first. Ava sailed past him, all elegance and grace. Isabella, wanting to imitate her sister's stage presence, tilted her chin up, lengthened her stride and stumbled over her own two feet. Niles' massive grip saved her from humiliating herself in front of their new business partners.

She flashed him a grateful smile. "Thanks."

"Almost like old times." He rubbed the small of her back and escorted her from the room.

Theo frowned at the exchange. Studying the trio departing his office, he recognized a connection between the gigantic man and Isabella. *Time to find out more about the Security Manager of Twin Springs. Before it's too late.*

His sister's anger continued buzzing around him, but he no longer listened to her words. Once she wore herself out, she'd be more receptive to his side of the argument. Maddy wasn't in the forefront in his mind. He could handle her. Usually. But could he handle the agreement he just made?

He remembered the kiss he'd shared with Isabella in the hot springs. What if he failed? What if, after one year, he couldn't turn her around?

He leaned forward in his chair. Even with Maddy in the room, he felt empty and alone. Placing his elbows on the desk, he rested his chin on his steepled hands. He'd struck the deal and the clock counted down, one year from today. A total of twelve months to win her heart, and save his. Three hundred and sixty-five days to figure out how the hell he had wronged her five years ago and to heal the pain he'd accidentally caused her. Then, perhaps, Isabella would fill the hole she left in his soul.

CHAPTER ELEVEN

The office door closed behind the trio and Ava grabbed her sister by the hand, dragging her from their father's office, out from behind the Front Desk, past the Bell Stand, and into a corner of the President's Hall. Inside the nook stood a bank of three private phone booths. Elegant in their day, a wall separated the booths and etched, bi-fold glass doors enclosed each booth with privacy.

Pressing on Isabella's shoulders, Ava forced her down on the white, wooden bench in the closest booth and stood in what little space remained, while Niles' great frame filled the doorway better than any door. "How's your face?"

Laying the back of her hand against her cheek, Isabella wasn't sure if the heat was from seeing Theo again or the slap. "Fine, she's a handful. Quick to flame broil." She rubbed the tender skin. "At least we have time to regain control of the hotel."

Ava waved her hands before her eyes. "What were you thinking?"

She snorted. "I didn't think she'd smack me. Usually I can tell when a dish is about to boil over, but her? No."

"Not that," Ava waived her off. "One year? That's all you gave us to work with?" With each word, she expressed her disbelief by moving her hands and arms in grand, flamboyant gestures. Her voice rose high in the tight space. "What can we do in twelve measly months? 'All or nothing?'" Her arms arched up and knocked the phone receiver off the wall. "We'll save the hotel?"

Isabella caught the hard plastic before it hit her in the head. "I thought you were all in on the idea. You're the one who said we'd sell him our shares." She replaced the receiver in its cradle. "You looked so sure."

"I was doing what I do best, hitting my cue. I was acting, feeling the moment, going with the scene. It is what I do, or did. Really Izzy, we're clueless about running this hotel."

Mutinous, Isabella folded her arms across her chess. "What does Theo know about running a hotel?"

"What's between you and him anyway?" Shrewdly, her gaze narrowed and focused in on her younger sister. "What's your story?"

Forgotten feelings rushed through her and yearning churned in the pit of her stomach. She despised Theo for returning and reawakening the emotions within her. Averting her eyes before they gave her away, she studied the phone hanging from the wall, clearly a left over from the 1980's with its gray, plastic frame and multiple push buttons. Since her father's death, she didn't want to feel anything, especially towards Theo. She glanced past her sister to Niles listening intently. Her cheeks flamed. "Nothing," she mumbled. "I don't want to talk about it."

"That's up to you. But we must talk about Twin Springs." Ava weaved her finger in the curled phone cord as it dangled lifelessly from the receiver. "Even this phone is broken!" Exasperated, she continued, "Not knowing how to manage the hotel is only the beginning of our problems. I walked the property this morning and spoke with the employees. Things weren't going well before Dad called the Beaumonts." She paused, uncharacteristically raking her hand through her long black hair. "Then, Dad got this harebrained idea to rebuild Twin Springs' tower." Her arms flew up. "The tower, for goodness sake."

It was too much. Everything tumbled in on top of Isabella. She pressed her hands over her ears. "Stop, stop. Just stop." She rubbed her temples with her fingertips. "What do you want to do? Sell him our shares?"

"No." Niles' voice rumbled from the doorway. "Don't do that. I can help you. I'll take care of you and Twin Springs."

Isabella's heart warmed. He was always there willing to help. Her father had made an excellent decision when he placed the security of the hotel within his capable hands.

He belonged to the Twin Springs family. Thus, his well-being fell under her and Ava's responsibility. "Your duties will be doubled now that Dad has passed. I don't want to add this to your burdens." She shook her head. He didn't deserve these pressures too. "It's not your problem. We'll handle it and figure out what to do."

The cubby lit up with Ava's smile. Affectionately, she patted him on the shoulder, "You're so kind. Of course, we'll need your help. But Isabella and I have to make this decision together."

Like a mountain, unable to move, Niles held his ground. "I understand, but I'm available if you need me."

Lowering her voice, Ava soothed him with her words. "I know you are and I'm sure we'll need to lean on you often over the next year. Would you give us a moment alone? So we can discuss things?"

He hesitated. Watching the two sisters, his expression hid within his beard. "Sure. Let me know how I may be of service." He turned and walked away.

Ava pulled the folded glass door closed and leaned back against the wall. "At least you know about running the kitchen."

Shame filled her and heat rushed back into Isabella's cheeks. She hesitated and fumbled with the Twin Springs' letterhead and pencils sitting on the small shelf below the phone. "I was kicked out of the kitchen."

Ava gasped, "What are you talking about? Who kicked you out?"

"Executive Chef Dubois, the new chef. That's how I found out about our new partners."

"How dare he! You've lived in that kitchen your whole life. You know more about how it works than he'll ever learn."

She raised her hand and effectively stopped her sister's tirade. "I appreciate your confidence in me." Avoiding her intense gaze, she hesitated in telling the truth. The extreme weight of failure compressed her lungs and the pressure in her chest returned. This time, not from the dream.

She rubbed her chest and confessed, "I don't know anything about running the kitchen. Yes, I've spent every waking moment there, but I was selfish and only focused on the cooking. Not looking at what Dad might have wanted or needed. Or even what the hotel might someday need. I haven't even finished my apprenticeship. What are we going to do?" She pressed her fingers against her eyelids to prevent the moisture prickling behind them from escaping. "Why did I agree to one year?"

Ava knelt before her sister and grasped her hands within her own. "No one knows more about cooking than you. I don't care what you think. Besides," she asserted, "Dad wanted you to follow your dream of being a great chef." A tiny, self-depreciating laugh escaped her lips. "Just like he wanted me to follow my dream."

Isabella tucked her feet up on the seat. Wrapping her arms around her legs, she rested her chin on her knees and thought about their situation. She needed to be honest with her sister. "I'm not ready to run the kitchens, let alone all of Twin Springs."

Ava's delicate shoulders slumped and she leaned back against the wall. "You're not ready? I have zero practical skills. But we don't have a choice in the matter. We're Fairbanks. It's our responsibility to care for Twin Springs and her employees." She contemplated for a moment. "We don't know anything about business, but Beaumont does."

Theo was dangerous and sneaky. Isabella had learned firsthand about the dangers of misplaced loyalties. He'd lured her in, until she had built up a false sense of security with him, then when she least expected it, he'd snuck up on her. She wanted him gone. She shook her head vehemently from side to side. "I don't trust him. We can't trust him with Twin Springs."

"Hear me out. Since his parents' death and taking over their holdings, he has tripled his family's net worth. He knows when to buy companies, how to grow companies and when to break them up and sell them."

"Exactly," said Isabella. "I don't trust him. He could take apart Twin Springs, rip her heart out and turn her into a swank hotel with no soul. Or he could decide she isn't worth the effort and close her doors. The Grand Dame doesn't deserve that."

Ava considered her sister's words. Suddenly, she straightened and tossed her luxurious hair back over her shoulder. She gave her sister a roguish grin. "Then let's use his expertise—his gift with business. Take the year and learn everything we can from him on how to run the hotel. Use him, his capital and his golden touch to put Twin Springs back in working order. Meanwhile, we'll learn everything we can about the inner workings of the hotel. You start with the stables, KidsCare, the Front Desk. I'll focus on the boutiques, shooting and archery range and other outdoor activities. That'll be a good start."

Isabella nodded, then, hesitated, "But what about your career on stage?"

"I—," Ava faltered and her gaze slid away. "We can talk about that later. I'll ask my agent for time off. With Dad's death and everything…what's a year, when it means keeping Twin Springs alive. Then, we'll have time to learn everything and take over."

Isabella stared at her sister, unsure what new role she played, but she knew if Ava had committed to a part then Theo was minced meat. She must swallow her distain for Theo. "I guess, I'm stuck with him."

CHAPTER TWELVE

Isabella greeted the new day gasping for air. She surged up to a sitting position, the visions from her childhood nightmare surrounding her. Her heart slammed against her ribs and she sucked in deep breaths. She dug her fingers into the covers around her. "Just a dream. I'm in bed. Safe. Just a dream," she repeated to herself.

She drew her knees to her chest and pressed her back against the antique headboard. The nightmare's ending result never deviated. She drowned.

She crawled out of bed sporting her favorite blue t-shirt. The bright yellow words imprinted across her chest declared "Sauciers Do It On The Fly." Dragging the sweat-soaked shirt off her body as she walked, she stumbled over a pair of her kitchen clogs as she made her way to the shower and attempted to wash away the remains of the dream. Afterwards, she threw on the first clothes touched by her fingers, eager to begin her first day.

With two thumbs up, she saluted the pictures of renowned chefs Leslie Revsin and Julia Child tacked on the wall next to her door. "I'm off to learn how to run the stables. Then I'll be one step closer to getting rid of Theo, jerk face, Beaumont," she declared to her heroes.

She slipped her arms into a soft, red checkered work shirt. "Wish me luck," she murmured, abandoning the confines of her room and the heavy weight of drowning in her sleep.

Theo marched up to the stables, muttering under his breath. "What the hell was she thinking? Running the stables? I'll be damned if she'll give up on her dreams." The trees opened up to a large clearing. Black horse fences knitted the wide pastures into a patchwork quilt, dotted by horses munching at mounds of hay within steel circles. Stable hands led more horses through their morning routine. The large, wooden barn stood before him, its green, metal roof reflecting the sunlight. Raising a hand to shield his eyes, he staggered to a stop and glared. "Who the hell puts stained glass windows through the upper roofline of a barn? A barn! Damn it." But he knew who. Ben. With his grand ideas of rebuilding the Grand Dame to her former glory.

Adjusting to the glare, he thundered forward while he examined the wide barn, with its long upper roofline broken up by cupolas with horse weather vanes. Below, two rooflines slanted off and were separated by double barn doors. There, appearing incredibly small within the wide framed opening, stood Isabella.

He stumbled at the sight of her. She was cute as a button in blue jeans that hugged the curve of her butt, just visible below a red checkered, cotton shirt that billowed in the breeze. Her honey blonde hair was stacked on top of her head and she'd tied a cute red bandana around it. He backed up into the shadowed forest, leaned against a tree and contemplated her, rocking back and forth in her white tennis shoes. "I'm just checking on her," he assured himself.

Liar, a voice whispered within his head and he felt like a stalker.

Stepping further into the barn, she ran up to a horse. "Freckles!" Her voice easily carried to him. Lovingly, she ran her fingers through the dark mane of the speckled horse. "I've missed you," she placed a kiss on his muzzle.

"Fine," he mumbled under his breath. "I'll give her space." He turned to leave but the horse snorted. Her laughter reached out to him and wrapped a silky fist around his heart. He couldn't help himself. He moved closer. And closer still.

"I've missed riding you."

At her words, he swallowed hard.

"I've missed the wind blowing through our hair. Missed brushing you. The smell of hay. I miss. . ." she thought for a moment. "Everything." She inhaled deeply, and crinkled her nose. "Now the manure, I could do without."

"Alright, Miss Isabella." Crawford, the Stables Manager moseyed up. Short and stocky, his wrangler jeans bowed like a horse shoe on his bent legs. His bottom lip stuck out where he'd tucked a wad of chew. He tipped his sweat stained cowboy hat, and revealed another sweat ring plastering thinning, nut-brown hair to his head. "I understand you want to learn how the stables work."

Theo's lips tilted up when Crawford spit a stream of black goop from his mouth and Isabella danced out of the way to avoid getting hit.

Without missing a step, he continued. "Currently, we have twenty-four horses. Sixteen stallions and eight mares. We lease the horses from the Lone Oak Farm and rotate them every three months. Fresh horses happy guests."

"Really." She ran her fingers through the speckled horse's mane. "I thought Freckles was our horse."

Crawford chuckled and a little dribble escaped the corner of his mouth. He wiped it with the back of his hand. "Naw, you girls were always partial to him. So we keep him around whenever you're back. Mrs. Oakes' orders."

Theo couldn't help himself. He stepped inside the building and stood behind her. Even in the stables, she smelled like vanilla.

Isabella stiffened and flipped around. "What are you doing here?"

"Just checking to see you're alright." And he was, he assured himself. Not stalking her.

"Sure," she muttered under her breath. "You didn't check to see if I was alright at the pool. Just walked away, laughing."

Not understanding her comment, his brows furrowed, but he didn't want to fight. He wanted peace. And if he was being honest with himself, he wanted her.

Clearing his throat, he reached out and grasped the hand of the man in front of him. "Crawford," he pumped his hand. "The stables look great. Clean. Well managed. Twin Springs can count on you."

He puffed up with the praise. "Mr. Beaumont. Pleasure to have you out here. Let's sit in the tack room, have a sip of good ole Blue Ridge white lightning."

"Normally, I'd love to." Theo clasped his hands behind his back because they wanted to touch Isabella. Even if it was just to guide her forward by placing a hand on the small of her back. "Don't want to interrupt the two of you. Just here to tag along."

She rolled her eyes. "Yeah right."

Crawford spit.

She squealed and sidestepped just in time.

The Stable Manager glanced down at the manure at her feet. "Miss Isabella, horses are messy. You'll have to understand that if you're going to manage T.S."

"It wasn't that." Her voice faded away at his disappointed gaze. "Yes, sir. You're right. Barns are messy but they have their own sense of beauty too."

"Well, I'll give you the nickel tour on how we run things here." He strode down the expansive walkway. Stalls lined each side and horses stuck their heads out, neighed and nudged the shoulder of his denim shirt. His daughter cast a little salute in their direction and hung a bucket of oats inside a stall. Then, she twisted one of the horses tails into a long, white braid that resembled her own thick braid hanging down her back.

Theo fell into step with Isabella, trailing behind the manager. He hated that she couldn't do what she loved. Just because she disliked him. "You don't have to do this you know."

The sound of Crawford's southern twang faded into the background.

She glanced up at him, "What?"

"Learn every job at Twin Springs. I can run the hotel."

"I'm sure you'd love that," she muttered from beneath her breath. "Why don't I just sign over my shares to you right now?"

He stumbled to a halt and held her up with a touch to her shoulders. "That's not what I mean. You don't need to manage everything. I'll take care of you. Take care of the hotel. The employees, everything."

"Why do men keep telling me that they'll take care of me?" She placed her hands on her hips and glared. "I'm not a helpless child."

Daggers shot from her gaze. He'd screwed up and scrambled to explain. "That's not it. I want you to stay in the kitchen. Cook. You love to cook."

She stepped closer, tipped her head all the way back to see up into his eyes and poked him in the chest. "Is that what you want? Me out of the way?" She poked him again. "I'm not leaving. You are."

"Look, you don't need to manage the hotel to contribute. Follow your dreams. Do something fun. Get back to the kitchens. Cook up a storm. Hell, run the kitchen. I don't care."

Her gaze narrowed and pinned him to the spot. And he realized that he'd messed up. Again.

"Get back to the kitchen," she mocked him, scrunching up her face. "Do you think working in the kitchen is easy? Or do you think that's where women belong? Do you want me barefoot and pregnant too?"

Her words were like a gut punch. Breath swooshed out of his

mouth. Isabella pregnant with his child. He could picture her with a rounded belly. She'd have one of those cute waddles. The vision stole his breath and left him wanting. Wishing.

The air around them was quiet, as if it was just the two of them. He glanced down at her belly and back up at her gorgeous, green gaze. Would their child have her eyes? He could only be so lucky. Her face flushed. It was then that he tore his gaze from her and glanced around. Stable hands had stumbled in to see what the commotion was about. Crawford's daughter stood there, with the horse brush limp in her hand. And Crawford's mouth hung open, tobacco juice dribbling down his chin.

He'd embarrassed her.

"I-I'm sorry. Excuse me." She rushed from the stables.

"Isabella, wait." Theo called out, but it was too late.

The Stable Manager walked with him out of the barn. "Some fillies are high strung. Need extra time. A gentle hand." He nodded his head as if he'd just imparted a tractor full of wisdom and slapped Theo on the back. "Sure you don't want a sip of hooch?"

Out of the corner of his eye, Theo thought he saw the unkempt man from the funeral. Quickly, he turned and strode towards the woods, but he'd disappeared before he was able to get a good look at him. He returned to Crawford's side. "Who was that?"

"Don't know." He spit on the ground. "Didn't see nobody."

CHAPTER THIRTEEN

he next day, even though the sun hadn't even peeked over the mountains, the nightmare woke Isabella and stole any hope for rest. She laid there and concentrated on controlling her breathing until her heart slowed to a steady beat. Only then was she able to roll out of bed.

She showered, scrubbed her face and secured her long, blonde hair in a twisted knot on top of her head. She wrapped a black bandana with little red cherries around her head and tied it in behind her ear.

She slipped on black pants, a button up white shirt, and sensible flat shoes. Slid her passkey in her back pocket. Her gaze lingered on her heroes' pictures by the door and she paused. "Yes, I'd love to hide in the kitchen and cook one of your recipes. But Twin Springs needs me. Time to conquer the Front Desk."

Stepping out of her room, she knocked over a small mason jar. "What's this?"

She lifted it up to eye level. It was filled with almost a hundred fireflies. "I haven't seen fireflies in a jar since we were kids," she muttered, turning it in her hand. "Not since Ava, Niles, Logan and I spent one summer collecting them." She surveyed the long, empty hallway. "Who would've left this for me?" The corners of her lips tilted up into a smile, "I'll release you all later." She tucked the jar inside the doorway of her room, and was back on mission.

She exited the elevator and skirted the Front Desk. Behind the counter, hidden from the view of the guests, was a myriad of computer screens, credit card readers, printers, and papers stacked and wrapped with rubber bands and sticky notes. "Oh, my."

Niles looked up from one of the computers. "What are you doing?"

"I'm here to learn the business."

He scoffed under his breath and adjusted the collar of his green Security Manager shirt with his beefy finger. "Paperwork isn't quite your thing. Never has been."

"Well, it is now," she lifted her chin.

"Alright," he nodded and scratched his thick beard. "Let me show you the ropes."

His thick fingers nimbly rapped against the keyboard. In her ears, his deep voice took on an auctioneer's tone as he flew through the instructions. "Easy."

"Easy," she parroted and her stomach dropped. Everything he'd said had flown over her head. "Can you explain that again?"

He snickered, "Dizzy Izzy," and leaned in over her, spreading his mass up against her back. "You find the guest portfolio by clicking here."

Resisting the urge to rub her ear, where his thick breath coated her skin, she sidestepped out from under his suffocating presence. Her feet caught on something and she tripped, pitching sideways. She grasped the counter and righted herself. "Oops."

He shook his head and continued. Picking up speed, he sped through the instructions. "Got it?"

"No," she pressed her fingertips against her eyelids to hold off the moisture building up. Why hadn't she helped her father more? Why did she allow the pull of the kitchen to prevent her from learning how to run Twin Springs?

Sucking in a deep breath, she straightened her shoulders and brushed away the tears. "Start again. Slower this time."

Talking as if he was tutoring a child, he again walked her through the process.

Brows furrowed, she clicked the keys and attempted to follow his directions.

"Is it true the hotel is closing?"

"What?" Distracted from her efforts, she said, "No way. Twin Springs will never close."

"From what I understand, the hotel is sinking financially. Even with Beaumont's money."

Her fingers fumbled. "What?"

He sighed heavily and took over the keyboard, "Maybe the Front Desk isn't for you."

"I'll take care of her," Theo's voice sounded like a deep, dark brandy pouring over ice.

She stiffened. Refused to even glance up at his traitorous face. "No. Niles is an extraordinary instructor. I'm catching on like wild-fire." She didn't know which lie was greater.

"I have no doubt that you're more than capable," he replied.

Surprised, she looked up. Theo was cool and collected in his charcoal black suit, crisp white shirt and black tie. Her heart thundered in her throat. *How dare he look so good!*

"Where's the Front Desk staff?" questioned Theo.

"Don't you know?" mocked Niles.

"Careful," murmured Theo, his voice soft.

Like two bucks, the men squared off and faced each other.

"Food poisoning." Niles crossed his arms and glared. "Some tainted food in the employee cafeteria. Half the hotel's maids are sick too."

"That's terrible," Isabella exclaimed.

"Great," muttered Theo. He gazed off into the distance, before adding, "Contact Maddy, she knows how to work a Front Desk."

"Wonderful," Isabella grumbled under her breath. "Even a sixteen year old can figure this out."

His lips dipped into a crooked grin that disappeared so quickly, she wondered if she'd imagined the softening of his face. "Between her, myself and Isabella, we've got the Front Desk covered." He turned and dismissed the other man.

"We're expecting a bus load of golfers for the Summer Classic. No way can the three of you handle a group of that size."

Niles' walkie-talkie clicked and a disembodied voice called out his name. He snatched it from his hip and grumbled into it. "Something's up at the spa."

"Let me know what's happening right way," replied Theo. He stepped into the space and turned his back. "We'll hold down the Front Desk." He touched Isabella on the arm. "Let me show you how this works. We have this same system in our hotels."

A tingling traveled up Isabella's arm and everything but Theo's silver gaze faded away. Tiny wrinkles had bloomed at the corner of his eyes in the last five years and she reached up to smooth them with her fingertips. Her hand halfway to his face, she stopped, shook her head and cleared it. "Someone else can teach me." She rubbed her moist palms against her jeans. "Anyone else."

"Here's our first guest," replied Theo. "Welcome to Twin Springs Hotel and Spa." Confidently, he greeted a couple and bantered back and forth with them while guiding her through the check-in.

A long line formed in front of them and flowed down the center of the lobby. Following his instructions, she checked in guests.

"You're a natural," he whispered and her fingers fumbled on the keyboard.

Maddy skirted the desk and took up sentry at the other computer. Her curls were captured into a bun at the nape of her neck and she looked professional in a long, black skirt and white, collared shirt. She glared over at Isabella but turned to greet the next guest with a wide, toothy grin.

Nibbling on her lip, Isabella navigated the check-in screen. "We have you down for a premium, king-size guest room," she informed a couple with graying hair. She forced what she hoped was a confident smile on her face.

Theo's voice buzzed beside her as he spoke with someone on a walkie. "Have Chef Dubois bring up an early tea service." He slipped the walkie back into a pocket inside his jacket. "If you click here, we'll upgrade Mr. and Mrs. Hillgrove to a junior suite for their wait."

"Oh," purred the wife, clutching her husband's arm and leaning against his shoulder. "That sounds wonderful."

"Thank you," replied the husband. "We have to leave before the group. Can we get a shuttle to the airport?"

Isabella resisted the urge to rub the bunched up muscles in her neck. "I'll transport you, myself," she assured. "Thank you for your patience."

Theo leaned in, placed his hand on top of hers and guided the mouse around. "Click here, and we'll add their request and a reminder."

Her hand trembled beneath his and she snatched it back. Heat rushed to her face. "I've got it," she protested to cover her body's traitorous reaction. Plastering a smile to her face, she handed the guests their keys and a map.

Guests buzzed at the Front Desk as Theo guided her through one check-in after the other. Even though she tried, they grew restless with her lack of speed. Beside her, Maddy efficiently and quickly worked and some guests jumped to her line as it dwindled down.

Isabella finished checking in a thirty something woman, already dressed for the greens. "Enjoy your stay and good luck in the tournament." After the woman walked away, she welcomed the next couple and checked them in. With Theo's help, she finished her line. Letting out a deep breath of relief, she leaned back against the counter and attempted to loosen the death grip her muscles had on her neck.

"You did great," he reassured her.

"Great?" Maddy jeered. "I've already had two guests back and fixed the mistakes you've made."

"I helped her with each one." He shook his head, negatively. "There weren't any mistakes."

"Excuse me," Mr. Hillgrove slid a key across the counter. "A couple was already checked into our room."

Isabella spun around, her stomach twisted. "I apologize," she stammered and looked down at the screen. Her mind blanked on what to do.

"I've got you, Mr. Hillgrove." Maddy's confident voice dispelled her youthful face. "There is a gorgeous view from a junior suite on the west side of Twin Springs. It'll be perfect." The keyboard clicked under her deft fingers. "Here are your new keys. I'll have a bellman move your bags and here is a coupon for you both to use at the spa."

"Wonderful," he smiled at the teen. "Thank you for your help." He joined his wife in line for tea.

Maddy turned towards her. "Look, some people just aren't able to handle the stress of the Front Desk."

"No. She didn't make any mistakes." Theo peered down at the screen. "I walked her through each one." He scrolled through. "Someone messed with the reservations. Maddy?"

"I didn't do it." The teen tapped her foot. "I'm telling you she messed up."

He called over a bellman. Rapidly, he clicked through the reservations and made changes, printed new keys and folio's. He looked up at the young bellman's expectant face. "Track down these guests, exchange their key's and deliver their bags to the correct rooms. I've arranged for welcome baskets to be put in each of their suites for the inconvenience."

Isabella's cheeks burned. "I-I don't know what happened." She'd been so distracted by his presence that she must have messed up. Mortified, she stepped back from the computer. "I'm sorry."

"Excuse me," a woman called out.

Isabella turned, red faced and ready to face a disappointed guest.

"Are you Ava Fairbanks' sister?"

Blinking rapidly, she nodded. "Yes, may I help you?"

A bright light blinded her and she raised her hand in defense.

"Why do you think Ashlee Hollingsworth shot herself on stage beside your sister?"

A woman with dark black hair and hawkish features stuck a mic in her face, behind her a man had a large video camera propped on his shoulder and pointed it at her.

"What? What are you talking about?"

"Let's start again." Moving in closer, the reporter angled her body so that she was also in the shot. "We are at the Twin Springs Hotel and Spa, where Broadway star Ava Fairbanks has taken refuge. This is her sister, Isabella Fairbanks. Mrs. Fairbanks, was your sister having an affair with her director, Ashlee Hollingsworth's husband?" Not waiting for her to reply, she added, "Do you think that's why Ashlee Hollingsworth shot herself on stage, spewing blood over your sister?"

Isabella gasped and stared into the lens of the camera. They were talking about Ava. Spouting horrible rumors about her. How dare they! Rage boiled her blood. "That's disgusting. Ava would never."

Theo rounded the counter and grabbed the camera man up by the arm. "This is private property. Time for you to leave."

"What's going on here?" At Ava's silky voice, everyone froze.

Everyone, except the reporter.

"Ava Fairbanks," she turned and bumped up against Theo, dislodging him.

"How long have you been sleeping with Director Hollingsworth? Did you tell his wife? Did you take pleasure in stealing the husband of a woman who paled in comparison to you? Did you feel victorious when she killed herself?"

"You're sick." Isabella rushed forward, the urge to scratch the reporter's eyes out overwhelming. "Don't talk about my sister like that."

Blood drained from Ava's face and her tall, willowy frame shook. "No. You don't understand. I—."

Isabella wrapped her arms around her sister's shaking body and propped her up. "Have you no decency? Her father just died!"

Theo's voice whiplashed through the reporter's questions. "Get out!" He drug the camera man by the collar across the lobby to the front door. Guests sat, eyes wide, with tea cups halfway to their open mouths. The elderly doorman opened the glass door just in time for Theo to toss the camera man through.

The young bellman hustled the reporter out behind him.

Standing on the veranda of Twin Springs, Theo stood with his legs spread and his hands on his hips. "Step one foot back on Twin Springs property and you'll be hearing from our lawyers." He addressed the young bellman at his side. "Make sure they leave."

Hugging her sister around the waist, Isabella couldn't believe her eyes. Quiet Theo. Straight laced Theo, had literally just thrown them out.

"Are you alright?" Theo held Ava's shaking hands between his. Rubbed them.

"Ava," Isabella hugged her sister. "What were they talking about?"

Her sister refused to meet her gaze. "I didn't. Please believe me. I didn't do the things they said."

"O.M.G." Gasped Maddy, jumping up and down like a fan girl gone wild. "You're AVA. The AVA. Broadway AVA. I love you. You sing beautifully." She turned to her brother. "Did you know?" Not waiting for an answer she swung back to the Fairbank's sister. "Please, please, please teach me to sing like you."

"Not now, Maddy," muttered Theo.

"Jacqueline," she shot back, slipping between the sisters and lacing her arm through Ava's. "You played a part from the 1920's, your costumes were just to die for. Do they let you keep them?"

Ava seemed to rally as Maddy guided her over to a couch before a fireplace. Her lips spread into a brilliant smile. "Only in my dreams," she replied.

Crestfallen, Maddy pulled her down to sit beside her and asked, "Not even the shoes?"

Ava's laughter rang out across the lobby. "Not even the shoes."

Worried, Isabella bit her lip, studying the two, their heads bent, deep in discussion. She knew Ava had slid into a part to hide her emotions.

"Don't worry," Theo stood beside her. "Maddy's exuberance will either exhaust her and she won't be able to think of anything else, or it will build her up so she's stronger."

"I can't believe the lies they were spreading." She looked up at him from beneath her lashes and grudgingly murmured, "Thank you."

He chuckled. "That was hard for you."

She lifted a shoulder. "I'm sure that when someone as rich as you dates, it hits all the major tabloids. You must have a lot of experience dealing with the paparazzi."

He sighed heavily. "There isn't much time, or energy, leftover when you're raising a teen by yourself. Dating wasn't a luxury Maddy allowed me."

"You were so forceful with them. Was the lawyer line a bluff?"

"No," his voice dipped. "After my parents' death, the press circled like vultures waiting for me to fail."

Isabella winced. He'd lost both of his parents at once, and still raised a rebellious young teen. She touched the sleeve of his jacket and gazed up into his smoky eyes. The years faded away. "I'm sorry."

He hesitated, then stepped in closer and gathered her hands up into his strong ones. Soothingly, he stroked her palm with his thumb. "Isabella, I—"

"I'm glad everyone here is having fun." Niles rolled his eyes. "We've got a big problem. The fire sprinklers went off in the spa. There's extensive damage. Five rooms flooded. The floors are buckling. Drywall and baseboards soaked. Finally, got them shut off. It's bad."

CHAPTER FOURTEEN

*A*nkle deep in water, the Fairbanks sisters attempted to soak water up in the long cotton strands of their mops. Over and over, they wrung out the mops in their buckets with a pull of a handle. Down the hall, wet vacs were sucking up even more water from the other rooms. The spa's once beautiful lounge looked like a cruise ship that had sunk. Water dribbled down the cream walls. The floors were wavy and buckled. Rods bowed under the weight of soaked curtains. The teal tufted chairs were pushed up against one wall and pillows floated.

Pausing, Isabella leaned against her mop. "Ava, why didn't you tell me about what happened last time you were on stage?"

Ava squeezed water out of her mop into the bucket. "It happened the same day Dad died. I was in my dressing room. I'd just given my costume to the police as evidence when you called to tell me about Dad's death. In a matter of days, we returned here, planned Dad's funeral and found out we didn't fully own the hotel. There just didn't seem to be a right time to share with you. And, to tell you the truth, I was glad that you hadn't had a chance to check the news and hoped that you'd never find out."

Isabella nodded. "Now, can you tell me what happened that day?"

Stiffening, her sister refused to lift her gaze. "During the closing act, the director's wife walked on stage and shot herself." She fought for the words that seemed stuck in her throat. "I didn't sleep with her husband."

Her sister's normally proud stature was bent, defeated.

Isabella's heart went out to her. How could people profit on other's pain by sensationalizing a tragedy? Would the world be persuaded by the tabloids' lies and hate her sister? "I believe you."

Ava lifted her head. "You do?" she whispered.

"Without a doubt." She surveyed her sister. Any other woman standing barefoot in ankle deep water and wearing rolled up blue jeans with a dark green Twin Springs t-shirt would've appeared dowdy. Not Ava. Her curves and unconscious sensuality moved the outfit into the column of down right sexy. She looked down at her own similar attire, semi-flat chest and decided that the sex-o-meter didn't even budge off zero. Clothes always took on a boyish flair on her skinny, five-foot-one frame.

She tilted her head and considered her sister's issues. "The problem is that you're naturally va-va-voom! Because of that, women instantly envy or hate you and men? Well, they find you irresistible. Then their egos cause them to misunderstand."

Ava laughed deep and low, sultry. "Misunderstand what?"

"That you have a moral compass that could withstand a hurricane and still point due north."

"Thank you." Her sister seemed to grow inches, just by her faith in her. "I should've told you but, with Dad's death, I just couldn't bring myself to burden you with my problems."

"Your problems are my problems. We'll weather this storm."

They mopped together in silence. "I sucked at the Front Desk."

"No," placing her fingertips over her mouth, Ava feigned mock horror. "Not you."

"Funny." Isabella nudged her mop with her own. "Why aren't you surprised?"

"Computers aren't your thing. You shine when you can use

your hands and creative talents. Like cooking. You were born to be a chef. Let me handle the Front Desk. I did it during high school."

"I thought you spent all of high school hanging out with Logan."

"Oh, I did. After all, you were busy in the kitchen." She paused, gazed into the distance, remembering. "Logan and I had such fun together." Her green eyes glittered with amusement and another sensual laugh escaped her lips. "Until we'd get caught. Our antics weren't so fun then."

"I assumed you two were an item."

"Logan?" Ava did a double take. "Never. He was like my paternal twin. We thought alike. Lived for adventure. If there was a tree that couldn't be climbed, we did it."

Joy filled Isabella's soul. The Ava she knew and loved was coming back. "I had such a crush on him."

"How could you?" Ava cast a roguish grin and tossed her long ponytail over her shoulder. Her midnight black hair floated down her back. "You were holed up in the main kitchen."

"How could I not? His thick, sandy hair…" Again, both girls leaned against their mops and gazed sightlessly.

"Those eyes. Bluer than a mountain sky in spring."

Both sisters sighed, then their eyes met and they bent over laughing.

Wiping away the tears, she giggled. "'Bluer than a mountain sky'?"

"Well, he's hot. Definitely man candy." Ava paused, and the laughter drained from her face. "Or was."

"What do you mean, was?" concerned, she clutched her sister's arm.

"Dale told me that he's been discharged from the Special Forces. Medically discharged. There was an explosion and he was burned."

"No," Isabella gasped. A lump formed in her throat and she shook her head with denial. "Not our Logan." She whispered, "How bad?"

"I'm not sure. I haven't seen him. I was coming to the Front Desk to tell you."

"What are you two doing?" Theo called out. His long stride consumed the distance between them. He'd shed his suit jacket but his tie was still high and tight up against his neck. He'd swapped his loafers for what looked like muck boots from the stables.

"Here comes trouble," muttered Isabella.

"He's not so bad," replied Ava. "I've never seen a man work so hard for something that won't be his in a year."

"You'd better believe it won't," she whispered back before he reached them.

He scowled down at her. "We have wet vacs to suck up the water."

"Yeah, but they're all being used." She bristled at his tone. "So we're doing what we can."

He pulled the mop from her hands. "You're wasting your time."

Isabella saw red. Life was so unfair. Her father was dead. Reporters hunted Ava. Logan was burned. And Theo was trying to steal Twin Springs from them. She grabbed ahold of the mop and tried to pull it back but he held it firm. "Who are you to tell me how to spend my time?"

"You're so frustrating." Theo attempted to tug the mop from her hands. "Dale and his maintenance crew will take care of the water."

"Dale has more important things to worry about." With a rush of adrenaline, she jerked down on the mop handle.

The end flipped up and long, wet strands of cotton slapped Theo in the face.

"Oh." Isabella's eyes widened at the shocked look on his face. "I—"

"Goodness." Ava's laughter flowed between them. "Such a fuss over a mop."

Isabella's small frame hitched with mirth but she pressed her lips together and held back the giggles. Theo was a sight. His shirt was soaked. Water dripped down his face and off his chin. His tie was like a soggy black tongue. Even his long eyelashes were tipped with droplets.

He lifted his tie by two fingers, stared and released the fabric. It flopped against his chest with a juicy slap. His steel gray eyes stared down at her.

Suppressing the laughter bubbles percolating within her chest, she unwrapped the bandana from around her head and used it to dab at his face.

His lids swept down. He stood still as a statue and allowed her to pat at the water.

Laughter laced her voice, "I didn't mean to swat you." She was inches from his face. So close, she could smell his musky scent.

His eyes flew open.

She felt scorched by the heat in his gaze. Her breath caught. Held. And the laughter faded from her lips.

"I'm going to go mop over there," Ava's voice doused them with frigid water.

Stiffening, he grasped Isabella's small wrist and cleared his throat. His voice was soft, husky. "I've got it." He lowered her arm, tugged the cloth from her hands and wiped his face.

Cheeks flaming, she moved back, avoiding his intense gaze.

He sucked in a deep breath. "What's more important to Dale than Twin Springs?"

A pillow floated by and she couldn't seem to spit out the words that needed to be said.

Ava's voice lowered. "His son, Logan, was wounded and medically discharged from the Army."

"Why didn't he tell me?" He studied the cloth in his hands. "I would've told him to go home. Be with his family."

Isabella looked up into his eyes. There was a deep sadness within the gray depths. "Dale's a proud man. I don't know if he knows how to stop working. Even for something as terrible as this. His family were the original owners of Twin Springs. Maybe he feels like being here is like being home."

Tucking the cloth into his pocket, he nodded.

Ava spoke up. "Logan's home from the hospital. I guess he has been for six months. Dale said he's badly scarred but, worse than that, he's lost his way. Doesn't know what to do with himself out of the military."

His brows furrowed. "Is there a position here that would fit his skills?"

"Sure there is." Excited, Isabella's voice picked up speed. "He's an amazing carpenter. Just like Dale." Her gaze skimmed the damage around them. "He can fix this. Give him a team of men and he'll go to work."

Theo assessed the destruction. "Are you sure? This is going to take more than just basic carpentry skills."

Raising herself up to her full height, she nodded, "I'm certain."

Theo's walkie squawked and he brought it to his ear and listened. "Got it. Bring them through."

The women looked at him expectantly. "The water damage company is here. So you hang up your mops."

"Wonderful," Ava handed him hers.

Awkwardly holding the mop, he added, "There's something else. This wasn't an accident."

"What do you mean?" Isabella questioned. "Of course it was. Twin Springs is old. Things break."

"That was Dale. Someone had fused the shut off valve. That's why there's so much water. By the time they figured out how to turn off the sprinklers, the damage was done."

"Never," replied Isabella. This was exactly why Theo couldn't take over the hotel. He didn't understand her or her people. "It must've rusted shut or something. No one would purposely hurt the Grand Dame. Most of our employees have worked here for generations. They love the hotel as much as we do."

"Perhaps, you're right." Theo's brows drew together. "I'll check into it further."

Ava called over her shoulder as she walked from the room, "I'll talk with Logan. The sooner we get him on the job the better."

Suddenly, Isabella realized she was alone with Theo. He stood uncomfortably close and she was at a loss for what to say.

"I have to meet them at the loading dock," he began, cleared his throat and attempted to tighten his wet tie. "Before I go, I wanted to apologize for whatever I did wrong five years ago."

"Whatever you did wrong." His words rolled around in her head. Like it was nothing. "Whatever you did wrong? So inconsequential that you can't even remember?" Rage replaced common sense. In one, swift motion, she reached down, lifted the hefty bucket full of dirty water and tossed it in his face. "That's what I think of your lame apology." She dropped the empty bucket at his feet, splashing them both and stalked off, not bothering to survey the damage she'd caused. In her haste, she bumped into Niles.

"What's going on," he grasped her by the arms and crouched down so that he could look into her eyes. "What did he say?"

"Nothing. He's just a jerk."

"Don't worry about him." He put his arm around her and guided her away. "He'll be gone soon and things will get back to normal around here."

"Good." Her mind reeled. *How could he not remember? He'd held me under, dragged me down to the bottom of the pool.* She ground her teeth together. *"Whatever" he did wrong?* She stumbled over something and his arm tightened. "Can't happen fast enough."

"You're right. I don't know how long the Grand Dame can survive under his care." Niles kicked a floating pillow out of the way. "If the spa's anything to gauge by. We didn't seem to have these problems before he arrived."

The big man's deep voice and Isabella's small one had carried to Theo. Water dripped in front of his gaze, as he watched the couple walk away. He pulled her headband out of his pocket and studied it in his hands. Rubbed one of the little cherries with his thumb. "She can't wait for me to leave."

He felt wretched. His heart burned where her words had

pierced clean through it and left a gaping hole. Options rolled through his brain. "Maybe she'd be better off without me," he forced the words out of his mouth. They tasted foul on his tongue. "What the hell did I do to make her hate me so much?"

Unsure how long he stared down at the little cloth, Theo gathered himself, wiped his face, and reverently folded it into a small square and slipped it into his back pocket. In the end it didn't matter if she hated him or wanted him to leave. He couldn't. He was bound—by a promise to take care of the Fairbanks girls. "Whether they liked it or not."

CHAPTER FIFTEEN

*I*sabella shifted under the covers. The dream formed around her, becoming incredibly real.

. . .Her black satin shoes made muted sounds on the kitchen's worn, wooden floor. With a careless flick of her wrist, she tossed her red fox stole onto the butcher block counter. Her feet ached from dancing on the small wooden platform in the Main Dining Room.

She paused. Supporting herself with the counter, she untied the t-straps on her shoes and kicked them aside. Humming a snappy tune, she held her arms out to her sides, hands flipped up, and danced a couple quick steps to the music stuck in her head.

With her movements, thousands of black beads shimmered over her emerald satin sheath dress and her matching headscarf fluttered to the floor. She scooped up the black satin scarf and brushed away any dirt from the green flowers embroidered on the fabric.

Laughing out loud at herself, she smoothed fine, blonde hairs back into the intricate knot high on the back of her head. She wrapped the headscarf back around her hairline, knotted it low and to the side of her head, just beneath her ear, so that one of the long ends floated to the front of her delicate, pale shoulder and one, to the back. Despite the late hour, she was too wound up to head to bed. She set to work on making a quick snack for herself. "Besides, what better way to end the day than to cook?"

A smile curved her red painted lips. Her fingertips lovingly caressed the black, iron fronts and silver trimmed doors of the row of brand spanking new Monarch ranges. She loved the improvements the General had made to the kitchen. "Imagine," she whispered, "being able to cook on stoves heated by gas, not coal." She longed to cook on the gray, iron top plates and sighed, "Absolutely a dream."

She gathered tins of dry goods and other supplies that she needed to make a quick batch of blueberry pancakes. "Perhaps I should run a plate up to the General's room as a late night surprise. After all, the dancing will not stop for hours yet and my father will remain with the guests until the last one retires."

The sharp clicks of boot taps on the wooden floor caused her shoulders to stiffen.

"What the hell do you think you are doing?" The Lieutenant's voice thundered and he grabbed her by the top of her arm. He swung her towards him, causing the beads on her dress to shimmer and sparkle through the air. "Women of your station do not work in the kitchens of Twin Springs."

His fingers sank into her upper arm and she bit back a sharp cry of pain. Tipping back her head, she glared. She resented the fact that he towered over her. She wrenched her arm from his grasp. "It is none of your business. You must be ossified touching me like that. Back off or I'll tell my father."

"The General?" His thin upper lip curled. "He's too busy hobnobbing with his wealthy friends to attend to the propriety of his Gems." He glanced down at the new emerald necklace surrounded by sparkling diamonds on her neck. He admired how the gem nestled between the swell of her silky breasts. His thin lips peeled back from his teeth and he jeered. "Your father needs me to run this hotel so that he can play with his friends. I assure you, I can hold my liquor better than any of the flops you know."

Insolently, her gaze raked over his overly slim, tall frame. Her lips curled up, taking note of the unfashionable way he continued to blouse his tan, wool trousers into the high black leather of his boots. "Even with the Great War over, you still consider yourself a military man? A man of action?" He assumed everyone still referred to him by his rank of Lieutenant as a sign of respect, similar to the General. Little did he know, she and her sisters addressed him as the Lieutenant to remind him of his place —well below their father. She held back a smile, reveling with secret knowledge.

His thick, wool suit jacket brought a perpetual sheen to his face that he constantly mopped up with his handkerchief. Darkened with the slick of sweat, his toe head hair didn't need pomade to remain smoothed back from his broad forehead. A shiver of revulsion rolled down her spine. "You're no longer a man of action and my sisters and I are of no matter to you."

Again, he seized her arm. His grip pulled her close and he bent his head down low, his blue eyes piercing hers. His thick and heavy breath wafted over her. The slightly sweet and foul smell of liquor churned her stomach and she turned her face away.

"Everything in Twin Springs is mine to monitor and take care of. It's my job. Especially you and your sister, Ruby. Unwed women are expected to modify their behavior so as not to sully the good name of their future husbands. Ame is the responsibility of that sap of a husband of hers. But you two," he licked his lips enjoying the view provided by the deep v dip of her gown. His other hand slid down her curves and pressed her tight against his hardened crotch. "One of you might be lucky enough to shelter under my last name. And I'll be damned, if you'll bring shame to my good name."

She pushed hard against his chest and broke from his hold. Gaining her release, she stumbled backward. Her stocking feet slipped, she lost her balance and fell backwards against the stove. Reaching out to break her fall, she pressed her hand against the hot stovetop. The sizzle and smell of burned skin filled the air. Crying out in pain, she blew on the singed skin of her palm.

The Lieutenant roared with laughter. "See! That's what happens when *you leave my protection. Learn from it little girl and stay out of the kitchen."* He turned on his heel.

She glared in the direction of his back, hating him as he marched from the room and chortled at her expense. . .

Isabella woke. The budding summer sun cast away the shadows with a warm glow. She rubbed her eyes and stared at the ceiling afraid to believe that it was morning. "I didn't dream that I was drowning."

She sat up and spoke louder, "It was a crazy dream but a new dream." Scrambling to her feet, she stood on her bed, pumped her arms, and wiggled her butt in a dance of joy. Pausing, she considered the dream. "Maddy must've planted a seed in my subconscious about the 1920's when she was talking with Ava. But who're Ruby and Ame?" she wondered. "And the General?" She tried to remember her lineage. "I think we did have a relative that served." It was just on the tip of her consciousness. "Wasn't he in WWI?" She shook her head and hugged herself. "It doesn't matter. Anything's better than drowning."

She jumped down from the bed and shoved the window up. Fresh mountain air flowed over her and cooled her face. She breathed in deeply. Leaning out, she spread her arms wide and shouted to the world, "I didn't drown!"

CHAPTER SIXTEEN

fter showering, she tugged on snug black pants and a black tank top. She gathered her long hair up in a loose topknot and trapped its thickness with the twist and snap of a hair tie. Around her hairline, she secured it with black bandana, spotted with white dots. Feeling guilty about sneaking down to cook, she addressed the faces of her two heroes, tacked beside the door. "I'll help with the KidsCare. I swear. But I just have to cook something. Today is such a wonderful day."

With a skip in her step, she tucked her kitchen notebook under her arm and exited her room. In the distance, a vacuum hummed as she slipped down the back staircase. Someone was always tending to the Grand Dame. She pushed aside her worries about running Twin Springs aside and charged down the stairs to the main kitchen.

With only the sparkle of the lights reflecting off the stainless steel world of the kitchen to greet her, the solitude surrounded her. Filling her lungs with deep, cleansing breaths, her lids fluttered closed and she enjoyed the peace. Bit by bit, the weight of her responsibilities lifted and her lids rose to the clean lines and simplicity of her surroundings. She placed her kitchen notebook on the counter and rubbed her hands together. "Time to cook something special."

She understood the therapeutic powers in creating a dish. While cooking, she could free her mind, deal with the emotions brought up by Theo's presence and work out a game plan. She washed her hands and pulled an apron over her head.

A movement at the swinging doors behind her surprised her. "A fellow early bird," she grumbled and sighed heavily. Disappointed at not having the kitchen to herself, she threw a quick good morning over her shoulder without bothering to identify who entered.

"Isn't it a little early for the breakfast shift," came a smooth voice from behind her.

She flipped around. *Theo, in her sacred place!* She jerked the apron's belt tight and tied it. "Shouldn't you be sleeping? Or stealing gifts from children?"

His lips twisted into a self-mocking grin. "I save that pleasure for Christmas."

"Isn't this how you like your women? In the kitchen?" If he'd just go away, then she wouldn't have to sort out the feelings swirling in her gut.

Theo groaned. "I didn't mean that. Forgive me and my stupid words. Give me a chance, and I'll help you learn everything you need to know about running a hotel."

She froze. Would he really? He was a natural leader, able to fill her father's shoes without a misstep. She wanted to learn, but from him? Had she allowed anger to consume her common sense? Out of the corner of her eye, she studied him. "It's barely dawn and you're in a button up dress shirt and pressed suit pants." She taunted. "Don't you ever bend?"

He leaned against the counter and crossed his arms. "I was just about to hit the sack after dealing with a little crisis."

"The spa renovation." Shame rolled in her stomach. She should've been checking on the progress instead of cooking.

"No. We have a team on that."

Must be personal, she decided. She hated to admit it, but dealing with his sister must be difficult. "Jacqueline?"

"No, a little ruckus in the ballroom from an event running long."

"Oh." Her gaze flowed over him. Exhaustion pulled at the corners of his eyes. A part of him still resembled the young man she remembered, his short hair was mashed against his head on one side and standing straight out on the other. She smothered a grin at the contrast he presented and averted her gaze down towards the floor. To his bare feet. "You can't be in the kitchen without shoes," she burst out. "The Department of Health would have a fit."

He glanced down and wiggled his toes. Looking back up, his gray eyes twinkled. "I don't see anyone here but you and me. I won't tell if you don't." He winked. "I was hungry and hoped I could scrounge something up."

Her heart stopped for a moment, then raced and slammed against her ribs. *Don't forget he's the enemy,* she chanted in her head. Stiffening, she half turned away and attempted to focus on the open pages of her notebook.

He stepped closer, leaned in and peered over her shoulder. "What's that?"

Her breath caught in her chest and she swallowed hard before replying. "Only my single, most treasured possession."

"Really." He leaned closer and placed his arms on each side of her.

Her hand shook when she flipped through the worn pages and her voice squeaked out a reply. "It contains recipes and diagrams for executing my favorite dishes."

His chest pressed against her back. "Anything in there for me?"

Scooting out of his embrace, she placed her palm over her fluttering stomach. "My stomach's grumbling. I must be hungry."

The ever present voice in her head mocked, *Liar.*

Leaning back against the opposite counter, his gaze scorched her. "I'm famished."

A faint breeze flowed through the kitchen and the pages of her notebook stirred and rolled over like waves in the ocean. Both of them rushed forward to protect the contents. But the breeze settled on a page deep within the back recesses. "Bueberry Pankaks" was scrawled across the top of the page in faded pencil.

She slapped her hand on the page and halted any possibility for more movement. "This sounds good."

He placed a hand on her shoulder and leaned in, "You need a little help with your spelling."

At his touch, her insides warmed, as if she had just enjoyed a favorite meal. *Remember, he's the enemy.* With a flick of her wrist, she smacked him in the arm, moved a little to the side and away from the heat of his body. "I was eight."

His brows rose. "You were lucky to be mentored by one of the Executive Chef's at such a tender age. Fantastic opportunity."

A snort escaped her lips. Delighted by his misconception, her face lit up. "Emma taught me how to cook." Involuntarily, her lips spread into a huge grin and laughter bubbled in her chest.

He leaned in, bringing his heat with him. "She must've been an incredible teacher." He cupped the side of her face in his palm. His voice lowered, and his hypnotic words encircled them in a private world far away from reality. "You've always had a beautiful smile."

Laughter caught in her throat and her ears pounded with the sudden beating of her heart. Sinking in the quick-silver of his gaze, she whispered, "Emma's just an old friend."

His head tipped down and she felt the warmth of his breath against her already inflamed skin. "Must've been a special friend for that wattage of a smile."

His gaze focused in on her lips and turned molten. The pad of his thumb trailed a blaze of fire across her full lower lip.

Surrounded by his heat, her body melted like butter in a hot pan.

"I missed you."

Her knees liquefied beneath her and she clutched the counter behind her to keep from sliding into a puddle at his feet. "Missed me?"

Her heart stepped back in time, and she remembered. Water had lapped at their heated skin. Snippets of their last time together clicked the stalled gears of her mind forward. Stollen kisses. Pulled under. Shocked. Dragged down. She choked. Her lungs had burned for air. Her hands clawed towards the blurry lights that floated above the water's surface, until she burst through. Winter air cooled the burning in her lungs. Cruel laughter had echoed off the hot springs water and left behind a heart broken by betrayal.

She stepped out of his reach and wished the cool air could freeze her heart. "Emma was a figment of my imagination." *Just like the love you offered me,* she recalled. "An imaginary friend, all made up in my mind."

He tucked his hands into his pockets and leaned against the counter. "I've never had an imaginary friend. Where did she come from?"

Relief flowed through her at his back to business attitude. *I can handle this. Just business.* She removed a silver bowl from the metal rack above her head and her hands trembled.

Before she could squash it, the renegade voice replied, *Liar, liar, pants on fire.*

CHAPTER SEVENTEEN

Theo couldn't drag his gaze away. Isabella stared down at the book. Her dark, thick lashes shadowed any chance for him to read the expression in her eyes. *I missed you? You idiot,* he mocked himself. *You scared her.*

Her petite body had stiffened and he felt her pulling even further away from him. The silence stretched between them. *Would she even reply? Is this how she'd spend the next year? Ignoring him? You shouldn't have touched her, pushed her,* he admonished himself, but his heart understood that he didn't have a choice.

Unsure what else to do, he shoved his hands further down into his pockets, to where he'd earlier stuffed the black fabric with cherries. He rubbed his thumb against the only piece of her he'd have, her bandana, and hoped she wouldn't completely shut off when she'd just begun to let him peek in to her life.

"My sister and I loved playing hide and seek in the attics. That's where I made up Emma."

Her voice sounded small, distant. As if her mind was far away. In a desperate attempt to pull her back, he asked, "Why the attics?"

Her attitude continued to cool and she placed distance between them to collect ingredients. Her attempts to be civil cut away pieces from his heart. "In the way old days, the staff of the wealthy guests roomed in the attics. The proximity of those rooms allowed the maids and nannies to attend to the needs of the affluent families without being underfoot. Once the well-to-do families no longer traveled with their own large staff, the attics became storage areas. Guests weren't allowed in top floors of the hotel so, we had the length of each wing to play and explore."

He enjoyed watching Isabella. Her black tank top and the matching black jeans hugged her in all the right places. Following the smooth motions of her dainty frame, his mouth grew dry. She didn't just cook, she danced. Tiny as one of the ballerinas on top of a music box, she moved through the kitchen. Raising up onto her toes for an ingredient before twirling away with it. Her fluid movements didn't hesitate, they were graceful and sure. This was where she belonged. Where she shined. His mind registered her words. Barely.

Her arms full, she laid out the ingredients on the steel prep surface. "The multiple rooms, with faded and torn wallpaper, begged for two little girls to play and explore. Stuffed with everything from family items being stored, to extra or broken furniture, to fully decorated Christmas trees waiting to be dragged out for the holiday season. The attics offered us a taste of freedom in a home invaded by strangers."

She dug into the front pocket of her jeans and pulled something out that she cupped within her hand. He could care less what the small treasure was. He wished that she would treat him like that. To be cared for by her. To be close to her. *God, you've lost it,* he reprimanded himself and tightened the tie against his throat.

She washed and dried the object on a linen towel. With the treasure, her delicately boned fingers measured a white powder and she tossed it into the bowl. Unwillingly, his gaze flung to a small box and identified the white substance as baking soda. She moved on to the salt, measured it with the dime in her hand and also tossed it in the bowl. His brows furrowed. Now he easily identified what she removed from her pocket. A nickel and a dime. *What the hell was she doing?* Amazed at her actions, he asked, "Why did you use coins instead of measuring spoons?"

She paused and stared down at the coins in her hand. Confusion knitted her brows and flowed across her features. "Just for old times' sake. But—" She blinked up at him, the green pools of her eyes wide. "I don't know. I guess my little girl's imagination didn't understand measuring spoons at eight."

She shrugged a dainty shoulder. "Anyway," with smooth, sure movements she added the rest of the dry ingredients, followed by the wet, "we loved to investigate the rooms with their tall doors. The decade old carpets showed threadbare tread marks but we didn't care. Alone in our wonderland, our imaginations blossomed and Ava and I transformed ourselves into anything we wanted. Sometimes we pretended we were pirates sailing on a great ship and the crooked floors resulted from the ship pitching from side to side. Ava threw herself into any part. It was serious business for her, playing make believe."

He couldn't imagine Ava as a little girl. But his mind filled with images of a young Isabella, a bundle of energy, running through the hallways with her thick mass of honey-blonde hair flying out behind her. Dust instead of flour would sprinkle her nose. *Did her laughter and excitement light the way? As it did when she was a teen?* He attempted to reign in his thoughts. *Ava. She was talking about Ava playing make believe.* "I'm sure it was. Her first experiences with 'treading the boards,' as they say."

Tipping her head to the side, Isabella considered his comment. "I guess it was." With a flick of her wrist, she cracked eggs on the side of the mixing bowl and continued her story. "We'd been playing hide and seek. Ava and I were mad because Dad had told us that we must let Niles play with us."

Remembered ire flowed into the edges of her speech. He smiled at the vision of two little girls' rebellion at an invasion. "A boy in your private wonderland? No way." He mocked.

Her gaze met his, and amusement twinkled in the green depths. "Exactly!" She waived a spoon at him. "It was our special place. I was hiding and looked over to find this girl staring at me. I followed Emma down to the kitchens and she taught me how to make blueberry pancakes."

One of his brows arched up. "How does an imaginary friend teach you to make pancakes?"

Heat flamed in her cheeks and she dipped her head and continued stirring.

He sighed heavily and regretted the embarrassment his question had caused her. He searched his mind to think of another topic. *Damn it, damn it, damn it.*

CHAPTER EIGHTEEN

sabella considered his question. How did an imaginary friend teach you how to cook? He must think she was a nut case. Everyone else did. The staff had started calling her Dizzy Izzy after her first adventure with Emma. Unable to come up with an intelligent reason, she answered with truth. Which was more than he deserved. "I was playing. Don't know. For years, she showed up in my mind and we played in the kitchens."

She folded in the blueberries and her lips curled up. "I guess Ava isn't the only Fairbanks good at playing make believe." She fired the cooktop and pulled a stainless steel pan down from the rack. She felt the heat from his gaze, watching her every move, and felt foolish for sharing so much. She had opened her personal life to the enemy. An uneasy silence settled on the kitchen.

"Why are you down here so early?"

With a ladle, she plopped down four perfect circles of batter. "I like it when the kitchen is quiet." *Or I used to,* she mused. Resentment coated her taste buds but she didn't remove her focus from the task at hand.

With a spatula, she turned up the corner of one of the pancakes and checked for the golden glow before flipping the pancakes, one by one. "Sometimes it's the best time to create."

He sniffed the air. "Smells wonderful."

Her heartbeat ticked up when he gave her a roguish grin. "Mouthwatering."

She grabbed two shiny black plates from the metal shelving and frowned, puzzled over what happened to Twin Springs' signature dishes. Shaking her head in wonderment, she plopped two pancakes on each of the ugly dark plates.

"You're in luck." She placed a precut template on top of each pancake and sprinkled them with powdered sugar. Deftly, she flipped off the template, leaving behind the signature TS logo on top of each pancake in powdered sugar.

"Sweet," he murmured. "I wondered how they did that."

Without comment, she removed her apron and tossed it into the soiled laundry bin. Then, she pulled down a large silver tray, almost as wide as she was tall. She placed a decanter of orange juice, glasses, the two plates, napkins and silverware on the tray. With the skill of a master, she balanced the tray on one arm and her shoulder and grabbed a silver boat of syrup with her free hand. Without looking back to see if he followed, she headed back out the swinging doors and turned right. She didn't stop until she reached the door of the Executive Chef's office at the end of the hall.

Theo jogged after her. "Let me help."

Her breath caught in her chest at his closeness within the narrow hallway. "I've got it. If you could just get the door." She felt foolish about how breathless her voice sounded. The heavy, oak door groaned in protest as he held it open for her. Careful not to brush against him, she maneuvered past.

He perused the room. Bearing the scars of time, a long, rectangular oak table filled the center. Surrounded by a mismatch of oak chairs, the table easily seated twelve. An unique, antique, roll top desk with a large pigeon hole hutch above, dominated the far corner. The desk sat upon a wide, circular, wooden platform that required a step up in order to reach it.

His voice filled with the awe of a little boy finding a hidden treasure. "I didn't know this room was back here."

Suppressing a smile, she bent down and placed the tray on the table. "Haven't you heard?" She lowered her voice to a mock whisper as she set the table for their breakfast. "This room is haunted. The kitchen staff murmurs tales of things moving by themselves, of strange sounds and the smell of burnt vanilla. Not for the faint of heart."

Theo leaned back against the wall and tucked his hands into the side pockets of his slacks. Suppressed laughter lightened his tone. "You don't say."

Realizing she had started to enjoy his company, she rolled her shoulders and eased the tension knotted under her skin. One year. She could do it. "Some of the staff is sure that it's the ghost of an angry head chef who doesn't want anyone in his sacred area. Others say it's the ghosts of two love torn employees. Few dare to come in this room." She glanced at him. "We could eat in the Main Dining Room, if you'd feel more comfortable. I wouldn't want you to have nightmares."

He grunted under his breath. "You don't seem scared. Have you encountered any ghosts in this room?"

She rested back against the edge of the table. "No, but Maude did. Scared her to death. As my dad told it, she ran up to him panting and shaking, her face ashen. His heart sunk, thinking a serious accident occurred in the kitchen. He held her shoulders and waited for her to calm down. Finally, after much coaxing, she controlled her breathing enough to tell him she heard grunts and moans coming from the back chef's room. Dad said, 'She did the sign of the cross across her chest and gasped out, Ghosts.' He burst into this room and caught two would be lovers in a very, let's say, delicate situation. It was one of his favorite stories." She snorted and laughed. "Not for the guests to hear, of course."

He chuckled with her and stepped up on the platform to examine the desk. "Did your Dad fire them?"

Her brows furrowed with confusion. "Who?"

"The kitchen staff." He pulled and rolled up the desktop. The boy in him itched to explore. "The ones caught in this room."

She observed the stiff man before her. *Of course his first consideration was to fire them. He's corporate. He'll never understand the Grand Dame.* "You can't fire family."

Startled, he looked up, his brows raised. "It was your sister in this room with someone?"

"Of course not," Isabella gasped, appalled at the idea. "Everyone at Twin Springs is family."

He ran his hands over the smooth wood of the desk. "Beautiful. You don't find pieces like this anymore. I take it Chef Dubois doesn't use this room to plan his menus." He pulled each tiny drawer out of the hutch above and explored the contents inside.

"Executive Chef Dubois," she corrected him. "I guess he doesn't. But the desk is beautiful. I used to play in here when I was a little girl. I'd pretend that I was the Executive Chef designing my menus. I almost busted my head open, rolling around in that chair and taking a digger off the edge."

"It does seem dangerous that it is up so high," he stated, stepping down. He pulled a chair out for her. "May I?"

"Thank you." She sat in the chair he offered. He helped her scoot in and an involuntary shiver ran down her frame as his chest brushed against her hair.

"Scared?" he mocked, and settled himself diagonally from her at the head of the table.

Of you or the ghosts? She spread her linen napkin across her lap and looked him straight in the eye. "Never. This is my home. Any strange happenings are a part of it and a part of me."

He drizzled maple syrup on his pancakes.

Intently, she watched him as he took a bite. Watched and waited. She couldn't help that her breath caught in the back of her throat.

He looked down at his plate, back at her, and his eyes widened in awe. "These are wonderful! Why aren't they on the menu?" His eyes rolled with pleasure. "They melt in your mouth."

"Just one of my recipes." She shrugged at him and attempted to hide her pleasure. "Not ready yet for the guests in the Main Dining Room." She shifted in her chair, happy with his reaction, but wary of his intense, steely gaze and afraid of sharing too much. "So what's the deal on your sister's name? Is it Maddy or Jacqueline?"

He chuckled. "Maddy. Definitely Maddy."

"Then why does she insist on being called Jacqueline?"

With his pancake laden fork, he drew a path through the syrup on his plate. "Well, when my parents died, Maddy went through a difficult time. She struggled, thinking she needed to be more. More perfect. More refined. More—" He took another bite and paused, considering. "I don't know how to explain it. Just more. She was kind of a wild child growing up." His lips spread into a wide, crooked grin and her heart skipped a beat.

"Always up to her ears in some kind of mischief." His smile faded away." Since the car accident that killed our parents, she tries to be perfect by dressing older, calling herself by her middle name. Anything to appear more refined and grown up. Her full name is Madison Jacqueline Beaumont. But she now demands for everyone to call her by her middle name, Jacqueline. It's my mom's name. The doctors I spoke to didn't feel it was healthy, her taking on Mom's name and dressing above her age. So, even though it ticks her off, I address her as Maddy. Hoping that it will sink in."

Resting her chin on her steepled hands, she listened. Unexpectedly, within this man across from her, she again remembered the young man she once knew. His humor, outgoing demeanor and the tall, broadening shoulders that hinted at the promise of the man within. She compared her memory to the man who sat before her now. Reaching across the table, she placed her hand on his. "I'm sorry. When did the accident happen?"

He studied her hand, so tiny and delicate sitting on top of his. "It was in the fall. Five years ago, actually right after my family left Twin Springs."

"Why didn't Dad tell me?"

"He didn't know we were an item at the time. We kept it all hush, shut. Remember? But he was terribly kind to allow my parents to be buried here, at my request."

He watched her digest the new information before capturing her hand within his. "What happened?" He drew her in close. "What happened five years ago? Why did you suddenly shut me out? What did I do to make you hate me?"

Wrenching her hand from his, she shot to her feet and began clearing the dishes. *I'm such a fool. He lies straight to my face with a smile on his lips.* Her response was rapid as gun fire. "Like you don't know."

"But—"

"I bared my heart to you. Told you about my greatest fear."

"What—"

"You thought it was a great joke didn't you? Dragging me under the water like that."

"No." He ran his hand through his hair, confusion clouding his gaze. "How—"

"Holding me under. I couldn't breathe. I was convinced that I was going to drown. When you let go of my ankle and I clung on to the side of the pool, I heard you laughing as you went into the woods. Do you know how many years it was until I could even go near a pool of water after that?"

"I—"

"Real funny wasn't it." Leaning across the table, she jabbed her finger into his chest. "A great laugh at my expense."

He growled deep in his throat and in an instant he skirted around the table and gathered her up by the shoulders. He crushed his lips to hers.

Isabella drowned in the warmth of his lips and the taste of his tongue. His arms held her under the waves of passion while the smell of vanilla swirled around them and filled her lungs.

He lifted his head and gazed down at her. "You're like a drug laced with vanilla." He rubbed her slightly swollen bottom lip with the pad of his thumb and studied her dark lashes laying against her milky white skin. "I just want to—"

"So this is how you plan on purchasing back your shares?" mocked a woman's voice.

Her eyes flew open. Maddy leaned against the door jam, looking glamorous. Isabella stiffened and pushed away. Heat rushed into her cheeks. *One year,* she reminded herself. *Don't forget he's the enemy,* she chanted. *Don't forget he's the enemy.*

"We'll discuss this later." Theo glared at his sister. "Next time you'll let me get out more than one word at a time." With quick strides, he grabbed Maddy up by the arm and dragged her away.

She heard the two of them arguing as she crumpled back into her chair. She bent forward and buried her face in her hands, the hotness of her cheeks warming her palms. "One year to regain control of my home," she promised herself. She inhaled and slowly exhaled, calming her heart. "One year to put up with him. Then, I will kick him out of my kitchen and my life forever."

Inhaling deeply again, she noticed the sweet scent of vanilla in the air and lifted her head. "That's odd. Someone else must've arrived early to the kitchens too." She grumbled to the empty room. "Looks like everybody's up early today."

Quickly, she gathered their dishes and piled them high on the tray before heading towards the door. Skidding to a stop, she froze in place. In the doorway stood Emma. Her head was tilted to the side, her lips curled up and welcoming, just like she remembered.

Immobile, Isabella gaped as her brain attempted to understand the vision before her. A white kitchen apron protected the handkerchief folds of Emma's pink dress. A bejeweled, gauzy, pink turban was wrapped around her head and allowed her upswept honey blonde hair to shine within its elegant setting.

A tingling began in Isabella's belly, spread throughout her limbs and grew in ferocity until her whole body shook. She lost all feeling in her arms and they fell limply to her sides. Only the shattering of the dishes crashing to the floor woke her from the daze.

She glanced down at the mess and then back up to the doorway. Emma had vanished.

"I'm losing my mind."

CHAPTER NINETEEN

The lights in the room dimmed and encased her mind in darkness, even though her eyes were wide open. She sunk to the wooden floor and buried her face in her hands. Rocking back and forth on the floor, her mind scrambled to process what she saw.

Emma.

She'd appeared right before her eyes. She clearly wasn't a young girl, as she'd once thought, but a very fashionable, petite woman. And she looked remarkably like her!

In the distance, she heard sounds of the breakfast shift moving around in the kitchen. She wasn't just a bumbling fool but, now, also a crazy one. Hands fisted, she pressed her knuckles into her eyes and rubbed. *First the dreams and now my imaginary friend is back.* "Please let it be the stress. Otherwise, I'm going mad."

She peeked between her fingers. The doorway was empty. Her hands slipped from her face. "Just a day dream," relief flowed through her voice. She crawled over to the broken dishes and checked the hallway. "A figment of my imagination."

She swallowed hard and held back the hysterical giggles that bubbled and threatened to escape her throat. "Brought on by my discussion with Theo earlier. That's all." On her knees amidst the shards, she painstakingly piled broken plates and cups back on the tray. "Just my overactive imagination."

A shadow cast over her and Niles filled the doorframe in his Security Manager uniform. "Who are you talking to? What happened?"

Startled, she let out a little squeak and clutched a sticky broken plate to her chest. "You scared me."

He rushed forward and she could've sworn the ground trembled. He grabbed her by the upper arm and hauled her up at an awkward angle. "Did Jacqueline hit you again? I swear if she did —" He left the sentence unfinished and reached forward, lifting her chin. "Are you alright? Did Theo hit you?"

She back peddled and searched for an excuse. "No, I just—" she studied her feet, unsure how to explain the broken dishes.

"Oh, Dizzy Izzy." Tutting under his breath, he stepped back. He ran his fingers through his shaggy brown hair and snickered. "Did you trip?" Amusement glittered in his gaze and he shook his head.

Suddenly released from his hold, she scrambled to find her balance and stumbled over his feet.

He barked with laughter.

Her cheeks flamed. Caught between being called crazy or clumsy, she chose the latter. Besides, he'd tease her incessantly if he knew that her imaginary friend had returned. Averting her head from his prying, she bent down and re-stacked the dishes on the large tray. Unfortunately, Niles and her sister possessed the uncanny ability of knowing when she lied. "Yeah, well what can I say?" she mumbled towards the floor. "I tripped and fell. Now there's a mess all over." She filled and hefted up the tray.

His gravely laugh rumbled.

She glanced up and saw his floppy green polo shirt literally shaking with the vibrations of his laughter. "You can stop now. It's not that funny."

"Of course you tripped. I should take this from you." As if the tray was a child's toy within his massive hands, he tugged it out of her grasp and placed it safely on the table. "Prevent future spills."

He shuffled closer. His gigantic frame dwarfed her and cut off the space around her. She stepped back and hoped to gain enough room to breathe.

He followed her. "Izzy, we need to talk about the Beaumonts and Twin Springs."

She waived him off. "Don't worry, Ava and I have a plan. Everything's going to be alright."

He stepped forward again. "You've been away. For the last few months I've worked with Theo over the phone. I don't think you girls understand what you are up against. Beaumont Industries is known for their underhanded dealings. He buys companies dirt cheap, breaks them up into little pieces and then sells them, devastating the employees and their families. There are rumors that he forced those companies to sell at below market prices by destroying their businesses."

He scratched at his thick beard. "I think he's doing the same thing here by sabotaging the hotel. Look at what's happened since he and his sister declared their ownership of Twin Springs. The broiler broke down. Twice we evacuated guests due to a faulty fire alarm and, lastly, the sprinklers in the spa. He's driving the hotel into the ground until you and Ava are forced to hand over your shares."

He bumped against her and grasped her elbow. "Also, there are the suspicious circumstances around the death of his parents. Ask the Sheriff. He's dangerous. You experienced how vicious and obnoxious his sister is. The way she slapped you? I'm sure she's off her rocker."

Her stomach rolled and her brain raced with the new information. "I don't trust him either. But do you have any proof?" With the heel of her hand, she rubbed at the ache building inside her chest. "We can't just accuse him of these things without evidence."

"I'll get you the proof." He leaned in, his muddy brown eyes only inches from hers. "You know, I have money. I want to help you. Twin Springs is my home too."

She rubbed his arm and shared a small smile, "Thank you. Let's get the evidence first. Besides, I don't want to take your money."

His voice rumbled from deep within his chest. "I'd do anything for you." He drew her within his arms and lifted her small frame off the ground. Once on face level with his massive height, he pressed his mouth against hers.

Lips sealed shut and unable to move within his bear hug, she dangled beneath his lips. His beard tickled her face and a giggle built inside her chest and spilled out against his puckered lips. "Um, Niles?" she mumbled against his lips. "I think you're great but this is kind of like kissing my brother."

Immediately, he released her.

She fell to the floor, stumbled a little and grasped the edge of the table to steady herself.

Towering over her, a florid flush rushed up his neck and under his beard.

Great! Now I've hurt his feelings. She wanted to bite her tongue and take back her reckless words. "I didn't mean to embarrass you."

He towered over her. "Embarrass me? Dizzy Izzy, there's no way you could embarrass me." With one eyebrow raised, he glanced down at the broken dishes, then back at her.

The ringing of his cell phone saved them both from further humiliation. He raised the phone to his ear and gave short, one-word responses to the person on the other end before hanging up. "Just another strange emergency within Twin Springs. Mr. Beaumont wants me to meet him in room two-forty-five. Nothing for you to worry about, Izzy. I'll take care of it and obtain the evidence you need."

She disposed of the dirty dishes and cleaned up her workspace within the kitchen. Her hands busy, all thoughts of Emma were wiped from her brain. Worry pulled at her. *Was Niles right? Did Theo undermine businesses so he could buy them dirt cheap? Was he sabotaging Twin Springs?* Nibbling at her lip, she wondered, *What was this new emergency?* "I'll be damned if anything else will happen to Twin Springs."

She wiped her hands and marched up to room two-forty-five. The door stood open. It was a standard room with two antique, four-poster beds and matching nightstands. The feather beds were layered with down comforters, soft throws and pillows, all in a palate of brilliant blue and mint green. The smell of fresh flowers filled the room, drawing her attention to a clear globe vase filled with the bountiful blooms of blue hydrangeas paired with the tall spikes of star shaped, white flowers.

The generous bathroom had double white pedestal sinks. She knew the tranquil scene was complete with a claw foot tub tucked into the corner.

Entering, she gasped. A cavernous hole attempted to consume the bathroom floor. Held back only by brass pipes and ropes, the tub teetered on the edge of the massive black opening that fought to suck it down. "Who did this?"

Dale Oakes, almost as old as the hotel, peered down into the hole with his legs spread and his thumbs hooked into the front pockets of his jeans. As the Head of Maintenance, he was easily identified from the rest of his crew because of his ever-present blue jeans, white t-shirt and dark blue work shirt. He shrugged in reply, "Darn if I know."

She picked her way around the white tiles that teetered on the edges of the hole and joined him, straining to see over his shoulder and down into the gaping space. "What happened?" Straightening, she maneuvered to get a better view and bumped against Niles.

Chewing on a toothpick, Dale shook his head. "Ya'll won't believe it, Miss Isabella. I've worked on the Grand Dame my whole life and I've never seen anythin' like it." He scratched the gray stubble on his chin and adjusted his tool belt. "Someone left the water on in the bathroom. Filled that there tub up until the combined weight of the tub an' the water caused a foot of the tub to break through the floor. The water was left on long enough that the floor gave through. Revealed a hidden space below."

"You're kidding me!" She surveyed the damage to the bathroom. One of the tiles wobbled, fell and was consumed by the blackness. Wanting to see more, she skirted around Niles and the double porcelain sinks. Her face flamed and she attempted to push his unexpected kiss from her brain. She'd have to fix things with him later. "Excuse me."

Holding the edge of the sink with one hand, she leaned forward and peered down into the darkness. Her eyes squinted and she leaned further to make out what laid beyond. Bumped slightly from behind in the tight quarters, she lost her grip and pitched forward.

Dale grabbed hold of her arm and prevented her from tumbling in headfirst. "Careful, Miss Isabella."

Niles harrumphed and muttered, "You really need to pay more attention, Izzy."

She flushed. "Sorry, clumsy of me. What's down there?"

"We're not sure." Niles leaned forward and assessed the black hole. "According to the floor plans, this room should be over the Grand Lobby. But that's not the lobby."

"A secret room!" She rubbed her hands together and her gaze glittered with excitement. "Lower me down."

"What?" Dale rocked back on his heels. "No way. You're not goin' down there, Miss Isabella." He shook his graying head emphatically. "I can't do that."

"Oh, sure you can." She gazed affectionately into his gentle blue eyes. "Please. I must see what's down there." She turned her best smile on him and grasped him by his work sleeve. "I'll just lay on my stomach. You can lower me down by my arms." She laid flat on the cold tiles and nodded up at him with encouragement, her arms raised. "No problem at all. See."

CHAPTER TWENTY

"No. Way. In. Hell," declared Theo.

Isabella scrambled to her feet and swayed at the edge of the gaping hole.

His heart roared in his ears and he rushed forward only to come to a stumbling halt when Dale pulled her back before he could reach her. "Damn it! You're just as stubborn as Maddy."

He slammed back the double doors to the bathroom and more tiles tumbled. Feet braced wide, he stood in the doorway of the bathroom with flashlights in his hands and a large coil of black rope wound around one of his shoulders. Fear coated his mouth and he swallowed the foul taste. He wanted to take the rope and tie Isabella to a chair. For her own safety. And his sanity.

He scowled at the two men. Before he could control his words, fury spewed from his lips. "What were you thinking? Were you going to let her go down there?" His gaze pierced each man. "Dale? Niles? We have no idea how deep the room is. It could be thirty feet just like the Grand Lobby."

Niles shrugged. Crossing his arms, he lounged back against a sink. "You all are the bosses. I'm just security."

"Who are you to decide what I can and can't do?" She balled her hands into fists and dug them into her hips. Her green gaze raked his body and glittered dangerously. "You'd better stay out or you might dirty your clean, white button up shirt or crumple your pretty tie."

After living with Maddy, he recognized the danger signs of a pissed off woman. Hands on hips, beautiful but pursed lips. Knife sharp tone. "I understand you're still mad at me." He risked his life by inching closer to her and handed a flashlight to Dale, then Niles. "But you have no idea how far down the floor is."

She stuck her hand out for a flashlight.

Instead he snagged her around the waist and dragged her back from the hole. Holding her on his hip, he ignored her shrieks and kicking. "Don't let her get any closer," he instructed Dale. The old man's brows raised, but Theo ignored his censure at his attempt to handle the situation. Instead, his gaze flickered to Niles. Unable to read his expression behind his damn beard, he gave a frustrated glare. He'd have to handle her on his own.

She bit down on his shoulder.

Gritting his teeth to hold back a grunt of pain, he dumped her into a chair. "Stop. Stop acting like Maddy."

Her cheeks pinkened and she crossed her arms and glared back at him.

He resisted telling her how damn cute she was when she was mad. It would just tick her off more. He rolled his shoulder and refused to give her satisfaction by rubbing it. "Stay here." He straightened his tie and calmed his breathing. She was small but mighty. Obviously, he'd picked the wrong tactic for handling her. He changed gears and implored her. "Please, stay here."

He tied one end of the rope to the shiny, black handrail in the hall and evaluated the strength of the aged, white spindles that held it up. Tugging on the rope, he decided that it would hold his weight. Aware that everyone was evaluating every move he made, he took his time and tied a knot in the rope every three feet to allow for hand and foot holds.

He peered down into the dark hole. Unquestionably not an accident, it confirmed his suspicions of sabotage. He needed to search for clues below before they were destroyed. He evaluated the two men in the room and realized he couldn't trust anyone associated with the hotel. *Except Isabella.*

Theo tossed the rope into the dark hole and listened. He grunted with satisfaction when he heard the soft thud of the rope hitting bottom. Placing a flashlight in the side pocket of his slacks, he lowered himself into the darkness.

Methodically, he worked his way downward hand over hand and pinched the rope between his feet. Stale air swirled around him, thick with dust. A couple feet above the ground, he released the rope. His feet found purchase on a soppy rug, slippery from the thick dust that turned into a muddy mess due to the water leak from the room above. He steadied himself and clicked on his flashlight.

Isabella's voice reached him through the darkness. "What's down there?"

He looked up and saw her delicate face, illuminated by the light from above, as she again peered down the hole. Attempting to see what was in the room, she flickered her flashlight from side to side and blinded him with the beam of light.

He might not fully understand his feelings towards her, but one thing was for certain—he didn't want her hurt. "Damn it, I can't be in two places at once, so someone needs to keep her back and safe." Exasperated, he shouted to the men above him. "Dale!"

"Don't worry," the older man's voice drifted down. "I've got her by the ankles."

Isabella gave him a triumphant grin and kept flashing her light around. She wiggled her head and shoulders further down into the hole. "What can you see?"

Her kerchief came loose from around her hair and fluttered down to him. He grabbed the bit of fabric before it hit the soggy ground.

Thick dust choked him and he coughed to clear his lungs. Frowning at the white polka dots on the black fabric, he shook the material out and tied the handkerchief around his nose and mouth.

Maybe if he appeased her, she'd stop sticking her head down the damn hole. "It appears to be a study or an office of some sort!" he shouted back.

"Really?" She shimmied further forward.

"Niles!" he yelled up. "You pull her back and keep her the hell away from the opening. You're Security. Secure her, damn it. Dale, get on the walkie and have someone bring a forty-foot ladder. That should be enough."

He heard a commotion above him. Dragged back and away from the hole by her ankles, Isabella cried out in frustration. Pausing for a moment, he listened to her giving Niles hell. Returning to the task at hand, he surveyed the room. It was about fifteen feet by twenty and paneled in mahogany. Mostly covered by sheets, the furniture formed eerie mounds in the middle of the room. His flashlight shone upon a huge mahogany desk. "A man's desk, despite the intricate carvings on the legs."

His flashlight beam bounced off glass encased shelves behind the desk. "Mementos." Above the keepsakes, three faces glowed and floated in the glass, staring back at him. Involuntarily, he jumped at the sight. Getting control of himself, he moved closer, his eyes narrowed, and studied the floating faces. "A reflection."

He shook his head at his own foolishness and turned to find the source. Dust sparkled in the beam of his light and he focused his attention on a large oil portrait that hung above the fireplace. He maneuvered around the covered furniture and across the room. The faces of three gorgeous women smiled back at him. Their pale green eyes glittered at him through the dust. One woman with hair black as midnight cut close and sharp at her chin, one with blazing red hair captured in a long bun at the base of her neck and one who was a mirror image of the woman he just ordered dragged from the opening above.

CHAPTER TWENTY-ONE

*L*ater that morning, Isabella waited in the Grand Lobby with Ava and Jacqueline. A portion of the wall next to the trio was cordoned off with red velvet rope hanging from brass poles. The staff buzzed with the news of a secret room being found and two bellboys hovered around their stand, waiting for the great reveal. Across from her lounged Maddy, scrunched down into her chair with her arms crossed.

"Isn't this cozy?" Isabella's gaze flickered over the guests. Families comfortably talked in the intimate settings created throughout the lobby by luxurious chairs and couches grouped around antique coffee tables or fireplaces. A massive rug of green leaves and soft flowers cushioned the guests as they wandered from those high back chairs and elegant couches to the long tables set up with china cups and plates. A baby grand piano played in the background as they stacked their plates with tiny, crustless sandwiches and soft, chewy pastries. "This is my favorite time of the day in the Grand Lobby, when the guests gather for the time-honored tradition of taking tea."

"Whatever." Jacqueline rolled her eyes. "We should offer a choice of ice tea too. Especially since it's summer. And I'm telling you," she pointed to a little boy with curly blonde hair, weaving his way between chairs, "that kid over there would rather have a tiny peanut butter and grape jelly sandwich with a soda. Or hot cocoa. Especially in the winter."

Astonished, Isabella shared a look with her sister. "Out of the mouth of babes. That's a wonderful idea."

"Just saying," replied Jacqueline. "How much longer?" she whined. "It's been forever since they went in there."

"I agree." Isabella sat up. "It seems like hours since Dale and Theo started working."

"They think the door's opening is right here?" Ava uncrossed her long, elegant legs and leaned in towards her sister.

"Yep," inserted Jacqueline. "I don't understand why we couldn't go down into the room with them." Slumping in her chair, she crossed her arms and pressed her chin into her chest. Her toe tapped with annoyance. "Theo sucks."

Again, Isabella nodded in agreement and then caught herself. "I hope they hurry. I'm supposed to help with KidsCare today." She clicked on her cell phone, checked the time and set a reminder alarm. "But I don't want to miss this."

Ava moved closer. "What did you see from above?"

Jacqueline leaned forward. Until, that is, she caught Ava's intense gaze and quickly resumed her teenager 'I don't care' attitude.

"I couldn't see anything specific," answered Isabella, ignoring the teen's huff in response. "Just shapes covered with dust."

The screeching of a saw pierced the air. Covering their ears, all three girls jolted to their feet. Startled guests turned in their seats at the commotion. Inch by inch a long saw blade sliced through the plaster and cut out a large rectangle in the shape of a door. With only a couple inches left to cut on both sides, the saw blade paused. The tips of two screwdrivers pierced through the drywall and the girls jumped back. The cutting resumed, until it finished off the last couple inches of the wall. Grunts and groans filled the air and the large piece of drywall was lifted out of the way.

Light poured from the Grand Lobby into the hidden room.

From within emerged two men covered from head to toe with a thick paste formed by water mixed with dust and drywall.

"Gawd!" Jacqueline waived the dust from in front of her face. "You're disgusting." Hands on her hips, she punctuated each word with a tap of her toe. "Someone's going to clean that room before I enter."

"You must be kidding me." Isabella compared the men covered with dirt and muck to the teen in her pristinely pressed pants, delicate shirt and impossibly high stilettos. Giggles bubbled in her throat. Unable to contain herself, her laughter filled the air and Ava chimed in.

Jacqueline glared back. "What's so funny?"

Shaking his head at the three women, Theo replied, "It's up to you if you want to go in or not, Maddy." He handed each of the sisters a flashlight.

The Fairbanks sisters stepped through the makeshift opening.

Jacqueline's face fell. She hesitated, unsure, and plucked at the edge of her pant pocket with her thumb. Then she rushed forward, snatched one of the flashlights her brother held and pushed past him. "Wait for me," she demanded. Chin held high, she plunged into the darkness. Heels and all.

Gradually, Isabella's eyes adjusted to the darkness. Everyone's flashlights reflected around the room, barely lit by the light from the Grand Lobby. She trailed her fingers through what must have been decades of dirt on a massive mahogany desk. "How long do you think this room has been shut up?"

"Not sure," said Theo. "It looks like a long time. Fifty years, maybe more. You had no idea it was here?"

"No," she glanced around. "I wonder how many times I've passed this wall and not realized there was something behind it."

An assortment of tarnished picture frames littered the long back wall. A dingy heap of fabric covered strange lumps and mounds and ran along a short bookcase that almost stretched the length of the wall under the pictures.

Maddy removed one of the sheets from a large, leather chair and a musty smell suffused the air.

Coughing on the kicked up dust, Isabella waived her hand in front of her face. Carefully, she picked her way towards the desk, stepping over broken tiles and drywall from above. The water leak had soaked the large rug that dominated most of the room. Due to the mixture of time, dust and water, the rug's colors were no longer distinguishable

Isabella examined the items on the desk. Ignoring the soaked and ruined papers, she focused on an ornate, black desk phone. She picked up the receiver from the brass cradle. The curved body felt heavy in her hand and proved the room was real. The receiver was covered in dirt and was dripping in places. Without pause or rational thought, she lifted it to her ear and listened. Dead silence. Laughing softly at her own foolishness, she carefully replaced the receiver before the slender brittle cord disintegrated. She reached out for a long, thin piece of wood, a little wider and longer than a ruler. Picking it up, she attempted to wipe the muddy goo away with her fingers.

Behind her, Ava gasped and she spun around, catching herself before she slipped on the slimy floor by grasping the desk. "What's wrong?"

Transfixed, Ava's body froze in front of a beautiful oil portrait. Its colors vividly reached out to the beholder even through the dust of time.

With the board still in her hand, she weaved her way past the debris and mounds of furniture and stood beneath the massive painting and held her sister's hand. A talented artist had painted the portrait. At first, she scarcely recognized one of the marble and wood fireplaces from the lobby. Instead of the current cream walls, a green, ivy wallpaper surrounded the fireplace.

What held the attention of everyone in the room wasn't the vivid colors, or the use of darks and lights, or even the obvious talent of the artist, but the subjects. Three women, frozen in time, reached out across the span of generations and captivated the onlookers with their enduring beauty.

"They look almost exactly like both of you." Maddy's silver eyes were wide with wonder. "The dark haired girl looks just like Ava, only her hair is chin length. And the blonde girl looks identical to you. Her hair is even kind of twisted up on the top of her head. She even wears a lace bandeau across her hair, like how you wear bandanas." She walked forward to get a better look. "Who's the redhead? Do you have another sister?" Quizzically, she glanced back over her shoulder.

Ava blanched and fell into one of the dusty chairs, shaking and oblivious to the cloud of dust caused by her actions. "I have no idea who the redhead is." Her voice lacked its usual projection and confidence. "Isabella's my only sister."

Speechless, Isabella gazed at the portrait. For the second time today, Emma grinned back at her. "It can't be." She shone her light directly upon the face of the blonde woman. "That's Emma."

"What?" exclaimed Ava. "That's your imaginary friend from when you were little?"

Enthralled, her eyes widening, Maddy's gaze swiveled from one sister to the other.

Isabella bit her lip. Too late to retract her hasty words, she instantly regretted her outburst. "Yes. You're going to think I'm nuts but this is the second time today that I've seen her." She hesitated, taking in everyone's shocked stares, but proceeded to describe how Emma had appeared in the doorway of the chef's room.

No one said a word. She shifted under their gazes and swallowed hard. Heat rose in her face and burned her cheeks.

"Wow, you guys have ghosts here!" Bouncing up and down, for once, Maddy looked and acted every bit of her age. Turning on her brother, she glared at him and hissed. "If you hadn't pulled me from the room, I might've seen her too."

Isabella never considered the possibility that Emma was a ghost. She scanned her memories, searching for clues. "I guess we do. She was supposed to be my imaginary friend. A figment of my imagination. I thought…I thought," she stammered, "I outgrew her, until today."

"Let's not get too carried away here," Theo's voice extinguished the excitement.

"You think I'm making this up?" She stiffened and moved further away from him. "I know what I saw."

"Yeah, she knows what she saw," agreed Maddy, her head bobbing up and down. "This is great!" Suddenly switching gears, her brows knitted together. "When did you out grow her? Do you think she'll appear to me?"

"They look like they're from the twenties." Dale moved forward and examined the painting. Rubbing the dust filled stubble on his chin, he replied, "Ya'll know, 1928 is when the Great Fire happened. It's when the tower burnt down and the General lost his girls."

"You're right." Isabella stepped forward. "I had a dream this morning about a General at Twin Springs. I thought we had a military man in the family. Do you think they could be his girls? What were they called . . . his Gems?"

"What girls? What General? What fire?" Maddy's head pivoted. She threw her hands in the air and started tapping her foot, kicking up more dust. "What gems?"

Dale coughed on the dust and waved his hand in front of his face. Thoughtfully, he hooked his thumbs in the front pockets of his jeans. "Might be. Might be."

Isabella took pity on Maddy. "If I remember it right, our ancestor, the General Rockwell, purchased this hotel from a local widow after World War I. He brought his wife and three daughters to live in the Tower of Twin Springs. On New Year's Eve in 1928, there was a great fire. Rumor has it that the General had installed a row of new stoves in the main kitchen and there was a problem with the gas hook-ups. The explosion shook the hotel, trembled down the gas lines and caused small fires throughout the property. By morning, the fires had consumed Twin Springs' distinctive tower, her stables and portions of her kitchens. People were lost that night, including the General's three daughters. All the family's personal items were lost when the fire destroyed the Tower. The remaining family relocated their living quarters to another wing of Twin Springs."

Isabella's phone alarm pierced the thick air. With a swift click and tap, she silenced the noise. She couldn't wait to get out of the room. She needed time to think. "I have to go."

"This is an awful lot of excitement for one day," added Theo. "Why don't we get cleaned up. I'll contact housekeeping. Perhaps we can get a brigade of maids in here to clear a bit of the dust away. Dale, can you secure the door? I'll tell Niles to make sure none of the guests decide to come exploring in here and also to secure the room above. We need to make sure everyone knows room two-forty-five is off limits. We can't have anyone else moving around up there until we repair the ceiling."

Relieved by his announcement, Isabella handed him her flashlight and scrambled from the room. Once clear of the hidden room and the painting, she paused and inhaled clean, fresh air. Realizing she still held the piece of wood, she used the sleeve of her shirt to wipe away the grime. Boldly etched words gleamed back at her from the brass nameplate. "The General."

CHAPTER TWENTY-TWO

Isabella rubbed her temples. The guests' children scrambled around on the KidsCare playground. Backdropped by white cottages, the playground's wooden towers were connected by swinging bridges, wooden ramps and walkways. Slides shot out of the bellies of the smaller towers. Her head rang from the kids' exuberant shouts and screams and she wanted nothing more than to return to kitchen and hide.

She raised up on her tippy toes to see over the taller children and checked on three little girls pumping their legs to make their swings go higher and higher. Other children raced around her, shouted and climbed back up ladders. She let out a deep sigh and checked her phone for the third time. "Time for snack and then one more hour."

Tucking her phone into her back pocket, she called out, "Come on everyone." She clapped her hands to gain their attention. "Snack time."

The children continued to shout and scramble through the maze of walkways. Isabella froze. Unsure what to do, she cupped her hands around her mouth and tried again. "Let's go everybody. Time for snack."

The kids continued to ignore her.

An ear-piercing whistle emanated from behind her and blanketed the playground in silence. Theo's long gait quickly brought him to her. "Snack time," his commanding voice rang out. "To the picnic tables. Now!"

She couldn't believe it. The kids clambered over each other to obey. Even the older boys. Frustration lacing her voice, she asked, "Why are you good at everything?"

"Not everything." His gaze warmed her. "I can't seem to get you to give me the time of day."

Unsure what to say to that, her mouth hung open. Was Theo flirting with her? With a snap, she closed her mouth. Over her dead body. But her belly fluttered and her cheeks warmed. "It's a quarter 'til five."

His lips actually curved up at her joke. Then broke open into a wide smile showing perfect, white teeth. Her knees went weak. "I've had a lot of practice rounding up kids. Thanks to Maddy and her friends."

Unsure what to say, she grabbed the basket of sandwiches, chips and juice boxes, and started setting them in front of each child. Reluctantly, she felt herself softening towards him. "It must be hard raising a teenager."

He chuckled, "Taming Maddy you mean." He shrugged. "Between her and our family business, there hasn't been time for anything else. Anyone else."

Her gaze flowed over him, his pressed suit. His shoes shined. Everything on him perfect. He was a single dad. Just like her father. She remembered the antics her and Ava had played growing up. Running free through Twin Springs. It must've been hard, all that responsibility placed on his shoulders at such a young age. Now, add the responsibility of Twin Springs.

He attempted to capture her gaze with his. "Isabella," his husky voice broke through her thoughts.

She glanced away, and placed another bag of chips before a child. "Yes."

"I'm sorry that I didn't return to Twin Springs sooner. Fix

things between us. I kept meaning to but things just got in the way."

The children's laughter and conversations couldn't mute the painful past that stretched between them. She didn't know what to say. A week ago, she would've snapped at him and told him to go to hell. But now, a different image of him started to form and she saw a man similar to her father. Who shouldered the responsibility of a little girl all alone.

Theo cleared his throat and tightened his tie. "Um, The Hillgroves will be ready for transport to the airport in an hour. Do you want one of the bellhops to drive them?"

She shook her head and attempted to push the image aside. "I promised that I'd do it."

He reached in the basket, grabbed the remaining chips and started handing them out. "Good. I've hired a new Front Desk clerk, Sheela. She seems very sharp."

Isabella gave a self-depreciating laugh. Where she'd struggled to even run one department of Twin Springs, he'd shined. Leadership came naturally to him and the employees respected him. She hated to admit it, but he was a better General Manager than she could ever hope to be. "I'm sure she's better than me."

She felt his gaze on her as she placed a juice box alongside each sandwich.

"You know, bookings are down. Even with the golf season in full swing. Perhaps we could bring more business in through the dining experiences."

She went to place the final juice box down but the seat was empty. His words floated to the back of her brain. She was missing a child. Quickly, she scanned the kids before her. Her heart leapt into her throat and the empty basket fell from her limp grasp. "One of the girls is missing!"

"What?" He glanced around. "Which one?"

"A little girl with short, dark hair and a big, pink bow in her hair. She was swinging over there." She pointed to the three swings. "Katie. Her name's Katie." Her heart raced like a freight train. "I must find her. Watch the kids. And call for help." Panic closing in on her, she searched the playground, checking every tower and hiding spot. She climbed down a ladder and Theo was waiting for her. "Did you find her?"

"Not yet," he replied. "I have an employee with the other kids. We're going need to call the parents."

"Give me a few more minutes to search." She clambered up to the tallest tower for a bird's eye view. And spotted movement. Between two of the cottages was a little girl, crying into her knees. Isabella pointed. "There she is!"

She slid down a slide and ran towards the little girl, Theo at her heels. She skidded to a stop, and kneeled before her. "Why are you hiding here?"

The little girl sniffled and raised her tear stained face. "The man said I could have a balloon if I followed him. But then he let them go." She looked up at the sky.

Isabella followed her gaze and caught a glimpse of multicolored balloons floating over Twin Springs' new tower. "Oh, Katie. I'm so glad you didn't go with him."

"What did he look like?" asked Theo, his face rock hard. "Can you describe him?"

The girl shook her head and tucked her face into her crossed arms.

"You're safe now," Isabella hugged her. "How about a snack? Maybe some cookies from the kitchens." Over the girl's head, her gaze met Theo's.

"I'll contact her parents and have them meet me in my office, if you'll take her for cookies and meet us there." He hesitated and she knew there was more. He was holding something back.

"What? What aren't you telling me?"

"I've been seeing this man." His gaze bored into hers. "Hanging out in the woods. I should've called the police after I first spotted him at the funeral."

She laid her hand over his and squeezed. There he was, taking responsibility again. Shouldering the blame when it wasn't his. "No, I should've kept a better eye on the kids."

CHAPTER TWENTY-THREE

Theo stood on the front veranda with Mr. and Mrs. Hillgrove, their luggage piled on a cart. He never wanted to tell a parent, ever again, that their child had been lost. The devastated look on the father's face, the mother crumbling into tears, even when her child was within her arms… He sucked in a deep breath and attempted to tame the feelings running rampant through him. He needed to face the facts. Someone was trying to destroy Twin Springs, one accident at time. And now that someone had tried to steal a child.

One of the hotel's vans crested the hill and began descending the long, steep driveway. "There's Isabella to pick you up." *She's driving a little fast,* he thought, as the van picked up speed. "I'll accompany you—" He broke off mid-sentence. The van careened down the hill at a break neck speed, swerving from side to side.

"It's going to hit the fountain!" shouted Mr. Hillgrove and his wife screamed.

Sure enough, the van headed straight for the large fountain in the middle of the circular driveway, hitting it with enough force that the hood crumpled upon impact and the top cherub broke off, shattering the windshield. A geyser of water sprayed over the van.

"Isabella!" shouted Theo, stumbling down the stairs. He

jumped over the hedge, rushed up to the car and jerked open the door. "Are you hurt?" He pushed the airbag out of the way.

Her face was dotted with blood where tiny shards of glass had slit her. There was a small cut in her hairline and blood dripped down her forehead. The statue had landed in the passenger seat. He jerked her bandana from his pocket and used it to stem the flow. "Stay still. Don't move."

"I've got it," she took the cloth from him and held it to her head.

Unmindful of the spray that soaked them, he ran his hands down her limbs, checking for broken bones. Images of his mother hanging from a tree branch plagued the back of his mind and his father's voice whispered, "*Take care of the girls.*"

Once again, he'd failed. Emotions clogged his throat.

The statue was only a few feet from smashing her. He could've lost her. He didn't think he could bear that kind of pain. He'd give up anything and everything to be with her.

"I'm fine." She started to uncurl herself from behind the wheel.

He pressed her shoulders back. "Wait for the ambulance."

"No," she shook her head. "Really, I'm fine." She climbed out. "I don't know what happened. I pushed on the brakes but the van wouldn't stop. Then the steering went bonkers."

She looked up at him, her eyes green pools of tears. "Did I hurt anyone?"

"No. Just the fountain."

Her giggle sounded hollow. "Never really liked those cherubs." She hugged herself, shaking from head to toe. "Creeped me out."

He couldn't take it anymore. He pulled her into his arms and held her tight against his chest. He didn't care if she felt the pounding of his heart. She'd scared the crap out of him. "Please, Isabella," he whispered into her hair. "Go back to the kitchen. I promise, when the time comes, I'll find you the best General Manager possible." He hoped it would be him, but he held back the words *pick me.*

A great shudder rolled through her body. "Alright."

His heart swelled and he squeezed her tighter. She'd be safe in the kitchens and he'd be one step closer to fulfilling his promise to Ben, when she fulfilled her dream and became an Executive Chef.

Ava rushed down the staircase. "What happened? Are you hurt?"

Unwillingly, he released Isabella to her sister's concerned embrace.

Niles thundered to a halt beside them. "What the hell happened?"

"Theo can tell you." Ava wrapped a protective arm around her sister. "I'm taking her up to her room."

Watching the women go, Theo felt a piece of him shatter. He'd almost lost her because he hadn't taken care of her. Robotically, he explained.

Scratching at his beard, Niles replied, "Just like your parents' car."

"What?" Theo's attention snapped to the other man. "What did you say?"

"Didn't the brakes fail in their accident too?"

Rage consumed Theo, blurred his sight and pushed caution to the side. He grabbed the larger man up by his shirt and threw him against the side of the van. "Don't you ever refer to my parents again. You don't know anything about them. Understand?"

Niles grunted.

Disgusted with himself, Theo released the man and walked away. His father would've been ashamed of his lack of control.

CHAPTER TWENTY-FOUR

The next morning, Isabella stood ready to man a position within the main kitchen. Automatically, she tugged a purple and pink mottled piece of fabric out of her pocket and tied it around her hairline to hide the cut in her hair. Her hands stilled. "Just like Emma." A chill ran down her spine and she shivered. "I must've been subconsciously copying her since I was a child."

Marc stood at his usual spot. Ready and waiting, he lounged against the stainless steel sinks in faded jeans and a white t-shirt. Casting him a pinched smile, she tied one of the green aprons over her cook shirt.

Turning his baseball cap backwards, he acknowledged her with a wink.

Executive Chef Dubois entered, strutting his large body up at the pass. "So, you're back," he sneered. "I heard you stormed out of the stables, failed miserably at the Front Desk and lost a little girl." He snickered. "Come to try your hand in the kitchen?"

All eyes were on her. Heat burned her checks, but she couldn't deny the truth in his words. "Yes, and I'm ready to work."

"I told Mr. Beaumont that I didn't want you. But he insisted." Dubois' beady gaze examined her from head to toe. "What makes you think that you're good enough to work in my kitchen, when you've failed everywhere else?" He sniffed. "Let's see." He fired a question off to her. "What's a mise en place?"

Used to the ritual from culinary school, she fired back an answer. "It's all the ingredients laid out that will go into whatever dish I'm preparing that night, Chef."

"Who's James Beard?"

Relieved with the simplicity of the question, her shoulders relaxed and she replied. "He was a food writer, cookbook author, teacher and an outstanding chef. He's considered one of the most highly regarded food writers in America. He hosted the first food program on television."

With lightning speed Chef Dubois followed her answer with another question, "What's crème brûlée?"

"Burnt cream," she promptly replied. "A baked custard topped with sugar that is caramelized with heat. The heat creates a dual-textured dessert consisting of a soft, creamy custard inside, yet a brittle sugar topping, Chef." Holding her breath, she understood that even though she owned part of the hotel, the chef ruled the kitchen. Without a good chef in charge, the possibilities of Twin Springs pulling out of the red were limited, if not impossible.

Executive Chef Dubois pursed his thin lips until they curled in, almost disappearing into his heavily jowled face. With a curt nod, he said, "You may remain." Catching her involuntary grin out of the corner of his eye, he added, "Try not to poison anyone. Gather your mise en place. You're preparing the crème brûlée for tonight's dinner service. Let's see how well you cook." He turned to the pass, grabbed the first ticket, and barked out orders to the kitchen crew.

Efficiently, she gathered the ingredients. Heavy cream, sugar, salt, egg yolks, vanilla beans and sugars. She ensured the cleanliness of all her equipment. Double-checked for any grease that might affect the sugar. Lining up her mise en place, she realized that she already worked at a disadvantage. Chef Dubois assumed that he handed her an impossible task. Crème brûlée required time to chill before firing them. Time she lacked unless she worked rapidly, yet carefully. Any mistakes with her cooking or timing and her desserts would fail.

She pulled a blue dry erase marker from the front pocket of her cook shirt and wrote her times on the stainless steel countertop of her workstation. Brows furrowed, she combined the cream and salt and brought the mixture to a simmer and added a little lemon.

Beads of sweat dripped down the back of her undershirt from the stifling heat. Using a wooden spoon, she stirred the ingredients together, then, removed the pot from the burner. She split the vanilla bean and scrapped the seeds from the pod before stirring them into the cream. She covered the dish, jotted down the time and let it steep while she began the process again for the next batch.

Returning the original pot to the heat, she brought the cream to a boil. Then combined the egg yolks and the rest of the sugar, and tempered the mixture into a hot cream. She strained the custard through a fine-mesh sieve and ladled the creamy dessert into the little, white ramekin bowls. While they baked in their water bath, she returned to the other batch.

Just in time, she removed the custards from the water bath, wiped them dry and set them in the refrigerator to chill. She continued the process over and over for each batch.

Chef Dubois called out, "You're up girl."

Everyone in the bustling kitchen heard the sneer in his voice and paused, their gazes filled with pity.

"Five crème brûlée for table ten, and three for table six."

Isabella ignored his tone, replying loud and clear, "Yes, Chef." She pulled out the chilled crème brûlée ramekins and evenly coated each custard with a thin layer of sugar. Using a propane torch she melted and caramelized the sugar before placing a minia-ture template of the Twin Springs logo over each ramekin and dusting them with confectioners sugar.

"Crème Brûlée up," Isabella called out, and brought her desserts up to the pass.

"Girl, don't be stupid. You think I'll let your food go to out to the guests without tasting it." Dubois' thick fingers pulled a tasting spoon out of a cup on the rack. "Bring up another, while I taste one of these."

Turning back to her station, she processed another while keeping one eye on Chef Dubois. She needed his approval to remain in the kitchens and help Twin Springs succeed. And to do the one thing she loved more than life—cook. Chef Dubois' test weighed heavily upon her shoulders.

He broke the thin crust of sugar with his spoon, placed a dollop of custard in his mouth and rolled it around. Swiftly, he turned and pinned her with his beady eyes.

She gasped.

Hatred poured from his gaze. Quickly, he shuttered his emotions, leaving her unsure if she imagined his anger or not.

"Adequate," he drawled. "You may remain. With the correct tutelage, there's a slight chance of you becoming a serious chef. Pick up your schedule tomorrow morning." He continued barking orders from the pass.

Face glowing, she gave a little, "Yes," and her small fist pumped the air.

Maude observed Isabella from her station. Smiling from ear to ear, she called out, "Congratulations, Izzy."

Chef Dubois shouted from the pass, "No talking. Work!"

After sending her friend a quick thumbs up signal, Isabella returned her focus to the next order. Exhilaration bubbled. Finally, she was one step closer to regaining full ownership of Twin Springs.

Part
Two

CHAPTER TWENTY-FIVE

1 5 June 1928

The General struts with his damn medal and tells his war stories to all the rich saps. Commiserating with the locals about their stupid hometown boy. Their hero. That lowly Private. The stories now grow in grandeur. About how the General and Private saved all. I should've been there. Damn it! The Medal of Valor should be mine!

It's the General's fault, the bastard, that I wasn't by his side and on the side of honor. His and Adriana's. But I taught her a lesson for seducing me and preventing me from fighting by the General's side that day.

I drowned her in the pond behind her home. Held her beneath the water, while I watched the light fade from her eyes. Her hands desperately scratched at my massive forearms for release. But I granted no mercy. Beneath the churning water, her lips parted, releasing the last of her air in what I like to remember as a goodbye kiss.

Adrenaline rushed through my body, igniting my senses. The

power I felt. My hands had decided her fate. That was the day I became a god walking the earth among mere mortals. Able to take whatever I wanted.

Only I know the secrets of the Grand Dame they call Twin Springs. I have plans. Even now, I create great wealth from within her great belly. Selling my moonshine to the rich and the thirsty in D.C. With my new fortune, I will finally destroy General Rockwell. I deserve Twin Springs and all her fruits. Perhaps, I deserve to taste all the General's Gems. Let them sparkle on my arm.

Lt.

CHAPTER TWENTY-SIX

*W*eaving between guests, Isabella speed walked through the Grand Lobby as fast as her short legs would carry her. She glanced down at the text from Theo.

"The housecleaning crew finished the room. Meet me there."

For the past week she'd lived in the main kitchen. Anticipation rushed through her veins and quickened her step. She rubbed her hands down her lemon colored cook shirt. Finally, she could search the room for clues as to why Emma appeared to her.

Dale and his crew had worked hard to repair the water damage and the hole in the wall of the Grand Lobby. Carefully, he'd cut back and removed the drywall from around the entrance. His efforts had revealed heavy double doors flanked by tall pocket side panels.

She admired the results. Painted a crisp, clean white, the original doors and molding blended well with the other archways and doors within the lobby. A stain glass palladium window was uncovered and curved high above the double doors. The window gleamed in the sunlight and reflected soft colors throughout the lobby and down upon the guests' heads.

"How could someone hide something this beautiful?

Dale even attached my discovery." Engraved with bold strokes, the mahogany and brass placard had been affixed at eye level on the right panel above a dark metal slot. She ran her fingertips over the etched words. They glowed in the sunlight and felt warm to her touch. Her heart pounded. Something once lost from her world clicked into its rightful place and happiness filled her. "The General. My great, great grandfather."

The smell of linseed oil permeated through the double doors. Shaking her head, she pushed away her fanciful musing and grasped the oblong doorknob. The dark metal felt cool in her hand. Preparing herself, she took a deep breath and opened the door to her past.

"I'm telling you how I want it." Maddy's voice pierced the air. She adjusted the bright pink scarf draped around her neck. "The awful dark molding and paneling must be removed. Empty the room completely. All this old junk can go straight into the trash. Think modern. Think clean lines. I want a bar across the back wall." She smoothed her hands down her silk black blouse and pants. "Sleek, shiny and black."

Dale held his aged hands out beseechingly in front of him. "Miss Maddy, I can't do that."

"Miss Jacqueline," she spit out. Not missing a beat, she continued. "Pink neon letters behind the bar with the bar's name." She lifted her hands up in front of her face, spread them wide and proclaimed, "Jacqueline's," drawing the word out as she spoke. "Along the front of the bar will be aluminum and clear plastic bar stools in the shape of martini glasses." She rubbed her hands together. "Perfect! A shot of modern into this dying old hotel."

Dale remained frozen like a deer caught in the sights of a twenty gauge shotgun. Ready to bolt, but unable. "You can't even drink," he sputtered. "What'd you want with a bar? And off the Grand Lobby, no less." He shook his graying head side to side.

"Dale," Isabella ignored the teen and stepped between them. "The doors are amazing. I can't believe they were here the whole time."

Released from Maddy's invisible hold, he adjusted his tool belt and inched towards the exit. "We only needed to peel back the layers. It was easy, since we were able to see the doorframes from the inside of the room. We found the door knobs in one of the desk drawers." He examined his team's efforts. "The crew from housekeeping did a fine job of cleaning up the General's room."

The door opened behind her and in filed her sister. Ava was a breath of fresh air with her jet black hair hanging in a long, smooth pony tail down the length of her back. Her cream blouse and designer slacks flowed with her movements and molded to her tall, slender body.

Even though Isabella loved and admired her sister, she realized that beside her, she resembled a squatty duck in her yellow cook shirt and black pants. "Hey, sis."

Her voice trailed off when Theo entered behind her.

With their arrival, Dale edged closer to the door. "If y'all don't mind, I'm goin' to check the progress on the room above."

Theo nodded, and the older man hastily escaped.

Secretly, she scrutinized Theo. Really looked at him. He crossed his arms and leaned nonchalantly against the wall, his ironed pants barely bending. His starched, white shirt outlined the muscular body beneath, stretched across his wide shoulders and glowed against his skin. His gray tie was thrust tight up against his throat and matched the charcoal of his eyes. Everyone else faded into the background.

Those eyes. She lost herself within the deep, dark pools of his gaze. His suppressed passion bubbled up from beneath the surface, soaked into her, coated her heart, stripped away her outer trappings, and bared her soul to his. His warm desire bandaged the pieces of her heart back together and she emerged a beautiful swan. Transformed. All with the power of his gaze.

Desire trembled through her body and she swayed towards his heat. Betrayed, her mind rebelled against the weakness. Her memories protested. The terrible laughter from the pool cackled in her ears, echoed in her consciousness and reminded her of the truth. He was the enemy.

She gritted her teeth and ripped the band-aid from her heart. The broken pieces of her own needs and desires bubbled up into her throat. She swallowed hard and tore herself away from his gaze. Without any other alternative, she buried the weakness beneath sure grit and determination and focused in on the secret room. The General's room.

Gone were the layers of dust. Mahogany and dark leather now gleamed in its place. She pulled lightly on a black, metal basket hooked to the inside of the door panel.

"For mail to drop into," murmured Theo. "Simple but ingenious at the same time. One of those mail slots would be handy at registration. Some guests still use the old mail slots at the elevators for their post cards home, but many drop them off with the Front Desk clerks."

Isabella surveyed the room. The once tarnished, silver picture frames across the back wall now glinted beneath the lights and stood out against the richly paneled wall. An assortment of hard-back books were stuffed in the glass bookcase beneath, while metal, toy vehicles lined the top of the bookcase. On the adjacent wall, the portrait hung above the fireplace, flanked on both sides by electric sconce lamps. A sitting area formed in the middle of the room from two man-size wing back chairs and a long leather couch. The huge, mahogany desk still dominated the right side of the room. The cast iron phone gleamed with a new black cord. She lifted the receiver to her ear. Her eyebrows rose with disbelief at the welcoming hum emitting from the ear piece. "Amazing."

Behind the desk, the glass enclosed shelves sparkled. She skirted around the desk and peered inside the cabinet to discover what time and dust had once concealed: an assortment of framed family pictures, an old baseball, and a white silk handkerchief embroidered with an eagle holding a flag within its talons. The words "forget me not" were embroidered beneath the outstretched wings. Behind the silk handkerchief sat a black and white wedding picture with the bride draped from head to toe in lace. Blissfully smiling, her tiny frame was almost childlike in stature and dwarfed by the size of her military husband at her side. To the right of the photo, a military medal slept on satin within a little box. She twisted an ornate metal key, unlocked and opened the cabinet door. Reaching in, she removed the box with the medal. Her eyes narrowed and she brought the box closer to examine the golden upside down star. The word valor was inscribed across the bar with an eagle sitting above it. A blue ribbon tab was attached to the medal. She rubbed her thumb gently across the sky blue ribbon laden with tiny white stars.

"It's the Medal of Honor," Theo stated in awe from behind her.

Not realizing he hovered behind her, she jumped slightly and bumped against him.

"I looked it up last night just to make sure."

"My father told me all the family heirlooms were lost in the fire." She laid the medal back in the case and picked up a circular metal disk hanging by a leather cord from a picture of the General and two other soldiers. She palmed the tag and with the pad of her finger traced the etching of her great, great grandfather's name along the top circle. GEN was etched across the middle and a barely discernible U.S.A. along the bottom arch. "It's the General's dog tag."

Looping the leather back over the edge of the picture frame, she examined another picture inside. Three men, one obviously the General, posed in front of a tank. A young Private, with a cocky grin, stood on top, while another military officer, indistinguishable due to the picture fading out from age, stood off to the right.

"Here's a picture of the General with President Woodrow Wilson at Twin Springs," Ava called out. "There's also one with Gloria Swanson the actress, and Coco Chanel the clothing designer."

"You're kidding me!" Maddy rushed over to examine the pictures. "He knew everyone. That's Jack Dempsey, the boxer." Squinting her eyes and leaning in, she pointed to another photo. "I think that's Duke Ellington leading the band on the stage in the Crystal Ballroom."

"I'm sure this is the General playing golf with Calvin Coolidge. And this appears to be a photo of him with his family." Ava waived her sister over to join her. Obviously, it was taken at Twin Springs on the front veranda between the two white pillars. "See the three sisters? The redhead is heavy with child and is standing arm in arm with her siblings. The General is flanking them on the right. They must be getting ready to go someplace. Behind them are two maids with suitcases at their feet."

"Or they just returned." Suddenly exhausted, Isabella collapsed on the couch. "So far nothing has answered my questions about Emma. The room has only revealed additional questions. So much to take in."

Her sister joined her. "I know, but it's something."

Isabella leaned her head back and stared up to where just a week before she'd dangled down through a wide hole trying to see into the darkened room. Now the hole was covered with fresh drywall, not yet taped or painted. "It's amazing how much everyone has done in such a short time."

Maddy flopped herself into one of the chairs and abandoned her heels by kicking them off. "I'm tired of looking at stupid old things." She stretched out her legs and let her arms hang over the sides of the chair. "Tell me about the General. The head landscaper told me that he heard this room held his greatest treasure, three rare and precious jewels. He was sure, once found, this great treasure would save Twin Springs and bring her back to her glory days. I don't see anything close to being rare jewels in this room. Just old junk."

Amusement glowed in Ava's gaze. "Not much was saved after the Great Fire. Growing up, when I asked my father about the fire, he shook his head and didn't reply. So last night I researched the General online while I pulled the night auditor position."

Isabella's eyes widened. "You pulled the night auditor?"

"Don't look so surprised. I'm more than just a pretty face. I can sit at the Front Desk and run the daily reports."

"Of course you can," stammered Isabella. "I just didn't know you wanted to. What about your acting?"

"I spoke to my manager. After what happened, I can't return to the stage. Not yet. He's giving me a year." Ava waived her sister's concern away. "Let's talk about the General. It was easy to find information on him from the Internet. Especially, since Theo told me he was a Medal of Honor recipient. The website on Medal of Honor recipients stated that General Benjamin Rockwell sired three girls, named Ruby Lynn, Amethyst, and Emerald Mae. Even society dubbed the girls as the General's three gems. By family, they were lovingly referred to as Ruby, Ame and Emma."

"Emma the blonde," added Isabella. "The redhead is our great, grandmother, Amethyst Fairbanks. Her infant son survived the fire but not her. Thankfully, he lived. Otherwise, Ava and I wouldn't be alive."

"Correct," her sister replied. "And Ruby is the one who looks like me."

"Emma," Isabella stared up at the portrait. "Our long lost aunt. I can't believe I mistook her for a young girl."

Theo walked over and stood beside her. "Notice how tiny she is. She's about the same height as you. I'd say pushing five foot in those heels."

"I'll have you know, I'm five foot one in my bare feet. Not all of us mere humans were blessed with long legs like each of you were."

His lips cured into an amused smile. Leaning in, his face only inches from hers, he whispered, "Prove it." He straightened and added in a louder voice, "Except for Ava, it appears puny women run in your family. The General's wife, Emma, and you."

Feeling once again like a squatty duck, she lashed out. "Puny?" Clenching her teeth, she ground out, "I'm not puny. I'll have you know, I can carry a ten gallon pot filled with cut potatoes and water."

He squeezed one of her biceps. "I guess there is some muscle in there." He chuckled.

Was he laughing at her? Quickly, she slapped his hand away, scooting closer to her sister and out of his reach. "Stop that."

Ava let out an exasperated sigh. "You were just a child too," she interrupted. "You can't blame yourself for not knowing."

Her face reddening, Maddy observed the interaction between Isabella and her brother. "You call me immature."

Theo switched the subject. "How did the General receive the Medal of Honor?"

"He and an injured Private strapped metal to a vehicle, drove it directly into enemy fire and protected our troops. Then, they fired on the Germans. Together, they destroyed two enemy machine gun nests and broke the advancement of the enemy forces. Even after being severely injured, he rallied his troops and sent the enemy packing. The Army promoted him to General and awarded them both the Medal of Honor." Ava shook her head. "Unfortunately, the Private died from his wounds and was awarded the medal posthumously."

"That's so sad," said Maddy.

"I know," replied Ava. "Do you want to hear something odd? The private's last name was Oakes."

Theo stiffened. "Oakes, as in Dale's last name?"

"Yes," replied Ava. "I wonder if he was related, a cousin or something. Dale never mentioned one of his ancestors received the Medal of Honor."

Theo's brows furrowed. "That is interesting."

"I thought so." Ava chuckled under her breath. "There was quite a stir in this room last night. The night auditor job can be pretty boring with the lobby quiet. For the past couple nights, I've listened to the maids chitchat and gossip with each other. Last night a scream pierced the stillness and one of the maids raced out of this room. She actually hid behind the Front Desk. Tears streamed down her face and she told me that one of the sisters had materialized out of the portrait and touched her on the shoulder. The other maids spilled out of the room laughing. They considered it quite the joke until they saw how upset their friend was."

"I heard the rumors," said Theo. "It's my fault. I wanted to reward the maids for all their efforts. Yesterday morning, I set them up with a complete body massages in one of the recently renovated rooms at the spa. I overheard the manager spinning tales to the maids about the General's three daughters. She claimed someone buried their ashes deep beneath the floorboards of this room. Now that the room has been revealed, their spirits were released to reap vengeance on all the staff who hadn't discovered how they died almost one hundred years ago."

Maddy shrieked. "Are they?" She tucked her bare feet up beneath her and far away from the floorboards.

Her brother chuckled. "No, so you can relax in your chair. But I should've put a stop to the nonsense when I heard the story."

"How did they die?"

"I don't know," said Isabella. "I just assumed they died in the fire. Perhaps it's time to try to figure that out."

"We have another problem," added Ava. "In the reports last night, I noticed a notation by the evening Front Desk shift. Guests have been reporting strange noises in the dead of the night. Already, five guests have checked out. One woman departed during teatime. She yelled across the lobby that she never intended to set foot in this haunted hotel again."

"That's not all," replied Theo. "The guest room above wasn't the only room with water left running. It just happened to be the room with the most damage. Three other guests returned to their rooms and reported the water running or a broken pipe leaving water damage. Dale has fans running in the affected guest rooms. The Front Desk has moved the guests to other rooms. I've upgraded their room type and issued drink and dining credits to help soften the inconvenience. I've ordered the maintenance crew to walk through any unoccupied rooms and suites and check for anything unusual."

"What's going on?" questioned Isabella.

"Well, it's not ghosts," he replied. "I asked Niles to look into the matter and find out if any of the staff is holding a grudge for something. Someone is undermining the hotel. I think they are trying to sink it one incident at a time."

Maddy let out a loud yawn and tossed her ringlets over her shoulder. "Can we talk about how I want to renovate this room?"

"Renovate this room?" inquired Theo. "What are you talking about?"

The teen jumped to her feet and with sweeping gestures she explained about turning the room into an upscale bar.

"Not happening Maddy." His tone was soft but his resolve was rock hard.

A thought suddenly occurred to Isabella. "Wait." She held her hand up. "That might not be such a bad idea."

Maddy squealed, jumped up and down and almost tipped her chair backward with her exuberance. She grabbed her by her hands, dragged her up and whirled her around. "See!" She taunted her brother. "I can see it now. 'Jacqueline's.' A bright pink and black theme. It'll be hot."

"The idea of a bar off the Grand Lobby is a wonderful idea. We could easily modify the Sitting Salon next door to this room. It also opens into the lobby. In the evenings, the guests could lounge in the comfort of the Grand Lobby with a glass of wine or liquor. Imagine, the grand piano playing softly in the background, guests winding down from their day and enjoying a drink before dinner or a light snack before retiring for the evening."

Vividly visualizing the scene Isabella created, Theo chimed in, "A polished oak bar, with brass beer taps. A couple comfortable sitting areas within the bar with deep leather couches and chairs for more intimate seating. You're right. The overflow of guests could spill into the lobby."

Her gaze glowed with the possibilities and her inner voice began to buzz. "We'd offer a lighter fare. Late night delectables only available from the Lobby Bar. A special blend of sweets, cheeses, breads and meats. Something special enough to entice the guests down out of their rooms for a little indulgence in the late evenings."

"And we'll call it—Jacqueline's." Maddy bounced up and down in her chair, excitement bubbling over.

"This is a lot to think over." Theo gave his sister a direct look. "We'll discuss the name, Maddy. Why don't you and Dale work up a proposal and present it. He can help you price out the costs. Perhaps, we can do the work in-house." Shifting subjects, he addressed Isabella. "Would you work up a couple sample menus for the new Lobby Bar?"

My first menu. A giddy thrill vibrated through her body and she barely controlled herself from imitating Maddy and bouncing up and down in her seat. "I—I'd love to."

Different ideas flashed through her mind. She gazed into Theo's steely eyes, somehow he believed in her. Even after her multitude of failures.

CHAPTER TWENTY-SEVEN

*L*ater that night, Isabella ambled through the varying shades of darkness, only broken by the hidden lights that cast a soft glow on the brick walkway. Lifting her face towards the starlit sky, she enjoyed the soft spray of raindrops upon her upturned face. She loved the solitude of after-hours.

Enveloped in a fluffy, white, Twin Springs robe, she approached the white picket fence that surrounded the Hot Springs pool area and halted at the matching gate. The opening was bookended by twin octagon bathhouses. She reached into a crack in the women's bathhouse outer wall, pulled out a small key and unlocked the gate. With a satisfied grunt, she slipped the key back into the hidy-hole and entered.

Soft lights gleamed up from the edges of the pool. The illuminated steam hovered above the still water. She rubbed her aching arms from helping Marc scrub the huge quantity of pots and pans left over from dinner service. Her body betrayed her. "So much for my declaration to Theo about not having puny arms."

The sound of her flip-flops slapping against her bare feet was drowned out by the rushing water of the large waterfall. "Besides, what good is it to be owner—" she corrected herself, "part owner, if you can't sneak into the Hot Springs pool late at night? After the rush of that dinner service, I need—" She shook her head. "No, I deserve a little pampering."

Dropping her robe on one of the white ladder-back lounge chairs, she kicked off her flip-flops and sat at the edge of the pool. The water swirled below. The underwater lights changed from blue, to green, to white and back again. Suddenly unsure of her decision, her heart felt heavy in her chest. "What am I afraid of? I swim in this pool every morning," she whispered to herself. Did the darkness subconsciously remind her of the last time with Theo? "He wouldn't dare mess with me. I'm a grown woman. Stronger, more mature, and tougher." Defiantly, she raised her arm to flex her muscles and winced with pain. Her arm fell to her side. "Maybe not so tough."

Nibbling on her bottom lip, she dipped a toe into the wet, welcoming warmth. She contemplated the powerful water and wanted to soothe her body within its heat, but she was still unsure. Pounding filled her ears from the strength of her heart beating within her chest.

"Isabella."

She paused, lifted her head. *Did the steam whisper my name?* She shook her head. *Foolish.* She leaned forward, braced herself and slid into the water. Embraced by its warmth, she trailed her arms through its weight, pushing it, feeling the water's drag and pull. "As long as I don't place my head completely beneath the surface, I'll be fine."

She floated over to one of the mini waterfalls, perched upon the smooth underwater shelf and allowed the water's pulsing force to soothe her aching shoulders and neck. A low moan escaped her lips. "How could something so comforting be so evil, so dangerous?"

The sensation of the cool rain falling lightly upon her face combined with the warm heat of the springs hypnotized her. Her eyelids drifted closed. The soreness abandoned her body. Finally, she relaxed.

CHAPTER TWENTY-EIGHT

*S*itting on the mossy seat and leaning back against the ivy, Theo watched her. The falling water of the waterfall blurred her image. At first, he thought she was a guest unaware that the pool was closed for the evening. Once she dropped the robe, his body instantly recognized hers. The silky feel of her skin pressing against him from his youth, invaded his heart and mind. "Isabella."

Bits of a green bikini struggled to cover her gorgeous curves. The water lapped against her soft breasts and he thirsted. His mouth suddenly dry, he swallowed hard. His fingers itched and his body throbbed. He hesitated, unsure if it was too late to make his presence known. Should he remain hidden or call out? He opened his mouth, but no sound came forth. He swallowed again, trying to moisten his vocal cords to speak.

The rushing, mini waterfall tumbled upon her smooth shoulders and moistened her neckline. The hot steam caused the falling blonde locks of her hair to curl and cling to her wet neck. Slipping beneath the water, he swam towards her. Under the water, her skin glowed in the light.

I'll just surprise her.

He reached out, brushing his fingers against her ankle and

surfaced before her. She flailed her arms and slipped beneath the water. Swiftly, he grabbed her by the arms and dragged her up. Chuckling, he received a dose of water to the face. His laughter stopped abruptly as she turned into a wild cat within his arms, flinging her arms wildly and kicking against him.

"Isabella, Isabella, it's me. Theo."

Digging her nails into his skin, she dragged them across his neck and chest. He inhaled sharply from the pain and released her, backing up out of the reach of her nails.

Her flailing feet brushed against the bottom of the pool. She gained her footing and pushed her soaked hair back from her face.

"What were you doing?" She turned on him and pelted him with her fists. "I hate you. I hate you." She pounded him.

"I didn't mean for you to go under. Isabella, I'm sorry."

"You're sorry? It's just like before." She pushed him away from her. "Anytime I let you get close, this is what you do. You take my greatest fear and shove it down my throat."

"I should've let you know I was there. I didn't mean for you to go under. I don't know what I was thinking." He raked his hand through his hair. "I just wanted to come up in front of you and… and… I don't know. I wasn't thinking."

Swallowing huge gulps of air, she struggled to catch her breath and calmed her racing heart. She glared at him as she attempted to rub away the pressure in her chest. "It's just like before. I shared with you, I opened my heart to you and told you about my dreams."

Theo stood still, stunned for a moment and at a complete loss of what she was talking about. He thought back, remembering the last time he was in this pool with her. He recalled her talking with him, telling him things. He was sort of listening, but he was thinking more about how to get her to let him touch her soft skin. He remembered that she smelled slightly of the hot springs but mostly of vanilla and the combination drove him crazy. *God, what did Isabella tell me? Something about the water. Yes. And something about a dream. A dream about…about…what?*

He remembered hearing someone coming and panicking. He didn't want to be caught with her by his father or, worse, her father. *A dream.* Suddenly it hit him. *A dream about drowning.* Shock and realization covered his face. "Oh my God, I'm sorry. I forgot."

"You forgot? You forgot?" she growled at him. "Did you also forget pulling me under the water then too? Holding me under?" Her growl intensified and she launched herself at him. One of her small fists latched onto his ear and the other a clump of his hair. She shoved his head under the water.

He choked on the warm, spring water. He circled one of his arms around her shoulders and the other under her knees. Holding her secured like a baby in his arms, he carried her squirming body back to the side of the pool and sat on one of the under water shelves with her upon his lap. Finally, he understood why she hated him. But he was at a loss as to how to prove his innocence.

"Look at me." He implored, as she struggled against him. "Please, look at me." Another growl rumbled from her chest, but she met his gaze. Her eyes resembled shards of cut green glass. "I swear, I swear on my life that I didn't pull you under the water all those years ago."

"Yeah, right."

"I swear. I wasn't even paying attention to what you were telling me."

Her eyes widened and she began struggling again.

"Please, I didn't mean it that way. I can't explain. I listened but I was, I guess you could say, caught up in the moment and not hearing your exact words." He looked beseechingly down at her. "It was stupid of me just now. Acting like a kid, coming up on you in that way. I'm sorry." He searched for understanding within her stunning face. How could someone hurt the beautiful creature before him? His eyes swept from her delicate face to her soggy hair in a knotted mess on the side of her head. She reminded him of a drowned kitten. And he left her unprotected. "Can you forgive me?"

"Release me and we'll see."

He eyed her warily. "Are you going to hit and scratch me again?"

She glanced at the ragged, red scratches across his body. Her cheeks glowed red. She turned her head away and mumbled, "We'll see."

Realizing her reply was more than he deserved, he released his hold.

She pushed herself away from him.

The hot springs water rushed between them and felt cold compared to the warmth of her body. She studied him, far out of his reach. He held his breath and waited.

"Don't touch me again," she spit out. "Promise me."

He closed his eyes. *Please don't ask me that.* Not knowing if it was a vow he could keep, he looked her straight in the eye and said, "I promise. On my honor as a Beaumont."

She swam over and perched herself on the shelf beside him, but not too close, maintaining more than an arm's length between them. Her breasts heaved against the water as she tried to calm her breathing.

Shame poured over his shoulders and flowed into his heart. *I did that to her.*

Leaning his head back against the rocks, he rubbed his face with his wet hands. Bile worked its way up the back of his throat, and he swallowed hard. "It won't happen again." His voice sounded hard and rough in his own ears. "I swear." He cleared his throat. "I'm sorry, Isabella. I swear on everything I love and hold dear that I didn't pull you under the water when we were younger."

"I heard you laughing, when I emerged," she whispered back.

"It wasn't me. Ask Maddy. She wouldn't leave my room so I could come back. She taunted me about telling Mom and Dad."

She turned towards him. "Then who was it?" Her eyes shimmered with unshed tears.

"I don't know. But it wasn't me. Maybe someone else was at the pool that night. Perhaps, whoever it was, hid behind the waterfall where we couldn't see him."

"Another person observed us? Listened to us? Someone other than Maddy?"

"Someone else must've been here." He felt sick with shame. To know he watched her earlier, just like the person who tormented her years before. His stomach rolled with revulsion. "A man would've stayed. Instead, I left you. And you faced whoever hid here alone. I'll never abandon you again, Isabella. I promise."

She leaned in and touched his hand beneath the water with her fingertips. "I believe you."

"Do you want to tell me again about your dream? I'll listen this time."

She snorted, "Yeah, right."

He racked his brain on how to help her understand and forgive him. How to mend the hurt that built up over time. "What if, I share something with you? A memory so painful that I've never told anyone else before?"

She remained quiet for a moment. "Maybe."

Tipping his head back against the smooth river rocks lining the pool, Theo closed his eyes. The rain fell lightly upon his face. "It happened five years ago." Held in for so long, the words clogged his throat. But he pushed them through. "We drove away from Twin Springs in a snowstorm. Miserable, I sat in the back seat trying to figure out what I did to make you give me the cold shoulder." With a wry twist of his lips, he cracked open an eye to look at her. "Guess I know now. Maddy chomped at the bit, giving me sly looks and tattling to my parents about us in the Hot Springs pool nights before. We wound our way down the steep mountain incline." Once he opened up to her, the dam broke and he couldn't hold the words, nor the emotions, back. His chest shuddered with suppressed sobs but the words flooded from his mouth. He told her about the car flying over the mountain, crashing through the trees. About waking and finding his father. "His last words were 'Take care of the girls.' And then he was gone."

Theo rubbed his face with his wet hands before he continued. "Then I looked up and found my mom. She too was dead." He averted his head. Tears ran down his face. He sniffled and wiped them away. Couldn't bear for her to witness his failure as a man and discover the terrified boy he hid beneath the surface.

He cleared his throat. "In the distance, the birds began chirping again and I heard Maddy crying. Climbing off the side of the car, I moved to comfort her. I sat next to her and pulled her into my arms. Sitting in the snow, I held her while she sobbed. Our parents were gone."

The scene cleared from his mind's eye. He could still hear Maddy weeping. His heart ached from the pain in his soul. Glancing around, he shook his head to clear the haunting sound. However, the crying wasn't Maddy, but Isabella.

"I'm so sorry, Theo." She reached out and grasped his hand. "I understand how much it hurts to lose your parents."

"You don't get it. I caused my parents' accident. I fought with my dad. Distracted him." Emotions welled up in him, threatened to consume him. "I killed them. It was all my fault."

"No," she squeezed his hand and scooted closer. "It was an accident. A terrible, unfortunate accident."

He listened to her words, but in his heart he knew the truth. He killed his proud, strong father. Murdered his beautiful, loving mom. He made Maddy an orphan. And no matter what he did or how hard he tried he could never right that wrong. He rubbed her hand with his thumb. Pushed down the emotions. Cemented them away to be dealt with later. The warm water flowed around them, circling them. "I'm sorry about your father, too."

Rain fell softly around them, enveloping them in a private world. She nodded. Sniffling, Isabella again told him about her dreams. Theo realized her trust was a precious gift. This time, he listened intently to her every word as he held her delicate hand within his.

CHAPTER TWENTY-NINE

Emotionally drained, Theo intended to pass by the Front Desk and continue up to his room. He raised a hand in greeting to the two young ladies working behind the desk and avoided Ava's intense gaze.

Noticing his damp hair, she called out, "Kind of late for a swim in the pool."

He halted mid stride, hesitated and turned back.

Ava leaned her elbows against the Front Desk's long, granite countertop, her long ponytail draping over her shoulder and brushing the black surface as she rested her chin in her hands. "It's kind of fun catching the hard nose, no nonsense Mr. Beaumont breaking the rules." Amusement crinkled the smooth skin at the corners of her eyes. In a low, stern voice she added, "Sir, the Hot Springs pool closes promptly at nine p.m."

He sighed and tugged at his cuff sleeves. "What makes you think I just came from the pool?"

Her spontaneous laughter filled the Grand Lobby. "Can you give me another reason why you are soaking wet, this late?"

"Do you interrogate all the guests who—"

A high-pitched scream pierced the air. He recognized the sound from his recently resurrected memories. "Maddy!"

He whipped around and raced towards the General's office with Ava trailing close behind.

Bursting through the doors, he scanned the office for his sister. In a chair with her knees pulled up tight to her chest and her arms wrapped around her black slacks, Maddy hysterically sobbed. Her pink scarf was discarded on the floor at her bare feet. A tall, well-built man in tattered jeans and a filthy work shirt leaned over her.

White-hot rage coursed through Theo. He grabbed the man by the collar and dragged him away. He pulled his arm back to smash the stranger's face in with his fist, but his arm froze in mid air, unable to proceed. The man before him, if you could call him that, was grossly mutilated by burns down the right side of his face. Sandy haired stubble covered the left side, while sparse patches of hair sprouted between the scars and razed skin on the right. The upper portion of his right ear shriveled and curved, melting back into his head.

"Too ugly to punch, huh? Even to protect this little girl?" the stranger taunted, before thrusting a stunned Theo away from him.

Ava placed her slender hand on Theo's shoulder and pulled him further away. "Theo, this is Dale's oldest son, Logan. He's the one who's been supervising the men remodeling the spa." She glided up to the burned man and kissed him on his mutilated cheek.

Logan jerked away, as if she scalded him. "Don't pretend, Ava. It's not funny." He limped over to the desk, turning the burnt side of his face away from everyone's view. He drew his baseball cap down low over his face and hunched up his shoulders. "Damn tinnitus causes ringing in my ears. I didn't hear the girl in the room. Otherwise, I wouldn't have entered."

Theo stared at him in shock. *My God how could a human being endure that much pain?* Embarrassed by his actions, he held out his hand, "Theo Beaumont. This is my sister, Maddy. I've missed you every time I checked in at the spa."

Logan ignored his outstretched hand for a moment and then

shrugged. He extended his mangled right hand and waited for his response.

Theo grasped the two fingers and thumb that constituted his hand. "A pleasure to meet you. Thank you for coming in to help with the repairs to Twin Springs."

His baby blue eyes glittered in response. "You say that now. Wait till I scare all the guests away."

Ava gasped, "Logan, don't say that."

Staring at the back wall, Logan refused to respond.

Disgusted by the humiliation his actions and Maddy's caused the burnt man, Theo zeroed in on his sister, still crying into her arms. "Maddy, come shake Logan's hand."

She shook her head and pushed her hands deep into her armpits. "No!"

He resisted the urge to jerk her up and force her to shake the burnt soldier's hand.

Wanting to defuse the situation and lesson everyone's embarrassment, Ava addressed the young girl. "Maddy, what were you doing in the General's room this late?"

"Great," she slouched further down in the chair, "now I have two older siblings. And my name is Jacqueline!"

Logan chuckled, enjoying her response. "Glad to see the girl's still got spirit, even after seeing my ugly mug."

"Shut up!" The teen refused to turn her head in his direction.

"Maddy!" Ava and Theo exclaimed.

The burnt man laughed harder and waved off the other two's protests. "Look little girl," he focused in on her out of the corner of his good eye. "Either you answer Ava or I'll come over there and ask you the question."

She sat straight up and words tumbled from her lips. "I was searching for the General's gems. In the painting, I noticed each of the sisters owned a beautiful piece of jewelry. I wanted to find them," she blurted out.

"What are you talking about?" Theo was completely exasperated with her attitude.

"The painting." She pointed up at the General's daughters. "The hair of Ava's twin is swept back by a ruby and diamond jeweled headband, Isabella's twin wears an emerald necklace surrounded by diamonds. The redhead wears a gorgeous amethyst and diamond necklace looped around her neck and dangling down her front. Each jewel matches each girl's name. I wanted to see if the General stashed the jewelry here in his room."

Logan refused to turn his face towards the painting, but Ava and Theo stood fascinated.

"She's right," replied Ava. "Each sister does own a stunning piece of jewelry."

"Doesn't mean the gems didn't burn up with the girls in the fire," inserted Logan. "Fire destroys everything of value."

Shocked, no one was able to answer him.

A knock sounded at the door. Cracking the door open, one of the Front Desk employee's poked her head into the room. "Mr. Beaumont, you wanted me to let you know when Mr. Cummings checked in."

Theo thanked her and she quickly closed the door.

"Who's Mr. Cummings?" asked Maddy.

Distracted, Theo removed the silver pen from his breast pocket and twirled the slender cylinder through his fingers. He took in Logan's dirty clothes. "Have I seen you? Out in the woods?"

"Maybe," grunted the man. "My family owns the farm next to Twin Springs."

His sister repeated the question. "Who's Mr. Cummings?"

Frustrated by his sister's pestering, he replied, "He's the investigator sent by the insurance company processing our claims. The company seems to feel that Twin Springs is filing fraudulent claims due to the unusual number of accidents reported."

Maddy blurted out, "they think we're lying?"

Ava's eyes narrowed. "They're questioning our claims?" She peeped out the door and noticed a balding, middle-aged man checking in. Closing the door she addressed the room, her head thrown back with confidence. "I'll take care of this."

Releasing her hair from its binding, she bent at the waist and flipped her hair over. She fluffed her silky black mane with her fingers. Flipping her hair back, she continued primping by releasing the top three buttons of her shirt. She pulled the fabric back at her shoulders and exposed the rounded tops of her full breasts. Opening the door, Ava became a completely different person. She rolled her hips forward and tipped her chin up and back. With the tip of her tongue, she wetted her top lip and rubbed her lips together. A sultry, welcoming smile curved her moist lips. Tossing a wink over her shoulder, she closed the door behind her.

"The insurance investigator will never know what hit him," replied Logan. Quickly, he escaped the room, leaving Theo to deal with his sister.

Theo's pen slipped from his loose fingers. "Don't ever do that, Maddy." He actually felt a little sorry for his fellow man. "Go to your room. We'll discuss how you acted later. Right now, I need to figure out if I am supposed to protect Twin Springs, Ava or the poor insurance investigator." He strode from the room.

CHAPTER THIRTY

Her hair still damp from the pool, Isabella shifted under the covers as the dream formed in her mind.

"Emma, did the Lieutenant hurt you?" asked Jean Claude Flamme, the Executive Chef of Twin Springs. He scrunched down to peer into her light green eyes, so different from his. He longed to pull her tiny frame close and comfort her, but he knew the dangers for her, and him, if he gave in to his cravings. The consequences of touching a colored servant like him, would be greater than a sore arm and a burn.

"It's nothing." She flexed her arm and moved it about. "I think." She blinked back tears and stared down at her throbbing hand.

"Let me see that." He took her small hand in his, noticing the stark difference between her pale skin lying across his large, ebony hand. Red and angry, the meaty part of her palm already bubbled in places. Reaching over her head, he pulled down a tin of lard. Twisting the lid off, he dipped his fingers into the pale yellow goo and smoothed a thick swab across her palm. Then, he wrapped a clean towel around her hand and wiped his hands off on another. Leaning closer, he flicked off the stove behind her. "You should know better than to confront the Lieutenant."

With his body mere inches from hers, her breath caught and held. Her gaze flowed over Jean Claude, admiring the high cheekbones in his handsome face and his broad shoulders looking strong in his crisp, white chef's jacket. He and his white jacket represented everything she wished for, but was not allowed to have or do.

Resentment built within her. "But why? Why can't I cook in the kitchen? I love cooking. The sounds, the smells, the energy. Cooking is like air to me. Essential to my life. You can be an Executive Chef and you're a colored man. Why can't I do what I want?" She held her towel wrapped hand close to her chest and beseechingly gazed up into his cloudy eyes. The pain in her hand was nothing compared to the pain in her heart.

Jean Claude compared his thin, black pants and white chef jacket to her finery. "We all have stations in life. There are things we can't change and the sooner we accept that fact, the better off we'll be."

Stumbling forward, she pressed her body closer to his. "Are you talking about us?" she whispered.

Turning, he strode away from her, creating a safe space between the two of them. He leaned against the wall. "I might as well be. You and I both know there can be no us. It doesn't matter what we feel, how great our love. It matters how society sees us."

Emma listened to his words, but her heart denied them. "I can't believe it. I won't." Her silk clad toe silently tapped on the wooden floor. Words flowed from her mouth, one after the other. "We're perfect together. We enjoy our love of creating with food. We—" She rushed forward, stepping in close to him with her eyes downcast. "Well, when you're near I can't think of anyone else. I'll be with no one else." Her words were warm in the air, hanging like the fragrance of vanilla that constantly surrounded her and followed in her wake.

Shaking his head to clear it, Jean Claude buried his hands deep in his front pockets. "You can't talk like that. You have a future. You'll marry a rich dandy just like the General wants. Just like your sister, Ame, did. "

"No!" She shook her head. "You're wrong!" Her cheeks flamed hot. "Ame didn't marry Everett for his money. She married him because he is soft spoken, gentle and smart." She sighed, thinking of her sister's young husband. "Everett's everything Ame ever wanted."

"And the fact that his family's stinking rich had nothing to do with it?" Jean Claude laughed, mocking her naive view. "Until now, nothing

has been denied to you and your sisters. But even the privileged few have rules. All you girls will marry. And just like your sister, Ame, those men will be from an upper crust family. Rich and white."

She considered his words. The cold-hearted truth rang true. "If we can't change my world, we can run away and I can live in yours."

He rubbed his hands across his face, searching for a way to make her understand. "What do you know of my world? Of constantly being aware of your lowered station, of biting your tongue when you know a faster and easier way to do something? If you do offer advice, the only response is to be slapped down and told not to mock your 'betters'. Then, to find out a few days later that the man who is so much better than you, is now toting your idea as his?" He looked off towards the sounds of the music. "Taking your office and your concepts as his own."

She gasped. "The General has never stolen an idea from anyone."

He gazed down at her sadly, resentful that he must burst her picture of the world. "No, he hasn't. The General's a good man but, outside this hotel, outside your little world, he's just that, a man. Slave to the dictates of society just like you and I. Even the great General couldn't weather the storm if one of his daughters married a colored man. You all would be shunned by the social elite. They'd no longer come to Twin Springs with their money and power and the Grand Dame would shrivel up and die, a forgotten old maid in the mountains."

Emma bit her lip, tears of frustration filling her eyes. "But you're only half black."

He laughed. Bitterness coated his tongue and filled his mouth. "There's no such thing as being half black. Just like there is no such thing as half dead. And that's what we'd be. Dead. If not literally, you'd be dead to everyone you know and love. Besides, what has my white half gotten me? Surely not you. You're so foolish. Go back to your perfect, pristine world where everything's handed to you. Be happy with what you have and stay away from me and out of my kitchen. There are things going on here that you can't handle and will never understand." He turned and strode away from her.

Suddenly chilled, she stood still and gazed after Jean Claude, his shoulders proudly erect as he disappeared from her small world and left her future dreary and bleak. She gathered up a fist full of fabric and beads and squeezed them tight. A part of her wanted to run to her room in the Tower, collapse on her bed and cry with frustration. But she wanted him more. She needed him. Without Jean Claude, her life felt bland and tasteless. "But, I love you." Her words sounded feeble in her own ears.

Jean Claude halted. Hanging his head low between his slumped shoulders, he paused, then, turned. Swiftly he returned to her, his long legs eating up the distance between them. He gathered her up by her delicate shoulders and brought her close to his heat. "Tell me how much you love me when we're not welcome in my world or yours. When you're so hungry you think your stomach is grinding against your spine in protest. When your children are teased, mocked and shunned. How great will your love for me be then?"

Pushing her against the wall, he dipped his hand into the v-neck of her dress and cupped her soft breast. Transfixed, they both stared down at her creamy white breast cupped in his hand. A glowing star laying in a nighttime sky. "How much do you love me?" His voice caressed her. "Realizing, that if I was caught touching you like this..." Lowering his head, he sucked gently on her nipple. His lips curved in sorrow as the blushing bud puckered in response. "Even if we were married, they'd hang me. Where would you be then, your belly swollen with my seed?"

"I don't care!" she declared, drawing his head down, pressing her lips to his.

His heart slammed against his rib cage in response to her touch, but he lifted his head from hers until their lips were separated by a breath. "You even kiss like a child," he mocked. "You want a taste of the real world? I'll give it to you." He ground his mouth down on hers.

She whimpered beneath his assault.

The sound of her distress squeezed his heart and tested his resolve. He couldn't do it. He couldn't harden his heart to her, even to teach her a lesson. His lips softened and his tongue delved into her hot sweetness, licking and tasting her as if she was one of the masterpieces he created in the kitchen. He kneaded her soft breast, gently plucking at the taut nipple with his thumb and forefinger.

Above the music emanating from the Main Dining Room, sharp clicks registered in the back of his mind. Caught up in the smell and taste of her, he ignored the warning sounds. Over the roar of blood rushing through his system and the beating of his heart, he heard Emma's name being called.

The fog of her within his head lifted. Opening his eyes, he was awe struck by her beauty. Her head tipped back, her black lashes rested lightly on the milky skin of her cheekbones and her breath was heavy out of her parted lips. Regretfully, he tucked her breast back into her bodice.

"Jean Claude, 'La Flamme', your flame burns me." She whimpered and tried to pull his head back down. "Please," she whimpered again.

Hearing the Lieutenant's sharp steps, he grabbed Emma by her unburnt hand and roughly jerked her.

Surprised, she called out, her eyes popping open, and she stumbled forward.

He placed his finger over her lips. "Shush," he whispered. "The Lieutenant will hear us." He tugged harder. "Come with me."

He dragged her through the kitchen and down the hall to an office that used to be his Executive Chef's office but now belonged to the Lieutenant.

"No." She dug in her heels and pulled back from his firm hold. "We'll be trapped. Then how will we explain being together?"

"Trust me," he replied, squeezing her hand.

She stared into his charcoal gray eyes, her heart beating so hard in her chest that she thought it might explode. But she trusted no other more than Jean Claude. She followed him into the Lieutenant's office and to a dead end.

Gently, so as not to make a noise, he closed the door shut behind them and locked it. Quickly, he crossed the room and stepped up on the platform where the Lieutenant's desk sat.

"What are you doing?" Emma questioned softly.

Ignoring her, he pulled a drawer out of the hutch above the roll top desk and stuck his arm into the cubby all the way up to his elbow.

Emma gasped as the whole platform moved and revealed a hidden room within.

He replaced the drawer and jumped off the platform, grabbing Emma's good hand and dragging her into the hidden room. Reaching out to the left, he flicked a switch and the room lit up by a solitary light bulb, dangling from a wire that ran across the ceiling and down one wall.

Eyes wide, she examined the room. The back wall was lined with floor to ceiling shelves. On the left, a plain, wooden desk was covered with stacks of money. Stretching high across the wall, above the money laden desk, hung a lone shelf stacked with books. On the right hand side of the room stood a scully sink and stove. Wooden crates filled with mason jars were stacked high in the middle of the room.

Jean Claude tugged her across the room and pushed her down behind one of the slap wood crates. "Stay here."

"No. No." Emma shook her head. "You'll be trapped in the other room." Huge tears rolled down her face and dripped off her chin. "The Lieutenant will kill you if he finds you in his office."

He removed the satin scarf from around her hair and gently wiped the tears from her delicate skin. "He'll kill us both, if he finds us together."

Her chest began to hitch with sobs. She shook her head and clutched his white coat within her fist. "Stay with me. Perhaps he won't look in here. We'll both be safe in here," she implored.

Dropping the satin fabric on the dirty floor beside them, he pried her small fist from his coat. Holding her hand gently within his, he kissed the tips of her fingers with his firm lips. "I can't take the chance that he'll find you. Don't you understand? I'd rather die than have you hurt." Inhaling her sweet vanilla scent, he kissed the tear silently rolling down her face. Tasting the salt of it, he leaned his forehead against hers. "I love you, Emma."

His shoulders slumped, defeated with his declaration. "I love you more than life." He drew back and stared into her beautiful green eyes, her black lashes glittering with tears. Tears for him. For them. "If you love me," he murmured, "stay here. Stay quiet and don't move. Don't move, no matter what you hear from the other room. Then, when you can't hear any sounds, still don't move. Wait. Wait until you hear the Tower's clock sound midnight and I come for you. If I don't return, then pull the metal lever beneath the light switch up and the door will open again." He gently, but firmly, squeezed her fingers. "Emma, do you hear me?"

"Yes," she answered, openly crying beside him.

"Good. Don't forget to push the desk back against the wall when you leave. Push it till it clicks. Do you understand?"

"Yes, yes, till it clicks," she repeated.

He heard a key rattle in the office door. "Quiet," he reminded her, pressing a finger against her lips before kissing her goodbye. Then, he left her.

He pushed the desk back just as the door opened to the office covering the sound of the click.

"What the hell are you doing in my office?" roared the Lieutenant, his boots ringing out as he crossed the floor.

"I came in to see you, Sir."

"You did huh, boy?" He smirked. "Then why was the door locked?"

Jean Claude shrugged. "It must have locked behind me."

"You want to lie to me boy? Do you think I'm stupid?"

Emma heard fists meeting flesh in the other room. She listened, horrified, as Jean Claude allowed himself to be beaten for her.

The Lieutenant bellowed, "Are you trying to steal from me?"

"No sir. Truly, the door was open when I entered." Jean Claude's voice sounded calm and steady when he replied.

Emma jumped when the thud of a body slammed against the desk on the other side of the secret door. She pressed her knuckles and the kitchen cloth tightly against her mouth so as not to make a sound.

"You want more of that boy?" the Lieutenant bit out. "Are you snooping where you shouldn't?"

"No sir. Miss Ruby asked me to get you. She had a question that only you could answer."

"You telling the truth?"

"Yes, sir!" Jean Claude's strong voice sounded out.

Silence filled the air. "Well, then."

She could tell the Lieutenant was satisfied by Jean Claude's answers. "Miss Ruby needs my help." His voice sounded smug to her ears. "Get the hell out of my office." The sound of a slap on skin vibrated through the door. "Don't you come in here again. Do you understand me?"

"Yes, sir."

She listened to the outer office door close. Letting out a sigh of relief, she quickly re-covered her mouth with her hands when the Lieutenant moved around outside. His boots scraped as he crossed the planked floor towards her and he stepped up onto the wooden platform. She held her breath, waiting to be discovered. The squeak of his chair and the rustling of papers sounded overly loud in the silence. Obviously, he wasn't in a hurry to see what her sister needed.

For what seemed like hours, she crouched down on the dirty wooden floor, her legs aching from her cramped position. Ever so gingerly, she shifted to sit more comfortably. Her back brushed against one of the crates behind her and the glass jars within chimed. She stilled, waiting, listening.

His movements were overly loud, as if they were both trapped inside a tin can. The tapping of a pencil on wood, the course sound of a match being lit, all blended in with the thick, beating drum of her heart throbbing inside her ears. The acrid scent of his cigar wafted over her, suppressing her senses. Softly, in the back of her mind, she hummed the song she danced to earlier.

Placing her moist forehead upon her knees, she rocked herself, the beads on her dress swaying with her. She squeezed herself tighter and tried to block out the sounds from the other room. Retreating into another world, she pictured herself and Jean Claude in their own restaurant cooking and creating marvelous dishes together. Fueled by her imagination, a magical world of smells and images swirled through her consciousness. And Emma waited. . .

CHAPTER THIRTY-ONE

ith the peal of a clock tower ringing in her ears, Isabella woke. She rolled over in her warm blankets and grabbed her cell phone from the antique bedside table, clicking it on to check the time. *Midnight.* "It can't be." Surrounded by darkness, she collapsed back into the pillows and brooded. "What a crazy dream."

Lightning flashed and lit up her room. The light rain she'd enjoyed earlier at the Hot Springs pool, now pelted hard against the windowpanes. She tasted Emma's fear in her mouth. "It was just a dream. Nothing more, just another dream.

"Dreams aren't real. They hold no power, no truth. Make believe." She dragged the covers over her head and mumbled to herself under the mound of blankets. "Get sleep. Only a few hours till breakfast prep. Need rest." Determinedly, she drew the covers tighter around her. "Just another dream," she sighed and yawned.

Images of Emma and Jean Claude filtered past her eyelids and her heart ached for them. "I wonder, did he come back for her?" She groaned and threw back the covers. "I have to see. I have to find out if the room is truly there."

She cast off her blue t-shirt and tossed it on the bed, pulled on a pair of black skinny jeans, one of her white tank tops and slid her feet into tennis shoes. She slipped her pass key and cell phone into her back pocket and secured her long hair, still damp from the pool, into a loose knot high on her head.

For the first time in her life, fear gripped her in its powerful grasp as she traveled down to the kitchen. Twin Springs seemed darker, less welcoming. The shadows within the corners of the hallway lengthened and whispered warnings to her. "It was just a dream. It was just a dream." She pulled open the stairwell door leading down to the kitchens. It felt heavy in her hand and emitted an eerie squeak. "Shake it off. Just a dream."

Her soft-soled shoes made no sound across the black and white blocked, vinyl kitchen floor. She progressed from the sleek, stainless steel counters, through the swinging doors and down the back hall towards the Executive Chef's room.

Pausing before the heavy oak door, she rubbed her breastbone with the heel of her hand. The smell of burnt vanilla filled her nostrils and she glanced over her shoulder thinking about the stove tops in the kitchen. Nothing was lit. She was sure of it. Turning back, she thrust the door open and surveyed the room. Her gaze locked on the large, pigeon hole desk. Taking a deep breath and squaring her shoulders, she crossed the room and stepped up on the platform. Pulling out the rolling chair, she sat down in front of the large, oak desk. For a moment she remained seated, staring at the different drawers, and thinking back to the dream. "It seemed so real."

But the particulars of the dream had already started to fade from her memory. She examined the hutch above the roll top desk. All the drawers were pushed in. She pulled out the middle drawer and reached into the hole behind the drawer, almost up to her armpit. She felt around. The tips of her trembling fingers touched the coolness of an oblong metal knob. Gasping, she snatched her hand back to her chest. In a weak voice she insisted, "It was just a dream."

Once again, she reached her hand into the drawer's opening, this time allowing her fingers to curl around the oval knob. She tugged. Nothing happened. She laughed under her breath and shook her head. "See, just a stupid dream. Just like the dream of me drowning. Nothing to be worried or afraid about. Dreams can't hurt anyone." An uneasy chuckle escaped her lips. "I'm clearly going crazy."

She started to remove her arm, but paused. Without conscious thought, she shoved her hand again into the hole and strained to reach all the way to the back, until she again grasped the handle, and twisted with all her might.

Silently and swiftly the platform moved. She grasped the desktop with both hands and planted her feet hard on the platform. When it came to a stop, she didn't move. Her breath came in quick gasps and her knuckles were white tipped from clutching the edge of the desk. Slowly, she released her clinched grip, stood and stepped down from the platform.

A darkened doorway loomed before her. She stared into the darkness. Then, without hesitating, she blindly reached into the doorway with her left hand and flicked the switch. The solitary light bulb, hanging from a wire, flickered and then lit the room with a yellow glow. Her legs gave out beneath her and she clung to the doorframe. "It wasn't just a dream."

A light layer of dust covered the objects in the room, but the floor was swept clean. Instead of crates, cardboard boxes were piled high in the middle of the room. The back wall was lined with wooden shelves similar to her dream, but they were filled with plastic gallon jugs filled with what looked like water. On the left was the same, simple, wooden table. The shelf above was laden with dusty books and draped with cobwebs.

Unlike in her dream, the desk below the shelf wasn't covered with stacks of money, but piled high with papers. She walked closer. Behind the mounds of paper, stood a large, wide screen monitor. Between the desk and the shelf, hung a cork-board with pictures. She placed her hands on the smooth wood of the desk and leaned forward. There was a photo of herself at her high school graduation. Dressed in her black cap and gown, she stood between her father and sister, smiling into the camera. Her eyes widened and moved to a snapshot of her and Ava as young girls, sitting proudly on the backs of two horses at the stables. Layers of photos of her and Ava were tacked to the cork.

Scattered amongst the pictures, someone thumbtacked an array of newspaper clippings. Yellowed with age and dated January 1st, 1929, the headline of one clipping read, "New Year's Eve Fire At Twin Springs, Tower Destroyed." She scanned the next clippings—a review of one of Ava's performances in high school and another on one of her performances on Broadway. Her eyes locked on a newspaper clipping covering the death of Theo and Maddy's parents. She gazed in disbelief at each picture, the words blurring before her. She shook her head. "How? Why?"

Then, she discovered a photo freshly printed on white paper, folded over and thumbtacked to the wall. It printed grainy, but she could clearly discern the photo's subjects and location. Of course she recognized the picture. She lived the moment captured in time only hours before. In black and white was a screen shot of herself in the pool with Theo. The two of them sitting side by side, talking. She stumbled back, as if she received a blow to the chest. She just stared at everything, digesting the implications. "Someone's watching us. All of us, and has been for a long time."

Isabella felt bare. All her secrets and special moments were now tarnished and stolen from her. She rubbed at the pressure building in her chest. "Who did this? What else have they spied on, and documented?"

Anger coursed through her veins. She leaned forward and scattered papers until she found a keyboard and mouse. She moved the mouse and the computer screen illuminated her face. She squinted, the glow of the computer overly bright in the dimly lit room. Live feeds of different rooms flashed across the screen. A picture of her sister, working the night auditor shift at the Front Desk, appeared. The screen shifted and the glow of the Hot Springs pool filled the screen. Next was a darkened room. She studied the screen, focusing in on the shapes. A large desk, couch and chairs. "The General's room!"

Moving on, the shiny counters of the kitchen filled the screen, then another darkened room. Isabella barely discerned the shape of an empty, rumpled bed. Horrified, she covered her mouth. "My room!"

The screen shifted and she observed Maddy, her usually tense body and uptight frame, soft with sleep. Fury boiled in her veins. "Someone's been watching Maddy!" Images from the Grand Lobby, Crystal Ballroom, Main Dining Room and Theatre filtered past and then repeated in an endless loop. She pulled out the desk's chair and sat hard. "What else are you up to?"

She focused in on the piles of papers stacked on the table. Pealing back the layers, she uncovered old and new floor plans of the hotel, guests' portfolios and receipts. Her elbow hit a pile of items and knocked them off the table. The sound of breaking glass filled the air. She leaned down, picked up the picture frame and hissed when she sliced her finger on broken glass. She snatched her hand back and checked her finger, before she reached back down. This time she carefully picked up the picture frame and shook off the broken glass. "It's the picture from the General's room, the one with the Private, the Lieutenant, and the General. Why would someone steal this?"

She placed the picture back on the desk. A drop of blood dripped from her finger onto the wooden surface. She wiped the blood on her black pants, then, sucked on her throbbing fingertip as she searched. Scooting her chair back, she pulled out the middle drawer in the desk. Inside she discovered her recipe book. Lying across it was a satin, black scarf embroidered with emerald threads. She rolled the satin scarf between her thumb and finger-tips and admired the beautiful design of swirled flowers. "Emma's scarf."

Astonished, she hauled out both items. Even though she held her own book and the scarf within her two hands, she couldn't believe they were here, real and together. "They were supposed to just be dreams. Fiction not fact. Just my over-active imagination. Not real."

Placing her recipe book on the pile of papers, she gently laid Emma's satin scarf over top. She was about to close the drawer when she caught sight of the edge of something tan shoved into the back of the drawer. Leaning sideways in her chair, she shoved her arm all the way back into the furthest corner. Grasping what felt like the spine of a book, she pulled it out. Curious, she examined the book, turning it over in her hands. It was old, the pages yellowed. A leather string was tied around it to keep the pages intact. With her fingertips and short nails, she tried to pry the knot apart. Unsuccessful, she bent down and, using her teeth, she tugged at the knot. The bitter tang of aged leather coated the tip of her tongue. Loosening the knot, she discarded the string. Gently, she opened the book. "It's a journal."

Her nose twitched. The smell of burnt vanilla once again filled the air around her. Squinting at the illegible scrawl, she scarcely made out the words across the first page. "5 June, 1928. Journal Entry."

"Fascinating," she mumbled. Electricity shimmered in the air. The fine hair rose on the back of her neck. She stiffened and fear froze her in place. The sound of heavy breathing reached her ears. Breathing from within the room and directly behind her. Instinctively, she turned. She felt a rush of movement and caught a glimpse of a dark shadow from the corner of her eye before pain exploded across her cheek and radiated into her brain. Manic laughter vibrated across her consciousness as she submerged into darkness.

CHAPTER THIRTY-TWO

Theo fell to his knees beside Isabella's unconscious form. His heart slammed against his ribs as he leaned down and checked her pulse with the tips of his fingers. A steady beat throbbed beneath his fingertips. The air rushed from his body in relief. Brushing escaped strands of her beautiful blonde hair away from her face, he laid the backs of his fingers against her forehead and found her skin cool to the touch. "Isabella. Isabella," he called softly.

His throat closed up. "Oh God," he prayed, "please let her be alright. Damn it, I love her." He sunk to the grimy, wide planked, wooden floor next to his woman. Tenderly, he gathered her into his arms and settled her on his lap. He loved her. How the hell did that happen? Love was dangerous. Love meant commitment. Love meant unbearable pain if he couldn't watch out for her. Losing his mom had taught him that lesson.

Tenderly, he stroked stray blonde hairs away from her face. Her face was a mess with the cut in her hairline and the nicks from the windshield. His swiftly indrawn breath penetrated the quiet room. Her cheek was turning mottled shades of purple.

"What happened to you?

Did you fall?" The pads of his fingers lightly prodded her

cheek, feeling for broken bones. Without prior thought, he leaned down and placed his lips lightly upon her bruise in a kiss. "Isabella, can you hear me?"

She stirred in his arms, drawing his attention. Gradually, her dark lashes lifted and her eyes opened, only to close again. Her arched brows furrowed and her hand rose to her cheek, knocking him in the side of the head.

Her eyes popped open. A "sorry," involuntarily left her lips.

She covered her face with her hands and softly murmured. "It hurts to talk. Why does my head hurt so bad?" She looked up into his face and stiffened within his embrace, scooting to the side and landing hard on her rump and back upon her elbows.

Theo's heart fell into the pit of his stomach. She didn't trust him. How could he protect her without her trust and confidence? Reaching out, he prevented her head from hitting the wooden floor by placing his hand between the back of her head and the floor. "Careful."

"Oh, my head is killing me." Moaning, she sat up and rubbed her temples with her fingertips. Holding her hands over her face, she rocked back and forth on the floor before peeking up at him between her fingers. "What happened?"

"You tell me." Spurred into action by the fact she remained on the cold floor, he bounded up and grabbed the over turned chair. Wood screeched against wood as he dragged the chair upright.

Isabella winced, covering her ears as a soft moan escaped her lips.

Appalled at the added pain he caused her, Theo took her comfort into his own hands. Hooking one arm under her knees, the other around her, he lifted her and placed her on the chair. "Forgive me," he whispered in her ear. "I didn't mean for the chair to scrape the floor."

Moist blonde hair tumbling around her shoulders, Isabella slumped in the chair with her elbows on her knees. Burying her face in her hands, she mumbled, "I don't know what happened."

He shoved his hands deep into his pockets to keep himself from touching her again. "How did you find this room?"

"What room?" Her head lifted and slowly she inspected her surroundings. As her eyes adjusted, she began taking in the scene before her. The boxes, the desk, and the solitary light bulb. Recognition pierced her aching brain. "Oh, my God, it's real."

"It sure is. Why didn't you tell me this room was here?"

She cracked a smile. "I didn't know it was." Then she told them about her dream.

Blood rumbled between Theo's ears at her lack of common sense. His voice roared across the room. "So you came down to investigate it! By yourself?"

She covered her ears, wincing with pain.

Lowering his voice, he continued. "Let me see if I understand this correctly." He ticked each point off with a raised finger. "You came down. In the middle of the night. And investigated a secret room by yourself?"

"It seemed like a good idea at the time." She lifted her shoulder in a slight shrug.

He rushed out and returned with a kitchen towel filled with ice. Holding the pack gingerly against her head, he asked, "Did you slip?"

Quickly becoming exasperated with his interrogation, she snatched the icepack from him and waved her free hand around. "Look around you. What would I slip on?" She glared at him from beneath her icepack. "Why would I come get anyone? I thought I was nuts, losing it, cuckoo." She twirled her finger next to her temple. "I didn't expect to find anything."

He surveyed the room for the first time. When he'd discovered Isabella splayed across the floor, all he had eyes for was her. Now, he was able to take in the surroundings. "Who put a computer in here?"

Isabella rolled her eyes, causing herself more pain. "Now you notice. That's not all." She gestured towards the wall with a flick of her wrist. "Check out the bulletin board. Then, look at what's on the computer."

He scrutinized the collage covered cork-board.

"It's all about you!" Worry creased his brow. "Your life, photos and clippings of you. Of your parents' deaths." Someone had been documenting her life. He looked closer. "What? I don't understand. There is a clipping on my parents' car crash, too. Who would do that?"

He pulled the newspaper clipping from the board and there was a crumpled picture beneath. A mature version of Maddy, complete with corkscrew curls and silver eyes, stared back at him. His hand shook as he tugged another photo from beneath a tack. "That's my mom," he announced. "And someone marked out her face with a red X." He felt the sudden urge to find the man responsible and beat him to a pulp.

Isabella jumped to her feet, and wobbled.

Quickly, he moved, and held her within the safety of his arms.

Bile climbed up the back of her throat from her quick movement. "I'm going to puke on you."

Undaunted, he moved his feet quickly back, out of firing range, but kept hold of her. "Go ahead, puke away. But next time, don't move so fast. You need to sit." He guided her back to the chair. "Stay," he ordered.

She tried to give him her best glare but it hurt too flipping much. "I'm not a damn dog," she mumbled. She tried to refocus on what he said before she attempted to move. "Are you sure it's your mom's picture?"

"There's no doubt in my mind. That's my mom." He tapped the picture with his fingertip. He continued to reply from between clenched teeth. "This picture used to be in my dad's wallet. I asked for it after the accident but no one could find it. I don't understand how someone could have it now."

"That's not all." She grasped his arm. "Look on the monitor. Someone's spying on us. Everyone. Look on the computer."

Slipping the picture in his breast pocket, he moved the mouse and the screen came alive. Eyes narrowed, he scanned the scenes flickering past on the monitor. A vein pulsed in his neck when he discovered Maddy's sleeping form softly outlined by the glow of her nightlight. His father's words echoed within his head. *"Take care of the girls."* He glanced from his sister, innocently sleeping, completely unaware of the evil watching her, to Isabella's beaten face. *"Take care of the girls."* The words vibrated through his body. *I failed.* His fist came down hard upon the table. "Who the hell is responsible for this?"

Surprised by the show of force, Isabella jumped.

He leaned forward on the table, cupping the back of his head with his entwined fingers as he tried to cage the rage burning beneath the surface. He wanted to find the person responsible for hurting Isabella and spying on Maddy. "Just a couple minutes with the unknown man would be enough to pull his guts up through his throat and out his fucking mouth," he ground out from clenched teeth.

Isabella's eyebrows shot up in her forehead.

"What happened, Isabella?" He brought his voice under control. He had to protect the ones he loved. "What happened to your face?"

Eyes wide, mouth agape, her astounded gaze met his. She paused, almost afraid to tell him.

"Tell me," he prodded. "I need to know it all." *Before I go insane.*

"Well, I was searching the desk. I'd already noticed most of the items on the board, and checked out the images on the monitor."

Leaning back against the desk, he crossed his arms and watched her with his eyes a dark storm cloud.

"I accidentally dropped some stuff off the side and shattered a picture frame."

Looking around, he bent down and scooped it up from the desk. "It's from the General's room."

"Yes," she replied, licking her lips. Unsure what the new Theo in front of her would do, she continued. "I cut my finger and was sucking on it when I noticed the middle drawer in the desk."

His voice deadly calm, he said, "So, you looked in there too, without calling me first."

"Well, yeah."

Her complete lack of concern over her own wellbeing infuriated him. *Maddy goes off halfcocked all the time and now Isabella. Damn it, they need to be careful.* He couldn't watch both of them at the same damn time. "Even after you saw all the clippings and discovered that someone was spying, you still decided to keep searching."

"Uh, yeah." She eyed him warily but continued. "I pulled out the middle drawer and I found my recipe book."

"Your recipe book was in here?" he asked, surprised. "What would someone want with it?"

"Hey, there are some pretty good recipes in there." She shifted her icepack. "But that wasn't all. I found the satin scarf. Can you believe it, the satin scarf."

Why the hell is she talking about clothes? Can't she stay on topic? He needed to know who hit her, then, he could find the man and beat the living shit out of him. He expelled an exasperated breath and gazed at the ceiling, focusing on anything to prevent him from ringing Isabella's neck himself. "What satin scarf?"

"The one from my dream, Emma's satin scarf." She glared at him. "You have to listen. My recipe book was laying in the drawer with Emma's satin scarf on top of it."

Completely at the end of his wits, he ground out, "Why the hell does that matter? I want to know how you ended up with the side of your face bashed in, not hear about some stupid satin scarf."

"I'm getting there!" she shouted back, wanting to hurl her ice pack at him, when her head pounded. "Don't you understand? Finding the scarf means that I'm not nuts. That my dreams, seeing Emma, all of it is real. That scarf is the same one from my dream, the one Emma's love removed from her hair and used to wipe her tears away." Unmindful of the pain it caused her, she jumped up and rushed over to the table. "That stupid scarf means I didn't dream everything up."

Prepared to grab the scarf and shove it in his face, she dug in the drawer. "Where is it?" The ice pack slid from her fingers. Her anxious hands scattered papers everywhere and she started pulling out the drawers. "Where're the satin scarf and the journal?"

Alarmed by her increasingly panicked movements, Theo placed his arm around her and drew her away from the desk. "Calm down," he soothed. "I'll find them." He guided her to the chair and handed her back the ice pack. "Let me search while you tell me what happened to your face. What does the journal look like?"

"It's leather, light brown. And has a leather string holding it together," she replied. "It's really old, from 1928."

He could care less about any journal, scarf, or her damn recipe book. He required information that only she could give him. "Tell me about your face," he prodded. Kneeling before her, he stared straight into the confusion clouding her gaze into stormy seas of green. "Focus on me and tell me what happened."

"I don't know. I was trying to decipher the journal and I heard something behind me. I turned and that's the last I remember, other than the pain."

He was right. Someone had hit her. Someone had actually punched Isabella. She didn't fall, or trip over anything. Someone struck her beautiful face with their fist. He pushed back the rage building within him and concentrated on getting the full story. Only then could he find the person responsible. He curled a strand of her soft hair around his finger, before tucking it behind her ear. His eyes never left hers. "You didn't see anything?"

"No. I only heard heavy breathing."

Leaving her just for a moment, he went over and searched the desk. All he could find was her recipe book and a long leather string. He returned and knelt in front of her. Brushing her hair back, he spoke softly, "I can't find the journal or the scarf."

"I'm not crazy," she whispered, looking as if she was about to break down and cry. "I swear."

"Look at me, Isabella." He tilted her chin up, held her free hand within his. "I don't think you are." He kissed the tips of her knuckles. "Whoever hit you must've taken them. But I did find this." He turned her hand over and laid the leather string across her palm before placing her recipe book at her feet.

Her fingers curled around the string, clenching the bit of leather tight in her fist. "That's the string that was tied around the journal. I swear. It's all true."

"I believe you," he replied, kissing her on the forehead.

Expelling a deep breath, she closed her eyes and whispered, "Thank you."

Her lashes swept up, revealing her troubled green gaze. "How did you know where to find me? How did you even know I was hurt?"

He had hoped she wouldn't ask. Now it was his turn to feel like a crazy fool. He rocked back on his heels and straightened, once again pushing his hands into his pockets.

"I couldn't find you, so I came looking for you."

She shifted the ice pack and tipped her head back to see his face. "How did you know I wasn't in my room?"

He hesitated before replying, "I knocked."

"I could've been a heavy sleeper and didn't hear you knocking."

He shuffled his feet and felt heat rushing to his face. "I used my pass key," he mumbled.

"You what?" Isabella asked, her voice deadly.

He knew that tone, the ah-shit tone. Obviously, he screwed up big time in her eyes. "I used my pass key. I wanted to check on you."

Finding Theo an easy target, she released her wrath over being spied on towards him. "You invaded my room. Simply walked on in and violated my space." Her voice trembled with anger. "Just like whoever was watching me."

Obviously, she didn't appreciate how difficult it was to insure everyone's safety. *Well, too bad.* "Yeah, I did. I whipped out my pass key and used it to enter your room. I looked for you in your bathroom, your closest, and I even looked under your bed. I needed to make sure you were safe. And I would do it again."

Surprised by the usually calm Theo's vehement display, she backed off. "What made you so sure you needed to check on me?"

"I just had this feeling." He splayed his hands wide before him. "I smelled burnt vanilla and I kept hearing your name whispered in my head."

"Burnt vanilla? You smelled burnt vanilla and thought of me?" She was suddenly appalled.

"Yes, yes I did. I went looking for you and when I couldn't find you in your room, I kept smelling the burnt vanilla and the smell grew stronger as I neared the kitchen. I followed the scent until I found you, in here and on the floor."

"Burnt vanilla, huh?" Isabella replied. "I think I remember smelling burnt vanilla right before I opened the door to the outer room. I almost didn't continue because of it."

Theo noticed that the ice had begun to leak through the kitchen towel. Removing the towel, he said, "Let's get you a real icepack and some pain killers." Even though he wanted nothing more than to hold Isabella all night, and perhaps do more, he knew she needed rest and a watchful eye. Besides, he made that idiotic promise not to touch her. Reluctantly, he suggested, "I'll find Ava. She can stay with you, so you're not alone tonight."

He'd failed to protect his girls. After he dropped her off, he'd spend the rest of the night correcting that mistake. He removed his cell phone from his pocket. "I'll call Niles and work out a plan to track who comes and goes out of the Executive Chef's office. We're going to keep this room a secret. That way, we might find out who knows about its existence and the person responsible for hurting you." He pinned her with a direct look. "Is that all?" he prodded. "Is there anything else you can tell me about who struck you?"

"I didn't see who it was. Only a shadow." She hesitated.

Desperate for any bit of information on her attacker, he coaxed, "Tell me."

"Laughing." She looked up at him, her eyes huge in her pale face. "Before I passed out, I heard laughing. The same horrible laugh that I heard at the pool the night someone dragged me under the water."

CHAPTER THIRTY-THREE

*H*ead throbbing, Isabella gathered up the items she needed for the meat station. Relieved to find herself alone, she hoped the quietness of the empty kitchen would sooth her aching head before the storm of dinner service. After she'd discovered the hidden room, her sister had spent the few hours left of last night with her. Deep sleep was impossible. Ava kept waking her every hour to check on her. The splitting headache and the lack of sleep made even the neon pink of her cook shirt cause the area behind her eyes to ache. "Maybe being punch in the head helped too."

Lightly, her fingertips felt her cheek, pressing and testing its new puffiness. She winced with the pain, then, shrugged. Guests expected an outstanding dinner service no matter what. She fired the burners but her mind shifted from cooking to the secret room. As a child, Twin Springs was a warm, welcoming place for her to grow and play. Surely, she and Ava had explored every nook and cranny of the huge hotel over their lifetime. But the discovery of the General's room, and now this new room, had squashed her beliefs.

Maude entered, whistling and dancing in her plastic, blue clogs. There was a definite bounce to her steps. The red and green chili pepper design on her cook shirt wiggled and rocked in tune with her boogie moves.

Isabella cringed at the high pitched tune and suppressed a grin, enjoying Maude's dance with her white toque hat wobbling on top of her head to the beat.

"Meat station huh?" Gathering up ingredients for the sauté station, she continued whistling. "You're early, as always."

"You too. It's early afternoon and here you are, happy and dancing." She turned fully, smiling at Maude.

"Dios mio, what happened to your face?" The older woman rushed over and enveloped her against her warm body.

Embarrassed by the attention, she turned her face away. She was at a loss for words, not knowing what to say to her oldest friend. "Nothing," she mumbled into her shoulder.

"Nothing?" Maude exclaimed, pulling back to examine her face. "Your beautiful face looks like blueberry cobbler, all puffy, black and blue. You tell Maude, what happened?"

She hesitated. When they decided to keep the hidden room secret, they didn't discuss what she would tell everyone about her bruised cheek. "I—well—I," she sputtered.

"Oh, my dear Izzy, los santos nos ayudan. I mean, Saints help us, you fell over your own two feet again didn't you?" She hugged her against her generously cushioned body and patted her on the back. "You really need to learn to be more careful."

Isabella didn't know if she should be relieved at being supplied with a handy excuse or insulted by Maude automatically attributing her bruised face to her clumsiness. She decided to go with the safest answer. "Yes, I was rushing up the stairs and slipped, hitting my face," came her garbled reply as she tried to extract herself from Maude's soft embrace.

"Should you be working? Take the day off, you're the boss."

She huffed and mumbled under her breath, "Yeah, right, I'm the boss." But, she replied, "No, I need to work. Need to be busy." *Besides, I'm creeped out from knowing someone watched me sleep and undress in my room. There's no way I could rest now.*

"If you're sure. The meat station is the busiest. Do you want to switch? I can take meats for you."

"No, I'll handle it." She cast her a grateful smile and kissed her on the cheek. "Thank you for offering though." Resting back against the counter, she attempted to shift the conversation from her face to Maude. "So tell me, what's with the happy tune?"

Her brown eyes sparkled with joy and she sighed, laying her hand over her great bosom. "I think mi Marcos is in love."

"Really?" Isabella leaned in. "Do tell."

Glancing about the kitchen quickly, she lowered her voice. "He won't tell me anything but he was out on a date last night." She gave Isabella a knowing nod. "With a girl."

She smiled at Maude's excitement. "Do you know what girl?"

"No, but when I gathered up his clothes from last night they smelled like perfume." She beamed with happiness and did a little jig in place. "Sweet, girly perfume."

Wanting to help her friend with the puzzle, she asked, "Do you know what kind of perfume his shirt smelled like?"

"Nope, just girly. Well, perhaps a little rich. That's it. It must be one of the guest's daughters." Her eyes widened. "I mean, it could be anyone. We all know about the no fraternizing with the guests policy. Probably, just one of the girls from town, now that I think about it." Busily, she began lining up her mise en place.

Isabella rolled her eyes and regretted the action when pain flashed through her skull. Instead, she patted her friend's hand. "Don't worry about me." *After all, I can't judge anyone about fraternizing with the guests since my time five years ago with Theo.* "Your secret is safe."

"Thank you." Maude squeezed her hands and danced with excitement.

"What the hell is going on?" Executive Chef Dubois roared. "If you're in my kitchen, you're working. Stop holding each other's hands and get to work."

"Yes, Chef!" they both shouted in unison.

Chef Dubois' massive body ambled over. His pudgy fingers reached out, lifted her chin and examined her face.

"Stick your nose in where it didn't belong?" he jeered, looking down his nose.

Maude raised her brows at his actions. "No, she fell."

He grunted in response and turned away to head up the pass. "If you're in my kitchen you'd better be ready to work." He turned back towards her, "Can you handle it girl?"

Her chin lifted. "Of course I can."

"We'll see, we'll see."

The rest of the kitchen staff filtered in and set up their work stations. Maude nudged Isabella as her son lumbered in wearing his usual jeans and t-shirt combo. He dug into his duties, filling the sink with soapy suds. Isabella shared a smile with Maude. Soon, all her time and thoughts were filled with focusing on the filling of orders. The six burners blazed, heating her face and causing perspiration to roll down her back. Chef Dubois' voice reverberated through her skull as he boomed out orders.

The crashing of dishes surprised her and she jumped, burning the palm of her hand on the hot stove. Hissing with pain, she shook and blew on her palm.

"Boy!" Chef Dubois roared. "Your head's been in the clouds all service."

She swore the kitchen floor shook as Executive Chef Dubois stomped over to Marc and grabbed him up by the front of his white t-shirt. "I'll not have stupidity in my kitchen." He shook his lanky frame. "You hear me boy?"

Shocked by Dubois actions, Isabella's fuzzy brain rebelled. She couldn't believe her eyes. What did Dubois think he was doing? He couldn't do that to her family. Her head throbbed and her vision blurred, darkening around the edges. "Stop it!" she yelled. The kitchen twirled around her and she thought that she'd pass out.

Dubois ignored her and continued to shake Marc. "I can help you get your head out of the clouds and come back down to earth," he admonished, spittle spewing forth with his angry words. Pulling back his arm, he raised his meaty hand high ready to strike.

Burnt vanilla filled her nostrils. Maude gasped beside her. Appalled by the scene unfolding before her, Isabella's head jerked back. No one else would be hurt today, not in her kitchen. "I said stop it!" Spatula in hand, she rushed forward and pushed between Chef Dubois and Marc. Tipping her head way back, she glared up at him and hissed, "Back off."

"Who are you to tell me what to do? You're just a make believe chef who thinks she knows what the hell she's doing." Dubois bumped her with his massive belly. "Move aside."

The fine hair on the back of her neck bristled at the obnoxious man's actions. "No." She brandished the spatula, tipped her head further back and glared up at him from the short distance. "I might not be an Executive Chef like you or maybe even a real chef, but you'll not treat my staff like this."

"*Your* staff?" he sneered. "You have no staff. You're just a figure head, soon to be pushed out."

The kitchen became deathly quiet. No one moved.

All rational thought left Isabella, only her rampant emotions remained. Unbridled words spilled from her, "They're my staff, and more than that, they're my people."

Fury trembled through her body. "You're fired Executive Chef Dubois." She jerked her thumb towards the door. "Get out. We don't need you, or your kind, here at Twin Springs."

"You can't fire me. You fire me and this hotel will fold up in days. I'm the reason people still come. They come to taste my food, to revel in its brilliance. You have no authority over me. Who's going to run the kitchen if I'm gone? You?" His spittle showered over her. "You can barely see over the pass. You're still wet behind the ears, not even finished with your training. You're nothing and have nothing to give the cliental, nor this kitchen."

Realization flowed over her as she wiped the spit from her face with the neckline of her pink shirt. Her people deserved better. "I said," she ground out between clenched teeth, "that you're fired. Get out of the kitchens and out of Twin Springs."

"We'll see what Mr. Beaumont has to say about this." Chef Dubois smirked at her and stepped back.

Theo's powerful voice carried across the kitchen. "I agree with her."

Gasping, she swiveled towards the doorway. Framed in the kitchen doorway was Theo. His hands were bunched in his side pockets and he appeared cool and collected. Perfect in his pressed black suit, a dark green tie clenched tight against his throat. She bowed her head, embarrassed by her lack of control. Perhaps Theo, with his even-tempered demeanor, could save the situation and bring Chef Dubois under control.

"You heard her," he stated calmly. "You're fired."

She lifted her head and his steely gaze locked with hers. It was then that she noticed the suppressed rage within his gaze. A vein on the side of his neck throbbed.

"When do you want him off the premises?"

Her jaw dropped. *He supports me?* Snapping her mouth closed, she appeared to grow almost two inches taller and faced Executive Chef Dubois. "By tomorrow morning."

Theo nodded in agreement. "That's it then." He shifted his gaze to the chef. "Be out by tomorrow morning. You can pick up your last check from my office before you leave."

Dubois sputtered, "You can't do this. You need me."

Theo walked over, his silver gaze deadly. "We have an Executive Chef right here," he tipped his head towards Isabella. "She has something that you'll never have."

"What's that?" mocked Chef Dubois.

"Passion. A passion for food and for people." Theo leaned forward, bringing his face only inches from Chef Dubois. Close enough to ensure only Dubois heard his words. "Don't ever touch what's mine again." Raising his voice, he added, "Now get out."

Executive Chef Dubois hastily stepped back from the unrestrained rage that emanated from Theo. Then, he gathered himself up and puffed his chest out, almost bursting the buttons of his chef jacket. "You'll regret the day you fired me," he warned Isabella and stomped away.

The doors swung closed behind him and silence filled the kitchen. Service was at a complete standstill. Then applause vibrated through the room. Every one of the kitchen staff that were once frozen, watching in horror at what transpired, were now clapping and smiling at her and Theo.

Everyone, that is, except one teenage boy. Marc hung his head, studied his feet and mumbled, "I'm sorry. I caused you to lose the Executive Chef."

"You didn't cause us to lose anything of value," replied Theo. "Maude," he called out. "Hold down the fort for a minute." He shifted his attention to Isabella. "I want to talk with you."

He seized her by the hand and she cried out. Theo loosened his grip and gently turned her wrist. He shook his head at the angry red burn, before he gazed deep into her eyes. "What am I going to do with you?"

Almost tut-tutting at her, he continued to shake his head in wonder. He pulled her over to the hand sink and ran her burn under cold water. He moistened a clean kitchen towel and wrapped it loosely around the burn on her palm, then he grabbed the medical kit from the wall and guided her back to the Executive Chef's room.

Sitting down beside her at the long, wooden table, he opened up the medical kit. His voice was deceptively quiet as he dug around for supplies. "Why didn't you tell me how bad things were in the kitchen?"

Her arm tingled where he held it still and dried the area around the burn. Warmth flowed up her arm and settled in her belly as she focused in on his question. She shrugged. "Every kitchen is different. Some are loud and frantic, with screaming and yelling. Others are quieter with a tense calm. A lot of Executive Chefs are loud and demanding. If you work in a kitchen, you have to develop a thick outer skin. It's imperative. But today, Dubois went too far. I really think he was going to hit Marc."

Placing cool antiseptic cream on her burn, he replied, "So you thought the best idea was to get between them." He loosely placed a bandage over the burn and secured it with medical tape. "You could've been hurt." He stared at her and she saw the anger hiding behind his gray eyes.

Then it hit her. She'd fired the Executive Chef of Twin Springs in the middle of dinner service. Twin Springs was at stake. "I'm sorry we lost our Executive Chef."

"I don't care about that." Theo studied her, looking at the shades of green, black and blue running across her cheek and up around her left eye. He hesitated, as if something was on the tip of his tongue just waiting to be said, waiting to be tasted. Breaking her gaze, he grabbed an ice pack from the kit, crushed the bag to activate its cooling properties and placed it along her cheek. "What were you doing at work today anyway? You should've been in bed, resting. You could have a concussion from the hit you took."

Her smaller hand replaced his, holding the ice pack. The cold numbed some of the aching in her cheekbone. Perhaps he was right. She should take better care of herself, but her needs came second to the problems of Twin Springs. "I could use some water and a pain med."

Muttering under his breath, he jumped up and grabbed a bottle of water from the mini fridge. He removed the cap and placed the water before her. Sitting back down, he dug around in the medical kit and withdrew a medicine bottle of ibuprofen. Reading the directions, he looked her up and down. "With your size, do you take the adult or child's dosage?"

Isabella prevented herself from rolling her eyes and suffering more pain. "Adult." She held her hand out and he dropped two pills into her palm. She popped them into her mouth and downed them with a swig of water. Leaning her head against the back of the chair, she closed her eyes. The consequences of her firing Chef Dubois crashed down upon her. Someone needed to run tonight's service and take over the kitchen until a new Executive Chef was hired. "I can't do it you know," she said softly.

"Can't do what? Fight a man twice your size," he harrumphed. "I know that."

She smiled ruefully, enjoying his company. "No, I can't run the kitchen. Executive Chef Dubois was right. I know how to cook, but I know nothing about actually running a huge kitchen. I'm not fully trained. I just love to cook. I'm going to fall on my face, just like at the Front Desk and KidsCare."

Scooting his chair closer, he drew Isabella and her chair between his strong thighs. "You can do it. You're intuitive and imaginative. You love the kitchen staff and they love you. Most of all, you love food."

Guilt filled her, tightening her chest. She allowed her emotions to run rough shod over what was best for Twin Springs. She closed her eyes, and shifted the icepack. "I'm not ready. I don't know anything about time schedules, planning big menus or ordering supplies. I can't handle the scheduling of banquets, breakfasts, lunches, dinners and room service. It takes years to grow and become a full-fledged Executive Chef. I'm not ready."

Gently, he placed his fingertip below her chin and guided her face forward until her eyes opened and met his. "Listen to me, really listen. I understand how you feel. I know you feel woefully inadequate, like the whole world is upon your shoulders. That others rely on your success or failure."

At his words, her stomach rolled with anxiety. She pressed her fingertips against her eyes and felt bile climbing up the back of her throat. Swallowing hard, she glared at him. "You're not helping."

He smiled, taking her hands lightly within his and stroking her knuckles with his thumbs. "Just listen. I felt the same way when my father died and I took over the management of Beaumont Industries. In the blink of an eye, I became the Chief Executive and owner, plus a single parent. Of Maddy, no less." He exaggerated his sister's name, wiggling his eyebrows at her.

A reluctant laugh escaped her lips.

"This is what I found. There will always be someone with more knowledge and experience than you. There will always be someone to place doubt and confusion in your mind. You have to trust your instincts, and go with what you feel is right. You, Isabella, have grown up around the kitchen of Twin Springs. You have trained everyday of your young life to one day run the main kitchen. From the day you cooked your first blueberry pancake until now, you were born to lead that kitchen. You've lived and breathed cooking. There's no one, no one, more qualified to be the Executive Chef at Twin Springs than you."

Gently, he kissed her. Her lips softened beneath his and he leaned in taking full advantage of her sweetness. She felt the power and the promise within his kiss, awakening and stroking a yearning deep within her soul.

The door burst open, banged against the wall and broke them apart. Her head rattled against the back of her chair and she groaned.

"I must learn to lock that door," he grumbled under his breath.

"How is she?" Maddy panted, out of breath. Wringing her hands and teetering on four inch spiked heels, she rushed over to Isabella and knelt beside her. "Oh my God, look at what Chef Dubois did to your face." Tears filled her eyes and she wailed, "I'm so sorry."

"I'm fine."

"No. You're. Not," the teen declared, flinging herself across her lap and hysterically sobbing.

Isabella glanced up at Theo, her eye's wide with wonder.

He raised his hands in male defeat.

Softly, she stroked the girl's long curls. "I am okay, Maddy. Really, I am."

"It's all my fault," wailed the teen. "You were hurt and Marc dropped the dishes. We're going to lose the hotel and—and I'm to blame." Her shoulders shook with her sobs. "It's my fault Chef Dubois punched you in the face." Her sobs grew louder. "The hotel's going to fail. I'm going to lose ownership of Twin Springs. It's all my fault. Just like before."

All at once, she became aware of the sweet perfume that surrounded Maddy like an expensive cloud. Suddenly, all the teen's blubbering made sense. "Oh, Maddy," she said knowingly. She smiled brightly at Theo. "Were you and Marc on a date last night?"

"Yes," she moaned into the crook of her arm.

"What?" Theo felt like he took a blow to the chest. "What date? I told you to go to your room last night." Disbelief filled his voice. "You're dating? Who told you that you could date?"

Ignoring her brother, she continued to cry and Isabella smoothed damp curls away from her youthful face.

"Listen to me." She shared a secret smile with Theo as she repeated the lie she told Maude earlier. "I tripped and hit my head last night. I wasn't punched by Chef Dubois."

He snorted at her explanation.

"You weren't?"

Isabella glared at him. "Shush," she admonished. "No. I wasn't. It's not your fault Chef Dubois was fired either."

"It isn't?" Maddy raised her head and looked at her with tear stains running down her face.

"No, it's not." She brushed away the tears. Things finally clicked into place and she understood Theo's earlier words. He was right. It was time for her to step up and run the kitchen. Ready or not. "Chef Dubois was overbearing and obnoxious." She looked at Theo over Maddy's head. "It was time for him to go. Just like it's time for someone who loves the Grand Dame to run the kitchen."

"Are you sure?" The teen sat back on her heels.

Isabella pasted a smile on her face. "One hundred percent," she replied, lying through her teeth as fear clawed her insides. "Twin Springs isn't going to fail. We are going to make sure of it."

She sniffled and wiped away the tears with the back of her hand. "We? As in you and I?"

Is this how it feels to have a younger sister? Being able to soothe her fears and enjoy someone admiring you. Wow, what was Ava complaining about? Having a younger sister is great. She briefly squeezed Maddy, and reassured her. "Yes, us together. We'll keep Twin Springs from failing."

"Well—" Maddy's eyes slid from Isabella's to her brother's and back. She inhaled deeply and rattled off, "If we are working together now, and you're now the Executive Chef, then I have some ideas. I think the food of Twin Springs should have a presence on our website. We should offer the menu, have weekly recipes, and specials. We should take up a charity, and have charity events. We should invite that critic guy my brother knows to taste your food—"

"Whoa, Maddy," interrupted Isabella. Her brain raced to keep up with the teen's exuberance. "I'm just getting used to the idea of being an Executive Chef. Slow down a little." She laughed. "Those are all fabulous ideas, except the last one. Let me finish this service and then we can sit down and talk about every one of your ideas."

"I agree," said Theo. He looked evenly at his little sister. "And while you're finishing the service, my sister and I will discuss my new rules on dating."

CHAPTER THIRTY-FOUR

Chaos, that was all Isabella could think when she returned to the kitchen. Guests' tickets spilled over and under the pass counter. Maude fumbled at the pass stuttering out orders as the chili peppers on her cook shirt trembled with fear. Broken black dishes still covered the floor and a skillet flamed out of control.

She processed the mayhem before her. *I must bring order back to the kitchen or we're sunk.* She clapped her hands twice to gain everyone's attention.

Panicked faces turned towards her.

"Alright. Let's pull it together. Marc, cleanup those dishes. Then, if anyone needs help, you're going to be the 'go-to' guy. They tell you what they need and you'll either go to get it or do it. Understand?"

He nodded, his coffee colored eyes wide as saucers.

She felt compelled to set the tone. Proper respect was an important part of a well-run kitchen. "Excuse me, do you understand?"

"Yes, Chef!" shouted Marc, propelled into action.

"Maude, collect those tickets off the floor and place them on the rail before we lose an order. Also, you're now handling the meat station."

"Gracias a Dios," she responded, making the sign of the cross. "I mean, yes, Chef." She scurried around collecting tickets before taking up her place at meats.

"Let's go people! Time to show that we have what it takes." She turned towards the pass, her cook shirt a bright pink star at the helm of the kitchen. Ready to grab the first order and call it out, she reached up to pluck the ticket from the rail. Her breath caught. *My God, I'm a good foot too short.* Rising to the very tips of her clogs, she stretched her arm out to its full length, straining with her fingertips to reach merely one. The tickets hung out of her range. Her arm fell to her side. "Useless."

She wanted to die inside. Chef Dubois was correct. She wasn't able to reach the tickets. She broke out in a cold sweat and bowed her head and mumbled, "Why can't I have long legs like Ava?" Her mind raced for a solution. "Marc, go and find me an empty crate from the storage room."

He trotted from the room, shouting, "Yes, Chef!" Returning quickly, he handed her a bright blue crate. She stepped up on the plastic box, snatched the first ticket and sounded off, loud and clear. She finished her order with, "Let's make magic, people!"

A resounding, "Yes, Chef!" filled the kitchen.

She worked the pass like a general, only leaving her position to fill in where needed due to her absence on the line. Her head throbbed and her palm ached, but she felt alive. More alive than ever before.

Using a small spoon, she tasted the roasted chicken with risotto. Satisfied, she plated it and then sent the dish forward. "Great risotto, keep it up."

"Thank you, Chef," rang out.

She heard the stations talking between each other, throwing out times and working in unison to make the dishes come together. Gone was the policy of no talking and the excellent quality of food coming to the pass showed the difference between communication and fear. She wobbled on the crate, grabbing tickets and passing plates through the pass. Leaning awkwardly forward, the shooting pain in her lower back rivaled the throbbing pain in her head. Just as when she cooked, a conversation hummed in her head.

Crunching? What is crunching back there? the voice in her head asked. She pivoted, her gaze honed in on Marc chopping onions.

"Marc, grab a sharpened knife. Can you hear how the knife is crunching and not slicing through the onions?"

"Yes, Chef."

She plated the next dish. Pausing to listen, she arched her back and massaged her knuckles against the small of her back. "Sounds better. Keep up the good work!" she shouted out.

Marc glowed with pride and started slicing another onion.

"Table up," she called to the wait staff.

A young woman on the wait staff came forward and stacked the plates on her large black tray. Blowing her midnight black bangs out of her eyes, the server hesitated before leaving, "Chef?"

"Yes, Diana," answered Isabella, popping up on tiptoe to see her over the pass counter.

She hefted the tray up on one shoulder, "I've heard more compliments in the Main Dining Room tonight than any time since Chef Dubois started here."

She flashed her a grateful smile, "Thanks for letting me know."

Taking a moment, Isabella twisted the cap off her water bottle and swallowed small sips while evaluating the activity around the kitchen. She liked how everyone worked together. She noticed Nick dropping fresh mushrooms in a sauce pan and did not hear the accompanying sizzle when they landed in the pan. "Nick," she called out. "Your sauce pan isn't hot enough. Did you hear a sizzle when the mushrooms hit the pan?"

"No, Chef."

"That's because you need to heat up your sauce pan more. Then you'll hear the sizzle when your ingredient hits the pan."

"Yes, Chef. Thank you, Chef."

She turned back to the pass, tasting, smelling and inspecting every dish before it left her kitchen. She lost track of time as she called out orders and passed the finished plates through.

We're done, that was the last order. Exhilaration pulsed through her. *We survived. I can't believe we actually did it.* Glowing with pride, she addressed the kitchen. "That's it everyone!" she called out. "Shut it down and let's cleanup for tomorrow morning." She smiled as shouts and high five's vibrated through the kitchen. Taking another swig of her water, she stepped down from the wobbly crate and noticed Theo leaning against the doorframe, his ankles crossed.

He straightened, clapping his hands as he moved towards her. His eyes glowed with pride. "Excellent job, Executive Chef Fairbanks. Reports from the dining room are superb about your staff's performance tonight."

"Thanks." Her heart swelled from his praise. "We just need to straighten up for tomorrow's breakfast service and then we'll be finished."

"No, you're not," he replied sharply. "I'm here to make sure you take some more pain killers and get much needed rest."

Stunned by his changed tone, she stepped back. She didn't want to lose the respect of her team. Not now, not after all they accomplished tonight. "I can't. I need to finish with the team."

"The team can finish up on their own." He grasped her by the arm to coax her from the room.

She scanned the kitchen. Even though everyone's heads were bent, concentrating on their tasks, she knew better—they heard every word being said. She realized what happened now, in the tug of war between her and Theo, would not only set the tone for future services, but also her place in their eyes. "No."

She wrenched her arm from his hold. "No. That's not the kind of Executive Chef I want to be. We're a team and we finish as a team."

He contemplated Isabella's stiffened shoulders and clenched jaw. Seeing her determination, he backed off. "Fine. I'll be back for you."

She worked with her team until every saucepan was wiped out, and every pot scoured. After the counters were sparkling clean and everything was back in its place, she said goodnights to everyone.

Maude lagged back. "I want to thank you."

Surprised, she turned towards her friend. "Thank me?"

"Yes, for mi Marcos. He was in the wrong but I couldn't believe what was happening. I'm ashamed to say, I was paralyzed in place. Thank you for standing up for my son."

Clasping Maude's hand, she squeezed it. "You would've stopped it. Don't think twice about what happened. Besides, how many times have you covered for me as I was growing up? I should be thanking you."

"Thanking me? Pshaw, what on earth for?"

She couldn't believe Maude didn't realize her worth and value in her life. Maude had remained by her side since she'd cooked her first blueberry pancake. "You were like a mom to me. Someone I could talk with about my problems after my mom died. You supported me with my cooking. You're the one who approached my dad about Chatham Institute of Culinary Arts."

Dabbing a tear with the corner of her apron, Maude answered, "And tonight you made us all proud. You're now the Executive Chef of Twin Springs."

She gazed around the main kitchen. Her kitchen. Joy filled her heart. She would've pinched herself, just in case she was dreaming, but her dreams were never this happy. "I can't believe it."

"I can. You belong in the kitchen cooking and guiding others."

She bubbled over with joy. "Thanks, I seem to have heard that from someone else today. Do you want to have a drink of wine and celebrate with me?"

Wringing her hands in her apron, Maude answered, "I can't. I need to go home and see if I can ferret out who my son was daydreaming about when he caused all the excitement tonight."

Thinking back to the teenager and her expensive perfume, she chuckled. "I can solve that mystery for you. It's Maddy."

"Maddy?" Maude echoed. "No way." She pressed her palms to her hot cheeks. "Perhaps I should have that drink with you."

CHAPTER THIRTY-FIVE

heo found Isabella in the Executive Chef's office sleeping soundly, with her torso resting across the large, oak table and her head nestled in the crook of her arm. He was stunned by her beauty. Her soft breath fogged the wine glass next to her hand, strands of her hair curled against her soft skin. Shaking his head at his impure thoughts and remembering his foolish promise to her at the Hot Springs pool, he quietly removed the partially full wine glasses. He picked up the empty wine bottle, examined the label and murmured, "It must've been some celebration."

He stacked the two wine glasses and the bottle on a tray with the other leftovers from her meal. Wine, cheese, and meats. A jealous green monster crept up his back, peered over his shoulder and wondered who the gorgeous woman before him celebrated with. Shaking it off, he looked down at her sleeping form. She deserved to celebrate. Placing all the dishes in the kitchen for the staff to take care of, he returned and glanced at the papers that were strewn around her.

He browsed through new menu plans for each of the hotel's restaurants. A Twin Springs room service menu was marked up with deletions and additions, written in her delicate flowing script. He was amazed. She had drawn diagrams that completely re-organized both the kitchen and the Main Dining Room to make them more efficient. "Busy girl."

Impressed, he glanced back down at her and resisted tucking a strand of her blonde hair behind her ear. Instead, he straightened up her papers and placed them in a neat stack on the table. He itched to open the secret door and re-examine the room. *It will have to wait. I owe it to her to wait so we can examine the room together.*

With the care of a lover, he hooked one arm under her legs and one around her back and held her closely to his chest. Vanilla. He inhaled deeply, filling his lungs with her scent and couldn't believe that his pounding heart didn't wake her. Instead, she settled into his embrace and burrowed her head in the bend of his neck and slept the whole journey back to her room. He juggled her to one side as he tugged his pass key out of his pocket and unlocked her room. Tipping sideways with her in his arms, he flipped on the light beside her bed.

Her room was a disaster. Items were scattered, drawers had been pulled out and dumped on the floor. Even the mattress had been tossed. "Holy shit!"

She jumped, her head knocking him in the chin. "What? Who?" Suddenly realizing Theo was holding her, she struggled in his arms. "Put me down."

"Wait." He put his pass key between his teeth and released her legs, allowing her body to flow down the length of his.

Her breath caught in the back of her throat, she was momentarily dazed within the circle of his arms. Gaining her equilibrium, she pushed back against his chest and glared up at him. "I told you not to use your key on my room."

He removed his pass key from his teeth and slipped it into his back pocket. He tested his jaw, evaluating the damage from her head. "You should register your head as a weapon."

"Sorry, but I told you—" she started as she turned, immediately shrieking. "What happened to my room? It looks like a tornado hit it."

Picking up a lacy bra hanging off the lampshade, he dangled it off his fingertip. "This isn't how you keep it?"

She marched over and snatched the bra from his hand. "Very funny." She began picking up her personal items and tucking them under her arm. "No, it's not. Who could've done this?" She picked up a picture of her with her sister and dad. Taken on the front porch of Twin Springs, it was the last time they were all together. The glass looked like a boot heel had smashed it. She choked back tears. "Why would someone do this?"

He assessed Isabella and her room. Her was face battered and bruised, all her possessions were scattered across the floor. The joy of achievement from earlier this evening was wiped away. "It could be from anger, revenge, or perhaps someone was searching for something. I don't know. But, I'll fix this. I promise."

"Searching for something?" She dumped all of her items on the couch and rushed over to her bed. She pushed the mattress the rest of the way off the box springs. "It's not here."

"What's not there?"

She ignored him, struggling to pull the headboard from the wall. He assisted her and watched as she searched behind the bed. Getting on her hands and knees, she lifted the bed skirt and looked under. "It's gone."

"What's gone? If you tell me, then I can help you search."

She sat on the edge of the box spring. "The leather string. The leather string that held the journal together. It's gone." Tears swam in her eyes. "I didn't imagine it all last night. Did I?"

Knelling down before her, he tipped her chin up to look at him. "Hell no. You didn't imagine anything." He gave her a half smile. "If you could see your bruised face, then you wouldn't be wondering."

Exhausted, she gazed into the smoky depths of his eyes. Her fingertips pressed on her cheekbone and she welcomed the pain she felt. Proof. Proof she wasn't crazy. The room was real, Emma was real, and someone real was trying to destroy her home.

Out of the corner of her eye she saw a shimmer of reflected light. Getting to her feet, she bent over and extracted a silver pen from under her couch. Theo Beaumont was engraved in bold powerful strokes along the side of the pen. "Your pen." Confusion weighed down her voice. "What's your pen doing here?" She looked at the pen and then back at him. Her voice gained strength. "You seemed so comfortable in using your pass key to enter my room. Now my room is trashed and I find your pen here."

She threw it at him. "Am I imagining that too?"

He caught the flash of silver as it bounced off his chest. "No." He studied the pen, rolling it over and over between his fingertips. The same pen his parents gave him for his high school graduation. "This is my pen."

"Maybe Niles is right. We didn't have these problems before you came." Her shoulders sagged. "Get out." Her voice sounded small and defeated.

His gaze probed hers, searching for understanding and a chance to explain. He took a step towards her. "Wait. I don't know how my pen ended up in your room. I didn't do this, Isabella."

"Just get out." Dejected she grabbed up more clothes and shoved them in the closet.

Theo placed a lifetime of yearning into one word. "Isabella."

"Now!" she shouted, the stress of the day shifting her emotions into high gear. Taking a moment to get herself under control, she repeated while averting her gaze, "Get out, now."

The pen might as well have pierced his heart. The gash from her words cut deep. He studied her, seeing everything he'd ever wanted standing right before him. The hotel meant nothing to him, just a means to be with her. And now he was further away from his goal than ever before. He didn't understand how his pen had ended up in her room.

He turned and grasped the door handle. "Deep down, you know it isn't me." A thought occurred to him, and he turned back.

"How could I have collected all those pictures? I was busy caring for Maddy. Running a business."

She evaluated Theo, his broad shoulders and long, lean frame held power and commitment. But more than that, she knew they held tenderness, and honesty. He didn't sneak around spying on people.

"Why would I cross out my own mother's face?"

She gasped. He was right. Before her stood a man who, when his parents died, faced great responsibility and shouldered it with dignity and strength. He didn't shirk his responsibilities—he met them head on. She'd witnessed the pain he still endured after losing his mother. Shame filled her.

He rushed forward and gathered her hands in his. "Do you really think that I could have hit you?"

Shame filled her even more. She'd accused him of terrible things. Unsure how else to ease the pain she'd caused, she wrapped her arms around his waist and mumbled into his chest. "I'm sorry. You're right. You couldn't have done this. You're not causing the accidents."

Theo's arms enveloped her in safety and she sighed against his chest. Enjoying his comfort and strength, she asked, "Who do you think it is?"

His chin jiggled against the top of her head as he spoke. "What about Logan?"

She pulled back and perched on the edge of her bed. "Never. Logan grew up with me. He, Ava, Niles and myself consider Twin Springs our home."

Theo gave a noncommittal grunt and began righting the room. He wanted to tell her that war changed men, but it wasn't worth upsetting her further. He picked up a very feminine piece of lace and discovered it was her panties. "Then who?"

She snatched the pair of undies out of his hand and threw them in a drawer. "I'd love to blame Chef Dubois. He's such a jerk." Quickly, she gathered up the rest of her underwear and bras. "But he hasn't been here long enough. Some of those clippings and photos were old."

She raced around the room, collecting items, while he righted the bed and made it. Once the room was under control, she stood there, wringing her hands. "Would you mind," she paused, and licked her lips. Clearing her throat, she tried again. "Would you stay with me? Spend the night?"

Blood rushed through him. Theo thought the top of his head might blow off at her words. Hot waves of need rolled through his body.

"I'm scared."

Like a splash of ice-water, her words cooled his desire. Someone had been watching her, hit her and broke into her room. Naturally, she was afraid. "I wouldn't want to be anywhere else."

She pulled a comforter and pillow off the bed and placed them on the couch. "Do you mind?"

Disappointment flooded his body. He eyed the short couch, but he'd accept any crumbs she'd give him. "Not at all."

"Thank you," she disappeared into the closet.

Slowly, he removed his jacket and folded it. Grasping ahold of his tie, she emerged from the closet and he almost choked himself. Her glorious, corn silk hair floated around her shoulders. She wore a short blue t-shirt that flirted with the curve of her bottom as she moved. His heart thundering in his chest, he read the phrase aloud, "Sauciers Do It On The Fly?"

Her face flushed to the most delicious shade of pink. "It's just a kitchen joke."

Enjoying her discomfort, he tugged his tie free and began unbuttoning his shirt. "Do what on the fly?"

"Nothing," Isabella mumbled, burrowing down under the sheets. From beneath her lashes, she watched him take off his shirt, revealing his lean, flat stomach. His muscles flexed as he laid his clothes on the floor in a perfectly folded pile. Only his slacks remained. A disappointed sigh escaped her lips when he climbed under the comforter without removing his trousers.

"Did you say something?"

"No, nothing," she answered, reaching up and flicking off the light. Moonlight blanketed the room in a soft glow. Knee's bent, he tossed under the covers, attempting to find a comfortable spot. Finally, he settled down with his legs hanging off the end by two feet.

"You can climb in with me."

Immediately, blood rushed into his loins. He swallowed hard and didn't trust himself to answer.

"Are you asleep?" she whispered.

"No." His voice was deep, husky.

But he didn't move. "Did you hear me? The couch is way too short. You can sleep with me."

Theo groaned. She didn't want him. She was concerned about his comfort. He sat up and waited for his body to calm, schooled his features into a calm facade. "If you're sure."

She pulled back the covers and he climbed in and laid flat on his back, stiff as a board, afraid that, if he moved, he'd brush against her and morph into a mangy dog, begging for any scrap of affection she handed out. Her sweet vanilla scent wafted over him, while he listened to her every sound. Her bottom brushed against him and he swallowed hard. Clenched his teeth. She tossed and turned some more before settling into sleep. *You promised not to touch her*, he reminded himself. *Beaumonts don't break promises.*

He lay there, unable to sleep with her soft body beside him, and made a mental list of things he needed to do. He didn't care how much money he needed to sink into the hotel she loved, he'd sell Beaumont Industries for her. Put everything on the line for her. And Maddy. He clenched the covers within his fist. He'd keep them safe or die trying.

Once her breathing had settled down and her chest rose softly, he turned his head. Her long, blonde hair splayed across her pillow. Ever so gently, he grasped a lock between his thumb and forefinger and rubbed. Buttery soft. He suppressed the urge to lift it to his nose and sniff. *Would it smell like vanilla too?*

Reluctantly, he let go. Her thick, dark lashes lay softly upon her milky white skin. Her rosy lips parted and he smothered a groan. Unable to shift his gaze from her beauty, he watched her until the morning sun brightened the room. Only then, did he slip from the bed. His mission was clear. Protect the woman he loved. At all cost.

CHAPTER THIRTY-SIX

*I*sabella opened her eyes and stretched, releasing a long yawn. She'd slept like a baby. The room was bright and she turned her head. Theo was gone, only a dent in his pillow remained. She frowned. "Damn."

"How late is it?" She grabbed her phone from the bedside table and clicked it on. "Two thirty!" She sprang out of bed and was halfway to the bath when she realized that her sleep had been dream free. No drowning. No dreams of Emma. Just restful slumber. "Thank you, Theo."

No time to waste, she showered then dug through the pile of clothes in the bottom of her closet. Sliding one leg into black pants, she then hopped on one foot while trying to slip the other leg through and pull her white chef jacket from culinary school from a hanger. She finished dressing and sped down the stairwell to the kitchen.

Her footsteps rang out within the stairwell as she muttered to herself, "Great way to start out your first official day as Executive Chef. You should be in hours earlier than everyone else and last to leave."

Exiting the stairwell, she skidded to an abrupt stop. Marc leaned against the swinging kitchen doors, blocking her way.

"Can't go in there." He said, examining his nails.

Lines creased her forehead. "What are you talking about?" She pushed to pass him.

His strong, young arm shot out and barred her way. "Nope. Can't go in yet. It's not ready."

"What's not ready?"

Shrugging, he refused to answer.

She evaluated the teenage boy for a moment and then sniffed the air. "Is that perfume I smell?" She sniffed closer to him. "It is!" She crossed her arms over her chest and tilted her head to the side. "Why, Marcos, are you wearing perfume?"

Heat rushed to his cheeks and he stuck his hands into the front pocket of his jeans and shuffled his feet. "Well, no, Chef. Not exactly."

Triumphantly, she rushed past him and called back over her shoulder, "Sucker!"

She stopped dead within the swinging doorway of the kitchens. Surprised at her abrupt stop, Marc plowed into her back and almost knocked her over. Grabbing the doorframe, she steadied herself. Before her eyes, her kitchen was under siege. The kitchen crew busily prepped for dinner service in the back portion of the kitchen, while the maintenance crew rolled other portions of the kitchen around.

Maude scurried up to her, wringing her hands in the green apron that blocked the multitude of red and green apples printed across her cook shirt. She cuffed her son lightly on the back of his head and knocked his baseball cap to the floor. "Marcos," she admonished, "you were supposed to keep her from entering."

He brushed his light brown curls back into place, scooped up his hat and shoved the cap down on his head. "I tried, Mom. Really I did." He jerked his thumb at her. "She tricked me."

"Tricked you?" Maude placed her hands on her mighty hips. "Just how did she trick you?"

Deciding to save Marc from further embarrassment, she asked, "What's going on in here?"

With a glare at her son, Maude replied, "It was supposed to be a surprise." She swept her arms out in front of her. "It's going to be just like we talked about last night. All hands were called on deck. Dale and his crew were called in first, then all the kitchen crew were called in. Promised time and a half if they came in early and helped to remodel the kitchen before today's dinner shift." She winked at Isabella. "I don't know what got into that man but he's pulling out all the stops to put this kitchen just the way you want it."

A group of men rolled a counter in front of her and she jumped out of the way. She spied Dale on his back underneath the front of the pass. His arm cranked away with one of his tools and he was half under and half outside of the pass window. She marched over to him and nudged his work boot with the toe of her shoe. "Dale, what are you doing?"

He poked his head out. His short gray hair stuck out in all directions. He rolled his toothpick around in his mouth thinking and glanced between her and Maude, who was violently shaking her head side to side. "Well now, Miss Isabella, you're gonna have to ask the big guy about that. I'm not at liberty to say just now."

"Big guy? Who's the big guy? You mean Niles?"

"Oh, no, ma'am. He is big, but he's not the one in charge of this."

"Theo?"

"Yes, ma'am."

"Theo did all this?" She was stunned. Everything was shifting and emerging as she had dreamed. "Where is the big guy?"

He confirmed with Maude before answering. "Well, now, Miss Isabella, he's in your office."

"Thanks!" She twirled on her heel and headed determinedly towards the Executive Chef office. She bobbed and weaved around the excited bedlam, back out the swinging doors and skidded to a halt in front of the door. A couple inches above the antique doorknob was a new, small, black oval circle. She felt the glassy surface in wonderment, then, twisted the knob to enter. The door didn't budge. Her brows wrinkled, "He locked me out?" She banged on her office door with her fist.

Theo's strong voice came from within. "Just a minute…

Good. I'm glad you're here." Letting out a deep breath, Theo adjusted his black tie. "Now, let me tell you what I've done." He sounded giddy. Almost like a little boy.

"I wanted to thank you for reorganizing the kitchen."

He pulled out a chair for her, seated her and then sat beside her.

"What's going on?"

He slid an ID card and a long, silver necklace across the table to her. "Those are yours. Each one is personal to you. The ID card is also a magna strip door card. It opens all hotel rooms on property in addition to the back of the house areas."

She picked up the necklace. From it dangled a silver medallion about the size of a quarter. One side was etched with the Twin Springs logo and her name, the other side was shiny black. "What's this? It's beautiful."

He gave her a delighted smile that reminded her of a kid on Christmas morning. "That's a RFID fob. A radio-frequency identification. It has a small chip and antenna within. The medallion will open your personal rooms and personal offices." He brought it over to her office door to demonstrate. "The door will open automatically from within when you turn the knob." He opened the door to demonstrate, and then closed it. "Also, the door should automatically unlock when you walk within three feet. If not, swipe the back side of your necklace in front of the reader." He tapped the shiny black circle with his finger, then, demonstrated by waiving the medallion in front of the shiny surface. Simultaneously, the lock clicked open and Isabella's cell phone buzzed.

She pulled her phone from the pocket of her chef's jacket and read the text message. "It says, Executive Chef office door open. That's amazing."

He smiled. "Another lock, just like this, is being installed on your sister's room, your room, Maddy's room and Ava's office.

That way, you'll receive a text message if anyone enters your room or your office. Also, it will add extra security to your personal areas until we find out who's sabotaging the hotel."

"Ava's office?" she questioned.

"Yes, I hope you don't mind. I asked her to be the Group Sales and Special Events Coordinator. At least, until she returns to the stage. I felt it was fitting that a Fairbanks should sit in the office with the most history, the most meaning to the family, so I gave her the General's room as her office."

Isabella's heart swelled. "Wonderful.

Are we the only ones able to access our rooms?"

He hesitated. "Well, no. I needed to factor in the maid service. But you will receive a text message saying the maids name when she enters your room. And for safety reasons, myself and Niles, as Security Manager, also have access." His smile wavered. "If you feel uncomfortable with me having access, I can change that."

Blushing, she stammered, "No, I'm—That's fine." She took a deep breath. "In fact, I feel better knowing you and Niles can get in if needed."

His voice was soft, "I asked Logan to do an extra sweep of your rooms and offices for hidden cameras. I figured with his Special Ops background, no one was better suited."

He held the necklace out to her.

"Would you mind, helping me put it on?" She turned and she could've sworn his hands trembled as he placed the necklace around her neck and clasped it.

She turned again. Her lips were only inches from his. "Thank you for doing all this. For staying with me last night." She reached up and kissed him. His lips were soft beneath hers but they didn't move. Confused, she stepped back. It was then she noticed his hands were balled into fists at his side. Heat rushed to her face, he wasn't interested. "Sorry, I just thought I'd thank you with a kiss." Once said, the words sounded stupid to her ears. She wanted to sink into the floor and die from embarrassment. She glanced around for something to shift his attention. "Let me show you how to open the secret door." Striding over to the desk, she showed him where to find the knob.

Silently, the platform slid open and revealed the darkened room. "That's amazing," he breathed out. "Where's the light switch?"

Reaching her arm around the corner of the door, she flicked the light switch on. "It's here."

The lone light bulb sputtered to life. This was the first time the two of them had time to really take in the room. The pale walls were cracked with age and the new, modern boxes seemed out of place. Some of the brown, wooden shelves sagged beneath the weight of the plastic jugs. To the right, Isabella spied a scullery sink and old, cast iron stove.

She squealed with excitement, drawing his attention from examining the rest of the room, and rushed over to the old sink and stove. Unmindful of the dirt and cobwebs, she stood on old, slatted wood mats, and ran her hands lovingly over the smooth, porcelain double sink and heavy, cast iron stove top. "Gorgeous."

She pulled an old copper pot from under the sink and declared, "A set pot for boiling water. How cool is that?" Grinning from ear to ear, she held the dingy, dented pot above her head like a trophy.

"I've lost her," muttered Theo. With an exasperated sigh, he turned to inspect the desk. He wanted to delve into the computer and papers, but the desk was now completely empty. The computer, all the papers, and pictures were gone. The only items left behind were the dusty, old books across the high shelf. "Damn it," he ground out. "The desk was cleaned out."

"What?" Isabella reluctantly placed her newly found toy on the floor and joined him. "Where did everything go?"

Theo raked his fingers through his hair. "I don't know. But I'm going to find out." He pulled his cell phone out of his back pocket, pressed a quick dial number with his thumb and lifted the phone to his ear. "Come down to the Executive Chef's office. Now." He slipped his phone back into his pocket and surveyed what was left.

"It's been wiped clean." He removed the middle drawer. "Everything is gone."

Isabella dragged out the chair and stepped up to reach the small bookshelf above the desk. "Not quite everything."

She examined the books, then, began bouncing up and down on top of the chair. Her voice filled with excitement. "You'll not believe what these books are." She brought down a volume and blew off the dust. "They're old cookbooks. This is a copy of Le Viandier by Guillaume Tirel." Reverently, she opened the book and quickly skimmed the pages. "It's in French!" she shouted triumphantly and hugged the dirty book to her chest. "Can you believe it?"

Steadying the chair underneath her dancing feet, Theo couldn't help but feel a little envious of the stupid old book. "Perhaps I could, if I knew what it was."

"It is an original 1892 edition. A very rare collection of recipes."

"How much is it worth?"

Appalled, she looked at him. "You can't sell this. It's priceless to me."

"What else is up there?"

Reluctantly, she leaned down and delicately placed the book on the table before she examined the bookshelf closer. "There are a couple more cookbooks. Most early 1900's." Carefully, she removed the books, examining each one before placing it on the table.

Glancing around the room, Theo wandered over to poke around the boxes. "This must have been the Chef's office at one time."

Isabella nodded and perused the books. "What's this?" She climbed up on the tabletop, in order to gain a few extra inches.

The old desk wobbled.

"Be careful," Theo warned.

Ignoring him, she reached up on her tiptoes. Something brown was wedged behind the cookbooks. She withdrew a leather bound book caked with dust and cobwebs. Amazed, she stared at it.

"Another treasure?" mocked Theo.

"It looks just like the journal I found earlier." Eagerly, she untied the leather string and examined the pages. "It is a journal," she declared. "Dated 1928 too. There are newspaper clippings of recipes, time schedules and hand written notes and recipes. It must have been the journal of the Executive Chef of Twin Springs."

"Who does it belong to?" he asked.

She thumbed back to the front of the journal. "J. C. Flamme."

Color drained from Theo's face. He croaked, "What was the name?"

Bewildered she glanced down at him. "J. C. Flamme"

"May I see it?" He reached out and his hand shook.

She noted a slight ashen tinge to his skin and handed him the journal. "Of course."

He held the journal just as reverently as she had held the Le Viandier book. He ran his finger across the author's name and turned the pages, carefully smoothing each page as he examined the journal. "J. C. Flamme was the brother of my mother's grandfather"

"You're kidding." She scrambled down and peered at the aged journal in his hands.

"He was a Chef in New Orleans, where my family comes from." He swallowed hard. "Is the hand writing the same as the other journal? The one you found before?"

Isabella leaned in and examined the writing. "No, the other writing was cramped and hard. This is more long and flowing. Do you know what this means?" She sat back on the edge of the desk. "Your great, great uncle was the Executive Chef here at Twin Springs." She thought for a moment and her eyes widened. "Why didn't I put it together before? J. C. Flamme is Jean Claude Flamme. He was the head chef with Emma," she gushed. "From New Orleans you said?"

Solemnly, he flipped the aged pages, and gave her a nod.

She covered her mouth with her hand. Eyes wide, she whispered from behind her fingers. "Jean Claude is La Flamme. Can you believe it? You're related to La Flamme."

"Who is La Flamme?"

"Only one of the most famous chef's in America. He was renowned for his French cooking and became Head Chef at the White House. I can't believe you're related to La Flamme." She looked at him with new found interest.

"It definitely explains my mother's long time interest in Twin Springs. Do you mind if I hold onto this? I'd like to show it to Maddy."

"Sure," she automatically responded. Then she hesitated. "But, may I read the journal too? With your permission of course, I want to examine his recipes."

He retied the leather string around his ancestor's journal. "Of course. I guess Maddy and I do have roots here."

Tucking the journal under his arm, Theo strode over to one of the boxes and pulled out a plastic jug. Popping off one of the lids, he sniffed. "You're not going to believe this."

She rushed over to him. "What is it?"

Theo held out the jug to her. "Definitely not water. Smell, but be careful. It'll knock you on your butt."

"May I see?" Isabella took the bottle from him and waved the fumes up to her nose with her free hand. She dipped the tip of her finger into the jug and touched it to her tongue. Recapping the bottle, she held it horizontally between her hands and shook it.

"What are you doing?"

"See the bubbles," she replied. "I am watching the size and time it takes for the bubbles to disappear. This is moonshine. High grade, at least one hundred ninety proof."

"How do you know how to do that?" he asked in awe.

"When I was at culinary school, one of the older instructors, Chef Chatham, kept a small jar of moonshine in the drawer of her desk. After a successful dish that I created, she brought me into her office to celebrate. She shared a shot of her uncle's special brew with me. We talked for hours about her uncle's secret still in the mountains of West Virginia. She told me bootlegging was how her family originally financed the upstart of the Chatham Institute of Culinary Arts."

"I don't believe it. People are still bootlegging?" He popped off the plastic lid from another bottle and sniffed.

Isabella shrugged and counted the bottles. "I guess so. Her uncle is still brewing."

"It is illegal right? Even though prohibition is over, brewing shine to sell is still illegal. Isn't it?"

"I'm pretty sure making moonshine is illegal if you want to sell it. Looking at the amount of bottles here, someone is making big enough batches to sell," said Isabella.

"But why's the moonshine here at Twin Springs? This is crazy. We're not in the prohibition era." Imitating her actions, Theo lifted and shook one of the plastic jugs. "These bottles aren't left over from the twenties. They're plastic and appear brand new."

"I count sixty gallons of shine." Isabella stepped back after examining the stacked boxes. "You know, I think there are some boxes missing from last night."

They scrutinized the pile.

"I'm not certain," he replied. "But one thing is for sure, we need to contact the authorities." He paused, perusing the amount of liquor. "Quietly, contact the authorities. We don't want this kind of publicity for the hotel."

The outer office door opened and Isabella's phone beeped, causing her to jump.

"Holy crap," Niles' voice rumbled as he stepped through the secret room's opening. "I had no idea this room was back here. What's all this?"

"That is what we are going to find out," replied Theo. "You told me you secured the Executive Chef's office."

"I did. Just like you told me to. My office installed a camera outside the door and I assigned a security team to monitor the footage around the property twenty four hours a day, seven days a week." He scratched his dark, massive beard. "Why? Did something happen?"

"Items are missing from this room," replied Theo. "I'm going to want to look at all of our security footage since your department installed the camera."

"Not a problem. I'll make sure they are available at your convenience."

Isabella handed Niles a jug. "Sniff that. If you're brave enough, take a swig. It's moonshine."

He swallowed a mouthful of the home brew. "It's smooth." He added between coughs, "But it has a bit of a bite at the end."

Amused, her eyes twinkled. "That'll put even more hair on your body. If that's possible." Placing the cap back on the jug, she returned it to one of the boxes. "Your family has lived here for generations right?"

Niles nodded.

"Have you ever heard of moonshine being made and sold in these mountains?"

"Not that I know of." He reached into one of the boxes. "I wouldn't mind taking some of that home."

She slapped his hands away.

Theo spoke up. "No one is taking anything. It's going to stay right here until we contact the ATF and they decide what to do with it."

Niles put the jug back. "You might want to contact the local sheriff first. He tends to get cranky if people don't respect his territory. I can call him if you want."

Isabella's cell phone alarm buzzed and she pulled it out, examining the alert. "I have dinner service." She automatically added, "When you are done in here, push the desk back." Her gaze met Theo's so similar to Jean Claude's from her dream. "Push it till it clicks."

CHAPTER THIRTY-SEVEN

After leaving everyone else to figure out the moonshine, Isabella pushed the kitchen door open to lead dinner service. She expected bedlam. Instead, the kitchen crew greeted her and busily prepped their stations. Everyone smiled and gave a quick, "Good afternoon, Chef," as she walked by. The kitchen was set up exactly how she'd diagramed it last night. *How did they get this all done?*

As she neared the pass, Maude clapped her hands and demanded everyone's attention. "I know you are all as proud as I am to have one of our own as the Executive Chef of Twin Springs." She turned to Isabella. "We have a gift for you."

Marc stepped up from behind his mom carrying a bundle of white.

Shaking out the bundle, Maude revealed a brand new, stark white, chef jacket.

Isabella reached out and ran her fingertips along the words sewn across the upper right side. Embroidered in Twin Springs' signature green hue was: Isabella Fairbanks, Executive Chef, Twin Springs Hotel and Spa. She hooked an arm around Maude's waist, one around Marc and hugged them tight. "Thank you." Her warm gaze flowed over her kitchen family, "Thank you all."

Thunderous applause broke out in the kitchen. Maude helped her undo her chef jacket from culinary school and slip on the new one. Isabella rubbed the embroidered Twin Springs logo on the mandarin collar with the tips of her fingers. "I can't thank you all enough." She addressed everyone. "Let's make sure all the guests in the dining room remember this evening's service. Let's send out food that not only satisfies their hunger and enhances their dining experience, but helps create a special memory for them to remember us by."

Taking a deep breath, she turned to the pass, ready to receive the first order.

Marc stepped up. "Allow me, Chef." Reaching down, he unclipped a metal step that extended the full length of the pass. He winked. "No more crates for you."

"Who did this?" she whispered in awe.

"The big guy," Maude reminded her.

She stepped up, easily able to reach the tickets and see over the pass to the wait staff. "I think I might just love that man."

CHAPTER THIRTY-EIGHT

ead bent, Isabella furiously scribbled notes across a yellow legal pad. Her first week as the Executive Chef was a whirlwind. Her petite frame was almost lost amidst the wide variety of ingredients strewn across the long, oak table. An abundance of fruits, cheeses, breads, and nuts piled high on the Main Dining Room's black dishes.

Hitching his tool belt higher on his hips, Dale emerged from the second newly discovered room and leaned against the once hidden doorframe. He looped his thumbs in the front pockets of his faded jeans. "Miss Isabella, I've got everything all hooked up if you want to come and take a look at your new office."

Moments went by. Isabella's brow furrowed, she shuffled a few ingredients, and mumbled under her breath.

He chewed on his toothpick and waited. "Miss Isabella?"

She raised her head and her gaze focused in on his image. "Yes?"

His toothpick shifted sides between his lips and he patiently repeated himself.

A surge of excitement built, rumbled through her frame and escaped in an excited squeal. She wiped her hands on a small white towel and her eyes sparkled. "Show me what you've done. And all within a week! You're amazing."

Dale shifted his weight and allowed her to enter first.

She rushed forward with a cheek splitting grin. "I guess we shouldn't call it a secret room any more, should we?"

"Nope." He moseyed in after her. "Not since Miss Maddy found out about it. That girl's mind's like quicksilver. Give her a new spot to think about and she's dreamin' up creative ideas on what to do with it."

She patted him on the shoulder, concern wrinkling the smooth skin on her forehead. "I'm sure she's keeping you and your crew hopping."

He pulled a cell phone out of a pocket on the side of his tool belt. "Mr. Beaumont gave me one of these." He wiggled the small black phone between his aged fingers. "Can't use my radio to talk with him about Miss Maddy's ideas anymore. 'Cause she kept breaking in and giving her input. Mr. Beaumont put his number in here, so all I have to do is press a button and it rings directly to him." He shook his head. "Miss Maddy wanted me to give her my," he paused, "digits?" He looked quizzically at Isabella. "Thank God Mr. Beaumont told me what they were."

She laughed. "Here, give it to me." She snatched the cell phone, swiftly inserted her number, handed it back to him and squeezed his hand. "Now you also have me to call if you need help with her."

"Thanks Miss Isabella. Love that girl, but she sure is a handful. Don't know how Mr. Beaumont does it. I've raised one strappin' boy and have another almost full grown. They were easier than her."

"I understand. But she does have wonderful ideas." She quickly added, "Sometimes. When she came in here and declared the secret room should now be the Executive Chef's office and the old Executive Chef's office should become a Tasting Room, I was floored. Can you believe it, a tasting room? What does she know about tasting rooms at her age? But she was right, and the rooms were probably originally designed to work that way. The long table is perfect for staff meetings. Once the boxes are moved and a working table is placed in the other room, the large open space is an ideal place for me to create in peace. Then, I can hold taste testing with other chefs, plus the wait and kitchen staff. Hosting a taste testing for the kitchen is a wonderful way for the kitchen staff to come together and learn at the same time. Or I can throw a crisp linen tablecloth on the long table and now Twin Springs offers an exclusive intimate dining experience for elite clientele, their family and personal guests. We can even offer private cooking lessons with the Executive Chef of Twin Springs." She grinned up at Dale and tapped her chest with the tip of her thump. "That's me. I'm the Executive Chef of Twin Springs."

The wrinkles around the edges of his eyes deepened with his smile. "Had no doubt you'd make it one day, Miss Isabella. None at all."

He rolled back on his heels and directed her attention to the room. "I think these two rooms were once one big room." He motioned at the wood floor. "See how the planks continue from one room to the next? The wall was placed in after the floor was laid."

She gave a non-committal response and turned to focus on the improvements he made in the new office.

The smell of cleaning solutions and fresh paint permeated the air. In his own unique ambling style, Dale showed her the updates. "We replaced the danglin' light bulb with these three hanging light fixtures." He reached over the boxes and pulled on one of the black light shades. "Once your work table is here, you can draw these lights closer or move them higher. We put in recessed lighting throughout the room to compensate for the lack of windows. The three shelving units across the back wall now have white doors with frosted glass fronts. Everyone chipped in to make this room come together. Even Niles personally painted some of those shelves for you."

She opened one of the glass doors and ran her fingertips across the newly painted, glossy white shelves. "I can't believe these are over a hundred years old."

"They made things right back then."

"I love how you painted the back walls of the shelves in green."

"Thought we should keep everythin' in line with the rest of the grand hotel." He stuck his used toothpick in the tiny front pocket of his jeans, replacing it with a new one. "The lightin' we placed inside each shelf will also help keep the room bright."

"It's beautiful and a wonderful place for me to keep my supplies and cooking tools. I love that we were able to keep the original stove and sink."

"Yep," Dale replied. "Gas stove fittings replaced and inspected. Ready for you to fire it up. Re-plumbed the double sink." He reached over to the wall mounted faucets. "Since back then there were separate hot and cold faucets, we switched it up for you. Now you have one faucet that adjusts to any temperature from cold to hot. And one that pipes out steaming hot water for your quick boilin' needs."

She threw her arms around him and balanced on her toes. "Thank you, Dale!" She hugged him tight. "I would kiss you on the cheek but you are too darn tall."

His cheeks flushed to a dark scarlet and he patted her awkwardly on the shoulder. "Wasn't anything, Miss Isabella. Still need to finish rewiring the walls and paint 'em the color you want. Or wallpaper them, if you like that better. Then we can place in the refrigerator you want. Won't be able to work on that till next week. Finishing up on the spa and General's room, then startin' in on the new Lobby Bar."

She waved a hand at him and followed him out of the room. "This is more than enough. Whenever you guys have the time. Again, thank you. You've been working overtime a lot lately."

He shrugged. "It's good to still be useful. Besides, the plannin' of the bar is finally getting my oldest out of the woods and back into the living world."

"How is Logan doing?"

"Well, the maids are not screaming every time they see him now." He tugged off his baseball cap and wiped his suddenly moist eyes on his blue work sleeve. "It'll take time. The war on terror left some pretty heavy scars on that boy." He replaced his cap. "Not just on the outside."

She gripped his sleeve within her small fist. "Let me know if there's anything I can do."

"Will do," he replied. "I think working on this beautiful old Dame will be the best therapy for the boy." He cleared his throat. "Well, Miss Isabella, if there's anythin' else you need, you just call." His smile widened around the toothpick. "Or send Miss Maddy. She seems to have a sixth sense for where I am."

"Thanks, Dale."

He opened the door just as Theo was about to knock. Looking the younger man up and down, he frowned at his black suit pants and pin striped shirt. Shaking his head, he stepped aside, allowing Theo to enter. "Sir."

Theo clasped Dale's hand and shook it. "How's it going?"

"It's a goin'." He winked at Isabella and closed the door in his boss' face.

heo lifted an eyebrow at Dale's unique exit. A part of him yearned for the older man's approval, but he shook it off and inched his tie closer to his throat. "A man of few words."

He shifted his attention to his main goal. Isabella. For once her boxy chef jacket was draped over a chair and not covering her delicious curves. Maybe he should burn the dumb thing. Perhaps then, her stunning little body would never again be hidden from his sight. The white tank top she wore skimmed her, curving in at all the best places. His body began to burn. His mouth was suddenly parched.

Hopelessly aware of how the swell of her silky breasts peeped out above the neckline of her tank top, his gaze devoured her. He yearned to dip his hand in, pluck out her breast and nibble on it. Unable to touch her soft skin, he suppressed a telling groan of misery and pathetically swallowed in an attempt to moisten his mouth and throat. Desperately, he searched his mind for a good reason for being there. Other than the obvious one, "I can't stay away from you."

"Did you say something?"

Shit, shit, shit, vibrated through Theo's brain. Did he groan out loud? Or worse, did he voice his thoughts? The heat drained from his loins and rushed to burn bright across his face. He reigned in his emotions and swiftly replied, "Not at all."

He pressed his weight into the balls of his feet to prevent them from shuffling and restrained his gaze from dipping beneath her chin. Suddenly, he realized they stood awkwardly just inside the door. *Crap.* His mind raced for a safe topic. "If you noticed, I did try to knock."

"He can be taught," she gently mocked and her lips curved into a generous smile.

His gaze shifted from her chin to her soft lips. The wattage of her smile spread warmth through his chest. He swallowed hard and forced words up through his throat. "How's your new office coming along?"

She tilted her head and little pools of green lights sparkled in her eyes. "It's wonderful. Truly, a dream office for any chef."

Searching his mind for a reason to stay, he asked, "I've wondered, how long have you wanted to be an Executive Chef at Twin Springs?"

She choked back a laugh. "That's like asking how long I've needed to breathe. It's an easy answer." Her voice lowered reverently as she replied, "Since I flipped my first pancake and realized that I love bringing someone else pleasure through my food." Self-deprecating laughter laced her voice and she shared a crooked grin with him.

He was entranced by her. Her effervescent zest for cooking. Her light hearted manner. Just her.

She looked up at him and her incredibly long lashes framed the passion glowing within the green glow of her gaze. "Now I understand how lucky I was. I grew up around the great chefs here. The exquisite food our kitchen delivered developed my taste buds at an early age." She licked her lips and continued.

He knew that he should be concentrating on her words but he was sidetracked when her pink tongue slid along her bottom lip until it glistened.

"Besides, no other chef I know, not even Leslie Revsin, enjoyed the tutelage of a ghost who helped create their love of cooking and food." She laughed.

Not knowing what the hell she just said, he laughed with her. Frantically his mind attempted to rewind her words, trying to focus in on a reply that wouldn't show the simpleton he'd just become. "Who's Leslie Revsin?"

She raised her hands to the heavens and declared, "I'm surrounded by amateurs." She winked and lowered her hands. "She's only one of my greatest idols and the first woman to run the kitchen of a major hotel. She took the helm of the Waldorf Astoria hotel in New York."

The passion of her words vibrated between them. He flexed his hands, itching to catch her by the hips and bring her closer. He regretted to his core, the promise he'd made at the pool. Instead, he showered her with his faith in her abilities. "You could take her."

She shook her head. "I'm not into competing against other chefs. Creating dishes for guests and people I love gives me a sense of accomplishment. When I design a dish, I have no sense of time. I'm caught up in mixing the flavors, the acids, the sugars and the tones of the food. Once finished, I can't wait to taste my new creation and then share it with others for their pleasure. I just hope my love affair with food comes through on the plate."

He'd sunk to the lowest level possible for a man. He watched this glorious woman come alive and burn bright right before him. And he was jealous. Jealous of food. A pitiful excuse of a man who'd promised not to touch the only woman who made his blood boil. His silence stretched between them.

Abruptly feeling uncomfortable with sharing so much of herself and his silence, she switched gears and shuffled over to the table. "Can we afford the renovations here plus the renovations of the spa?"

Thank God! Finances, debt, money issues, he chanted in his head. He knew talking about money would help cool down his fever. That, and perhaps only looking at her forehead. Her chin was obviously too close to her lips. "The funds from the insurance claims will eventually offset the costs. Besides, the newly discovered rooms were virtually untouched by time. We pay the maintenance crew no matter what and the other improvements that we made were pretty minor."

"I understand Ava assisted with handling the insurance investigator."

Finances or thinking of her sister. Either worked to keep him from disgracing himself by falling to his knees and begging for her to share her body with him. Remembering Ava's distinct style in handling Twin Springs' little problem, he chuckled. "Yes, she did. I felt privileged to see her in action. The investigator was putty in her hands. One moment she was a somewhat nutty but very sexy woman spinning him around her fingers, the next she became a tragic waif and Mr. Cummings actually comforted her for the losses at Twin Springs. Amazing."

"That's Ava. The first woman was her part as *Sally Bowles* in the Broadway musical *Cabaret*. The second, from her performance as the young orphaned Cosette from *Les Miserables*."

Astonished by Ava's talent, he shook his head. "Towards the end, I felt sorry for Cummings. From now on, I'm going to keep a close eye on your sister and warn my buddies."

"Don't worry. The real Ava is nothing like either of those characters. What about the new Lobby Bar, can we afford it?"

He shrugged. "I shifted some personal investments. We will be fine."

"How will Ava and I ever buy out your and Maddy's shares if you keep having to invest more of your money into Twin Springs?"

Not wanting to discuss the possibility of her sending him away, he ignored her comment and strode over to the table covered with food. "What are you doing here?"

"Working out the menu for the Lobby Bar."

Mountains of food were piled on the table. Effortlessly, he identified the easy ones like white bread, nuts, some kind of yellow cheeses, and of course fruits. "Seems like a lot of food for a bar menu."

"The menu is not only for those drinking at the bar," Isabella answered. "Since the guests spill over into the Grand Lobby, I wanted to include selections for families to purchase as a snack or light meal from late afternoon until midnight. This will allow guests to select sandwiches, soups and sweets in addition to the finger sandwiches that we offer during teatime. Your sister had the wonderful idea of adding PB & J to the selection we serve at afternoon tea for the kids who don't like cucumber or cream cheese sandwiches."

Better and better, he thought. Talking about Maddy completely banked his fire. "Of course she did."

"Now they'll be able to order other items children enjoy, too, like hot dogs and chicken tenders. At the same time," she added, "I want to offer small plates for couples to share while enjoying late night drinks together. Dishes that will complement the tones of the fine whiskeys, wines and beers we offer."

"How do you accomplish that?"

"Well," her eyes scanned the table. "For example, the breads. We will offer bread freshly baked daily. Fresh bread has a milky aroma." She broke a loaf of bread, inhaled and swept the piece under his nose.

His eyes widened. "It does!" He perched on the edge of the table. "I never noticed that."

"And you're related to La Flamme. It amazes me."

He felt the black slick of failure coat his heart and lifted his shoulders in defeat.

"Close your eyes," she commanded.

His heart accelerated and all thoughts of Maddy, finances and failure flew from his brain. "Why?"

CHAPTER FORTY

*I*sabella's breath caught but she'd committed herself. "Just close your eyes." She watched his dark lashes hesitate and lay still on his high cheekbones. She ripped off a bite size piece of bread. Unwillingly, her voice lowered to a husky whisper. "Open your mouth."

She slipped the bread between his parted lips and felt the heat of his breath as she placed it on his tongue. At her boldness, her heart slammed against her ribs and she snatched her hand back before her fingertips were caught between his firm lips. "Fresh bread tastes almost like popcorn or similar to toasted hazelnuts."

Momentarily entranced by his full lips, her eyes skimmed the hard plains of his face. From his strong jawline, to his high cheekbones, to his thick, black lashes. His eyes opened. Their gazes locked. His smoky gaze penetrated her defenses. Unconsciously, she leaned in towards the heat he generated.

"Amazing," he replied and stepped closer.

Skittish, she broke away from his intense gaze. "Combine the flavors of certain nuts and cheeses, and we'll have a beautiful dish."

"How so?"

His husky voice warmed her and goosebumps bloomed across

her chilled skin. "We pair fresh walnuts with the dish, they're not as bitter." She sucked in even breaths to calm her beating heart, then scooped up a handful of walnuts, shook them and moved them around in her hand with a finger. "Notice the color of the skin?"

"Yes."

"Fresh walnuts have a thin, tan skin." Breathless, she placed a walnut in his mouth.

His lips caught the tip of her finger.

Ever so slowly, she watched her finger slide from his warm, wet mouth. Her heart was a moth, beating against the constraints of her chest to burn within his flame.

Yearning to burn with him, her legs melted. She leaned in and whispered, "Sweet and moist."

"Yes, very sweet," he groaned deep within his chest. "I can't Isabella. I promised you."

Their lips inches apart, she felt his muscles tense. She trailed her fingertips down his arm and wished he'd caress her. Her breath mingled with his. "What promise?"

His fingers dug into the fabric covering his thighs. "The vow I made at the pool. My promise not to touch you."

She no longer cared about promises. Not the promise she made to herself to stay away from him, or whatever foolish promise he made to her. Only he could quench the insistent need within her body. She craved his heat. His strength. She needed him. Theo Beaumont. The boy who'd stole her heart years ago and the man before her who made her body burn and come alive.

She moved closer, in between his thighs, and freed her heart to flutter closer and closer to his heat. Not caring if her heart was consumed by the flame of his spirit, she pressed her softness against the strength running through his hard body. "Theo, don't you realize," she rubbed her palm over his thudding heart, "every time we are in the same room, I feel your presence touching me." Reaching up, she traced a trembling fingertip across his smooth bottom lip. "Every time you speak to me, I feel stroked by your words. Every time you look at me I feel caressed by your gaze."

His eyes reflected back at her as molten pools of steel. "Please stop." He groaned from deep within his soul. "I promised you and the top of my head will explode from the increased pressure your words and touch are inflicting upon my resolve. I must keep my promise. It's all I have. If I'm unable to honor my vow to you, I'm nothing. Unmanned."

"Theo," she whispered, her lips a breath away from his, "I'll release you from that vow. If you'll promise me one thing."

His body vibrated against her with need. "Oh, God." He squeezed his eyes shut and brought his trembling body under control. His eyes opened and resolve shone from his gaze. "Anything."

She pressed her lips against his mouth and her words spelled out her desires against his lips. "Promise me, you'll never stop touching me."

He jerked her close, delved into her sweetness and she tasted his flavors. His fingers laced into the bun of her hair and he cradled her head within his palm. He tasted sweet as he licked and devoured her mouth.

He stood and she clung to him, unwilling to move away from him even for a second. Relief flooded through her when he lifted her and wrapped her legs around his middle. Carrying her, he continued to ravish her mouth as he walked over and locked the door.

She smiled against his lips, "No Maddy today?"

He placed her on the edge of the table. "No Maddy. Only us." Blindly, he reached behind her and pushed food out of the way.

Subconsciously, she heard food and dishes scattering across the table and crashing to the floor.

Reverently, he laid her back and slowly released her glorious hair. He splayed the thick softness around her head with his tapered fingers. His hands spanned her ribcage, slowly lifting her tank top, skimming her smooth, silken skin with his lips as he went. Pulling it up and over her head, he cast the fabric aside. Reaching down, he undid the snaps on her jeans and slid them down her luscious legs.

From above her, he viewed her beautiful body laid out before him. His gaze feasted on her creamy white skin, barely concealed by her silky bra and panties. He studied the fabric covered with little dots of pink, blue, green and yellow. His brow rose. "Polka dots, huh?"

"I thought they were happy."

He gazed down appreciatively, "Well, they're certainly making me very happy."

Her laughter flowed over him. "If I knew that I'd be modeling for you, I would've worn my black lace."

He released her bra and freed her breasts to his gaze. Cupping their softness in each hand, he bent forward, licked and nibbled on each nipple until they rose to a rosy peak, and her head tipped back with rapture. "It's you, Isabella, I want to see. I could care less what you're wrapped in. You're beautiful." He puckered a kiss on one rosy nipple, "My Isabella," then the other. "My beauty." Then he trailed kisses down to her belly button and her body shivered. "My Bella."

His hands skimmed down her body, effortlessly removing her panties. With care, he dipped into her moist softness. Twirled his fingers between her soft folds and his thumb massaged her silky nub.

She writhed with the pleasure of his touch and her knees raised to grip his hips.

Placing her small hand on his, she halted him. Extending her arms, her fingers busily worked on the little buttons of his dress shirt. She slid the fabric away and ran her hands along the muscled groves of his shoulders. Her heart ached from the angry red scratches across his chest.

"I'm so sorry," she murmured and placed soft healing kisses along each scratch.

He drew her hands from him and lightly held them high above

her head. "They're nothing compared to the pain of waiting for you. I didn't bring protection but that doesn't mean I can't bring you pleasure."

"I'm protected. So, wait no more," she whispered.

Spurred into action, he ran kisses along her neck as he released himself from his pants. Skimming his hand along the curve of her bottom, down to the nook behind her knee, he raised her leg up and pressed himself within her silky sheath. Steadily, he rocked against her softness.

Her heart thundered and her breathing quickened into short gasps. Only then, with his own heart racing, Theo accelerated his strokes and surged forward. The fragrance of fresh vanilla flowed over their entwined bodies and their souls blended and melded into one.

Exquisite pleasure coursed through Isabella and she trembled, then, shuddered. Finding his release within her throbbing body, Theo leaned his forehead against hers. Their bodies slick with sweat, he kissed the bruises high on her cheekbone.

Except for the sounds of their mingled breathing, silence filled the room around them. Then the doorknob jiggled.

CHAPTER FORTY-ONE

Isabella's eyes popped wide open. "Maddy," she whispered, her voice frantic and ending in a high-pitched squeak. "Move." She slapped her hands against his bare shoulders and urgently pushed at him.

Not wanting to leave her warmth, Theo momentarily hung his head. He groaned with frustration, "Sometimes being a big brother sucks."

His comment drew a narrowed glare and shushes from her. Spurned into action by another jiggle of the doorknob, he released her and tugged up his pants. At least he was able to enjoy the sight of her sexy body bouncing around on one foot as she attempted to put her panties on and pull her tank top over her head simultaneously.

Muffled voices outside the door argued and a knock sounded at the door.

In the process of buttoning up her jeans, she flipped her massive hair back, and gave him a panicked look. "Hurry," she whispered.

He watched her vain attempt to cleanup the scattered food from around the room. Using her small hands, she brushed bits of food and pieces of broken china from the chairs. Getting down on her knees, she cupped her hands and scooped the smashed dishes and food into the trashcan.

What's she doing? Momentarily shocked by her panicky movements. He walked over and crouched down. Taking her hands in both of his, her paused her frantic movements. "Don't worry, Maddy can't tattle to my parents."

She smacked him on the arm. "That's not funny," she hissed. "It matters to me." Lowering her voice, she added, "News like this will spread through Twin Springs like wild fire. The staff will look at me with knowing smiles and looks. They'll assume this is how I earned my new position." She shoved the metal trash can into his hands. "Now move it, help me cleanup this mess!"

Confusion fogged his brain. He couldn't help but wonder if she was ashamed of being caught having sex or if she was ashamed of being caught having sex with him. An ill feeling filled him, as if his heart turned to lead and sunk to his stomach. "If you want our relationship to be kept a secret then by God that's what will happen." Even if her wish contradicted everything he was working towards.

He swept the ruined food into the trash, while she stacked what remained of the black plates. She placed the trashcan along the wall, just in time for her cell phone to give a warning ping and the door to open.

Looking back over his shoulder, Niles' gigantic frame entered the room.

Ava's angry voice followed him. "I don't think we should go in her office without her permission."

"She won't care," he replied, drawing the fabric of his green shirt forward and brandishing the Security Manager insignia. "I'm head of security here at Twin Springs. The sheriff wants to confiscate the moonshine now. Don't you Sheriff?"

Isabella donned her chef jacket and cast a polite, pasted-on smile towards her unwelcome guests.

Stunned by the scene before him, Niles abruptly stopped, causing a pile up of people behind him. "Your hair's down." Dumbfounded, he stared at Isabella. "You haven't worn your hair down since you were a little girl."

Ava skirted around him. "What are you talking about?" She surveyed the room, taking in Theo leaning against the table, his arms crossed, displeasure clearly written across his face and Isabella nervously fiddling with the ends of her hair. "Oh, my," she breathed at the sight before her.

"I don't have all the time in the world. Show me this secret room and your moonshine." A crabby voice emanated from the hall. "I need to get back to the station." Sheriff Briggs, chest puffed out, strolled into the room followed by a disgruntled teenage boy draped from head to toe in black leather. Moving at his own pace, Logan filed in behind.

"Well, looks like there was quite the food fight in here," said the Sheriff.

The young boy snickered behind him.

Sheriff Briggs cuffed the boy in the back of the head. "Shut up, son."

Logan took up a solitary stance lounging against the door-frame. He resembled a homeless man in his tattered black Beatles t-shirt and hole filled jeans.

"Why didn't you answer the door?" Niles questioned, still confused.

"Why do you think?" snickered the young boy.

Great, just great, thought Theo. How would he control some stupid kid and the Sheriff from spreading what they saw?

Isabella's smile wained and heat rushed into her cheeks.

He flexed his fingers and then balled them into fists, wanting to knock all their heads together for embarrassing her. But he understood protecting her was more important.

He'd failed her once and he'd be damned if he would again. He needed to remain above the fray, control the situation and not allow his personal feelings to interfere with taking care of her. Later, by whatever means necessary, he'd control the damage. Theo stood, drawing himself to his full height, and commanding the attention of the group. His steely gaze scanned the room, impacting each intruder with its intensity. "We were in the other room and didn't hear you knock." The no-nonsense tone in his voice dared anyone to argue.

The teenager slinked back in response, muted.

Niles' face flamed red above his beard and he shoved his hands into his pockets.

Taking Theo's cue, Ava moved forward, further into the room. With a wide, sweeping gesture, she directed everyone's attention to her and away from Isabella and Theo. "Sheriff, the boxes are right through here." Casting him a dazzling smile, she linked her arm with the Sheriff's, drawing his attention from the room and over to her stunning face. With a wave of her hand, she gestured for the teenager to follow, "You too, Wyatt. Right through here."

Theo watched the groups' reaction to Ava's efforts. Wyatt pushed his greasy black hair back out of his dark eyes and followed, his downcast face twisted and sullen. Warily, Theo eyed the teenager, assessing him. He made a mental note to keep the boy away from Maddy. Niles refused to make eye contact with him or Isabella. He did an abrupt about turn, exited out into the hallway and slammed the door closed behind him.

Logan sidestepped out of the doorway before the door closed on top of him. Silently he limped, trailing behind the crowd, pausing only to bend down and reach under the long, oak table. With his mutilated hand he scooped up a polka dotted piece of fabric and handed Isabella her bra. "You might need this," was his only comment as he passed.

Humiliated, her cheeks flushed pink and she glared at Theo. She scurried after the group, while shoving her bra into her coat pocket.

He let out an exasperated sigh and joined them.

Sheriff Briggs stood in the middle, rocking back on his feet, legs spread as he surveyed the room full of boxes. "Lookie what we have here," he drawled, pulling out a pack of gum from the side pocket of his tan, tactical pants. Taking his time, he removed a stick and folded it into his mouth. "Tryin' to quit smoking," he winked. At the snort emanating from the lanky boy behind them, he smoothly responded, "Shut up, son," and returned his attention to Isabella. "My son's here to help carry boxes to the truck. Just ignore him."

Relief filled Theo when he noticed Isabella give the Sheriff a little smile for his comment, as she placed her hands into the front pockets of her chef jacket. Only for the relief to be replaced by exasperation when her shoulders stiffened and she quickly removed her hands almost causing her bra to fall out.

Color flared to her cheeks and she glared at Logan. "Why are you here?" she inquired, frustrated by his earlier actions.

"What? You don't think I'm not man enough to carry a few boxes?"

"No, I didn't mean that. Of course not," she sputtered. "We have staff in the kitchen who could help."

He tipped his sandy blonde head towards Theo. "Someone didn't want a lot of people knowing about the moonshine. Somehow, he thinks he can keep secrets within Twin Springs."

"Logan, play nice," admonished Ava.

The boy snickered and the Sheriff's accompanying reply rang out, "Shut up, son."

Theo shook his head. He thought dealing with Maddy was tough, but nothing compared to this group. "Enough," his authoritative voice called out. Ready to remove the attention from Isabella, he extended his hand, "Sheriff, I haven't had the pleasure of meeting you yet."

"Not true."

Searching his memory, his brow creased, "We've already met?"

"Yep." The Sheriff chopped at his gum, appraising him. "I

responded to the scene of your parents' accident. My first vehicular fatality on the job as the new Sheriff." He pumped Theo's hand. "Quite a sight. Your sister shiverin' in the freezing air, surrounded by deep snow. And you holding her, no coat, not even a shirt. Always wondered what happened to your shirt."

An icy cold flowed through his veins, chilling him, and he dropped his hand without answering.

"Never found that van. Niles said you inherited quite a fortune. With your parents gone."

An uncomfortable silence filled the room. The Sheriff continued without missing a beat. "Understand ya'll having some trouble round here, not meaning the shine. Seems since you Beaumonts have taken over, Twin Springs has been having a hell of a time."

Theo's eyes narrowed to gray slits. "What are you implying?"

"Niles tells me strange things been happening around here." The Sheriff nodded towards Isabella. "Those bruises look pretty fresh." He assessed Theo, looking him up and down. "We don't take to our women being hurt here."

Rage coursed through Theo. Staring at the hick Sheriff, an immense hatred filled him and mindlessly propelled him forward. Only Isabella urgently tugging on his sleeve stopped him. Gathering his emotions and mentally holding himself apart from the scene, he pushed aside his anger for a later time.

Besides, allowing his feelings to run wild was a luxury that he was no longer allowed. Pulverizing the Sheriff would just piss him off and perhaps motivate him to accuse and prosecute Twin Springs for illegally selling moonshine. That would be a rash and foolish move. No matter how good slamming his fist into that blowhard, dick faced Sheriff would feel. Stoic, he waited for Isabella to tell the Sheriff the damning facts. She didn't see who hit her, he found her in a secret room, following a scent that no one else smelled. Combine those facts with the Sheriff's current view towards the Beaumonts and he would be sleeping in a jail cell later tonight.

Isabella spoke up, "Really, it's not like that. Not at all. I fell."

The boy snorted.

"Shut up, Wyatt," she fired back at the teenager. "I didn't know you and Niles were such good friends."

Stroking the handle of his gun, the Sheriff watched Theo. "Yep, poker buddies. Lose a bundle to him monthly. Hard to read his face, 'cause of that damn beard."

"Sheriff," said Ava, patting Theo on the arm. "Why don't you come look inside the boxes and give us your opinion?"

Snapping his gum, the Sheriff reached down into a box and withdrew one of the jugs. Popping the lid, he took a swig and wiped his mouth with the sleeve of his uniform. "That's some fine shine. Going to be a damn shame to pour it down the drain."

His son snorted.

Swiftly, Ava asked, "Do you confiscate a lot of shine?"

"From time to time. This used to be a wet county. When my pop was just a boy, he told me everybody used to brew themselves up some white lightning. Everybody except the Lutheran preacher, he made the barrels." Sheriff Briggs slapped his leg, laughing at his own joke, as his gum hung out the side of his mouth. Controlling his laughter, he continued, "It's the cold mountain springs. The water cools the stills' coils. Plus, the thickly wooded hollers make it difficult for us law enforcement to track down where they're brewin'. Used to call the Feds, but too much paperwork. Easier to just dispose of the shine at the station. Never found a stash this big. Say, you don't know how it came to be here?"

"No," replied Isabella. "We didn't even know this room was back here."

"Mighty strange," he replied, shifting the crotch of his pants. "I'll be needing to speak with your employees. See if I can get to the bottom of this. Can't have bootleggers thinking they are getting the best of me, now can I. Don't worry, once it gets cold and the leaves start fallin', I'll be able to track a still this big down mighty quick. They can't hide the smoke when the leaves drop." He smacked his son hard on the back. "Alright, grab a box and let's get these loaded up. Got work to do."

"We'll get out of your way then," replied Ava. She draped an arm around her sister's shoulders and led her towards the door. Stealthy, she removed a chunk of bread from Isabella's hair, pressing it into her palm. A broad smile lining her face, Ava kissed her on the cheek. She tossed Theo a sultry wink and exited the room in grand style.

CHAPTER FORTY-TWO

2 7 December 1928

Evil fucking whore. She let him touch her. I have proof. Found her scarf, right there next to the crates.

She's forced my hand. Now I must kill both her and her colored lover. It's all her fault. She seduced him with her scent, the curve of her breasts, her silky, long blonde hair. She spread her legs for him. Opened herself up to him. Soiled herself and now she's of no good to me. I'm going to kill her just like Adriana. They'll rot in Hell together. Filthy whores! Every single one of them.

I'll bide my time, wait and watch until she spreads her legs again. Then, I'll catch her with her lover and destroy the bitch who dared to cast me aside.

Lt.

CHAPTER FORTY-THREE

The next morning, Isabella sat in her new Executive Chef's office typing her menu ideas into the new computer that Theo had ordered for her. Earlier, she'd propped open the outer office door and now she enjoyed the warm summer breeze flowing from the loading dock, through the kitchen and down the hall. Bouncing to the beat of the music emanating from her earbuds, she danced in her chair, only pausing her work to sing the song's chorus into her impromptu microphone—the mouse from her computer. Fully into her performance, she froze when she felt something touch her shoulder. "Spider!"

A panicked shriek escaped her lips. Propelled into action, she jumped from her seat while frantically dusting off her shoulder. Feeling a large presence in the room, definitely greater than a spider, she whirled around and was ready to fight. Relief filled her at the sight of Niles, a big teddy bear in his usual uniform. She placed a hand over her chest and rubbed the fabric of her chef jacket to still her panicked heart. "You frightened me."

"You never cease to surprise me. That was quite the performance."

"I—well—I—" she stuttered. Not wanting to elicit a Dizzy Izzy response from him, she replied, "Yeah, it's all the rage in the New

York club scene." She shifted from foot to foot. She never enjoyed the knowing looks that he gave her when she messed up. He felt like a disapproving older sibling.

His deep laugh broke the silence. "I'm sure it is. You'll have to share those moves with me later. Can we talk? I need to show you something."

"Must be important. You just finished the night shift and must be dead tired. What's up?"

His beefy hand withdrew a flash drive from the pocket of his khakis. He flipped her chair around, sat down straddling the chair backwards and leaned forward to maneuver the mouse. "Just let me insert this into the back of your computer. You know, I'd never want to purposefully hurt you. I feel a deep responsibility towards you and Ava since your father passed. My greatest wish is to help you regain Twin Springs and for the Grand Dame to thrive."

Amazed, she listened to his words. She couldn't recall Niles ever sharing so much with her, baring his soul and sounding so sincere. She remembered him as a child, bigger than most but always around. She'd never considered that all that hair concealed such a huge, caring heart. She beamed at him and rubbed his arm with affection. "You're a kind hearted soul and an asset to not only Twin Springs, but also to my sister and me."

Intrigued, she rested her hand on his shoulder and bent forward to see the screen. "Is this one of those YouTube videos?" She flashed him another smile. "The puppy ones are my favorite."

He shook his head. "No. Something else. I discovered it when Theo told me to pull up Twin Springs' security footage."

Her eyebrows furrowed as Theo's fuzzy image popped up on the computer screen. "What?" Curious, she peered into her friend's molasses brown eyes. "What's this?" She leaned in further. Theo stood in the back hallway, entering what seemed to be the original Executive Chef's office. After a few moments he appeared back in the hallway and slowly closed her office door.

Niles reached forward, zooming the picture in with a click of the mouse.

Theo turned. Facing the camera, he tucked a leather journal under his arm. Maniacal laughter trailed behind him as he strolled away and out of the camera's view.

She jerked back from the computer screen. Her legs shook beneath her and shock vibrated through her body. Her hands clapped over her ears and her eyes squeezed shut. Her mind rebelled at the thought. A terrible niggle of doubt raised in the back of her mind. *How could it be Theo?* "No. It can't be. Can't be the same awful laughter as at the pool. He said—he told me." Unable to continue, she shook her head. The laughter echoed through her mind, tormenting her and driving her mad. "Stop it. Please just mute it or something."

Niles pressed mute and rose. He rubbed her back and gazed down at her, his eyes soft with concern. "I hate doing this to you." His finger tapped the screen. "Look at the date and time in the corner. It's the date the journal disappeared from within this room. The date your face was smashed in." He bent down and gathered her in his arms. "I'm sorry, but I promised you proof."

Disbelief sucked the air out of her lungs. Her chest hitched and she couldn't catch her breath. She struggled out from under his embrace and rubbed her breastbone with her knuckles. Unwelcome tears ran down her face and dripped from her chin. She'd let Theo touch her. Actually, told him to touch her. Almost begged him to take her. Her stomach churned, remembering. He was so blasé about people knowing. Did he time it for the greatest effect, knowing the Sheriff and everyone else would discover them? "I think I'm going to be sick."

She stumbled, righted herself and ran to the sink, just in time to lose the contents of her stomach. She leaned forward against the sink, head down, sweat and tears dribbling off her nose. Her voice vibrated with raw emotion, "I just can't believe it."

She turned on the water and rinsed out the sink. The mechanical motions allowed her to put her brain in neutral. She cupped her hand under the water and rinsed out her mouth. Unable to face the computer screen or Niles, she trailed her fingertips over the antique sink, taking comfort in the curves and coolness of the porcelain. She ached to lay her hot cheeks upon the sink's cold surface and go back in time to ten minutes ago, when she was happy. But there was no going back. She dragged the black kerchief from her hair and soaked the cloth with chilly water until her fingers felt numb and stiff. She twisted and squeezed out the water and welcomed the coolness of the cloth against her face. Not bearing to see the pity in Niles' eyes, she continued to face the sink. "Thank you for showing it to me."

"I'm sorry to hurt you."

"You—" Her voice cracked. Her heart burned with pain. She kneaded her lip with her teeth before taking a deep steadying breath and continuing. "You've always been a true friend to my family. To me. You cared for my father when he was sick. How can I hold you responsible?" She shrugged. "At least now I know."

"Perhaps Theo holds you responsible for how his family was treated here at Twin Springs. Isabella, you can never truly know someone else's heart."

She remembered Emma's dream with her chef and their undeniable love. Tears welled up in her eyes from the unequivocal love Emma and Jean Claude shared. A love she now would never know. "Perhaps," she choked out, dabbing at her eyes with the sleeve of her chef's jacket. She recalled how Jean Claude protected Emma with his life, not caring about the punishing blows he received to keep her safe. Her family didn't beat La Flamme but how was Theo to know? The beating did happen here at Twin Springs. Also, the most traumatic experience of Theo's life, the death of his parents, was connected to Twin Springs. The world around him irrevocably changed after his family drove away from the hotel. He was no longer carefree, but filled with duty and responsibility and unable to finish college with his friends. Anger and resentment could twist a mind. She took a deep breath, centering herself. "Perhaps he does blame Twin Springs for everything."

CHAPTER FORTY-FOUR

"Who blames Twin Springs for everything?" asked Theo, striding in.

Isabella twirled to face him, blanched and froze in place. Without uttering a word she studied Theo, soaking him into her heart with her gaze. The breadth of his shoulders in his pressed, button-up shirt, with his ever constant tie high and tight against his throat. His tan pants were pressed and snapped with each of his steps. On any other man, his clothes would scream nerd, desk jockey, or uptight jerk. But on Theo, the clothes morphed into a cloak of strength and confidence that radiated from his core.

Greeting her, he cupped the back of her head with his hand and kissed her firmly upon her mouth.

She stiffened within his embrace and slid her mouth away from his.

Tension flowed through the air. Filled the room. Theo raised his head and gazed down at her. His brow wrinkled with concern and his gaze grew dark and heavy. "What happened?"

She stepped away from him. Separated herself from his strength, his heat. She sensed his gaze resting upon her, questioning. Her heart throbbed with loss and she kept her own eyes cast down, afraid he or Niles would discover the pain she concealed.

She heard herself say, "Show him." Her voice sounded foreign and distant in her ears, as if it emanated from the other room, instead of from her own mouth.

Mutely, Niles cued up the video and replayed it.

Curious, Theo stood alone. He watched the computer screen with his hands tucked into his front pockets.

She saw his body jerk when he identified the person on the screen as himself. After the video ended, maniacal laughter continued to vibrate off the walls. "Is this what upset you?"

Her silence coated the air.

Still not facing her, his shoulders slumped and his head bowed. "Was that the same laughter you heard at the pool and in this room the night you were hit?"

Unable to speak over the emotions bottled up in her throat, she confirmed with a nod. Her heart thundered against the confines of her chest, frantically trying to reach out to him.

Not hearing a response, he turned and spread his arms apart, palms raised, questioning her. The stormy shadows of his gaze silently questioned her. Still receiving no response, his arms dropped hopelessly to his side. He'd lost her.

She recognized the deep sadness within his gaze. His pain coursed through her and stole her breath. Pierced her soul. For Isabella, the time between her heartbeats lengthened. Before her stood a combination of the young man she had once known in her youth and the man he matured into. She reflected back upon the first time they met, on his playfulness and unabashed love of life, to the present day man before her, forced too soon into adulthood and responsibility. Now she understood, Theo abandoned his childhood and freedom to raise Maddy. Without resentment, he supplied his little sister with love, and understanding. And, she was certain, with an abundance of tolerance. He showered her with so much love and support that Maddy felt safe enough to venture out on her own and enabled her to become an adventurous, free thinker who plowed through life without the fear of making mistakes or criticism. The monster from whom that laugh emanated, who held her under the water, was incapable of generating that level of love and compassion.

The more she considered him, the more her heart quickened. Even today, Theo cared for everyone within his sphere. Generously, without asking for anything in return, he gave love, support and commitment to those around him. He strode forward to repair and renovate Twin Springs and gave freely of his time, his efforts and yes, his money. Even after his and Maddy's own financial stability was threatened. Deep in her heart she understood, video or not, that he would protect his Twin Springs family with as much furor as his ancestor. The hotel was a part of his family too. His mother had understood this fact. Obviously that was why she had invested in the hotel. By doing so, she'd irrevocably tied Theo and Maddy to the Grand Dame.

She knew, without a doubt, that this man standing before her, cloaking himself in uptight clothing, was all she ever wanted. The only question that remained was, did she love him enough to believe in him?

Her heartbeats thundered in her ears. A smile spread across her face and with two quick strides, she launched herself into the safety of Theo.

Surprised, he wrapped his arms around her. He enveloped her within his strength, lifted her high in the air and close to his heart.

She pressed her hot cheeks into the crook of his neck. The pressure on her chest lifted and she breathed freely. "I don't care what I saw." She burrowed her face against his neck. "I don't care what evidence comes forth. I don't care if your pen was in my room. I don't care what's on that stupid video. I know you, Theo Beaumont. You didn't take the journal. You didn't hit me. Not you. I believe in you."

Tightening his embrace, Theo rocked back. He drew her closer and kissed the softness of her hair. He swallowed hard. His voice was rough and course with pent up emotions. "You rock me to my core, Isabella. To have you say that you believe in me? It almost brought me to my knees," he whispered into her hair. "No one believed in me. Not my father. Not the board when I replaced him. No one. I strove to prove myself, but it was too late. My parents died convinced that I was immature and reckless. I lost my parents before I could prove my worthiness to them. I've spent every waking moment trying to make up for the fact that I caused the accident. I fought with my father and distracted him. It's my fault my mother removed her seatbelt. No matter what I do, I can't bring them back. I can't give Maddy back her parents. But to know you believe in me, fully and willingly, is more than I deserve." He squeezed her tighter, crushing her lips with his.

At his words, tears streaked tracks down her face. She cupped his face within her palms and separated their lips only enough to whisper, "You didn't cause the accident that killed your parents. Just like you didn't hit me. We need to find proof. Perhaps if we start at the beginning, at the pool, then we'll discover who's sabotaging the hotel."

He rested his forehead against hers. "We'll start at the beginning. I'll talk with Maddy. Perhaps she saw something when she followed us to the pool that night."

Niles made a sound and drew their attention.

Remembering that they had an audience, he reluctantly loosened his hold and allowed her to slide down and away from the safety of his body. His fingertips tilted her chin up, so that he could look into her face. With care, he ran his thumb under each of her eyes and gathered up the tears. He kissed her lightly on the eyelids and her bruised cheek. "Play it again." Moving closer, he studied the video. "When was this taken?"

"The night that Isabella discovered the secret room. The night someone hit her and stole the journal." Niles pointed to the time and date stamp in the corner of the screen.

"How do you know what day the journal was stolen?"

Niles stiffened. "It has to be that date. You have the missing journal in your hand."

Theo considered Isabella, hooking his thumbs in the side

pockets of his slacks. "Even with this, seeing me with your own eyes, you still believe in me?" he asked in awe.

"Yes, I know in my heart it was not you."

With lightning speed, he grasped her chin and again kissed her soundly on the mouth, tasting her softness and breathing in the belief she held for him. Looking into her dewy gaze, he whispered, "Thank you."

Niles harrumphed deep in his throat.

Straightening, he confronted the large man. "I can give you three different reasons why I know that's not the night someone hit her and stole the journal." He ticked a finger in the air. "One, my hair is not wet from my time with her at the pool. Two, I have my silver pen in my front pocket which shows this was taped after she so kindly found it and gave it back." He smiled ruefully at her, squeezing her hand. "Three, that's Flamme's journal. The one she," he nodded towards her, "found after the room was cleaned out. You can see how the pages are bulging from clippings and it is tied together with a leather cord. The cord for the other journal was stolen from her bedroom after she was hit."

Niles leaned in and examined the footage again. Turning, he held out his hand, "I'm sorry, but I needed to be sure."

Shaking his hand, Theo nodded. "I understand needing to be sure. Were you able to get all the footage together from the last two weeks?"

"Yes," Niles answered. "You and Isabella are the only ones viewed coming out of the Executive Chef office alone. I'll email the video files to you."

"Great. If you don't mind, I have some things I'd like to discuss with Isabella."

Niles pulled out the flash drive and palmed it in his massive fist. "No problem."

Thoughtfully, Theo watched him depart. "How long have you known him?"

CHAPTER FORTY-FIVE

"Niles?" Isabella tucked a loose strand of hair behind her ear. "Forever. His father was the Security Manager here at Twin Springs. Why?"

Theo shrugged. "He doesn't seem to fit in within the grandness of the hotel. How did he become Security Manager?"

She leaned back on the desk, thinking. "Well, he served with the Marines for a while as an MP. When he returned, Dad gave him a job in the security office. At that time, George was the manager. After forty years of service to the Grand Dame, George passed away and Dad promoted him to head of security."

"Hmmm," replied Theo. "Enough of him." He grabbed her by the hands and raised them to his lips. He gazed into her beautiful green eyes, while pressing kisses to her delicate fingers. "I have a surprise for you."

"You do?" At the warm look in his eyes, her heart slammed against her chest. "What is it?" She thought for a moment. Then, she gave him a sly look. "Does your surprise have anything to do with food? Perhaps a taste testing?"

He chuckled. "Not in the way you are thinking. I have a friend that I've known since my bad days in college. I asked him to come to Twin Springs for tonight's service."

"I'd love to cook for your friend." She smiled with genuine happiness and excitement. It warmed her heart that he considered her food good enough to invite a long time friend to dine at the hotel. "Would the two of you prefer to dine in the Main Dining Room or would you like me to make up our new Tasting Room so that you can dine privately and catch up?"

He gathered her into his arms, lifted her and nibbled on her neck. He couldn't resist touching her when she was within reach and released her only to work on undoing the buttons on her boxy chef coat. "You don't understand. He's kind of famous in the culinary world. I asked him to come here as a favor."

Trying to concentrate on his words, she slapped his hands away and stepped back. His nearness confused his words and muddled her brain. "What do you mean he's famous in the culinary world? Is he an Executive Chef? Or a Pastry Chef? Are you trying to hire him? Or do you want me to interview him for a job?"

Grinning down at her, he gathered her close again. "Interview him? No. He's a food critic that writes for moderncuisine.com.

A feeling of dread weighed her down and she froze in his embrace. "A food critic?" Her voice was deceptively soft. "You asked a food critic to come and evaluate my food?"

He flashed her a Cheshire cat grin. "Exactly! Think of the press for Twin Springs when he gives you a glowing review. It's just what we need to create buzz, excitement. And bring in more guests."

"You're so sure he'll give me a good rating?"

"Of course he will."

Her voice was deadly calm. "Because he's your friend?"

Suddenly unsure of what he did, Theo shuffled his feet. His brow furrowed. "No, he'll be honest with his review. My friend or not, he has a reputation to protect. But how could he not love your food?"

A sickening dread coated her throat and she whispered, "What's his name?"

"Butch McKinley."

She pushed hard against his chest and walked away. "Are you kidding me?" Panic and horror pressed down on her chest, drowning her lungs with fear.

"Are you alright? You look really pale." He maneuvered her to the desk chair and shoved her head down between her legs. "Sit down for a moment. Don't lift your head yet. You looked like you were going to pass out."

He grabbed her moist kerchief off the table, drenched the fabric under the cool water at the sink and rang it out. He crouched down before her, moved between her legs and pressed the cool cloth to her wrists and her cheeks. "What happened?" He was amazed at her reaction. "I thought you'd be excited."

For the second time that morning, she held a wet cloth to her cheeks to cool them. Self-doubt flooded her consciousness. Chef Dubois was correct. She had nothing to offer Twin Springs' clientele. She hadn't even finished cooking school. Without her diploma, she was a fraud. Her skills were not up to Butch McKinley's level of judgment. How could he put her in this predicament? She was supposed to have a year. A year, damn it! Before she assumed the responsibilities of running the kitchen. She looked up at him. "Are you insane? Butch McKinley is known as the Red Butcher. And it's not because he chops up meat. It's because he chops up Executive Chefs. Even the most refined and seasoned chefs quake in terror when any tall, redheaded man enters their restaurants. Why? Just in case he's the Red Butcher. The joke around the culinary world is that more redheaded men are served the best meals of their lives because the Executive Chef's think they're Butch McKinley." She grasped the front of his dress shirt in her fists and shook him. "You've just ordered up and signed the execution order for Twin Springs. My cooking and recipes are not up to his level."

He chuckled, his eyes crinkling at the corners, and tried to extract her fists from his shirt.

Her eyes widened and her brows rose. "Are you laughing at me?" she shrieked.

Realizing he made a major error, he swallowed back the laughter bubbling up his throat. "No, no, not at all. Butch is a great man. He'll give you a fair review."

She shot to her feet and paced the room. "You have to call your friend and tell him that you've changed your mind." She whirled around with her arms crossed. "Whip out your cell phone and call him now."

He spread his hands out in front of him, palms raised. "I can't."

"Yes, you can," she spit out, crossing the room and tapping him on the chest with her finger. "Pull out your damn cell phone and call him. Kindly thank him for offering to come but tell him we need to postpone his trip to a time in the future."

"But—"

"I'm not talented enough to present my food to the Red Butcher."

"You—"

"I'm clumsy. Everything I do goes wrong and in the end I muck it up."

"I—"

"Why do you think they call my Dizzy Izzy?"

He growled deep in his chest and placed his hand lightly over her mouth, momentarily silencing her.

Isabella's eyes widened with shock and then narrowed to little green chips of ice.

"We're not going to do that again." He released her mouth. "Listen to me, I can't call Butch and tell him not to come." He rubbed her arms. "He already left and will be here this afternoon."

She deflated. "No, he can't be."

He smiled reassuringly. "I don't know who started calling you Dizzy Izzy. That name doesn't reflect the talented, gorgeous woman standing before me. To me, you're Bella. You're intelligent, courageous in the kitchen, and a dynamic visionary creating outstanding dishes. Bella means beautiful, graceful and, without a doubt, lovable. You stood up to a man twice your size to defend Marc. You kicked him out of the kitchen. You're my brave Bella. I wish I could breathe belief into you and enable you to see how truly special you are. Trust yourself and your abilities. But if you are not willing to trust yourself yet, then trust me. Trust that I believe in you, that I see beneath your fear and worries to the truly amazing woman you are."

She froze as his belief flowed over her, filling her lungs. "Okay," was all she could say.

He beamed down at her and kissed her on the forehead. "Good girl. I'll ask your sister if she will show Butch around Twin Springs and occupy him until dinner service. She can distract any man for any length of time. If that doesn't work, I'll sick Maddy on him. Then, you'll have hours to prepare. Don't worry. It's going to be great. You're going to be great." His cell phone rang and he pulled it out, glancing at the number. "It's Dale. Maddy must be bugging him with another notion of hers. I have to go before she tears down a wing of the hotel for some crazy idea in her head. You'll be great, my Bella." He tilted her chin up and kissed her lightly on the lips. "I believe in you too."

He left her office and she stared after him. "The Red Butcher eating in my dining room." Time stilled and she stood immobile, planted in the same spot where he left her.

"Chef, Chef." Marc repeated, snapping his fingers before her dazed eyes. "We have a problem."

CHAPTER FORTY-SIX

"What?" Isabella focused in on Marc. She grabbed his hand before he snapped his fingers again. "What?"

"Mom wanted me to get you." He was already turning, expecting her to follow. "There's a problem in the kitchen."

"A problem?" she echoed, trailing after him, feeling dazed after her talk with Theo. She shook her head to clear it. "What's up?"

"You look kind of pale. Maybe it's best if Mom tells you."

She refastened the buttons on her chef jacket. Heat from the unusually warm morning flowed over her as she followed the teen. Today promised to be a scorcher. She made a note to close the loading dock's doors before the kitchen became unbearable to cook in. As she walked, she ran through Twin Springs' dinner menu in her head, mentally weighing each course, examining it, and testing its viability. She wanted to become Theo's Bella more than anything, to make him proud. To save the hotel. Marc held the kitchen door open for her to enter. "Thank you."

The kitchen was unusually quiet and extraordinarily hot. Where the staff was usually prepping for breakfast service, there was nothing. Instead, they leaned back against the counters sipping from water bottles or quietly talking to each other. She understood Marc's intensity and sensed a problem. It wasn't hard to find Maude. She wore a cook shirt covered with slices of bacon with faces, arms and feet. Shaking her head at the crazy pattern, she quickly crossed the room. "What's going on?"

Busily wringing her hands in her apron, at first Maude didn't answer, her mouth just opened and closed. Finally, her voice squeaked out, "Follow me." She turned and rushed to the back of the room where the large, walk-in freezer stood. She cranked the silver handle, held the door open and motioned for her to enter.

Giving a quizzical look, Isabella entered and stepped into a wet puddle. Two inches of water covered the entire floor. She was struck by the warmness within the freezer. Very warm. Thousands of dollars of dripping wet meats surrounded her. In her head, she calculated the loss and the urgency of tonight's service. Her heart plummeted into the pit of her stomach. "How much meat is in the refrigerator?"

Unable to meet her eyes, Maude again replied, "Follow me."

With her insides twisting into a sick ball, she trailed behind. Maude opened the massive walk-in refrigerator door. A foul odor and intense heat greeted them. "How did this happen?"

"I don't know. I came in and the doors to the walk-ins were wide open. I closed them so that the smell didn't reach the dining area."

Unable to believe her eyes, Isabella reeled with astonishment. "Everything seemed fine last night."

Mopping her brow with her apron, Maude replied, "That's right. We cleaned up, left for the night. They must've shut down some time after."

"Theo was right, someone wants us to fail. And they might have just succeeded." Dazed and confused, she stared at the rotten food. She couldn't trust the quality of anything. How could her teams prepare for breakfast and dinner service? "Oh, no." Her chest clenched. Tightened. "The Red Butcher," burst from her lips.

"What did you say?"

Forgetting all Theo's advice, Isabella struggled to breath as her chest tightened into a hard ball. "The Red Butcher," she repeated, gasping for air. "He's critiquing tonight's dinner service."

Maude crossed herself. "Dios Mio, what are we going to do?"

Bending over, legs spread, hands on her knees Isabella chanted Theo's words. "Smart, brave, courageous." Little by little, her breathing calmed. Thinking, she remained motionless. "Forget Dizzy Izzy. I'm Brave Bella."

She rose, realizing what she needed to do. With the demeanor of a General, she issued orders. "Get Dale. Have him see if he can fix the walk-ins. Tell him to report directly to you or me with the results. Then check Twin Springs' other two restaurants that handle the lunch services and see if their walk-ins are working. If they are, see how much food they can spare. We need to begin prepping and serving the breakfast buffet with their extra ingredients. Let me know what they say. Right away. Hopefully, between the three kitchens, we'll have enough for the dinner service also.

"Marc," she called out.

The teen jogged up to her. "Yes, Chef."

She rattled off commands and her voice grew with confidence. "You and the rest of the crew clean out these walk-ins. Get them ready to receive food. Bring in the wait staff to help. All hands on deck.

"I'll call the suppliers and find out how fast they can ship fresh meats, cheeses, vegetables, and fruits. Then, I'll revamp tonight's menu with what we can get." She dashed back to her office and pulled up the phone numbers of Twin Springs' suppliers on the computer.

CHAPTER FORTY-SEVEN

*H*ours later, Isabella clicked off and pocketed her cell phone. She scratched out the last supplier's name on her list. Her ears burned from their anger. Twin Springs' accounts were six months or more overdue with every supplier. Some had threatened legal action for failure of payment. The last woman had laughed at her request for help. She threw the pencil across the room, and squeezed her fist. "Chef Dubois, if we hadn't already kicked you out, I'd wring your neck." Could Dubois have snuck back and disabled the walk-ins? "I wouldn't put it past him."

Defeat seeped over her, coating her tongue in a foul bitterness. "Our reputation is ruined. No one will help," she whispered. She placed her elbows on the desk and rubbed her temples. "There must be a way. I just need to find it."

Deep inside she wished for her father. He'd know how to handle the suppliers. She leaned back and rubbed her breastbone with her knuckles. At Maude's soft knock, she glanced up and a glimmer of hope filled her.

"Chef."

"Tell me," she waived her in. "What were the results?"

"Dale and Logan are both working on fixing the walk-ins. The crew cleaned out and sanitized both the freezer and the fridge. The other kitchens are sending over the food they can spare."

"Good, good," replied Isabella. "As soon as the food comes in, have the crew begin prepping what they need for the breakfast buffet. Let's go see how Dale is doing."

The two women entered the back of the kitchen. Dale had squeezed his body behind one of the gigantic, metal walk-ins.

Unsure how to help, Maude backed herself up out of the way and began muttering to herself in Spanish while kneading the fabric of her apron between her fingers like rosary beads.

Isabella pushed up her sleeves and attempted to squeeze herself behind the deep freeze. She straddled Dale's legs and poked her head in above his twisted body.

"That's not going to help," said Logan from behind her. "You're just blocking his light." He carried a clamp light in one hand and a metal cylinder in his other. He plugged in the light and clamped it high on the back of the walk-in, washing the entire area with light. Hooking an arm around Isabella, he held her against the giant, faded, red tongue of his grimy Rolling Stones t-shirt and hauled her out of the way.

An involuntary squeak escaped her lips. She glared at him and took up space beside Maude, irritated by his heavy handedness. "I just want to see how everything is going. Besides, your shirt smells as if it hasn't been washed since the seventies. Twin Springs has a reputation to protect, Logan."

He ignored the two women's presence entirely and held up a lime green tank. "I have the Freon."

"Almost finished repairin' the fitting."

Isabella heard a few grunts and muttering as Dale worked in the tight space.

Logan grit his teeth and rubbed his hand against the nubby, crimson patches of scar tissue and hair on his cheek. He grimaced as if in pain. "Dad, come on out and let me finish it."

"Nope, I've got it. Hand over the Freon and let's get her pumped back up."

After attaching everything, Dale slithered out. "That should do it, Miss Isabella." He rubbed his hands on the dark red rag he'd removed from his back pocket. "Give it some time and she'll be workin' good as new."

"What happened?" She once again peered behind the big, metal box.

Logan replied, "It looks like someone poked holes in the Freon lines for both the fridge and the freezer. Slowly, the Freon leaked out. If the door hadn't been left open to speed up the process, you might've served spoiled food to the guests without realizing it."

"Surely, I'd have noticed it by the smell," said Isabella, aghast.

"The way I'm thinkin'," replied Dale, "the food would've spoiled slowly over time. You might've realized, but some of the less experienced kitchen staff mighta not noticed the food was slightly off."

"Oh no, you're right," she replied. "How are the walk-ins at the other restaurants?"

"All in working order," replied Logan. "I just checked them out."

Deep relief filled her. At least they wouldn't need to close Twin Springs until new walk-ins were installed. "It was odd that only these were messed with. Maybe someone just wanted this kitchen to fail." Wanted her to fail. Dubois! "Could someone have vandalized it a while ago? Say, around the time Dubois left?"

"You think he's behind this?" questioned Theo, entering the room.

"Well, not only was he a pompous jerk, but I just found out that he hasn't paid any of our suppliers for at least the last six months."

"What?" he shouted. "Not possible. I've gone over Twin Springs' books for the last year. All the suppliers have been paid."

She shook her head. "They insist the opposite. They've attempted to contact Chef Dubois for payment. For months now, he didn't return their calls. Every supplier cancelled all future food shipments and are refusing to work with us ever again."

"How much are we talking?" asked Logan.

"For six months," replied Theo, quickly calculating, "we're close to the half million mark. Chef Dubois made himself a nice little nest egg at the expense of Twin Springs."

"That much?" Isabella's mind reeled at the news. "He was a slimy jerk."

Placing his arm around her, Theo attempted to sooth her, "We'll think of something. Don't worry."

Strong, dependable Theo. She wrapped her arms around his waist and whispered, "What are we going to do?"

"Call that obnoxious Sheriff, unfortunately. Don't worry. We'll figure this out." He brushed her hair back and lifted her chin. "If I clear the debt with the suppliers, will they be able to get a shipment of food in today before the dinner service?"

"No," she gripped the lapels of his jacket. "We can't take even more money from you. There has to be another way."

"Twin Springs is a part of my family too. Let me help."

Reaching up on tiptoe, she kissed him. "Thank you. We'll pay you back, I promise."

"Are you good for today's dinner service?" asked Logan.

Reminded of their audience, Isabella flushed and moved out of Theo's embrace. "He's right. Even with the food from the other kitchens, we're still short for tonight."

"And I invited the, what did you call my friend, the Red Butcher to dine tonight."

She rubbed her temples, thinking. "I have to admit, when I pulled up the suppliers list I was surprised that we weren't using local companies or farms," she murmured. "We've always bought local."

"Maybe, Dubois knew a local would've let the cat out of the bag," added Dale.

"Perhaps," replied Theo.

Isabella looked up and met Dale's faded blue eyes. "Fresh, locally grown produce." A glimmer of hope filled her. "Your family owns the largest farm in the area." Her voice grew in strength as an idea began to form fully. "In fact, as an original part of Twin

Springs, your farm, Lone Oak, provided fresh milk, produce and meat for the kitchen."

"You own a farm that large, Dale?" inquired Theo.

"Yep," he replied. "Born an' raised in the same house."

"Why do you work here, instead of working your farm?"

Taking his baseball cap from his back pocket, Dale twisted the hat in his large hands. He paused, studying his cap, before replying. "My older brother was the farmer. I loved working with wood and fiddlin' with machines. When he died, the farm went to me." He placed the cap on his head, his blue eyes soft with remembered sadness. "I guess, I'm lucky to be blessed with a woman who likes playin' in dirt."

Isabella remembered the story of Lone Oak Farm. Each generation gave birth to two boys, and with each generation only one boy survived past the age of thirty-five. At the entrance to the farm stood one lone oak instead of two oaks on each side of the road. With each birth of a younger son, the mother planted an additional oak tree. But when one of the sons passed away the young tree also withered away. She wished she had stopped Theo before he asked Dale about his farm. Then she might've prevented the sorrow washing over the gentle older man before her. She knew Dale and his wife hoped that they'd broken the curse, since Logan returned from war hurt but alive. Needing to shift from the painful subject, she asked, "Do you think your wife can help us?"

Thoughtfully, he chewed on his toothpick. Everyone watched as he rolled it around in his mouth. "Miss Isabella, I can't speak for my wife. The farm's her baby. I learned long ago not to come between a woman an' her baby."

Marc entered the kitchen and joined his mom. He glanced over at Logan and visibly jolted, startled by his appearance. The young boy glanced down at the floor and mumbled to his feet, "Hi, Logan. Heard you were back. Um—good to see you again."

Logan's body twitched and vibrated at the boy's presence and the sounds of the kitchen filling up with people. "I'll talk to mom." His voice sounded raw and broken. He drew his baseball cap down low over his face and maneuvered his body so that his burnt side faced the wall, away from human eyes. "I'll talk to mom," he repeated, and a bead of sweat trickled down his face. Without waiting for anyone's confirmation, he spun around. Even with a slight limp in his gait, his long legs ate up the floor as he quickly departed.

Isabella's soulful eyes followed him. Her heart was heavy with his pain, but hopeful for his mother's help. She turned back to the men. "Dale," she asked, "would you look over the kitchens and make sure we don't have any other surprises?"

He nodded.

"Thanks," she murmured, her mind zooming ahead, hopeful. "The kitchen crew and I will examine the ingredients we have. Until I hear from Mrs. Oakes, I'll work up a special menu using what we have. Marc," she called out, "why don't you work with me?"

Without hesitating, the teen's excited voice replied, "Yes, Chef."

She smiled at his exuberance.

Theo grasped her by her arm and drew her close so that only she heard what he wanted to say. "I'm sorry that I added to your worries by inviting my friend. I should've asked you first."

Reaching up on her tiptoes and cupping the back of his neck with her hand, she guided his head down to hers. "It is alright," she whispered against his soft lips. She kissed him and lingered beneath his lips. "Together, we'll make it work. We're a family here at Twin Springs." Reluctantly, she released him and turned way. With Marc in tow, she walked away.

Theo stared after her. "That's my girl." The whispered phrase escaped his lips without prior thought.

"About time," muttered Dale as he hitched up his tool belt.

Theo's smile twisted with amusement at the older man's comment. "Some of the best wines take the most time. Isabella was well worth the wait."

"So what are you goin' to do about it?" questioned Dale, rolling his toothpick between his fingers.

Surprised by his willingness to chat, Theo adjusted the neck of his tie. "To start, I need to pay off the suppliers."

"Chicken shit," Dale muttered under his breath.

Theo's head whipped around sure he hadn't heard him correctly. "Pardon me?"

"Ya heard me," replied Dale. "Youth is wasted on your generation. All talk and no action. Someone is goin' to scoop up that girl if you're too big of a dumb ass to pin her down." He shoved the toothpick into his pocket, turned his back on him and strode out of the kitchens. Leaving Theo to stare after him slack jawed.

CHAPTER FORTY-EIGHT

With her inner voice humming in her head, Isabella and Marc huddled at the large, oak table. Together they hashed out the menu for that evening's dinner service with the Red Butcher.

Her pencil tapped the pad of paper. The menu contained a vegetarian selection, and a meat selection. That is, until the meat ran out. Then the selection narrowed dramatically to pasta. Finished, she slipped her pencil into the narrow pocket on the sleeve of her chef jacket. "These are all the ingredients we have to work with."

Marc hunkered down, examining the list and the menu with her. "It's not much."

Tucking a piece of blonde hair up into her cherry red headband, she replied, "You're right, it is pitiful but it's all we have." She clicked her phone and checked the time. "We only have three hours until dinner service. We have to make-do."

Maude burst into the room, the bacon people on her shirt heaving with her large bosom as she fought for air. "Izzy, I mean, Chef," she gasped. "You must come to the loading docks."

Jumping up, Marc placed his arm around his mom, supporting

her weight with his arms. "Are you sick Mamasita?" Concern laced his voice. "Sit down. Your face is really red."

"Of course I'm not sick." She slapped his concern away with impatience. "Just need to catch my breath." She grabbed one of Isabella's and her son's hands. "You're not going to believe it."

Isabella stared at Maude, wondering if the stress of the morning had impaired her friend. Another horrible thought crossed her mind, what if something else broke? Cautiously, she asked, "Believe what?"

"Mamasita calm down. Take deep breaths and tell us what you are talking about."

"I can't. You have to see it." She dragged each of them by the hand from the Tasting Room down the back halls to the loading docks. With a grand gesture she pushed open the loading dock doors.

Isabella skidded to a halt behind her and bounced forward as Marc plowed into her back.

"Sorry, Chef," he exclaimed.

Struck speechless by the sight before her, Isabella didn't hear his apology. Three of Twin Springs' white paneled vans were backed up to the loading docks. The Kitchen Crew busily carried crates of fresh produce from the backs of two, and white packages of fresh meat from the other.

Maude clutched her by the arm and danced a little jig, the bacon people swaying with her excitement. "It's a miracle. Mrs. Oakes told the drivers whatever Twin Springs needs, if her farm has it, then it is yours. She called the other farms in the area and everyone opened their gates to Twin Springs. Over and over the drivers heard things like, 'Twin Springs supported our family during the hard years', 'Twin Springs employed my daughter and helped pay for her college', 'Twin Springs didn't fire my father when he was too old to perform his duties and let him work with dignity into his golden years'."

Tears welled up in Isabella's eyes. Suddenly, she realized tonight's dinner service wasn't about her and her sister regaining ownership of the hotel. It wasn't even about Twin Springs. Her making tonight's dinner service a success was about the community surviving. Twin Springs wasn't the heart of the community. She had it wrong all along. The people from the community and surrounding farms were the real heart. And the Grand Dame supplied the life-blood that pumped the heart and kept the community alive. She gazed through tear soaked eyes as crates of fresh eggs, squash, corn, tomatoes, blueberries, asparagus, and meat were pulled off the trucks. The generosity of the community's heart overwhelmed her. They supplied more than she'd ever imagined possible. She laced her fingers with Maude's. "You're right. It's a miracle."

"Si, it is." Maude mopped her own eyes with her apron. "They all wanted to give back to Twin Springs."

Marc rubbed his hands over his forehead. "Women. You cry at everything. Happy, sad, corn, fruits, anything." He pushed forward to help unload. "I'll help get an inventory. So you can revamp that awful menu we just created." He cast her a jaunty little salute.

"That would be great." She leaned into Maude and whispered, "You have an outstanding boy there."

"Gracias. He's not so bad."

"He's going to be a great chef one day. He has the drive and is not afraid to experiment with food." She gave her a quick hug. "He's wonderful, just like his mom."

Maude glowed with pride. "I almost forgot," she gasped. "I was so excited about the trucks that I haven't shown you."

"Shown me what?" she asked. "Did something else break?"

She shook her head. "You need to see the Main Dining Room."

Once again she hauled her by the hand and guided her through the busy kitchen, this time to the Main Dining Room.

Maude paused before the swinging door, trying to catch her breath as she patted her chest. "Your sister and Maddy worked all day on this," she said, holding open the door for Isabella to enter.

The wait staff rushed around the room before her. Gone were

the dark, heavy draperies that covered and concealed the great arched windows. In their place were bright drapes in golds, greens and soft creams. Sunlight cast a golden hue throughout the room, creating a warm and welcoming feeling. As if she was in a dream, she walked up to one of the round tables and glided her fingertips across the new table linens. The dark purple tablecloths were replaced with crisp white.

Isabella glowed with pride as her sister gracefully strolled across the room towards her, wearing a form fitting, midnight black dress.

"What do you think?" Ava smiled at her stunned face.

"It's beautiful."

"Maddy and I wanted the dining room to reflect you and your cooking. Warm and giving, but at the same time quiet and elegant. Not dark and cold like Chef Dubois."

Where there used to be black plates on each table there now laid white porcelain plates delicately etched with flowers buzzing with tiny bees and butterflies, intertwined with the dark green Twin Springs logo. Each table was graced with a low laying candle surrounded by fresh flowers. In awe, she asked, "How did you put this together so quickly?"

"It wasn't hard," replied Ava. "It was just a little re-staging. Just like in the production of a play. Move this here, add a little of this, swap a little of that. You know Twin Springs never throws anything away. Everything was in the attics. We just needed to send the drapes downstairs to laundry, wash and sanitize the plates. Do you remember these plates?" Her sister held one up to show her. "Generations of Twin Springs' guests have used these plates."

She admired the beautiful place setting. Mixed in with some of the cups, saucers, and plates was the older chinaware, stamped with Twin Springs' Tower Logo. A feeling of rightness filled her. "Yes, it's good to see them gracing the tables of the Main Dining Room once more."

"Maddy wants to sell Twin Springs' signature dishes in one of the gift shops and online. She said we could market it as 'Take a little Twin Springs home with you'."

"That's a wonderful idea." She hugged her sister. "I can't believe you did all this. It's so warm and inviting and brings back so many memories."

"Isabella, the dining room represents you and the hotel. It represents all of us."

Leaning down, she smelled the low laying flower arrangement in the middle of the table. "The flowers are a beautiful touch."

"I wish I could take credit for picking them out. Delivery trucks pulled up from the local florist dropping off mounds of fresh flowers. June said she heard Twin Springs was in need." She raised an arched brow, "Something about the Red Butcher."

Isabella chuckled. "News travels fast. Didn't Theo tell you about his friend Butch and ask for your help?"

"Not yet."

"Be ready. Theo invited a friend of his. Unfortunately, he's a famous critic in the culinary world, also known as the Red Butcher." She filled her in on his reputation.

"Well, we will have to see if I can help butter him up for you." Ava smoothed her curves and batted her eyelashes.

Laughing at her sultry display, Isabella replied, "Keep Maddy away from him. Who knows what will come out of her mouth." She surveyed the dining room. The tables looked crisp, the stemware sparkled and the flowers were elegant and inviting. The room glowed with geniality and elegance, a true reflection of the Grand Dame. "The dining room is perfect." Hugging her sister's curvaceous form, she whispered, "Thank you."

"You deserve it kiddo." Ava squeezed her back. "You deserve your dream. We're going to knock this Red Butcher's socks off."

"Yes, we are. But I'd better figure out a menu that will also satisfy his taste buds."

"When you finish the menu, email it to me and I'll have it printed and placed in the folios for this evening's dinner service."

Isabella squeezed her once more before sprinting back to her office. Marc was already there, ready and waiting.

"Here's what we have." Handing her a paper, he stared over her shoulder as she examined the list.

Biting her bottom lip, she inspected the new inventory. After a moment, her eyes rose and her face glowed with excitement. "We can work with this. Let's create a menu that will tame the Red Butcher."

CHAPTER FORTY-NINE

The pressure within Isabella's chest intensified with each step through the kitchen. She'd placed her heart into creating tonight's menu, pillaging her recipes and ideas until she bared her soul through the menu for all to judge. Even though the effort had sucked almost all the courage from her slender frame, she wanted to be brave for Theo. For herself.

Everyone relied on her to deliver a successful service. Her sister, Theo, the kitchen crew, the community and of course the Grand Dame herself. More than anything, she yearned to prove herself worthy of their faith and support.

She straightened her white jacket. Lovingly, her fingers brushed over the embroidered words, "Executive Chef, Twin Springs Hotel and Spa." Aiming to live up to the title, she stepped up on the metal platform in front of the pass and turned to face the kitchen crew. Their faces were taut with fear.

The wait staff squeezed in around the edges of the kitchen. Everyone's attention was glued on her. Concern wrinkled the corners of their eyes and the skin on their foreheads. They stared at her, with their collective breath held, and waited.

Her knees shook and she feared her legs would buckle beneath the weight. From deep within, she forced out a confident smile.

She scanned their faces, examining each one, feeling their tension. Both the kitchen and wait staff understood the significance of tonight's dinner service. They recognized the power of the Red Butcher's review for any restaurant, let alone for the Main Dining Room they loved. They huddled together and waited for her to lead as the General led. She looked out among them, conscious that her dreams and Twin Springs' troubles were secondary. Today, the community demonstrated what they'd realized all along and what she'd only recently learned. The people before her were what kept the hotel alive and relevant.

These people were the General's true jewels and greatest treasure.

She spoke and her voice flowed over the crowd gathered in the kitchen. "Today has once again shown me how important each of you are. Most of you are second, third or even fourth generation staff. Your ancestors, along with mine, have cared for and loved the Grand Dame that others refer to as Twin Springs. Entire generations have spent every waking moment pumping life into her old bones. As will our descendants after us. Without you, she's an old shell with wandering halls and tall ceilings. Your efforts breathe life into her. Without each of you, she would live no more and would become an old woman left to die in the Blue Ridge Mountains. Her beauty would fade and she'd wither away. Forgotten.

"Today, our community came together to demonstrate their belief. Their belief in you and me. They love this grand old lady as much as we do and realize that, when the Grand Dame is strong, she supports the community and helps it to thrive.

"It's not important who stands at this pass guiding you for today's dinner service. What matters is you. Each and every one of you. Your families' and my family's future depend upon our performance tonight.

"On the other side of that wall are the guests we serve. Our ancestors have strived for centuries for those families to feel at home within these walls, just as we have. At every service, our goal is to create a memory for our guests and to give them a peek into the heart of the Grand Dame. I'm going to be up front with you. Tonight, we have a critic experiencing Twin Springs' dining for the first time."

A hiss filled the room.

She raised her hand.

The room quieted.

"He's a guest just like all the others we welcome into our home. In fact, Mr. McKinley is an invited guest." Her lips curved at the shock on their faces. "Let us not see him tonight as a critic. Let us see him as an old friend and embrace him the same way we welcome all our families. Let's give Mr. McKinley and everyone dining tonight the best meal of their lives. And let's show the community around Twin Springs that their generous actions and contributions were appreciated and put to the best use. Does each of you have the new menu for your station?"

"Yes, Chef."

"All stations prepped and ready?"

Their voices rose in answer to her question, "Yes, Chef."

"Then let's make this an incredible meal for our guests."

They roared as one, "Yes, Chef!"

Not sure if all their efforts were for naught, she turned to pull the first ticket of the evening from the rail. For the next hour, she and the kitchen crew worked in unison. Like a well-tuned machine, the kitchen churned out dish after dish. She scrutinized each plate as if it belonged to the Red Butcher.

Midway into service, she glanced up from the dish she inspected and regarded the white tickets lining the rail like soldiers. They were in the weeds. Orders piled up faster than the staff could roll out the dishes. She looked over the kitchen and searched for a weak spot, a place to improve upon or a station to switch to and help the efficiency. But the backup wasn't due to the staff not performing their jobs well, the new menu caused it. The kitchen worked with a handicap, due to the lack of time required for the crew to learn the new menu and perform at top speed. Therefore, the orders were taking a little longer than usual. She stepped down from the pass and walked the line, checking in with each station, to instruct and answer questions. Confident with the results, she resumed her position at the pass.

"Chef, we have a count of ten on lamb," Maude called out from the meat station.

A crash sounded behind Isabella. She spun around. Maude, hands on her mighty hips, stood frowning over her son. Marc picked up an overturned tray of raw lamb from the floor and deposited the now soiled meat into the trash bin.

Maude shouted, "Chef, make that a count of 6 on lamb!"

Isabella made direct eye contact with the teen. "Are you alright?"

Cheeks pink, he hung his head. "Yeah, sorry Chef. I know we are working with limited supply."

"It happens. The kitchen is a busy place with a lot of moving parts. You'll find your sea legs," she joked. "Just get back into the game and work hard to ensure a great service."

"Yes, Chef." He bounced forward like a gangly puppy, ready to please.

She shook her head in wonder at his exuberance. Resuming her duties, she glanced up to find her sister's green eyes staring at her over the pass.

"He's here."

The Red Butcher. Her mouth gaped between open and shut, searching for a reply.

Taking pity on her, Ava asked, "Do you want me to get you 'a water' for the kitchen?"

Her question snapped Isabella out of her daze. 'A water' for the kitchen was code for a stiff drink of alcohol. She felt a giggle inching up the back of her throat. Only her sister could make her laugh at a moment like this. "Thanks for the offer. I'm good. How are things on the floor since the Red Butcher showed?"

"As far as I can tell, the dining room is running smoothly. Do you want to see what he looks like?"

Intrigued, she stepped down from the pass and joined her sister at the swinging doors that lead to the Main Dining Room. Ava's head high and Isabella's low, the girls nudged the swinging door open and peeked through the crack. She studied the Red Butcher, from his flaming red hair that was cut short and tight around his ears, to his large oval belt buckle that gleamed silver in the candlelight, down to the luxurious black leather cowboy boots on his feet. On any other man the eclectic fashion combo would be an odd contrast against the expensive black suit. Somehow, he carried the combination, exuding male confidence and charm. The Maitre' D guided him to a table central to the dance floor, yet private from other guests. The Red Butcher folded his long, lean body into the chair and perused her new menu. "I always wondered what the Red Butcher looked like. Somehow I imagined him with a cleaver dripping with blood."

"He's one good looking, tall glass of water," Ava's response almost purred in her ear.

She nodded. Suddenly, she was staring straight into gorgeous blue eyes. The Red Butcher's eyes. Like children, she and Ava jumped back and hid behind the swinging doors.

Her chest heaving with excitement, but not wanting to be heard in the dining room, she swallowed a laugh and glanced over to her sister. "I should return to the kitchen. Obviously, spying isn't one of my skills."

Ava straightened her black pencil skirt, fluffed her sleek black hair and hitched her breasts up higher so they swelled a little more over the square cut neckline of her dress. "Let me go and use some of my skills with our new friend."

She snorted with laughter. Quickly, she covered her mouth with her hand and compared her boxy chef jacket to her sister's sexy dress. Lowering her hand, she said, "Be good now."

Ava's full lips spread into a sultry smile. "Aren't I always?" She gave a throaty chuckle and skirted around her sister. Hips swaying in the wind, she sailed through the swinging doors and headed straight towards the Red Butcher.

Watching her, she admired her confidence. "She's going to chew him up and spit him out."

Isabella washed her hands before rejoining the pass. She continued inspecting the dishes and sending them through to the awaiting wait staff. Lost in the rhythm of her work, she pulled the next ticket from the rail. Transfixed, she stared at the top of the ticket where the waitress circled and checked a capital C. She contemplated the critic's ticket as the blood drained from her body, causing her arms to feel weightless and powerless. Her voice shook and cracked as she started to call out the order. Taking a cleansing breath, she centered herself and restated the order. "Order: one prime rib app and sweet potato bisque, fire the prime rib."

Sensing a change in the atmosphere, the crew's, "Yes, Chef," was hesitant and delayed.

Pushing her shoulders back and plastering a reassuring smile on her face, she turned and spoke to the crew. "Just an order for a guest everyone."

"Yes, Chef!" they shouted in reply.

Later, two dishes were slipped back up to the pass by one of the servers. Startled, she studied the returned prime rib and bisque. Only half of the prime rib was eaten and barely any of the bisque. Suddenly, it dawned on her that the dishes belonged to the Red Butcher. Her eyes widened with horror and she looked through the pass to Diana. "He didn't like them?"

Diana blew her dyed black bangs out of her eyes and raised her hands in bewilderment. "Said he was ready for his lamb."

Dread filled Isabella. Perhaps, Chef Dubois was right all along. She wasn't ready. She shook off the black thoughts and nodded. "No problem." Over her shoulder, she called out, "I need one lamb on the fly. Tell me we have one left, Maude."

"Yes, Chef. Right up, Chef."

She inspected and passed through two more orders before passing the lamb to Diana's awaiting hands.

Diana placed the dish on her tray, and brought it swiftly up to her shoulder. Turning on her heel, her feet slid out from under her. She crashed to the floor with the Red Butcher's lamb. A deathly silence filled the kitchen.

Isabella rushed around the pass and almost slipped herself from a slick spot on the checker board tile. Grease. *How did grease get on the floor in front of the pass?* Gripping Diana's elbow, she helped her stand. "Are you hurt?"

She dusted off her black skirt and white shirt. "I'm so sorry, Chef, I don't know what happened."

"It's not your fault, there's grease on the floor."

"Grease?" Diana wobbled on her feet.

"Why don't you sit down." She guided her over to a plastic crate near the back of the kitchen. "Marc, clean up that spot and, Maude, another lamb on the fly."

"Last lamb, Chef. We're 86'd on lamb." In record time, Maude prepared the Red Butcher another dish.

Isabella checked the temperature, plated the lamb with grilled asparagus and drizzled the red wine sauce around the edges of the plate. With her towel, she ensured that none of the sauce touched the sides or underside of the plate before passing the dish through to Diana. "Are you sure you feel up to finishing the service?"

She forced a smile and her chin lifted a notch, "Switch servers now? And tip off the Red Butcher that there was a problem? No way!"

Nodding, she watched Diana carefully turn with her filled tray and pass through the swinging doors into the dining room.

Isabella continued to send orders through to the other servers.

"He sent the dish back."

She glanced up and noticed tears welling up in Diana's eyes. Isabella's voice clogged, and she had to clear her throat before she could answer. "What?"

"I asked him if something wasn't to his liking and he just shrugged. He ordered the cornmeal trout, followed by the cobbler." She pressed her lips together, and waited for Isabella to reply.

She wanted to run, to run and hide. *So much for my creativity and intuition.* She failed. She wasn't ready or brave. The proof stood before her eyes. She had nothing to offer the clientele or the kitchen. She wished she had a tower to run and hide in like Emma.

Blankly, she stared down at the stainless steel counter top. Wide eyed, her reflection gazed back at her. The green eyes passed down from generation to generation were filled with defeat. She thought of Emma. Between the Lieutenant and society, she didn't stand a chance at attaining her dream of becoming a chef.

Unlike Emma, she was surrounded by people who loved and believed in her. Who wanted her to succeed. How could she allow her own fears, Chef Dubois' words or the Red Butcher to deny her from attaining her dream? She muttered, "Damn it, no more fear, no more worries. I will achieve my dream, if not today and in this service, then tomorrow or the next day."

She straightened to her full height, rising up on her toes for good measure. From this point forward, nothing would hold her back from being an Executive Chef, or from saving this community and Twin Springs. "If the Red Butcher wants the cornmeal trout and the blueberry cobbler, then it's our job to deliver."

She shouted out the new order and sent it through along with other orders. The Kitchen regained their rhythm and worked in sync. The rest of the service passed like a dream. Her inner voice hummed, the camaraderie of the crew swirled around her and the wait staff passed guest comments through the window. All flowed like warm water. Serving the last dessert, she called out, "Shut it down."

Clapping and beaming she stepped down from the pass and exchanged handshakes and hugs with everyone. Only the Red Butcher sent back dishes. All the other guests raved about their new menu. Her crew worked hard and deserved to celebrate. "An extraordinary service, everyone. No matter what happens, we overcame great odds together. Let's clean up and prep the kitchen for tomorrow's breakfast service."

High fives and hugs continued to be exchanged around the kitchen.

"Isabella." Theo touched her shoulder.

Grinning from ear to ear and enjoying the exuberance within the kitchen, she turned and wrapped her arms around his waist. "We did it. We finished the service." Her relieved words flowed over his chest.

He drew her away from him. "The Maitre' D said he wants to talk with you."

"Who?" She rocked back and forth enjoying the safe warmth of his embrace.

"Butch McKinley." His voice flowed down to her. "AKA, the Red Butcher."

CHAPTER FIFTY

A small "Oh" escaped from her lips. Isabella turned and surveyed the kitchen, noting the excitement and happiness of her family. The Red Butcher wanted to speak with her. Her insides quaked but she understood meeting with guests was not uncommon for the Executive Chef. She tried to rationalize but, deep down, she knew. The Red Butcher had sent back every one of her dishes because he enjoyed fresh meat. Fresh Executive Chef meat, served up in a white chef jacket with a cherry red bandana on top. Knowing the Red Butcher didn't want to swap recipes, she drew in a deep breath and steadied herself before exhaling. "Alright. Where is Mr. McKinley?"

"Butch is still in the dining room. Do you want me to go with you?"

In a slight daze, she shook her head. "No, I can handle him."

Automatically, her feet moved, one in front of the other, towards the Main Dining Room. Halting behind the swinging doors, she unbuttoned and alternated the sides of her double-breasted chef jacket to cover the incidental stains. She patted her hair back into the topknot. Thinking twice, she removed the cherry red kerchief from around her hair, dabbed any shininess from her face and slipped the piece of fabric into her back pocket. She took a deep breath and pushed forward through the doors. There before her, sitting at the table typing on his tablet, was the man who had sent back all her dishes. The Red Butcher.

As she approached, the redheaded man glanced up at her and stood. He drew out a chair at his table and assisted Isabella by scooting her chair in.

She didn't want to like this man. It felt petty but she resented his gentlemanly display. The Red Butcher was not allowed to be a gentleman. Especially after he had sent back her food.

"Thank you," she murmured. She watched him tuck his long legs under the white tablecloth and noticed that his knees came very close to touching the underside of the table. She looked for the cleaver that he would use to destroy what little career she had.

Squaring her shoulders, she held out her hand, "I'm Isabella Fairbanks, the Head Executive Chef at Twin Springs."

"Butch McKinley. Glad to meet you too ma'am," his voice held a slight western twang.

She wanted to roll her eyes at his accent, sure it was just a facade to lure her into feeling safe. But southern manners prevailed. It took every inch of her resolve to not begin her sentence with "bless your heart". Instead she opened with, "Thank you for coming to Twin Springs. We're honored to have you as our guest." She wondered if the heat of her lie had burnt off her taste buds.

Butch smiled knowingly at her. "I have to tell you," he drawled, "I was genuinely surprised when Theo called and asked me to critique the dinner service here at Twin Springs." The dining room filled with his good-natured laugh. "Most restaurant owners shy away from me coming to their establishments. I expected to receive a follow up call, telling me it was not a good time. But none came."

Her fingers smoothed a corner of the white tablecloth. She tilted her head and unwillingly shared a slight smile with him. "Believe me, if I'd known in time, you would've received that call."

Butch shouted out another laugh. The wait staff hovered, casting coveted glances towards the couple. "I have to tell you, I very much enjoyed the welcome committee you sent out. The attractive black haired woman is your sister right?"

"How could you tell?"

"Only sisters could have such matching gorgeous, green eyes."

Traitorous heat rushed to her face and she realized her cheeks flamed red. "They run in our family."

"Lucky you." Studying her, Butch hesitated. "Out of respect for Theo, I'm going to give you a choice. I don't have to publish my assessment. I can delete everything I just noted." He paused, evaluating her, searching for answers in the pale green depths of her eyes. "Or you can let me write my review, good or bad, and have a real critique of your restaurant. You'll finally know what your abilities are."

She cleared her throat. "I—"

He held up a hand. "Hear me out first before you decide. If the critique is bad, as you understand, the review will, in all actuality, destroy Twin Springs."

Her eyes widened. To hear her fears spoken out loud, and so casually by the man who controlled the destiny of Twin Springs, stole her breath.

"If the review's good, are you prepared for what will come of that? Of the notoriety, the increase in business? I know it sounds so good. Success. But I've seen great budding chef's destroyed because they were not ready for the pressure, for the sudden increase in bookings, for the calls from magazines and newspapers." He paused, analyzing how her fingers continued to play and pluck at the table linens.

The Red Butcher actually gave her an option. She couldn't believe it. Perhaps chivalry wasn't dead. Maybe deep down inside the Red Butcher was a gentleman. Abruptly aware of his intense gaze, she quieted her nervous fingers by placing them in her lap. "Thank you for the offer. It's unbelievably decent of you to give me the choice."

She considered his words, weighing the pros and cons. Twin Springs could stay as she was, limping along, quietly seducing guests to come to the mountains and stay within her walls. But what if— What if what the Red Butcher wrote could save the Grand Dame? Save the community?

Or his review could kill Twin Springs. She glanced around the dining room that the wait staff had scrambled to ready for him. She thought of the community and kitchen crew who'd pulled together to make the evening's dinner service even possible. The right choice formed clearly in her mind.

"Mr. McKinley—"

"Butch," he inserted.

"Butch, then. Thank you for your gracious offer. But, I must decline. After all, Twin Springs has graced these mountains for over two hundred years. She survived the depression, the Japanese diplomats interned here during World War II and a great fire. Twin Springs never shrank from her duties to the guests, her employees or the community. In fact, she always rose to the occasion. And I must do the same. So, please write your review. Good or bad."

Suddenly, she felt light and free. Her chest expanded and she was able to take in a deep, cleansing breath. "We welcome you to stay as long as you like." She cast him a brilliant smile. "We have a gorgeous breakfast buffet in the morning. Take the waters at the Hot Springs and pick up some cool, refreshing bottled water for the drive home."

She placed her hand over Butch's and squeezed. "Whatever your review is, Twin Springs can handle it. We welcome the review and you."

She rose and Butch followed her cue, shooting forward to pull out her chair for her.

"I need to help prep the kitchen for tomorrow. But, please sit as long as you like, enjoy the music and dance with the other guests." Isabella again offered her hand. "Thank you for providing a critique of our dinner service." She shook the Red Butcher's hand and walked back to the kitchen with a slight spring in her step.

CHAPTER FIFTY-ONE

heo's gaze narrowed in on Butch McKinley studying Isabella as she departed. His college buddy pulled out a small tablet and typed in additional notes. He regretted calling Butch. He should've known better than to listen to one of Maddy's hare brained ideas. It was just that sometimes her ideas were good. Perhaps, even great. Those times had lulled him into accepting another idea. Until he'd been kicked in the balls when her latest brainstorm went to shit. *Time to pay the piper.* He came up behind his college friend, "Don't get too attached. She's mine."

Butch turned and grasped Theo's hand in a hearty handshake. "Just adding some additional notes before they fly out of my mind. One thing's for sure, successful review or not, you discovered a jewel in that girl. She is absolutely three stars on the Michelin scale."

He chuckled, smoothing his black tie down his shirt. "Butch, you can't judge women on a restaurant rating system."

The tall man shrugged. "We all have our own scales. Do you think she can handle what will come with my review?"

Theo glanced around them, checking to see if anyone could hear their conversation. He studied him with leveled eyes. "That bad, huh?"

Butch gave a non-committal reply.

His warm gaze flowed over Isabella before she disappeared behind the swinging doors. "She can handle anything. Let's go to my office and share a drink."

"I'd love to but I need to write this review while the flavors are still fresh."

"Whatever you write, thank you for coming. I know you have a lot going on with your family."

"Any time Theo. You know that. We're a long way from college huh? How's that demon-child, little sister of yours?"

He scratched his head with his knuckles before replying, "Sassy as always. Maddy's like watching over a prize filly. I'm trying to keep her in the gate and rested for the real race."

Butch laughed. "More like a prize bull. Don't try to sugar coat it, you keep her hidden for the protection of others."

"I won't tell her you said that."

Splaying his hands out in front of him in mock horror, Butch replied, "Hell no. I don't need one of her sharp horns goring me. But," he smiled thoughtfully, "I might come back to visit Isabella's sister."

"Good luck there. I have a feeling the rivers run deep beneath that beautiful face."

Butch gazed off into the distance, lost in a memory. "I watched her perform on Broadway one time. Her voice pierced my rock hard soul. It's a waste of Ava Fairbanks' talent to be here."

Theo resisted the urge to waive his hand in front of his friend's face. He had seen that sappy look before, on the poor insurance investigator. He sure didn't expect his friend to fall so quickly under Ava's spell. "That good, huh?" he joked, mocking his friend and snapping him out of his daze. "There's one thing I've learned. The Fairbanks sisters have a mind of their own." Unwillingly, his gaze was tugged towards the kitchen.

"Don't they all?" Reluctantly, Butch added, "It was great seeing you. But, I need to head back to my room and write this review."

"When will it be published?"

"I'll finish the review up tonight and email it out. It'll be posted by the morning."

"That fast." He grasped Butch's hand again. "Really, no matter what you write, thank you for taking time out to come."

"The pleasure was mine. Really Theo, too much time has passed."

Their eyes met and he realized the last time they were together, Butch had saved him from falling into a deep, dark abyss after his parents died. "You're right, too much time has passed."

He nodded. "I'm glad to see that you've decided to start living. For a while there, I thought you intended to throw you life away and turn into a lonely old man. About time you realized that your parents never intended for you to put your life on hold and sacrifice your happiness for Maddy's. Anyway. When you have time, let's get together and catch up. Bring beer and your girl." Butch flashed a lazy half smile. "Bring the singer and I'll owe you forever."

Theo hoped his mouth didn't hang open from Butch's rant. Only a buddy could slug you in the stomach and consider it an act of brotherly affection. Pushing the thought aside, he clasped Butch on the back and jerked him forward for a quick man hug. "Find your own women," he joked.

Butch gave a deep laugh. "Will do, will do."

Theo watched his friend walk away. He didn't care what tomorrow brought. Tonight was a stunning success. Perhaps after that beer, he'd share with his friend what an amazing feat Isabella pulled off tonight. Now, she deserved to celebrate and enjoy the moment.

He mulled over Butch's statement about his parents. Did he put his life on hold by trying to protect his sister, wanting to give her the best life possible? Perhaps. What else was he supposed to do? His parents were dead. Besides, the last time he put himself first and fought for what he wanted, his parents died. Butch must be wrong, he was living.

Or was he really just chicken? After all, Maddy hadn't

prevented him from returning to Twin Springs over the past five years. He did. Maybe it was time he started living for himself and his own happiness. He pulled his phone out, his heart slamming against his ribs, as he texted Isabella. "Meet me in the Crystal Ballroom in an hour. Wear your best dress." He waited for her response.

"Best dress?" She texted back, "You assume I have one. You get what you get."

Feeling alive, he slipped his phone back into his pocket. Then he removed his black tie and loosened his collar. Moving his neck from side to side, he tested the newly found freedom. "Only an hour to prepare. Isabella performed miracles today, let's see what I can do."

CHAPTER FIFTY-TWO

*E*nveloped by one of the fluffy, white Twin Springs robes, Isabella studied her reflection in the floor length mirror. She'd finished showering. Exhaustion pulled at her from the roller coaster day but her stomach fluttered with excitement. Her first real date with Theo.

Unwilling to admit how tired she really was, she examined herself. Moving closer to the mirror, she pulled at her skin with the tips of her fingers. She looked worse than usual. Her pasty white skin showed the pressure from the tense day. Holding the edges of her robe closed with one hand, she reached inside her robe with her other hand and hitched up her tiny breasts, attempting to imitate her sister's actions from during the dinner service. She tipped her head to the side and scrutinized the results before releasing her boobs in exasperation. "It's no use, my breasts are minuscule, just like the rest of me."

Life was so much easier when she hated Theo. She didn't have to put her feelings out on the line. She could immerse herself in her love of cooking. Maybe she should cancel rather than allow Theo see how truly terrible she looked. It was useless. Besides, did she really deserve more than one miracle in a year or a month, let alone in a single day?

In the voluminous robe, she trudged across her bedroom and threw her closet door open. An array of different shades of black jeans and tank tops stared back at her. She glared at them. "Wear your best dress," she muttered. "My chef jacket with heels would be the closest thing to a dress I have.

"Ava!" Why didn't she think of her sister before? She created illusions every night for the stage. Once, she'd transformed herself into a decrepit old woman. If Ava performed awe-inspiring theater magic nightly, surely she could create some kind of miracle with her. Ava was the key, her only hope. She grabbed her phone from the bed, "SOS," she texted to her sister. "Meeting Theo. Look like crap."

"Got your back. Be right there," her sister responded.

Ava would handle the makeup, but what about clothes? She stared miserably at her wardrobe. "Theo's used to beautiful women. Gorgeous, tall, slender women that actually own a dress." She kicked at the sneakers lining the floor. "Women who own a pair of heels.

"Why do I even need to dress up?" She jerked a pair of black jeans off the shelf and put them on under the robe. She began pulling clothes from her closet, holding them up to herself before tossing them on the floor. "Argh! I suck at being a girl." Flopping down on top of the pile, she buried her face in her hands. "He should just take me as I am." *But would he?* A tear escaped and trailed down her cheek. She wiped it away with the back of her hand and texted, "Said to wear best dress. Don't have one."

Her phone beeped back. She glanced down at the text from her sister.

"Don't even think about wearing your black slacks."

She threw the phone at her bed. It bounced off and dropped on the floor. She went over, kicked the phone under the bed and fell face first on the soft bedspread. Grumbling to herself and not caring that her hair soaked the bed linens around her, she waited with her arms and legs splayed out.

When her sister knocked, she didn't budge. Barely lifting her head a couple inches, she called out, "Come in."

Ava, the magician, breezed into the room ready to save the day. With a dress bag over one shoulder and a bulging black hobo bag over the other, she assessed her little sister. "Are those black pants I see peeking out from under that robe?"

"I'm hopeless," she mumbled into the mattress. "What kind of a woman am I?" She rolled to her side and noticed how beautiful and put together her sister looked, even at the late hour. "If it wasn't for us both having matching green eyes, my lack of feminine wiles would prove that I was adopted. I'm a pitiful excuse for a woman. I don't even understand how the other girls make themselves pretty. How could Theo ever love someone like me? I don't wear makeup. My daily skin care routine includes a bar of soap, warm water and a washcloth. The same bar of soap I use to clean my body. My hair isn't constantly piled on top of my head because I consider the hairdo sexy or elegant, but because scooping my long hair up into a ball and strapping a rubber band around the mass is easy, efficient and keeps the long strands from falling into the food I prepare."

She yanked the oversized sleeves of the robe up to reveal her hands. "Look at these hands! Red and raw from working with hot water in the kitchen." Frowning, she sniffed the back of her hands. "Wonderful! My hands still smell from the onions I chopped up for tomorrow's breakfast shift." She rubbed the pads of her fingertips against her cheek. "Yep, rough and dry. Nails? I have none." She flopped back, face down. "I have nubs," she moaned into the mattress, her voice muffled. "Just like my legs. Nubs."

Ava's musical laughter flowed out. "Is this the girl who just single handedly saved Twin Springs?"

"That girl gets to wear jeans and tennis shoes," came her garbled response. "Besides, we don't know yet if the Red Butcher liked any of the dishes he ordered."

"Pshaw," replied Ava. "I know when a man likes what he sees and that man was in love with everything served to him."

She rolled over and faced her sister. Hope seeped into her heart. "Do you think so?"

"Oh yeah. That man took one bite and fell in love. For a moment there, I thought he was lost to the world around him."

"Right, sure." She rolled to her back and looked up at the coffered ceiling. "What did you do, hide under the table and watch him?"

"Of course not. Maddy and I dressed up as wait staff and worked the Main Dining Room."

A gasp escaped her lips. "You. Did. Not."

"Yes. We. Did." She placed items from her soft, leather hobo bag on the antique desk. "We watched him for the entire service. Not a big deal. It was just like being part of a play. I made some great tips."

The bravery of her sister always amazed her. "Maddy too?"

Ava lounged on the side of the bed. "You should've seen her. She definitely throws herself fully into any situation. Full steam ahead. That's Maddy. By the end of the shift, she found a half dozen ways to improve the service, make it faster and easier for the wait staff."

With an unladylike snort, Isabella burst out laughing. "I don't doubt it."

Her sister gave two quick tugs on the pant leg of her black jeans. "Let's get you ready for the ball, Cinderella. Come sit in the chair at the desk." With a grand flourish of her arms, she added, "Let me work my magic."

Isabella's stomach rolled, making her feel sick. "Oh God," she moaned. "Shoot me now."

"Now, now," Ava tut-tutted. "Take off those awful jeans."

She did as her sister ordered and slumped in the chair, listening while Ava kept up a steady monologue of behind the scene stories from the plays she performed in.

With a round brush and blow drier she blew Isabella's long, wet hair until dry. "You're like one of those dolls we owned as kids. You know, the ones where you pulled the hair and more and more came out to make it longer." Then she curled and secured her hair in huge rollers around her head.

She removed a plastic tube and squeezed thick, green goo on Isabella's face and smoothed the grainy green mixture around with her fingertips. "Stay still."

"It's cold." She clamped her lips together to keep the muck out of her mouth. "Smells funny."

"Too bad." Ava smoothed the goo on Isabella's hands and slipped her green hands into plastic bags. She rambled on as Isabella's face tightened into a hard mask. She tapped her fingertips on the hardened green shell and grunted with approval. Removing the plastic bags, she squeezed gel on the back of her hands. "Okay, you're ready. Go into the bathroom and wash your hands. Then use a warm, wet washcloth to soften and remove the mask. Hurry back."

Hardened to a dark grey, the mask pruned her young face. At risk of cracking her face, she mumbled a non-committal reply and rushed to the bathroom.

When she returned, Ava patted the chair and motioned for her to sit. "Turn around in the chair and tip your head back," she commanded.

"Yes, ma'am," Isabella said as she complied. Her sister moisturized, concealed and smoothed a base coat of foundation on her face. "Do you do this every day?"

"Not to the same extent. But yes, I do take the time to make up my face every day." She clicked sharp tweezers.

Isabella eyed the shiny steel warily. "What are you going to do with those?"

"Just a touch up here and there." Quickly, she plucked a hair from one of Isabella's eyebrows.

Jumping back as if burned, she rubbed her offended eyebrow with the heel of her hand. "What the heck is that? A torture device?"

Her sister looked at her adoringly, as if she was a young kid who just said something cute. "I love how we are sisters and yet we are so very different. No, it's not a torture device. But beauty is pain. So suck it up."

Warily, she leaned back again. "Just leave me some eyebrows when you're done."

For thirty minutes Ava worked her magic. She removed the huge rollers, backcombed, twisted and twirled Isabella's hair into an elegant knot high on her head.

"Don't look yet," she admonished before adding another coat of mascara. "I covered up the bruises the best I could. They developed some very interesting hues of green and bluish black. So, you can still see them slightly underneath. If I had my theater makeup with me, I could've done a much better job." She tossed the mascara back on the table and waived her hands in front of Isabella's face until the mascara dried sufficiently.

She withdrew a round bottle of perfume from her bag. "With the vanilla undertones, this fragrance is perfect for you." She misted the air around her chair.

Immediately, Isabella coughed and gaged as the mist coated the inside her mouth. She desperately wanted to spit out the offending flavor. "I think you've ruined my greatest asset, my taste buds."

"You should've closed your mouth. Wipe your tongue on the sleeve of your robe if you have to. Just don't look in the mirror. Better yet, close your eyes, while I grab your outfit."

She shifted in her seat and rubbed the knobby fabric of her robe back and forth across her tongue.

"Stay right there and keep your eyes closed." Ava crossed the room and unzipped the garment bag. Carefully, she removed the dress from inside. "Stand up." She moved closer. "Hold on to me and step in. Keep your eyes closed."

A soft cloud surrounded her. She heard Ava zip up the back of the dress. "Does it fit?"

"Yes, I borrowed the dress from Maddy. She's closer to your size." Ava adjusted the neckline and ran her hands down the length of the dress, tugging it into place. "Okay, go ahead and look."

The woman in the mirror wasn't pitiful, but beautiful. Isabella's breath caught in her chest and she exhaled it. Like a sleepwalker, she moved over to the full length mirror and hesitantly reached out to touch her refection. The sweetheart neckline sparkled with hundreds of little crystals. The waist nipped in and the silver chiffon flowed over her hips, dipping low before floating around her legs. Her green eyes sparkled like jewels in her face. They were lightly lined with a smoky dark liner and her long lashes appeared impossibly long. The Twin Springs' medallion nestled between the rising swell of her breasts.

"Just a few extra touches." Ava adorned Isabella's ears with long, sparkling earrings that almost brushed her bare shoulders. Bending down, she slipped straps of silver on her feet.

"Now you're ready." She straightened and stood behind her sister, admiring her creation in the mirror. "Beautiful as always."

Transfixed by her own image, Ava's words didn't register. "I can't believe-that-is-me." She stepped forward towards the mirror. One of the high heels snagged on the carpet and nearly dumped her.

Ava reached out and caught her before her face hit the mirror.

Clutching her sister's arm, she glared down at the offensive shoes. "How do you walk in these?"

"Slowly, delicately, and very, very carefully. One foot, heel to toe, in front of the other," advised Ava.

Hesitantly, she moved forward. "Slowly," she murmured. "Delicately, heel to toe," she repeated out loud.

Swallowing back laughter, Ava smiled wide. "You're a natural!"

She grinned and strolled her version of 'delicately' around the room, murmuring to herself. Exhausted from the effort, her shoulders slumped. "Do I have to wear high heels?"

Ava's eyes widened with horror. "Yes! Look at what they do to your legs." She reached forward and lifted the hem of her dress. "Those are not nubs."

She glanced down and was completely taken by surprise. Her legs appeared endless in the stilettos. "Not too shabby."

"Not too shabby?" repeated Ava. "Theo is going to weep and kiss the floor when you walk in."

Two wishes granted in one day. First, completing the most difficult service of her life. And now, the unbelievable chance to outshine any woman Theo ever dated. That was the most she dared to hope for. She wanted Theo to desire her. And then, just maybe, someday, even to grow to love her. Perhaps if her luck held, he might even grow to love her as much as she loved him. "Then I guess I am ready."

"Just a minute." Ava ran over to her bag and pulled out her cell phone. "I want to get a picture. I might never get you in a dress again."

CHAPTER FIFTY-THREE

Teetering on Maddy's borrowed stilettos, Isabella progressed down the hallway from her room. Her right hand rubbed along the wallpaper, just in case she hitched forward and needed to catch herself. She muttered her sister's instructions under her breath. "Heel to toe. Heel to toe."

Her admiration for Ava grew in leaps and bounds after the excruciating amount of time and effort she expended to just reach the elevators. She grumbled, "No way in hell, am I taking the stairs."

Stretching her legs into an extraordinarily wide step, she avoided the crack along the elevator's threshold and wobbled into the elevator. She rode down two floors to the Grand Lobby and the steel doors parted before her. She paused, gathered her courage, grasped the side of the elevator door and cautiously hobbled out. Thrilled with her progress, she beamed at the young woman working behind the Front Desk.

The Front Desk clerk swallowed a gasp with an awkward cough and covered her mouth with the tips of her fingers.

Florid red spread across Isabella's face, and she mumbled under her breath. "Dumb heals. I hate you." She waived her hand at the young woman, "I know. I'd laugh too. Just bear in mind this is my first time walking on stilts."

Continuing past the Front Desk, she extended her hands out to her sides for additional balance. "I've got this."

The melody from the baby grand piano flowed through the Grand Lobby and washed over her. The soft lights cast a dreamlike glow and illuminated her beauty to those around her. Concentrating on remaining upright, she missed the bellhops' dazed faces and slack jaws. Ensnared by her beauty, they dropped back and stared longingly after her. At a snails pace, she turned the corner into the Presidents Hall and stumbled towards the Crystal Ballroom. Trailing after her, one of the bellhops shook the fog from his brain, rushed forward and held open the ballroom's tall doors. With a sigh, they whispered closed behind her.

At the top of the double staircase leading down to the ballroom floor, Isabella paused and steadied her breath. The lowered sidelights allowed the huge chandelier to cast tiny pin points of light, that glittered and gleamed around the ballroom. Graceful, white French doors lined the opposite wall and led out to the back patio. Night stars back dropped and twinkled through the high windows arching across the tops of the French doors. Petite tables with curving, elegant legs huddled together around the edges like debutants waiting for a turn on the dance floor, all bare-topped and empty, except for one.

At the far right edge of the dance floor stood one, lone table, draped with crisp white linens. A bottle of champagne chilled in a silver ice bucket and was surrounded by two crystal glasses and small platters of cheese, soft breads and chocolate covered strawberries.

Searching for Theo, Isabella's gaze swept the room. The fragrance of roses filled the air, but there were none to be seen. Not a soul remained in the room but her. She wished for her cell phone to check the time. "Am I too late? Did Theo already leave?"

The piano's love song seeped through the closed doors and pierced her consciousness. Its passionate melody swirled around her and weighed down her heart until it felt leaden within her chest. Gradually, she realized the price of her grand makeover. She was too late. She missed her opportunity with Theo. She hung her head and gripped the banister. Her mind filtered through the process of her transformation and weighed the time spent. She zeroed in on the culprit. The mask and the stupid tweezers. She knew it. "All that crap for nothing." She resisted stomping her feet with frustration. *What? Theo couldn't wait another ten minutes?* She tapped her toe and almost fell on her ass. Holding on to the handrail for dear life, she muttered, "If I risked my life in these damn heels and he doesn't show up, I'll kill him."

A sound to her right attracted her attention. Her breath caught and hope filled her heart. She straightened and pushed her chest out and chin up as per her sister's instructions.

The door to the theatre slammed opened and two teenage boys burst out. The skinny adolescents ogled her. They snickered, elbowed each other as they tromped across the dance floor and exited out the left side doors.

I can't believe this! Instantly deflated, she stared after the boys. "I wasn't important enough to wait for?"

Unwelcome tears gathered in the corners of her eyes. Furious with fate, she blinked back the moisture and turned to leave. Her spiked heel turned in under her but she caught herself before she fell. "I'll never wear heels again."

"Wait!"

She stilled and carefully turned around.

Theo entered the ballroom through the back patio's French doors. He abruptly stopped and stared at her, an odd bundle of flowers in his hand. Speechless, his gaze brushed over her.

Warmth seeped through her limbs. As time stretched between them, and under his intense gaze, she began to fiddle with her dress.

"You're beautiful." Purposefully, he strode towards her.

Pleasure coursed through her. "All worth it," she decided.

"Even the tweezers." She picked her way down the staircase and across the dance floor, whispering, "Heel to toe, heel to toe."

"Did you say something?"

Appalled, she shook her head. "No. Nothing at all." She took stock of the man before her, admired his wide shoulders in his black jacket, his white collar crisp, open and loose against his strong jaw.

Sheepishly, he presented her with a battered array of flowers. "I have no idea what they are. Don't tell the landscaper, I pulled them from the walkway outside."

"Thank you." She studied him over the blossoms. He seemed different. He wore the same clothes from earlier, but something had changed. She couldn't put her finger on exactly what. Just more relaxed, less uptight. Whatever the change was, she felt more drawn to him than ever.

"I won't tell." She winked, buried her nose in the multi colored blooms and enjoyed their blended fragrance. "They're gorgeous."

"No, you are." He laced his fingers with hers. "Let's celebrate." He guided her over to the table and poured champagne into two tall, fluted glasses. He held one out to her.

She placed the bouquet on the table and accepted the crystal glass.

Raising his glass to her in a toast, Theo said, "To you, Isabella. A woman who treats everyone around her as family, whose love and creativity knows no bounds."

She beamed. "And to you. A man who saves the day, and protects the women in his life. Your father would be proud."

"Your confidence in my ability to protect you and Maddy means more to me than I can say. I'll strive to never let you down." Clicking his glass against hers, somehow Theo was able to wash the bubbly champagne down his suddenly constricted throat.

Quizzically, she mulled over his words. Did he actually doubt himself? He was their rock. The backbone of their little group. "I see you chose one of the fruit, nut and cheese platters that will be available for the Lobby Bar."

"Yes, I seem to have grown quite fond of fresh bread and walnuts lately." He gave her a heated look over the rim of his glass.

She smiled. Her heart skipped a beat and began to beat even faster thinking of that night in her office.

Music faintly flowed in from the Grand Lobby. Theo held out his hand to her. "May I have this dance?"

She started to extend her hand and place it in his but at the last moment she snatched it back. She didn't think her sister's instructions on walking in heels applied to dancing in them. She nibbled her lip.

"What's the matter?"

Staring down at her silver strapped nemesis, Isabella shook her head. She didn't want him to realize how pitiful she was in the woman department. "Nothing." Mustering up her courage, she flashed him a brilliant smile. "I would love to dance."

He gathered her into his arms and swung her around.

Unprepared for the sudden move, her feet tangled beneath her and she pitched to one side, almost toppling over. Automatically, his strong arms tightened and he prevented her from completely embarrassing herself.

"Did you hurt yourself?" Theo asked, his voice laced with concern.

Great! Now he'll know. Perhaps I should stop pretending to be more than I am. She refused to meet his gaze. She wasn't an actress like her sister. Just a girl who worked in the kitchens. She sucked in a deep breath. *No more faking!* "No. It's these damn shoes," she muttered, looking down at them. "Beautiful, but completely impractical."

"Poor Isabella, being a girl is pretty hard huh?" He lightly mocked her and squeezed her tight.

Relief flowed through her. *He understands.* Completely ready to give up her farce, words gushed from her mouth. "You have no idea. Do you have any clue about what women go through to prepare for a date? I didn't. My sister's ruthless when it comes to beauty."

Theo flung his head back and shouted with laughter.

Brows furrowed, she cast him a suspicious look. "Perhaps you don't understand after all," she grumbled. "Men. What do you all know about the time and effort it takes for a woman to look beautiful?" Thinking about how desperately hard she tried to please him, she growled, "It's not funny."

Tipping his head back down, he laid his forehead upon hers. "Isabella," her name was soft upon the air, "you're perfect just the way you are."

Caught up in her own tirade, she continued. "It was awful," she declared. "Ava kept repeating over and over, 'beauty is pain'. Then she told me to walk heel to toe. Delicately," she drew the word out for emphasis. She lifted her skirt and brandished the offending shoe. "How do you walk delicately heel to toe on this skinny little spike?"

His shoulders shook but he gallantly held back the laughter. "I have no idea."

She threw her hands up in the air, causing her to wobble on the skinny heels. "Exactly my point. Men don't have a clue."

Theo bent down on one knee.

Her breath caught and he gently lifted her right foot by the back of the ankle. Grasping his shoulders, she steadied herself.

He pulled the back strap of the silver heel forward, sliding it across her delicate arch and off her foot. "I'm removing these devices of torture." He bent further down, lifted her foot up to his mouth and pressed his warm lips, in a kiss, to the top of her bare foot. Then he turned his attention to her other foot.

Her heart almost exploded from her chest. Chest heaving with the emotions he released, her gaze slid up his body as he stood until she stared up into his molten eyes.

The straps of silver dangled from his index finger. His full lips twisted into an amused smile. "Should we put them down the garbage disposal?"

His gentle deed humbled her. Touched her to the core. Waiting for her heart to stop slamming against her ribs and her breathing to slow, she examined her nemesis hanging from his finger. Greatly tempted, she considered his idea. "Only if you want to face the wrath of your sister. Those are her shoes."

"Then perhaps we will just leave them here." He turned and placed them on one of the chairs. Then he kicked his own shoes off and shoved them under the chair. "There, now we are both on even footing." Once again, he held out his hand. "Are you ready?"

Isabella glided into Theo's arms. The chandelier sparkled down on the couple as they slow danced across the ballroom's glistening wooden floor. Oblivious to time, she swayed comfortably in the strength of his embrace and listened to the tattoo of his heart.

"It was awfully presumptuous of you to tell me to wear my best dress," she whispered and glanced up at him through her lashes. "The closest thing to a dress that I own would be wearing my chef jacket with pumps."

Theo stopped mid step, threw his head back and clasped his hands to his heart. "My God. Don't do that to me. You're going to give me a heart attack. I'll be dreaming of you in your chef jacket all night." His warm gaze pinned her to the spot. "Your gorgeous legs, the jacket barely covering that stunning bottom of yours. Lord, help me."

Her face flamed as if she just finished cooking in front of a six burner stove top on high. "Stop talking like that," she admonished.

Enjoying her discomfort, he gathered her once again close within his arms. "I'm going to dream of holding you tight like this." His hands slid down and cupped the curve of her buttocks. Leaning back, he lifted her off her feet and up against his hardened frame. "Of my hands slipping down over your chef jacket, then up and under it until I am holding your silky skin just like this."

"A guest might see us," she whispered.

"I don't care." Her lowered his head and tasted the champagne on her lips. Wanting, needing more, he delved into her softness.

Isabella burned. The heat of his touch stoked a fire deep inside her. The fire he had built and lit earlier. Somewhere in the back of her mind, a great clock struck midnight and beautiful singing drifted into the Crystal Ballroom from the direction of the theater.

Reluctantly, Theo lifted his head and allowed her body to slide down the length of him until her bare feet found purchase on the wooden dance floor. "Your sister's serenading us?"

"Hmmm," she murmured and placed her cheek against his chest. "I haven't heard her sing in years. I forgot how beautiful her voice is."

"Perhaps I should be on my best behavior with her close by." He guided her over to the table and pulled out a chair for her. Again, he bent down to a knee.

"Oh no, don't put those things back on my feet."

Theo smiled. Holding both of her hands in his, he gazed deep into her eyes, searching for something. An answer to a question only he knew.

"Theo?"

"I've loved you since the first time I saw you walking across the Grand Lobby." He swallowed hard. "I want to wake up every morning with you snuggling beside me and go to bed every night holding you in my arms. I want to grow old with you," He drew a small, velvet, black box from his pocket. He cracked it open and presented her with an emerald ring lying in a bed of diamonds.

"Isabella Fairbanks, will you marry me?"

CHAPTER FIFTY-FOUR

Theo watched Isabella's eyes flutter between the velvet box and him. She gaped up at him, unable to speak. The sparkle and happiness from earlier had disappeared from her face. *Shit.* This wasn't going at all the way he planned. *See,* he told himself. *You're not meant to live for the moment. You're a planner. You stake out what you want, develop a plan and conquer. This live by the seat of your pants idea was shit.* He considered plowing his fist into Butch's mouth the next time he offered his insights. *And Butch was a critic. I'll critique his ass with my boot.*

I—I—," Isabella shuddered.

Desperately, he floundered for any tool or weapon within his arsenal with the ability to sway her towards accepting him.

"Are you sure you want me?"

Not want her? He was astounded by her question. No, he didn't merely want Isabella. Not at all. He desperately needed Isabella. She was everything to and for him. Like oxygen, water and food. She was his trifecta. Without her in his life, he would shrivel up and die, a lonely, tight ass scrooge. Was that it? Was that her hesitation? She didn't realize how much he loved her, wanted her, needed her. Was the girl blind? He'd only stumbled over himself trying to please her, and spend time with her. But if she needed words not actions, then he'd give them to her.

Lowering himself to both knees, he held her hands within his. Fervently, he gazed into her eyes. "Want you? How could I not want you? I love that compact, little body of yours, your perfect breasts, and rounded butt. I love your smell." He searched his soul for the right words. The words she needed to hear. "You're spontaneous and creative. You have a huge heart. You are accepting of others, even my obnoxious little sister. " He laid all his cards out for her to see. "You accept me for the tight ass I am. Isabella, I feel alive when I am with you. I think about you constantly. When I'm not with you, I feel like a part of me is missing."

"Theo—" Silent tears slipped down her face.

Theo kissed the droplets away, attempting to stop the flow. At a loss for words, he added, "I swear, I'll never ask you to wear heels ever again."

"You promise?" she whispered.

"I promise."

She shared a watery smile. "Then what can a girl say, but yes."

Triumph coursed through his veins. Ready to conquer the world, he gathered her up into his arms, kissed her as the fragrances of vanilla and roses intertwined and swirled around them.

Isabella's hands shook within his grasp. He was lucky Maddy brought the ring with her to Twin Springs. He'd tried to get his little sister to hand over the ring, no questions asked. An impossible task. Finally, he swore Maddy to secrecy and explained why he needed Mom's emerald ring. Obviously, she shared with Ava, hence the serenading. "This ring belonged to my mother. It wasn't her wedding ring, I saved that for Maddy. But she wore this ring every-day. I've always felt a kinship to it," Theo said, slipping the ring on her finger. The ring almost reached from the base of Isabella's finger to her knuckle. "I know the emerald's a little large on your delicate hand. If you don't like it, we can select another one together."

She held her hand out and admired the ring. "No, I love it." The cushion cut emerald sparkled. As did the diamonds, surrounding the green stone, inlaid into the platinum band. She moved her hand from side to side and the emerald sparkled and winked back. The ring felt warm against her finger. "It feels right."

He didn't want anything to mess up his future relationship with her. A smart business man tied up all the loose ends and sealed the deal. *This time with a kiss*, he thought. "I have something else for you. You could call it a pre-wedding gift." From within his jacket he pulled out and handed her a folded stack of papers.

Quizzically, she glanced up at him and unfolded the papers. "What is it?"

"It's my company's shares of Twin Springs. I signed our shares back over to your family. This is my wedding gift to you."

An anguished, "No," pierced the air.

Isabella jerked up from her seat.

Maddy's head, her curls sticking out in every direction, popped up from behind a grouping of tables. Dressed in a silky, pink pajamas set and slippers, she raced over to Isabella and Theo.

"What the hell's wrong now?" He grabbed his sister by her shoulders and searched her face, trying to evaluate the situation. This wasn't one of Maddy's usual freak-outs. Her gray eyes were wild with fear. "What's the matter?" He hugged her tight. "What happened? Are you hurt?"

Maddy wrenched herself out of her brother's embrace. She snatched the papers from Isabella's hands and ripped them in half. "You can't give her our shares of Twin Springs and make me leave." She continued to rip, "Do you hear me, you can't make me leave!" Sobbing, she ripped the last of the papers into tiny pieces. "I won't go. This is the last place I remember being happy. This is the last place I remember being a family." She threw herself into her brother's arms.

Shocked, he held his little sister as she cried into his shoulder. Why hadn't Maddy talked with him about how she felt? If she didn't tell him these things, how could he fix things for her?

Women confused the hell out of him. "I'm not sending you away after I marry Isabella. I don't believe in boarding schools."

She glared up at her brother. "I'm not going to a boarding school," she ground out.

Smoothing her curls, Isabella sighed, "She wasn't talking about being sent to a boarding school."

"Of course she was. She thinks once you and I marry, that we will send her away."

Maddy shoved him back. "You're so stupid."

"What's wrong? Here I am trying to sooth you and you go all three year old on me."

"Stop it, both of you." Suddenly, Isabella understood how he felt shouldering the responsibility of being the only adult in the situation. "Believe me, Theo. You're way off base." She returned her attention to his little sister. "Nothing is going to change. Contract or not, Twin Springs is your home now." She reached out for Theo's hand, dragging him close. "We are your family now."

Theo re-evaluated the situation. He had misunderstood his sister's problem, but he definitely perceived added benefits to marrying Isabella. From now on she could interpret girl-speak for him. *Fan-fucking-tastic. Life on easy street.*

Maddy wiped her nose with the back of her hand. "No, you and my brother are a family now. And I am alone."

"No, we're all family," she insisted.

"Are you sure?" tentatively asked Maddy.

"I'm positive." She smiled and wiped the tears from the teen's face. "All of us are a family. You, your brother, my sister and me. All of us."

"So you can't make me leave then, right?" Maddy's voice hitched. "If we are a family, even if you own all of Twin Springs. No matter what?"

"Even if I did own all of Twin Springs, I wouldn't force you to leave. I love you as much as I love my sister. I don't want your family's shares of Twin Springs." She stared straight into Maddy's tear soaked eyes. "Besides, the Grand Dame needs you. Look at the life and innovative, young ideas you've brought to every part of her. Not only do we all love you, but she needs you."

Oh no, thought Theo. *Don't do it, Isabella.* He laid a hand on her shoulder, attempting to stop her. "Isabella," he warned.

"Really?" Maddy asked, ignoring her brother.

"Really. Look how the guests enjoy your new ideas at Tea Time. Once the Lobby Bar is finished, the Grand Lobby will not be just for taking tea anymore. Look what you and Ava accomplished in the Main Dining Room. You belong here."

"Now you did it," said Theo. He stood back, arms crossed, ready for battle. He glanced down at Isabella. She might understand girl-speak but she didn't have a clue on how Maddy's mind worked. But she had a hell of a heart and he loved her for it.

Maddy gave her brother a sly look. "See, I belong here. So you and Dale better start listening to me more."

He dragged his warm gaze from Isabella and focused on Maddy. "Now, that part, we will have to take under discussion."

"Take her up to her room," prompted Isabella. "Reassure her, and make sure she is safely in bed." She tugged the ring from her finger and held it out to him, in the palm of her hand.

"What?" Pain pierced his heart. *What just happened*, he wondered and searched her face for the answer. "Why?"

She pressed the ring into his hand. "It's all too much for Maddy. We need to slow down."

His brows rose. "Slow down? If we went any slower, we'd be stopped."

She refused to meet his gaze. "Then perhaps we should stop. For Maddy. To protect her."

He felt the tug between responsibility for his sister and desire for Isabella. "This is not how I pictured this evening ending," he growled.

She shook her head. "Maddy needs you. We will have many other nights."

Theo cupped the back of her neck and guided her forward for a quick but satisfying kiss. "I love you," he whispered. "This isn't over."

She watched Theo leave with his arm around his little sister. Even as the distance widened she heard Maddy informing him about her newest ideas on updating and modernizing Twin Springs.

With Maddy's shoes dangling from her fingers, Isabella entered her bedroom. She tossed the offending shoes on the couch and fell backwards on her mattress. "Theo loves me and we have all the time in the world to be together." Concentrating on that delicious thought, she fell into a deep sleep. In the beautiful dress, she floated away on a cloud of chiffon.

CHAPTER FIFTY-FIVE

Swaying to their own rhythm, Jean Claude Flamme and Emma slow danced. Bending down, he kissed the silky crown of golden curls piled on her head. Unmindful of his bruised and swollen shut eye, he surveyed their surroundings with his one good eye. The kitchen's scuffed, wide plank floor served as their dance floor. Stoves and butcher block counters crowded in around them and the aroma of the evening's service lingered in the air. She deserved more. A woman with her beauty and stature merited celebration by all. Not being hidden away and kept in the dark. She deserved a man capable of placing her in a setting that would allow her to sparkle and bloom for all to admire. She deserved more than his station in life could give her. After all, Emma was more than he deserved.

He pressed his hand against the small of her back and drew her in closer. He enjoyed the sensation of her petite body moving against his frame as her chiffon dress swirled between their legs. He knew the Lieutenant sniffed around. So many eyes in Twin Springs. So many were willing to expose his and Emma's secret for their own personal gain.

An honorable man would walk away, leave Emma and Twin Springs. But he wasn't honorable. He was weak. Weak for her. And a coward inside, afraid of life without her. He understood the consequences of their actions but selfishly he craved any moments possible with her. Even if their moments were tainted by back rooms and secret rendezvous. He rubbed a loose tendril of her hair between his thumb and forefinger and enjoyed the satiny feel. "Soft as corn silk. You glitter in your dress more finely than any jewel." Any jewel he deserved to touch, he reminded himself.

Reaching up, she cupped his bruised face.

An involuntary hiss released from between his lips. Embarrassed, he attempted to smile. But the pressure from his swollen and bruised lips caused fresh cracks to form and bleed across his mouth.

Quickly, Emma drew back her hand. "I'm sorry. I'm so very sorry that you were hurt because of my stupidity. My naiveté."

Before replying, he dabbed at the blood with his cooking side towel. "Thankfully, the Lieutenant didn't break my hands. Without the use of my hands, I can't cook. If I can't cook then I couldn't remain at Twin Springs. I couldn't steal these moments with you. Besides, I'd endure any pain to keep you safe." She was dainty and small, he thought, noting the delicate bone structure of her face and shoulders. His chest ached with pain at the possibility of the Lieutenant catching them together. The Lieutenant's rage would overwhelm him. He worried that in the midst of a fit the Lieutenant would lose sight of the fact Emma was the General's daughter, until it was too late. Overcome with the outrage of Emma letting a colored man touch her, yes, the Lieutenant would kill her. The thought of the Lieutenant's fists smashing her face or his hands touching her body filled him with horror. A violent anger boiled within his body and begged to be released. Without anyone to stop him, the Lieutenant would kill Emma. The image of her dying almost brought him to his knees. "I'd give my life for you."

"But I don't want you to." She hugged him tight and mumbled into his jacket. "Why cannot people just let us live our lives?"

He smoothed his hands down her back. She lived in a sheltered world. Where the General was all powerful and protected her well. The world outside of Twin Springs was beyond her comprehension. "People are always in other people's business. They get pleasure from judging others. It allows them to feel good about themselves while causing someone else pain. It's a story as old as time, and I don't think it'll ever change."

She listened to his words. "I hate them. I hate those people. Why can't they let us live and love in peace?" She nuzzled into him as he squeezed her tighter within his embrace.

"Tonight's New Year's Eve," she whispered. Laying her head on his chest, she enjoyed the steady beat of his heart. "Tonight's the night wishes are made and granted. I wish we could run away together. I wish we could run far away. Go west and discover a plot of land where no one lived around us for miles. Then, we could live in peace. We could have babies together." She clutched him closer as they swayed. "I want to have your babies, to feel them grow inside of me. To have your hand on my stomach so you can feel the baby kick as my sister's husband does with her rounded belly. We could watch our children grow until they too have babies for us to coddle and play with. That is my wish."

Her dream world didn't exist. Not even in the talkies played nightly in Twin Springs' theater. He must protect Emma. Protect her from the Lieutenant, and from being ostracized by society. Keep her safe from her own naiveté. He made a noncommittal grunt that rumbled within his chest.

The movement tickled Emma's ear and her lips curled up in response. "My sister will have her baby soon," she spoke softly. "The General will have his heir. One that he can form and mold any way he wants. Perhaps then he'll let Ruby and I follow our dreams. Then my wish must come true."

Shaking his head from side to side, he replied, "You must stop dreaming. Enjoy what we have for now. One day you'll find a man and forget about me." His heart ached from his own words but he recognized that they must be said.

Anger coursed through her body and caused her voice to rise. "I'm not a child, needing to be protected and coddled. I know my own mind, and I am telling you, Jean Claude Flamme." Emma shouted, "Never. Never, will I allow another man to touch me. Never."

Fearful of listening ears, he desperately tried to calm her. "Shush," he admonished, placing a fingertip over her lips.

Standing still, he strained to hear beyond the silence. In the distance the distinctive click of the Lieutenant's boots sounded against wooden floor planks.

"Oh my God," she gasped, the blood draining from her face. "The Lieutenant heard me. He'll discover us. Together."

His time with her had ended. Now her safety was his only concern. "Run Emma. Run and hide where you did last time."

She refused to budge. "I can't leave you again," she whispered. "We'll go to my father. He'll understand."

"There is only one option. You must hide." Not waiting for her permission, he dragged her down the hall towards the office. From the sharp clicking of the Lieutenant's boots, he could tell the Lieutenant was definitely now in the kitchen.

"It's too late. You'll be trapped. He will kill you if he finds you in his office again."

"I'm not going in. You are. Go hide in the secret room. I'll come for you, like last time."

They paused outside the heavy, wooden door. "No." Her voice was firm. "We will have my dream. I want my wish. I'll hide in the secret room but you take the train tonight and run." She lifted the emerald necklace from around her neck and pressed it into his palm. "Take my necklace and purchase a place for us. Send word of where you are and I'll join you."

He shook his head. "No, you deserve a better life. You deserve more than I can give you."

He watched as Emma folded his ebony fingers over the necklace. It warmed his palm from being nestled against the heat of her body.

"Jean Claude, this is my heart that I'm placing in your hand. Don't break my heart. You run. Run and find us a safe plot of land where we can make babies and grow old together."

"Emma," he growled unwilling to leave her.

She reached up and held his strong face between her palms. She pressed a soft kiss upon his lips. A tear rolled down, blending between their lips. Leaning back, she memorized his features. Tilting her head slightly, her pink tongue licked the saltiness from her lips. She dazzled him with her smile. "Jean Claude Flamme, it's New Year's Eve, tomorrow will be 1929. Anything is possible. The world is new, bright and shiny. Make a place for us. Promise me."

He looked down at her pleading face. His fingers tightened on her shoulders, the need to shake her into reality was great. He wanted to rant at her that just because hemlines were raised and you feel free without your tight undergarments that doesn't mean that the world has changed. Then, he gazed into her beautiful eyes and everything within him transformed. Her usually light green eyes were darkened with fear. But a dazzling flame sparkled from deep within her. She still believed. Believed in them.

He would fight. Fight for Emma and their future. The consequences be damned. His decision made, Jean Claude knew there was no more time for discussion. He pulled out his key ring. The jingling keys sounded overly loud in the long hall. Quickly, he opened the door and pushed her inside. "Put one of the chairs under the handle so he can't follow you. I know another way. I'll get you out." Lingering precious moments, he kissed her one last time, pushed her inside, slammed the door and re-locked it. He tossed the keys through the open transom above the door. Just in case he lost the battle. Then she could escape. The time for running had passed. Only her safety remained. Ready for battle, he accepted what fate required of him.

The Lieutenant's roar of anger filled the hall and vibrated off the walls.

The inability of being free to cast his own mark with destiny, burned and raged within him. Drawing from a lifetime of oppression and control, he released the pent up rage within his soul and answered with a battle cry of his own.

CHAPTER FIFTY-SIX

The Lieutenant's furious roar filled the hall. Emma shuddered. Jean Claude didn't escape. They were both trapped. She'd delayed him with her foolish wishes and hopes. And now the Lieutenant knew their secret. She froze when she heard Jean Claude's answering roar. She cried out in anguish, "No, Jean Claude! Hide with me!"

She scooped up his key ring. Her fingers shook uncontrollably as she inserted the key in the lock. She must let him in. She turned the key, unlocked the door and pulled.

Jean Claude wrenched the door from her grasp and slammed it closed. "Damn it Emma. Lock the door and don't come out. Hide."

On the other side, she heard the two men struggling. Unlike last time, Jean Claude fought back. She recognized that he fought for his life. And hers. He fought for their future. He no longer had a choice but to try and grant her wish. She twisted the key and locked the door. Quickly, she pulled a chair over and wedged it under the black oval doorknob. "Forgive me Jean Claude."

Emma stepped back. Covering her ears, she tried to block out the dreadful sounds of bones pounding flesh behind the door. The weight of the men slammed against the door and the chair wobbled precariously under the force. "The chair won't hold!"

Panicked, she searched for something else to block the door. Anything.

"The table." She grasped the edges of the enormous table and pulled. It wouldn't budge. She wasn't strong enough. "No use." Her frantic gaze flitted from one piece of furniture to another. The desk was secured to the platform. There was nothing else left in the room to block the door.

Emma's back slid down the length of the door, until she crumpled in a useless heap on the wooden floor. Her shoulders slumped and sobs shook her tiny frame. "I failed, Jean Claude." She looked over to the table. "I'm not even strong enough to move a table."

She stilled. "But I can remove one of the leaves and jam the board in the crack beneath the door." She scrambled to her feet, reached beneath each side of the table and unlocked one of the leaves. She slid the end of the table out and removed one of the five foot long boards. She dragged the leaf over to the door, shoved the edge of it under the door and pushed until it stuck.

Little by little, the noise on the other side of the door hushed. Her breathing came hot and quick in her chest as she inched closer, pressed her ear against the wood and listened. A terrifying silence greeted her. She whispered, "Jean Claude?"

The Lieutenant's harsh laugh filled her ears. "Come on out, Emma."

Keys jiggled on the other side of the door.

"If you go away, I won't tell the General," she bargained.

The Lieutenant's voice softened, "I just want to help you."

His voice was so close, she whimpered deep in her chest. "I don't need your help."

Manic laughter vibrated her ear. "Emma, you're confused. No one taught you the rules. I can help you with that."

Why won't he go away? Her father would never allow anyone to treat her this way. "I'm the General's daughter. I order you to go away!" She slapped her hand uselessly against the door.

The click of the lock vibrated through her brain. She reared back and fell hard on her elbows. The chiffon of her dress floated up around her like a cloud. "Go away," she sobbed.

"Your colored lover is dead." He sang the words almost like a maddening child's verse. Taunting with his voice high and shrill, " You

let him rut between your legs. Filthy whore, I'll show you what a real man feels like."

He killed Jean Claude. Her heart ripped from her chest and a high pitched wail emitted from her soul. Wrapping her arms around her knees, she rocked herself back and forth. Lifting her head, she stared at the door. "I hate you! Somehow, I'll make you pay for this sin."

The black doorknob slowly turned and horror inked a path across her soul. Panic raced through her veins and forced her to move. She scrambled up and rushed over to the roll top desk. Panting with fear, she reached back behind the desk, curled her fingers around the back edge and pulled. But her soft soled shoes just slipped on the waxed, wooden floor. The desk refused to budge. Quickly changing positions, she braced her shoulder against the wall. Her feet braced against the outer leg of the desk and her fingers once again curved around the desk's hutch. Using all her strength, she pushed. "Why won't you move?"

The Lieutenant whistled a low jazz tune through the door.

She glanced back at the door, and watched the knob slowly move from side to side.

His singing continued to flow over her.

Suddenly, the knob rattled violently.

Insane with panic, she buried her hands within her hair and pulled. "How did Jean Claude move the desk? What did he do?" She closed her eyes and pictured the desk on that day. On the left, the top two-cubby drawers of the hutch above the roll top desk were open, with slips of paper falling out of one. On the right, only one drawer laid open. The one on the end. She remembered he removed the middle drawer. Tears of relief formed in her eyes. She yanked out the middle drawer and stuck her arm into the hole where it laid. The tips of her fingers felt a tiny lump of steel and she tugged at the knob. Nothing happened. She pulled the handle again, harder this time, and braced her other hand against the hutch for leverage. Again, the desk refused to budge.

The door handle rattled and stilled.

Slowly she turned her head and glanced back towards the door. Perhaps he left. She straightened, turned fully towards the door and listened for the taps of his shoes.

The Lieutenant punched the door.

She jumped. Her body stiffened and her breath froze. Why doesn't he understand? "I'm the General's daughter. He wouldn't dare touch me."

The Lieutenant's body weight hit the office door.

The door groaned in protest and she fell back against the desk.

With his weight, he struck the door again and again as the doorframe shuddered in response to the blows.

Urgently, her breath came in panicked gasps. She flipped around and stuck her hand back into the empty drawer space. She grasped the knob, jerking it clockwise. The platform beneath the desk slid open and she clutched the edges of the desk to steady herself. Gathering her skirts, she darted behind the desk. Using both hands she thrust the lever under the light switch down. Pressing her hands over her mouth, she watched the desk slowly move back until it clicked into place.

Safe behind the wall, she heard the office doorframe shatter and give way.

Maniacal laughter permeated through the wall. "Foolish girl. Don't you think I know about that room? Even the great General does not know that room exists. But I do. You're trapped." He cackled. "I found your scarf," his sing song voice rang out. "On the floor. I've been waiting, watching. Only a matter of time. I knew you could not stay away from your lover. Filthy whore." The laughter continued.

Dread leadening her heart, the lever slowly rose. She sprang forward and pressed her entire body weight down upon the slender, iron handle. Her paltry weight was her last defense from his rage. She waited. Listened. The lever slowly inched up and cut into her hands. Whimpering, she pressed harder.

She twisted her head from side to side and searched the secret room for an escape route. The wooden floor was empty. The crates had been removed. Across the room, she noticed a faint light. Part of the shelving was pushed in, and a crack of light glowed from beyond. The lever continued to move and cut deeper into her hand. Jean Claude had said that he knew another way. Was that it?

Blood throbbed in her ears and her frightened heart attempted to burst from within her chest. She released the lever. Reaching down, she gathered her chiffon skirts and raced towards the light. Focusing on it, she rushed forward and pushed the bookcase with all her might. It opened and revealed a stone staircase that curved downward. Holding her skirts high, she started down the staircase towards escape.

Strong fingers laced through her topknot and dug into her scalp. She swayed back and forth on the top step, arms flailing, her forward momentum suddenly halted.

"Where do you think you are going little girl?" asked the Lieutenant.

Pulled by her hair, her body was jerked backward. She clawed at the stairwell walls to stop her reverse momentum, scrapping her heels and nails on the stone stairs and walls. Her hair ripped from her scalp and tears sprung into her eyes.

"You want to know what a real man feels like?" he asked, and ground his mouth on hers.

Sure her neck would snap, she strained against his strength. He dragged her head back further and further and forced his thick tongue into her mouth. She choked beneath his onslaught. Instinctively, she bit down and blood tainted her mouth.

The Lieutenant howled above her and backhanded her.

Fiery pain blazed a trail across her face and her world exploded into brilliant sparks of lights.

"Filthy slut." Bloody spittle sprayed across her face. He repeatedly backhanded her, pausing only to spit out a bloody chunk of skin.

Her face swollen and bruised, Emma mumbled incoherently.

He held her by the hair. "What's that, bitch?"

Between split and bloody lips, she whispered, "If you leave Twin Springs, I won't tell the General you hit me. Just let me go. I won't tell a soul."

High above her the Lieutenant's voice sounded far off and distant. "Don't you understand, you stupid bitch? There isn't going to be anyone to tell." He backhanded her again.

"Jean Claude," she moaned.

"You want to join your lover?" he questioned. "Then I am at your service." Effortlessly, he lifted her small body high above his head, "Join him in Hell," and he threw her down the stairwell.

Emma's world spun out of control. Her small body bounced against the stone steps, tumbled down the last few, hit a dirt floor and rolled against something metal. Blood and dirt filled her mouth. The metallic taste was no longer foreign and strange on her taste buds. Instinctively, she smacked her lips and tried to moisten her mouth with spit. One word roared through her muddled mind. Escape. Her father would save them. He would protect her and Jean Claude. "I must escape. Escape and find the General."

Arms shaking with effort, she raised herself up from the dirt floor and lifted her head. It felt thick and heavy on her slender neck. With a trembling hand, she brushed her dirt and blood filled hair away from her face. Head throbbing, she attempted to concentrate on where she was. Lit only by a string of bare bulbs, a cavernous room surrounded her. The air chilled her skin. She was deep beneath Twin Springs, in an underground chamber. In the distance, she heard the faint sound of rushing water.

Feeling disoriented, she grasped the metal object to lift herself up. Her skin singed on the hot pipe and she gasped with pain. She attempted to focus on the brass monstrosity before her. Even she knew what it was. "A still? There's a still under Twin Springs?"

She shook her head and pitched forward precariously as dizziness wafted over her. She was trapped in a large room filled with crates, empty mason jars and a great, wooden table. Wild laughter sounded off in the distance, bouncing off the stone walls until it permeated her hazy brain. "The Lieutenant."

Discovering a hidden strength, she lifted herself up on her wobbling legs. Pain exploded in her head. The immense room spun and tilted. The edges of the room darkened around her. Swaying on her feet, she pressed the palms of her hands to her temples. Only one of her shoes remained, her silk stockings bunched up around her ankles. Desperate for escape, she stumbled forward and righted herself against one of the wooden uprights supporting the underground room. Leaning against the jagged beam, she kicked off her shoe and removed her stockings, pushing them off with her feet.

"Emma," he called down. "Emma." His words filled the room and surrounded her.

His voice propelled her into action. She stumbled forward and spied a tunnel. Her only hope for escape. Focusing on the archway, she felt her way along the stone walls of the cavern. Her breathing was harsh and labored as she staggered into the tunnel.

Leaning heavily against the wooden pillars and dirt walls, she worked her way down the tunnel. Abruptly before her, it forked. "Left or right?"

The Lieutenant's distinctive footsteps rang out on the stone steps.

She stumbled on the hem of her long dress and fell hard on her knees and hands. The air knocked out of her, she waited, and listened. She rose up on her knees. A sweet odor filled her nostrils. "Gas. My God, it's gas." She scuttled backward. Again, her feet tangled in the folds of her dress and hindered her escape. She twisted her body over to crawl, not caring the direction she headed.

The Lieutenant's insane laughter rang out in the distance. "Say goodbye to Twin Springs, Emma."

A whimper escaped her throat. In the distance she heard the Tower's clock beginning to strike its midnight tune. She pivoted, her body screaming with pain as she gained her feet. Hitching her gown up around her waist, she ran for her life down the left fork of the dark tunnel. The air stilled and the fine blonde hairs stood on the back of her neck. Emma stiffened with a primal fear that she didn't quite understand. Her mind screamed, Run!

But she had nowhere left to go. Before her rose an impregnable wall of fallen rubble, blocking her escape. Reality dawned. She'd never feel Jean Claude's strong arms around her again. She'd trapped herself at the end of the tunnel. She turned, her bare feet kicking up dust from the dirt floor, and looked back towards where she came. Like a mouse in a maze, afraid to retrace her steps but unable to move forward.

A vibrating rush of air exploded through the tunnel and propelled her backwards on the dirt floor. Twin Springs shuddered. Emma lay unconscious. Unmindful of the rocks that fell around her, sealed her in, and removed her last hope of escape. Her long, blonde hair was no longer in an intricate top knot, but wild and loose around her shoulders. Escaped locks splayed across her face and covered the fresh bruises that bloomed high on her cheekbones with vibrant hues of blue and purple.

Just an hour earlier, she'd laughed in delight as her long, flowing party dress twirled between her and the man she loved. Jean Claude Flamme. She'd tasted the sweetness of champagne from his kisses, caressed the hardened length of his body against her softness. Sensed her beauty reflected in his inflamed gaze. Never again. She'd failed. Failed herself and her love. Now, her chiffon dress was bunched up around her legs, torn and covered with a fine mist of dirt.

The final bongs of the clock struck midnight. The dusty air stilled and settled around her. Without making a sound, a spider web of cracks formed in the tunnel walls. Leisurely, the warm spring water, with which her family's fortune was made, seeped down the dirt walls and darkened them. Rising around her, the water enveloped her in warm, loving arms and held her until the last breath left her body. Her once bright, blonde hair, darkened and wet, reached out along the water's surface. Emma floated within the water's embrace until time and love no longer held any meaning for her. . .

CHAPTER FIFTY-SEVEN

*C*hoking for breath, Theo woke. The vivid dream filled his senses. His mouth was tainted with the taste of Emma's blood and dirt. Yet, his lungs gasped for air. *Is this how Isabella felt growing up with these nightmares?* he wondered. Drowning in her sleep, only to experience the horror again night after night.

He leaned back against the pillows, unwilling to fully admit how the dream rocked him to the core. Emma didn't stand a chance. She was a sheltered girl, completely unprepared for true evil. He felt for Emma. The Lieutenant lied to her. He didn't kill La Flamme.

He understood Jean Claude's sense of duty and honor towards protecting those he loved. How did his ancestor continue living knowing that he'd failed to protect the love of his life? How did he cope with losing Emma forever? Did he sell the emerald and wait for her to join him? What did he think when she never arrived? Or did he know of Emma's death? Did he leave Twin Springs because he couldn't stand the pain of being there without her? Did he later kill the Lieutenant and run away? Unanswered questions jumbled Theo's brain.

Something about the necklace bothered him. He'd seen it before. Swinging his legs over the side of the bed, he sat there for a moment with his head in his hands, thinking. The moment Emma held the necklace in her hand resonated with him. Squeezing his eyes, he tried to concentrate on the dream but the details quickly faded away. The painting. He needed to study the necklace in the painting. A strange sense of urgency filled him. He must go to the painting now.

Quickly, he slipped into his jeans and tossed on a shirt. Pocketing his phone and master key card, he went down the stairs towards the General's Room. Giving a quick salute to the night auditor, he paused when he spotted Logan in the Grand Lobby. He'd covered his dirty t-shirt with an equally soiled green and blue flannel shirt. He could smell the man from three feet away. "What are you doing here so late?"

Logan pressed his lips together and glared, irritated by his question. "Working. What do you think?"

"This late?" repeated Theo.

Logan ran the remaining fingers of his mutilated hand through his blond hair, dark with grease. "Bite me, Theo. I have more than half of the spa up and running, ready to receive paying guests. Why the hell do you care when I work?"

Surprised at Logan's tone, Theo stepped back. "It just seems odd."

One of the night auditors moved around the Front Desk. Keeping her eyes trained on the ground, she passed them. Logan watched the girl avoid him, her gaze averted. He bit back, "Yeah, well, my whole damn life is odd now." He scowled at the girl's back. "But the Grand Dame always needs tending."

A pang of guilt filled Theo. Of course Logan worked at night. Less prying eyes. "Then I will let you be."

He used his key card to gain access to the General's Office. His cell phone beeped as he entered. He placed his phone on buzz, so as not to be disturbed. He sniffed the air. The smell of fresh roses permeated the room. He glanced around and didn't notice any freshly cut flowers. "This room constantly smells like roses since it became Ava's office. She must pack the drawers with the damn things." He suppressed a chuckle. "Bet the General would love that."

Theo crossed the room to the portrait. He ignored the buzzing of his phone in his pocket. The painting was more important. He stared up at Emma. Jean Claude's woman. The necklace held an amazingly large emerald in a square cut and surrounded by diamonds. He thought back. What was it about seeing the emerald in Emma's hand? Why did the image strike a chord within him? He'd seen a similar emerald in a woman's hand. He racked his brain.

An image of Isabella, holding his mother's emerald ring in the palm of her hand, flashed in his mind. It was the same square cut as the one in the painting. "That's it. My mother's ring. Emma's necklace. They're the same emerald. Someone removed the emerald from the necklace and placed it into a ring."

He should have realized it sooner. "My family has owned the necklace all along."

Another memory niggled in the back of his mind, from his last time at Twin Springs. His mother was showing someone her emerald ring. She stood at the top of the stairs and spoke with someone about her family's history. "Who was it?"

His phone buzzed again. Annoyed, he pulled it out and glanced down at the message. "Executive Chef office door open." He stared at the text bewildered. "Why is she working so late?"

His unanswered questions converged. He remembered whom his mother showed the ring to. He knew who was responsible for sabotaging the hotel. The room filled with the smell of burnt vanilla. His heart froze and he tasted the heady fear from the dream. "Isabella."

CHAPTER FIFTY-EIGHT

Reaching out with her left hand, Isabella flipped on the light switch and flooded her new office with light. The bookshelf was cracked open and a faint light glowed from beyond the gap. On unsteady legs, she crossed the room, reached out and pushed the rest of the bookshelf forward. She stared down a stairwell carved out of rock, rubbing her breastbone with the heel of her hand. "Exactly like the dream."

Now, she understood how her dreams ended. She whispered, "I'm going to drown exactly like Emma. Following in her footsteps, repeating her mistakes and denied a life with my true love, my soul mate."

The faint sound of metal clanging on metal reached her from below. She glanced down at her phone, at Maddy's text. "Meet me in your office. Please, I must talk to you. Only you. Don't tell my brother."

She squeezed the cell phone tight in her fist. "No. I'm not going to die. That's not my destiny, damn it."

Mocking her words, an oily, black fear slid down her spine as she stared down the stone stairwell. Every bone in her body told her not to go. *What if Maddy needs me?* That possibility propelled her forward. She gathered up her long, chiffon skirt. In her bare feet, she padded down the cold, rock steps. After a couple feet, she spied something pink on the stairs. She rushed forward and picked it up. A pink slipper. Her hands trembled. "Maddy," she breathed.

Determined, she tucked the slipper under her arm, gathered up her skirts and continued. As the stairs curved, the change in temperature caused goose bumps to bloom over her bare arms. *I must be far below Twin Springs.* Progressing even further, the damp cold seeped into her bones. The clanging grew louder and was joined by the calls of a bird. She slowed her steps and rounded the corner at the bottom of the stairs.

Back dropped by the faint sound of rushing water, a parrot sang a soulful jazz song.

The dress fell from her numb hands. Before her loomed a large cavern, encased by rock walls and complete with a working brass still. Dangling from black cords, bare bulbs crisscrossed the ceiling and lit the room. In the middle of the room was a rectangular wooden table covered with full plastic jugs. Piles of empty plastic jugs lined the floor. Stacks of fifty pound sugar bags and cardboard boxes filled the corners of the room. Across from her gaped the mouth of a tunnel, shored with aged, wooden beams and upright supports.

A black iron cage dangled from the wooden cross beam. Housed within the cage, a lone bird stood sentry. He plucked at what little feathers remained on his scrawny neck and chest and gray and red feathers floated down and littered the floor below.

Spying Isabella, he attempted to spread his gray wings. His head feathers brushed against the top of the cage and his wings bent against the bars and he released a high pitched screech. Quieting down, he folded his wings, grasped a plastic jug cap in his claw and chewed on the edges. Canting his head, he contemplated Isabella, his pupils swiftly widening and then shrinking to pinholes. "Get the fuck out," cried the bird in a gravelly male voice.

Stunned, she stepped back, feeling as if she had stumbled down the rabbit hole and her life had tumbled out of control. She shook her head at the surreal scene and squeezed her eyes shut. "Must be a dream."

Dropping the pink slipper, she pressed her face into her hands and rubbed her eyes with her fingertips.

The bird shrieked and drew her attention. His feathers flattened. Trembled. His dark pupils expanded as he hunched down. His breathing deepened and a low growl emitted from his black beak.

The hairs raised on the back of her neck. Her gaze shifted from the gray parrot over to the tunnel entrance and the faint hope of finding Maddy's mischievous face faded away.

There stood Niles. Backlit by the light from the tunnel, his face was cast in shadows but his brown eyes gleamed in the darkness. Moments passed as they studied each other. Leisurely, he crossed the room and set a jug on the table.

"Welcome to my little factory." He made a grand gesture with his arm. "Thank you for coming. Have a drink with me and experience the true wealth of Twin Springs."

She lifted her foot, inched it backwards on the dirt floor and felt for the stone steps behind her. Desperately trying to act casual, she forced her face to soften, and cast him a brilliant smile. "Niles, you saved Twin Springs!"

Dazed for a moment, he echoed, "Saved Twin Springs?"

"Of course." She lowered her hands and clutched mounds of fabric within her fists. "With all the money this still could bring, Twin Springs will never need to worry—" Spinning around, she lifted her skirts and sprinted up the staircase.

Her head jerked back and her hands clawed the cold air. Pain seared her as Niles' huge fist dragged her back by the hair. "No!" she screamed.

She wouldn't die like Emma. She refused. Clawing at his hand, she dug her fingernails into his skin. *History will not repeat itself.*

With a fist full of her hair, he dragged her across the room and threw her down on the dirt floor.

A cloud of dust filled her mouth. She coughed and spit,

searching the room for a weapon, any weapon. For a way to escape.

"Save Twin Springs," he scoffed, looming over her. The bare light bulbs illuminated him from above and transformed his huge body into its true form, grotesque and monstrous. "Why would I do that?" Strolling towards the table, his maniacal laughter trailed behind him and vibrated off the walls. "Why? When I've done my best to destroy the bitch!"

"Destroy the bitch," echoed the parrot.

Niles chortled under his breath. "Yeah, destroy the bitch." He picked up a jug and swished the clear liquid within. "You were supposed to turn to me when things went wrong. But you never could do anything right, could you? Instead, you turned to him." Never taking his eyes off her, he took a swig from the jug and wiped his mouth with the back of his sleeve. "Evil fucking whore. Spread your legs for him, didn't you? Right there on the table."

She estimated the distance between her and the stairwell. She wouldn't make it. She shifted, ever so slightly, and judged the distance to the entrance of the tunnel.

He mimicked Theo, "'I caused my parents accident. I fought with my dad and distracted him.' Give me a fucking break. What a whiner. Theo should have died with his parents. I should've rammed their car with the Twin Springs van, not just forced them off the road."

Isabella gasped.

He waived the jug in front of him, again trying to imitate Theo's voice. " 'Knowing you believe in me is more than I deserve,' " he mocked. "Theo's not a man. He's a pissant. Real men don't talk that way."

He hocked a loogie and spit it out on the dirt floor. "I wanted to puke. Where's your hero now, Izzy? He did give me some good info though. Didn't know Maddy spied on you two at the pool that night. Had to grab her. Couldn't have her ruining my plans for you and Twin Springs. Did you like the text I sent you? Knew you would scurry to her aid. You're a stupid bitch."

Fury filled her. No one touched her family. "Where is she," demanded Isabella.

Swinging the jug in his hand, he sauntered over and bent down beside her. Rocking back and forth on the balls of his feet, he considered her. "Wouldn't you like to know." He held out the jug. "Have a drink with me and I might tell you."

She turned her face away.

He cackled with delight and she flinched as the laughter from the pool surrounded her.

Abruptly, his laughter stopped. "Drink."

"Drink, drink, drink," chanted the parrot, bobbing up and down.

She shook her head. "Never."

"I said have a drink with me," he ground out. He grabbed her hair and pulled her head back over his bent knee.

Shocked, she screamed out with pain and he pressed the jug against her lips and poured.

She choked and her throat burned as moonshine spilled down her throat. She struggled against him. Clawed at his arms.

He paused and grinned.

Coughing, she gasped for air. Hatred glittered in her gaze.

"Don't you like it?" His chest shook with mirth when she pressed her lips together and refused to reply.

"You don't? Why, this is fine shine. Sells for high dollar." He hummed in the back of his throat. "It's an acquired taste though." With a fist full of hair, he jerked her head back. "You'll get used to it."

Prepared, she clamped her lips shut and squeezed her eyes closed.

"You think that will stop me," he muttered, releasing her hair. His thick hand pressed down over her nose and blocked her air.

Her eyes wide but lips still clamped, she struggled, scratching, kicking and bucking her body until her lungs were empty. Finally, her lips parted and she gasped for air, only to welcome shine flowing over her lips and down her throat. She choked and struggled against his strength, fighting for oxygen.

Jug empty, he shoved her off his lap.

She rolled over into a muddy puddle of shine, hacking and struggling for gulps of air.

"You always were so fun to torment," he placed his boot on the curve of her butt and kicked her away. He turned and tossed words over his shoulder as he strutted back towards the table. "A little nudge here," he threw the now empty jug into a pile. "A strategically placed foot there and you'd tumble over. Clumsy little Isabella. My very own Dizzy Izzy," he taunted.

His back turned, cautiously she crouched on the dirt floor. Unlike Emma, she was ready to fight. Ready to fight for her, Theo and Maddy. She wobbled up to her feet and the room tilted. Decision made, she turned, stumbling, and sprinted towards the tunnels. But her feet tangled in the long dress and she landed hard on her hands and knees.

Niles tossed back his head and cackled.

The parrot imitated his insane laughter.

"See," he chortled. "Dizzy Izzy."

Unsteadily, she once again worked until she was standing upright. Laboriously, hand over hand, she gathered her skirts high above her knees. *Run!* Her mind screamed.

Her limbs moved as if they were swimming through thick molasses. Leaning heavily against the wall as she went, she stumbled down the tunnel.

"Go ahead and hide. There's nowhere to go. Especially not for a little girl who's afraid of water." His manic laughter followed her, vibrating off the tunnel walls.

She lurched and swayed on her feet. The string of lights shifted in and out of focus as she followed them. Yards felt like miles within the underground tunnel. With the dream vivid in her memory, she searched for Maddy and a way out. She halted at a fork in the tunnel. Leaning against a wooden upright, she pressed her forehead against the dirt wall. Closing her eyes, her alcohol infused brain strained to remember the direction Emma had traveled to a dead end. "Left or right?"

Bending over, she stuck two fingers down her throat. Her stomach heaved and emptied its contents on the dirt floor. Wiping her mouth with the back of her hand, she noticed a white, plastic pipe running along the base of the tunnel. She picked up her skirts and followed the pipe.

The tunnel ended, opening up to a huge cavern and she stumbled to a halt before an underground river that roared and rushed past her. She swayed at the edge of the churning water. Trapped.

"Izzy," Niles' voice boomed through the tunnel. "I see you can't handle your liquor." His laughter rang out. "Ready or not, here I come."

Bare bulbs ran along the sides of the dark, underground river. Choking from panic, her chest hitching for air, she scanned the white crested and frothy river for a boat or something to float on. On the opposite bank, ran a rocky ledge. There perched Maddy, soaking wet and shivering, with her head bent and arms wrapped around her pajama clad legs. She cupped her hands and shouted, "Maddy!"

The teen lifted her head. Wet curls were plastered against her ashen face and her lips were visibly blue.

"Stay there!" she yelled over the rushing river. Time was short. "I'm going to wade across the river!"

She pulled the cumbersome dress over her head and dropped it on the bank. The river must empty out somewhere. "Don't move. When I reach you, we'll make our way down the ledge and out of the tunnels."

In her bra and panties, Isabella sat on the side of the bank and slowly lowered herself in, gasping as the freezing mountain water seeped into her bones. Sliding in completely, the water lapped against her chin and stole her breath. Tipping her head back, she waded across, her feet sliding on the slippery rocks lining the riverbed.

The rushing water fought against her with every step. Something brushed her foot. She stopped dead. Shivering uncontrollably, she peeked over her shoulder towards the tunnel's wide, black mouth. No one was there. But Niles couldn't be far behind. She worked her way forward again, teeth chattering. "Almost to the other side. Just a few more feet."

Again, something brushed her foot. She screamed and attempted to run through the deep water, her chest jerking with panic.

A hand snaked around her ankle and dragged her under the water's raging surface.

Water poured into her lungs. A bare bulb glinted high above the water and winked at her in the distance. She clawed her way towards it but the hand held her inches below the shiny surface. She kicked wildly to free herself but remained anchored to the river's rocky bottom.

She looked down, into Niles' mad gaze. He smiled, bubbles escaping from between his toothy grin. His iron grip tightened and he jerked her further below waves.

Desperately, she kicked hard, aiming for his smug face, and the heel of her foot connected with hard flesh. She was free. Her head broke the water's plane and she sucked air into her lungs as the current carried her swiftly downstream and further away from Maddy. Reaching out hand over hand, she fought against the river's pull and swam towards the rocky ledge.

The power of the current smashed her body against a boulder and forced the air from her lungs. Water rushed around her, over her head as she clung to the outcropping. Her feet peddled beneath her, sliding on the slick riverbed as she worked to thrust herself above the rushing water. She dug her feet in, arched her back and rose above the waves. Clambering high on the boulder, she rested her cheek against the rough surface. Her body was numb but she was only feet from the rocky ledge. "I'm so close. I think I can grab the edge and climb up."

She reached out, straining to stretch her arm and fingertips towards the ledge. "Just a little more."

A mountain of a man erupted from the river and split the water before her eyes. Water pouring off his face and dripping from his beard, Niles grinned. His white teeth glistened within his brown beard. With one massive hand, he grabbed her by the throat, lifted her up and slammed her body down under the water.

She thrashed. Her nails raking down his hairy arms and her feet kicking against his body.

Feral, he shook her under the water and played with her like a dog with its favorite toy. Over and over, he lifted her and allowed her to gasp for air before shoving her back under.

She sensed the life leaving her body. Her nightmares blended with reality. Her arms weakened and fell lifelessly away from her body, sinking down to the rocky riverbed. Her limp knuckles brushed back and forth against the bottom. Theo's face flashed before her, the startled look on it when she'd smacked him with the mop, the pride in his gaze when she'd finished her first service, and his lips curved into a smile as he held her foot in his hand. She couldn't leave him.

Her fingers curved around a large rock, and she palmed it. Using the last of her strength, she surged up and struck Niles hard in the temple.

Shocked, Niles' mud brown eyes stared at her. His smile faltered and his huge hand released her throat. Then, he crumbled before her.

Free of his grasp, she fought to stay above the rushing current and sucked air into her lungs. She kicked off the boulder and her cold fingers latched onto the rocky ledge. Clinging to the edge, she turned her head and watched Niles' lifeless form float downstream.

With the freezing mountain water rushing by, she began the arduous task of pulling herself out of the water. Her arms shook as she painstakingly attempted to swing her leg over the edge. After the third attempt, her foot hooked. Her body was so cold and numb from the water that she didn't feel the skin on her inner thigh scrapping against the rough rock as she hoisted herself up and over. She lay on the side of the bank and wept with relief.

"Isabella."

She quieted. Listened.

"Isabella."

Her head rose.

Again, a male voice called her name, echoing in the chamber.

She scrambled up to her hands and knees and stared downstream, searching for Niles. She picked up a rock and clutched it high above her head ready to fight.

"Isabella. Isabella, where are you?"

"Theo." She dragged herself up. Hugging the smooth, rocky wall, she worked her way upstream towards his voice. "I'm here," she croaked out.

In the opening of the tunnel, stood Theo, tall, strong. "I see you!"

His usually pressed suit was rumpled and the button's didn't line up on his white shirt. He was a mess. The corners of her lips tilted up. "My hero." Relieved, she slumped against the wall. Her wet body shivered uncontrollably in the cold, underground air.

"Don't move!" he yelled. "I'll swim out and get you."

Fear pierced her heart. "No, the river will suck you downstream."

"What?" he shouted back over the roaring water. Unable to hear her, he removed his clothes and started slowly across.

With supreme effort, Isabella turned her trembling body and slid down the wall until she perched on the edge. She wrapped her arms around her knees and tried to control the movement of her limbs.

He never took his eyes off her as he picked his way across the river. The water slapped against his chest and he slipped and disappeared under the churning surface.

"Theo!" she cried out, her heart leapt into her throat. Desperately, she scanned the water, waiting for him to break the surface.

With a spray of water he emerged further down the stream. The river beating against him with every stroke, gradually, he labored his way back until he reached her. He grabbed her up in his arms and squeezed her tightly, leaning back only to place kisses across her face. "Are you alright?" He smoothed back her wet hair so that he could see her face.

"Yes." Her body shuddered with cold.

He held her face between his palms and kissed her, searing her lips with his love. "Thank God." He crushed her to his chest. "I'm never going to let you out of my sight again. I'm going to keep you by my side. Safe."

Her lips blue, shaking uncontrollably, she soaked in what little heat his body offered. She had to tell him the truth about his parents. "It was Niles." Her teeth chattered out each word. "All this time, it was him. He did everything. The sabotaging of Twin Springs." She wrapped her arms around him. "He killed your parents."

His body jerked as if he'd been shot. "What?"

Tears rolled down her face. Tears for him. She squeezed him tighter. "He was driving the van that forced your family off the side of the road. It wasn't your fault. It was Niles."

Theo shuddered. His mother's beautiful face floated before his eyes and his throat clogged with emotions. He opened his mouth to speak but couldn't. Couldn't find the words. Then anger rushed in. Warmed him. Gave him purpose. "Where is he?"

Her arm shaking uncontrollably, she pointed downstream. "He's gone. The water took him."

Robbed of the chance of ripping Niles apart himself, he glared at the rushing water. Isabella shuddered in his arms. The cold water had numbed his body from the chest down. He could only imagine how cold she must be. He needed to get her warm. To safety. "Let's get you home." He tugged her forward, placing her limp arms around his neck. "Can you hold on?"

At first the water seemed almost warm against her frozen body. Then, the deep cold sunk into her bones. Gritting her teeth against the pain, she nodded, tightening her hold around his neck and threading her fingers together for a firmer grip.

"Wrap your legs around my waist." Her body was like a block of ice, even against his chilled skin. "I need to get you warm and fast. Whatever happens, don't let go." He looked into her eyes, "No matter what, you hold onto me. Do you understand?"

Teeth chattering, she nodded. "Thank God you came." She wasn't sure if she could've made it back across the water alive. She squeezed him, drawing warmth from his body to hers. Everything was going to be alright. He'd get her across. Niles was dead. Twin Springs would live on. Another thought niggled at the edges of her frozen brain. "Wait!" She slid her legs down and away from his warmth. "You must save Maddy first."

CHAPTER FIFTY-NINE

The roar in Theo's head muted the sound of the rushing river. "Maddy? What are you talking about?" Her words sunk in as the water churned against them.

Isabella pointed upstream towards a huddled form. "We have to save her."

Following her outstretched hand, he spotted his little sister in the distance. She was slumped over on the ledge. Motionless. He scarcely recognized her silky, pink pajamas. They'd been soaked and darkened with water.

"Take care of the girls." His father's voice howled through his brain.

How could he save them both? He couldn't bear losing either one. He loved them. How could he choose between Isabella and Maddy?

"Go get Maddy." Her teeth chattered involuntarily. "I can make it back across."

He hesitated. His heart and mind torn in two. Maddy was the weaker of the two. Should he take her first? Or should he take Isabella across and come back for his little sister? His gaze searched his sister's crumpled body, hoping for movement or any sign of life. Could she survive that long?

"Go now," Isabella ordered, her voice slurring. "I'll meet you on the other side."

Perhaps she was right. Reluctantly, he released her.

She shuddered and turned away.

"No." He couldn't abandon her again. He couldn't handle living with the knowledge that he could've prevented her death but he'd made the wrong choice. He wouldn't live that way, half alive like Jean Claude. "No," wrenched from his soul. He reached out and grasped her by the arm and dragged her back. "I'm not leaving you. We'll do this together."

Staring into her glassy eyes, he wrapped her arms around his neck and held her tight against his body. Slowly, he pushed his way against the current and towards Maddy. His feet struggled with each step to keep from slipping. When he reached his sister, he shifted Isabella. "Hold on to the side so that I can pull her down."

Isabella didn't reply.

He glanced down. Her was head bent and her wet blonde hair trailed in the current. Her arms floated lifelessly at her sides. Only his arm had prevented her from being swept down the river. Tightening his hold, he grabbed Maddy's motionless body with his other arm, dragged her off the shelf and against his chest. Pinning Isabella between him and the rocky edge, he worked his free arm around his sister until he'd anchored her to his other side. Then, he focused on one goal—getting both the girls across the river. Alive.

Carrying the two women he loved more than life, Theo stumbled across the river. The weight of each girl created added drag against the raging current. With each step, he fought for their lives and chanted the mantra, "Take care of the girls. Take care of the girls."

The freezing water turned his feet into blocks of ice, weighing him down. He gritted his teeth to prevent them from chattering against the bitter cold. "One more step." The burning, tingling sensation in his arms had stopped. Now, he couldn't feel them at all. They were numb. His heart thumped against its icy cage. Had he dropped them? He glanced down at Maddy's limp form, "Another step. One more," checked on Isabella, her head rocking against his body with each step. "Half way there."

His feet slipped beneath him and pulled the trio under the churning water. He tightened his hold and dragged his feet along the rocky riverbed until he was able to regain his footing. He dug his feet in, righted himself and surged up out of the water. He squeezed the girls, trying to force water out of their lungs as he struggled against the current. Finally, he reached the other side.

He laid his little sister on the bank and rolled Isabella up next to her. Shivering, his skin ashen, he pulled himself up out of the water and crawled over to his girls.

Maddy moaned and rolled herself into a ball, shivering uncontrollably. But Isabella didn't move. Still as death, she laid there, her skin almost translucent. Theo's heart slammed against his chest. He leaned over her soundless mouth before pressing his ear to her chest. Nothing. "No! Come on Bella, breath for me." He tilted her chin up, pinched her nose and breathed against her frozen lips. Clasping one hand over the other, he pumped her chest. "Don't leave. Please." Two more quick breaths. He listened again. Silence. Openly weeping now, he pressed her chest over and over. Blew into her mouth. Pressed again. "Please. Come back. I need you. Please don't leave me."

When she didn't move, he hung his head. His shoulders racked with sobs and a low keening cry escaped his soul. He bent down to give her one last kiss.

Sputtering, Isabella gaged and water spilled from her lips. His heart soared and he tilted her on her side. "That's it, Bella. Breath. Live for me."

When the racking in her body subsided, he rolled her back and cradled her in his arms.

Her breathing labored, Isabella lifted her small hand and touched his face. "I guess I do get true love," she murmured in a raspy voice.

"We both do," he replied, pressing kisses all over her face. "I'll love you forever, my Bella." Her body went limp and she passed out with a smile on her lips.

Theo gazed down at the two people he loved more than life, their matching purple lips and blue tinged skin. "We have to get you warm." He gathered his girls close. His legs shook beneath him as millions of pin pricks pierced his skin, burning him. Strengthening his resolve, he lifted them once again in his arms.

Someone was behind him. He felt him.

He loosened his hold and allowed his girls to slip back onto the dirt floor. His frozen fingers curved into fists and Theo turned. Ready to fight.

"Whoa!" Logan's hands flew up in defense. "It's just me." He knelt next to the girls and checked the pulse on the side of their throats.

Theo joined him and began rubbing their arms and legs to bring back circulation. "Help me."

After a few moments of rubbing, Logan said, "We need to get them warmed up. Now. Get dressed and we'll carry them to the spa and warm them there."

As Theo attempted to drag his pants up his wet, cold legs, he watched Logan take his dirty flannel shirt off and wrap it around Maddy's body. All his irrational mind could think was, *Maddy would freak if she knew what she was wearing.*

CHAPTER SIXTY

rapped in a mint green blanket, Isabella enjoyed the warmth from the fire. She'd slept late into the afternoon but Theo still insisted she take it easy in the General's room with Ava. The sounds of afternoon tea being served in the Grand Lobby filtered into the room. She lifted a warm teacup to her lips and listened to the guests moving about and enjoying the summer day. Last night thousands of needles had pricked her skin as Theo and Logan warmed her and Maddy in the teak tubs at the spa. She doubted she'd ever feel warm again.

"I love tea time," she murmured to her sister.

Sitting across from her, Ava mixed the cream and sugar in the bottom of her cup before pouring tea over top. "After all, taking tea is an art," Ava's voice twinkled with laughter. Her eyes flowed over her little sister who lounged on the couch before her. The laughter fled from her face and her expression became sober. "I'm thankful we didn't lose the two of you last night." She looked up at the painting of the General's three daughters. "I couldn't bear losing my sister," she stated, rubbing her face with shaking fingers.

The General's doors flew open, and Maddy rushed in wearing a denim shirt with flowered silk shorts. Quickly, Isabella placed her teacup on the table before the teen threw herself into her arms.

"I'm so happy that you're alright." Maddy squeezed Isabella tight. "So very glad you weren't hurt. He made me text you," she wailed.

Following his little sister, Theo brought in a tray of crustless sandwiches, pastries and tea for everyone. He placed the tray on the table between the girls. He monitored his girls as his sister blubbered all over the woman he loved. "Maddy, you need to slow down. The doctor said for you and Isabella to relax today."

A little jealous of how quickly the young girl bounced back, Isabella smoothed Maddy's curls and held her close. She whispered in her ear, "My heart would break if something happened to you."

The teen pulled back and grinned. "Yeah, that would suck." She winked, kissed Isabella on the cheek and whispered back, "Right back at you."

Theo leaned against the edge of the General's desk, looking as if he didn't have a care in the world in his jeans and open collared shirt. "How did you end up in the tunnels?" he asked. "I put you to bed."

Maddy kicked off her shoes, lifted an edge of Isabella's blanket and snuggled in. "Well, I was sneaking down to meet Marc in the kitchens. I was late because I was spying on the two of you. So when I finally showed, he was gone. That was when I saw Niles acting strangely and decided to follow him."

"Maddy," Theo growled. "You're going to be the death of me." He rubbed the back of his neck with his hand. "It looks like Marc and I need to have a man to man talk."

"Don't be too hard on them," croaked Isabella.

"What's wrong with your voice?" asked Maddy, drawing back. She noticed the black and blue bruises covering her throat and gasped.

Isabella pulled the collar of her shirt closed.

"Is that from when he tried to strangle you?" asked Maddy

Ava choked on her tea. "Niles tried to strangle you?"

Maddy sat forward, the blanket falling from her shoulders, and filled Ava in on what she'd witnessed. "And then, I guess, I passed out."

At the end of Maddy's tale of the events, Theo put down his teacup before he crushed it in his hand. "I should've protected you. From now on, let's have one unbreakable rule. No one wanders into a dark tunnel without me. Promise?"

Ava laughed.

"Promise," said Maddy and Isabella in unison.

Tightly, Maddy hugged Isabella, causing her to wince from the pressure on her throat. "See, we're just like sisters. We even think the same." She sighed with happiness, snuggled closer and began munching on a crustless PB & J sandwich.

"Stop smothering her. Let her breath," Theo called out.

"It is fine." Isabella smiled and patted the teen on the leg. "Stay with me. If feels good to have everyone here. I didn't know if I would see any of you again." She squeezed Maddy's and her sister's hands. "None of us thought it was Niles." She looked up at Theo. "Anyways, I wouldn't want to be any other place but here having tea with all of you."

Limping in, Logan stood quietly next to the door. His green and blue flannel shirt was back on his body, covering a slightly yellowed t-shirt screen-printed with the word 'Credence', a peace sign and an army helmet with a Suzie Q patch.

Happy to see him, she called out, "Logan! Come in and sit with us."

Surprise flowed across his scarred features at the joy in her voice. He canted the burnt side of his head towards the wall. "Just checking in on you two. How are you feeling after your ordeal last night?"

Swiftly, Theo crossed the room and shook his mutilated hand. "Thank you for your help last night. I'm sorry about how I treated you when I first saw you. For a brief moment, I wondered if you were the one sabotaging Twin Springs."

Astonished at the accusation, he blinked. "I—I understand."

Isabella's hand flew to her throat. "Never did I think it was you. But, then, I didn't think it could have been Niles either." She glanced over to Ava. "We grew up with both of you. Played with you when we were children, attended school together."

Ava nodded. "Played doctor." She winked at Logan and her laugh lit up the room.

Theo shook his head. "You Fairbanks sisters never cease to amaze me." Shifting the topic, he added, "I just received a call from the Sheriff. They haven't found Niles' body yet. But, the Sheriff says that it takes time. A body can travel quite a distance or get caught under a bank and never be found."

Isabella shuddered, thankful it wasn't her or Maddy who'd floated down the river.

"They did find Chef Dubois," said Theo.

"What do you mean?" asked Maddy.

Theo eyed his sister. "Perhaps you should leave the room."

Maddy huffed and crossed her arms tight against her body. Glaring at her brother, she replied, "Stop treating me like a child."

"After what Maddy went through, she deserves to know it all." Isabella squeezed the teen's hand. "She can handle it. Tell us what happened."

Reluctantly, he continued, "The Sheriff found Chef Dubois dead on the side of the road. Appears the chef lost control of his car and it plunged down the side of the hill."

Logan moved further into the room, towards the painting. Their banter flowed around him.

"Just like Mom and Dad," muttered Maddy.

"That's terrible." Isabella drew her closer.

"No. Not just like Mom and Dad." Theo's voice hardened. "He was an embezzler. Chef Dubois was nothing like our mom and dad."

Logan interrupted them. "Dad finished checking the still in the cavern. Disabled it and shut it down. Pretty old still. I'd say some parts were ninety plus years. But there'll be no more homemade brew at Twin Springs."

Theo leaned against the fireplace mantel. "The Sheriff and his son will be over later to confiscate the jugs."

"I'm sure he will," replied Ava. "I wonder how much of that shine actually makes it down the drain."

"Did you look down the other tunnel?" asked Isabella.

"Yes." Distracted, Logan's head swiveled between the painting and Isabella. "We removed the rocks from this side of the cave in. Over time the water had receded and we found Emma's remains. After the ME gives her a once over, we'll be able to bury her."

Isabella thought about Emma and Jean Claude's struggles, of all the obstacles against their love. "I want her buried in the family plot."

"That is up to you and Ava," replied Theo. "Or, if you want, we can bury her next to Jean Claude. I know the cemetery he's buried in."

She considered the idea. "Is there any way we can have Jean Claude moved to Twin Springs? It only seems right. The two of them side by side in the family plot. Finally together and at home."

"I'm sure Jean Claude would want to lay beside his love forever. I'll contact the necessary government agencies and start the process right away," replied Theo.

"Thank you." She paused, another thought entering her mind. "Unless Jean Claude is buried next to his wife, then it wouldn't be right."

He shook his head. "He never married."

"Then yes, let's have them both buried here." She focused on Logan. "Were there any concerns about the tunnels and cavern being under Twin Springs?"

Logan stared up at the portrait.

She waited for his answer. "Logan?"

He pulled his gaze from the painting. "What?" He tilted his burned side towards the portrait and away from everyone else in the room. "Sorry. What did you say?"

She repeated her question.

"I looked the cave and tunnels over. Actually, the large room is to the left of the loading dock. There's nothing but grass over it. Doesn't affect the structural integrity of Twin Springs at all. The tunnel continues down beside the road and follows it for a while. If you want, we can shore up the tunnel with metal supports. I wouldn't suggest destroying it with the river and springs so close by. The state inspectors want to come and look at it tomorrow but it should be alright. By the way, what do you want to do with the parrot?"

Isabella shuddered thinking of the large, gray parrot that mocked her. "It was terrible. The poor thing was trapped in a cage too small for him."

Logan spoke up. "He's a beautiful bird. Lots of spirit for the conditions that he has lived in. Got one hell of a colorful vocabulary. Needs someone willing to care for him though. Sings jazz. I've never heard a bird sing the blues before. I can take him to the aviary until we find a home for him."

Ava piped up, "I'll take him."

"Are you sure?" asked Isabella. "Shouldn't you check him out first?"

"A bird that sings the blues? How can I resist? He can sit in this office with me. Besides, I have never met a male, bird or otherwise, who I couldn't tame."

Logan grew quiet, his eyes once again drawn to the portrait.

"If you're sure." Isabella's focus zeroed in on Logan. "Are you okay?" She swore his cheeks turned red before he replied.

"I'm fine. Still amazed by everything."

"We all are," replied Theo.

"It was the perfect set up, brewing moonshine under Twin Springs." Logan rubbed his whiskers. "One of the ways bootleggers were tracked down and caught was the light of their still in the dark of the night or the smoke of the still during the day. Drew the Revenuer's straight to their stash. At one time, these mountains were lit up at night with the light of stills. But, whoever built this still vented up through the pipes in the kitchen. The smoke didn't stand out from any of the other kitchen vents pumping out smoke in the 1920's. The bootleggers stored their stash in the big cavern and transported it by boat down river or packed it out through the loading docks. Who'd notice or think twice about an extra box or two leaving the back of the hotel."

"Niles said there weren't any bootleggers in these parts. I guess that was another lie," stated Isabella.

"Lied through his beard," replied Logan. "Oh yeah, almost forgot." He pulled out a piece of paper that he'd tucked behind his back. "I found this online. The Red Butcher posted his review."

Springing up, Ava snatched the paper from his hand. "Let me read it." She stood scanning the paper.

Biting her lip and waiting, Isabella stared up at her sister.

With a toss of her gorgeous black hair over her shoulder, Ava stepped forward onto an imaginary stage to read the review out loud to her small audience. "'I had the distinct pleasure to dine in the Main Dining Room of Twin Springs Hotel and Spa. Few restaurants surprise me and even fewer delight me. The dining experience presented by the Main Dining Room of Twin Springs is one of a kind. Diners realize they're in for a special treat as soon as they enter the elegant and spacious dining area. Guests step back in time. They're welcomed by true southern hospitality from a softer point in time of our history. The decor is soft and appealing. It's a delight to discover a historic dining room that has remained true to its roots. When other restaurants try to morph themselves and conform to every passing trend—'" Ava paused and bowed to Maddy, "That's our doing," she stage whispered before continuing. "'The staff is attentive to the every need of the clientele without feeling intrusive.

"'But it was the cuisine that brought tears to this Rocky Mountain boy's eyes. The prime rib appetizer was seared to perfection. The lamb and asparagus were unbelievably fresh and sweetened with just a touch of red wine sauce.

"'Proud of my heritage, a part of me mocked the selection on the menu touted as 'Blue Ridge Mountain favorites'. I decided to put this selection up against one of my dearest hometown dishes.

With great reluctance, I returned my lamb and ordered the corn-meal dusted trout paired with corn and potato hash, sided with yellow and green zucchini slaw.

"'With my first bite, I was materialized back in time to my nana's kitchen table. The farm fresh ingredients sang for me through every mouthwatering bite. My mind couldn't believe what my taste buds declared, freshly caught mountain trout breaded and cooked to perfection. My nana would've been proud to call that dish her own.

"'I glanced about to my fellow diners and watched in amazement as families and couples enjoyed their meals, sharing bites with each other as they discovered a hidden delight within the dishes presented to them.

"'Rarely do I encounter a budding chef with such innate talent. Poised and self-assured, Executive Chef Fairbanks never faltered or became belligerent when I sent back not one but three dishes in my quest to find hidden talent and discovered her natural flair for blending flavors, tones, and color to please the palate. With her own sense of style, Executive Chef Fairbanks exudes a passion for food that weaves savory magic through every dish.

"'Yes, I'd traverse the Blue Ridge Mountains time and time again for another bite of Executive Chef Fairbanks' delicious cuisine. Next time, I'll bring my nana.'"

Stunned, Isabella looked around the room. "I can't believe it."

"I can." Bursting with pride, Theo lifted her hand and kissed it. "Now we just need to wait and, hopefully, the reservations will start pouring in."

Holding her hand within his, he bent down to one knee. He reached into his pocket and pulled out a small, black velvet box. "I've already begged for Maddy's permission. She was a fierce negotiator and I've had to give her Dale's telephone number as part of the deal. But she's all in on us becoming a family." He opened the box and the emerald ring glowed in the light of Isabella's eyes. "So I ask again. Bella, will you marry me?"

She glanced at Maddy. Her hands clasped to her chest, the teen nodded. "Will you take us both?"

"Yes!" Isabella surged forward, held Theo's face between her palms, and kissed him. "Yes. Yes."

He slipped the ring on her finger. "Now and forever." Grasping her by the back of the neck he finished with an earth shattering kiss.

Isabella's inner voice sighed.

The teen rolled her eyes. "They're engaged. They'll be sucking face all the time now."

"Maddy," gasped Isabella, pulling away.

"What?" asked Maddy. "At least he did it better this time. You should've seen my brother last night. All thumbs. He was such a dweeb. Flowers. Champagne. Dancing. I thought I was going to gag."

"Oh my! Let me see," burst out Ava. She shoved the review at Logan's chest and all but pushed Theo aside. She squealed with glee. "Congratulations! Gorgeous ring. And an emerald, how fitting."

"It was my mother's ring," replied Theo. "Do you recognize the emerald?"

Isabella stared down at her hand. "Should I?"

He glanced up at the painting. "Emma gave her necklace to Jean Claude for him to purchase a new life for them. Unfortunately, they never had that life. Someone in my family must have reset the emerald in a ring, adding some of the diamonds surrounding the emerald to the band."

"After all this time. Your family owned Emma's necklace all along," murmured Isabella.

"Yes, and now it's home where it belongs." He planted a possessive kiss on her lips.

"Wonderful," said Ava. "I'll be planning my first wedding at Twin Springs."

"This calls for a celebration." Theo rounded the desk and lifted a plastic jug out from behind it. "I stashed a couple bottles." He laid out four small shot glasses and filled them. "About two fingers of this should be enough."

Isabella waived her glass off. "Please, I don't think that I'll be drinking anytime soon."

Maddy sprang forward, arm outstretched. "I'll take hers."

He replaced a shot glass in the cabinet, firmly retorting, "No, you will not."

"Fun sucker," Maddy muttered, slumping back on the sofa.

Theo passed out the shot glasses. "To the women of my life, may all your dreams be filled with happiness and may all your wishes come true. And to Twin Springs, may her arms welcome many generations to come."

Ava sipped her shot. "Wow! That'll curl your toes."

"Smooth, and neat," added Logan, tipping his glass at the portrait.

Ava looked up at the three women. "I wonder if we will ever know what really happened to the other two sisters."

"I think we should find out," replied Isabella. "But for now, at least we found Emma. Perhaps she and Jean Claude will be at peace."

Theo pulled her up to him and brushed his lips across hers. "I love you. I'll never let you go." He inched his lips from her soft mouth. "I will love you always. I promise." He smiled against her lips. "You know I always keep my promises." He sealed his declaration with a soul searing kiss.

"See! I told you." Maddy rolled her eyes. "Sucking face."

CHAPTER SIXTY-ONE

1 December, 1928

How stupid can they be? I mock their pitiful efforts. Do they not realize how much I've done for them? I was the catalyst for all the success they now possess. It was I who pulled this pile of bricks from the brink of disaster. I turned Twin Springs into a sensation with the press and seduced the rich to once again visit this ancient monstrosity.

How can it be, that they do not realize my power? I'm the one who grants the success and prosperity they so richly enjoy. At any time, I can destroy the Grand Dame. Destroy them. Mark my words, they'll regret not noticing me. They'll regret not giving me the recognition that I deserve. All three of the General's daughters will cower at my feet. Even the General's proud Ruby. It's time that she learns her place.

Then, I'll take all his Gems from him. One by one. Just like he tried to take my manhood from me. We'll see who's the greater man.

Lieutenant Clayton Porter
Future Proprietor of Twin Springs

HELLO, MY BOOK-LOVING FRIEND, THANK YOU.

Dear Reader,

I hope you fell in love with Isabella and Theo's journey—and with the secrets of Twin Springs.

The story continues in **Book Two, *Sleepwalking with Ruby,*** and concludes in **Book Three, *Haunted by Amethyst,*** the final chapter of *The Mystery of the Three Gems* trilogy.

Want early access to my newest mysteries, short stories, and behind-the-scenes inspiration? Subscribe to my newsletter and become part of my reader circle, where I spill the tea about ghosts, grit, and the heartbeats behind every story. My subscribers always get sneak peeks before anyone else!

If you love books, laughter, and a dash of chaos, join my **Book-Loving Friends** Facebook group. It's where readers and I share favorite reads, twisty mysteries, and plenty of fun during live chats and giveaways. The tea's always hot—and there's always a chair waiting for you.

Every mystery needs a witness, and I'd love to hear from you! If *Visions of Emerald* touched your heart, please take a moment to leave a quick review. Even a single line helps other readers discover their next great escape.

Scan the QR code for all the links in one spot — my reader circle, the Book-Loving Friends Facebook group, review page, and more. One scan and you're in.

Keep reading, I've included a sneak peek into *Sleepwalking with Ruby* just for you. I hope you love Ava and Jaxon's love story as much as I do.

I'll keep the kettle warm until next time—
Love,
~ **Dee**

One scan and we will be Book-Loving friends.

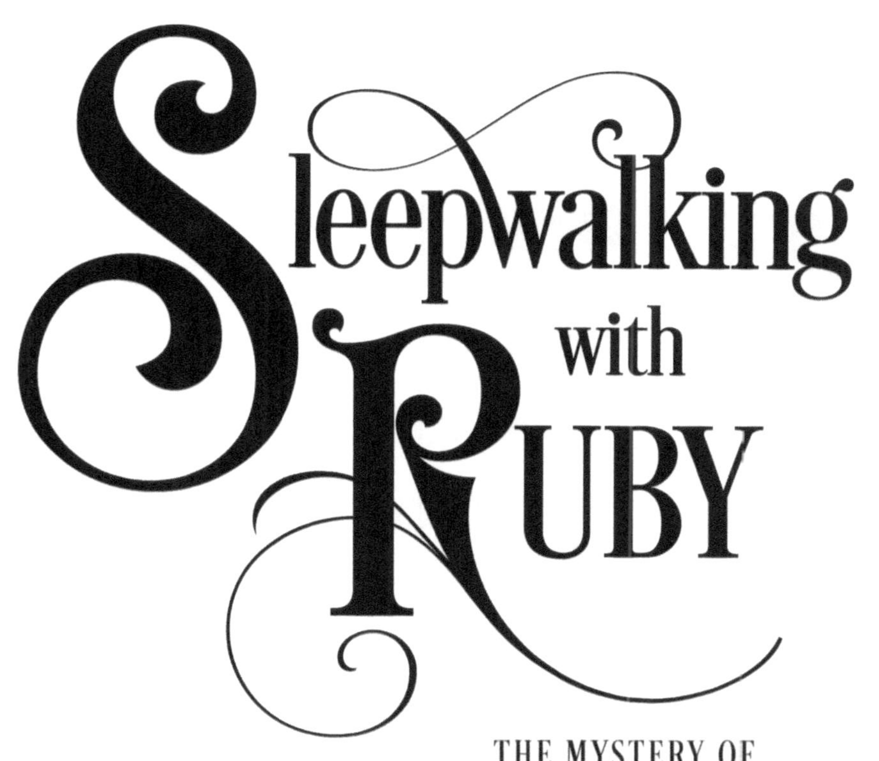

THE MYSTERY OF
THE THREE GEMS, BOOK TWO
A TWIN SPRINGS TRILOGY

DEE ARMSTRONG

CHAPTER ONE

*2*8 September, 1928

Year after year, I watch the all mighty General preen before his public and those adoring sops that make an annual pilgrimage to Twin Springs just to bask in his glory. He wears the invisible uniform of widower proudly across his chest and the brainless women melt around him, for him. He holds everything that a man desires within his palm. Women, presence, recognition, power, family and wealth. Much more than he deserves. Much more than any man deserves. Anyone, except me.

I followed the General from the Great War to the backwoods of the Blue Ridge Mountains. Even after he left me behind for the mission that granted him so much glory. After my service, he turned away in distaste at the prospect of making me a partner and gave me kitchen servants to command. He thought that would put me in my place. Perhaps even placate me. His strategic move gave me my first advantage. It was in the kitchens that I discovered the secret passageway to the tunnels.

Within the cavern and tunnels under Twin Springs, I've created the greatest empire known to man. Bootlegging liquor is my own little pot of gold. Money is the answer, the great equalizer. No matter your birthright, if you have enough cash then Kings and Generals will bow down to you. Running moonshine is better than Greenbacks and I'm well on my way to becoming the next Rockefeller from selling it to the thirsty masses in D.C. and Richmond.

Next, I'll begin syphoning off the General's money, one mishap at a time. Once he hits rock bottom, I'll break him by seizing his most priceless possessions. Twin Springs and his three daughters, his Gems. With a little tutelage, Emma will become a proper wife. And Ruby, with her thick black hair, luscious body and sultry voice, I've decided to let her live. How I lust for her when she sings. I'll keep her high in Twin Springs' tower, my own little song bird. As for their older sister, Amethyst, I'm still going to kill her and her unborn babe. I have no choice, the powerful must rule.

Lt. Porter

CHAPTER TWO

PROLOGUE

"If Mommy's now an angel, do you think she's watching us?" Izzy mumbled the question around the thumb that she refused to remove from her mouth.

Ava Fairbanks wanted to pretend she didn't hear her sister. Her chest ached when they talked about Mom. But Izzy was only six and it was her job to take care of her. After all, she was a full two years older. Unsure what to say, she entwined her fingers between her sister's and squeezed. "Look up."

Both girls lay beneath the enormous Christmas tree that stood tall and proud in the middle of Twin Springs' Grand Lobby, the sprawling hotel their family owned and lived in. Boxes wrapped in bright holiday paper guarded the edges, keeping them safe inside their own little world. A few late night guests walked by chattering, utterly unaware of the hiding, PJ clad little girls.

The scent of freshly cut pine tickled Ava's nose, she breathed in deeply and pointed up to where hundreds of little white lights twinkled within the branches. "I think, that when our family goes to heaven, it's their job to watch over us." Quickly, she wiped away the tear that slipped from the corner of her eye. "Just like those lights shining down on us."

Izzy sucked hard on her thumb, her brows furrowed. She rubbed the seam of her pink flannel pajamas between her fingers like it was a blanket. "Do you think they'll tattle on us for playing here?" Her words sounded even more child-like around her thumb.

Ava's laughter flowed up through the branches and lit up their secluded world with its magical sound. "Naw, they have more important things to do."

Her little sister snuggled closer to her side and she wrapped her arms around her and stared up at the lights. "I wish one was Mommy, then we could talk to her anytime we wanted," she whispered. She picked out the brightest light, tucked high up in the branches and pretended it was her mother watching over them. Ava's lids grew heavy and the combination of her sister's warm body and the grand piano playing softly in the background lulled her into a helpless sleep.

A silver mist weaved a path down through the branches and hesitated over Izzy. Deep in sleep, her lashes lay upon her milky white skin and her long, blonde hair covered her shoulders like a thick blanket. Izzy's thumb sucking sounds were barely discernible within the late night quiet of the lobby. The haze encircled the little girl's arm and tugged until her thumb burst out of her mouth with a pop.

Moving on to Ava, the mist hovered over the length of her body and smoothed the wrinkles in her blue PJ's, covered with little white clouds. Raising and lowering in tune with her breathing, it reached out and swept her long, black hair away from her sleep, softened face. Leisurely, it lowered and melded with the slumbering girl.

• • •

Moving with a grace well above her tender age, Ava stepped onto the wooden stage of Twin Springs' Theatre. The clouds on her pajamas glowed brightly under the floodlights. She flipped her long hair over her shoulder and shook her head allowing it to flow down her back and shimmer under the sidelights' muted glow. Her body swayed in time with a tune playing in her head. From under her lashes, she stared sightlessly upon the empty seats of her audience and a low, jazz song flowed from her lips.

From the depths of her young soul, she belted out a tune of sadness, love and loss. Her juvenile frame rolled with the highs and lows of the melody until the crescendo where she flung her arms out, tipped her head back and hit a high note.

Angels wept when the magnificent clarity of the sound touched heaven.

Lowering her chin, Ava's eyes cleared and her arms dropped limply to her sides. Startled, she blinked and glanced around. The stage lights blinded her and she raised her arms to block the glare. "How?"

At the edge of the stage, her father and Izzy stared up. Her little sister's green eyes were huge in her face and her soggy thumb hung out of her slack mouth. Their father studied her through wet eyes. His normally tall, strong form was buckled as he held back emotions. Tears ran unchecked down his cheeks and dripped off his jawline. Sucking in a deep breath, he rubbed his hands over his face and wiped away the moisture.

Unsure of what had just happened, Ava's chin trembled and she swallowed hard. "Daddy?"

Silence stretched between them and a deep fear crept into her heart.

"I—." His eyes met hers and he scrapped his fingers through his bright russet hair, searching for words. "I don't know where you heard that song, but you have a gift. A beautiful, one of a kind gift."

Relief flooded her thin frame. Everything would be alright. She had no idea how she'd ended up on the stage or knew the words to the song that she'd just sung. All she remembered was the heady scent of roses, golden eyes, and a desire so deep to sing again that it rocked her soul.

CHAPTER THREE

Sergeant First Class Jaxon Wolfe pushed his night vision goggles up onto his helmet, leaned into his sniper rifle and adjusted the thermal scope. Through the vision of the special scope, the darkened city below transformed from the night visions goggles' shades of grays and greens into a brilliant palette of oranges, yellows, purples and blacks. Zero white. White meant the shit was hitting the fan. Indicated fire.

He panned up and down the street, checking for heat signatures before zeroing in on the squatty, flat roofed, two-story building that his team had just entered. Things were quiet, just like he liked it.

Time ticked in his head and he checked the horizon. They were inching up on morning prayers, where the whole city would come alive with loudspeakers broadcasting the call to kneel. His Special Forces teammate crouched down at the door, rifle ready, protecting the back of their team inside. As a result of his thermal scope, Jaxon's view of Woody was just an orange outline with shades of bright yellow along the hottest points of his body. The sandy ground below his feet was a brilliant shade of purple and the building at his back a combination of muted tangerine walls and purple uprights.

Through one of the windows, he spotted his team's orange bodies filtering by, one after the other, in a silent dance. Tagging each other as they infiltrated the building searching for Tango one and Tango two. Get in, grab the bad guys, alive, if possible, sweep up any intel, and come home alive. That was the mission.

They were lucky for the intel. Not often did a member of the press give up information and expect nothing in return. His mind shifted to the gorgeous, tall blonde, who'd given them not only the names of the terrorists but the location and best time to hit the target. If he hadn't seen Doc pull his shoulder on the last drop, he would've thought he'd stayed behind just to cozy up to her.

The team paused before another window on the second floor and Jaxon frowned. "Bad spot," he murmured. "Keep moving, stay out of the kill zone." He suppressed the urge to break radio silence and tell them to move ass. They understood their jobs.

Below him, Woody's orange form moved. He stood and checked his wrist.

"Steady," Jaxon whispered, knowing full well his teammate couldn't hear him unless he clicked his mic on.

"Sixty seconds till exfil," Woody murmured into his throat mic.

"Damn it," grumbled Jaxon, annoyed with the break in protocol. Woody was such a surfer boy, all golden blonde, smiles and lots of action with the girls. "Thank God, my sister refused to date another guy from my team."

Adopted or not, JD was Jaxon's sister. Her childhood had been rough, jerked from orphanage to orphanage, her mother dead and never having known her father. He'd be damned if one of his teammates would jerk her feelings around too. Not even the good-hearted surfer boy, Woody. His heart picked up a beat when Woody's orange form checked the target pack on his wrist. If he didn't pull his shit together, they'd need to switch his nickname to surfer girl.

Woody's yellow head scanned the area around him and Jaxon shifted his position as an uneasy feeling joined the sweat beads rolling down his back. His instincts screamed. "Shit."

The orange blobs of his team mates scattered from the window and his headset went crazy. The team sounded off, breaking up and chopping each other's sentences into indiscernible nonsense. Woody jerked the door open to join the fight when the code word "Avalanche," was shouted. BOMB.

The floor under Jaxon's feet trembled and shades of white with black edges spread across the building's walls, casting out the oranges and purples with the heat of fire. Woody's orange form was dragged into the doorway, only to be expelled in a ball of bright white. One by one, his team stumbled from the building, their once orange forms consumed in a white haze, edged in black. Their screams pierced the desert air.

Men spilled from the surrounding buildings, flashes of white expelled from the barrels of their guns, peppering his team's burning forms with bullets. Automatically, Jaxon fired, taking out target after target as his team dropped, one after another, and rolled until they laid in white heaps on the purple ground. From the edges of his sight, their forms cooled from white to black, even as he killed the men running towards them. He took out eight more men. "Shit, there are too many of them."

Jaxon activated his Command Net by squeezing the pressel on the fore grip of his rifle. "Request Kinetic Strike on target," he shouted, as he dropped five more bad guys. "In thirty seconds."

Making a choice he'd forever doubt, Jaxon jerked down his night vision goggles, abandoned his perch, and thundered down the staircase. "Double time it, damn it. Your team needs you."

In the time it took him to get street side, only one team member remained alive. He sprinted across the street, his footfalls muted by death screams. The ground was hazy with smoke and the stench of burning flesh permeated the air.

His right side on fire, Woody gained his feet and staggered forward. Quickly, Jaxon took out two more men before he reached his friend. He rolled Woody in the dirt to extinguish the flames and a bullet pierced his thigh but Jaxon didn't even notice the sting, his adrenaline was running so hot. Grabbing Woody with by the collar with one hand, firing from the hip with his rifle, he pulled him to safety. Behind them, the Predator drone dropped fire, as the desert sun rose and the speakers spouted morning prayers.

CHAPTER FOUR

cres of rolling, emerald green hills were dotted with white gravestones, each denoting a fallen soldier. All equal in death, their wars blurred together, creating waves of white that expanded as far as the eye could see. Arlington National Cemetery, where America's heroes were laid to rest.

Each team of six horses pulled a fallen comrade, forming a long train of flag covered caskets, bringing not one, but eight soldiers to their final resting place. Their hooves clopped against the pavement, amid the suppressed sniffles of their loved ones, seated in rows before open graves.

Jaxon glanced over to where Woody stood rigid under a tree in his Army Service uniform. Just like all the soldiers present, his dark blue pants with their thick yellow stripe were bloused into the tops of his combat boots. On his black jacket, his medals gleamed in the morning sun. A green beret skimmed the top of his head and folded over towards his right ear.

That was where the similarities ended. The tree struggled to shade Woody's razed skin. Beneath his beret, a part of him still resembled the surfer boy the team had joked about but the other half was shriveled into a horrific mask of pain. Florid, biting scars enveloped the right side of his face and ate a path that flowed like molten lava down his neck and disappeared under his collar. More scars tacked the corner of his right eye into a half closed position. Only three fingers remained on his right hand and his right ear had melted into his head.

Failure roiled in Jaxon's gut, coating the lining with a black sickness. His disgust with himself was so great that he thought he might throw up and he adverted his eyes to the back to the crowd. If he hadn't trusted his shit instincts and believed the intel was prime, then his brother-in-arms wouldn't have been marked for life.

He spied the Geezers in the back row and groaned. Family. Always there, whether you wanted them or not. Out of respect, his father wore his stark Navy whites and Jaxon's uncle wore his Army dress greens. They were present not only for him, but also for the fallen. Once a soldier, always a soldier.

To cover the shame eating him alive, he grumbled under his breath, "Damn it." Now, they were witnesses to the pain and destruction caused by his bad judgment. "Why did they come?"

They glanced up, and the sympathy in their eyes almost brought him to his knees.

He searched the crowd for his adopted sister. Not seeing her, he breathed a sigh of relief and mumbled, "At least JD isn't present to witness the roll call of the dead. My friends. The ones that her worthless piece of shit brother couldn't protect when they needed him the most."

Their Company Commander stood and shouted out from the list of names to account for his men.

"Sergeant Gonzalez."

The call to report was met with dead air.

"Sergeant Jack Jose Gonzalez. Report!"

Pure silence. For one heartbeat. Two. Then a third. Not even the wind dared to answer for the missing as Gonzo's casket was lowered into the ground.

"Warrant Officer McCormick."

Muffled sniffles filled the silence.

"Warrant Officer Rodney Thomas McCormick. Report!"

The silence of the fallen cut away another jagged piece of Jaxon's soul and Roddie's casket also disappeared.

As the names of the dead were called, Jaxon waited for his name, bracing himself, hoping to be strong and not allow his voice to crack. To honor them with what little strength he had left.

"Staff Sergeant Borland."

His widow swayed with grief and her father grasped her around the waist before she collapsed.

"Staff Sergeant Oscar Borland. Report!"

Muted by death, silence coated the air as Stretch's casket descended.

"First Sergeant Wolfe."

"Here Sir!" He called out, his voice gravely but firm.

"Staff Sergeant Fitzgerald."

In the stillness, Fitz's widow did her best to hold back the tears and make her husband proud. Their two small girls stood at her side in their black dresses, with white bobby socks and shiny black patent leather shoes. Their blonde hair was pulled back into ponytails.

"Staff Sergeant Alan Liam Fitzgerald. Report."

Fitz's casket was lowered. His oldest reached up and clutched her mother's hand. Her small voice reached out to Jaxon, "Is that Daddy?"

Her mother's shoulders shook and all she could do was nod.

Jaxon stood tall and stared straight ahead, his jaw rock hard but inside he was crumbling into a heap and pushing back tears.

"Sergeant First Class Landon St. John."

"Here Sir!" The Doc called out from behind.

Jaxon turned. It was then that he noticed the shiny, blonde hair of the reporter. The beautiful bitch who'd given them the intel. She dared to stand among the grieving, right alongside Max's widow when his name was shouted next. Their fingers were laced together. Side by side, they swayed in the breeze like the thin branches of a willow tree. Both draped in black, one woman with shockingly flaming red hair spilling down her back, the other with hair the color of wheat, captured into a low ponytail at the nape of her neck. The reporter's cornflower blue eyes met his and he clenched his teeth to smother the snarl that begged to erupt from his throat.

His blood boiled and his hands flexed. He wanted to rip the traitor to shreds but he had to hold steady. He couldn't further disgrace his brothers by causing a ruckus at their funeral. On the open graves of his comrades, he swore to never trust a woman again. Especially a beautiful, lying bitch like the one before him.

"Sergeant First Class Oakes."

Woody refused to answer. Instead, he turned and limped away.

Bagpipes whined out the bars of Taps and Jaxon stayed until the bitter end. His heart wrenched when the gray smoke from the twenty-one gun salute back-dropped the row of widows clutching folded American flags to their chests. They flinched with each shot.

Like dominoes, one after another, their necks bent and they surrendered to their sorrow, weeping into the red, white and blue cloth. Only one widow refused to break. Max's wife. She stared sightlessly towards the horizon, the tips of her russet hair fluttering in the breeze.

It's my fault their husbands are dead. Their kids are fatherless. His brothers had believed in him. Trusted his damn instincts that the intel was good. *I failed them.*

Once all the other mourners had left, Jaxon placed a shiny, new quarter atop the curve of each headstone. In remembrance. In respect. Special Forces Green Berets, celebrated as the quiet professionals. "How could the country mourn for soldiers they didn't know, on a mission they'd never hear about?"

They're forgotten because of me.

Today, he'd shed his uniform for the last time. Fold up his green beret and shove it in the back of a drawer. He didn't deserve to wear either ever again.

CHAPTER FIVE

For a fleeting moment, Ava Fairbanks thought she was sleepwalking. Again. But even her dreams couldn't conjure the cliché of the man who lounged before her.

If only Director Terrence Hollingsworth realized what a laughable image he presented, draping himself against the proverbial casting couch. His tan pants left nothing to the imagination. In one hand, he brandished a cigar between stained fingers, while the fingertips of his other hand stroked his chest where the overly tanned skin was strategically revealed. As a Broadway star, Ava preferred to live in the dream world of the theatre. But Hollingsworth's office was a living nightmare.

Windowless, the room reeked with smoke. The illumination of a lone lamp and the glowing tip of his cigar hovered around him like a golden sickness.

The air glittered with her mocking laughter and she shook her head at the stage scene he presented. She tilted her head back and stared down at the little man. "Is this how you greet all your actors?"

"*The* AVA," the thick, sticky sap of his voice clung to her. Tainted her. The lamp's light lit up the delight on his thin face and he licked his lips. "Such a big night for you. I understand a movie producer has tucked himself into the back seats."

Her heart ticked up at the news. *Keep it together*, she ordered. *This is your big chance. You hold this production together and let it ride out its run. Don't let some self-important jerk ruin it for you, for everyone.*

"With your green eyes, and," he licked his lips, his stare penetrating, "that luxurious, jet-black hair, you'll go far in this business. That is, if you're the lead for tonight's opening."

Her stomach rolled with revulsion. She crossed her robe tighter over the costume for her first act, a simple cornflower blue, plaid dress with a white bow collar. Out of the corner of her eye, the gleam of a steel desk appeared to be the only safe haven. Refusing to allow him the pleasure of knowing he made her skin crawl, she skirted around his desk and gracefully draped herself in his chair. "Who else would be the lead?"

"Why, your understudy of course."

Her insides shook at the possibility. *Can't let it happen.* She spread her lips into a broad smile and hid her fear behind false bravado. "My understudy couldn't sing her way out of a wet paper sack. She wouldn't do the part of Charity Rae justice. With her as the lead, *The Rise of Rae* would fold and the crew would be out of work."

Leaning forward, Hollingsworth ground his cigar into the smiling face of a 1940s pin up girl that lounged in a tiny sailor suit at the bottom of his glass ashtray. He smacked his thin lips. "She and I came to an agreement just yesterday. It's my decision as the director."

Twisting the many silver rings on her fingers, her body's desperate demand to step out onto the stage built inside her. Like manna from Heaven, performing brought life, healing, and substance to her existence. On stage, reality faded to the background and was replaced by the warmth of bright lights and the heartbeat of the audience. Entrancing the audience with her acting was like sipping from the fountain of youth and she thirsted for one more drink. She couldn't, no wouldn't allow him to steal her dream. "I earned the lead for this production. You can't remove me."

Shaded an unusual color of blue by the contacts he wore, his eyes lowered and his gaze flowed over her body, making her feel cheap and dirty. Keeping his eye on her, he picked up a gold plated lighter from the table before him and clicked it open, closed, open. He snapped it shut, tossed it back on the table, and patted a spot on the couch beside him. "Ava. You and I need to come to an understanding before opening call. Don't you understand? I have final say. I'm the director." His voice descended to a sticky-sweet timbre. "I have all the power."

Across the expanse of his desk, she examined him. Anger bubbled within her, but she masked her emotions beneath a calm façade. She lifted the lid of a mahogany humidor box and selected a cigar at random. Acting as if she didn't have a care in the world, she unwrapped the cellophane wrapper, slid the cigar under her nostrils and inhaled its unique aroma. "Smells like crap. Just like what you're trying to sell me. "

His eyes narrowed and he bit out, "That's an eight hundred dollar cigar."

Picking up a pair of stainless steel cigar cutters, Ava observed how the sharp blades cut though the circular hole when squeezed. She palmed the clippers and rolled the cold metal over and over in her palm. "I'm a million dollar actor. Here to entertain the audience. Not you."

Hollingsworth surged to his feet and barked, "Who the hell do you think you are?" He slapped his palms on the leather blotter of his desk and leaned forward across the expanse. "You have a choice. Join me on the couch or, hell," he rapped the desk with his knuckles, "here on this desk, and you'll open tonight's performance. Otherwise, your understudy will replace you when the curtain goes up."

Her laughter cascaded off the walls of the little room.

Heat inched up his face.

"No man control's my destiny. No man has say over what I do. Not even the mighty Director Terrence Hollingsworth."

She rose and circled the desk until she stood in front of him. "The investors cast me as lead in this production, not you. They cut your check and mine. Besides—." Once again, she slid the cigar through the metal cutter and regarded him through her thick lashes. Her look was bitter cold. "Touch me and this will be your dick." She snipped the cigar in half and the pieces tumbled to the floor. "That should get through to both of your little brains."

She tossed the cutter on the desk and in one fluid movement turned to exit the room.

A rush of air behind her was the only warning.

Hollingsworth slammed into her and pinned her between his long body and the door.

The impact stole the breath from her chest and her forehead bounced off the wooden door. Dazed and unable to think, shock shuddered through her slender frame. Then rage. This was a part she'd never play. But her arms were trapped between her body and the hard door. She struggled to free herself. Fury scalded her cheeks and blood pounded in her ears. She ground out between clenched teeth, "Get off me. Now!"

He pressed his lips against her slender neck. She felt his hot, moist breath as he branded her with small, stinging bites along the unprotected length of her throat, until his lips lingered just above her earlobe. The stench of his cigar breath flowed over her. Slowly, he raised the back of her robe.

Then the hem of the blue dress beneath.

A chill snuck under the layers, followed by a shaking that started in her knees and trembled uncontrollably through her frame. Color washed from her face and an unbearable cold settled into her bones. She bucked but he held her firm, trapped against the door.

He slid his moist palm over her hip and down her flat stomach.

His other hand reached up and squeezed her around the throat, restricting her airway.

Her legs weakened. Fear so primal and primitive descended upon her, dug it's claws into her throat and stole her ability to speak.

His hand slipped into the front of her panties and he pulled hard, ripping them.

Her body jerked to cast him off and horror inked a black path into her heart and pumped it with a fist of terror. Lack of air caused the edges of her sight to darken.

Beneath her cheek, a light rap sounded on the door and a flicker of hope rooted within her frozen heart. She opened her mouth to call out.

But nothing happened.

From the other side of the door, a meek voice barely penetrated the thickness of the wood. "Terrence? Darling, are you in there?"

The Director stiffened and his hold loosened.

Seizing the moment, Ava shoved back with her arms and knocked him backward. She wrenched open the door. Light and fresh air flooded inside.

Whipping around, her mind rebelled and she struggled to cope with what had almost happened. Her breath was heavy and fast in her chest as she looked down at Hollingsworth, who'd landed on his ass.

Slack jawed, he stared past her at the person in the doorway.

Heat surged into her pale cheeks and rage vibrated within her. She swung her slender leg back and kicked him as hard as she could in the balls.

He writhed and rolled on the ground at her feet.

Satisfaction filled Ava and warmed her chilled body. "I'm calling the police and then the investors. One of us will be leaving. It won't be me."

She turned and faced her rescuer but the "thank you" froze on her lips. Ashlee Hollingsworth, the Director's timid wife, had saved her with a simple knock on a door. Her natural, flat, mouse brown hair had been curled and twisted up and now framed the horror on her tiny face.

Behind her stood Roger, the backstage hand. His mouth gaped open before he collected himself and mumbled, "Five minutes Miss Fairbanks. Five minutes 'till curtain call."

For the first time in her life, Ava wished she was sleepwalking and could wake. But her nightmare had only just begun.

ACKNOWLEDGMENTS

As with everything in life, nothing worth having is created in a vacuum.

I would like to acknowledge the superstars in my life. They're my balcony people. The ones who believed in me when my own faith faltered. The ones who supported me with my dream of writing.

First and foremost, I would like to thank God for giving me such a great hunger to create.

My father, who when I told him that I wanted to write novels, treated me as if I was already a successful published author.

My mother, who gave me the love of reading and checks every page for errors that I've missed.

My husband, who has supported me unconditionally, pushes me for excellence and threatens to send me to the "cabin" if I'm allowing the silly stuff to derail my writing dream. (Once, I rented a cabin to write in for a week. I was so lonely that I came home after one day.)

My daughter, Kasie, who kept the light lit in the window and rejected the naysayers. One of my greatest cheerleaders.

My daughter, Lacey, my voracious reader. She read every version and spread the word on my books. Another one of my greatest cheerleaders!

My son, Kody, who stuns me with his imagination and his natural storytelling. One day, my son, you too will write, and the world will be better for it.

My Developmental Editor, Tessa Shapcott. She pushed me to

write the best stories possible and, with her British whit, challenged me and allowed me to grow while lifting my spirits.

Copy Editor Shannon Eversoll, who fine-tunes everything to a professional shine. Checking all those P's and Q's.

This book wouldn't have been the same without each and every one of you.

I have been truly blessed.

-Dee

ABOUT THE AUTHOR

Dee Armstrong writes thrillers and romantic suspense with a paranormal twist — stories that squeeze the heart, rattle the nerves, and still leave room for love, laughter, and sass. She pits tough heroines against bad guys you'll love to hate — with twists that keep the pages flying and endings that fight for hope.

A former U.S. Air Force Russian linguist and three-time Taekwondo Black Belt National Sparring Champion, Dee believes the vulnerable should be protected and justice must be fierce—because the past never stays buried, and the truth never sleeps.

When she's not writing about danger and desire, Dee is chasing after her littles, sipping tea on the porch, and plotting against the weeds in her garden.

Find her at www.DeeArmstrong.com or @DeeArmstrongAuthor for sneak peeks, behind-the-scenes chaos, and stories that leave a fingerprint on your heart.

instagram.com/dee_armstrong_author
facebook.com/DeeArmstrongAuthor

www.ingramcontent.com/pod-product-compliance
Lightning Source LLC
Chambersburg PA
CBHW031614180726
48284CB00005B/1545

Melissa Foster

Liebe gegen den Strom

Die Bradens in Peaceful Harbor

Die Autorin

Melissa Foster ist eine preisgekrönte *New-York-Times-* und *USA-Today*-Bestsellerautorin. Ihre Bücher werden vom *USA-Today-Bücherblog*, vom *Hagerstown Magazin*, von *The Patriot* und vielen anderen Printmedien empfohlen. Melissa hat mehrere Wandgemälde für das *Hospital for Sick Children*, eine Kinderklinik in Washington, D. C., gemalt.

Besuchen Sie Melissa auf ihrer Website oder chatten Sie mit ihr in den sozialen Netzwerken. Sie diskutiert gern mit Lesezirkeln und Bücherclubs über ihre Romane und freut sich über Einladungen. Melissas Bücher sind bei den meisten Online-Buchhändlern als Taschenbuch und E-Book erhältlich.

www.MelissaFoster.com

Melissa Foster

Liebe gegen den Strom

Die Bradens in Peaceful Harbor

LOVE IN BLOOM – HERZEN IM AUFBRUCH

Aus dem Amerikanischen von Rita Kloosterziel

Deutsche Erstveröffentlichung
2019 bei World Literary Press, MD, USA
© 2016 der Originalausgabe: Melissa Foster
© 2019 der deutschsprachigen Ausgabe: Melissa Foster
Lektorat: Judith Zimmer, Hamburg
Umschlaggestaltung: Natasha Brown

ISBN: 9781948868327

*Für Elise, weil unsere Crazies so
viel Spaß zusammen haben.*

Vorwort

Mir hat es riesigen Spaß gemacht, Sam und Faith dabei zuzusehen, wie sie lernen und wachsen und sich unausweichlich ineinander verlieben. Sie stehen inzwischen ganz oben auf der Liste meiner Lieblingsfiguren, und ich hoffe, dass Sie sie ebenso lieben werden wie ich!

Wenn Sie über Neuerscheinungen immer auf dem Laufenden bleiben möchten, bestellen Sie doch meinen Newsletter unter: www.melissafoster.com/Newsletter_German

Die Serie über die Bradens ist Teil der Reihe *Love in Bloom — Herzen im Aufbruch*, mit jeder Menge Familie und jeder Menge Romantik. Viele der Helden und Heldinnen früherer Liebesgeschichten begegnen uns in späteren Romanen wieder, sodass Sie keine Verlobung, keine Hochzeit oder Geburt verpassen. Am Ende dieses Buches finden Sie eine Liste der kompletten Reihe.

Sehen Sie sich auch bei den *Readers Goodies* um, der Seite mit den Bonbons für treue Leserinnen. In englischer Sprache finden Sie dort Familienstammbäume, Checklisten für die verschiedenen Serien, die empfohlene Lesereihenfolge sowie den Link zum essenziellen *Love-in-Bloom*-Guide, in dem Sie alles über Ihre Lieblingshelden und -heldinnen erfahren können: www.melissafoster.com/Reader-Goodies

Viel Spaß beim Lesen!

Melissa Foster

Eins

Es gab Grenzen, wie lange ein Mann eine Hochzeitsfeier ertragen konnte, bevor er zu viel trank oder sich mit einer anschmiegsamen Frau davonmachte, um all dieser Reinheit zu entkommen. Sam Braden stand mit einem Drink in der Hand da, begutachtete die Auswahl an weiblichen Gästen und überlegte, welche der beiden Alternativen er wählen sollte. Möglicherweise würde es sowohl aufs Betrinken als auch auf die Damenbegleitung hinauslaufen.

»Wenn du die Brünette willst, nehme ich die Rothaarige.« Ty, sein jüngster Bruder, wies mit dem Kinn zur Bar. Abgesehen davon, dass er ein weltberühmter Bergsteiger und Fotograf war, war Ty auch oft genug Sams Gefährte bei seinen nächtlichen Ausschweifungen. »Es sei denn, eine reicht dir nicht. Für den Fall würde ich mich für eine der Staley-Schwestern entscheiden.«

Sam schnaubte. *Haben wir doch alles schon hinter uns.*

Sein Blick fiel auf zwei Blondinen, die über die Tanzfläche auf sie zukamen. Vor einem Monat hatte er etwas mit der gehabt, die ihn gerade mit den Augen verschlang, und die Rothaarige, die Ty eben beäugt hatte, hatte sich zu ihrer heißen, schweißgetränkten Balgerei dazugesellt. Dann wanderte sein

1

Blick zu der sexy Brünetten, die an der Bar stand und aussah, als würde sie am liebsten darüberspringen und sich dahinter verstecken, wenn sie nur wüsste, wie. *Faith Hayes.* Den ganzen Abend hatte er versucht, sie nicht anzusehen, aber es war aussichtslos. Sie arbeitete in der Arztpraxis von seinem Bruder Cole. Faith war süß und lieb und schlau, und … Sam sollte sich lieber nicht vorstellen, wie er sie auf die Bar legte und lauter schmutzige Dinge mit ihrem hinreißenden Körper anstellte.

Nein, ganz sicher nicht.

Immer wenn er sie ansah, immer wenn er an sie dachte – *also an jedem verdammten Tag* –, kam dieses Gefühl in ihm hoch, mehr zu wollen als ein paar Quickies. Er wollte sie nicht nur auf die Bar legen, er wollte sie auch mit zu sich nach Hause nehmen. Das an sich war schon seltsam, denn Sam nahm nie eine Frau mit in sein Blockhaus. Aber die Hälfte seiner Besuche in Coles Praxis waren nichts weiter als ein Vorwand, um einen Blick auf Faith zu erhaschen. Er verstand nicht, was ihn so an ihr faszinierte. Schließlich bevorzugte er normalerweise Frauen, die schnurstracks mit ihm ins Bett steigen wollten und sich dabei sehr geschickt anstellten, aber er konnte nicht leugnen, dass sich etwas in ihm regte, sobald Faith in der Nähe war. Er zwang sich, den Blick abzuwenden, und betrachtete stattdessen die Tanzfläche, wo Cole, sein ältester Bruder, mit seiner frisch angetrauten Frau Leesa tanzte. Gleich dahinter sahen sich sein jüngerer Bruder Nate und dessen Verlobte Jewel tief in die Augen. Machten sie eigentlich je etwas anderes? Früher hatte sich Sam geschüttelt bei dem Gedanken, sich zu binden – *außer natürlich an ein Bett.* Aber es war nicht zu übersehen, wie glücklich seine Brüder waren, seit sie sich verliebt hatten, und in letzter Zeit hatte er das Gefühl, etwas zu verpassen.

Die große Blonde drängte sich an Sam und versperrte ihm

dabei den Blick auf Faith. Sie blinzelte ihn mit keckem Augenaufschlag an, während sich ihre Freundin an Ty heranmachte. »Ihr Jungs seht einsam aus.«

»Guten Abend, die Damen«, sagte Sam geschmeidig und lenkte seine Aufmerksamkeit wieder auf die hübschen Frauen, die definitiv wussten, wie sich ihr Körper zum Wohle der Menschheit einsetzen ließ.

»Tänzchen gefällig?«, fragte die Blonde und Sam folgte ihr auf die Tanzfläche wie ein Hund dem Stöckchen.

Musik und Tanzen kamen für Sam gleich nach Wildwasser-Rafting. Als Besitzer von »Rough Riders«, einer Firma, die Abenteuerurlaube mit Raftingtouren anbot, stand er ständig unter Dampf, aber ein ordentlicher Beat besänftigte seine innere Unruhe. Und Sam war immer ein wenig rastlos.

Die Blondine bewegte sich sinnlich in seinen Armen und erinnerte ihn an all die Gründe, warum er heute Abend einer Frau den Vorzug vor dem Alkohol geben sollte. Bei diesem Gedanken ging sein Blick wieder zu Faith, die nach wie vor an der Bar stand, sich an einem Getränk festhielt, das höchstwahrscheinlich nichts weiter als Limonade war, und einen Finger nervös am Rand des Glases entlangfahren ließ, während sie … *ihn beobachtete?* Sams Lippen verzogen sich zu einem Lächeln und Faiths Blick huschte davon. Sie wurde immer hinreißend flatterig, wenn er Cole in seiner Praxis besuchte, und obwohl er es wahrscheinlich nicht tun sollte, bereitete es Sam ein diebisches Vergnügen, mit ihr zu flirten.

Cole schob sich vor ihn und versperrte ihm die Sicht auf Faith. Er warf seinem Bruder einen drohenden Blick zu. *Bloß nicht, Junge*, signalisierte er.

Es gab keinen Zweifel: Sam liebte Frauen und alle um ihn herum wussten es. Er liebte ihren Duft, das Gefühl ihrer weichen Körper an seinen festen Muskeln, ihre zarten Züge, die Laute, die sie auf dem Höhepunkt der Leidenschaft ausstießen. Aber neuerdings machte es ihm keinen Spaß mehr, sich ein Stelldichein mit irgendeiner beliebigen Frau auszumalen. Seine Gedanken kreisten nur um Faith, und er wollte all das mit ihr erleben, statt sich etwas zusammenzufantasieren.

»Sam!«, sagte Cole strafend.

Sam schüttelte den Kopf, um das Durcheinander darin zu vertreiben, und lachte leise, als er seine Aufmerksamkeit wieder der Frau zuwandte, mit der er tanzte. Seine Hände fuhren über ihren Rücken. *Mmh.* Sie fühlte sich gut an. Unwillkürlich wanderte sein Blick wieder zu Faith, die in ihren Drink starrte. *Bestimmt fühlst du dich noch viel besser an*, war der erste Gedanke, der ihm in den Sinn kam. Es war jedoch der zweite Gedanke, der ihn überraschte: *Ich frage mich, woran du gerade denkst.*

Ich hätte nicht zu dieser Hochzeit kommen sollen. Faith sah zum hundertsten Mal an diesem Abend auf ihre Uhr. Sie hatte sich vorgenommen, nach dem Abendessen noch eine Stunde zu bleiben. So gehörte es sich schließlich, wenn der Chef heiratete, obwohl sie am liebsten auf der Stelle gegangen wäre. Berufliche Verpflichtungen außerhalb der Arbeitszeit waren ihr sowieso unangenehm, aber hier war sie nicht nur von Leuten umgeben, die sie kaum kannte, zu allem Überfluss schienen ihre dummen Hormone auch noch unablässig *Ich will Sam Braden* zu flüstern. Lieber Himmel, im Moment hasste sie sich selbst. *Sieh ihn dir doch an, wie er mit dieser Frau tanzt, diesem stadtbekannten*

Flittchen. Er hatte fast den ganzen Abend getanzt und dabei kaum eine Frau ausgelassen. Sie standen praktisch Schlange, um in seiner Nähe zu sein. Und warum auch nicht? Er war nicht nur nett und charmant, sondern auch groß, dunkel und unverschämt gut aussehend. Derart gut aussehend, dass selbst einer intelligenten Frau wie Faith der Kopf wie leer gefegt war. In seinen Armen über die Tanzfläche zu schweben, war der Traum aller Frauen in Peaceful Harbor. Aller Frauen außer ihr.

Jedenfalls meistens.

Ich sollte wirklich eine Tequilaflasche köpfen. Oder gehen. Da sie nach einer Flasche Tequila nicht mehr würde nach Hause fahren können, kam sie zu dem Schluss, dass sie besser ging.

Außerdem hatte sie die perfekte Ausrede, sich ein bisschen früher zu verabschieden als die anderen Gäste. Für den nächsten Tag hatte sie eine Autowaschaktion organisiert, um Geld für eine Online-Selbsthilfegruppe zu sammeln, die sie gegründet hatte. Sie hieß WAC, Women Against Cheaters, und richtete sich an Frauen, die schlechte Erfahrungen mit untreuen Männern gemacht hatten.

Mit Typen wie Sam.

Sam schaute auf und – *Oh Gott, lass mich auf der Stelle tot umfallen* – ertappte sie dabei, wie sie ihn anstarrte. *Schon wieder.* Sie wandte sich ab und hoffte, dass er es nicht wirklich bemerkt hatte, obwohl seine Augen wie Laserstrahlen waren, die ihr ein Loch in den Rücken brannten. Natürlich hatte er es bemerkt. Es konnte gar nicht anders sein. Sie leckte sich ja förmlich die Lippen nach ihm. Dass sie ausgerechnet den Mann anhimmelte, der schon mit den meisten Frauen in Peaceful Harbor geschlafen hatte, wenn man den Gerüchten Glauben schenkte, ging ihr mächtig gegen den Strich. Abgesehen von seinem unverschämt guten Aussehen gehörte er genau zu der Sorte

Mann, die sie am allerwenigsten wollte oder brauchte.

Doch sie konnte nicht anders: Sie musste ihn einfach heimlich beäugen. Dabei ging es ihr wie allen Frauen hier, die nicht mit ihm verwandt waren: Sie fühlte sich von ihm angezogen wie eine Motte vom Licht. Er war *hinreißend*. Männlich. Kräftig. Und dieses Lächeln. *Heiliger Strohsack.* Sie fächelte sich Luft zu. Sein Lächeln allein reichte, um ihr den Atem zu rauben. Alle Bradens sahen gut aus, aber Sam hatte etwas Raues und Rätselhaftes. *Etwas Gefährliches.*

Zu gefährlich für sie. Und das war okay, weil sie sich ja gar nicht mit ihm einlassen wollte. Jedenfalls nicht so, dass sie sich eine feste Beziehung zu ihm vorstellte. Mit einem Mann wie Sam konnte man keine feste Beziehung eingehen, und sie würde nicht das Dummchen sein, das es versuchte. Ihr reichte es, ihn mit Blicken zu verzehren und so zu tun, als sei er ihr egal.

Oh Mist! Da kam er geradewegs auf sie zu. Er überquerte die Tanzfläche, als gehörte ihm die Welt, bewegte sich selbstsicher, entschlossen und konzentriert, während die Blondine und ein Dutzend anderer Frauen ihm nachstarrten. Dabei sah er sie die ganze Zeit unverwandt an, als wollte er sie mit Blicken ausziehen. Faith bekam weiche Knie. Seine dunklen Augen waren schmal und verführerisch und schillerten vor Verruchtheit. Unter dem teuren Smoking wirkten seine breiten Schultern noch massiger und kräftiger. Die obersten Knöpfe seines Hemdes waren offen und erlaubten ihr einen Blick auf seine gebräunte Haut und einen Schimmer von Brusthaaren. Er sah aus, als sollte er eigentlich lässig ausgestreckt auf einem Sofa liegen, von Frauen umschwärmt. Wie ein Gott.

Wie ein Gott? Wie albern ist das denn?

Faith war keineswegs eine graue Maus, die keinen Mann abbekommen hatte. Sie war Single, weil sie es so wollte, schönen Dank auch. Bei der Wahl ihrer Männer hatte sie bisher kein gutes Händchen gehabt und außerdem waren Männer einfach bescheuert. Sie logen und betrogen, was das Zeug hielt, nur um ihr schließlich alle Schuld in die Schuhe zu schieben. Seit sich JJ, ihr letzter Freund, dem ungeschriebenen Gesetz »Männer müssen fremdgehen« gebeugt hatte, nach dem das männliche Geschlecht zu leben schien, hatte sie die Auswahl potenzieller Kandidaten ausschließlich auf langweilige, etwas nerdige Männer beschränkt.

»Faith.«

Sams tiefe Stimme glitt über ihre Haut und grub sich in ihre Erinnerung. Für später, wenn sie alleine in ihrem Bett lag und an ihn dachte. Auch das hasste sie. Warum, oh, warum nur musste er solch ein notorischer Frauenheld sein? Konnte er nicht so sein wie seine Brüder Cole und Nate? Treu bis in alle Ewigkeit?

Er berührte ihren Arm, und es war, als verbrenne ihre Haut.

»Oh. Hi, Sam.« Das klang doch locker und beiläufig, oder? Er war so groß, stand so dicht bei ihr und roch nach Sonnenschein und Hitze und Männlichkeit.

Na prima. Jetzt geht mir deine Männlichkeit nicht mehr aus dem Sinn.

»Möchtest du tanzen?«, fragte er.

Ja. Nein! Bleib bei deinen Langweilern, Faith.

Sam war alles andere als langweilig. Draußen in der Natur ging er jedes Wagnis ein, das sich ihm bot. Und abends feierte er, laut und ausgelassen. Nein, damit wollte sie nichts zu tun haben.

»Nein danke.« Sie nippte an ihrem Drink und wünschte, es wäre Tequila statt Whiskey Cola. Und sie wünschte, sie wäre zu Hause, statt neben dieser menschlichen Hitzewelle zu stehen.

Er zog die Augenbrauen zusammen. »Sicher? Ich habe dich den ganzen Abend noch nicht auf der Tanzfläche gesehen.«

»Sind dir schon die Mädels ausgegangen?« *Lieber Himmel, habe ich das laut gesagt?*

Ein entspanntes Lächeln breitete sich auf seinem Gesicht aus. Er wirkte nicht beleidigt, sondern eher … *amüsiert?* Er sah sich im Raum um. »Nein, eigentlich nicht. Da sind ein paar, mit denen ich noch nicht getanzt habe«, sagte er und richtete seine Schokoladenaugen wieder auf sie. »Aber ich möchte mit dir tanzen.«

Sie trank ihren Whiskey Cola in einem Zug aus, damit ihr das »Okay« nicht herausrutschte, das ihr auf der Zunge lag, und stellte das leere Glas auf die Theke. »Danke, aber ich wollte gerade gehen.«

»Das wäre aber schade.« Sein Blick wanderte langsam über ihren Körper, sodass sie sich verletzlich und nackt vorkam.

Nackt mit Sam Braden. Plötzlich schien ihr Innerstes in Flammen zu stehen. Offenbar war es ihm nicht entgangen, denn seine Augen wurden schwarz wie die Nacht.

»Du siehst heute Abend unglaublich schön aus, und es ist Cole und Leesas großer Tag. Du solltest hierbleiben«, er beugte sich etwas näher zu ihr, »und mit mir tanzen.«

Mit diesen butterweichen Knien würde sie sowieso nicht weit kommen. *Unglaublich schön?* Faith hatte oft genug zu hören bekommen, dass sie hübsch sei. Aber *unglaublich schön?* Das ging wohl doch ein bisschen zu weit. Typisch Sam Braden, der Süßholzraspler. Sam Braden, der die Grenzen austestete.

Sie musste zugeben, dass er diese Anmache perfekt beherrschte. Seine Augen waren nur auf sie gerichtet, während sie die Blicke fast aller Frauen im Raum auf sich spürte, als fragten sie sich, was sie hatte, das sie nicht hatten. Oder vielleicht wollten sie sie auch einfach umbringen. *Jep.* Das war's wahrscheinlich.

»Die Hochzeit war wunderbar«, brachte sie mühsam hervor, »und ich freue mich für Cole und Leesa, aber morgen Nachmittag veranstalte ich am Harbor-Park eine Autowaschaktion. Deshalb sollte ich jetzt wirklich gehen, ich muss noch einiges vorbereiten.«

Sam trat näher. Seine Finger fuhren federleicht über ihren Arm, schickten einen Hitzeschwall direkt in ihr Gehirn und verursachten einen Kurzschluss.

»Am Harbor-Park?« Die rechte Seite seines verführerischen Mundes hob sich zu einem neckischen Lächeln. »Aber der Abend ist doch noch lange nicht zu Ende. Du kannst nicht gehen, ohne wenigstens einmal mit mir zu tanzen. Nun komm schon. Denk nur, wie Cole sich freuen würde, wenn er sieht, dass du dich amüsierst.«

Er war wirklich hartnäckig. Vielleicht sollte sie einfach nachgeben und mit ihm tanzen. Sie hatte keine Lust, eine weitere Trophäe in der langen Reihe von Sams Eroberungen zu sein, aber schließlich wäre es nur ein einziger Tanz. Dann könnte sie nach Hause gehen und er würde sich irgendeiner anderen Frau zuwenden. Dieser Gedanke war wie ein Stoß in die Magengrube.

Ihre blöden Hormone bahnten sich wieder einen Weg an die Oberfläche. *Du hast ja wirklich nett gefragt.* Vielleicht las sie einfach viel zu viel in diesen Tanz hinein. Es war schließlich kein Date.

Aber er starrte sie unbeirrt mit diesem »Ich will dich flachlegen«-Blick an, der so typisch für ihn war. Genau denselben Blick hatte er an diesem Abend schon mehreren anderen Frauen zugeworfen.

Mehreren. Anderen. Frauen.

Grundgütiger! Warum überlegte sie überhaupt, ob sie mit ihm tanzen sollte?

Es war seine Hand, die an ihrem Arm entlangfuhr, bis sie zitterte und ihr gleichzeitig ganz heiß wurde. Und diese Augen, die nur sie zu sehen schienen und ihr das Gefühl gaben, ungeheuer wichtig zu sein. Sie war Sam nicht wichtig. Ihr Verstand wusste das, aber ihre Eierstöcke hatten diesen Teil ihres Gehirns offenbar fest im Griff und zermalmten ihre intelligenten Zellen.

Faith warf einen Blick auf die Tanzfläche und sah Cole, der Leesa etwas ins Ohr flüsterte. Sie waren so ein schönes Paar und Cole war so ein freundlicher Chef. Vielleicht sollte sie doch ein bisschen länger bleiben. Sie musste ja nicht mit Sam tanzen. Sie konnte einfach mit ihm reden, bis es ihm langweilig wurde und er zur nächsten Frau weiterging.

Coles Miene wurde ernst und auch Leesa schaute zu ihnen herüber. Er sagte etwas zu ihr und steuerte dann mit einem wütenden Blick auf Sam und sie zu. *Mist.* Das war nicht gut. Schließlich war er ihr *Chef.*

Du lieber Himmel. War sie völlig verrückt geworden? Sie konnte doch nicht mit dem Bruder ihres Chefs tanzen!

»Also …« Panik stieg in ihr auf, als Cole näher kam. Cole respektierte sie, aber ihm war nicht entgangen, wie nervös sie wurde, wenn Sam in der Nähe war. Er hatte sie mit hochrotem Kopf dasitzen sehen, wenn Sam ihn in der Praxis besuchen kam und ihr im Vorübergehen Komplimente machte. Dass er sie jetzt dabei ertappte, wie sie seinen Bruder anhimmelte, war das Letzte, was sie brauchen konnte. »Ich muss wirklich gehen, aber danke, dass du gefragt hast, Sam.« Sie drehte sich auf dem Absatz um und eilte davon, bevor sie die Nerven verlor.

Zwei

»Hör auf, dich wie ein trotziges Kind zu benehmen, und such dir irgendjemand oder irgendetwas anderes«, fauchte Cole, während Sam Faith nachsah, die aus der Tür schlüpfte.

Sam war verwirrt. Es passierte selten, dass ihn eine Frau abblitzen ließ, schon gar nicht, wenn er sie zum Tanz aufforderte. Dass Faith Nein gesagt hatte, bescherte ihm ein merkwürdiges Gefühl in der Magengegend. Der Drang, ihr nachzugehen, war stärker als alles, was er jemals empfunden hatte, aber Cole, der mit einem wütenden Blitzen in den Augen vor ihm stand, hielt ihn zurück.

Und vielleicht tat sein Gewissen auch seinen Teil dazu.

»Reg dich ab, Bruderherz.«

»Abregen? Sam, sie ist meine Angestellte. Sie ist klug und kompetent und sehr gut in ihrem Job. Das Letzte, was sie braucht – und das Letzte, was ich brauche – ist, dass du ihr die Karriere versaust.«

Seufzend fuhr sich Sam mit der Hand übers Gesicht und wünschte, er könnte verstehen, warum seine Gedanken ständig um Faith kreisten. Sicher, sie war sexy, aber das traf auf viele andere Frauen auch zu. Vielleicht hatte Cole recht und er war wirklich einfach nur trotzig, denn die Gefühle, die in seinem

Innersten an ihm nagten, passten eigentlich gar nicht zu ihm.

Er warf einen Blick zu der Tür, durch die sie gerade verschwunden war, und fragte sich, warum sie davongelaufen war. Wegen Cole? Oder seinetwegen? Warum interessierte es ihn überhaupt? Hier waren so viele andere Frauen. Bei einem derart reichhaltigen Angebot fiel es ihm normalerweise schwer, sich zu konzentrieren, aber jetzt beherrschte ein einziges Bild seine Gedanken: der Ausdruck in Faiths Augen, kurz bevor sie sich zum Gehen gewandt hatte. Es war ein entschlossener, fast ängstlicher Blick, und das beunruhigte ihn. Er war ganz sicher kein Furcht einflößender Typ.

Ach nein? Okay, auf jemanden wie Faith wirkte er vielleicht Furcht einflößend. Zu den soliden Schlips-und-Kragen-Typen, auf die sie wahrscheinlich stand, gehörte er nun wirklich nicht.

»Vielleicht hast du recht«, räumte Sam ein.

Coles Miene entspannte sich ein wenig.

»Ich will ihr Leben nicht durcheinanderbringen. Es ist nur so, dass sie ... mich fasziniert.«

»Halb Peaceful Harbor fasziniert dich, Sam.«

Er schnaubte verächtlich. *Wenn du wüsstest!* Die Frauen, mit denen er sich traf, *faszinierten* ihn nicht. Sie törnten ihn an. Das war etwas ganz anderes, wie er selbst erst in diesem Moment begriffen hatte. »Faith ist irgendwie anders.«

»Du hast recht. Sie ist tabu, und du wolltest schon immer genau das haben, was du nicht haben kannst.« Cole legte Sam den Arm um die Schulter und wandte sich mit ihm der Gästeschar zu. »Sieh dich um. Eine ganze Horde von Frauen, die nur auf eine Gelegenheit warten, mit dir zu turteln. Die Auswahl ist riesig. Aber wenn es um meine Angestellten geht, lässt du gefälligst deinen Reißverschluss zu, verstanden?«

Sam sah sich im Raum um. Bisher hatte ihn sein Image als

Frauenheld noch nie gestört. Im Gegenteil: Er war sogar stolz darauf. Sam war gut zu den Frauen, die sich auf ihn einließen. Er behandelte sie mit Respekt und gab ihnen in den wenigen Stunden, die sie gemeinsam verbrachten, das Gefühl, etwas Besonderes zu sein. Als er nun jedoch den Blicken einiger hübscher Gäste begegnete, verspürte er nicht den gleichen Drang wie sonst. Was Faith gesagt hatte, ging ihm nicht aus dem Kopf: *Sind dir schon die Mädels ausgegangen?* Im Moment ging ihm alles gegen den Strich, auch Coles Witzeleien, die er schon viel zu oft gehört hatte. Und obwohl er es selbst kaum glauben konnte, ging ihm sogar sein Ruf gegen den Strich.

Nach Damenbegleitung stand ihm jetzt nicht mehr der Sinn. Sam wandte sich wieder der Bar zu und fragte sich, wie viele Drinks es brauchen würde, bis er aufhörte, an Faith zu denken.

Faith fuhr geradewegs zu ihrer Wohnung. Sie warf ihre Schlüssel auf die Couch, stapfte in die Küche, öffnete den Gefrierschrank und steckte den Kopf hinein.

»Wenn du das Bananeneis suchst: Das habe ich aufgegessen.«

»Ich brauche kein Eis«, sagte sie zu ihrer besten Freundin Vivian, die übers Wochenende zu Besuch war. »Nur Abkühlung.«

Vivian hüpfte auf die Küchentheke und baumelte mit den Beinen. »Oh, das klingt interessant. Heißt das, dass die Hochzeitsfeier nicht nur furchtbar bescheuert war?«

Faith knallte den Gefrierschrank zu. »Die Hochzeit war

wunderschön, genau so, wie ich es erwartet hatte. Das Ganze fühlte sich an wie eine private Zusammenkunft von Coles engsten Freunden und Familie. Und dann waren da noch ungefähr sechs Dutzend weibliche Singles, die sich um Sam drängten.« Sie verdrehte die Augen.

»Sexy und single, das zieht Frauen an«, neckte Vivian.

»Das machte es auch nicht besser. Ich habe dir ja gesagt, dass ich nicht hingehen wollte.« Faith seufzte. »Wenigstens ist es vorbei, ich kann es abhaken und mich auf die WAC-Aktion vorbereiten.« Vor zwei Jahren, nach einer schmerzlichen Trennung und nach zu viel Alkohol und zu wenig Schlaf, hatte Faith das Online-Forum für Frauen eröffnet, die betrogen worden waren. Vivian hatte sie dabei unterstützt und ermutigt. Als Faith am nächsten Morgen verkatert aufgewacht war und den Schmerz über die Trennung immer noch so intensiv empfand wie vor dem Alkoholrausch, hatte sie beschlossen, dass das Forum eine gute und sinnvolle Idee war. Ursprünglich wollte sie nichts weiter, als Frauen einen sicheren Ort zu bieten, an dem sie sich über das Unrecht, das man ihnen angetan hatte, austauschen konnten. Schon bald hatte sich daraus eine landesweite Community von Frauen für Frauen entwickelt und mittlerweile gab es Ortsgruppen in verschiedenen Städten. An der morgigen Autowaschaktion würden Mitglieder aus ganz Maryland teilnehmen. Mit dem Erlös sollten die Kosten für Internetauftritte und irgendwann die Neugestaltung ihrer Website bestritten werden.

»Du hättest mich als deine Begleitperson bei der Hochzeit anmelden sollen, so wie ich es dir gesagt habe«, meinte Vivian. »Ich hätte dich daran erinnert, wie heiß du aussiehst. Also, nun erzähl schon. Ich weiß doch, dass du mir was verschweigst. Du siehst aus, als hättest du mit jemandem rumgeknutscht und würdest dir wünschen, dass es nicht beim Rumknutschen geblieben wäre.«

Schön wär's. »Diese Hochzeit war ein Arbeitstermin, mehr nicht. Ich sehe nicht ein, wieso wir *beide* unsere Zeit dafür opfern sollten.« Sie ging in ihr Schlafzimmer. Vivian folgte ihr auf den Fersen.

»Sam hat mich zum Tanzen aufgefordert.« Sie nahm ihren Schmuck ab, und während sie ihr Spiegelbild betrachtete, fragte sie sich, was Sam wohl gesehen hatte, als er so nahe bei ihr stand, dass er ihr unter die Haut hätte kriechen können. Eigentlich dachte sie, sie hätte sich selbst und ihre Reaktionen unter Kontrolle gehabt, aber jetzt, wo sie Platz zum Atmen hatte und die Luft nicht mehr voll von *ihm* war, fiel ihr ein, was sie zu ihm gesagt hatte. *Sind dir schon die Mädels ausgegangen? – Echt cool, Faith.*

Vivian verschränkte die Arme und ihr Lächeln wich einem ernsten, finsteren Blick. »Du hast doch nicht mit ihm getanzt, oder?«

»Nein, ich habe nicht mit ihm getanzt.« Vivian hatte den letzten Sommer bei Faith in Peaceful Harbor verbracht und hatte Sam einige Male im Whispers, einem Nachtclub, in Aktion gesehen. Im Laufe dieses Sommers hatte sie auch seine super-sexy Brüder unter die Lupe genommen – so formulierte sie es selbst, nicht Faith. Faith hatte Vivian von ihren Fantasien über Sam erzählt, war aber mit ihrer Freundin einer Meinung, dass Sam nicht der richtige Mann für sie war.

Faith zog sich Shorts und ein bequemes Shirt an und wich Vivians Blick aus. Sie waren seit Ewigkeiten beste Freundinnen. Sie stammten beide aus Oak Falls in Virginia, waren dort aufgewachsen, und Vivian lebte immer noch dort. Gemeinsam hatten sie aufgeschürfte Knie und Tanzveranstaltungen in der

Schule und gebrochene Herzen durchgestanden, und nachdem Vivians Ex sie hintergangen hatte und JJ in seine Fußstapfen getreten war, waren sie noch näher zusammengerückt. Der feste Vorsatz, sich nie wieder betrügen zu lassen, stärkte ihre Verbindung.

»Gut, denn so nett und großzügig Sam und seine Familie auch sein mögen: Seine persönliche Definition von Großzügigkeit ist sehr individuell. Und das brauchst du nun wirklich nicht, Faith. Es kann nur mit einem gebrochenen Herzen enden.« Vivian nahm Faith bei der Hand und zog sie ins Wohnzimmer. »Lass uns über morgen reden. Dann denkst du nicht die ganze Zeit daran, dass du nicht mit ihm getanzt hast.«

»Ich bin nicht an Sam interessiert. Ich sehe ihn nur gerne an. Und er riecht gut.« *Was ist bloß los mit mir?*

Vivian hob ungläubig eine Braue. »Niemand belässt es beim Ansehen und Schnuppern.« Sie ließ sich auf die Couch sinken und zog Faith zu sich herunter. »Du weißt, dass ich nur das Beste für dich will. Und dieser Mann ist nichts für dich. Männer wie er sind der Grund, weshalb du den WAC gegründet hast.«

»Ich weiß. Mach dir keine Sorgen. Ich bin gegangen, okay? Ich habe nicht mit ihm getanzt. Und außerdem kann ich es nicht fassen, dass du über meine Eisvorräte hergefallen bist. Kannst du mir mal sagen, wie ich jetzt die Lust auf etwas anderes wegschieben soll? Welches Gegenmittel bleibt mir noch, wenn kein Eis mehr da ist?« Faith griff nach dem Ordner mit den Details zu ihrer WAC-Aktion.

»Das Gegenmittel heißt Vibrator, meine Liebe, und den schiebst du nicht *weg*, sondern ...« Vivian wackelte anzüglich mit den Augenbrauen. »Er lebt in deiner Schublade, also kann er dich nicht betrügen. Er hat keine Augen, um anderen Frauen hinterherzusehen, und kann deinem Selbstwertgefühl nicht den Boden unter den Füßen wegziehen. Und das Beste von allem? Du kannst so oft kommen, wie du willst, ohne dir Sorgen machen zu müssen, dass er seine Munition verschießt, bevor du fertig bist.«

Sie hatte recht, aber ... »Vermisst du es nicht, in den Armen eines Mannes zu liegen?«

Vivian verdrehte die Augen. »Als wären diese Typen, mit denen du dich abgibst, echte Männer! Das sind sie nicht. Sie sind eher wie Platzhalter, für den Notfall. Sie sind nichts weiter als ein Vorspiel für richtige Männer.«

»Das ist nicht wahr! Sie sind nett und zuverlässig, und sie würden niemals eine andere Frau ansehen, geschweige denn eine Frau betrügen.« Seit sie nach Peaceful Harbor gezogen war, hatte sie nur ein paar Männer kennengelernt. Und keiner von ihnen hatte auch nur die geringste Ähnlichkeit mit Sam Braden.

»Langweilig.« Vivian warf ihr blondes Haar mit einem Kopfschütteln über die Schulter. »Da halte ich mich lieber an meinen batteriebetriebenen Freund mit drei Geschwindigkeitsstufen.« Sie nahm ihr Handy heraus und grinste. »Lass uns Charley fragen.«

»Halt meine Schwester da raus! Wahrscheinlich seziert sie gerade eine Krabbe oder so etwas.« Sie streckte die Hand nach dem Handy aus, doch Vivian sprang mit dem Telefon am Ohr vom Sofa auf. Charley war fünf Jahre jünger als Faith und studierte Meeresbiologie. In diesem Sommer hatte sie eine Teilzeitstelle bei der Brave Foundation in Harbourside in Massachusetts, wo auch ihr College war, und abends arbeitete sie in einer Bar. Sie ging fast nie aus und hatte definitiv keine Zeit für solche Albernheiten.

»Char! Hey, wie geht's dir?« Vivian grinste Faith an,

während sie lauschte.

Sie bedeckte das Mikrofon mit der Hand und sagte: »Sie seziert keine Krabbe. Sie ist bei einem Lagerfeuer.«

»Wirklich? Schön für sie. Sie braucht mal eine Pause.« Faith öffnete den Ordner und fügte hinzu: »Sag ihr, dass ich sie lieb hab, und erzähl ihr nicht, warum du –«

»Faith hat gesagt, sie hat dich lieb«, sagte Vivian zu Charley. »Und sie will wissen, ob du meinst, dass die Männer, mit denen sie ausgeht, langweilig sind.«

Na prima! Faith und Charley redeten nicht oft über ihre Männergeschichten. Abgesehen von dem Altersunterschied war Charley immer so beschäftigt, dass sie bestenfalls mit halbem Ohr zuhören konnte, wenn Faith das Thema Männer ansprach – im Gegensatz zu Vivian, die ihre Verabredungen stundenlang analysieren konnte.

»Sie sagt, sie sind schlau«, sagte Vivian enttäuscht.

»Danke, Schwesterherz!«, rief Faith.

»Und du sollst nicht zulassen, dass das Arschloch von JJ dich von Leuten fernhält, die keine Krawatte tragen.«

»Werde ich mir merken«, sagte Faith halbherzig, aber ihre Gedanken wanderten sofort wieder zu Sam. Sie hatten nie mehr als ein paar Worte miteinander gesprochen, wenn er Cole in der Praxis besuchte. *Und das war fast jede Woche.* Bis zum heutigen Abend. *Ein Mann wie Sam braucht keine Worte.*

Leider sprach er die universelle Sprache der Lust und die richtete er an jede Frau in seiner Nähe.

Drei

Nach einer unruhigen Nacht, in der Faith jeden Traum – und jeden wachen Augenblick – durchdrungen hatte, lief Sam noch vor dem Morgengrauen seine tägliche Runde und ging dann früh ins Büro von Rough Riders, um sich den Papierstapel vorzunehmen, der sich auf seinem Schreibtisch türmte. Sein Unternehmen wuchs derart rasant, dass er kaum Schritt halten konnte. Wenn Ty zwischen seinen Klettertouren und Fotoaufträgen in der Stadt war, hatte er ihm immer geholfen, und Sam hatte jahrelang keine zusätzlichen Hilfskräfte benötigt. Letztes Jahr hatte er Patrick Fisher angeheuert, den jüngeren Bruder von Nates Verlobter Jewel, und seit diesem Sommer hatte Patrick eine Vollzeitstelle. Vor ein paar Wochen hatte er einen weiteren Mitarbeiter einstellen müssen, um die wachsende Zahl der Kunden und die anfallenden Reparaturen an den Booten bewältigen zu können. Tex Sharpe erwies sich als eine perfekte Ergänzung ihres Teams, aber Sam brauchte außerdem jemanden fürs Büro. Sein Schreibtisch war übersät mit Einverständniserklärungen, Beschreibungen künftiger Abenteuertouren, Rechnungen und dem anderen Kleinkram, der regelmäßig anfiel. Ganz zu schweigen von den Vorbereitungen für das alljährliche Rough-Riders-Barbecue. Er war schon seit Wochen auf der Suche nach einem geeigneten Kandidaten, aber die meisten Bewerbungen taugten nichts, und außerdem gab es viel zu viele andere Dinge, um die er sich kümmern musste.

Er wischte sich mit dem Unterarm über die verschwitzte Stirn und blinzelte in die Sonne. Vermutlich war es fast zwölf. Um zehn hatte er sich mit Tex getroffen, und gemeinsam hatten sie die Boote kontrolliert und gereinigt und die Ausrüstungen sortiert, während sie die Details für das Barbecue besprachen. Patrick hatte sich derweil um die Kunden gekümmert. Sam hatte gehofft, dass die körperliche Arbeit ihm helfen würde, seine Gedanken von Faith abzulenken und ihn vergessen zu lassen, was sie gestern Abend gesagt hatte. *Sind dir schon die Mädels ausgegangen?*

Grinsend schleppte er das Boot, an dem er gerade gearbeitet hatte, in das Bootshaus zurück. Gestern Abend hatte sie hinreißend ausgesehen in diesem eng anliegenden Kleid. Faith war etwas ganz Besonderes, so viel stand fest. Wenn er sie in Coles Praxis sah, war sie immer schrecklich nervös, und dann schleuderte sie ihm das entgegen, als er sie zum Tanz aufforderte? *Sind dir schon die Mädels ausgegangen?* Glaubte sie, dass er alles anmachte, was nicht bei drei auf den Bäumen war?

Dieser Gedanke nervte ihn.

Sein Handy klingelte und er zog es aus der Tasche. »Hey, Ty. Wie geht's?«

»Dasselbe wollte ich dich fragen. Du bist gestern Abend früh verschwunden.«

»Ich wollte heute Morgen zeitig anfangen«, erwiderte er.

Sam tippte Tex auf die tätowierte Schulter und deutete mit dem Daumen über die Schulter auf den Parkplatz.

Tex sah ihn mit seinen ernsten dunklen Augen an und nickte.

Sam ging Richtung Parkplatz und lächelte, als sein Blick auf sein Motorrad fiel. Normalerweise fuhr er seinen Truck, aber heute Morgen hatte ihn eine Rastlosigkeit umgetrieben, für die die Freiheit, die das Motorrad ihm bot, genau das Richtige war.

»Als ob dich das jemals davon abgehalten hätte, dich zu amüsieren«, sagte Ty spöttisch. »Willst du mir sagen, was los ist?«

»Nicht wirklich«, murmelte Sam und nahm seinen Helm vom Motorrad.

»Cole war gestern Abend ziemlich genervt. Ist er dir auf den Geist gegangen?«

Über die Bemerkungen seines Bruders hatte Sam die ganze Nacht gegrübelt. Als würden ihn die Frauen faszinieren, mit denen er schlief. Was war faszinierend an einer Frau, die sich einem Typen an den Hals warf? Verdammt, sie hatten nur ein einziges Ziel. Sie wollten ein bisschen Spaß, genau wie er auch. Sie alle spielten das gleiche Spiel. Unterschiedliche Gesichter, unterschiedliche Namen, die gleiche unverhohlene Anmache. Nicht, dass er sie nicht schätzte. Sex war besser als jede Droge, aber seltsamerweise war es gestern Abend nicht seine bevorzugte Droge gewesen. Bis jetzt war er noch keiner Frau begegnet, die in ihm den Wunsch weckte, sie besser kennenzulernen oder sich um sie zu bemühen.

Als er sich auf das Motorrad setzte, dachte er: *Außer Faith.*

»Hey, Alter, bist du noch dran?«

Tys Stimme zerrte ihn aus seinen Gedanken. »Tut mir leid. Mach dir keine Sorgen um Cole. In den Flitterwochen hat er genug Zeit, die ganze Sache zu vergessen. Vermutlich liegt er in diesem Moment in Treats Resort auf Tahiti am Strand, mit einem Drink in der einen Hand und Leesas Hand in der anderen.« Ihr Cousin Treat Braden besaß Hotelanlagen auf der ganzen Welt und hatte Cole und Leesa großzügigerweise einen Aufenthalt in einem Resort ihrer Wahl angeboten.

»Wahrscheinlich. Was machst du gerade?«, fragte Ty. »Hast du Lust auf eine Kletterpartie oder bist du mit Papierkram beschäftigt?« Er war für ein paar Wochen zu Hause, bevor er sich an seine nächste Bergbesteigung machte, und wie Sam konnte er kaum jemals stillsitzen. Außer Frauen gehörten Wandern, Motorradfahren, Rafting und Klettern zu ihren gemeinsamen Interessen.

»Keine Zeit, tut mir leid. Ich fahre nach Hause, um zu duschen, und heute Nachmittag hab ich schon was vor. Sollen wir uns heute Abend treffen? Im Whispers? Um acht?« Obwohl ihr Bruder Nate das Tap It besaß, eines der beliebtesten Restaurants mit Bar in der Stadt, gingen Sam und Ty gern dorthin, wo es Live-Musik und Horden von weiblichen Singles gab und die Argusaugen der Familie nicht jede ihrer Bewegungen verfolgten.

Eine Stunde später war er frisch geduscht und immer noch verwirrt von seinem ungezügelten Interesse an Faith, doch Sam war wild entschlossen, herauszufinden, was ihn so an ihr faszinierte. Und diesmal würde er sich nicht abwimmeln lassen. Er stieg in seinen Truck und fuhr zum Harbor-Park. Zwei Frauen in Bikinis hielten Schilder hoch, die auf die Autowaschaktion der Women Against Cheaters hinwiesen, und wiesen Sam einen Platz in einer der beiden langen Auto-schlangen zu.

Wie bitte!? Women Against Cheaters?

Er reihte sich hinter einer blauen Limousine ein und suchte das Gelände nach Faith ab. Junge Frauen in knappen Shorts und Bikinioberteilen, einteiligen Badeanzügen oder mit Shorts und Tanktops bekleidet seiften Autos ein und wuschen, schrubbten und spritzten die Fahrzeuge ab. Normalerweise hätte sich Sam zurückgelehnt und ihren Anblick genossen, allerdings war es nicht der Anblick, den er suchte.

Hatte er etwas falsch verstanden, als Faith gesagt hatte, dass sie am Harbor-Park eine Autowaschaktion veranstalten würde? Als er an der Reihe war, blieb eine vollbusige Blondine vor seinem offenen Fenster stehen und lächelte ihn an.

»Danke, dass Sie an unserer Autowaschaktion teilnehmen. Am besten schließen Sie Ihr Fenster, damit Sie nicht nass werden.«

»Danke«, sagte er geistesabwesend und suchte weiter nach Faith. Schließlich entdeckte er sie auf dem Parkplatz. Sie starrte konzentriert auf ihr Handy. Ihre Haare waren zu einem Pferdeschwanz zusammengebunden, und sie trug ein pinkfarbenes Bikinioberteil und weiße Shorts, die jeden Zentimeter von Sams Körper aufweckten. Er stieg aus dem Wagen und fragte sich, was sie so fesselte. Eine Nachricht von einem Freund? Bei dem bloßen Gedanken spannten sich seine Muskeln an.

»Sir? Ihr Fenster?«, erinnerte ihn die Blondine.

Sam nahm sie kaum wahr. Mit einem gedankenverlorenen »Dankeschön« reichte er ihr den Schlüssel und lenkte seine Schritte in Richtung Parkplatz. Und Faith.

Die Autowaschaktion war vielversprechend angelaufen, sie hatten von Anfang an gut zu tun gehabt. Faith war zufrieden mit der Beteiligung. Sie genoss es, endlich einigen der anderen WAC-Mitglieder zu begegnen, nachdem sie sie bisher nur online kennengelernt hatte. Es war schön und zugleich erschreckend, dass schlimme Erfahrungen sie zusammenbrachten. Die Bande, die sie aufgrund ihrer schmerzhaften Vergangenheit geschmiedet hatten, waren intensiv und dauerhaft, und nachdem sie die Frauen nun persönlich getroffen hatte, war ihr Wunsch, ihnen zu helfen, noch stärker.

Sie hatte schon lange nicht mehr so viel Spaß gehabt. Nachdem sie ein paar Bilder in die Gruppe gepostet hatte, freute sie sich darauf, mit den anderen Frauen weiterzuarbeiten. Sie schob gerade ihr Handy in die Tasche, als Lira, eines der Mitglieder aus einer benachbarten Stadt, mit besorgtem Blick auf sie zukam.

»Alles in Ordnung?« Faith wusste aus ihren Online-Diskussionen, dass Lira einen Tiefschlag erlitten hatte, von dem man sich nicht so leicht erholte. Ihr Ehemann, mit dem sie drei Jahre lang verheiratet gewesen war, hatte sie nicht nur betrogen. Er hatte sie ausgerechnet mit ihrer eigenen Schwester hintergangen, die ihnen als Babysitter aushalf. Als Gegenleistung fürs Babysitten hatte Lira ihre Schwester ihr Auto benutzen lassen. Jetzt stand sie ohne Mann und ohne Betreuung für ihr Kind da, und als wäre das nicht schon genug, hatte ihr Ex, kaum dass er aus der gemeinsamen Wohnung ausgezogen war, sämtliche Zahlungen eingestellt. Auch seine achtzehn Monate alte Tochter Emmie hatte er seit Wochen nicht mehr gesehen.

Lira zupfte nervös am fransigen Saum ihrer Shorts herum, die ungefähr so alt aussahen wie ihre hauchdünnen Flip-Flops. Sie hatte glattes dunkles Haar, das ihr immer wieder über die Augen fiel. Sie strich sich eine Strähne hinters Ohr und sagte: »Kann ich dich einen Moment alleine sprechen?«

»Natürlich.« Faith führte sie weiter von den anderen weg. »Stimmt etwas nicht?«

»Ich wollte dich fragen, ob du weißt, an wen ich mich wenden könnte, um eine kostenlose Therapie zu bekommen. Ich laufe meinem Ex ständig über den Weg, und außerdem habe ich kaum genug Geld, um meine Rechnungen zu bezahlen. Das alles wächst mir allmählich über den Kopf. Es geht nicht nur um das, was in der Vergangenheit passiert ist. Meine Schwester ist ein Teil von Emmies Leben, aber ich finde den Gedanken unerträglich, dass meine Tochter denken könnte, was meine Schwester gemacht hat, sei okay. Und ich möchte nicht, dass sie an die falschen Männer gerät, wenn sie älter ist, so wie es bei mir war. Wenn ich mit jemandem reden könnte, der sich mit solchen Sachen auskennt, würde mir das vielleicht helfen, klarer zu sehen.«

»Oh, Lira. Es tut mir leid, dass du so eine schwere Zeit durchmachst, aber Emmie kann sich glücklich schätzen. Du willst den Kreislauf destruktiver Verhaltensweisen durchbrechen, und der Wille ist der erste Schritt, um dieses Ziel zu erreichen.« Sie umarmte Lira und ging in Gedanken die Namen der Therapeuten durch, an die Cole ihre Schmerzpatienten überwies. Leider hatte sie keine Adressen parat, die lagen alle in Peaceful Harbor. »Hast du mal mit deiner Versicherung über eine Therapie oder eine andere Art von Beratung gesprochen?«

Lira wurde rot vor Verlegenheit. »Ich bin nicht versichert. Ich musste meinen Job aufgeben, weil ich dabei so wenig verdient habe, dass ich mir keinen Babysitter leisten konnte. Und in der kleinen Stadt, in der ich lebe, finde ich keine neue Vollzeitstelle. Es ist aussichtslos. Ich habe jetzt einen Teilzeitjob, und der wirft genug ab, um für Emmie eine Krankenversicherung zu bezahlen, aber für mich reicht es nicht.«

Es war eine Sache, die Geschichten der WAC-Mitglieder online mitzubekommen. Lira gegenüberzustehen, die Angst in ihren Augen zu sehen und die Scham in ihrer Stimme zu hören, war jedoch etwas ganz anderes. Faith hatte einen Kloß im Hals – und schwor sich, noch mehr zu tun, um den Frauen zu helfen.

»Hast du es beim Sozialamt versucht?«

Lira schüttelte heftig den Kopf. »Ich traue mich nicht. Mein Ex will zwar anscheinend nichts mit Emmie zu tun haben, aber meine Schwester arbeitet beim Sozialamt, und wer weiß, was sie mit diesen Informationen anfangen würde. Ich weiß, dass sie Emmie liebt, aber ich kann nicht riskieren, dass sie es irgendwie gegen mich verwendet.« Ein gezwungenes Lächeln umspielte Liras Lippen. »Ist schon okay. Ich dachte nur, dass du vielleicht jemanden kennst.«

»Ich werde mit meinem Chef sprechen und ein paar Möglichkeiten checken. Ich bin mir sicher, dass wir eine Lösung finden.« Sie umarmte sie wieder. »Kann ich jetzt noch etwas für dich tun? Wo ist Emmie?«

»Meine Mutter lebt ungefähr eine Stunde von uns entfernt. Sie ist gekommen, um meine Schwester zu besuchen, also passt sie auf sie auf. Es ist nicht ideal, aber es ist ja nur für ein paar Stunden und ich hatte keine andere Wahl.«

»Und dann bist du hier? Statt Zeit mit deiner Mutter zu verbringen? Könnte sie dir finanziell helfen?«

Wieder schüttelte Lira den Kopf. »Wo, glaubst du, hat meine Schwester gelernt, sich wie eine Schlampe aufzuführen? Und wo, glaubst du, habe ich gelernt, mich auf so schreckliche Männer einzulassen? Meine Mutter ist nicht gerade die Stabilste, aber sie und meine Schwester lieben Emmie wie verrückt. Ich weiß, dass sie bei ihnen in guten Händen ist. Und außerdem brauchte ich das alles hier.« Sie warf einen Blick über die Schulter auf die anderen Frauen, die lachten und scherzten, während sie die Autos wuschen. Dann sagte sie zu Faith: »Die Mädels in der Gruppe sind so wichtig für mich. Egal, wann ich mich in einem der Foren anmelde, da ist immer jemand zum Reden, der versteht, was ich durchmache.«

Faiths schwoll das Herz vor Freude, als sie hörte, dass ihre Bemühungen Früchte trugen. Sie hatte es selbst erlebt, wie die Mitglieder des WAC sie nach ihrer Trennung von JJ über manche Nacht voller Verzweiflung hinweggerettet hatten. Dass Lira es aussprach, machte es jedoch noch realer.

»Ich bin froh, dass du gekommen bist, und ich werde versuchen, dir eine Überweisung für einen Therapeuten zu verschaffen. Du machst dich gleich nach der Autowaschaktion auf den Heimweg, oder? Du gehst heute Abend nicht mit uns weg?«

»Ich kann nicht. Ich muss zurück zu Emmie. Eigentlich kann ich mir das Benzingeld für die Fahrt gar nicht leisten. Danke, Faith. Ich sage es wirklich nicht gern, aber ich bin froh, dass dein Freund dich betrogen hat, denn sonst hättest du den WAC nicht gegründet.«

Während Lira sich in Richtung Damentoilette verabschiedete, überlegte Faith, wie viele der anderen Mitglieder davon profitieren würden, wenn ein Fachmann als Anlaufstelle zur Verfügung stünde, den sie sich tatsächlich leisten könnten. Allmählich nahm eine Idee in ihrem Kopf Gestalt an, und sie wandte sich mit neuer Entschlossenheit wieder der Autowaschaktion zu. Wenn Faith eine Idee ausbrütete, war sie wie ein Hund mit einem Knochen, und wenn es darum ging, anderen zu helfen, war sie noch entschlossener.

Mit schwungvollem Schritt steuerte sie auf den Truck zu, der sich gerade in die Reihe gestellt hatte – und blieb wie angewurzelt stehen, als sie Sam sah, der an der Beifahrertür lehnte.

Er lächelte, und Emotionen breiteten sich Zentimeter für Zentimeter über seine Gesichtszüge aus, bis sie seine Augen erreichten und zu Glut verschmolzen. Faiths Puls raste, ihre Gedanken wirbelten durcheinander. Warum war er hier? Und warum sah er sie an, als sei sie eine *seiner* Frauen, eine der *Auserwählten*? Sie schluckte mühsam und versuchte, seinen Körper nicht mit Blicken zu verschlingen. Es war aussichtslos. In seinen verblichenen dunklen Jeans und dem eng anliegenden schwarzen Tanktop, unter dem sich jeder verdammte Muskel in seiner massigen Brust abzeichnete, war er eine Augenweide. Sie versuchte, ihn nicht anzustarren, aber seine Arme … Sie stellte sich vor, dass eine Frau genau spürte, wo sein Körper endete und ihrer begann, wenn sie in diesen Armen lag. Solche Arme vermittelten ein Gefühl von Sicherheit und Zugehörigkeit und sorgten dafür, dass sich eine Frau von Kopf bis Fuß warm und gut fühlte. Und solche Arme waren stark, stark genug, um sie zu packen und dann entschlossen und heftig ganz tief in sie –

Was zur Hölle mache ich da? Offensichtlich war es schon viel zu lange her, dass sie dieses spezielle Bedürfnis befriedigt hatte, wenn sie auf diese Weise an Sam dachte.

Sie stakste über den Parkplatz, ein wenig genervt, weil er ihre Autowaschaktion als Treffpunkt nutzte. »Sam? Was machst du hier?« Einige der Frauen sahen interessiert zu. Sie warf einen Blick auf seinen Truck. Hilary saß auf dem Fahrersitz.

»Das hier ist eine Women-Against-Cheaters-Aktion, stimmt's?« Seine aufreizend üppigen Lippen verzogen sich zu einem teuflischen Grinsen. »Kannst du dir einen besseren Ort vorstellen, um knackige Frauen kennenzulernen? Jeder weiß doch, dass eine verschmähte Frau im Bett etwas beweisen muss.«

»Du lieber Himmel! Du bist –«

Er lachte. »Ich mach doch nur Spaß, Faith. Sei nicht so verkniffen.« Er hielt gerade lange genug inne, dass sie sich fragte, ob sie tatsächlich zu verspannt war. »Die logische Antwort auf deine Frage wäre: Um meinen Wagen waschen zu lassen.« Er trat näher – und sie machte unwillkürlich einen Schritt zurück.

»Du bist wahrscheinlich der Grund, warum die Hälfte der Frauen in dieser Stadt der Gruppe beigetreten ist.«

Verwirrt sah er sie an. »Wovon redest du? Seitensprünge sind nicht meine Art.«

»Ha! Und die Erde ist eine Scheibe. Ich muss arbeiten.« Sie wollte an ihm vorbeifegen, doch er packte sie am Arm und drehte sie unerbittlich zu sich.

»Faith, ich betrüge Frauen nicht. Lieber Himmel, denkst du so von mir?«

Sie blickte auf seine Hand und wünschte, der Stromschlag, der sie durchfuhr, würde sich nicht so gut anfühlen. »Ach, komm schon, Sam. Du brauchst es nicht zu leugnen. Es ist ja nicht so, als würde ich dich verurteilen.« Sie entwand sich seinem Griff und vermisste seine Berührung sofort. Sie hasste es, ihm diese Dinge zu sagen. Sie dachte nicht gerne an Sam, weil sie nicht an ihn denken *sollte*. Aber er war immer da und der Gedanke an ihn hielt sich hartnäckig in ihrem Hinterkopf. Der süße Kerl, der in der Praxis mit ihr flirtete, der sexy Tänzer, den sie bei seinen abendlichen Streifzügen durch die Stadt gesehen hatte, und der Mann, der sie gestern Abend gebeten hatte, mit ihm zu tanzen.

Die Sorte Mann, die mich verletzen würde, wenn ich es zuließe.

Sein ernster Blick haute sie fast um. »Ich betrüge *nicht*. Ich würde niemals eine Frau absichtlich verletzen, Faith. So bin ich nicht. Wie könnte ich überhaupt? Ich habe seit der Highschool keine Freundin mehr gehabt.«

Sein Zorn überraschte sie, aber es waren der Schmerz und die Verwirrung in seinen Augen, die dafür sorgten, dass sich ihr Magen verknotete. Glaubte er wirklich, dass es einen Unterschied machte, ob er in einer festen Beziehung fremdging oder ob er reihenweise Frauen flachlegte? Wusste er nicht, dass sich die Frauen, mit denen er geschlafen hatte, wahrscheinlich mehr erhofft hatten? Oder war das alles nur eine Fassade, die er da aufbaute? Ein Spiel, das er spielte?

Ach, was soll's. Natürlich war es eines seiner Spielchen, und dafür hatte sie keine Zeit.

»Tut mir leid. Ich hätte das nicht sagen sollen. Jetzt muss ich mich wieder an die Arbeit machen, sonst geraten wir in Verzug.« Sie zwang sich, wegzugehen, und hoffte inständig, dass sich ihr heftig pochendes Herz bald beruhigen würde.

Im nächsten Atemzug war er neben ihr, streifte sein Hemd ab und stopfte es in die Gesäßtasche seiner Jeans. Faith wurde fast schwindelig beim Anblick seines muskelbepackten Oberkörpers.

»Was …?« Sie schluckte hastig, bevor sie tatsächlich anfing zu sabbern. »Was hast du vor?«

»Helfen.« Er tauchte eine Hand in einen Eimer und holte einen triefenden Schwamm heraus. Mit der anderen Hand schob er seine Sonnenbrille vom Kopf auf die Nasenwurzel und sah Faith an, sodass sich ihr Gesicht in den Gläsern spiegelte. Sie fühlte sich wie hypnotisiert.

Na wunderbar. Sie brauchte diese Brille, verdammt.

»Du gehörst nicht zur Gruppe«, sagte sie. Wenn er meinte, dass er ihre Aktion nutzen konnte, um eine Frau abzuschleppen, war er schief gewickelt.

»Nein, aber du gehörst dazu, und ich möchte in deiner Nähe sein.« Er zuckte mit den Schultern und begann, seinen Wagen einzuseifen.

Ihr Herz setzte einen Schlag aus. *Du dummes, dummes Herz.* Das war Sam, der Schmeichler, wie er leibte und lebte. Für ihn war sie nichts als eine weitere Eroberung. Dass eine Frau nicht auf ihn hereinfiel und ihn zurückwies, war er nicht gewohnt. Ihr Verstand durchschaute ihn sofort und wusste, warum er so tat, als sei er unwiderstehlich von ihr angezogen. In ihrem Innersten kam sie jedoch nicht dagegen an, dass sie sich warm und gut fühlte, weil der Held ihrer nächtlichen Fantasien sie begehrte.

»Oh, ein Helfer, und noch dazu ein so ansehnlicher! Hallo, ich bin Brittany.« Brittany winkte, doch er beachtete sie kaum.

»Nett, dich kennenzulernen, Brittany«, sagte er, ohne den Blick von Faith zu wenden. »Ich dachte, ich könnte Faith ein bisschen unter die Arme greifen.«

»Hat die ein Glück!«, sagte Brittany und sah vielsagend zu Faith herüber.

Seite an Seite mit ihm zu arbeiten war vollkommen unmöglich, solange er halb nackt war und seine prachtvollen Muskeln spielen ließ. Es juckte Faith in den Fingern, seine Brustmuskeln zu berühren. Sie waren einfach zu schön. Am Bauch zeigte sich dieses verführerische V, das geradewegs in Richtung Gefahrenzone wies. *Genusszone?* Das waren die Muskeln, die keine Bezeichnung brauchten außer *Muskeln, die einer Frau den Verstand rauben.*

Alles an Sam raubte ihr den Verstand, von seinem Lächeln, das sagte: *Ich bin ein richtig netter Typ*, über seine Augen, die sagten: *Ich möchte dich unter mir spüren*, bis hin zu dem Grübchen direkt links neben seinen Lippen, von dem sie wünschte, sie hätte es nicht bemerkt.

Sie musste weg hier, und sei es nur, um genug Sauerstoff in ihr Gehirn zu bekommen, damit sie wieder wie ein normaler Mensch funktionierte.

»Dann helfe ich dem anderen Team.« Faith ging zu der zweiten Reihe von Autos und spürte, wie Sams nachdenklicher Blick jedem ihrer Schritte folgte.

Sie versuchte, ihn gar nicht zu beachten, aber das Gelächter von Sam und den Frauen war kaum zu überhören, während sie ein Auto nach dem anderen wuschen.

»Was macht er hier?« Vivian kniff die Augen zusammen.

»Er hat gesagt, er will helfen.« Sie wusste nicht, warum sie ihrer Freundin verschwieg, dass er *ihr* helfen wollte, doch es war, als wollte sie diese Worte einfach nicht hergeben.

»Okay. Er ist ein netter Kerl, aber lass nicht zu, dass er dich in seinen Bann zieht, Faith.«

»Also bitte. Für wie dumm hältst du mich?«

»Hm, du siehst ihn gern an und er riecht gut. Und mein Vibrator kommt überhaupt nicht zum Zug«, sagte Vivian ironisch. Sie packte Faith bei den Schultern und starrte sie so fordernd an, wie es sich nur eine beste Freundin erlauben durfte. »Glaub mir. Mit Ansehen und Schnuppern fängt es an, aber bis zum Berühren und Küssen ist es nicht weit. Und dann ist er tief in dir vergraben und du rufst laut seinen Namen.«

Sie spürte, wie ihre Wangen bei dem Gedanken brannten.

»Und dann …« Vivian senkte die Stimme. »Und dann duftet er irgendwann nach dem Parfum einer Anderen und hat immer weniger Interesse an Sex mit dir. Der Mann, der dir einst das Herz gestohlen hat, langweilt sich. Und derweil hast du dich verliebt, in ihn oder in den Sex mit ihm oder in was auch immer. Das alles nimmt kein gutes Ende.«

In den nächsten Stunden gingen Faith die Worte ihrer Freundin nicht mehr aus dem Kopf. Sich an all die Gründe zu erinnern, warum Vivian recht hatte, war nicht so einfach, wenn sie gleichzeitig mitbekam, wie Sam nicht nur beim Autowaschen half, sondern sich auch ernsthaft mit den Frauen unterhielt. Seit einer Stunde redete er mit Lira, während sie beide einen Wagen nach dem anderen einseiften, abspülten und polierten. Was konnte er schon mit einer dieser Frauen gemeinsam haben?

Kriege ich hier irgendwas nicht mit?

Es war ihr peinlich, aber sie hatte, nachdem sie ein paar Bilder auf Facebook hochgeladen hatte, nach Sams Facebook-Account gesucht. Er hatte kein eigenes Profil, nur eine Fanseite für Rough Riders, die kaum etwas über ihn preisgab. Sie wusste nicht, warum, aber sie hatte angenommen, dass er in den sozialen Medien allgegenwärtig sein würde.

Hilary tauchte plötzlich neben ihr auf. »Sam ist schon den ganzen Tag hier.«

Für jemanden, der nur auf der Suche nach einer Gefährtin für ein Schäferstündchen war, zeigte er sich seltsam einsatzbereit. Und für jemanden, der als Einziger in Peaceful Harbor Raftingtouren anbot, opferte er verdammt viel Zeit für diese Autowaschaktion, vor allem, da in ein paar Wochen das Rough-Riders-Barbecue stattfinden sollte. Jeder in der Stadt sprach davon. Hatte er nicht schon genug damit zu tun, seine Firma zu leiten oder sein eigenes Event zu organisieren?

»Sexy Typen bedeuten normalerweise nichts Gutes, aber er ist wirklich total süß«, sagte Hilary und starrte zu Sam hinüber.

»Kann sein. Wenn man auf solche Typen steht.« *Du weißt*

schon: vollgepackt mit Muskeln, Schlafzimmerblick und wahrscheinlich mit einem gigantischen Schwanz, der dir einen Orgasmus nach dem anderen beschert.

»Hm?« Hilary lachte. »Meinst du die Typen, die einen zum Lachen bringen und mithelfen? Oder meinst du die Typen, die so knackig gebaut sind, dass einem blinden Mädchen die Tränen kommen würden?«

Heimlich beäugte sie Sam, der gerade neben einem Auto kauerte und die Stoßstange schrubbte. Bei jeder Bewegung wölbten sich seine Rückenmuskeln und seine sonnengebräunte Haut schimmerte in der Nachmittagssonne. Er wandte sich in ihre Richtung, und sie konnte seinen Blick tatsächlich fühlen, bevor er seine Brille hochschob. Er lächelte und hob das Kinn, als wollte er sagen: *Hey, Baby* – das war natürlich *ihre* harmlose Fantasie, die sich da zu Wort meldete. Hitze durchströmte ihren Körper, aber es waren die Schmetterlinge in ihrem Bauch, die sie innehalten ließen.

»Beides, nehme ich an«, sagte sie leise, aber Hilary war schon verschwunden. Faith war allein. Sie starrte Sam an, der ihren Blick erwiderte. Trotz ihrer Bedenken musste sie lächeln, was er mit einem strahlenden Lächeln quittierte.

»Sammy!«, rief eine der Frauen.

Langsam streckte er seinen großen, kräftigen Körper. Seine Bewegungen waren anmutig und ruhig wie die eines Panthers, und selbst als Lira den Schlauch auf seinen Rücken richtete und ihn von Kopf bis Fuß nass spritzte, zuckte er nicht zusammen. Seine Augen waren unbeirrt auf Faith gerichtet, als ein übermütiges Lachen erklang, das Faith mitten ins Herz traf. In diesem Lachen könnte sie sich verlieren.

Sam wandte sich ab, unterbrach den Blickkontakt und jagte die kreischenden Frauen. Er schnappte sich den Schlauch, den

Lira immer noch festhielt. In diesem Moment hätte Faith am liebsten mit Lira getauscht. Oder vielleicht wollte sie nur spüren, wie sich seine großen Hände um sie legten.

Er hatte genug Frauen, die ihm nachliefen. Sie wandte sich ab und fühlte sich ein wenig ... tja, wie fühlte sie sich? Enttäuscht? Eifersüchtig?

Ein kalter Wasserstrahl traf sie und sie schrie auf. Sams Lachen folgte ihr, als sie wie wild auf Zehenspitzen umherhüpfte, in dem verzweifelten Versuch, dem Wasserstrahl zu entgehen. Es war hoffnungslos und schon bald war sie pitschnass.

Sie war Sam nicht gewachsen. Er war zu schnell, zu zielsicher.

Für den Bruchteil einer Sekunde wurde sie schwach und fragte sich, ob sie ihm wohl jemals gewachsen sein würde.

Nach der Autowaschaktion blieb Sam noch da, half beim Aufräumen und hoffte, ein paar Minuten mit Faith allein zu ergattern. Er hatte sie den ganzen Nachmittag lang beobachtet. Sie zeigte eine unglaubliche Mischung aus Entschlossenheit und Konzentration, wenn sie mit Kunden zu tun hatte, Fotos machte und sie auf Facebook und Twitter und Gott weiß wo sonst noch veröffentlichte und ansonsten Autos wusch und abspritzte wie alle anderen auch.

Nachdem die anderen gegangen waren, wartete er darauf, dass Faith ihr Gespräch mit Vivian beendete, einer scharfzüngigen Blondine, mit der sie besonders eng befreundet zu sein schien. Die Blicke, mit denen Vivian ihn den ganzen Nachmittag über bedacht hatte, waren alles andere als wohlwollend gewesen, und jetzt gerieten die beiden offenbar aneinander. Faiths Gesicht sah abgehärmt aus, ihr ganzer Körper wirkte angespannt. Sam wollte ihr keine Unannehmlichkeiten bereiten, daher zog er sich in seinen Truck zurück. Er nahm sein Scheckheft aus dem Handschuhfach, und als er wieder ausstieg, umarmte Vivian die Freundin gerade, während Faith reglos dastand. Als sich Vivian schließlich verabschiedet hatte, ging Sam über den Parkplatz.

Er hatte Faith heute mindestens ein Dutzend Mal dabei ertappt, wie sie ihn beobachtete, aber jetzt senkte sie wieder den Blick, als er näher kam. Er fragte sich, ob das an ihm lag oder ob Vivian etwas damit zu tun hatte.

»Danke, dass ich heute mithelfen durfte.«

»Soll das ein Witz sein?« Endlich hob sie den Blick und sah ihn mit ihren schönen dunklen Augen an. »Du hättest nicht den ganzen Tag bleiben müssen. Vielen Dank.«

»Hat Spaß gemacht.« Er zog sein Scheckheft aus der Tasche. »Ich würde gerne an die Gruppe spenden.«

»Sam.« Sie schüttelte den Kopf.

»Was ist? Ich habe den ganzen Tag damit verbracht, alle kennenzulernen. Wusstest du, dass Brittany ihren Freund nur eine Stunde, nachdem sie eines Morgens zur Arbeit gegangen war, mit einer anderen Frau im Bett erwischt hat?«

»Ja, aber ich hätte nicht gedacht, dass du es auch weißt.«

»Ich auch nicht.« Das brachte sie zum Lächeln. Wie sehr liebte er das Leuchten, das dieses Lächeln in ihre Augen zauberte. »Diese Frauen haben viel durchgemacht. Sie haben mir erzählt, dass ihr aus dem Erlös der Waschaktion die Gebühren für eure Website und möglicherweise ein Upgrade bezahlen wollt.«

»Ja, das war der Plan.« Ihre Stimme wurde wieder ernst. »Es ist schlimm, wenn ein Mann eine Frau betrügt. Dadurch kommt sie sich klein und unwichtig vor. Als sei alles, was sie vorher mit ihrem Partner hatte, nichts mehr wert.«

»Das klingt, als wüsstest du, wovon du redest.« Hatte ein fieser Kerl sie betrogen? Und ihr das Gefühl gegeben, sie sei klein und unwichtig? Der hässliche Gedanken schnürte ihm den Hals zu. Sam wusste, wie sich das anfühlte. Obwohl er damals erst sechzehn Jahre alt gewesen war, hatte es ihn bis ins Mark getroffen.

»Ich überlege auch, wie ich Therapeuten, Berufsberater und dergleichen ins Boot holen kann, die helfen oder vielleicht eine Erstberatung oder Ähnliches anbieten könnten. Vielleicht können sie uns einen Rabatt geben oder der WAC könnte einen Teil der Kosten übernehmen. Aber das sind lauter Zukunftsvisionen.«

Ihr grimmiger Gesichtsausdruck und die Tatsache, dass sie nicht auf seine Bemerkung einging, sie wisse wohl, wovon sie rede, machten ihm klar, dass sie nicht mit ihm darüber sprechen wollte.

»Das ist ein großes und wichtiges Unterfangen.« Er öffnete sein Scheckbuch und begann, einen Scheck auszustellen.

»Sam, bitte nicht.«

Ihr schneidender Tonfall überraschte ihn. Er schob seine Sonnenbrille hoch und versuchte, ihren Gesichtsausdruck zu deuten. Entschlossenheit? Frustration? Er war sich nicht sicher, aber es war definitiv nicht das Ich-will-dich, das er sich erhofft hatte, als er sich auf den Weg zum Harbor-Park machte.

»Das ist wichtig für mich, Sam, es ist kein Spiel. Ich möchte diesen Frauen helfen, während du sie nur erobern willst. Ich habe hart daran gearbeitet, diese Gruppe aufzubauen, und will nicht, dass du sie nutzt, um Bettgenossinnen aufzureißen.«

Ihre Worte trafen ihn hart. »Du hast wirklich keine gute Meinung von mir, nicht wahr?« Er schüttelte den Kopf und überlegte, was er als Nächstes sagen sollte. »Faith, ich bin nicht der, für den du mich hältst.«

»Dann hast du also nicht fast jede Frau in der Stadt herumgekriegt? Oder hast manchmal gleich mit zweien gleichzeitig geschlafen? Diese Gerüchte scheinen mir nämlich ziemlich stimmig zu sein.«

Zum ersten Mal, seit Sam sich erinnern konnte, brachte er es nicht fertig, es mit einem Lachen abzutun, als er mit seinem Ruf konfrontiert wurde. Er zuckte innerlich zusammen. Nicht, weil er sich für seine Taten schämte, sondern weil es ihm aus irgendeinem Grund wichtig war, was Faith von ihm dachte.

»Faith.« Er wusste nicht, was er sagen sollte, stattdessen nahm er sie am Ellbogen und führte sie zu seinem Truck.

»Was machst du?«

»Ich möchte dir etwas zeigen.« Er holte sein Handy aus dem Handschuhfach und reichte es Faith.

Verwirrt runzelte sie die Stirn.

»Sieh es dir an. Es ist nicht passwortgeschützt.«

»Sam ...« Sie hielt ihm das Telefon entgegen und er schob es sanft zu ihr zurück. Dabei legte er seine Finger über ihre.

»Bitte ...«

»Nein. Sam, ich werde mir nicht ansehen ...«

Er nahm ihr das Handy ab und öffnete die Liste der eingegangenen Anrufe.

»Ich möchte nicht wissen, wer dich anruft. *Mein Gott!*« Sie trat einen Schritt beiseite, doch er packte sie behutsam um die Taille, zog sie zurück und drückte sie fest an seine Brust.

Einen Moment lang war sie wie erstarrt, dann schien sie gegen ihn zu schmelzen. Er war sich nicht sicher, aber es fühlte sich an, als würde sie den Atem anhalten.

»Gib mir zwei Minuten. Das ist alles, worum ich dich bitte.« Dabei wollte er so viel mehr als zwei Minuten. »Dann kannst du davonlaufen.«

»Okay«, hauchte sie atemlos.

Oh ja, sie fuhr auf ihn ab. Sie fühlte sich so warm und verlockend an, dass er einen Moment lang vergaß, was er ihr zeigen wollte.

»Sam!«

»Entschuldigung.« Er scrollte durch die Liste. »Welche Namen siehst du?«

»Ich komme mir vor wie ein Voyeur.«

»Lies einfach die Namen vor.«

»Ty, Shannon, Tex, Tempe ... Sam, was soll das?«

»Das wirst du gleich sehen.« Er rief die Liste seiner Apps auf. »Was siehst du?«

»Sam!« Sie wand sich und versuchte, sich zu befreien.

Er hielt sie nur noch fester. Sie fühlte sich zu verdammt gut an, als dass er sie einfach loslassen wollte.

»Kein Snapchat. Kein Facebook Messenger. Nur ganz normale Sachen.« Er scrollte zum Internet und zeigte ihr den Browserverlauf. »Und keine Pornoseiten, keine ...«

Sie drehte sich in seiner Umklammerung, und ein Stromstoß durchfuhr ihn, als er die Mischung aus Lust und ungläubigem Staunen in ihrer Miene sah. Kurze Zeit war er wie benebelt, und sie nutzte die Gunst des Augenblicks, sich aus seinen Armen zu befreien. Er unterdrückte den Drang, sie wieder an sich zu ziehen.

»Und was soll ich damit anfangen?« Die Entschlossenheit war in ihre Stimme zurückgekehrt. »Es ändert nichts an dem, was du bist oder was du tust.«

Sie hatte recht und diese Erkenntnis traf ihn wie ein Stoß in die Magengrube. Sie war nicht irgendeine Frau, die er aufreißen wollte. Sie war klug und respektierte sich selbst genug, um Abstand von Männern wie ihm zu halten. Dieses Selbstvertrauen, diese Überzeugung, dass sie mehr verdient hatte, machte sie noch faszinierender.

»Ich möchte nur, dass du siehst, dass ich kein Schwein bin, das Booty-Call-Nummern auf dem Handy speichert oder

Nacktaufnahmen oder ähnlichen Mist auf Snapchat teilt. Ich bin, wer ich bin. Ich baue keine Fassade auf. Ich verstecke nichts vor dir, Faith, und ich versuche auch gar nicht zu leugnen, dass ich kreuz und quer durch die Betten gewandert bin.«

»Und was willst du mir damit sagen?« Sie verschränkte die Arme wie eine Barriere zwischen ihnen.

Er erinnerte sich an Coles Worte und wusste, dass sein Bruder recht hatte. Faith konnte es nicht brauchen, dass er ihr Leben vermasselte. Und der Ausdruck in ihren Augen, alles, was sie sagte, jedes Signal, das sie aussandte, zeigte ihm, dass sie diese Überzeugung teilte. Aber eine Stimme in seinem Kopf mahnte ihn, nicht aufzugeben. Faith hatte ihn fasziniert, seit er ihr das erste Mal begegnet war. Er hatte sie jedoch in der Kategorie »zu süß für Sam« einsortiert. Nun allerdings verspürte er das Bedürfnis, die Grenzen dieser Kategorie zu durchbrechen.

Vielleicht lag Cole wirklich richtig mit seiner Einschätzung. Er wollte das, was er nicht haben konnte. Wie zum Teufel sollte er wissen, warum er Faith plötzlich in die Arme nehmen und die Sorge von ihrem wunderschönen Gesicht küssen wollte? Er wollte die Süße schmecken, der er versucht hatte zu widerstehen, und ihr beweisen, dass er nicht der war, für den sie ihn hielt.

Aber so vieles von dem, was sie gesagt hatte, stimmte. Wie sollte er sie dazu bringen, es mit ihm zu versuchen? Mist, so hatte er sich den heutigen Tag nicht vorgestellt.

»Ich denke, ich will dir sagen, dass du vielleicht eine wundervolle Geschichte verpasst, wenn du ein Buch allein nach seinem Einband beurteilst.« Er warf ihr einen letzten Blick zu, bevor er hinzufügte: »Danke, dass ich an etwas so Wichtigem teilnehmen durfte. Es war mir eine Ehre, die Frauen kennenzulernen. Ich wünsche ihnen alles Gute.«

»Er hat nicht einmal versucht, die Tatsache zu vertuschen, dass er mit so vielen Frauen geschlafen hat.« Faith zwängte sich in ihre Jeans und streifte ein seidiges Top über, während Vivian in ihrer Schmuckschatulle nach Ohrringen suchte.

»Ich weiß nicht, was du von ihm erwartet hast, aber ich muss sagen, ich bin überrascht. Wie viele Männer würden den ganzen Tag dableiben *und* dir ihr Handy zeigen?« Ihre Augen weiteten sich, als sie Faith die Ohrgehänge reichte. »Ach du liebes bisschen. Das war wahrscheinlich sein Wegwerfhandy.«

»Was ist denn ein Wegwerfhandy?« In einer halben Stunde waren sie mit einigen Frauen aus der Gruppe zu einem Drink verabredet.

»Weißt du nicht, was ein Wegwerfhandy ist? So etwas benutzen Drogendealer, damit die Polizei sie nicht aufspüren kann.«

»Vivian, Sam ist doch kein Drogendealer.« Sie betrachtete sich im Spiegel. »Sehe ich sexy aus?« Sam hatte gesagt, sie sei verkniffen, und sie wollte ihm auch in diesem Punkt das Gegenteil beweisen. Sie war total entspannt. Auf eine sehr kontrollierte Art und Weise.

»Oh nein. So gehst du heute Abend nicht weg.« Vivian zog Faith das Top über den Kopf und warf es aufs Bett. »Was hat unser notorischer Schürzenjäger über unsere Gruppe gesagt?«

Faith sah ihre Freundin mit ausdrucksloser Miene an. Sie fand es nicht richtig, Sam einen *Schürzenjäger* zu nennen, nachdem er sich solche Mühe gegeben hatte, sie vom Gegenteil zu überzeugen. Andererseits ließen sich seine zahllosen Frauenbekanntschaften nicht leugnen.

»Er meinte, betrogene Frauen seien die besten im Bett, weil sie etwas beweisen müssten. Aber das war nur ein Scherz.« Nachdem Sam sich verabschiedet hatte, hatte sie eine halbe Stunde gebraucht, um die Fassung wiederzuerlangen. Als er sie an seine Brust gedrückt hatte, hatte er sich einfach himmlisch angefühlt. Sein kräftiger Arm hatte ihre Taille umfangen und sie in der Wärme seines Körpers gefangen gehalten. Und dann diese Muskeln! Fast war sie bereit gewesen zu glauben, dass all diese Gerüchte über ihn nicht stimmten. Doch dann waren diese wohlwollenden Gedanken zerplatzt wie eine Seifenblase, als er zugab, dass sie der Wahrheit entsprachen.

»Da hat er aber unrecht. Wir waren die Besten im Bett, noch bevor wir etwas beweisen mussten. Da siehst du, dass er keine Ahnung hat.« Vivian zog Faith ins Gästezimmer.

»Es war nur ein Witz. He, was soll das? Ich bin noch nicht fertig mit Anziehen.«

»Ich gebe dir was von mir. Heute Abend werden wir die Männer in dieser Bar aufmischen und sie dann richtig schön hängen lassen. Und dafür können sie sich bei Sam Braden und seinen dummen Kommentaren bedanken.« Vivian nahm einen schwarzen Lederminirock aus dem Schrank und warf ihn Faith zu. »Zieh den an.«

»Wie bitte? Da passt nicht einmal mein linkes Bein rein, geschweige denn mein ganzer Hintern.«

»Anziehen. Sofort.«

Während Faith den Minirock überstreifte, durchwühlte Vivian ihren Koffer.

»Perfekt.« Sie hielt ein cremefarbenes, leicht durchsichtiges Baumwolltop hoch. »Das ist Rock Chic. Mit dem U-Boot-Ausschnitt zeigst du genug Haut, um heiß auszusehen, aber nicht nuttig. Mit dem Lederrock und den Plateausandalen siehst du aus, als würdest du ständig so rumlaufen.«

Faith zog das locker geschnittene Top über den Kopf und sofort rutschte es ihr von der Schulter. Sie streifte ihre Hochhackigen ab und betrachtete sich im Spiegel.

»Super! Ich fühle mich richtig gut darin. *Sexy.* Kein Wunder, dass du solche Sachen anziehst. Dieses Outfit ist wie eine Vitaminspritze fürs Selbstvertrauen.«

»Willst du mal richtig auf sexy machen?«

Faith sah an sich herab. Mit diesen Klamotten entfernte sie sich ein wenig aus ihrer Komfortzone, aber nicht so weit, dass sie sich nicht wohlfühlte. Wenn Vivian nicht dabei wäre, hätte sie das Top wahrscheinlich zur Jeans getragen, aber der Rock gab ihrem Selbstbewusstsein einen richtigen Schub, das konnte sie nicht leugnen.

»Noch sexyer? Soll ich das Rockbündchen umschlagen, damit man meinen Hintern vorblitzen sieht?«

»Ach was, setz einfach deine schwarz gerahmte Brille auf. Damit siehst du sowieso schon heiß aus und dann noch dieses Outfit? Wie ein kluges Sexkätzchen.«

»*Will* ich überhaupt wie ein kluges Sexkätzchen aussehen?« Sie biss sich auf die Unterlippe und dachte darüber nach, wie sie wirken wollte. Die Brille hatte sie noch nicht einmal auf Rezept bekommen, sie hatten sie letzten Sommer nur zum Spaß gekauft.

»Ja, dann kannst du dich von einem Club voller Typen anstarren lassen und Sam vergessen.« Vivian plusterte Faiths dunkles Haar auf. »Du könntest dir einen Müllsack überziehen und würdest immer noch sexy aussehen. Du bist wunderschön. Dieses Outfit betont das einfach nur. Und deine Brille gibt dir das gewisse Extra, das wir normalen Frauen nicht haben.«

Faith lachte. »Normal? Du siehst Julianne Hough zum

Verwechseln ähnlich. Gegen dich bin ich gar nichts.«

»Du hast eine Brille, die ›Finger weg‹ signalisiert, und einen Körper, der mit ›Nimm mich‹ lockt. Außerdem bist du klüger und hast einen besseren Job.« Vivian arbeitete in einem Bekleidungsgeschäft in Oak Falls.

»Du hättest dir auch so eine Brille kaufen können«, erinnerte Faith ihre Freundin. »Du liebst deinen Job genau wie ich, und ich bin nicht schlauer. Ich habe nur länger die Schulbank gedrückt als du. Gehen wir also davon aus, dass wir beide sexy sind, auch wenn du *heißer* aussiehst.« Dieses Spiel, bei dem sie sich gegenseitig Komplimente machten, spielten sie die ganze Zeit. *Wie alle Frauen*, dachte Faith. »Aber das ist alles nicht wichtig. Was zählt, ist, dass du und ich ein tolles Team sind, und dank unserer hervorragenden Planungsfähigkeiten hatten heute alle viel Spaß.«

Vivian folgte ihr ins Badezimmer, wo sich Faith schminkte und ihre sexy Bibliothekarinnenbrille aufsetzte. Sie hatte sie im letzten Sommer nur zweimal getragen, aber Vivian hatte recht – in Kombination mit dem Outfit hatte sie was.

Vivian stellte sich neben sie an den Spiegel und begann, sich die Wimpern zu tuschen.

»Lira hat gefragt, ob ich jemanden wüsste, der eine kostenlose Therapie anbietet. Ich überlege, ob wir die Angebote des WAC erweitern könnten.«

Vivian sah sie über ihre Wimpernbürste hinweg an. »Du kannst keinen Therapeuten anheuern, falls es das ist, was du meinst. Das kostet viel Geld. Und so viel Geld hast du nicht. Es ist ein *kostenloses* Forum, das weißt du doch.«

»Nein, jemanden anstellen geht nicht. Aber vielleicht könnten wir uns mit anderen Gruppen zusammentun, die Frauen helfen, und Therapeuten finden, die eine kostenlose

Telefonberatung anbieten. Dann wäre es eventuell möglich, Rabatte oder Gruppentarife einzurichten.« Auf jeden Gedanken folgte eine ganze Lawine weiterer Ideen. »Oder vielleicht finden wir einen Therapeuten, der bereit ist, Skype-Sitzungen abzuhalten, einzeln oder in der Gruppe.«

»Meinst du das ernst?«

»Ich glaube schon. Schließlich kann sich nicht jeder solche Hilfe leisten. Die arme Lira hatte schon Mühe, das Benzingeld für die Autofahrt zusammenzukratzen, um an unserer Aktion teilnehmen zu können, und sie ist nicht einmal krankenversichert. Ich würde ihr wirklich gerne helfen, einen Job zu finden.«

»Gehst du da nicht ein bisschen weit?« Vivian legte ihre Schminksachen beiseite und sagte: »Wie soll das gehen? Sie lebt in einer anderen Stadt.«

Faith konnte ihre Aufregung nur mühsam unterdrücken. Die Aussicht, das Forum um weitere Hilfsangebote zu erweitern, machte sie ganz zappelig. »Aber wir müssen einfach versuchen zu helfen. Überleg doch mal, wie viele andere Forumsmitglieder in einer ähnlichen oder noch schlimmeren Situation sind. Ich meine ja nicht, dass wir eine riesige Organisation oder so etwas aufbauen sollten, aber vielleicht können wir auf der Website Jobangebote in den einzelnen Bundesstaaten veröffentlichen. Ich habe das noch nicht alles genau durchdacht, aber ich glaube, ich bin da auf der richtigen Spur.«

Vivian zerrte sie aus dem Badezimmer und griff sich ihre Handtaschen vom Tisch. »Du hast diesen ›Ich mache das sowieso, egal, was Vivian dazu sagt‹-Blick in den Augen. Reden wir unterwegs weiter darüber.«

Ein Abend mit den Frauen und ihrem neuen Projekt war vielleicht genau das Richtige, um sich Sam aus dem Kopf zu schlagen.

Im Whispers war es laut und voll, so wie Sam es mochte. Das war genau das, was er brauchte, um sich Faith aus dem Kopf zu schlagen. Es gefiel ihm gar nicht, wie sie nach der Autowaschaktion auseinandergegangen waren. Nachdem er online eine Spende an die Gruppe überwiesen hatte – weil er den Frauen, die er im Harbor-Park kennengelernt hatte, ebenso helfen wollte wie Faith –, hatte er den größten Teil des Abends damit verbracht, sich einzureden, dass er aufgeben sollte. Faith brauchte ihn in ihrem Leben nicht.

Es war Stunden her und seine Gedanken kreisten immer noch um sie. Das Gefühl ihrer glatten Haut verharrte auf seiner Handfläche, als hätte sie ihn gebrandmarkt.

Sam versuchte, sich auf die Band zu konzentrieren, die am anderen Ende der Tanzfläche spielte. Kaum hatten er und Ty das Whispers betreten, wurden sie auch schon von einer Gruppe von Freunden umringt. Nun saßen sie dicht gedrängt in einer Tischnische. Sam war eingeklemmt zwischen Jennifer, einer vorlauten Brünetten, und Tia, einer ihrer ebenso vorlauten Freundinnen. Er hätte wer weiß was für einen Drink gegeben, aber in der Nische war kaum Platz für alle, und außerdem waren seine Arme rechts und links auf der Rückenlehne der

Sitzbank ausgestreckt.

»Wie wär's mit einem Tänzchen, Sam?« Jennifer fuhr ihm mit dem Finger über die Brust.

Er war nicht in der Stimmung, mit jemandem zu tanzen, außer mit einer einzigen Frau, und ausgerechnet an die sollte er besser nicht denken. Das machte ihn nervös. Andererseits wäre ein Tanz eine gute Gelegenheit, aus der engen Nische herauszukommen.

Einen Arm um Jennifer geschlungen, drängte sich Sam durch die Menschenmenge zu einer Stelle näher an der Band. Jennifer schlang ihm die Arme um den Hals und nutzte jeden Hüftschwung im Takt der Musik, um seinen Körper wie zufällig zu streifen. Normalerweise wäre Sam auf ihre verführerischen Bewegungen eingestiegen, aber Faith war ihm unter die Haut gegangen. Die Dinge, die sie gesagt hatte, hatten ihn zutiefst getroffen. *Es ändert nichts an dem, was du bist oder was du tust.*

Verdammt. Was war los mit ihm? Sie war nur eine Frau von vielen.

Eine sexy, kluge, ehrgeizige Frau, die wahrscheinlich der Schmerz dazu getrieben hatte, den WAC zu gründen. Der Gedanke, dass ihr jemand wehgetan haben könnte, machte ihm zu schaffen. Faith war nicht wie Jennifer oder Tia oder die anderen Frauen, mit denen er sich umgab. Sie gingen das Risiko ein, ohne dabei irgendwelche Erwartungen zu hegen. Sie boten sich an und hatten dabei nur eine einzige Gegenleistung im Sinn: Sex für Sex. Und keine von ihnen konnte Faith das Wasser reichen.

Faith hatte Klasse. Sie brachte sich selbst Wertschätzung und Respekt entgegen. Sie war eine Frau zum Heiraten. Die anderen waren Frauen fürs Bett. Und genau deshalb hielt sich

Faith von ihm fern. Eine Ehe hatte er noch nie auf dem Radar gehabt. Doch seit er sie bei Coles Hochzeit gesehen hatte, wollte er mit anderen Frauen nichts mehr zu tun haben.

Warum um alles in der Welt schraubte er sich immer weiter in diesen Morast? Er sollte Faith vergessen, statt sie immer mehr zu begehren.

Er schlang seine Arme um Jennifers sexy Körper und versuchte, sich in ihr zu verlieren. Sie war warm, weich und schön kurvig. Aber ihr Parfüm war ihm zu aufdringlich und sie war ziemlich groß, mindestens eins siebenundsiebzig. Normalerweise störte ihn das nicht, im Gegenteil: Es brachte ihre Münder näher zusammen, immer eine heiße Sache. Aber nachdem er Faith im Arm gehalten hatte, so zierlich, so weiblich, so perfekt, fühlte sich alles an Jennifer falsch an.

Jemand stieß ihn von hinten an und er warf einen Blick über die Schulter. Da war die Frau, die seine Gedanken gefangen hielt, in den Armen eines anderen Mannes. Sam spürte, wie sich sein Innerstes zusammenzog. Er hatte kein Recht, irgendwelche Ansprüche zu erheben, aber dass sie da war, dass sie nahe genug war, um sie zu berühren, und dass sie verdammt heiß aussah, reichte aus, und schon wollte er sie ganz für sich haben.

»Entschuldigung.« Faith hob ihre schönen dunklen Augen und schnappte nach Luft. »Sam.«

Selbst ihre Stimme stellte seltsame Dinge mit ihm an. Sie ließ ihn *nachdenken*. Über die Dinge, die sie gesagt hatte, und über das, was er gefühlt hatte, als er sie gehalten hatte. Und sie trug eine Brille mit schwarzem Rand – bei den meisten Frauen ein sicheres Mittel, jeglichen Sexappeal zu zerstören, aber bei Faith? Bei ihr sah sie rebellisch und zugleich unglaublich sexy aus.

»Faith.«

»Ich wollte nicht …«

Jennifer legte ihre Hand auf Sams Wange und zog sein Gesicht zurück zu ihrem.

»Sam, hier bin ich.«

Er war sich der Frau in seinen Armen nur allzu bewusst, als sie ihn zwang, seine Aufmerksamkeit von Faith abzuwenden. Er schaute wieder nach hinten und sah den Hinterkopf des Mannes, mit dem Faith tanzte. Faith spähte um die Schulter des Typen herum und begegnete Sams Blick. Am liebsten hätte er sie abgeklatscht, aber er hatte Jennifer im Arm und Faiths Partner – Ihr Date? Ihr Freund? – drehte sich um und musterte ihn kritisch.

Sam war nicht in der Stimmung, sich mit irgendjemandem anzulegen, weder mit einem dahergelaufenen Idioten noch mit der Frau, die sich so hartnäckig an ihn klammerte. Als das Lied zu Ende war, hörte Jennifer nicht auf, sich an ihm zu reiben, worauf er normalerweise sofort eingestiegen wäre. Aber Faith verschwand in der Menge, und er gab den Versuch auf, sie aus seinen Gedanken zu verbannen, egal, ob sie mit ihrem Freund da war oder nicht.

Er nahm Jennifer bei der Hand und führte sie zum Tisch.

»Ich wollte noch weitertanzen«, maulte sie.

»Tut mir leid, Jen.« Am Tisch fing er Tys Blick auf. »Ty, holst du Jen einen Drink?«

»Klar. Setz dich dort hin, Schätzchen.« Ty wies mit dem Kopf auf die andere Seite der Nische.

»Danke, Bruderherz.« Er trat einen Schritt zurück, überlegte es sich dann anders und zog seine Brieftasche hervor. Er holte ein paar Zwanziger heraus und reichte sie Ty. »Nur für den Fall.«

»Im Ernst? Vergiss das Mittagessen im Mr. B. morgen nicht. Shannon fährt am Mittwoch wieder.« Ihren Eltern gehörte das Mr. B., ein Lokal mit Mikrobrauerei im Jachthafen, und ihre jüngste Schwester, Shannon, war nur für Coles Hochzeit ein paar Tage nach Hause gekommen.

»Ich werde dort sein.«

Sam drängte sich durch die Menge. Mit einer Größe von über eins achtzig war es ihm ein Leichtes, das Meer von Menschen nach Faith abzusuchen, aber die Suche wurde noch einfacher, als ihr liebliches Lachen durch die Luft wehte. Sam folgte dem entzückenden Klang über die Tanzfläche zu einem runden Tisch, an dem Faith mit mehreren Frauen saß, die er bei der Autowaschaktion gesehen hatte. Der Typ, mit dem sie getanzt hatte, war verschwunden. Vielleicht gab es doch einen Gott. Faiths sonnengebräunte Haut schimmerte im gedämpften Licht. Ihr Haar lockte sich verführerisch auf ihren Schultern und dann diese Brille ... In diesem Outfit sah sie aus wie eine faszinierende Mischung aus Playboymodel und Wissenschaftlerin, eine heiße Kombination. Aber es war nicht das Zucken unter seinem Reißverschluss, dessen er sich im Moment am deutlichsten bewusst war. Es war der dringende Wunsch, mit ihr allein zu sein, ihre ungeteilte Aufmerksamkeit zu genießen und wieder mit ihr zu *reden*.

Welchen verdammten Zauber übte sie auf ihn aus?

Er konnte nicht zulassen, dass sie in dieser Kategorie »zu süß für Sam« blieb. Vielleicht sollte er die Finger von ihr lassen, aber nicht, ohne vorher zu beweisen, dass er nicht der war, für den sie ihn hielt.

»Hey, Sam ist hier!« Brittany sprang vom Tisch auf und umarmte ihn.

Er erwiderte die Umarmung und wünschte, es wäre

stattdessen Faith gewesen, die ihn so begeistert in Empfang nahm. »Wie geht's, Britt?«

Faith sah von ihrem Gespräch auf. Die Luft zwischen ihnen knisterte und brannte und die Grenzen der »zu süß«-Kategorie verwischten vollkommen.

Faith umklammerte die Stuhlkante und schärfte sich ein, dass der Sexprotz, der vor ihr stand, nicht der richtige Mann für sie war. Aber dieses Lächeln, dieses Grübchen und diese wilden dunklen Augen waren auf sie gerichtet und sie dachte an ihr Gespräch auf dem Parkplatz und an seine Behauptung, er sei niemand, der Frauen betrüge. Sie hatte ihm all diese unbarmherzigen Sachen an den Kopf geworfen. Wie konnte sie so nur so dreist sein? Er war der Bruder ihres Chefs. Was hatte sie sich bloß dabei gedacht?

Als sie im Whispers angekommen waren, hatte sie sich in ihrem Outfit cool und sexy gefühlt, aber jetzt zupfte sie am Saum ihres kurzen Rocks. Sie war gekleidet wie eine der Frauen, mit denen er sich normalerweise umgab. Würde er sie so sehen? *Möchte ich, dass du mich so siehst?*

Ihr Puls raste bei diesem Gedanken. Er machte sie ganz verrückt.

Vivian beugte sich vor und flüsterte: »Nein. Lass dich von seiner Ausstrahlung nicht täuschen.«

Widerstrebend wandte Faith den Blick ab und schaute auf die Tanzfläche. Sie hatte die Frau gesehen, mit der er getanzt hatte. Groß, mit einer beeindruckenden Oberweite, *hinreißend.* Warum stand er hier an ihrem Tisch und nicht bei ihr?

»Wir haben viel Spaß zusammen«, sagte Brittany.

»Bei unserem Mädelsabend«, setzte Vivian hinzu. »Stimmt's, Faith?«

Faith sah sie böse an, dabei sollte sie ihr dankbar sein, weil sie versuchte, sie in der Spur zu halten. Sie mochte Vivian wirklich sehr, aber sie brauchte keinen Babysitter. Sie konnte auf sich selbst aufpassen, wenn es um Sam ging. *Wahrscheinlich.*

Er ging um den Tisch herum, musterte sie unverhohlen und hielt ihren Blick mit seinen glimmenden dunklen Augen fest. Sie wagte kaum zu atmen und konnte keinen klaren Gedanken fassen. Vielleicht brauchte sie doch einen Babysitter.

Er streckte ihr eine Hand entgegen. Seine schönen, langen, kräftigen Finger lockten sie. »Ich werde dich nicht allzu lange von deinen Freundinnen fernhalten«, sagte er selbstbewusst, als hätte sie gar keine andere Wahl, als mit ihm zu gehen.

Sie starrte auf seine Hand, als sie die ihre bedeckte und einen Stromstoß in jeden einzelnen Finger schickte.

»Willst du mit mir tanzen?«

Stille hallte in ihren Ohren wider. Die Frauen an ihrem Tisch schienen ebenfalls den Atem anzuhalten, als er ihre Hand mit sanfter Bestimmtheit hochhob und sie aufstand. Sie bemühte sich, ihre Gehirnzellen wieder zum Laufen zu bringen – keine leichte Aufgabe, wenn man einem so wunderschönen Wesen gegenüberstand, das sie ansah, als wollte es sie verschlingen. *Ja bitte.*

Er legte ihr besitzergreifend den Arm um die Taille, während er sie mit einem Selbstvertrauen zur Tanzfläche führte, das sie faszinierte. Die Menge teilte sich für sie, und plötzlich waren sie von Paaren umgeben, die sich im langsamen Takt der Musik wiegten. Sams kraftvolle Arme zogen sie an seinen harten Körper. Grundgütiger, sie hatte recht gehabt. In seinen Armen fühlte sie sich weiblich und geborgen.

Er starrte sie aus scheinbar schwindelerregender Höhe an. Seine dunklen Augen glitzerten vor Wärme und Leidenschaft und gaben ihr das Gefühl, den ganzen Tag auf diesen Moment gewartet zu haben. Ein weicher Haarflaum schimmerte auf seiner sonnenbraunen Haut, und ein jungenhaftes und irgendwie auch sinnliches und männliches Lächeln umspielte seine Lippen.

Sie sollte etwas sagen. Irgendetwas. Aber sie konnte sich nicht erklären, wie sie hier in seinen Armen gelandet war. Es war so unglaublich leicht, sich von ihm mitreißen zu lassen. *Nur ein Tanz.*

»Du siehst wundervoll aus.« Seine Stimme war tief und eindringlich wie alles an ihm.

»Danke.« Sie wurde sich bewusst, wie sich seine feste, heiße Taille an ihren Handflächen anfühlte. Wie sich seine Oberschenkel an ihre drückten, wie seine Brustmuskeln ihre Brüste streiften. Ihre Nippel stellten sich auf und sie zog sich ein wenig zurück, aber seine Hand auf ihrem Rücken ließ sie nicht ausweichen.

Ein wissendes Lächeln spielte auf seinem Gesicht. »Nur ein Tanz«, versicherte er, als könnte er ihre Gedanken lesen. »Ich hatte nicht erwartet, dich hier zu sehen.«

»Ja, ich bin nicht oft hier«, antwortete sie wahrheitsgemäß. Sie war schon ein paarmal im Whispers gewesen, aber normalerweise zog sie Clubs vor, bei denen es nicht so offensichtlich um Fleischbeschau ging. Sie hätte sich ausrechnen können, dass Sam hier sein würde. Warum hatte sie nicht daran gedacht, als sie überlegten, wo sie nach der Autowaschaktion hingehen sollten? Wahrscheinlich lag es daran, dass Sam vor einem Monat, als sie den Abend geplant hatten, für sie in die

Kategorie der Unberührbaren gehörte, jemand, an den sie gar nicht erst denken sollte. In dieser Kategorie gab es niemanden außer ihm und er füllte sie mühelos aus. Und machte es Faith damit praktisch unmöglich, *nicht* an diese verdammte Kategorie zu denken.

»Dann habe ich heute Abend ja Glück.«

Der Druck seiner Hände wurde fester, während sie tanzten. Als sie ihren Rhythmus gefunden hatten, glitt eine Hand wie von selbst ihren Rücken hinauf, die andere fand ihren Platz weiter unten. Seine Bewegungen waren anmutig und männlich zugleich, wie Sex in flüssiger Form. Wenn das alles war, was sie sich zugestand, ein Tanz, ein paar Minuten in seinen Armen, wollte sie es genießen. Sie gab sich der Musik hin und saugte das Gefühl in sich auf, ihm ganz nah zu sein. Sie schlang die Arme um seinen Hals und sein Blick wurde noch dunkler. Sein Lächeln bekam etwas Sündiges. Mit geschlossenen Augen lehnte sie die Wange an seine Brust und lauschte dem sicheren und festen Schlag seines Herzens. Dass sie schon feucht war und ein gefährliches Spiel spielte, blendete sie aus. Warum sollte sie wegen weniger Augenblicke ein schlechtes Gewissen haben?

Seine Hand legte sich unter ihrem Haar um ihren Nacken. Ja, oh ja. Das fühlte sich *so* gut an.

Er beugte sich herunter, und sie spürte seinen warmen Atem am Ohr, als er sagte: »Sprich mit mir, Faith.«

Er sagte ihren Namen so, wie er sie ansah, als sei sie wichtig und schön. Und das erweckte die Schmetterlinge in ihrem Bauch zu neuem Leben.

»Ich überlege gerade, wie du es geschafft hast, mich zu diesem Tanz zu überreden.«

»Du willst hier in meinen Armen sein.«

Diese Augen! Denen entging wohl nichts. Und er hatte

verdammt noch mal recht.

»Vielleicht«, gab sie zu, »aber komm jetzt bloß nicht auf dumme Gedanken. Wie du schon sagtest: nur ein Tanz.«

»Warum sträubst du dich so dagegen, Zeit mit mir zu verbringen?« Wenn seine Augenbrauen so schräg standen wie jetzt, wirkte sein Blick todernst.

»Ich werde keine weitere Kerbe an deinem Bettpfosten sein, Sam.«

Sam sah sich mit gespielt unschuldiger Miene in der Bar um. »Siehst du hier irgendwo einen Bettpfosten?«

Faith musste unwillkürlich lächeln. »Du weißt schon, was ich meine.«

»Vergiss den Bettpfosten. Aber es gibt keinen Grund, warum wir nicht tanzen, reden oder Zeit miteinander verbringen können.«

Warum klang es alles so einfach, wenn er es sagte? Wusste er nicht, dass allein dieser Tanz mit ihm sie zum Schmelzen brachte und sie sich dafür ein bisschen hasste?

»Sam.«

Er legte die Hände um ihren Hinterkopf. Wow, das fühlte sich unglaublich an.

»Faith.«

Da schmolz sie weiter dahin. Und um ihren Slip war es endgültig geschehen.

Nein. Sie wollte sich nicht in die Schar der Frauen einreihen, die sich von Sam um den Finger wickeln ließen. Sie straffte die Schultern und warf ihm einen Blick zu, der hoffentlich sachlich und kühl wirkte.

»Wir tanzen gerade«, sagte sie. »Und wir reden.«

»Geh mit mir aus«, sagte er im gleichen Tonfall, in dem er sie zum Tanzen aufgefordert hatte. Es war keine Frage, sondern eine sanfte, aber bestimmte Forderung.

»Nein danke.« Gut. Kurz und bündig und ohne Verhandlungsspielraum.

Er hob amüsiert die Augenbrauen. »Du willst mit mir ausgehen, Faith.«

»Nein, will ich nicht.« *Oje, was für ein verwirrendes Netz von Lügen wir weben, um unser Herz zu schützen.*

»Oh doch«, sagte er leichthin. »Und du wirst es tun.«

Für eine unendliche Zeitspanne hielten seine dunklen Augen sie gefangen, bevor er ihren Kopf besitzergreifend an seine Brust führte. Eigentlich sollte seine Unterstellung sie wütend machen, aber er fühlte sich so gut an. Sie schloss die Augen, während eine Stimme in ihrem Kopf sie verspottete. Seine Schultern unter ihren Händen waren kräftig und locker. Er wirkte ruhig und gelöst wie eine Sommerbrise. Im Gegensatz zu ihm war sie so angespannt wie eine Sprungfeder, die jeden Moment losschnellen konnte.

Als der Song zu Ende war, fuhr Sam ihr mit der Hand über den Arm und verschränkte seine Finger mit ihren. Wortlos hob er ihre Hand und küsste sie. Dann hielt er sie an seine Brust und zog Faith an sich.

»Noch einen Tanz«, flüsterte er an ihrer Wange.

Sie spielte mit dem Feuer. Wie konnte sie da etwas anderes tun, als dahinzuschmelzen?

Sam wollte nicht, dass der Tanz endete, doch der Beat verklang unerbittlich und alles, was ihm blieb, war die Begierde, die durch seine Adern rauschte, und der dringende Wunsch, Faith besser kennenzulernen. Sie sah zu ihm auf wie ein Reh, fasziniert und gleichzeitig verängstigt. Er wusste, dass sie zu ihren Freundinnen an den Tisch zurückmusste. Schließlich hatte er versprochen, sie nur kurz zu entführen, obwohl er sie am liebsten nicht wieder hergegeben hätte.

Ihre Finger waren immer noch ineinander verschränkt. »Wie wär's mit einem Spaziergang?«, platzte es plötzlich aus ihm heraus. *Ein Spaziergang?* Er hatte keine Ahnung, woher dieser Gedanke kam.

»Was?« Ihre Augen weiteten sich verwirrt.

»Ein Spaziergang. Gehen. Das ist das, was die Leute mit ihren Beinen tun, wenn sie von einem Ort zum anderen unterwegs sind. Lass uns hier abhauen und am Strand entlanglaufen. Ich möchte nur mit dir reden, Faith. Mehr nicht.« *Mehr nicht* würde ihm alles an Zurückhaltung abverlangen, aber Zeit mit ihr war ihm wichtiger, als sie anzumachen.

Sie starrte ihn an, als hätte er den Verstand verloren, und

vielleicht war das tatsächlich der Fall, doch er wollte sie kennenlernen. Es war seltsam, aber Faith sagte Dinge, die ihn zum Nachdenken brachten, und Sam war nicht der Typ, der gerne innehielt.

»Ich kann nicht einfach verschwinden, Sam.«

»Eine halbe Stunde, länger nicht.« Das Whispers befand sich am Ende von Dunes Landing, einer Sackgasse mit Aussicht auf das Meer. »Die anderen werden noch hier sein, wenn wir zurückkommen, und sie können uns von der Terrasse aus beobachten, wenn sie mir nicht trauen.« Hoffnung keimte in ihm auf, als sie über seinen Vorschlag nachzudenken schien.

Dann warf sie einen Blick zu dem Tisch, an dem ihre Freundinnen saßen. »Ich kann nicht.«

»Doch, du kannst.« Er hob ihr Kinn, damit er ihr in die Augen sehen konnte. »Ich steh auf diese sexy Brille.«

»Ach so, du versuchst also doch, mit mir anzubandeln.« Sie stieß sich von ihm ab, aber er hielt immer noch ihre Hand und zog sie erneut an sich.

»Vertrau mir, Faith. Wenn ich mit dir anbandeln wollte, würde ich mich nicht mit einer halben Stunde zufriedengeben – und du auch nicht.«

Sie holte zittrig Luft und das gefiel ihm. Es gefiel ihm sogar sehr.

»Sam«, sagte sie schon etwas weniger entschlossen.

»Barfuß im Sand. Ein lockeres Gespräch. Das ist alles, worum ich dich bitte. Ich verspreche, nichts anderes zu versuchen.« Der Drang, ihren verführerischen Mund zu küssen, war so stark, dass ihm die Lippen brannten, aber er würde diesen Wünschen gerne entsagen, wenn nur etwas mehr gemeinsame Zeit dabei heraussprang.

Sie kniff die Augen zusammen und er ließ ihre Hand

widerwillig los. »Keine Tricks, kein Druck. Bei der Ehre der Bradens.«

»Ehrlich?« Sie lachte.

»Ehrlich.« Sams Vater war früher bei der Armee gewesen und seine Mutter hatte ihren Kindern mit jedem Wort Liebe, Loyalität und Aufrichtigkeit vermittelt. Auch wenn er Frauen reihenweise vernaschte, wusste er doch, dass in seiner Familie immer alle füreinander da waren, egal, was er und seine Geschwister taten. Als er den Zweifel in Faiths Augen sah, verspürte er das überwältigende Verlangen, dass auch sie diese Gewissheit erleben möge.

Diese Erkenntnis traf ihn mit der Wucht eines Schnellzugs.

Faith blickte auf ihre Hände, und als sie ihm in die Augen sah, war er sicher, dass sie ihn zum Teufel jagen würde. Er wünschte sich diesen gemeinsamen Spaziergang so sehr, dass es ihm eng in der Brust wurde. Seine Arme kribbelten nervös, während er sich das Hirn zermarterte, was er sonst noch sagen oder tun könnte, um etwas Zeit mit ihr zu ergattern. Und dann berührte sie seine Fingerspitzen mit ihren und betrachtete ihn mit einem halb lächelnden, halb ernsten Gesichtsausdruck.

»Gib mir eine Minute.« Sie steuerte auf den Tisch zu, an dem ihre Freundinnen saßen, und Sam blieb mit einem Hoffnungsschimmer zurück, an dem er sich festhalten konnte.

Sie lehnte sich über den Tisch und alle Frauen beugten sich vor und lauschten. Alle nickten lächelnd, außer Vivian, die erst Sam einen mörderischen Blick zuwarf, um gleich darauf Faith anzufunkeln. Sam musste sich zurückhalten, um nicht zum Tisch zu stürzen und Faith vor allem zu schützen, was Vivian ihr entgegenspuckte. Aber dazu hatte er kein Recht. Er würde sich nie zwischen Faith und ihre Freundinnen stellen, und als Faith sich zu ihrer ganzen zierlichen Größe aufrichtete und

Vivians Hand drückte, wappnete er sich dagegen, dass sie ihrem Spaziergang eine Absage erteilen würde.

»Es ist ja nur ein Spaziergang.« Faith war sich nicht sicher, ob sie sich selbst oder Vivian davon überzeugen wollte. Sie hatte ein schlechtes Gewissen, weil sie diesen Spaziergang überhaupt in Betracht zog. Schließlich sollte dies ein Mädelsabend sein und Vivian würde morgen wieder abreisen. Aber sie *wollte* gehen, und außerdem hatte Vivian, bevor ihr die Erfahrungen mit ihrem letzten Freund die Lust auf Männerbekanntschaften genommen hatten, Faith oft genug allein zurückgelassen, um mit einem Typen zusammen zu sein, den sie an einem gemeinsamen Abend kennengelernt hatte. Sam hatte Faiths Neugier geweckt. Wie viele Männer in Peaceful Harbor hatten sie zu einem Spaziergang eingeladen? Bisher kein einziger.

»Er hat versprochen, nichts zu versuchen.« Faith war sich nicht sicher, ob sie deswegen enttäuscht oder erleichtert war.

»Er ist gefährlich für dich, Faith. Du fühlst dich zu sehr zu ihm hingezogen, und sind wir doch mal ehrlich: Es sind Leute wie er, die unsere Gruppe zusammengebracht haben. Warum könnt ihr euch nicht hier unterhalten?«, bettelte Vivian.

Sie dachte an Lira und an all die Gründe, warum sich die Frauen überhaupt gefunden hatten. Sie wusste, dass Vivian auf sie aufpasste, und sie wusste, dass Vivian recht hatte. Sam stellte eine Gefahr für ihre Gefühle dar. Da war jedoch ein Flüstern, das sie in die andere Richtung lockte. Sein offener Blick, als er sagte, dass er niemals eine Frau absichtlich verletzen würde, hatte sich ebenso in ihr Gedächtnis gebrannt wie die

Aufrichtigkeit in seiner Stimme, als er ankündigte, dass er ihrer Gruppe mit einer Spende helfen wollte. Ein Teil von ihr, der stärker war, als sie geahnt hatte, klammerte sich voller Hoffnung an diese Bilder und wollte sie wie eine Krankheit sezieren und analysieren. Und es gab nur eine Möglichkeit, das zu tun. Bei einem Spaziergang mit Sam war ihre körperliche Sicherheit nicht gefährdet, nur ihre Gefühle. Und außerdem: Wenn er versuchen sollte, sich an sie heranzumachen, würde sie dann nicht alles wissen, was sie wissen musste?

»Na, komm schon, lass sie gehen«, drängte Brittany. »Er ist so ein netter Kerl.«

»Du hättest sein Gesicht sehen sollen, als ich ihm erzählt habe, dass mein Freund seine *andere* Freundin zu einem Abendessen bei Bekannten mitbrachte, zu dem er mich schon eingeladen hatte.« Hilary trank einen Schluck von ihrem Drink. »Ehrlich, er sah aus, als wollte er dem Kerl den Hals umdrehen, und dabei kennt er mich nicht einmal.«

Vivian warf einen skeptischen Blick in Sams Richtung. »Tatsächlich? Vielleicht steckt mehr in diesem Typen, als ich ihm zugetraut hätte.«

»Jep.« Hilary lächelte Faith an. »Geh nur, aber ich möchte alle Einzelheiten erfahren, wenn du zurückkommst.«

»Seid ihr sicher, dass es euch nichts ausmacht? Das sollte ja eigentlich ein Mädelsabend werden und –«

»Wenn du wirklich gehen willst – und ich glaube, du willst –, dann geh.« Vivian tippte auf ihre Armbanduhr. »Aber du bist angezählt und ich nehme dich beim Wort. Schließlich willst du doch dieses Outfit nicht den ganzen Abend nur an ihn verschwenden.«

Ihr Outfit. Oje. Sie war so in ihre Gedanken verstrickt, dass sie den knappen Rock und das Top ganz vergessen hatte, das ihr viel zu weit über die Schulter rutschte.

Mit zusammengekniffenen Augen versuchte sie, erneut das Selbstbewusstsein heraufzubeschwören, mit dem sie sich auf den Weg zum Whispers gemacht hatte. Sie hielt dieses Selbstbewusstsein fest und öffnete die Augen. Zu ihrer Überraschung überlief sie ein aufgeregtes Kribbeln, als sie an sich herabsah. »Okay, bin in einer halben Stunde zurück.« Als sie sich umdrehte und den Blick auf Sam richtete, war ihr Kopf wie leer gefegt. In ihren Gedanken gab es nur noch diesen Mann – gut aussehend, entschlossen, *gefährlich*?

Er legte eine Hand behutsam um ihren Arm, während er neben ihr herging. Verließ sie tatsächlich gerade das Whispers in Begleitung von Sam Braden? Die sehnsüchtigen Blicke der Frauen, an denen sie vorbeikam, bestätigten es, und das mulmige Gefühl in ihrem Bauch sagte ihr, dass es vielleicht keine gute Idee war. Sie verlangsamte ihre Schritte, aber Sams nachdrückliche Berührung trieb sie vorwärts.

Faith spürte die Abendluft auf ihrem Gesicht und die angenehme Kühle rüttelte ihren Verstand wach. Sam war nur ein Mann und dies war nur ein Spaziergang. Sie versuchte, die Hitze zu ignorieren, die seine Hand ausstrahlte, seinen erdigen, maskulinen Duft und die Art, wie er sie ansah, als sei sie alles, was er sich je gewünscht hatte.

Klug wie sie war, schob sie diesen Gedanken gleich zur Seite. Sam wollte nicht nur eine *einzige* Frau, egal, was sein Mund mit den verlockend vollen Lippen zum Besten gab.

An der Strandpromenade angekommen, kniete er sich neben sie, ergriff mit seiner großen, warmen Hand ihre Wade und drohte, die paar Gehirnzellen zunichtezumachen, die sie ihrem Verstand gerade abgerungen hatte.

»Halt dich an meiner Schulter fest. Dann helfe ich dir mit

deinen Schuhen.«

Keine Frau, die ihre Sinne beisammenhatte, konnte einem sexy Mann widerstehen, der zu ihren Füßen kniete. Sie stützte sich auf seine Schulter, während er ihr die Schuhe auszog und sie beiseitestellte.

»Du hast süße Füße«, sagte er, während er seine eigenen Schuhe auszog und sie neben ihre stellte.

»Tatsächlich?«

»Ich mag die Skittles auf deinen Zehen.« Seine Hand wanderte wie von selbst zurück zu ihrem neuen Zuhause, ihrem Arm, und sie traten auf den kühlen Sand.

»Skittles?« Sie sah verwirrt auf ihre Zehen hinunter und zuckte zusammen. Sie hatte völlig vergessen, dass sie ihre Fußnägel in verschiedenen Farben lackiert hatte. »Oh mein Gott, sie sehen wirklich aus wie Skittles.«

»Die mag ich am liebsten.« Eine Brise wehte vom Wasser her und zerzauste sein dichtes dunkles Haar, was ihn unglaublich sexy wirken ließ.

»Bestimmt nicht. Das ist nur einer deiner Anmachsprüche.« Sie schüttelte den Kopf und lachte leise, während sie am Ufer entlanggingen.

»Nein, das ist kein Anmachspruch. Ich mag Skittles wirklich am liebsten.«

Schweigend gingen sie nebeneinander her. Vom Meer her wehte eine weitere Brise, doch in der Hitze, die von Sam ausging, wurde es Faith nicht kalt.

»Also«, sagte sie nervös. »Worüber willst du reden, nachdem du mich hierhergelockt hast?«

»Über alles«, sagte er leichthin. »Über dich.«

»Über mich? Ich bin doch langweilig.«

»Du bist alles andere als langweilig. Erzähl mir vom WAC.

Warum hast du damit angefangen?« Er sah sie erwartungsvoll an.

»Ach, du weißt doch, wie so was geht. Eine schlimme Trennung, zu viel Tequila und eine beste Freundin, die auf mich eingeredet hat.« Sie versuchte, das Thema so beiläufig wie möglich abzuhandeln. Für ihn war es wahrscheinlich nichts anderes als ein beliebiger Gesprächsstoff.

»Nein, eigentlich weiß ich nicht, wie so was geht. Ich habe dir gesagt, dass ich seit Jahren keine Freundin mehr hatte, und Dates sind auch nicht meine Sache, also habe ich keine Ahnung, wie eine wirklich schlimme Trennung aussieht. Was ist passiert?«

Sie überlegte einen Moment. »Dates sind nicht deine Sache? Was meinst du damit?«

»Du erzählst mir deine Geheimnisse und ich erzähle dir meine.« In seinen Augen funkelte eine spielerische Fröhlichkeit und der Kontrast zu der Hitze, die sein Körper aussandte, warf sie ein wenig aus der Bahn.

»Da gibt es nicht viel zu erzählen.«

»Du hast eine Gruppe für Frauen gegründet, die betrogen worden sind. Vermutlich steckt eine Geschichte dahinter, aber du musst sie nicht mit mir teilen. Ich dagegen bin wie ein offenes Buch. Möchtest du wissen, warum ich mich nicht auf Dates einlasse?«

Nein. Vielleicht. »Sicher. Lass mal hören.«

»Wahrscheinlich bist du schon mal dem einen oder anderen Klassenclown begegnet, oder?«

Das war nun wirklich nicht das, was sie erwartet hatte, aber sie blockte nicht ab. »Ich glaube schon.«

»In jeder Highschool-Klasse gibt es einen, und bei jedem Klassentreffen schlüpft er in dieselbe Rolle, die er während der

Schulzeit hatte.«

»Okay.«

»Tja, dieser Typ bin ich nicht.« Er verstummte und sie sah zu ihm auf.

»Das war's? Das ist deine Geschichte?«

»Nein. Ich habe nur überlegt, wie ich es dir erzählen soll, und dann wurde mir klar, dass es mich unreif aussehen lässt, also habe ich aufgehört.« Er blickte aufs Wasser hinaus, und die Verspieltheit, die sie eben noch wahrgenommen hatte, schien sich wie ein Nebelschweif aufzulösen.

»Weißt du nicht, warum du dich nicht auf Dates einlässt? Oder bist du zu unreif, um dir die Wahrheit einzugestehen?«

Er drehte sich um und sah sie mit einem Hauch eines Lächelns an. »Du nimmst kein Blatt vor den Mund, oder?«

»Keine Ahnung. Kann sein. Ich versuche nur, dich zu verstehen, aber du bist kompliziert. Es ist, als hätte man eine Liste mit Symptomen und versuchte, eine neue Krankheit zu diagnostizieren.«

»Das hört sich schrecklich an. Ich bin keine Krankheit. Ich war noch nie krank und … das ist einfach furchtbar.« Er kicherte und brachte sie damit wieder zum Lächeln.

»Nein, ich meine nicht, dass *du* die Krankheit bist, sondern … Okay, du hast recht. Bei Blödsinn werde ich schnell unleidlich.«

»Weil du betrogen wurdest?«

Ihre Kinnlade klappte herunter und er hob abwehrend die Hand.

»Hey, fair ist fair. Bei mir hast du auch nicht um den heißen Brei herumgeredet.«

»Ja, und? Was willst du hören? Dass ich schlechte Erfahrungen gemacht habe?« Sie fühlte sich verletzlich, und das war kein Gefühl, das sie besonders schätzte.

Er berührte ihre Hand und Bedauern überschwemmte sein Gesicht. »Es tut mir leid. Ich wollte dich nicht ärgern. Ich möchte dich einfach besser kennenlernen, und zwar nicht nur das Hier und Jetzt, Faith. Ich möchte wissen, was dich zu der Frau gemacht hat, die du bist.«

Sein Geständnis kam völlig unerwartet und stimmte sie versöhnlicher. Aber die nagende Frage, *warum* er sie kennenlernen wollte, ließ sie nicht los. Schweigen breitete sich zwischen ihnen aus, während sie weiter am Strand entlanggingen, und sie unterdrückte den Drang, ihn zu fragen. Sam war eben Sam, er war so, wie er war, und hatte nur ein einziges Ziel.

Ihr Schweigen wurde nur vom Rauschen der Wellen und dem schwachen Klang der Musik in der Ferne unterbrochen.

Nach ein paar unbehaglichen Minuten sagte er: »Also, lass mich überlegen … warum halte ich mich von Dates fern?«

»Du musst es mir nicht sagen.« Sie schämte sich ein wenig wegen ihrer heftigen Reaktion.

»Möchte ich aber. Als Kind war ich ganz schön frech, wie der Klassenclown, nur anders.«

»Kann ich mir kaum vorstellen«, neckte sie.

Er hob eine Augenbraue, und sie war sich nicht sicher, ob er sie auf den Arm nehmen oder herausfordern wollte.

»Ich war immer bereit, die Regeln zu brechen und Risiken einzugehen. Ich habe mich davongeschlichen und am Strand Gitarre gespielt oder bin auf Partys gegangen.«

Wieder schwieg er, und sie wagte nicht, ein einziges Wort zu sagen. Sie wollte wissen, wie er sich selbst einschätzte.

»Natürlich wussten die anderen Kids Bescheid. ›Frag Sammy‹, haben sie immer gesagt. ›Er macht es bestimmt. Er macht alles.‹«

»Klingt nach einer bequemen Ausrede.«

»Bequem? Kann sein. Aber, hey, dass ich so war, wie ich war, hat verhindert, dass ich verletzt wurde.« Die Muskeln in seinem Kiefer spannten sich an.

»Ich kann mir kaum vorstellen, dass du jemals Verletzungen davontragen könntest. Du wirkst zu selbstsicher, zu ...«

»Zu was?«, sagte er herausfordernd. »Zu unverbindlich? Könnte sein. Hast du schon mal von Wabi-Sabi gehört?«

»Wabi was?«

»Wabi-Sabi. Es ist ein Teil der alten japanischen Kultur. Vereinfacht gesagt bedeutet es, Schönheit in Unvollkommenheit und in der Entwicklung – Altersflecken, Falten, Risse, Verfall, Wachstumszyklen. Ganz allgemein gesprochen akzeptiert und feiert diese Denkrichtung die Authentizität, indem sie anerkennt, dass nichts andauert, nichts fertig und nichts perfekt ist.«

Sie hatte das deutliche Gefühl, eine Seite von Sam kennenzulernen, die er nicht oft zeigte, und die Tiefe dessen, was er sagte, überraschte sie. Meist wirkte er wie ein unbeschwerter Bursche, der nicht über das Hier und Jetzt hinausdachte.

Du verpasst vielleicht eine wundervolle Geschichte, wenn du ein Buch allein nach seinem Einband beurteilst.

»Meine Kunstlehrerin an der Highschool hat mir davon erzählt, zu einer Zeit, als ich es am dringendsten brauchte. Der winzige Teil, den ich damals aufgenommen und mir so zurechtgebastelt habe, dass er zu meiner Situation passte, hat mir geholfen, ein paar Dinge loszulassen. Leider habe ich mir erst Jahre später die Zeit genommen, um herauszufinden, was Wabi-Sabi wirklich bedeutet. Als Teenager habe ich nur mitgenommen, dass ›nichts für immer bleibt‹.« Er schüttelte seufzend den Kopf. »Das hat es mir leicht gemacht, das Motto ›Sam macht alles‹ zur Lebensphilosophie zu erklären«, sagte er düster. »Ich spiele diese Rolle schon so lange, ich habe sie nie in Frage gestellt. Die Leute haben immer von mir erwartet, dass ich den Spaßmacher gebe, der sich nicht festlegt. Versteh mich nicht falsch, ich habe diese Rolle gerne gespielt. Ich liebe mein Leben und es hat mir wahrscheinlich viel Herzschmerz erspart.«

Er blieb stehen, setzte sich in den Sand und zog sie zu sich hinunter. Sie fragte sich, warum er in der Highschool eine Philosophie wie Wabi-Sabi gebraucht hatte.

»Die Sache ist die, Faith: Bis vor Kurzem habe ich gar nicht realisiert, dass ich eine Rolle gespielt habe.«

Er klang so ernst, so nachdenklich, dass sie die Hoffnung in sich aufkeimen spürte, all dies möge für ihn kein Spiel sein. Faith winkelte die Beine an. Dabei schob sich ihr Rock Stück für Stück höher und Sams Blick folgte ihm bei seiner Wanderung, ruhte dann auf ihrem Oberschenkel und ließ ihr Innerstes flattern und warm werden. Als er den Blick hob und sie ansah, erkannte sie Dunkelheit und Sünde, die von etwas noch Verlockenderem überdeckt wurden, etwas, dem sie sich nicht entziehen, das sie aber auch nicht definieren konnte.

Atmen, atmen, atmen.

Ihre Beine berührten sich, ihre Gesichter waren nur wenige Zentimeter voneinander entfernt. Ihr Körper schrie nach seiner Berührung, ihr Mund sehnte sich nach seinem Kuss, aber ihr Verstand war nicht bereit, sich diesem wilden Ritt anzuschließen. Ruhig, ohne Unsicherheit, ohne Eile, ohne Erwartungen sah Sam sie an, und Faith erkannte, was sie gefangen hielt. *Aufrichtigkeit.*

Für Faith war Aufrichtigkeit lebenswichtig. Sie brauchte sie dringend. Bisher waren ihr nur wenige Männer begegnet, die bereit waren, einer Frau gegenüber offen und ehrlich zu sein, und hier war Sam. Er hatte ihr sein Handy gezeigt, um ihr etwas zu beweisen, und jetzt offenbarte er ihr, wer er war.

»Warum?«

Er runzelte die Stirn. »Warum es so lange gedauert hat?«

»Nein, das verstehe ich. Aber warum bis vor Kurzem?«

Er sah aufs Wasser hinaus, dann schaute er ihr in die Augen. Die Luft zwischen ihnen pulsierte und ließ sie noch enger zusammenrücken. Sie fuhr sich mit der Zunge über die Lippen. Ganz bestimmt würde er sie gleich küssen. Sams Blick wanderte zu ihrem Mund und verharrte dort, während er sich über die Lippen leckte und sie vor Erwartung bebte. Sie konnte ihn nicht küssen, sie durfte ihn nicht küssen, aber als er sich näher zu ihr beugte, scherte sie sich nicht darum, was sie tun oder lassen sollte. Je dichter sein Mund an ihrem war, desto lauter rauschte das Blut in ihren Ohren. Als er sagte: »Ich glaube, jetzt bist du mit dem Erzählen dran«, brauchte sie einen Moment, bis seine Worte zu ihr durchdrangen und ihr klar wurde, dass es keinen Kuss geben würde.

»Faith?« Vivians Stimme durchbrach das Knistern in der Luft. »Bist du das?«

Ihr Kopf fuhr herum. Als sie die Frauen auf sich zukommen sah, sagte sie schnell zu Sam gewandt: »Tut mir leid.« *Dass ich dich fast geküsst hätte? Dass ich so aussah, als wollte ich es? Dass meine Freundinnen dazwischenfunken?*

Er griff nach ihrer Hand. »Geh mit mir aus«, sagte er hastig.

»Ich … ich kann nicht.« Sie wusste, wie gefährlich es war, mit Sam auszugehen, und Vivian hatte recht. Sie war zu sehr von ihm eingenommen, um kluge Entscheidungen zu treffen.

»Ein einziges Date.«

Ihr war klar, dass er eine Absage nicht hinnehmen würde, aber sie traute sich selbst nicht über den Weg, wenn es um Sam

Braden ging. »Du stehst doch normalerweise nicht auf Dates.«

»Ich sitze auch normalerweise nicht am Strand und unterhalte mich.«

Die Stimmen ihrer Freundinnen kamen näher. Faith stand auf und klopfte sich den Sand von den Beinen. Bei der Vorstellung, mit ihm auszugehen, wirbelten ihre Gedanken durcheinander, und sie war gleichermaßen geschockt und aufgeregt.

»Die Leute ändern sich nicht, Sam.«

»Warum meinst du, ich müsste mich ändern? Ich betrüge Frauen nicht. Das habe ich dir ja schon gesagt.« Als er näher trat, stockte ihr fast der Atem. »Ich unterhalte mich gern mit dir, Faith. Ein einziges Date.«

Brittany kam auf sie zugelaufen. Hilary und Vivian folgten ihr auf dem Fuße.

»Ihr seid schon eine ganze Stunde hier draußen«, sagte Brittany. »Wir haben uns Sorgen gemacht.«

»Sie haben sich Sorgen gemacht. Ich wusste, dass Sam nicht über dich herfallen würde«, sagte Hilary. Und fügte lächelnd hinzu: »Es sei denn, du hättest es gewollt.«

Sams Blick hielt ihren gefangen. In ihrem Kopf ging alles durcheinander. *Ein einziges Date.*

Vivian hakte sich bei Faith unter und sagte: »Komm schon. Ich will tanzen. Tut mir leid, Braden. Das ist ein Mädelsabend. Wir haben dir doppelt so viel Zeit gegeben wie verabredet. Du kannst von Glück sagen, dass du es nicht mit uns zu tun kriegst.«

Die Frauen zogen Faith den Strand entlang zum Whispers. Sie drehte sich um und sah Sam, der sich nicht von der Stelle gerührt hatte. Er hob die Hand und winkte ihr mit einer kaum merklichen Geste zu – und ihr kam es vor, als stünde ein winziges Stück von ihr dort neben ihm.

»Na endlich.« Shannon glitt von ihrem Barhocker und umarmte Sam. »Ich dachte, du würdest uns versetzen.«

Er küsste seine jüngste Schwester auf die Wange. »Würde ich das jemals tun?«

Shannon hob die dunklen Augenbrauen. Sam, Cole, Ty und Shannon hatten dunkles Haar wie ihr Vater, während Tempest und Nate nach ihrer blonden Mutter kamen.

Sam ging um die Bar herum und gab seiner Mutter Maisy einen Kuss auf die Wange. »Hi, Ma. Du siehst gut aus.« Er liebte ihren Stil. Mit ihren langen Flatterröcken und bunten Oberteilen sah sie aus, als sei sie unterwegs zu einem Barbecue am Strand oder zu einem Hippiekonzert.

Seine Mutter streckte die Hand aus und streichelte ihm die Wange. »Danke, Schatz. Schön, dass du hier bist.«

Sam klopfte seinem Vater, Thomas »Ace« Braden, auf die Schulter. »Wie geht es dir, Pop?«

»Ich habe die meisten meiner Kinder unter einem Dach – also ist es ein großartiger Tag.« Im Gegensatz zu den wilden Locken seiner Frau trug Sams Vater sein Haar immer noch so kurz wie zu seiner Zeit bei der Armee. »Ty und Tempe sind in der Küche und holen Sandwiches. Sie sind gleich wieder da.

Willst du was trinken?«

»Gerne, eine Cola bitte.« Er kletterte auf einen Barhocker und richtete seine Aufmerksamkeit auf Shannon. »Du fährst also zurück zu Onkel Hal? Wie kann es sein, dass du jetzt seit Monaten an einem Projekt arbeitest, das eigentlich nur ein paar Wochen dauern sollte? Braucht ihr wirklich so lange, um das Leben der Füchse zu erforschen?«

Shannon hatte die letzten Monate auf der Ranch ihres Onkels in Weston in Colorado verbracht, während sie an einem Projekt zur Überwachung von Rotfüchsen in den Bergen gearbeitet hatte.

»Bist du aber neugierig. Das habe ich echt nicht vermisst, als ich weg war. Du weißt doch, wie es ist«, sagte sie ausweichend, als Ty und Tempest mit Tabletts voller Sandwiches durch die Schwingtüren aus der Küche kamen.

Sam sah Shannon fragend an und sie grinste. Was zum Teufel führte sie im Schilde? »Hat das etwas mit Steve Johnson zu tun?«

»Ach, komm schon. *Steve?* Er ist ein Einsiedler. Überhaupt nicht mein Typ.« Sie winkte ab, aber die Röte auf ihren Wangen erzählte eine andere Geschichte.

Sam und seine Brüder hatten immer auf Shannon und Tempe aufgepasst, und es gefiel ihm gar nicht, dass sie sich vielleicht auf einen Mann einließ, den er nicht … *Was?* Den er nicht ermahnen konnte, seine Schwester gut zu behandeln? Großer Gott, er führte sich genauso auf wie Cole, wenn es um Faith ging. Allerdings war er so sehr an seine Rolle als großer Bruder gewöhnt, dass er sich nicht zurückhalten konnte. »Ihr beide habt aber ganz vertraut ausgesehen bei der Hochzeit von Rex und Jade. Sei einfach vorsichtig, okay? Schließlich sind wir nicht da, um ihn zu vermöbeln, wenn er sich danebenbenehmen sollte.«

»Du weißt, dass ich erwachsen bin, oder? Was du gerade gesagt hast, ist für mich der beste Grund, mit ihm auszugehen.«

»Shannon«, sagte er warnend. *Verdammt.* Sie hatte immer schon ihr eigenes Ding gemacht. Darin war sie ihm sehr ähnlich, doch jetzt konnte er sich plötzlich vorstellen, wie sich Cole auf der Hochzeit gefühlt haben musste. Kein gutes Gefühl.

Sie beachtete ihn gar nicht, sondern begann, mit ihrem Vater zu reden.

»Hey, Sammy.« Tempest stellte ein Tablett mit Sandwiches auf die Theke und nahm ihn in den Arm. Sie strich sich ihr langes blondes Haar hinters Ohr, als sie neben ihm auf einen Barhocker kletterte. »Ich arbeite an einem neuen Song, bei dem es um unvollkommene Schönheit geht. Ich denke, er wird dir gefallen. Immerhin betonst du ja immer, dass alle Dinge um uns herum einzigartig schön sind.«

Tempest war Musiktherapeutin und schrieb immer wieder neue Lieder. Von allen Geschwistern war sie die Ruhigste und Besonnenste. Sie war auch diejenige, die seine Überzeugungen am ehesten ernst nahm.

»Ich würde den Song gerne hören, wenn du fertig bist.« Dann fiel ihm etwas ein. »Hey, Tempe, kennst du Therapeuten, die Frauen, die gerade eine Krise durchmachen, ihre Hilfe ehrenamtlich anbieten würden? Oder vielleicht einen Rabatt gewähren könnten?«

Sie sah ihn fragend an. »Ich kann herumfragen. Warum?«

Er war nicht bereit, dieses Thema anzuschneiden. »Für eine Freundin.«

»Okay, ich werde mich erkundigen.« Sie beugte sich näher zu ihm. »Aber was viel wichtiger ist: Stimmt es, dass du hinter Coles Mitarbeiterin her bist?«

Sam starrte Ty an.

»Nein, ich war's nicht.« Ty lachte.

»Das habe ich auch gehört«, sagte Shannon. »Ist es ein Geheimnis? Jewel hat mir erzählt, dass du gestern Abend das Whispers in Begleitung von Faith verlassen hast. Ich glaube, Chelsea hat es ihr gesagt. Wenn du es also geheim halten wolltest, ist es dir nicht gelungen.«

»Lieber Himmel«, murmelte Sam. »Wir haben das Whispers nicht gemeinsam verlassen. Wir sind nur am Strand spazieren gegangen.«

»Spazieren gehen. So nennt man das also heute?«, witzelte sein Vater. Alle lachten, während Sam leise vor sich hin brodelte.

»Was gibt es da zu lachen? Und nein, Pop, so nennt man *das* heute nicht. Mit Faith ist das nicht so.« Sam hatte die Zähne so fest zusammengepresst, dass er fürchtete, sie würden abbrechen.

»Junge, du gehst doch sonst nicht spazieren.« Ty schüttelte den Kopf.

»Coles Mitarbeiterin Faith?«, fragte ihre Mutter mit einem freudigen Funkeln in den Augen. »Sie ist so ein süßes Mädchen, Sammy. Sei gut zu ihr.«

»Ja, Faith. Und, Mom, war ich jemals nicht gut zu einer Frau?«

»Natürlich nicht, Schatz«, sagte seine Mutter. »Ich meinte nur … na ja, sie ist Coles Mitarbeiterin. Du solltest vorsichtig sein. Das könnte kompliziert werden.«

»Hat Cole dir bei der Hochzeit nicht gesagt, dass du dich von ihr fernhalten sollst?«, fragte Tempest. »Jedenfalls hat er mir das erzählt.«

»Ist in dieser Familie denn nichts heilig?« *Das ist das*

Problem. Alles in ihrer Familie war heilig. Sie beschützten sich gegenseitig und diejenigen, die sie liebten, als gelte es das Leben. Für Cole war Faith eine treue Mitarbeiterin und damit offenbar so etwas wie ein Familienmitglied.

»Schatz, wir passen doch nur auf dich auf«, versicherte ihm seine Mutter.

»Wir passen auf *sie* auf«, korrigierte Shannon. »Sammy braucht niemanden, der auf ihn aufpasst.«

Wieder biss Sam die Zähne zusammen. Warum störte es ihn plötzlich, dass seine Familie so offen über alles sprach? Er kannte das ja schon seit Ewigkeiten. Kaum, dass Faith mit seinem Namen in Verbindung gebracht wurde, meinten sie, sie müsse *beschützt* werden. Das gefiel ihm nicht, es sei denn, er wäre derjenige, der sie beschützte.

»Du hast recht, Shannon. Auf mich muss niemand aufpassen, aber ich werde auf Faith achtgeben, keine Sorge.« Sam nahm einen Bissen von seinem Sandwich und dachte über alles nach, während seine Familie ihn ansah, als sei er von einem anderen Planeten.

»Was hast du da gesagt?«

Ty und Tempest tauschten einen Blick, den Sam nicht deuten konnte.

»Es ist lange her, seit du so etwas gesagt hast, Schatz.« Seine Mutter griff über die Bar und berührte seine Hand. »Es kam etwas überraschend, das ist alles.«

»So etwas habe ich dich noch nie sagen hören.« Shannon grinste.

»Du warst damals noch zu klein, Shan«, sagte Tempest, während sie Sam unverwandt ansah.

Es war höchste Zeit, das Thema zu wechseln. In der Vergangenheit herumzustochern war nie eine gute Idee. Sam war fest davon überzeugt, dass man nicht lebte, wenn man nicht nach vorne blickte. Und so jemand wollte er verdammt noch mal nicht sein.

»Wo ist Nate?«, fragte er.

»Er ist mit Jewel bei Krissys Tanzvorführung. Dabei fällt mir ein: Du kommst doch zu ihrer großen Vorstellung, nicht wahr?«, fragte seine Mutter.

»Bis dahin sind es noch fast zwei Monate, aber keine Sorge. Ich möchte sie auf keinen Fall verpassen.« Krissy war Jewels vierzehnjährige Schwester. Die Fishers gehörten praktisch zur Familie. Der Vater der Kinder war bei einem Bootsunfall ertrunken und ein paar Jahre später war ihr ältester Bruder Rick in Afghanistan gefallen. Er war Nates bester Freund gewesen, und Nate musste mit dem Wissen leben, dass er Rick den Befehl zu der Versorgungsfahrt gegeben hatte, die ihn das Leben gekostet hatte. Obwohl Nate schon jahrelang in Jewel verliebt gewesen war, hatten seine Schuldgefühle ihm so lange im Weg gestanden, bis es fast zu spät war.

»Gut«, sagte seine Mutter. »Hinterher essen wir hier zusammen mit Jewels Familie.«

Dann wandte sich das Gespräch dem Projekt zu, zu dem Shannon bald nach Colorado zurückkehren sollte. Sie berichtete von ihrer Arbeit und erzählte ihnen das Neueste von ihren Cousins und Cousinen aus Colorado.

»Onkel Hal veranstaltet immer noch wunderbare Grillabende«, sagte Shannon. »Die Cousins aus Trusty kommen auch öfters dazu, und es macht riesig Spaß, Zeit mit ihnen allen zu verbringen. Ich kann es noch gar nicht fassen, dass so viele von ihnen inzwischen verheiratet sind, Babys haben oder verlobt sind.«

»Wird aber auch höchste Zeit.« Maisy sah jedes ihrer Kinder

liebevoll an. »Eure Generation ist so darauf konzentriert, mehr, mehr und mehr zu bekommen. Ich mache mir Sorgen, dass dabei die Familie ins Hintertreffen gerät.«

Tempest wackelte mit dem Zeigefinger. »Mom, wir treffen uns fast jede Woche zum Mittag- oder Abendessen. Wie kannst du dir Sorgen machen? Wir alle lieben unsere Familie.«

Ihre Mutter griff nach der Hand ihres Mannes. »Ich meine nicht unsere Familie, Liebling. Eure eigenen Familien. Nichts ist schöner, als zu dem nach Hause zu kommen, den man liebt, oder eine eigene Familie zu gründen.«

Ihr Mann zog sie an sich und gab ihr einen Kuss. »Eure Mutter wünscht sich Enkelkinder.«

Maisy lachte. »Ist das so schlimm?«

»Mich brauchst du nicht anzusehen«, sagte Ty und warf Sam einen Blick zu. *Kommt nicht in Frage*, schien er zu sagen.

Sam überlegte krampfhaft, wie er Faith dazu bringen könnte, sich mit ihm zu verabreden, daher hörte er nur mit halbem Ohr zu.

»Ich will Kinder«, sagte Shannon. »Viele sogar. Nur jetzt noch nicht.«

»Ich auch. Wenn ich mich verliebe, hoffe ich, dass meine Liebe genauso tief ist wie bei dir und Dad«, sagte Tempest zu ihrer Mutter. »Ich bin überzeugt, dass es bei uns allen so kommen wird.« Sie stieß Sam an. »Auch bei dir und Ty.«

Sam war sich da nicht so sicher. Er konnte fast jede Frau haben – aber die einzige Frau, die er wollte, fand ihn vollkommen inakzeptabel. Diese schmerzhafte Erkenntnis hätte ihn dazu bewegen sollen, sie in Gedanken abzuhaken, aber er fühlte sich zu sehr von Faith, ihrer Aufrichtigkeit, ihrer Verletzlichkeit und ihrer Intelligenz angezogen. Verdammt, sie hatte ihn geködert, ohne es überhaupt zu versuchen.

Er sah sich um, spürte die Liebe seiner Familie, dachte an ihre Neckereien und die handfeste Liebe, die regelmäßig wie Medizin verabreicht wurde, wenn es einer von ihnen für notwendig hielt. Er dachte an ihre bedingungslose Unterstützung, an ihre Großzügigkeit, die Freunden, Familie und Fremden gleichermaßen zuteilwurde. All das liebte er an ihr, und plötzlich wurde ihm klar, dass dies nur ein paar der Eigenschaften waren, die Faith für ihn so anziehend machten.

Er schaute aus dem Fenster auf den Jachthafen, und als er die Boote betrachtete, die in den Hafen einfuhren, hatte er das Gefühl, als würde auch er seinen Kurs ändern. Einen neuen Weg beschreiten, aus der Strömung ausbrechen, die ihn schon so lange in eine bestimmte Richtung getrieben hatte, dass er ganz vergessen hatte, dass er die Wahl hatte. Er wollte frei sein, um stromaufwärts schwimmen zu können. *Zu Faith.*

»Eins ist sicher«, sagte sein Vater, während er die Theke abwischte. »Wenn euch die Liebe findet, womit ich fest rechne, wird sie eure ganze Welt verändern. Mit der Liebe ist es wie mit dem Alkohol. Du denkst, du willst nur einen kleinen Schluck, aber wenn du erst einmal davon gekostet hast« – er warf Sam einen Blick zu – »und zum ersten Mal *echte* Liebe unter Erwachsenen erlebst, die jeden deiner Gedanken gefangen hält, wirst du alles dafür tun, um mehr davon zu bekommen. Du willst ganz darin eintauchen.«

Montags ging es im Zentrum für Schmerztherapie in Peaceful Harbor immer hektisch zu, und nun, wo Cole in den Flitterwochen war, hatte Faith noch mehr Patienten zu versorgen als sonst. Mittlerweile war es nach drei Uhr nachmittags und Faith war den ganzen Tag von einem Untersuchungsraum zum nächsten gehetzt. Sie kam fast um vor Hunger. Aber selbst das laute Magenknurren und die Flut von Patienten, um die sie sich kümmern musste, hatten Sam nicht aus ihren Gedanken vertreiben können. Gestern Abend hatte sie gehofft, dass er noch einmal ins Whispers zurückkehren würde, aber er war nicht wieder aufgetaucht. Als Vivian und sie nach Hause gekommen waren, hatten sie sich die Website angesehen und festgestellt, dass ein anonymer Spender fünftausend Dollar überwiesen hatte. Sie wusste, dass das Geld von Sam sein musste. Wer sonst sollte einen solchen Betrag für ihre Sache lockermachen? Vivian behauptete felsenfest, dass es ein Trick von Sam sei, mit dem er sie in sein Bett locken wollte. *Ein sehr teurer Trick.* Faith war jedoch nicht davon überzeugt. Vivian hatte seinen aufrichtigen Blick nicht gesehen, als er angeboten hatte, den Scheck auszustellen.

In ihre Träume hatten sich widersprüchliche Gedanken an Sam gemischt, und als sie aufgewacht war, hatte sie sich gereizt und aufgewühlt und noch verwirrter gefühlt als sonst. Wenn der Abschied von Vivian am Morgen und der hektische Arbeitstag nicht reichten, um sie von Sam abzulenken, musste sie sich wohl oder übel damit abfinden, dass er ihr ständig durch den Kopf geisterte.

Sie versuchte, ihre Aufmerksamkeit auf ihren Patienten zu lenken. »Sie können sich jetzt wieder anziehen, Mr. French. Wir sehen uns dann in drei Wochen wieder.«

»Danke, Faith. Ich kann es kaum erwarten.« Er zwinkerte ihr zu und Faith schüttelte lächelnd den Kopf.

»Mit dem Flirten sollten Sie besser vorsichtig sein. Ich glaube nicht, dass es Mrs. French gefallen würde.«

Er winkte ab. »Meine Betty weiß, dass ich nur Spaß mache.«

»Einen schönen Tag noch, Mr. French.« Faith verließ den Raum und schloss die Tür hinter sich. Sie machte sich hastig ein paar Notizen und legte die Patientenkarte dann in die Ablage an der Tür.

»Kommst du klar?« Dr. Jon Butterscotch war Coles Partner und ein wahres Energiebündel. Um acht Uhr in der Früh war er ebenso wach und lebhaft wie um Mitternacht. Faith hatte ihm schon bei so vielen Notoperationen assistiert, dass sie es wissen musste. Mit seinem blonden Haarschopf, der immer aussah, als hätte er ihn nur schnell mit den Fingern glatt gestrichen, seiner Dauerbräune und einem Lächeln, mit dem er auch die anspruchsvollsten Patienten bedachte, sah er aus wie ein Surfer, der sich als Arzt verkleidet hatte. Hinter dem jugendlichen Äußeren verbarg sich jedoch einer der hellsten Köpfe – und ein Verstand, der einem doppelt so alten Mann Ehre gemacht hätte. Wie Cole nahm Jon seinen Job ernst, und er war stolz darauf, seine Patienten als Individuen zu behandeln, nicht als *Fälle*. Ein Grund mehr für Faith, ihn zu respektieren.

»Ein bisschen hungrig, aber ansonsten geht's mir gut.« Es verging kein Tag, an dem Faith dem Allmächtigen nicht für ihren Job dankte. Menschen zu helfen war immer schon ihr Traum gewesen, und die Medizin faszinierte sie. Die Stelle als Arztassistentin bot ihr beides, ohne dass sie dafür ein langes und kostspieliges Medizinstudium absolvieren musste. Sie hatte sich immer vorgestellt, dass sie ihren Abschluss machen, in ihrem Beruf Fuß fassen und JJ heiraten würde, ihren betrügerischen Ex-Freund. Aber das Leben machte, was es wollte, und stellte bisweilen die besten Pläne auf den Kopf.

»Hattest du keine Mittagspause?« Jon griff in seine Tasche und reichte Faith einen Energieriegel. »Du hättest mir Bescheid sagen sollen. Du weißt doch, dass ich davon immer ein paar in der Tasche habe.«

»Vielen Dank. Ich wollte dich nicht stören.« Sie dachte an die Liste, die sie gestern Abend zusammengestellt hatte, um die Aktivitäten des WAC auszuweiten, und an ihr Gespräch mit Lira. »Jon, kennst du irgendwelche Therapeuten, die pro bono arbeiten? Zum Beispiel für eine Wohltätigkeitsorganisation?«

Er runzelte die Stirn. »Auf Anhieb fällt mir niemand ein. Brauchst du professionelle Hilfe?«

»Nein, es ist nicht für mich.« Während das Wartezimmer voll war, wollte sie nicht erklären, was es mit dem WAC auf sich hatte, also sagte sie bloß: »Es ist für eine Freundin von außerhalb der Stadt. Sie hat nicht viel Geld.«

»Oh, dann fragst du am besten Brandy. Sie kann dir sagen, wen wir in unser Überweisungsnetzwerk aufgenommen haben. Ich bin sicher, dass sie dir weiterhelfen kann.« Er griff nach der Türklinke eines weiteren Untersuchungszimmers und sagte: »Viel Glück! Ich hoffe, du findest jemanden für deine Freundin. Und danke für deinen Einsatz hier. Du leistest gute Arbeit. Ich werde auch Cole davon erzählen.«

Faith konnte nicht aufhören zu grinsen, auch als er schon im Untersuchungsraum verschwunden war. Während ihrer Praktika hatte sie genug hochnäsige und egozentrische Ärzte kennengelernt, um sich darüber klar zu sein, dass sie mit ihrer Stelle bei Cole und Jon wirklich Glück gehabt hatte. Sie verstaute das Kompliment in ihrem Gedächtnis und schlüpfte in die Küche, um schnell den Energieriegel zu essen.

Brandy, die Kollegin vom Empfang, steckte gleich darauf den Kopf zur Tür hinein. »Faith, da ist ein Patient ohne Termin. Er sagt, es sei dringend. Und er will nur von dir behandelt werden.«

Faith hatte Mühe, nicht entmutigt die Schultern sacken zu lassen. Für den Rest des Nachmittags musste sie die Patientenliste im Zwanzig-Minuten-Takt abarbeiten.

»Ist er einer von Coles Patienten?«

Brandy nickte.

»Okay, ich kümmere mich gleich um ihn. Brandy, kannst du mir bitte eine Liste der Therapeuten aus der Gegend um Pleasant Hill aus unserer Datenbank geben? Ist aber nicht eilig.«

»Ja, mache ich«, sagte Brandy. »Raum sechs. Tut mir leid.« Sie eilte den Flur hinunter.

Ich liebe meinen Job. Ich liebe meinen Job. Ich liebe meinen Job. Lächelnd und mit neuer Motivation ging sie zu Raum sechs. Der Halter für die Patientenmappen war leer. Na prima. Sie hinkte mit ihren Terminen eh schon hinterher und stand nun ohne Informationen über den Patienten da. Kaum hatte sie die Tür geöffnet, setzte sie schon zu ihrer üblichen Vorstellung an.

»Hallo, ich bin Faith, und ich …« Ihr klappte die Kinnlade herunter, und ihre Stimme verhallte zwischen dem lauten Pochen ihres Herzens und der Hitze, die der Mann auf dem Untersuchungstisch ausstrahlte. Er war mit nichts als einem schwarzen Slip bekleidet und betrachtete sie mit einem Lächeln, bei dem ihr schwindelig wurde. Wenn sie Brandy erwischte, konnte die was erleben!

»Sam«, flüsterte sie und legte sich dann die Hand vor die Augen. »Warum bist du hier?« *Oh mein Gott. Nicht hinsehen. Nicht noch einmal hinsehen.* Unwillkürlich schoben sich ihre Finger ein wenig auseinander und sie wagte noch einen Blick. Sie konnte einfach nicht anders. Er saß da, als wartete er nur darauf, dass sie über ihn herfiel.

»In *Unterwäsche*?« Sie schloss die Augen.

»Brandy sagte, dass ihr eure Patienten normalerweise anweist, sich für die Untersuchung frei zu machen.«

Wie schaffte er es, so ruhig und selbstsicher zu sein, wenn sie sich kaum auf den Beinen halten konnte?

»Ja, bei Patienten machen wir das! Und die ziehen einen Kittel über. Warum hast du keinen Kittel an?«

»Damit all meine männlichen Reize verborgen sind?!« Er lachte ein wenig. »Wie kann ich dich davon überzeugen, mit mir auszugehen, wenn ich dir in einem Papierkittel gegenüberstehe?«

Atmen, atmen, atmen.

»Ach, komm schon, Faith. Es ist doch nicht anders, als wenn ich Badezeug anhätte.«

So sah ein Mann in Badezeug aber normalerweise nicht aus. Nun, kein Mann außer *ihm* natürlich. Das war verrückt. Wie konnte es sein, dass er sie dermaßen durcheinanderbrachte? Sie musste sich zusammenreißen und die Situation ganz professionell betrachten. Damit konnte sie umgehen.

Aber kann ich mit ihm umgehen?

»Außerdem«, sagte er, »habe ich dir gesagt, dass ich nichts zu verbergen habe. Ich bin keine Mogelpackung. Bei mir kriegst du das, was du siehst.«

Sie ließ die Hand sinken, sah ihn an und errötete am ganzen Körper. Es gab eine ganze Menge von ihm zu sehen. Er war hinreißend. Zu hinreißend. Und zu sehr von sich überzeugt. Seine breite Brust war herrlich, gebräunt, mit einem Hauch von Haarwuchs und so perfekt geformt, dass sie sie genau erkunden wollte. *Mit dem Mund.* Sein Duft war berauschend und machte sie ein wenig schwindlig. Sein Blick wanderte langsam von ihren Augen zu ihrem Mund, von dort zu ihrer Brust bis hinunter zu ihren Zehen, und sie spürte seine sinnliche Inspektion, als hätte er jeden Zentimeter ihres Körpers berührt.

»Meine Güte, Sam. Willst du, dass ich keinen klaren Gedanken mehr fassen kann und gefeuert werde?«

Er griff nach ihrer Hand und zog sie zu sich hin. Genau. Zwischen. Seine. Beine.

Heilige Mutter des Himmels und der Erde und wer immer sonst noch zuhören mag, bitte, bitte, bitte macht, dass ich nicht anfange, zusammenhanglos herumzubrabbeln.

»Ich sorge dafür, dass du keinen klaren Gedanken mehr fassen kannst?«, fragte er mit einem verführerischen Funkeln in den Augen.

Faith atmete tief durch. Klar, dass er sich sofort auf diesen Teil ihrer Frage stürzte, während er die Sache mit dem Gefeuertwerden geflissentlich ignorierte. Die Situation drohte zu entgleiten. Sie musste die Kontrolle übernehmen.

Kontrolle über Sam Braden. Bei dem bloßen Gedanken wurde ihr ganz schummrig.

Sie zwang sich, sich wie die professionelle Mitarbeiterin zu benehmen, für die ihre Chefs sie hielten. *Mein Chef.* Panik breitete sich in ihrer Brust aus. Sie straffte die Schultern und hob das Kinn.

»Wo bist du verletzt?«

Ein schelmisches Lächeln zeigte sich auf seinem schönen Gesicht. Wie konnte ein einzelner Blick ihren Körper dazu bringen, vor Bedürftigkeit zu zittern?

»Am Bein.«

»An der Wade? Am Oberschenkel?« Ihre Fragen klangen knapp und sachlich und ihre Stimme hörte sich zum Glück nicht atemlos an.

Eine Augenbraue zuckte hoch. »Am rechten Oberschenkel.«

Peinlicherweise zitterten ihre Hände, als sie seinen muskulösen Oberschenkel berührte. Oh, das fühlte sich gut an. Heiß und fest und … Sie räusperte sich. »Hier?«

»Ein bisschen weiter oben.« Sein durchdringender Blick hielt sie gefangen, während sie ihre Hand an seinem Oberschenkel weiter hochschob. »Noch höher«, sagte er.

Gleich bekam sie keine Luft mehr. »Hier?«

»Noch ein bisschen höher.« Der Mann war reine Sünde und Verführung, und sie war verrückt, dass sie jedes seiner Worte gierig aufsog.

»Sam.« Oje. Da war sie, die Atemlosigkeit, die sie befürchtet hatte. *Verdammt.* Sie war nicht eines seiner Groupies, die bei seinem Anblick in Ohnmacht fielen. »Sam Braden! Bist du überhaupt verletzt?«

Er legte eine Hand auf ihre, die andere auf sein Herz. »Und ob! Gestern Abend hast du mich abgewiesen.«

»Also wirklich! Du solltest dich nicht so wichtig nehmen.« Sie versuchte, ihre Hand wegzuziehen, aber er hielt sie fest und sah ihr unverwandt in die Augen.

»Vielleicht sollte ich dich nicht so wichtig nehmen, aber das funktioniert nicht.«

Oh mein Gott. Sie war nervös und erregt und genoss seine Aufmerksamkeit viel zu sehr. Sie hielt seinen herausfordernden Blick stand, aber es war alles zu viel. *Er* war zu viel. Plötzlich lachte sie laut los. Sie hielt sich die Hand vor den Mund, aber es half nicht. Sie war vollkommen hysterisch.

Sam wusste, dass es riskant gewesen war, sich für Faith bis auf die Unterhose auszuziehen, aber er wollte ihr beweisen, dass er nicht der war, für den sie ihn hielt. Und sie zum Lachen zu bringen, war doch sicher die beste Methode. Er hatte sich vorgestellt, dass sie losprusten würde, kaum dass sie ihn im Untersuchungsraum sah, und war überrascht gewesen, als sie es nicht tat. Dieses hysterische Lachen war erfrischend, kam es doch von der zurückhaltenden und vorsichtigen Frau, die im Moment die Fäden zu seinem sorgsam gehüteten Herzen in der Hand hielt.

Er wollte sie jedoch nicht noch mehr in Verlegenheit bringen. Daher sprang er rasch vom Untersuchungstisch und streifte seine Jeans über. Faith sah zu, wie er sich anzog, und brach dabei immer wieder in Lachen aus. Wenigstens sah sie ihm jetzt geradewegs ins Gesicht.

»Ich glaube, mir hat deine erste Reaktion besser gefallen. Diese hinreißende Röte war wirklich sexy.« Er zerrte sich das T-Shirt über den Kopf, trat zu ihr und sah ihr in die Augen. Mit dem Daumen wischte er ihr eine Lachträne von der Wange.

Sie leckte sich nervös die Lippen, spannte den Kiefer an, um weitere Lachsalven zu unterdrücken, und schaute ihn an. Ihre

Wimpern waren unglaublich lang und ließen sie unschuldig und klug aussehen.

»Ich habe mich geirrt«, sagte er. Heiterkeit, gespannte Erwartung und Verlegenheit lagen in ihrem Ausdruck und machten ihm bewusst, wie schnell sein eigenes Herz schlug. Er hatte dieses Organ nicht mehr wahrgenommen, seit er ein Teenager war und sein Herz in tausend Stücke zersprungen war. Die Erinnerung daran, wie Keira ihm erzählt hatte, dass sie mit einem Kerl aus ihrer Heimatstadt geschlafen hatte, überrollte ihn, gefolgt von der schmerzhaften Erinnerung an den Tag, an dem er erfuhr, dass sie weggezogen war. Damals war er ein dummer Junge gewesen, verrückt nach einem Mädchen aus der Nachbarstadt. Dank seiner verdrehten Auffassung von Wabi-Sabi hatte er diesen Teil seines Lebens tief in sich begraben. Er fragte sich, ob seine Kunstlehrerin gewusst hatte, dass sie ihm die Bestätigung an die Hand gab, seine Gefühle völlig zu verdrängen.

Am Abend von Coles Hochzeit hatte etwas in ihm klick gemacht. Vielleicht lag es an dem, was Faith gesagt hatte, oder vielleicht lag es einfach nur an Faith selbst. Was auch immer der Grund gewesen sein mochte, er konnte nicht ignorieren, was er fühlte. Er wollte Faith und er wollte für sie ein besserer Mann werden.

»Dein Lachen ist wie eine Droge und ich möchte mehr davon.«

»Sam«, sagte sie leise. »Du bist Coles Bruder. Er ist mein Chef.«

»Das stimmt, und er schätzt dich sehr und er liebt mich. Wir passen also perfekt zusammen.« Er wusste, dass er in Bezug auf Cole ein Risiko einging, aber Cole machte sich Sorgen, dass er Faith verletzen könnte, dass er einmal mit ihr schlief und sie dann links liegen ließ. Eine Frau links liegen zu lassen gehörte jedoch gar nicht zu seinem Konzept, jedenfalls nicht, wenn es um Faith ging. Wenn Cole wüsste, was er fühlte, würde er ihn ermuntern, da war er sich sicher.

»Du stehst nicht auf Dates und ich hüpfe nicht durch fremde Betten«, erwiderte sie bestimmt. »Wir passen überhaupt nicht perfekt zusammen.«

»In mancher Hinsicht hast du recht.«

»Genau.« Sie wandte sich ab, doch er nahm sie sanft am Arm und drehte sie zu sich.

»Du hast Angst, verletzt zu werden. Faith, ich gebe dir mein Wort, dass ich dich nicht verletzen werde.«

Sie verdrehte die Augen, eine ablehnende Geste, die ihn schmerzte.

»Sam, glaubst du wirklich, dass Leute Beziehungen eingehen und dabei schon genau wissen, dass sie sich gegenseitig verletzen werden?«

»Nein«, antwortete er. »Aber ich denke, beim Fremdgehen hat man die Wahl. Nichts zwingt jemanden dazu, fremdzugehen. Es bedarf einer bewussten, freiwilligen Entscheidung – werde ich den Menschen an meiner Seite verletzen oder nicht? Das ist etwas, worüber du dir bei mir keine Sorgen machen musst. Ich betrüge niemanden und werde dich niemals absichtlich verletzen.«

»Sagt der Mann, der von sich behauptet, seit der Highschool keine Freundin mehr gehabt zu haben.«

»Sagt der Mann, der weiß, was er will.« Die Worte klangen schärfer, als er beabsichtigt hatte, aber sie waren aufrichtig, genau wie seine Gefühle.

Die leise Spur eines Lächelns umspielte Faiths Lippen. »Du bist es nicht gewohnt, zurückgewiesen zu werden, oder?«

»Ganz schön direkt.« Er fuhr sich mit der Hand durch die Haare. »Nein, aber das ist nicht der Punkt. Ich stelle Frauen nicht nach, Faith. Wenn ich zurückgewiesen werde, drehe ich mich normalerweise um und verschwinde. Aber dir bleibe ich auf den Fersen und dabei geht es mir nicht nur um Sex.«

»Ich bin eine Herausforderung.« Sie hob das Kinn, als hätte sie ihn längst durchschaut. »Früher oder später werde ich dir langweilig werden, und dann geht es mir wie einem deiner Groupies und ich sehne mich nach einem Mann, den ich nicht haben kann.«

»Das wird nicht passieren.«

Sie verschränkte die Arme, und er konnte sehen, dass sie immer noch nervös war, immer noch Ja sagen wollte, obwohl ihr Verstand sie davor warnte.

»Ich bin wirklich spät dran, Sam. Ich kann keine Spielchen spielen. Wir passen einfach nicht zusammen. Ich mag dich, das ist wohl offensichtlich. Du bist heiß und lustig und klug und viel zu gefährlich für jemanden wie mich. Ich kann mein Herz nicht noch einmal aufs Spiel setzen.«

Es tat ihm weh, ihr Geständnis zu hören. »Faith, warum denkst du immer noch so schlecht von mir, nach allem, was ich dir gesagt habe?«

»Willst du eine ehrliche Antwort?«, fragte sie.

»Nur zu. Ich bin immer ehrlich, also kann ich auch ehrliche Antworten verkraften.«

»Du bist immer ehrlich? Wie bei deiner Oberschenkelverletzung?«, zog sie ihn auf.

»Die Verletzung ist echt.« Er klopfte auf sein Herz. »Aber wie sollte ich dieser Versuchung widerstehen? Vielleicht habe ich nie wieder die Gelegenheit, mich von dir anfassen zu lassen.«

»Du bist wirklich unglaublich.« Sie lachte. »Um den heißen

Brei herumzureden ist so gar nicht dein Ding, oder?«

»Nein. Und wie gesagt: Dabei bin ich immer ehrlich. Bitte erkläre mir, warum du mich für einen Schuft hältst.«

»Ich halte dich nicht für einen Schuft.« Sie seufzte, als fiele es ihr schwer, offen zu sein, doch Sam hoffte, dass sie seine Frage aufrichtig beantworten würde.

»Ich habe Angst, mit dir auszugehen. Ich weiß, dass wir viel Spaß zusammen hätten, aber ich möchte nicht eine der Frauen sein, die sagen, dass sie mit Sam Braden ausgegangen sind. Ich möchte nicht das erleben, was jede zweite Frau in der Stadt am eigenen Leib erlebt hat. Ich bin mehr wert als ein Abklatsch zahlloser früherer Dates. Ich habe zu hart daran gearbeitet, um mein Selbstvertrauen wiederherzustellen, nachdem ...« Sie schluckte schwer. »Ich habe endlich wieder Boden unter den Füßen und das kann ich nicht aufs Spiel setzen. Nicht einmal für dich.«

Faith hatte Mühe, so lange die Fassung zu bewahren, bis Sam gegangen war. Selbst als er endlich verschwunden war, starrte sie noch lange auf die geschlossene Tür, bevor sie tief durchatmete.

Was zum Teufel ist da gerade passiert? Sie war so überrascht gewesen, dass sie ganz vergessen hatte, ihn zu fragen, ob er hinter der Spende für den WAC steckte.

Es klopfte an der Tür und gleich darauf spähte Brandy ins Zimmer. Ihre glatten dunklen Haare fielen ihr über die Schultern. Sie war ein zierliches kleines Ding, zuckersüß und im Moment ziemlich schuldbewusst und verlegen.

»Hallo. Es tut mir leid. Sam hat mich gebeten, dir nicht zu

sagen, dass er der Patient ohne Termin war, und er ist Dr. Bradens Bruder und so nett und –«

»Schon gut, Brandy. Ich weiß, dass er sehr überzeugend sein kann.«

»Er ist so süß! Und diese Stimme«, sagte Brandy verträumt. »Seid ihr zwei ein Paar? Es schien ihm ungeheuer wichtig zu sein, dich zu sehen.«

»Nein, wir sind kein Paar«, sagte Faith rasch, um jeden Klatsch im Keim zu ersticken.

»Oh, ich dachte nur … tut mir leid. Übrigens, deine Patienten warten. Soll ich ihnen irgendwas sagen?«

»Nein. Ich werde gehen und mich für die Verzögerung entschuldigen, und jeder kommt dran, egal wie lange ich bleiben muss.«

Nachdem Brandy ihr die Liste mit Therapeuten gegeben hatte, nach der sie gefragt hatte, machte sich Faith wieder an die Arbeit. Um halb sieben verabschiedete sie sich von dem letzten Patienten, und als sie die Praxis schließlich verließ, war sie körperlich und geistig erschöpft. Sie fragte sich, ob es richtig gewesen war, wie sie mit Sam umgegangen war. Eigentlich wollte sie ihn nicht jedes Mal vor den Kopf stoßen, doch wenn sie mit ihm zusammen war, hatte sie Angst, es nicht zu tun.

Sie ging über den Parkplatz zu ihrem Auto und war überrascht, ein Notizheft mit einem einfachen weißen Einband unter ihrem Scheibenwischer zu sehen. Sie schlug es auf und las die handgeschriebene Notiz.

Faith,

ich frage mich, was du sehen würdest, wenn du nicht wüsstest, was man sich über mich erzählt. Würdest du mich dann so einschätzen, wie du es jetzt tust? Bist du bereit, deine Zukunft auf das zu verwetten, was du in mir zu sehen glaubst? Wenn ja, ignoriere diese Nachricht und mache weiter wie bisher. Ich verspreche, dich nie wieder zu belästigen. Wenn du jedoch nur die Spur eines Zweifels hast, wenn du fühlst, was ich fühle, wenn wir zusammen sind, dann gib mir eine Chance und geh zu Chelsea's Boutique.

Sam

»Oh mein Gott, Sam. Was machst du bloß?«

Sie las seine Nachricht zweimal. Er ließ nicht locker, und das machte sie neugierig und aufgeregt. Sie fuhr zu der hübschen Boutique, in der sie bisher nur ein paarmal gewesen war, und als sie vor der Tür parkte, fiel ihr auf, dass ihr der Gedanke, nicht hinzufahren, gar nicht in den Sinn gekommen war. Ihre Nerven standen in Flammen, als sie die Glastüren öffnete und den Laden betrat, ohne zu wissen, was sie erwartete.

»Hallo, Faith«, sagte Jewel, die an der Kasse stand. Sie kam mit einer großen Tüte hinter der Ladentheke hervor. »Die soll ich dir geben.« Mit einem seltsamen Blick in den Augen reichte sie Faith die Tüte. »Und das hier.«

»Danke.« Faith nahm die Tüte und den Umschlag entgegen. Sie hatte ganz vergessen, dass Jewel, die Verlobte von Sams Bruder, die Boutique führte.

Jewel musste ihre Beklommenheit gespürt haben. »Beides ist von Sam«, sagte sie und machte sich wieder an die Arbeit. Faith war dankbar, dass sie den Umschlag öffnen konnte, ohne dabei beobachtet zu werden. In dem Umschlag befand sich eine weitere handgeschriebene Nachricht.

Hi, schöne Frau,

Schön? Sie musste schmunzeln.

danke, dass du dich bis hierher auf mich eingelassen hast. Wahrscheinlich hast du immer noch deine Arbeitskleidung an und möchtest sie so schnell wie möglich loswerden. Da du dich entschieden hast, hierherzukommen, statt nach Hause zu gehen, dachte ich, du würdest dich über etwas Bequemeres freuen. Du kannst dich in der Anprobe umziehen. Such dir auch ein Paar Sandalen aus. Sie sind bereits bezahlt.

—S

Du hast mir etwas zum Anziehen gekauft? Sie sah zu Jewel hinüber, die lächelnd den Schlüssel zum Anproberaum hochhielt.

Als Jewel sie zu einer Kabine führte, sagte sie: »Ich glaube, ich finde das genauso spannend wie du. Was läuft da zwischen euch beiden?«

»Nichts.« Die Lüge schmeckte bitter. Da lief ganz bestimmt etwas, aber wie sollte sie es erklären, wenn sie es selbst nicht verstand?

Jewel öffnete die Tür zur Kabine und strich sich eine blonde Strähne hinters Ohr. »Wenn du meinst.«

»Was hat Sam gesagt?« Am liebsten hätte sie Jewel gefragt, wie Sam wirklich war, wenn er sich nicht in einem Club herumtrieb oder eine Party unsicher machte. War er der Mann, den sie gerade kennenlernte, oder war das alles nur Fassade?

»Nicht viel. Er kam herein und hat ein Outfit ausgesucht, das hat fast vierzig Minuten gedauert. Er hat sich wirklich Zeit genommen. Dann reichte er mir ein paar Dinge, die ich dir geben sollte, und als ich gefragt habe, warum, meinte er, ich würde es bald genug erfahren, wenn er Glück hätte.« Jewel zwackte mit den Augenbrauen. »Und? Hat er Glück?«

»Nicht so, wie du meinst.« *Vierzig Minuten?*

»Nun, wenn es hilft, kann ich dir sagen, dass ich Sam schon mein ganzes Leben lang kenne, und ich gebe große Stücke auf ihn.«

»Auch wenn er, ähm, nicht sehr wählerisch ist bei seinen Bettgenossinnen?« *Du lieber Himmel, habe ich das wirklich gesagt?*

»Okay, das ist ein kleiner Wermutstropfen, aber er hat das größte und freundlichste Herz, das man sich vorstellen kann. Keine Ahnung, warum Sam so ein Schürzenjäger ist, aber ich habe ihn lieb, so wie er ist. Ich meine, es gibt doch viele, die nichts anbrennen lassen, stimmt's?«

»Ja, wahrscheinlich«, erwiderte Faith halbherzig. »Ich bin allerdings nicht so«, sagte sie dann mehr zu sich selbst als zu Jewel.

»Willkommen im Club. Ich hatte null Erfahrung, vor Nate. Ich weiß nicht, was zwischen dir und Sam ist, aber ich kann ehrlich sagen, dass ich noch nie gesehen habe, wie er sich um eine Frau bemüht, außer wenn er … na ja, du weißt schon.«

Leider wusste sie nur zu gut, was Jewel meinte. Sie schlüpfte in die Umkleidekabine und las noch einmal Sams Nachricht. Trotz ihrer Bedenken fühlte sie sich wertgeschätzt, als sei sie etwas Besonderes. Alles, was er tat, war überraschend und, wie sie zugeben musste, auch durchdacht. Sie zog die Sachen hervor, die er ihr gekauft hatte: kein hautenger Fummel, wie sie befürchtet hatte, sondern Shorts aus Jeansstoff und ein hübsches rosafarbenes Top, das weich wie eine Wolke war. Woher wusste er ihre Größe? *Jewel.* Sie betrachtete sich im Spiegel und fühlte sich … wichtig für ihn.

Oje.

Sie sank für einen Moment auf die Holzbank in der Kabine und ließ den Gedanken sacken.

Als sie schließlich in ihrem neuen bequemen und niedlichen Outfit aus der Kabine kam, wartete Jewel bereits in der Schuhabteilung auf sie. »Sam hat schon bezahlt, also such dir ein Paar aus.«

»Meine Güte, ich komme mir vor wie Julia Roberts in Pretty Woman, nur dass meine Sachen bequemer sind. Und natürlich ohne diese Prostituiertennummer.«

»Du meinst, du hast das Gefühl, verwöhnt zu werden?«

»Ja«, sagte Faith, während sie die Schuhe betrachtete. »Genau das ist es. Oder vielleicht ist es noch mehr als das. So etwas hat noch nie ein Mann für mich getan. Ich habe das Gefühl, als sollte ich all diese Sachen von Sam nicht annehmen.«

»Normalerweise würde ich dir ohne Zögern beipflichten, aber für ihn ist das wirklich ungewöhnlich. Ich denke, es bedeutet, dass du ihm alles andere als egal bist. Ehrlich gesagt wüsste ich gern, was er für dich auf Lager hat. Er hat so geheimnisvoll getan.«

»Du meinst also nicht, dass ich komplett verrückt bin, weil ich nachgegeben und seine Nachrichten nicht ignoriert habe?«

»Überhaupt nicht.«

Dadurch fühlte sie sich nicht mehr ganz so fremd in ihrer Haut. Sie wollte auch herausfinden, was Sam vorhatte. Sie entschied sich für reizende perlenbesetzte Sandalen.

»Eins noch.« Jewel zog einen weiteren Umschlag aus ihrer Hosentasche, trat wieder hinter die Theke und holte eine Kapuzenjacke von Rough Riders hervor. Über dem Logo stand der Name Faith.

»Ich muss gestehen, dass ich ein bisschen neidisch bin«, sagte Jewel, »dabei habe ich den besten Mann von ganz Peaceful Harbor.« Sie umarmte Faith schnell und wünschte ihr Glück.

Als Faith den Laden verließ, fragte sie sich, ob Jewel nicht vielleicht falsch lag. Sie kannte keinen einzigen Mann, der sich so viel Mühe geben würde, um eine Frau dazu zu bringen, mit ihm auszugehen. Damit war Sam durchaus im Rennen um den Titel des besten Mannes von ganz Peaceful Harbor, oder? Oder würde ihm seine Vergangenheit immer im Weg stehen?

Sie hoffte inständig, dass dies nicht nur ein Spiel für Sam war, denn als sie in ihrem süßen neuen Outfit und der Kapuzenjacke mit ihrem Namen zum Auto eilte, merkte sie, dass sie ganz aufgeregt war. In der Abgeschiedenheit ihres Autos riss sie den Umschlag auf und las die dritte handgeschriebene Nachricht.

Hey, Baby.

Baby? Im Laufe von drei Nachrichten war er von Faith zu schöne Frau und schließlich zu Baby übergegangen. Und obwohl sie wusste, dass sie ein paar Kleidungsstücke und einige handgeschriebene Zettel nicht überbewerten sollte, genoss sie das Gefühl, etwas Besonderes zu sein.

Ich wette, du siehst sexy aus und bist nervös, und vielleicht wirst du sogar ein bisschen rot. Ich wünschte, ich könnte es sehen. Ich weiß, du hattest einen harten Tag, also will ich dich mit dem Rest nicht mehr lange aufhalten. Geh runter zum Jachthafen — oder scher dich nicht um mich und geh nach Hause. Ich bin froh, dass du bis hierhin mitgemacht hast.

—Sam, dein Date, wie ich hoffe.

Date? Er stand nicht auf Dates. Und woher wusste er, dass ihr die Röte ins Gesicht gestiegen war? Seine Nachrichten waren ebenso unwiderstehlich wie er selbst. Während der Fahrt zum Jachthafen schärfte sie sich immer wieder ein, dass er ein Frauenheld war. Als sie sich Harbour Overlook, einer Fußgängerbrücke über der Straße, näherte, traute sie ihren Augen nicht. Dort hing ein großes weißes Schild, auf dem mit großen roten Lettern SAG JA ZU SAM! aufgesprüht war.

»Grundgütiger, Sam.« Sie hielt am Straßenrand und machte ein Foto mit ihrem Handy. Als sie unter der Brücke hindurchfuhr, hatte sie eine Gänsehaut auf den Armen. Er hatte sich für sie so viel Mühe gegeben, obwohl sie ihn mit wenig schmeichelhaften Worten zurückgewiesen hatte. Das sprach Bände. Entweder war er bereit, alles Erdenkliche zu tun, um eine Frau zu erobern, oder es lag ihm wirklich etwas an ihr. Allmählich freundete sie sich mit der Idee an, tatsächlich mit Sam auszugehen, als sie zur nächsten Ampel kam.

An der Ecke standen zwei Schilder. Auf einem zeigte ein Pfeil in die Richtung, in der ihre Wohnung lag. Darunter stand: SICHERER WEG NACH HAUSE. Auf dem zweiten Schild wies ein Pfeil zum Jachthafen. HIGHWAY TO HEAVEN stand darauf. Sie musste lachen, als sie ein weiteres Foto machte und dann in die Straße zum Hafen abbog. Dort wurde offensichtlich, wie weit Sam Braden zu gehen bereit war, um sie zu überreden, ihre Meinung zu ändern. Auf dem Schild über dem Hafeneingang prangte in großen Leuchtbuchstaben: F. MR. B. BITTE. S. Sie fragte sich, welche Beziehungen er hatte spielen lassen, um die Aufschrift zu ändern.

Sie fuhr über den Parkplatz zu der Straße, die zum Mr. B. führte, und fragte sich, warum er all das auf die Beine stellte, nur um sie zum Brauhaus seiner Eltern zu lotsen. Von außen sah das Mr. B. genauso aus wie sonst. Faith zupfte ihr Top unter der Kapuzenjacke von Rough Riders zurecht und sah sich auf dem Parkplatz vor dem Lokal um. Plötzlich war sie nervös. Sie trug Sachen, die Sam nicht nur ausgesucht, sondern auch bezahlt hatte, und würde gleich das Restaurant betreten, das seiner Familie gehörte! Er hatte sich wirklich bemüht, ihr alles so behaglich wie möglich zu machen. Der Gedanke gefiel ihr, aber es fühlte sich immer noch seltsam an. Aufregend und romantisch, aber ganz anders, als sie es gewohnt war.

Im Mr. B. war es laut. Die Tischdame warf ihr einen kurzen Blick zu und ihre Augen weiteten sich. »Faith?«

»Ja.« Faith schluckte schwer.

»Bitte folgen Sie mir.« Die energische Brünette ging schnell auf die Bar zu.

Sam war nirgendwo zu sehen, aber sie erkannte Mr. Braden und lächelte ihn an. Sie war schrecklich verlegen.

»Bitte sehr«, sagte die Tischdame, drehte sich auf dem Fuße um und ließ Faith stehen, die Sams Vater ansah.

»Hallo, Faith. Wie geht's?« Er kam um die Bar herum und sogleich fiel ihm das Rough-Riders-Logo auf ihrer Kapuzenjacke auf. Wenn er lächelte, hatte er das gleiche Grübchen wie Sam, direkt unter seinem linken Mundwinkel.

»Gut, danke. Wie geht es Ihnen, Mr. Braden?«

»Heute ist ein magischer Abend hier im Mr. B. Ich freue mich, dass Sie kommen konnten.«

»Tatsächlich?« Oh nein. Das war ihr einfach so herausgerutscht. Sie war zu nervös. Für den Rest des Abends sollte sie besser den Mund halten.

»Er lachte und sein Lachen erinnerte sie an Sam. »Tatsächlich, junge Dame. Sam wird begeistert sein, dass Sie hier sind. Er war den ganzen Abend das reinste Nervenbündel.«

»Plauder nicht Sams Geheimnisse aus«, sagte Sams Mutter, die hinter Faith auftauchte. »Hallo, Liebes. Kommen Sie, ich bringe Sie zu Sam.«

Faith hatte Mr. und Mrs. Braden von dem Moment an gemocht, als sie sie letztes Jahr in Coles Praxis kennengelernt hatte. Sams Mutter war lebhaft, hatte dichte, blonde Locken und sah in ihren weit fallenden Tops aus wie ein Hippie. Sein Vater dagegen war viel konservativer und ruhiger, aber immer herzlich und freundlich.

»Nach oben?«, fragte sie und folgte Mrs. Braden durch eine Reihe von Türen erst in die Küche, dann durch eine schwere Stahltür und eine Treppe hinauf.

»Aufs Dach.« Sams Mutter senkte die Stimme und flüsterte: »Sam hat sich mächtig ins Zeug gelegt. Ich habe ihn noch nie so aufgeregt gesehen. Ich bin froh, dass Sie doch noch gekommen sind.«

Faith kam sich vor wie in einem Traum und schwebte von einer Überraschung zur nächsten, während Glück und Nervosität alles wie mit Feenstaub besprühten. Der Aufwand, den Sam getrieben hatte, schien alle zu erstaunen, und sie staunte auch. Damit, dass Sams Mutter sie auf dem obersten Treppenabsatz in den Arm nahm, hatte sie jedoch am allerwenigsten gerechnet.

»Viel Spaß. Und, Faith?«

»Ja?« Sie hielt den Atem an und wartete auf eine unangenehme Wahrheit, etwa: *Lassen Sie sich nicht von ihm täuschen. Er ist eben Sam.*

»Bitte brechen Sie meinem Jungen nicht das Herz. Er kann hart wie Stein sein, aber er hat einen weichen Kern.« Sie tätschelte Faith die Wange, wie ihre eigene Mutter es unzählige Male getan hatte, und stieg die Treppe hinunter, während Faith die Tür anstarrte.

Hinter dieser Tür war Sam.

Sam, der Sam mit dem weichen Kern. Sam, der sich mächtig ins Zeug gelegt hatte. Der Mann, der nicht auf Dates stand und sagte, dass er eine Frau nie betrügen würde. Der Mann, der glaubte, dass nichts ewig hielt. Der Mann, der gestern Abend am Strand eine ganze Stunde lang mit ihr geredet und alle Register gezogen hatte, um sie hierherzubringen. Sam, der Mann, von dem sie geträumt hatte, um den ihre Fantasien gekreist waren. Und jetzt stand sie vollkommen durcheinander da und wusste nicht, ob sie die Tür öffnen oder weglaufen sollte.

Sie sah die Treppe hinunter. Es wäre so einfach, zu ihrem Auto zurückzugehen. Viel einfacher, als sich den Emotionen zu stellen, die auf sie einstürmten, und die Leidenschaft zuzulassen, die sie nicht wahrhaben wollte. Aber einfach war langweilig, oder? Vielleicht mochte sie es doch nicht einfach, weil sie Sam mochte.

Sie wandte sich zur Tür, nahm all ihren Mut zusammen und schob sie auf.

Weiße Lichter beleuchteten eine hüfthohe Mauer, die die Dachfläche begrenzte. Faith trat nach draußen und hielt die Tür offen, während sie den für zwei Personen gedeckten Tisch bestaunte. Auf der roten Tischdecke lagen Leinenservietten bereit, zwischen einigen mit glänzenden Metalldeckeln bedeckten Schüsseln stand eine Flasche Wein und in einem Kerzenleuchter brannten drei wunderschöne Kerzen. Die hellen Flammen flackerten im Abendwind. Sam saß mit dem Rücken zu ihr und spielte auf der Gitarre, während er auf das Meer hinausblickte. Einen Moment lang lauschte sie der friedlichen Melodie, die aus seinen Fingerspitzen strömte, und als sie näher trat, glitt ihr die Türklinke aus der Hand und die Tür fiel mit lautem Krachen ins Schloss.

Sam drehte sich um, und seine dunklen Augen füllten sich mit Hitze, als er aufstand. In seiner Jeans und dem engen schwarzen Hemd sah er teuflisch schön aus. Er lehnte die Gitarre an die Mauer. Von der Terrasse unten schwebte leise Musik zu ihnen aufs Dach und bot einen sexy Hintergrund für Sam, der sich mit fließenden Bewegungen auf sie zubewegte. Wie konnte so viel geballte Kraft gleichzeitig anmutig und männlich wirken?

»Faith.« Ihr Name glitt ihm wie Seide von den Lippen, als er ihre Hand nahm.

Bei seiner Berührung empfand sie ein ungewohntes Gefühl der Geborgenheit, wie gestern Abend, und das überraschte sie.

Sein Mund verzog sich zu einem warmen Lächeln. »Ich bin froh, dass du gekommen bist.«

Ihr Körper fühlte sich zugleich elektrisiert und wie aufgelöst an, als sie eine Woge der Gefühle erfasste. In wenigen Tagen hatte er ihr mehr von sich offenbart als manche Leute in einem ganzen Jahr.

»Ich bin auch froh, dass ich gekommen bin.«

Neun

Sam fuhr Faith mit dem Daumen über den Handrücken. Er konnte den Blick nicht von ihr wenden und war sich mit jeder Faser seines Körpers der Hitze zwischen ihnen bewusst.

»Du siehst noch schöner aus, als ich es mir vorgestellt habe.«

Ein rosiger Schimmer überzog ihre Wangen. »Ich kann nicht glauben, dass du mir etwas zum Anziehen gekauft hast.«

»Ich hatte Angst, dass du dich nicht auf ein Treffen mit mir einlassen würdest, ohne dich vorher umzuziehen. Und dann hatte ich Angst, dass du es dir anders überlegst, wenn du erst einmal zu Hause bist, und dann hätte ich ganz allein hier oben gesessen und mich nach dir gesehnt.« Er beugte sich vor und gab ihr einen Kuss auf die Wange, während er ihren weichen, weiblichen, einladenden Duft einsaugte.

Sie atmete scharf ein, als seine Lippen ihre Haut streiften.

»Ich hatte überlegt, dir eine Jeans oder ein Kleid zu kaufen«, sagte er. »Aber wenn ich an dich denke, sehe ich Behaglichkeit, Anmut und dein anziehendes Selbstbewusstsein, und all das ist heißer als eine figurbetonte Jeans oder ein kurzer Rock.«

Ihre Augen weiteten sich ein wenig. »Das alles siehst du, wenn du an mich denkst?«

»Das ist nur ein Bruchteil dessen, was ich sehe. Mir ist noch nie aufgefallen, dass Kleidung etwas sehr Persönliches ist, bis ich in Jewels Laden stand und überlegte, worin du dich am wohlsten fühlen würdest. Natürlich wusste ich, dass du hinreißend aussehen würdest, egal was du anhast, aber darum ging es nicht.«

»Du hast dir so viel Mühe gemacht.« Sie fuhr mit dem Finger über ihren Namen auf der Kapuzenjacke.

Dass er die Jacke so schnell mit ihrem Namen beschriften lassen konnte, war nur möglich gewesen, weil ihm jemand einen Gefallen schuldete. Als er sie nun darin sah, so sündhaft süß und unglaublich sexy, wusste er, dass sich die Mühe gelohnt hatte. Am Nachmittag, als er umhergefahren war und die Schilder aufgestellt und alles für den Fall organisiert hatte, dass sie sich tatsächlich auf seine Einladung einließ, war etwas mit ihm passiert. Die ganze Zeit über hatte er versucht, Abstand von ihr zu halten und sie vor ihm zu schützen. Schließlich war selbst sein eigener Bruder davon überzeugt, dass sie vor ihm beschützt werden musste. Ein paar Wochen vor der Hochzeit hatte er eine Veränderung an sich selbst festgestellt. Beiläufige Tändeleien interessierten ihn nicht mehr, aber Faith? Sie beherrschte seine Gedanken Tag und Nacht, so sehr er auch versuchte, sie daraus zu verbannen. Heute hatte er seine Gefühle einmal genauer unter die Lupe genommen und erkannt, dass es ihm die ganze Zeit über nur um Faith gegangen war. Sie hatte sein Herz geködert, und weil er so fest entschlossen gewesen war, sich fernzuhalten, hatte er sich nicht erlaubt, es zu sehen. Jetzt war er nicht mehr bereit, das beiseitezuschieben, was sich richtig anfühlte, oder den Menschen zu ignorieren, der ihn Dinge fühlen ließ, von denen er nie geglaubt hätte, dass er sie fühlen würde. Er wollte nicht nur beweisen, dass er nicht derjenige war, für den sie – und alle anderen – ihn hielten. Er wollte noch mehr. Er wusste, dass er sich mit Faith nicht nur ein bisschen vergnügen wollte. Und er wollte, dass sie sich das ebenfalls wünschte.

»Eigentlich glaube ich, dass ich mir längst noch nicht genug Mühe gegeben habe.« Er trat näher und nahm ihre Hand. Das Funkeln der Lichterkette spiegelte sich in ihren Augen, als sie zum Tisch gingen. Aller Aufwand war es wert gewesen, nur um ihr wundervolles Lächeln zu sehen.

»Es ist wie ein Turm, für uns ganz allein. Das wäre doch alles nicht nötig gewesen.«

»Doch, das war es.« Er schenkte zwei Gläser Wein ein. »Du hast mir einen Korb gegeben, als ich mich wie jeder ganz normale Typ mit dir verabreden wollte.«

»Du bist kein ganz normaler Typ, Sam. Du bist der Bruder meines Chefs, und du verkörperst alles, wovor ich Angst habe.«

Er nahm ein Glas, prostete ihr zu und hoffte, dass sie ihre Ängste irgendwann hinter sich lassen würde. »Auf zwei Leute, die nicht perfekt zusammenpassen.«

Sie lächelte. »Ich kann gar nicht glauben, dass ich darauf anstoße.«

Ihre Gläser klirrten leise aneinander, und während Faith ihren Wein trank, weidete sich Sam an ihrem Anblick.

»Kein Mann hat mir je etwas zum Anziehen gekauft. Außer meinem Vater, aber das zählt nicht.«

»Dann fühle ich mich geehrt, dass ich der Erste bin. Das passt, denn schließlich bist du mein erstes richtiges Date.« Bevor sie einwenden konnte, dass dies kein richtiges Date sei, nahm er sie in die Arme und sagte: »Tanz mit mir.«

Mit gerunzelter Stirn legte sie ihm die Arme um die Taille.

Sam nahm ihre Hände und legte sie sich um den Hals. »So mag ich es lieber. Weil wir uns dann noch näher kommen.« Er sah ihr in die Augen, während sie sich in einem langsamen, sinnlichen Rhythmus bewegten.

»Wir tanzen«, sagte sie leise. »Auf einem Dach mit funkelnden Lichtern und Musik und Kerzenlicht. Sam, das ist bestimmt das Romantischste, was jemals jemand für mich getan hat.« Sie lächelte ihn an, doch er spürte, dass sie immer noch unschlüssig war, was sie beide anging.

»Du hast gesagt, dass du mehr wert bist als ein Abklatsch dessen, was ich mit zahllosen anderen Frauen in Peaceful Harbor gemacht habe. Ich habe keiner von ihnen jemals etwas zum Anziehen gekauft oder sie quer durch die halbe Stadt gelotst, um mich zu finden, oder sie zum Brauhaus meiner Eltern gebracht. Nur dich, Süße.«

Sie errötete und lehnte die Stirn an seine Brust. »Du hast mich ›Süße‹ genannt.«

Er lachte. »Ja.«

»Ich kann nicht anders, ich muss dir diese Frage einfach stellen.« Ihre Miene wurde ernst. »Nennst du alle deine Mädels so?«

Er wusste, dass ihr sein Ruf gegen den Strich ging, doch er hatte sich nicht klargemacht, dass er jeden ihrer Gedanken durchdrang. Er konnte ihr nur aufrichtig antworten: »Nein, Faith. Und ich habe keine ›Mädels‹.«

Sie nickte, die Stirn immer noch in nachdenkliche Falten gezogen. »Und wenn ich heute Abend nicht aufgetaucht wäre?«

»Das wäre richtig blöd gewesen. Stell dir nur vor, was ich von Nate zu hören bekommen hätte. Jewel erzählt ihm garantiert, was ich getan habe.«

Sie lachte, und er war froh, dass sie ein wenig aus der Deckung kam.

»Waren heute Nachmittag noch mehr nackte Männer in der

Praxis?« Er liebte den Hauch von Verlegenheit in ihren Augen, der kurz aufblitzte und ebenso schnell wieder verschwand.

»Du warst nicht nackt, und nein, zum Glück waren keine nackten Männer dabei.«

Sie fuhr sich mit der Zungenspitze über die Lippen und am liebsten hätte er ihren Weg mit seiner eigenen Zunge nachvollzogen. Aber er hatte sich vorgenommen, es langsam angehen zu lassen. Er war fest entschlossen, ihr zu beweisen, dass er nicht nur eins im Sinn hatte – aber je mehr er versuchte, nicht daran zu denken, desto mehr fiel ihm auf, dass sich ihre Oberschenkel berührten und ihre Brüste gegen seine Brust drückten.

»Du siehst mich an, als wäre ich nackt«, flüsterte sie kaum hörbar.

»Tatsächlich? Tut mir leid.« Er wirbelte sie herum und sie lachte, ein süßes, melodisches Lachen, von dem er mehr hören wollte.

Sie drehte sich zu ihm zurück, schlang ihm die Arme um den Hals und sagte: »Nein, es tut dir nicht leid.«

»Es tut mir leid, wenn es dir unangenehm ist, aber ich kann nicht aufhören, dich anzusehen. Du bist wunderschön.«

»Sam.« Sie senkte den Blick. »Du machst mich verlegen.«

Er hob ihr Kinn und sah ihr in die Augen. Wie von einem Magneten fühlte er sich über die unsichtbare Grenze gezogen, die er sich gesetzt hatte, um sich selbst in Schach zu halten. Seine Hand schob sich hinunter bis zu der Stelle, an der ihre Wirbelsäule begann. In seinem Denken war sie schon sein, aber sein Herz wusste, dass es nicht so einfach werden würde.

»Ich möchte dich nicht in Verlegenheit bringen.«

Ihre Lippen teilten sich mit einem Seufzen, und er unterdrückte den Drang, diese verdammte Grenze zu überschreiten und sie endlich zu küssen, zu schmecken, ihr sein Zeichen aufzubrennen. Er hatte die letzten drei Tage ununterbrochen an sie gedacht und jetzt hielt er sie in den Armen und konnte sie nicht einmal küssen.

»Erzähl mir etwas über dich, Faith. Hast du Brüder oder Schwestern?«

»Ich habe einen jüngeren Bruder und eine jüngere Schwester. Mack lebt in Oak Falls in Virginia, wo wir herkommen. Und meine Schwester Charley studiert Meeresbiologie in Harborside, Massachusetts.« Allmählich wurden ihre Bewegungen fließender und entspannter.

»Aha, du bist die Älteste. Deshalb bist du so besonnen und diszipliniert.«

»Weil ich die Älteste bin? Und an welcher Stelle kommt ein ungezogener Bursche wie du im riesigen Braden-Clan?« Ein spitzbübisches Funkeln blitzte in ihren Augen auf.

»Ich bin das zweite Kind, der typische Unruhestifter. Ist das nicht offensichtlich?« Er fuhr mit der Hand über ihren Rücken und spürte, wie sie unter seiner Berührung erzitterte. »Vielleicht solltest du das wilde Tier in mir zähmen.«

»Wäre es nicht schade drum?« Sie sah ihn unverwandt an. »All die Mädels hätten keinen ungezogenen Burschen mehr zum Spielen.«

»Du bist ein sexy kleines Ding, nicht wahr?« Hitze flammte in ihm auf. »Wäre das so schlimm? Wenn sie ohne ihn dastünden?« Seine Hand glitt zurück in die Kuhle direkt über ihrem Hintern.

Ihr Atem ging schneller, ihre Hüften schoben sich nach vorne und ihre leisen Worte klangen verführerisch: »Sag du es mir. Was willst du?«

»Dich.« *In meinem Bett, auf meinem Schoß, auf meinem Boot.*

Er wollte mit ihr zusammen sein, einen Raum mit ihr teilen, sie halten, mit ihr reden – und sie lieben. Dieser letzte Punkt war nichts Neues, neu waren allerdings die ernsten Gefühle, mit denen er seit der Hochzeit gerungen hatte und die mit jedem Wort, das sie sprachen, stärker wurden.

»Warum?«

Er begegnete ihrem neugierigen Blick. »Weil du klug und bedacht bist und dich in eine sichere kleine Luftblase zurückgezogen hast, um nicht verletzt zu werden.« Er legte ihr die Hand aufs Herz und spürte das wilde Pochen unter seiner Handfläche. »Aber du möchtest berührt und geliebt und geschätzt werden. Und ich mag es, wenn du aus der Sicherheit deiner Luftblase herauskommst und dich auf Zehenspitzen dorthin schleichst, wo Sammy ist.«

Sie lächelte und zupfte mit den Zähnen an ihrer Unterlippe.

»Weil ich dir die ganze Zeit widerstanden habe«, sagte er, während er ihren Blick gefangen hielt. »Und das will ich nicht mehr.«

Sie löste sich ein wenig von ihm. »Ich springe nicht mit dir ins Bett.«

»Das ist nicht das, was ich will.« Er lächelte. »Jedenfalls nicht heute Abend.«

»Sam!« Sie trat halbherzig einen Schritt zurück, doch er hielt sie fest. Sie sollte die Wahrheit hören. »Also ist das alles nur ein Mittel zum Zweck?«

»Nicht zu dem Zweck, an den du denkst, Faith. Nicht nur für Sex.«

»Okay.« Sie wandte den Blick ab.

Er verfluchte sich schweigend, weil er es vermasselt hatte, aber wie konnte er vor ihr verbergen, dass er sich zu ihr hingezogen fühlte, wenn es das Letzte war, was er wollte?

»Ich versuche, ehrlich zu sein. Wie kannst du erwarten, dass ein Mann dich ansieht und dich nicht berühren und küssen möchte? Du bist die verführerischste Frau, der ich je begegnet bin. Einen Moment bist du besonnen und zurückhaltend und gleich darauf selbstbewusst und herausfordernd. Und du treibst mich auf die wunderbarste Weise in den Wahnsinn, bist hellwach und scharfzüngig und einen Wimpernschlag später ängstlich und ausweichend. Aber willst du wissen, was mir am meisten zusetzt? Dass deine Augen mich verschlingen, während deine Worte mich umbringen.«

»Sam«, flüsterte sie. Ihre Hände glitten über seine Brust bis zu seiner Taille, heiß und verführerisch, während sie sich kaum merklich zur Musik wiegten und ihre Körper sich an jedem möglichen Punkt berührten.

»Deine Augen sind so voller Hunger und voller Bedenken. Ich möchte deine Bedenken lindern und deinen Hunger stillen.«

Sie schluckte schwer. Zu wissen, dass er ebenso eine Wirkung auf sie hatte wie sie auf ihn, spornte ihn an.

»Ich dachte, wir könnten zu Abend essen, uns kennenlernen, nicht mehr. Jedenfalls heute nicht, obwohl ich nicht aufhören kann, mir vorzustellen, dich zu küssen. Es ist nicht so, dass ich dich heute Abend oder morgen oder nächste Woche in mein Bett locken will. Aber …«

Ihr Herz pochte wild an seiner Brust. Ihre Finger gruben sich in seine Taille und entzündeten Blitze der Lust in seinem Innern. Sie blinzelte zu ihm auf, ihre Augen waren dunkel wie der Nachthimmel. Er spürte ihre Nähe mit jedem Nerv seines Körpers, schmerzlich und überdeutlich. Es war unmöglich, sich noch eine Sekunde länger zurückzuhalten. Er musste einfach wissen, ob es ihr so ging wie ihm.

»Was fühlst du, Faith?« Seine Stimme war rau von zurückgehaltenem Verlangen. »Was willst du, jetzt, in diesem Moment? Gibt es einen Teil von dir, der nicht hier sein will? Möchtest du reden? Oder möchtest du aufhören, dir Sorgen zu machen, aufhören zu hungern und endlich erleben, wie wir uns anfühlen? Ein. Einziger. Kuss.«

Ihre Augen weiteten sich vor Überraschung und verengten sich gleich wieder. Ihr Blick war erfüllt von ungezähmtem Verlangen. Wortlos stellte sie sich auf die Zehenspitzen, und er packte sie und drückte ihren süßen Körper an seinen. Der Kuss war gierig und unordentlich, fordernd und drängend, als ihre Zungen zusammenstießen, um noch mehr zu fühlen und noch mehr zu nehmen. Sie schmeckte nach Nacht und Lust und nach Dingen, für die er keinen Namen wusste, die jedoch sein Herz anschwellen ließen. Ihre hinreißenden Rundungen schmiegten sich an ihn, machten ihn hart und hungrig nach mehr. Seine Hände glitten über ihren Rücken und entlockten ihr ein lüsternes Stöhnen. Er hatte Mühe, sich unter Kontrolle zu halten. Seine Hände sehnten sich nach ihrer heißen Haut, er wollte dieses verführerische Stöhnen hören und dabei ihren nackten Körper unter sich spüren und tief in ihr vergraben sein.

Ihre Hände fuhren über seine Brust und drückten gegen seine Brustmuskeln, während ihre Hüften seine harte Männlichkeit pulsieren ließen. Er schob eine Hand unter ihr Top und tastete sich an ihrem Rücken entlang, so sehr sehnte er sich nach einer unmittelbaren Verbindung ohne etwas dazwischen. Ein sündiger Laut glitt über ihre Lippen und löste ein Stöhnen aus seiner Kehle. Wie sollte er ihr widerstehen? Wie konnte er sie vor ihm schützen, wenn sie jeden seiner Gedanken verzehrte und jeden seiner Schritte beeinflusste?

Faith war schockiert, wie begierig sie auf die sinnliche Freude reagierte, die ein Kuss von Sam jeder Faser ihres Körpers bescherte, und versuchte, sich von ihm zu lösen. Ihr Verstand bekam die Botschaft jedoch nicht mit, und sie stellte sich auf die Zehenspitzen, um ihm noch näher zu kommen und den Kuss noch tiefer werden zu lassen. Seine Hände waren groß und heiß, brandmarkten sie durch ihre Kleider hindurch und ließen die Stelle zwischen ihren Beinen schmerzlich anschwellen. Mehr, sie wollte mehr. Sie klammerte sich an seinen Hals, kämpfte gegen den Drang an, ihn wie einen Berg zu erklimmen und ihn nach und nach genüsslich zu verzehren. Aber seine Eltern waren ganz in der Nähe, und wenn sie einmal ihre Beine um seine Taille geschlungen hatte, würde sie ihn nie wieder loslassen.

Oh nein, nein, nein. Sie musste sich zurückhalten. Sie konnte sich nicht auf ihn einlassen. Er hatte ihr die Gehirnzellen vernebelt. Wieder einmal. Allmählich wurde das zur Gewohnheit, erst seine Blicke, dann seine Worte, dann seine Berührung und jetzt das ... dieser köstliche, unglaubliche, perfekte Kuss. Sie wollte nicht sein Spielzeug für eine Nacht sein und wissen, dass er sich ein oder zwei Tage später an die Fersen einer anderen Frau heftete.

Aber sein wundervoller Mund, der sie so geschickt verwöhnte, war zu köstlich. Sie konnte nicht widerstehen. Seine Zunge strich wild über ihre, und als wüsste er genau, was sie brauchte, wurden seine Bewegungen weniger fordernd. Sein Kuss wurde weicher und langsamer und verlieh dem Wort Folter eine ganz neue Bedeutung. Seine Zunge umspielte ihre, während seine Hände an ihren nackten Rücken gepresst waren.

Die quälende Zärtlichkeit seines Kusses überschwemmte jeden Punkt ihres Körpers mit Wohlbehagen – die Knie, Hüften, Brüste. Sam übernahm die Kontrolle, ohne Gewalt, ohne sie zu beherrschen und ohne die Verbindung zu lösen, sodass der Kuss umso süßer wurde.

Er schob beide Hände unter ihr Haar, und dann umrahmten seine großen, kräftigen Hände ihr Gesicht, während er sich zurückzog – nicht ohne vorher noch eine Spur zittriger Küsse auf ihren Wangen, dem Kinn und schließlich wieder auf ihrem Mund zu hinterlassen.

»Das war …«, flüsterte er an ihren Lippen, bevor er seinen Mund wieder an ihren presste. »Mach die Augen auf, Faith. Schau mich an. Sei bei mir.«

Seine eindringliche Bitte ließ sie die Augen öffnen, und bei der Art, wie er sie ansah, als hätte er sein ganzes Leben darauf gewartet, sie zu küssen und sie so zu halten, wurde ihr schwindelig. Sie sank wieder auf die Fersen. Ihre Beine trugen sie kaum noch, aber ihr Körper fühlte sich an, als sei sie auf Speed. Die Sehnsucht, mit der sie sich nach einem weiteren Kuss verzehrte, war so heftig, dass es fast wehtat.

Er lehnte seine Stirn an ihre und ein zufriedenes Lächeln umspielte seine Lippen. »Möchtest du gehen?«

»Nein.«

Ein Hitzeblitz zuckte in seinen Augen. Ebenso schnell jedoch trat etwas Warmes in seinen Blick, ein Gefühl, das weniger drängend, weniger sündhaft, aber genauso machtvoll war, und er legte seine Lippen wieder auf ihre.

»Gott sei Dank.« Seine Stimme war voller Verlangen.

Sie wollte all das – seinen Kuss, seine Berührung –, aber sie hätte fast die Zügel aus der Hand gegeben. Er musste wissen, wo ihre Grenzen waren. »Aber mehr geht nicht.«

»Mehr nicht«, wiederholte er.

Sie schüttelte den Kopf, und er schloss sie in die Arme und drückte sie. Seine Wange ruhte auf ihrem Haar, und sie hatte das Gefühl, als könnte sie gut und gern den Rest ihres Lebens so verbringen.

Ihr Magen knurrte und sie stöhnte.

»Wahrscheinlich kann ich nicht so tun, als sei das dein Hunger nach mir, oder?«, neckte er.

Wenn du wüsstest!

Nach einem weiteren süßen Kuss setzten sie sich an den Tisch. Ihr Herz pochte immer noch wie verrückt. Sam nahm die Deckel von den Schüsseln und eine köstliche Mahlzeit aus Lachs, gedünstetem Gemüse und gebackenen Kartoffeln kam zum Vorschein.

Sie unterhielten sich und aßen, und Faith erinnerte sich daran, dass sie ihn fragen wollte, ob er der Gruppe die Spende überwiesen hatte.

Sam hielt inne, die Gabel schwebte auf halbem Weg zum Mund in der Luft. »Ja. Du wolltest den Scheck ja nicht direkt annehmen und ich wollte gern helfen.«

»Aber Sam, das ist viel zu viel.«

»Ich glaube kaum, dass es ein Zuviel gibt.« Er spießte ein Stück Lachs auf und steckte es sich in den Mund.

Sie hatte keine Ahnung, wie man dieses Spiel spielte. War es ein Spiel?

Er legte seine Gabel beiseite, nippte an seinem Wein, nahm dann wieder ihre Hand und rückte mit seinem Stuhl näher zu ihr.

»Faith, was nützt mir der Erfolg, wenn ich ihn nicht dazu verwenden kann, anderen zu helfen? So hast du es doch auch gemacht. Du hast das gesamte Programm aufgebaut. Das muss dich jede Menge Zeit, Energie und Geld gekostet haben.«

»Ja, hat es, aber das, was ich durchgemacht habe, hat mich angetrieben.«

»Warum kannst du nicht akzeptieren, dass ich helfen möchte?« Seine Reaktion war überraschend heftig, und sie zwang sich, genauer hinzuhören. »Du hast mir gesagt, dass Männer wie ich der Grund sind, dass diese Frauen der Gruppe beigetreten sind. Ich habe noch nie eine Frau betrogen und werde es auch nicht tun. Ich denke, ich habe das ziemlich deutlich gemacht, aber trotzdem möchte ich ihnen helfen. Der Gedanke an das, was Brittany oder Hilary oder du oder Vivian oder die anderen Frauen erlebt haben, ist unerträglich.«

Sie wollte seine Aufrichtigkeit nicht wahrhaben, aber ihr wurde klar, dass sie gegen sich selbst kämpfte, gegen das, wovor sie Angst hatte, anstatt Sam zu glauben. Und das wurde keinem von beiden gerecht.

»Du weißt sicher, dass Liras Leben momentan auch ein bisschen chaotisch ist«, sagte er. Faith war überrascht, dass er über Liras Situation Bescheid wusste. »Ich denke, wir können uns gegenseitig helfen.«

»Oh?«, fragte sie neugierig. Noch vor ein paar Stunden hätte sie wahrscheinlich mit einem ironischen *Ach ja?* reagiert.

»Sie hat viel Erfahrung im Büromanagement, und ich brauche jemanden, der bei Rough Riders die Verwaltungsarbeit erledigt, die Sponsoren koordiniert und bei der Organisation des alljährlichen Barbecues hilft.«

Ihre Augen weiteten sich hoffnungsvoll. »Meinst du, du könntest ihr vielleicht einen Job geben?«

»Ich könnte mir eine längere Probezeit vorstellen. Wir werden sehen, wie es läuft. Wenn sie so gut ist, wie ihr beruflicher Werdegang vermuten lässt, wird sie schon lange unterbezahlt, und ich bin mir nicht sicher, ob sie weiß, wie viel sie wirklich wert ist. Aber mach dir keine Sorgen. Wenn es klappt, ist sie bei Rough Riders gut aufgehoben. Mit Sozialleistungen und allem Drum und Dran.«

Hatte er schon mit Lira darüber gesprochen? »Das ist dir wirklich wichtig, nicht wahr?«

»Ja, klar. Ich wurde dazu erzogen, anderen zu helfen. So habe ich es mein ganzes Leben lang gehalten. Warum ist das so schwer zu glauben?«

»Vielleicht, weil du nicht zur Autowaschaktion gekommen bist, um zu helfen.« Sie hob eine Augenbraue und das brachte ihr ein sexy Lächeln ein.

»Du hast recht, aber deshalb kann ich trotzdem den aufrichtigen Wunsch verspüren, zu helfen. Wenn mir das egal wäre, hätte ich keinen weiteren Gedanken daran verschwendet.«

Was sie als Nächstes sagen wollte, kam ihr nicht leicht über die Lippen, aber nach allem, was er heute Abend für sie und für die Gruppe getan hatte, schuldete sie ihm dieselbe Aufrichtigkeit, mit der er ihr begegnete – selbst wenn es peinlich war.

»Ich habe dich an dem gemessen, was ich über dich gehört hatte, Sam. Es tut mir leid. Das war nicht fair.«

»Dann lerne mich besser kennen. Finde heraus, wer ich wirklich bin.« Er sah sie erwartungsvoll an. »Geh mit mir aus, Faith.«

»Darüber haben wir doch schon gesprochen. Dates sind nicht deine Sache und –«

»Und du springst nicht gleich mit jedem ins Bett. Ich hab's kapiert. Das sollst du ja auch nicht. Ich bin dabei, mich zu ändern. Ich würde gerne mit dir ausgehen. Mein ganzes Leben lang habe ich alles abgeblockt, was nur entfernt nach einer emotionalen Bindung aussieht, aber bei dir kann ich es nicht abblocken. Du gehst mir unter die Haut, und ich möchte meine Gefühle nicht ignorieren.«

»Du willst nur mit mir ausgehen? Sam, ich kann nicht …«

Plötzlich lag sie in seinen Armen, ihre Körper prallten aneinander, sein Mund eroberte ihren und küsste ihre Sorgen fort. Er ließ den Kuss tiefer werden, als wollte er sie spüren lassen, wie heftig sein Verlangen nach ihr war. Er hielt sie, als gehörte sie schon ihm, und wieder fühlte sie sich begehrt, sexy und unglaublich geborgen, sodass ihre Entschlossenheit fast dahinschmolz.

»Sam«, flüsterte sie und berührte ihre brennenden Lippen. Eigentlich sollte sie sich wohl darüber ärgern, dass er ihr mit einem Kuss das Wort abgeschnitten hatte, aber sie war ihm überhaupt nicht böse. Sie hatte diesen Kuss gebraucht.

Er nahm ihr Gesicht in beide Hände. In seinen Augen spiegelte sich reine, unverfälschte Besessenheit und etwas, womit sie nicht gerechnet hatte: Hoffnung. »Denk nicht drüber nach.« Er sah sie unverwandt an. »Zerpflück es nicht, und steck mich nicht in eine Schublade, in die ich nicht hineingehöre. Das hier ist richtig. Ich weiß, dass du es auch fühlst. Du wirst dich nicht auf mich einlassen, wenn ich dir nicht treu bin, und ich will es für dich, für mich. Ich will das mit dir. Ich will dich, Faith. Ich möchte niemanden küssen außer dich, und ich will verdammt noch mal nicht, dass du einen anderen Mann küsst.«

»Du bist ein großes Risiko, Sam. Und ich weiß, dass es schrecklich ist, das zu sagen.« Die Worte brachen nur so aus ihr hervor, ohne dass sie vorher darüber nachdachte. »Wenn du mich betrügst, wäre das eine schreckliche Demütigung. Und ich muss hier leben und arbeiten. Ich kann nicht einfach alles stehen und liegen lassen und davonlaufen.«

Während sie aufgeregt auf und ab ging, erinnerte sie sich an den Schmerz, der sie überschwemmt hatte, als sie ihren Ex-Freund mit einer anderen Frau ertappt hatte. Sie wog das Risiko, sich auf Sam einzulassen, gegen den Sog der Begierde ab, der in ihr tobte.

»Ich werde dich nicht verletzen«, versprach er.

»Ich glaube dir, dass du keine bösen Absichten hegst, aber du könntest einen Fehler machen. Und mein Job, mein Leben, alles hier ist im Moment so gut.« Sie ging weiter auf und ab, viel zu aufgewühlt, um ihn anzusehen.

Als hätte er geahnt, dass sie den Blickkontakt mied, schloss er die Lücke zwischen ihnen, umrahmte ihr Gesicht wieder mit den Händen und zwang sie, ihm in seine alles verzehrenden Augen zu blicken.

»Ich werde niemals die sehr schlechte Entscheidung treffen, dich zu verletzen. Vertrau mir, Faith, und ich verspreche dir, ich werde dich nicht enttäuschen. Hab Vertrauen in mich«, flüsterte er, und möge der Herrgott ihr beistehen: Sie wollte es. »Ich werde nicht nur dafür sorgen, dass dir nicht der Boden unter den Füßen weggezogen wird, sondern ich werde dein Leben auch verbessern.«

»Du bist ein echtes Verkaufstalent, voller Verheißungen.« Ihre Worte klangen neckend, aber in ihrem Innern war sie kurz davor, sich aus ihrer sicheren kleinen Welt in die Arme des größten Risikos sinken zu lassen, das sie jemals eingegangen war, und sie wollte nicht verzweifelt nach Halt suchen müssen. »Ich brauche vollständige Transparenz, Sam.«

»Absolute Klarheit, versprochen.« Sein unerschütterliches Selbstbewusstsein bestärkte ihren Wunsch, ihm jedes Wort zu glauben.

»Weißt du überhaupt, was das bedeutet?«

»Ich habe vielleicht bisher einen Bogen um feste Beziehungen gemacht, aber deswegen bin ich noch lange kein Idiot.« Er nahm ihre Hand und führte sie zu der Brüstung, von der aus sie einen Blick aufs Meer hatten. Er legte ihr den Arm um die Taille. Sie passte perfekt an seinen muskulösen Körper, als sei er nur für sie gemacht.

»Was siehst du?«, fragte er.

»Das Mondlicht, das sich auf der Wasseroberfläche spiegelt. Es ist friedlich.«

»Es scheint friedlich zu sein. Aber sobald du dich in ein Boot setzt, lieferst du dich der Natur aus. Und Mutter Natur kann im Handumdrehen zuschlagen. Für mich ist das ein Risiko, das es wert ist, in Kauf genommen zu werden, weil ich weiß, dass ich mit allem umgehen kann, was sie mir um die Ohren haut.«

Er sah Faith durchdringend an.

»Wenn du mich anschaust, hast du Angst, einen Fuß in das Boot zu setzen. Aber du brauchst keine Angst zu haben. Ich weiß, dass du mit Stürmen oder Windböen nicht umgehen kannst, und ich würde niemals riskieren, dass du mich nie wieder so ansiehst, wie du es tust, wenn du über das hinausblickst, was dir über mich zu Ohren gekommen ist. Dann sehe ich Klarheit und Verstehen aufblitzen – und gleich darauf werden deine Augen wieder trübe und du ziehst hastig die Schwimmweste über. Du brauchst keine Schwimmweste, Faith. Ich passe auf, dass du nicht untergehst.«

Jedes seiner Worte traf wie ein Pfeil mitten in ihr Herz. Das tiefe Gefühl, das sie in seiner Stimme hörte, konnte man nicht vortäuschen.

»Macht es dir keine Angst, Sam, dass du dich plötzlich an eine Frau wie mich binden möchtest? An jemanden, der sich davor fürchtet, verletzt zu werden?«

»Mich zu binden jagt mir eine Höllenangst ein. Aber mich an dich zu binden? Nein, Faith, du bist die einzige Frau, an die ich mich binden will. Ich habe dreißig Jahre gebraucht, um das herauszufinden.« Seine Lippen verzogen sich zu einem warmen Lächeln.

»Willst du nicht mit jemandem zusammen sein, der jeden Abend feiert? Jemand, der wild ist und vielleicht noch eine andere Frau einlädt, mitzumachen? Denn das würde ich nie tun. Ich teile nicht gern.«

Er blickte zum Himmel hinauf und fluchte leise, wirkte aber nicht wütend. Es war eher so, als würde er sich selbst ermahnen. Als er ihr wieder den Blick zuwandte, waren seine Augen todernst.

»Ich schäme mich nicht für meine Vergangenheit, Faith. Alles, was ich getan habe, jede Entscheidung, die ich getroffen habe, jedes Stelldichein hat mich hierhergeführt. Diese Frauen, mit denen ich mich zusammengetan habe, gehören nicht zu der Sorte Frauen, die ich mein Eigen nennen möchte. Verstehst du nicht, was los ist?«

Verstehen? Sie konnte ja kaum atmen.

»Ich will mit dir zusammen sein. Ich möchte das fühlen, was ich gerade fühle, und mehr, und das geht nur mit dir. Du bist die einzige Frau, die mich interessiert, niemand sonst. Und wenn du meinst, ich würde dich jemals mit einem anderen Mann oder einer anderen Frau teilen, dann liegst du falsch. Und vor allem möchte ich nicht, dass du dir Sorgen machst, dass ich fremdgehe. Niemals. Du sollst in deinem Herzen wissen, dass ich dir mein Wort gegeben habe. Und mein Wort ist härter als Stahl.«

Seine Aufrichtigkeit zerschlug ihren Entschluss, Distanz zu

wahren und sich nicht auf ihn einzulassen, in tausend Stücke. Sie holte zittrig Luft, wollte näher bei ihm sein, wollte, dass die Gewissheit, die er verkörperte, wahr und echt war, und schob ihre Ängste beiseite. Vivian würde ihr den Kopf abreißen oder, schlimmer noch, ihm den Kopf abreißen, aber Faith konnte sich nicht ihr ganzes Leben lang vor dem fürchten, was vielleicht passieren würde. Und sie konnte ihre Entscheidungen nicht von den Überzeugungen anderer Leute abhängig machen.

Als sie ihm nun in die Augen sah, erkannte sie eine weitere Facette des Mannes, die er nach und nach enthüllte. *Er kommt aus seiner Deckung.* Und den Mann, der sich da zeigte, mochte sie sehr.

»Okay.«

»Okay?« Seine Augen weiteten sich.

»Okay, ja, aber …«

Er hob sie hoch und wirbelte sie herum, küsste ihren lachenden Mund schnell und hart.

»Kein Aber«, sagte er.

»Sam.« Lächelnd schlang sie ihm die Arme um den Hals und er legte ihre Beine um seine Taille. »Ich bin nicht einfach.«

»Was du nicht sagst!« Er küsste sie wieder.

»Ich bin auch ganz schön desillusioniert.«

Er küsste sie noch einmal und lächelte immer noch. »Gut, dass ich so geduldig bin.«

»Wenn du mir wehtust, werde ich dich kastrieren.«

»Baby, wenn ich dir wehtue, dann habe ich es auch verdient.«

Faith musste ihn einfach wieder küssen, und als ihre Münder zusammenfanden, hatte sie das Gefühl, von der Welt abgeschirmt zu sein, geborgen und geachtet im Auge des Sturms.

Zehn

Am Dienstagmorgen wachte Sam mit dem Gefühl auf, als könnte er die Welt aus den Angeln heben. Angesichts der Stapel, die sich auf seinem Schreibtisch türmten, war das eine gute Sache. Er schrieb Faith zwei Nachrichten und machte sich dann daran, das in den Griff zu bekommen, was bei Rough Riders anstand. Er fühlte sich so energiegeladen wie lange nicht mehr und erledigte in kurzer Zeit einen guten Teil der Arbeit. Zum Schluss skypte er mit Lira, um sie auf den neuesten Stand zu bringen.

»Das jährliche Barbecue ist ein wichtiges Ereignis bei Rough Riders. Firmensponsoren stellen Ausrüstung für unsere Abenteuertouren zur Verfügung. Manchmal bieten sie auch Unterkünfte an, je nachdem, welche Ziele wir ansteuern, in der Hoffnung, dass unsere Kunden in Zukunft ihre Ausrüstung kaufen. Wir laden frühere, aktuelle und potenzielle Sponsoren zum Barbecue ein, um ihr Interesse zu wecken und sie als Sponsoren zu gewinnen oder zu halten. Ich schätze, es ist wie ein Geschäftsessen, nur eben für Leute, die nicht in einem Büro arbeiten, sondern in der freien Natur. Wir laden alle ein. Wie bei den Sponsoren bekommen auch frühere und aktuelle Kunden und potenzielle Firmenkunden eine Einladung, zu denen wir Kontakte knüpfen wollen«, erklärte Sam. »Außerdem ist das Barbecue eine gute Gelegenheit, einander kennenzulernen. Wenn also alles klappt und du nicht noch vor dem Event bei Rough Riders das Handtuch wirfst, kannst du die Leute treffen, mit denen du sonst nur am Telefon zu tun hast.«

»Oh, ich werde sicher nicht das Handtuch werfen«, sagte Lira. »Ich kann es gar nicht erwarten, loszulegen. Aber ehrlich gesagt wusste ich gar nicht, dass es bei den Unternehmen einen so großen Markt für solche Touren gibt.«

»Unternehmen tun alles, um ihre Führungskräfte bei der Stange zu halten, und sie mit High-End-Abenteuern zu verwöhnen, entwickelt sich immer mehr zu einem Trend. Wir wollen erreichen, dass Rough Riders die einzige Firma ist, die ihnen in den Sinn kommt, wenn sie so weit sind«, erklärte Sam. »Du wirst dich mit früheren und potenziellen Sponsoren und Kunden in Verbindung setzen und mit denen, die noch nicht auf die Einladung geantwortet haben. Und dann bringst du Ordnung in das Finanzchaos, das ich angehäuft habe.«

Liras dunkle Augen weiteten sich vor Aufregung. »Es juckt mir in den Fingern, mit der Arbeit anzufangen. Ich habe mir die Dokumente angesehen, die du gestern Abend geschickt hast, und könnte mir vorstellen, wie du die Finanzen besser organisieren kannst. Ich bringe meine Gedanken zu Papier und schicke es dir. Und dann fange ich gleich an, herumzutelefonieren.«

»Du klingst ebenso begeistert, mit der Arbeit zu beginnen, wie ich mich freue, sie abzugeben.«

»Ja, das bin ich. Vielen Dank, dass du mir diese Chance gibst, Sam. Und danke, dass ich für den Anfang von zu Hause aus arbeiten darf. Du kannst dir nicht vorstellen, was das für mich bedeutet. Ich werde dich nicht enttäuschen.«

Sam hatte sich ihre Empfehlungsschreiben angesehen und hatte das Gefühl, dass sie recht hatte.

Nach dem Anruf schob Sam seinen Stuhl vom Schreibtisch weg und dachte an Faith. Sie hatte noch nicht auf seine Nachrichten geantwortet, aber er wusste, dass sie wahrscheinlich mit ihren Patienten beschäftigt war. Und so sollte es ja auch sein. Er war zu aufgekratzt, um stillzusitzen, daher ging er nach draußen und sah sich die große Gruppe junger Leute an, die sich im Laufe der letzten Stunde eingefunden hatte. Ein Dutzend Boote war bereits im Wasser, ein typischer Sommertag bei Rough Riders. Eins war jedoch anders. Vor einer Woche hätte er sich mitten unter den Bikinidamen getummelt und sich in ihrer Aufmerksamkeit gesonnt, die nun Tex zugutekam. Aber Sam war ganz in Gedanken an Faith versunken. Ihre süße Stimme, ihr verlockender Duft und das Vertrauen, das sie letzte Nacht in seine fähigen Hände gelegt hatte, waren alles, woran er denken konnte, und er hatte nicht vor, das zu vermasseln.

Er stand am sandigen Ufer und sah zu, wie die Frauen Tex umschwärmten. Sie strichen ihm mit dem Finger über Arm und Schultern, bestaunten seine Tattoos und umgarnten ihn mit aufreizendem Gekicher, das sie ihm hinwarfen, wie man einem hungrigen Bären Fleischbrocken hinwirft. Während Sam sie beobachtete, fiel ihm auf, dass er ihre Körper gar nicht begutachtete oder überlegte, welche der Frauen wohl später im Club auftauchen würden, wie er es früher getan hatte, bevor sich Faith bereit erklärt hatte, mit ihm auszugehen. Heute zählte er nur, wie viele Kunden auf die verbleibenden Boote verteilt werden mussten. Mit großer Neugier und ungläubigem Staunen nahm er wahr, wie rasch sich seine Einstellungen geändert hatten. Tex legte einer Blondine den Arm um die Schultern und nickte Sam mit einem albernen Lächeln auf dem Gesicht zu, das ihn aus seinen Gedanken riss. Tex war zu Rough Riders gekommen, nachdem seine Firma pleitegegangen war. Da er früher selbst Wildwassertouren angeboten hatte, war er an diese Vergünstigungen, die mit dieser Art von Unternehmen einherging, gewöhnt und freute sich offensichtlich darüber.

Besser du als ich. Der Gedanke war so fremd, dass Sam innehielt. Gleich darauf ließ er sich diese Worte noch einmal durch den Kopf gehen, diesmal mit mehr Nachdruck, und plötzlich schien ein Teilchen in ihm an die richtige Stelle zu rücken, als hätte es nicht gewusst, dass es nicht dort lag, wo es hingehörte, bis der ungewohnte Gedanke es lostrat.

Mit einem zufriedenen Lächeln drehte er sich um, um nach Patrick zu sehen, der einer Gruppe von Teenagern half, in die Kajaks zu steigen. Er war groß und schlaksig gewesen, als Sam ihn im letzten Sommer eingestellt hatte, mit blonden Haaren und den glatten Wangen eines Jungen. Im Laufe des Jahres war er mehr zum Mann geworden. Er trug sein Haar an den Seiten kurz, oben war es etwas länger. Er hatte breitere Schultern, seine Figur ähnelte nun eher der eines Erwachsenen. Außerdem hatte er inzwischen einen Bartansatz und einen Satz Autoschlüssel. *Sechzehn.*

Mit sechzehn Jahren hatte Sam seine Jungfräulichkeit verloren, hatte sich mit Haut und Haaren in ein Mädchen aus einer benachbarten Stadt verliebt, das ihm schließlich sein jugendliches Herz gebrochen hatte. Er dachte selten an diese Zeit in seinem Leben, aber jetzt fragte er sich, wie sehr diese Trennung seine bisherige Lebensweise beeinflusst hatte.

»Na, Alter.« Tys Hand landete schwer auf Sams Schulter und riss ihn aus seinen Gedanken. Mit seinen sechsundzwanzig Jahren, in Boardshorts und ohne Hemd, mit langem, dunklem Haar, das ihm in die Augen fiel, passte Ty genau zu diesen sorglosen, kecken Mädchen – so, wie es sein sollte. Bei seinem Anblick wurde Sam klar, dass er mit fast einunddreißig, einer aufstrebenden Firma und einer einzigen Frau, die sein Herz gefangen hielt, einen neuen Weg eingeschlagen hatte und endlich in die richtige Richtung unterwegs war.

»Hallo«, sagte Sam. »Ich habe dich gar nicht kommen hören.«

»Tja, was ein echter Ninja ist …« Ty wies mit dem Kinn zu den Frauen, die die Zehen ins Wasser tauchten und kicherten, während Tex ihnen mit den Schwimmwesten half. »Warum hilfst du diesen bezaubernden Damen nicht, die Schwimmwesten anzulegen? Sie werden von Jahr zu Jahr heißer.«

Sam dachte an Faith und sagte: »Das tut sie wirklich.«

»Von wem redest du?« Ty hob eine Augenbraue.

Sam ging zum Bootshaus, während Ty ihm auf den Fersen folgte. Er packte ein Ende eines Ruderboots. »Ich bin mit Faith zusammen. Pack mal mit an, ja?«

Sie trugen das Boot zum Wasser und auf dem Rückweg sagte Ty: »*Mit Faith zusammen?* Sammy, für ein flüchtiges Abenteuer riskierst du, dass dir Cole an die Gurgel geht? Was ist los mit dir? Er reißt dir den Kopf ab, kaum dass er nach Hause kommt.«

Dass Ty Faith mit einem flüchtigen Abenteuer in Verbindung brachte, machte Sam wütend. Er nahm ein weiteres Ruderboot und wies Ty an, das andere Ende anzupacken. »So ist es nicht.«

»Was ist nicht so? Cole kommt nächste Woche wieder. Wenn du dich also an sie ranmachen willst, solltest du dich beeilen.«

Sie trugen das Boot nach draußen und setzten es am Wasser ab. Eigentlich hätten die Boote ebenso gut im Bootshaus bleiben können, aber Sam brauchte die Ablenkung. Er hatte einen unglaublichen Abend mit Faith verbracht, und wie durch ein Wunder hatte sie zugestimmt, mit ihm auszugehen – nur mit ihm. Sie hatten noch lange auf dem Dach gesessen, und nachdem sie gegangen war, hatten sie sich bis fast ein Uhr morgens eine Nachricht nach der anderen geschrieben. Sam hatte die halbe Nacht wach gelegen und an sie gedacht, und als er aufgewacht war, galt sein erster Gedanke nur ihr. In ein paar Stunden, die sich wie ein ganzes Leben anfühlten, würde er sie wiedersehen. Das Letzte, was er jetzt wollte, war, über den Kerl zu sprechen, der ihn gewarnt hatte, die Finger von Faith zu lassen.

»Ty, mit Faith bin ich nicht auf ein Abenteuer aus, also sag das besser nicht noch einmal. Ich mag sie sehr, und du weißt, was es bedeutet, wenn ich so etwas sage. Ich werde das nicht vermasseln und werde auch nicht zulassen, dass Cole es vermasselt.«

Sein Bruder fuhr sich mit der Hand über das Gesicht und blinzelte einige Male, als hätte er ein Gespenst gesehen. »Meinst du das ernst? Ich meine, Faith ist heiß, aber sie passt eigentlich nicht in dein übliches Beuteschema.«

»Ich meine es sehr ernst, und ja, du hast recht. Sie ist nicht wie die Frauen, mit denen ich mich normalerweise vergnügt habe, weil ich mich mit Faith eben nicht nur vergnüge, Ty. Faith ist von nun an die einzige Frau in meinem Leben. Und Cole nehme ich mir vor, wenn er von seiner Hochzeitsreise zurückkommt.« Jemand rief Sams Namen, und er sah hinüber zu den jungen Frauen, die gerade in die Boote stiegen. Eine Brünette, die ihm zuwinkte, kam ihm irgendwie bekannt vor. Er konnte sich nicht an ihren Namen erinnern, aber er hatte ein paarmal mit ihr gefeiert. Er winkte zurück und wandte sich wieder seinem Bruder zu.

»War sonst noch was?« Sam verschränkte die Arme. Er war gereizt und hatte das Bedürfnis, Faith zu beschützen.

Ty ging kopfschüttelnd auf und ab. »Und was heißt das jetzt? Bist du raus aus dem Rennen? Sam, überleg es dir. Ich bin mir sicher, dass Faith großartig ist, aber willst du wirklich Tag für Tag dasselbe essen, nachdem du jahrelang jeden Abend eine andere Köstlichkeit probiert hast? Machst du dir keine Sorgen, dass dir langweilig wird?«

Sam biss die Zähne zusammen. »Langweilig? Auf keinen Fall. Ich kann es nicht erklären, aber es passiert etwas, wenn ich mit ihr zusammen bin. Und wenn ich nicht mit ihr zusammen bin? So wie jetzt? Dann schleppe ich Boote durch die Gegend, weil ich nicht still sitzen kann. Ich kann es kaum erwarten, sie zu sehen. Wann habe ich mich jemals so gefühlt?«

»Noch nie, soweit ich weiß. Mist, Sam. Erst Nate, dann Cole, und jetzt du? Alle umgefallen wie die Fliegen.«

»Ich bin überhaupt nicht umgefallen. Ich weiß, das ist ein Schock. Für mich ist es auch ein Schock, aber was ich für sie empfinde, ist …« Er suchte verzweifelt nach dem richtigen Wort – *riesig? gewaltig? alles verzehrend?* – und entschied sich endlich für etwas, von dem er wusste, dass Ty es verstehen würde. »Du kennst doch das Gefühl, wenn du beim Klettern den Gipfel erreichst?«

Ty nickte vorsichtig.

»Das ist unbeschreiblich, stimmt's? Und zu überwältigend, um es zu ignorieren. Und ich möchte es nicht ignorieren, Ty.« Er lächelte und dachte daran, wie er Nate gesagt hatte, er solle zusehen, dass er seinen Hintern hochkriegte und sich um Jewel kümmerte. Damals hatte sich Sam nicht vorstellen können, jemals in einer ähnlichen Situation zu sein. Und jetzt konnte er sich nichts Besseres denken.

Faith hatte zu wenig geschlafen, doch sie stand trotzdem unter Strom. Dafür sorgte schon Sams Nachricht, die er ihr frühmorgens geschickt hatte – *Guten Morgen, meine Schöne* –, gleich gefolgt von: *Ich vermisse dein süßes Lächeln.* Selbst seine Nachrichten ließen ihr Herz wie wild pochen. Sie wusste, dass sie vorsichtig sein und versuchen musste, einen kühlen Kopf zu bewahren, wenn es um Sam ging. Seine Frauengeschichten sprachen schließlich ihre eigene Sprache. Aber das war leichter gesagt als getan, denn alles, was er tat und sagte, haute sie einfach um. Seine Aufrichtigkeit und seine Entschlossenheit, sie für sich zu gewinnen, hatten sie überrascht, aber eigentlich waren es ihre eigenen Gefühle, die sie überwältigten. Sie musste nur an die Feuersbrunst denken, die ihren Körper erfasste, wenn sie zusammen waren, und schon war sie ganz scharf auf ihn.

In der Praxis ging es wieder einmal zu wie im Taubenschlag, aber wenigstens hatte Brandy heute eine Mittagspause für sie eingeplant und angeboten, ihr etwas zu essen mitzubringen, damit sie für den WAC recherchieren konnte.

»Brandy«, sagte Faith in die Sprechanlage. »Ich bin im Pausenraum, wenn du mich brauchst.«

Faith stellte ihren Laptop auf den Tisch, zog ihr Notizbuch heraus und begann, die Liste der Frauenorganisationen zu durchforsten, die sie sich aufgeschrieben hatte.

»Ah, hier ist meine süße Freundin also.«

Beim Klang von Sams Stimme schnellte ihr Kopf in die Höhe und das Wort *Freundin* verursachte ein wildes Flattern in ihrem Bauch. »Sam? Was machst du hier?« Er kam mit einer Tüte von Jazzy Joe's Café und einem Lächeln auf den köstlichen Lippen um den Tisch herum. Oh, wie liebte sie seine Lippen!

Sie hatte Frauen sagen hören, dass sich bei einem Kuss Himmel und Erde um sie drehten, aber keiner der Küsse, die sie bisher erlebt hatte, hatten auch nur annähernd solche Gefühle ausgelöst. Bis jetzt, bis zu Sam. Er küsste so, wie er alles tat: selbstsicher und gebieterisch, mit ein wenig Raffinesse und einer Menge Verführung.

»Mit dir zu Mittag essen.« Er beugte sich herunter und küsste sie. »Mm. Ich habe deine Küsse vermisst.«

Ich habe alles an dir vermisst. »Sam«, flüsterte sie. »Wir können hier in der Praxis nicht herumknutschen.« *Auch wenn ich es gerne täte.* Sie hatte sich seine Küsse immer und immer wieder in Erinnerung gerufen und wahrscheinlich grinste sie jetzt wie eine liebestrunkene Idiotin. Aus diesem Grund war sie Jon bisher aus dem Weg gegangen. Dieser Mann hatte ein untrügliches Gespür für Liebesgeschichten. Er hatte geahnt, dass eine ihrer Buchhalterinnen verliebt war, bevor die Frau selbst es wusste, und Faith hatte keine Lust, ihm auseinanderlegen zu müssen, dass sie mit Coles Bruder zusammen war. Wie Cole reagieren würde, wenn er es erfuhr, bereitete ihr schon genug Sorgen. Auf jeden Fall waren Küsse im Pausenraum keine gute Idee.

»Herumknutschen? Ich habe dir nur einen Begrüßungskuss gegeben. Das ist so üblich unter Leuten, die zusammen sind.« Er setzte sich neben sie, wickelte ein Sandwich aus und legte es vor sie hin, als hätte er ihren chaotischen Tag nicht gerade auf die verlockendste Weise auf den Kopf gestellt.

»Was ist mit Jon?« Ihre Gedanken wirbelten wie wild durcheinander. Sam in der Praxis beim gemeinsamen

Mittagessen war ein bisschen viel auf einmal.

»Butterscotch? Den habe ich gerade auf dem Flur gesehen.« Er griff nach ihrer Hand. »Hast du Angst, er könnte dahinterkommen, dass wir zusammen sind? Er soll bloß nicht wagen, sich uns in den Weg zu stellen.«

Lieber Himmel, sie liebte diese arrogante Seite an ihm, obwohl sie sie eigentlich schrecklich finden sollte.

»Sam, das hier ist mein Job.«

»Ich mache doch nur Spaß. Jon sieht das bestimmt ganz locker. Es ist ja nicht so, als hätten wir Sex auf dem Mittagstisch.« Seine Augen sprühten Feuer. »Es sei denn, dir gefällt so was.«

Sie verbarg das Gesicht in den Händen und stieß ein atemloses »Oh mein Gott« aus. Bei dem Gedanken an Sex hier auf dem Tisch überrollte sie eine Hitzewelle. Mit Sam! Wahrscheinlich konnte sie den Tisch nie wieder ansehen, ohne daran zu denken.

»Wo ist das Problem? Hätte ich vorher anrufen sollen? Ich kenne mich mit Dates nicht so gut aus, aber ich lerne schnell.« Er lehnte sich zurück und sein Blick wurde ernst.

»Dafür, dass du nicht auf Dates stehst, machst du deine Sache ganz gut. Ich bin nur ein bisschen nervös wegen der Arbeit. Ich liebe meinen Job und möchte nichts riskieren. Ich bin sicher, dass es gut geht. Oder zumindest hoffe ich, dass es gut geht. Jon weiß, dass ich nicht tun würde ... was du gesagt hast.«

Zumindest nicht, wenn wir nicht allein in der Praxis sind. Sam hatte ganz sicher magische Kräfte, sonst würde sie sich jetzt nicht Dinge vorstellen, die ihr vorher nie in den Sinn gekommen wären.

Seine Lippen verzogen sich zu einem teuflischen Lächeln.

»Was auch immer du gerade denkst, mach weiter.« Er rückte näher und schob ihre Beine zwischen seine. Seine Hände fuhren an ihren Schenkeln entlang, während er seine Wange an ihre drückte und mit einer rauen, verführerischen Stimme sagte: »Du siehst gerade so heiß aus. Ich würde dir gerne diese OP-Sachen vom Leib reißen und mich an deinem Körper sattessen.«

Faith hatte das Gefühl, dahinzuschmelzen. Sie umklammerte verzweifelt die Stuhlkante und hoffte, dass sie nicht als wimmerndes, bettelndes Etwas auf dem Boden landen würde.

»Uuups, entschuldige«, flüsterte er. »Wir wollten uns ja anständig benehmen.« Er drückte ihr einen Kuss auf die Wange, dann richtete er sich auf und nahm sein Sandwich, während sie versuchte, einen letzten Rest an Fassung zusammenzukratzen.

»Du solltest etwas essen. Du hast nur noch« – er sah auf die Wanduhr – »eine Dreiviertelstunde Zeit.«

»Stimmt«, brachte sie mühsam hervor. Sie räusperte sich, und Sam reichte ihr den Getränkebecher, den er mitgebracht hatte. »Danke.« Nach drei großen Schlucken atmete sie wieder normal, aber ihre Gedanken kreisten immer noch um das, was er gesagt hatte. Würde sie sich jemals daran gewöhnen? Würde sie sich jemals an *ihn* gewöhnen?

»Was machst du gerade?« Er zeigte auf ihre Notizen und den Laptop.

Ein weiterer großer Schluck, und dann schob sie die schmutzigen Gedanken zumindest so weit zur Seite, dass sie nicht wie eine lüsterne Irre klang. »Ich habe dir doch erzählt, dass ich nach weiteren Möglichkeiten suchen wollte, den WAC-Mitgliedern zu helfen. Ich habe eine Liste von Frauenorgani-sationen zusammengestellt, die Therapeuten, Berufsberater oder sogar juristische Hilfe anbieten.« Sie blätterte die Seite um und zeigte ihm eine andere Liste. »Das sind Therapiepraxen, die mit Wohltätigkeitsorganisationen in ganz Maryland zusammenarbeiten.«

»Ist der WAC eine gemeinnützige Organisation?«

»Nein. Als ich das Forum gegründet habe, hätte ich nie gedacht, dass etwas anderes dabei herauskommen würde als ein Austausch im Internet.« Sie rief die Website auf ihrem Laptop auf und zeigte ihm den Monitor. »Die Mitgliedschaft ist kostenlos und wir erhalten eine Handvoll Spenden. Nicht in der Größenordnung wie deine, sondern gerade genug, um einen Teil der Kosten zu decken. Wir haben erst vor Kurzem damit begonnen, Veranstaltungen wie die Autowäsche zu organisieren, bei denen wir uns tatsächlich persönlich begegnen. Ich hatte noch keine Zeit, alles durchzudenken. Die Idee, unseren Mitgliedern noch mehr anzubieten, kam mir erst am Wochenende, aber es fühlt sich gut an, es zumindest zu versuchen.«

»Es sieht so aus, als hättest du schon große Fortschritte gemacht. Eine gemeinnützige Organisation seid ihr nicht, also seid ihr vermutlich eine GmbH?«

Sie knabberte an ihrer Lippe und schüttelte den Kopf. »Nicht einmal darum habe ich mich gekümmert.«

»Du hast also die Domain und das Hosting erworben, aber den WAC nicht als Unternehmen angemeldet?«

Wieder schüttelte sie den Kopf und wand sich innerlich.

»Nun, da sind ein paar Sachen, die du tun solltest, um dich vor möglichen Klagen zu schützen. Hast du einen Wirtschaftsanwalt?« Plötzlich klang er sehr geschäftsmäßig, ganz anders als der sexy Verführer, der sie eben noch angesehen hatte, als wollte er sie verschlingen.

Und diese Seite an ihm gefiel ihr sehr.

»Nein, noch nicht. Aber ich schreib es gleich auf meine Liste.« Sie nahm einen Stift und kritzelte *Wirtschaftsanwalt* in ihr Notizheft.

Sam zog sein Handy heraus und scrollte durch seine Kontakte. »Faith, du musst den WAC unbedingt als Unternehmen registrieren lassen, nicht nur, weil ihr Spenden annehmt. Wahrscheinlich haftest du auch von Gesetzes wegen für alle möglichen Dinge. Ich weiß nicht, ob du rechtliche Probleme bekommen könntest, wenn du online Ratschläge gibst oder auf andere Hilfsangebote verweist, die du nicht persönlich geprüft hast, aber wir müssen sicherstellen, dass du geschützt bist.«

Dass er *wir* sagte, verursachte ein Flattern in ihrem Bauch, und ihr Herz vollführte einen glücklichen Tanz. Sie konnte nicht glauben, dass sie sich über die rechtlichen Aspekte überhaupt keine Gedanken gemacht hatte. Es machte Sinn, den WAC als Unternehmen anzumelden, zumal Sam so viel Geld gespendet hatte. Normalerweise betrugen die Spenden nicht mehr als ein paar Dollar. Sein Beitrag war mehr als großzügig und würde lange reichen, vor allem jetzt, wo Rechtskosten anfielen. Aber was er tat, um sicherzugehen, dass *sie* richtig geschützt war, bedeutete ihr noch mehr.

»Ich frage mal bei meinem Kumpel Brent Holloway nach. Wir sind zusammen aufgewachsen und sein Büro ist in der Stadt.« Er hob den Finger, als Brent sich meldete. »Hey, Brent, hier ist Sam.« Er hörte einen Moment schweigend zu. »Ja, ich habe den Papierkram bekommen, danke. Ich hinke ein bisschen hinterher, aber ich kümmere mich gleich darum. Hör mal, kannst du mir einen Gefallen tun? Meine Freundin betreibt ein Online-Forum …«

Er erläuterte Brent, worum es ging, und Faith schwelgte

wieder in der Leichtigkeit, mit der ihm das Wort *Freundin* über die Lippen kam.

»Das ist prima. Warte mal.« Sam hielt sich das Handy vom Ohr weg und fragte leise: »Wir könnten am Donnerstag um halb sieben kommen. Klappt das?«

Wir? »Ja, klar. Vielen Dank.«

Er beugte sich vor und küsste sie. Mit einem neckenden Glimmen in den Augen flüsterte er: »Freundin«, und gab ihr einen weiteren raschen Kuss, bevor er sich wieder seinem Gesprächspartner zuwandte.

Nachdem er den Anruf beendet hatte, sagte er: »So, das wäre geklärt. Ich könnte dich am Donnerstag nach der Arbeit abholen und dann gehen wir zusammen hin. Brent wird dir gefallen. Er ist ein großartiger Kerl.«

»Hört sich gut an. Vielen Dank.«

»Gerne. Du brauchst auch eine betriebliche Versicherung. Wir werden mit Brent darüber reden. Unser Kumpel Phil D'Amato kann dir sicher ein günstiges Angebot machen.« Er sah sie fragend an und sie erwiderte seinen Blick mit weit aufgerissenen Augen. »Ist das okay? Oder mische ich mich zu sehr ein?«

»Zu sehr einmischen? Sam, dich sollte man nicht unterschätzen, und das finde ich wunderbar. Du hast mir Mittagessen gebracht und im Handumdrehen meine Organisation auf die richtige Spur gesetzt. Es ist mir ein bisschen peinlich, dass ich nicht selbst an all das gedacht habe. Normalerweise achte ich darauf, dass alles seine Ordnung hat, und dann kommst du und erkennst sofort, dass ich Mist gebaut habe.«

Lächelnd berührte er ihr Gesicht. »Du hast keinen Mist gebaut. Du hast dich einfach auf die Aspekte konzentriert, auf die du dich konzentrieren solltest, nämlich die Hilfe für andere. Ich habe viel Erfahrung mit Unternehmen und den Pflichten, die du als Eigentümer übernimmst. Bei Rough Riders handelt es sich um eine andere Art von Unternehmen, aber der gesetzliche Rahmen ist bei allen Firmen ähnlich.«

»Du solltest mein Geschäftsführer sein«, sagte sie halb im Scherz.

»Das ist alles deins, Baby. Dein Unternehmen, dein Forum, deine Ideen. Ich helfe nur ein bisschen.«

»Ich kann einfach nicht glauben, wie sehr du mir hilfst.« Sie beugte sich näher zu ihm, sie sehnte sich nach seiner Nähe.

Er rutschte auf seinem Stuhl ein Stück nach vorne, so nah, dass sie ihn hätte küssen können, wenn sie sich nur einen Zentimeter weiter vorgelehnt hätte.

»Glaub mir, Faith. Ich wollte schon so lange nah bei dir sein, und als diese Barriere gefallen ist, haben sich alle Schleusen geöffnet. Jetzt wirst du mich nicht mehr los, und wenn ich eine Grenze überschreite« – seine Augen verdunkelten sich verführerisch – »musst du mich zurückhalten.«

Seine Nähe, seine Worte und sein durchdringender Blick jagten einen Schauder der Leidenschaft durch ihren Körper. Er war so nah, dass sie goldene Flecken in seinen Augen sehen konnte. Ohne einen weiteren Kuss würde sie den Rest des Tages bis zu ihrer abendlichen Verabredung nicht durchstehen. Ihr Herz klopfte, ihr Verstand bettelte *Küss mich* und ihr Gehirn gab den Versuch auf, die Zügel in der Hand zu halten. Sam strich sich mit der Zunge über die Unterlippe und ein bedürftiges Stöhnen drang aus ihrer Kehle. Was war mit der besonnenen Frau passiert, die sie immer gewesen war? Sie fühlte sich wie eine Süchtige und wollte mehr von ihrem besten Stoff.

»Küss mich schnell, Sam, bevor jemand kommt …«

Ihr letztes Wort wurde in einem heftigen und eindringlichen Kuss erstickt. Sie krallte die Finger in sein Hemd, um nicht von der Woge der Gefühle mitgerissen zu werden. Gerade, als sie dachte: *Dafür lohnt es sich, Ärger zu riskieren*, verlangsamte Sam das Tempo und bedachte sie mit einer Reihe von trägen, umwerfenden Küssen. Sie berührte seine raue Wange und schob ihre Finger in sein Haar, als sie sich voneinander lösten. Sie war benommen, ihre Lippen kribbelten wie der Rest ihres überhitzten Körpers.

»Entschuldigung«, sagte sie und zog verlegen ihre Hände zurück. »Ich liebe deine Haare und wollte das schon so lange machen. Ich konnte einfach nicht anders.«

Er sah sie an, wie sie noch nie jemand angesehen hatte. Als wollte er sich in sie fallen lassen. *Atmen, atmen, atmen.*

»Du brauchst dich nicht dafür zu entschuldigen, dass du mich angefasst hast«, sagte er liebevoll. »Ich möchte, dass du mich berührst.«

Und ich sehne mich danach, dich zu berühren. Sie schüttelte den Kopf, versuchte, die schmutzigen Gedanken wegzuschieben und sich auf Sam zu konzentrieren. Sie wusste seine Großzügigkeit zu schätzen, aber er sollte wissen, dass sie diese Hilfsbereitschaft nicht von ihm erwartete.

»Nach allem, was du gestern Abend auf die Beine gestellt hast, habe ich irgendwie ein schlechtes Gewissen. Ich hoffe, du meinst nicht, dass du immer mehr für mich tun müsstest, weil ich Angst hatte, mich auf dich einzulassen. Du hast mich überzeugt, Sam. Du kannst aufhören, all diese Dinge für mich zu tun, und einfach du selbst sein.«

Er ließ eine Hand in ihren Nacken gleiten und zog sie näher an sich. »Ich glaube, zum ersten Mal in meinem Leben bin ich einfach nur ich selbst.«

Elf

Am Abend stieg Sam mit einem seligen Grinsen die Treppe zu Faiths Wohnung hinauf. Ihr zweites Date kam ihm wie ein Meilenstein vor. Für ihn war es tatsächlich einer. Ihm war klar, dass er sie möglicherweise überrumpelte, aber er konnte nicht anders. Sie hatte wirklich eine Art von Schleuse geöffnet, von der er nie gewusst hatte, dass es sie gab, und er ließ sich einfach von der Strömung mitreißen. Gleichzeitig versuchte er, die süße Faith aus ihrer Sicherheitszone zu locken und ihr Vertrauen zu gewinnen, indem er ihr zeigte, dass er Spaß haben und sich ganz züchtig benehmen konnte. *Obwohl ein bisschen Unzüchtigkeit immer nett ist.*

Faith öffnete die Tür, und das Lächeln blitzte auf, das er so sehr liebte. Dieses Lächeln, das ihre schönen dunklen Augen strahlen und ihren Atem ein wenig rascher gehen ließ. Das Lächeln, das sein Herz aufgeweckt hatte.

»Sam«, sagte sie träumerisch.

Ihre Stimme und ihre lächelnden Augen zogen ihn an wie ein Magnet. Sie hatten sich gerade erst vor ein paar Stunden gesehen und schon war er wie ausgehungert nach ihr. Sein Arm legte sich um ihre Taille, und in dem Moment, bevor sich ihre Münder vereinten, schlossen sich ihre Augenlider flatternd. Er liebte diese Momente, in denen sie nicht auf der Hut war und er sehen konnte, dass sie nicht an seine Vergangenheit dachte und überlegte, wie diese Vergangenheit zu seiner Gegenwart passte. Nein, in diesen Sekunden dachte sie nur daran, wie gerne sie mit ihm zusammen war. Er labte sich an der Süße ihres Kusses und kämpfte gegen den Drang an, ihn tiefer werden und sie alles fühlen zu lassen, was er zurückhielt. Es war ein Kuss voll göttlicher Ekstase, ein Kuss voller Verheißung auf das, was kommen würde – Vertrauen, so hoffte er, und mehr. Er musste auf Distanz gehen, um nicht die Grenze zu überschreiten, die er sich gesetzt hatte, aber sein Körper drängte vorwärts. Alles an ihm drängte voran, seit er sich seine Gefühle für Faith eingestanden hatte. Für einen Mann, der Jahr um Jahr von einer Frau zur anderen gezogen war, der immer auf derselben Ebene, immer im selben Bereich geblieben war, stellte das eine große Veränderung dar.

Seine Zunge fuhr über ihre und die Berührung versengte seine Haut.

Sich mit Faith vorwärts zu bewegen, war so viel besser als alles, was er sich hätte vorstellen können. Er fühlte sich lebendig, konzentriert, inspiriert. Als sich ihre Lippen voneinander lösten – seine schmerzten und brannten sofort nach mehr –, wusste er irgendwie, dass nur Faith diese Wirkung auf ihn haben konnte.

»Hey, Süße«, sagte er, als sie die Augen öffnete. »Wie geht es dir?«

»Jetzt geht es mir besser.« Ihre Hände, die zu Fäusten geballt an seiner Brust lagen, zitterten, und er bedeckte sie mit seiner eigenen kräftigen Hand.

Ihr Blick senkte sich auf ihre Hände und sie flüsterte: »Entschuldigung«, als sie ihre Finger ausstreckte.

Er küsste sie wieder, zärtlicher als eben. »Du musst dich nicht entschuldigen, wenn du mich berührst, weißt du noch?« Er ließ den Blick über ihren Körper schweifen und stellte fest, dass sie über ihrem eng anliegenden weißen T-Shirt die Rough-Riders-Kapuzenjacke trug, die er ihr gegeben hatte. Sie zitterte in seinem Arm. »Ist dir kalt?«

»Heiß ist mir. Heiß, heiß, heiß«, flüsterte sie.

Er lachte. »Das ist wohl ein Kompliment, nehme ich an. Du siehst wirklich sexy aus.«

Sie sah an sich herunter und spielte nervös mit der langen Halskette, die zwischen ihren Brüsten baumelte. »Meinst du, das ist okay? Ich war mir nicht sicher, aber du sagtest ja, ich sollte bequeme Sachen anziehen.«

»Ja, das ist prima.« Er gab ihr einen weiteren schnellen Kuss. »Bist du so weit?«

Sie räusperte sich und sah auf seine Hand, die immer noch besitzergreifend an ihrer Taille lag.

»Tja, vermutlich muss ich dich loslassen. Verdammt, ich hasse das.«

Sie lachte und stupste ihn spielerisch in den Bauch. Nach einem weiteren Kuss ließ er sie widerwillig los. Als sie ihre Handtasche von einem Tisch bei der Tür nahm, sah er sich in ihrem Wohnzimmer um. Es war genau so, wie er es sich vorgestellt hatte, ordentlich und feminin, mit Kissen mit Blumenmustern auf dem Sofa, einem Bücherregal mit Sachbüchern über Medizin und vielen Romanen – *für deinen schlauen, sexy Verstand!* – und ein paar Grünpflanzen vor den Balkontüren.

»Okay, fertig.« Sie drapierte sich den Schulterriemen quer über den Oberkörper, sodass ihr T-Shirt zwischen ihre Brüste gepresst wurde.

»Diese Tasche gefällt mir«, neckte er.

Sie verdrehte die Augen, als sie durch die Tür gingen. »Typisch Mann.« Seine Hand legte sich um ihre Taille und sie sagte: »Hast du Angst, dass ich verschwinde?«

»Ich stecke nur meinen Claim ab. Du warst doch diejenige, die Exklusivität wollte. Hast du es dir anders überlegt?«

»Kommt nicht in Frage, Mr. Braden, aber fair ist fair.« Sie legte ihm ihrerseits den Arm um die Taille, während sie die Treppe hinuntergingen. »Du bist zweimal in der Praxis aufgetaucht. Die Folgen kannst du ausbaden, wenn Cole nach Hause kommt und mich feuert, weil ich mich mit seinem Bruder eingelassen habe.«

»Das ist doch bestimmt kein Grund, dich zu feuern.«

»Wir werden sehen.«

»Ich habe ihm schon eine Nachricht geschickt, dass wir reden müssen, wenn er wiederkommt. Mach dir keine Sorgen. Du kannst dich immer auf mich verlassen.«

Sie sah ihn mit einem neugierigen Blick an, als sie zum Parkplatz gingen. »Auch wenn ich dich fallen lasse? Oder würdest du ihn dann bitten, mich zu feuern, nur um dich an mir zu rächen?«

»Falls du mich fallen lässt?« Er stahl sich einen weiteren Kuss von ihren köstlichen Lippen. »Klar! Und wie ich mich an dir rächen würde.«

»Du bist unmöglich. Wohin fahren wir?«

»Wart's ab. Ganz oben auf meiner Liste von ›Dingen, die ich noch nie mit einer Frau gemacht habe‹ steht eine Fahrt mit dem Motorrad.« Er wies auf sein Motorrad.

»Wir nehmen dein Motorrad?« Sie trat einen Schritt zurück. »Sam, das habe ich noch nie gemacht.«

Er zog sie wieder an sich. »Mach dir keine Sorgen. Du

musst dich einfach nur an mir festhalten.«

»Und was ist, wenn ich loslasse?«

»Warum solltest du?« Er nahm einen Helm vom Rücksitz und stülpte ihn ihr über den Kopf. »Mein Gott, Faith. Damit siehst du wahrhaftig noch heißer aus.«

»Jep, ich möchte wetten, dass der Helm meiner Frisur den richtigen Pfiff gibt.«

»Vertrau mir. Deine Haare werden perfekt aussehen.« Faith quietschte, als er sie um die Taille packte und sie auf das Motorrad hob. »Wow, wenn du so auf meinem Monster sitzt … Das ist gefährlich. Baby, du kannst von Glück sagen, wenn ich es heute Abend schaffe, die Finger von dir zu lassen.«

»Wir wollten uns doch anständig benehmen, oder?«, sagte Faith, als sich Sam vor sie auf den Sitz setzte. Allerdings war anständiges Benehmen das Letzte, was sie im Sinn hatte, als sie sah, wie sich sein graues Hemd über seinem breiten Rücken spannte und sich darunter jeder Muskel bis hinunter zur Taille abzeichnete. Sogar sein schwarzer Gürtel sah heiß aus. Und sein Motorrad? Sein *Monster*? Sam hatte nicht zu viel versprochen. Zu sehen, wie er mit seinen kräftigen Beinen rittlings darauf saß, ließ die unanständigen Gedanken nur so sprießen.

»Anständiges Benehmen. Ja, ich erinnere mich. Es ist pure Folter, aber ich erinnere mich. So, jetzt leg die Arme um mich.«

»Bist du aber herrisch«, neckte sie und schlang ihre Arme um ihn. Er packte sie an den Unterarmen und zog sie nach vorne, bis ihre Schenkel weit gespreizt waren und sich ihre Brüste an seinen Rücken schmiegten.

»Perfekt. Halt dich fest. Lass nicht los, dann passiert dir nichts.«

Das Motorrad erwachte zum Leben und schickte aufregende Impulse zwischen ihre Beine, zu ihren Brüsten und überall dazwischen. Sie hatte keine Ahnung, wohin sie fahren würden, und sie hatte schreckliche Angst vor dieser Höllenmaschine. Aber sich an Sam zu klammern und zu spüren, wie sich die Vibrationen des Motors von seinem auf ihren Körper übertrugen, war wie ein vielversprechendes Vorspiel. Als sie aus der Parklücke hinaus auf die Straße einbogen, drängte sie sich noch näher an ihn, und als er die Straße hinunterbrauste, wurden die Vibrationen noch intensiver und ihre Angst wandelte sich in Aufregung.

Während sie durch die Stadt flogen, klammerte sich Faith an Sam fest und spürte jeden seiner Muskeln. Seine Bauchmuskeln regten sich unter ihren Händen, und sie musste einfach die Finger spreizen, um noch mehr von ihm mitzubekommen. Sam hatte recht. Diesen köstlichen Mann würde sie nicht fallen lassen. Sie fühlte sich wacher und freier als je zuvor, als er an Chelsea's Boutique, dem Jachthafen und Mr. B. vorbeifuhren. Die Zeichen, die Sam nur für sie aufgestellt hatte, waren verschwunden, aber die Erinnerung an diese Nacht würde nie verblassen.

Faith war es egal, wohin sie fuhren, als sie die Stadtgrenze hinter sich ließen. Dies war die aufregendste Fahrt ihres Lebens.

Kurz darauf hielten sie vor dem Whiskey Bro's, einer zwielichtig aussehenden Bar, kurz vor der Brücke, die nach Peaceful Harbor führte. Faith war schon oft daran vorbeigefahren. Wie jetzt parkten dort immer mehrere Motorräder. Durch die Fenster drang kein Lichtschimmer und sie sah, dass sie von innen mit schwarzer Farbe bemalt waren.

Oje!

Vor der Bar standen zwei Männer mit langen Bärten. Beide trugen Jeans, Stiefel und Lederwesten. Bisher hatte Faith solche Lederwesten nur in Filmen gesehen. Sam stieg ab, legte seinen Helm auf den Sitz und lächelte sie an.

»Alles okay?«

»Ähm, nein.« Ihr Blick ging zwischen der Bar und Sam hin und her. »Gehen wir da rein?«

Er half ihr, den Helm abzunehmen, und legte ihn auf dem Gepäckträger ab. Er lächelte, als sei dies das beste Date aller Zeiten. Er nahm ihr Gesicht in die Hände und schaute ihr in die Augen. Sie saß immer noch auf dem Motorrad, und wenn es nach ihr gegangen wäre, hätte Sam sich wieder vor sie gesetzt und sie wären zurück in den Stadtteil gefahren, in dem sie sich wohler fühlte.

»Ja, hier gehen wir rein.« Er ließ seine Hände unter ihr Haar gleiten, bauschte es auf und schob ihr eine lose Strähne hinters Ohr. »Wunderschön wie immer.«

Er nahm ihre Hand, um ihr vom Motorrad zu helfen, aber sie spannte die Beine an und weigerte sich, abzusteigen.

»Sam«, sagte sie gereizt. »Ich kann da nicht reingehen. Das ist die Art von Bar, um die mein Vater einen riesigen Bogen machen würde.«

Er packte sie an der Hüfte, während sie sich in seinen Händen wand.

»Stopp! Lass mich runter.«

Er tat es und hielt sie nun an seinem unglaublich kräftigen Körper gefangen.

»Wie war das mit dem Buch, das du nur nach seinem Einband beurteilst?«

Sie schaute über die Schulter und schauderte bei dem

Gedanken, dort hineinzugehen. Sie stellte sich die Typen vor, die wahrscheinlich Frauen verkauften für … sie wusste nicht für was. Ein Motorrad vielleicht? Natürlich war das ein Vorurteil, das auf Gerüchten beruhte, aber trotzdem. Sie war eine kluge Frau und kluge Frauen stürzten sich nicht kopfüber in riskante Situationen. Ihr Vater hatte sie vor solchen Orten gewarnt und sie vertraute seinem Urteil. Sie dachte noch darüber nach, als Sam ihr Kinn hob, sie zärtlich küsste und sie mit seiner sanften Berührung beruhigte. Das machte sie nur noch nervöser, denn kluge Frauen verloren sich nicht in einem Kuss. Oder?

Als er den Kuss tiefer werden ließ, hatte sie das Gefühl, als würde ihr Körper Stück für Stück mit seinem verschmelzen. *Oh ja, kluge Frauen verlieren sich sehr wohl in Küssen und in dem Gefühl deiner rauen Hand auf meiner Wange und in deinem verführerischen Duft.* Als ihr dieser Gedanke durch den Kopf schoss, riss sie die Augen auf und löste ihre Lippen mit einem Ruck von seinen.

»Oh nein, du kannst mich nicht mit deinen lustvollen Küssen locken.«

Er lachte, ließ sie aber nicht los. »Faith, glaubst du, ich würde dich jemals an einen Ort bringen, an dem dir Gefahr droht?«

»Nicht absichtlich.«

»Genau. Und wenn wir jemals an einen Ort kämen, der sich als unsicher erweist, was meinst du, würde ich dann tun?«

»Mich meinem Schicksal überlassen und davonlaufen?« Sie wusste, dass das nicht stimmte, aber sie war derart nervös, dass sie gar nicht nachdachte, was sie redete. Sams Augen verengten sich. Er fand ihre Antwort offensichtlich nicht lustig. »Ich weiß, dass du mich beschützen würdest, Sam, aber …« Sie warf erneut einen Blick auf die beiden bärtigen Männer, die ins Gespräch vertieft waren.

»Vertraust du mir?«

Sie holte zitternd Luft. »Ich vertraue dir. Aber welche Bar malt ihre Fenster schwarz an?«

»Die Art von Bar, in der ich herumhänge, wenn ich von der Außenwelt in Ruhe gelassen werden will.« Er verschränkte seine Finger mit ihren und küsste ihre Fingerknöchel, während sie den Parkplatz überquerten. »Außerdem hast du gesagt, dass du keinen Abklatsch dessen wolltest, was ich mit anderen Frauen gemacht habe.«

»Ist das wirklich der einzige Ort, an dem du noch nicht mit einer Frau geschlafen hast?« Bei dem Gedanken wurde ihr erst recht mulmig.

»Nein, Baby. Das hier ist einer meiner Lieblingsorte, und weil du mir so viel bedeutest, möchte ich ihn mit dir teilen. Und zufällig ist es tatsächlich ein Ort, an dem ich noch nie mit einer Frau zusammen war. Das war doch eine deiner Bedingungen, oder?«

Bedingungen? War das wirklich so bei ihm angekommen? Als ob sie eine Sonderbehandlung verlangte? Entgeistert blieb sie stehen.

»Sam, als ich das sagte, meinte ich es ganz allgemein. Ich wollte einfach nicht zu einer langen Liste von Frauen gehören, die du aufgerissen und mit denen du geschlafen hast, um bei nächster Gelegenheit weiterzuziehen. Ich meinte damit nicht, dass wir uns nur an Orten aufhalten können, wo du noch nie mit einer dieser Frauen warst.«

»Ich weiß.« Sein Blick war warm und nachdenklich. »Faith, ich weiß, dass es für dich schwer wird, wenn wir in der Stadt ausgehen, was wir irgendwann tun werden, weil ich unsere Beziehung nicht verstecken will. Aber dieser Ort ist wirklich etwas Besonderes für mich. Aber wir werden uns von der Stadt fernhalten, bis ich sicher bin, dass du mein wahres Ich siehst, wenn du mich anschaust, und nicht den Typen, für den du mich gehalten hast, als ich dich zum ersten Mal gefragt habe, ob du mit mir ausgehst.«

»Du machst dir also Sorgen, was passiert, wenn wir uns zusammen in der Stadt zeigen?«

Er seufzte, aber sein Blick war ernst. »Jetzt ist mehr Klarheit in deinem Blick als noch vor zwei Tagen. Du siehst mich an, als würdest du *mögen*, wer ich bin, und als wolltest du mit mir zusammen sein. Ich liebe das. Ich sehne mich danach. Aber ich weiß, dass die Frauen, die uns in Peaceful Harbor über den Weg laufen, wahrscheinlich mit mir flirten, egal ob wir zusammen sind oder nicht. Weil sie mich eben als den Mann kennen, der flirtet. Ich kann damit umgehen und angemessen darauf reagieren, aber ich möchte nicht, dass du in mir wieder *so einen Typen* siehst, nur weil sich ein paar bedeutungslose Leute danebenbenehmen.«

Was konnte sie dazu sagen? Er war gnadenlos in seiner Aufrichtigkeit und das machte ihn noch unwiderstehlicher. Sie stellte sich auf die Zehenspitzen und küsste ihn.

»Danke, dass du dir Gedanken über meine Gefühle machst. Ich habe versucht, nicht darüber nachzudenken, aber jetzt, wo ich weiß, dass du so bewusst und so im Einklang mit mir bist, ist es ein bisschen einfacher.« Sie warf erneut einen Blick auf das Whiskey Bro's. »Okay, ich bin dabei. Sehen wir uns deinen besonderen Ort einmal an.« Er drückte sie an seine Seite, ihren neuen Lieblingsplatz. »Kriege ich einen coolen Namen, wie sich das für eine Motorradbraut gehört?«

»Nur den, den du schon hast.«

Sie sah zu ihm auf. Sein Blick hatte etwas Besitzergreifendes. »Bradens Braut.«

Zwölf

Sam war nicht sicher, welche Reaktion er von Faith erwartet hatte, als er sie *Bradens Braut* nannte. Eine bissige Bemerkung vielleicht? Jedenfalls nicht die eifrige Zustimmung, die sich auf ihrem Gesicht spiegelte. Ihr strahlendes Lächeln, die Leidenschaft in ihren Augen und sein wachsender Wunsch, sie in aller Öffentlichkeit als *seine* Freundin zu zeigen, entfachten seinen Beschützerinstinkt. Er verstärkte seinen Griff um ihre Taille, als sie sich dem Whiskey Bro's näherten.

»Guten Abend, meine Herren«, begrüßte er die beiden Männer, die am Eingang standen.

Sie nickten stumm und der Größere der beiden hielt ihnen die Tür auf. Sam sog den vertrauten Geruch von Testosteron, Leder und Kameradschaft ein, mit einer unterschwelligen Note von erbitterten Konkurrenzkämpfen. Verdammt, er liebte diese Bar. Hierher kam er, um über Geschäfte, Motorräder, Sport oder alles Mögliche zu reden, ohne sich dabei als toller Hecht beweisen zu müssen.

Musik, Gelächter und Stimmengewirr schlugen ihnen entgegen und mindestens zwanzig neugierige Augenpaare waren auf sie gerichtet. Sam spürte, wie Faith neben ihm erstarrte. Er beugte sich vor und gab ihr einen Kuss auf den Scheitel.

»Ich pass auf dich auf«, sagte er. Er selbst machte sich zwar keine Sorgen um ihre Sicherheit, aber er konnte sich vorstellen, wie beängstigend die tätowierte Meute mit ihren Bandanas auf die süße Faith wirken mussten.

Er führte sie über die abgetretenen und zerschrammten Holzdielen zu einem Tisch neben dem einfachen, chaotisch aussehenden Tresen. Was sie wohl von diesem Ort halten mochte? Er zog ihr einen Stuhl hervor und drückte ihr beruhigend die Schulter. Ihm war klar, dass eine solche Bar für sie etwas völlig Neues sein musste, aber sie war keine verwöhnte Prinzessin – und das war eine der Eigenarten, die er an ihr mochte. Sie war *echt* und sprach aus, was sie dachte. Wenn sie es zuließ, konnte sie diesen Ort und seine Besucher ebenso lieb gewinnen wie er.

»Hallo, Braden, wie sieht's aus?« Die Stimme von Bullet Whiskey klang so rau wie sein Name. Er schlug Sam auf den Rücken, und bevor der antworten konnte, lächelte er Faith an und sagte: »Hallo, Schätzchen.«

»Faith, das ist Bullet Whiskey. Ihm und seiner Familie gehört die Bar.«

»Hallo. Nett, Sie kennenzulernen.« Sie lächelte Bullet an. Ihr Blick glitt über seine bunt tätowierten Arme bis zu einem Schlangenkopf, der unter dem Kragen seines Hemdes hervorlugte. Sie sah ihn fragend an, aber in ihrem Blick lag etwas Schelmisches, das bei Sam jedes Mal ein Flattern im Bauch auslöste. »Bullet ist ein interessanter Name. Haben Sie viele Menschen umgebracht oder fahren Sie sehr schnell?«

Sam lachte, aber insgeheim war er stolz, weil er wusste, wie unbehaglich sie sich fühlte. Trotzdem hatte sie den Mut gefunden, einen Mann aufzuziehen, der eine Handbreit größer war als Sam und bestimmt zwanzig Kilo schwerer.

Bullet fuhr sich mit den Fingern durch den Bart, während sich ein Lächeln auf seinem Gesicht ausbreitete. »Schätzchen, ich denke, die einzige Antwort, die du wirklich hören willst, ist, dass ich zu schnell fahre.« Er zwinkerte ihr zu. »Was kann ich euch bringen?«

»Faith? Wein, Bier, Limonade?«

Sie berührte seine Hand, die immer noch auf ihrer Schulter lag. »Was nimmst du?«

»Für mich nur Cola. Ich habe heute Abend kostbare Fracht an Bord.« Das brachte ihm ein weiteres warmes Lächeln ein.

»Ich nehme das Gleiche, bitte.«

»Kommt sofort«, sagte Bullet.

Sam zog sich einen Stuhl an den Tisch und setzte sich.

»Wow, eine echte Biker-Bar«, sagte Faith über die Musik hinweg und sah ihn mit großen Augen an.

»Ja, eine echte Biker-Bar«, sagte er amüsiert. Er beobachtete, wie Faith die rauen Holzwände betrachtete, mit ihren Nummernschildern, Biker-Logos, Flaggen und anderen Erinnerungsstücken wie einem Banjo, alten Schwarz-Weiß-Fotos, auf denen Verwandte der Whiskey-Brüder auf ihren Motorrädern zu sehen waren, und Ankündigungen bevorstehender Touren. Ihr Blick blieb an jedem Gegenstand haften, bevor er zum Tresen schweifte, wo Neonleuchten grellbunte Lichtakzente setzten. Etwa dreißig Männer und Frauen saßen an den Tischen oder drängten sich um den Billardtisch im hinteren Teil der Bar. Die drei Bandmitglieder mussten um die fünfzig sein. Sie trugen verblichene Jeans und schwarze Stiefel, die Frau eine Lederhose und mit Nieten besetzte Boots. Sie alle hatten schwarze Hemden mit einem rot-weißen Logo an.

»Es gefällt mir«, sagte sie beiläufig. »Es ist definitiv anders, aber Bullet scheint nett zu sein, ganz und gar nicht, was ich erwartet hatte. Ich dachte, er würde abweisend sein oder so. Das hört sich furchtbar an, oder?«

»Nein, das hört sich ehrlich an.« *Und das ich liebe an dir.*

»Kommst du oft hierher?«, fragte sie.

»Nicht oft. Alle paar Wochen.« Sam hatte das Whiskey Bro's zufällig entdeckt, als er nach dem College nach Peaceful Harbor zurückgekehrt war. Damals hatte er eine Tour auf seinem Motorrad unternommen und war auf der Suche nach einem Ort gewesen, wo er einen klaren Kopf bekommen konnte. Seitdem war er immer wieder hierhergefahren.

»Warum? Ich meine das gar nicht kritisch, aber warum ist eine Bar so weit außerhalb der Stadt dein Lieblingsplatz, wenn es nicht weit von zu Hause so viele Alternativen gibt?«

»Jeder braucht seine kleinen Fluchten.« Er nahm ihre Hand in seine und war heilfroh, dass sie sich wohler fühlte. »Außer vor dir. Von dir brauche ich keinen Rückzugsort.«

Sie senkte schüchtern den Blick, dann sah sie ihn an und neigte den Kopf, als versuchte sie, ihn zu verstehen. »Aber dein Leben scheint so voll und interessant zu sein, mit deinen Abenteuertouren, deinen Freunden, deiner Familie.«

»Mein Leben ist voll und es ist großartig, aber manchmal ist es zu viel.« Niemandem sonst hätte er ein solches Geständnis anvertraut, aber er wollte, dass Faith wusste, wer er wirklich war, und das bedeutete, dass er nichts vor ihr verbarg. »Es ist schön, hierherzukommen. Niemand erwartet etwas von mir, ich muss mich nur zurücklehnen, kann reden oder einfach chillen.«

»Wie seltsam. Ich kann mir gar nicht vorstellen, dass du dich entspannst. Du bist immer beschäftigt.«

»Nicht immer«, sagte er. »Das alljährliche Barbecue bei Rough Riders steht vor der Tür, und ich bin davon ausgegangen, dass du mein Date bist, aber ich sollte dich der Form halber lieber fragen, oder? Wirst du mit mir hingehen? Ich hoffe, dass wir uns zwischendurch mal von den anderen zurückziehen und allein sein können.« Er konnte nicht widerstehen: Er musste sich einfach zu ihr beugen und fragen: »Möchtest du das, Faith Hayes?«

Die Luft zwischen ihnen knisterte und ließ seine Gefühle an die Oberfläche schnellen. Er liebte diesen Blick an ihr, wenn sie aussah wie eine Tigerin im Käfig, als wollte sie spielen, müsse sich aber zurückhalten. Er testete sie aus, schob ihre Grenzen Stück für Stück ein wenig weiter. Den Anschein von Sitte und Anstand zu erwecken, war verdammt hart, denn sie war sexy und verlockend und sein Verlangen nach ihr war größer, als sie sich vermutlich zu erträumen wagte.

»Magst du kein schlüpfriges Gerede?« Er hielt ihren Blick fest und genoss es, dass ihr für einen Moment der Atem stockte.

Sie antwortete mit einem leichten Achselzucken, bei dem sich ein bisschen Gleichgültigkeit und ein bisschen *Dazu will ich lieber nichts sagen* mischten. Er ließ seine Hand in ihren Nacken gleiten, der ihm schon so vertraut vorkam. Wenn er sich vorstellte, mit den Lippen darüberzufahren, die zarte Haut sanft zwischen die Zähne zu nehmen und daran zu zupfen und zu saugen, bis sie nach mehr bettelte ... *Platz, Bursche.*

»Keine Sorge«, beruhigte er sie. »Ich werde dich nicht verderben.«

Sie starrte ihn an. Es schien, als schlummerten Weiblichkeit und Lust hinter einer Art unsichtbarer Mauer aus verbotenen Früchten. Gerade, als er dachte, sie würde sich abwenden, brach sie das Schweigen.

»So süß und unschuldig, wie du denkst, bin ich gar nicht.« Ihr Ton war reine Verführung. »Ich sage diese Dinge auch ... *in meinem Kopf.*« Langsam und lockend strich sie ihm mit der Fingerspitze über die Unterlippe. Da wusste er, dass sie sich genauso in das *Wir beide* verstrickt hatte wie er.

»Wenn du dir Mühe gibst, kannst du es bestimmt auch hören.« Plötzlich presste sie ihren Mund auf seinen und – *oh ja, verdammt* – ihre Zunge drängte sich fordernd zwischen seine Lippen. Der überraschende Kuss elektrisierte ihn und schickte einen heißen Stromstoß nach dem anderen durch seinen Körper. Als sie sich mit einem Ruck von ihm löste, ließ sie ihn hart und voller verzweifeltem Verlangen nach mehr zurück.

Sie legte einen Finger an ihre Lippen, als würden sie ebenfalls nach einem weiteren Kuss brennen, und fragte: »Und? Hast du es gehört?«

Bevor er sein Blut dazu bringen konnte, wieder nach oben zu fließen und sein Gehirn zu versorgen, brachte Bullet ihre Getränke. Er beugte sich zu Sam und sagte leise: »Bear würde gerne eine Runde Darts mit dir spielen. Ist das okay für dein Mädel hier? Sonst sag ich ihm, dass er sich jemand anderen suchen soll.«

Faith blinzelte ein paarmal und ihr Lächeln wurde breiter. »Ich liebe Darts«, sagte sie, ohne den Blick von Sam zu wenden. »Von mir aus kannst du gerne spielen. Wenn du willst, können wir mit mehreren spielen, dann bin ich in deinem Team. Ich meine, wenn es dir nichts ausmacht. Ich bin ziemlich gut.«

Bullet war genauso verblüfft wie Sam. »Du spielst Darts?«

Sie nickte aufgeregt. »Mein Vater hat es uns allen beigebracht und am College habe ich die ganze Zeit gespielt.«

»Verdammt, Braden. Wo hast du diese süße kleine Dame so lange versteckt?« Bullet nickte Faith zu. »Wenn du spielen willst, stellen wir was auf die Beine.«

Sam sah sie so überrascht und zugleich so lustvoll an, dass sie sich wie der heiße Feger fühlte, in den sie sich allmählich zu verwandeln schien. Sie hatte keine Ahnung, woher dieser Kuss gekommen war, aber der Drang, die Kontrolle zu übernehmen, hatte sie urplötzlich überkommen. Die Grenzen zu durchbrechen, die sie sich selbst gesetzt hatte, und ihn zu küssen, bis ihm schwindelig wurde, war ein herrliches Gefühl. Und dieser Kuss – lieber Himmel, jeder Kuss mit ihm – ließ ihren ganzen Körper vor Lebendigkeit kribbeln. Die Atmosphäre in dieser schwach erleuchteten, abgelegenen Bar, in der sie niemand kannte, war gefährlich und wie elektrisiert und weckte in ihr den Wunsch, tatsächlich *so* zu sein.

»Tut mir leid. Ich hoffe, ich habe dich nicht in Verlegenheit gebracht«, sagte sie zu Sam.

»Machst du Witze?« Er beugte sich vor und sagte: »Ich habe jedes unanständige Wort in deinem hübschen kleinen Kopf gehört.«

»Ach du lieber Gott. Ich kann gar nicht glauben, dass ich das gesagt habe.« Plötzlich brach übermütiges Lachen aus ihr hervor. Auch Sam musste lachen. »Es ist dieser Ort. Hier kennt mich niemand, also ist es einfacher … zu *spielen*.«

»Wir sind gar nicht so verschieden, du und ich.« Sams Blick wurde ernst. »Ich habe mein ganzes Leben lang gespielt, weil es das war, was man von mir erwartet hat, und ich war zu sehr darin verstrickt, um zu erkennen, dass ich eine Rolle gespielt habe. Und du bist dein ganzes Leben lang vorsichtig gewesen, weil du dich so definiert hast. Vielleicht ist das Whiskey Bro's der perfekte Ort für uns beide.«

Sie betrachtete den Mann hinter dem Tresen, mit seinen Armen, die über und über mit Tattoos verziert waren, und einem Bartschatten, der ebenso dunkel war wie der von Sam. Er hörte der Band zu, sein Kopf bewegte sich im Takt. Er hätte ebenso gut einer der Barkeeper im Whispers sein können. Dann sah sie sich verstohlen im Gastraum um. An den Tischen saßen Leute in Jeans und Lederjacken, und ein Paar in der Nähe der Band schien ebenso in seiner eigenen Welt versunken zu sein wie sie und Sam. Zu ihrer Linken hockte eine Gruppe stämmiger Burschen, von denen einer vollkommen kahl war, ein anderer hatte einen dichten Kinnbart und einen imposanten Schnurrbart, ein dritter hatte kurz geschorenes Haar und tätowierte Schultern. Im Vergleich zu ihnen wirkten die anderen an diesem Tisch ziemlich unscheinbar. Abgesehen von einem stummen Kopfnicken, mit dem Sam, Bullet und selbst *sie* begrüßt wurden, ließ man sich offenbar in Ruhe. Ihr Vater hatte ihr eingeschärft, dass Biker gefährlich waren, und sie war einfach davon ausgegangen, dass er recht hatte. Nun musste sie sich eingestehen, dass er keineswegs recht hatte. Der zufriedene Blick in Sams Augen und ihr neu entdecktes Gefühl der Freiheit sprachen eine deutliche Sprache. Sie hatte diesen Ort und die Menschen hier falsch eingeschätzt, so wie sie Sam falsch eingeschätzt hatte – und war dabei von den Ansichten anderer Leute und ihren eigenen verqueren Vorstellungen ausgegangen.

»Kein Wunder, dass es dir hier gefällt«, sagte sie. »Jetzt kann ich es verstehen. Es ist schön, wenn man nicht ständig auf der Hut sein muss.«

»Also kein Buch mehr nach seinem Einband beurteilen?«, fragte er mit einer hochgezogenen Braue und sandte ihr mit seinem Blick seine geheime Botschaft.

»Nein, die Zeiten sind vorbei.«

»Bones!« Faith zuckte zusammen, als der Mann hinter dem Tresen plötzlich losbrüllte. Er nickte dem kurzhaarigen Mann mit den tätowierten Schultern zu. »Du bist bei mir. Dixie!« Er wies mit Kinn auf eine Kellnerin, die sie noch gar nicht bemerkt hatte. Sie trug enge Jeans und ein knappes T-Shirt, auf dem WHISKEY BRO'S stand. Ihr flammend rotes Haar fiel in sanften Wellen über ihre Schultern und reichte ihr fast bis zur Taille.

»Ja, liebster Bruder?«, sagte sie grinsend.

»Du bist bei Braden und Bradens Braut«, antwortete der Barkeeper.

Ihr Herz machte einen Sprung. *Bradens Braut.*

»Sie heißt Faith«, rief Sam ihm zu. Er stand auf, zog Faith hoch und legte ihr den Arm um die Schulter.

»*Bradens Braut* gefällt mir«, sagte sie leise.

Er beugte sich vor und gab ihr einen Kuss auf die Nasenspitze. »Ich will nur, dass alle wissen, wer du bist. Außer dass du *meine* Braut bist, meine ich. Ich muss dir ein Sweatshirt besorgen mit ›Bradens Braut‹ drauf.«

Peng! Und schon hatte sie sich noch ein bisschen mehr in ihn verknallt.

»Der Barkeeper heißt Bear. Bear, Bullet, Bones und Dixie sind Geschwister.«

»Woher haben sie bloß diese Namen?« Sie hatte schon von Biker-Namen gehört, aber sie war neugierig, wie sie entstanden.

»Bones ist Arzt«, erklärte Sam. »Bullet war bei den Special Forces.« Als Dixie den Blick auf sie richtete, verstummte er.

Sie ließ lässig eine Kaugummiblase platzen, während sie ein Serviertablett auf der Theke abstellte und dann geradewegs auf Faith zukam. Dabei schwangen ihre Hüften wie bei einem Model auf dem Laufsteg und ihre schwarzen Stiefel mit den hohen Absätzen gaben bei jedem Schritt ein entschlossenes

Klack von sich. Schließlich blieb sie vor Faith stehen, verschränkte die Arme vor der Brust und musterte sie mit unverhohlener Neugier von Kopf bis Fuß. Faiths Nervosität flackerte wieder auf und sie war froh über Sams Arm um ihre Schultern.

»Hi, Dix. Wie geht's?«, fragte Sam.

Dixie richtete ihre schönen grünen Augen auf Sam, dann wieder auf Faith und dann wieder auf Sam. »Seit wann kenne ich dich, Braden?«

»Seit ein paar Jahren«, sagte Sam beiläufig.

Ihre Augen verengten sich. »Und wie viele Frauen hast du hierhergebracht?«

Oh Gott. Jetzt kommt's. Das ist nicht wirklich ein besonderer Ort, oder?

»Keine«, sagte er mit dem gleichen coolen Selbstbewusstsein, mit dem er alles tat.

Dixie sah Faith wieder mit ihren grünen Augen an und hörte gerade lange genug auf, auf ihrem Kaugummi herumzukauen, um ein breites Lächeln erstrahlen zu lassen, das ihre perfekten perlweißen Zähne zeigte. Sie war umwerfend, trotz ihres polterigen Auftretens. Faith hielt den Atem an und wartete darauf, dass sie die nächste Bombe zündete.

»Verdammt, Mädel«, sagte Dixie. »Du musst schon etwas ganz Besonderes sein, um an diesem Ort Arm in Arm mit diesem Mann aufzutauchen.« Sie zerrte Faith aus Sams Armen und drückte sie an sich. »Willkommen im Whiskey Bro's. Höchste Zeit, dass jemand das Leben dieses Mannes aufmischt. Er hat schon viel zu viele Jahre verschwendet.«

Faith konnte sich nicht vorstellen, dass Sam auch nur eine Minute seines Lebens verschwendete. Er sprudelte nur so vor Energie und musste ständig etwas tun, irgendwo hinfahren, irgendetwas sehen.

»Dixie Whiskey«, sagte Sam. »Ich möchte dich ganz offiziell meiner Freundin Faith Hayes vorstellen.«

»Dass sie deine Freundin ist, war wohl kaum zu übersehen, so wie du mit ihr rumgeknutscht hast und allen zeigst, dass sie dir gehört.« Sie wies auf seinen Arm, der nur darauf wartete, sich wieder bestimmend um Faiths Schulter zu legen. »Aber ihr zwei seid wirklich süß zusammen.«

Faith wurde es warm ums Herz, als sie das hörte. Sam war ein intensiver und rätselhafter Mann, und sie war das genaue Gegenteil. Sie war selbstbewusst und hielt sich eigentlich für jemanden, mit dem man Spaß haben konnte. Aber das, was sie unter Spaß verstand, und Sams Lebensstil hätten kaum unterschiedlicher sein können. Vermutlich fragten sich die Leute, was er an ihr fand, so wie sie selbst es ja auch getan hatte. Je besser sie ihn jedoch kennenlernte, desto mehr wurde ihr bewusst, dass sie doch gar nicht so verschieden waren. Und jetzt, als sie sich aus Dixies Umarmung löste und den Stolz in Sams Augen sah, verstand sie, dass es egal war, was die Leute über ihre Beziehung dachten.

Dixie umarmte Sam. Dann legte sie einen Arm um Faith und zog sie von ihm weg. »Wir sind Teamkollegen. Du, ich und Sam gegen meine Brüder, diese Angeber. Denen werden wir's zeigen.«

»Gerne.«

Dixie warf einen Blick auf ihren Namen oberhalb des Rough-Riders-Logos auf ihrer Kapuzenjacke. »Er macht keine halben Sachen, wie?«

Faith grinste.

»Sam ist einer von den Guten. Davon gibt es nicht viele.«

Nein, davon gibt es wirklich nicht so viele. Faith hörte Sam lachen und ihre Blicke trafen sich. *Du kannst von Glück sagen, wenn ich es heute Abend schaffe, die Finger von dir zu lassen,* sagten seine Augen. Aber in ihrem Kopf war sie diejenige, die diese Worte aussprach.

»Junge, Junge, euch hat's aber wirklich schlimm erwischt«, meinte Dixie leise. »Du musst diesen Mann mit nach Hause nehmen und ihm die Kleider vom Leib reißen, bevor ihr es hier auf dem Boden treibt.«

Faith riss ihren Blick von Sam los, während sich das Bild in ihr Hirn brannte, wie sie Sex auf den Holzdielen des Whiskey Bro's hatten. Erst der Pausenraum in der Praxis und jetzt hier. War denn kein Ort vor ihrem fiktiven Sexleben sicher?

Sie bemerkte Sams Gegenwart hinter sich, bevor sie seinen Arm spürte, der sich fest um ihre Taille legte. Sie lehnte sich an ihn und fühlte sich so geborgen und glücklich wie lange nicht mehr. Sie liebte es, dass Sam nicht versuchte, sie für sich einzunehmen, wie Typen es normalerweise bei den ersten Dates taten. Er war einfach nur *Sam* und das war so viel mehr als genug. Sie sammelten sich bei der Dartscheibe, und Sam stellte ihr Bear vor, während sich Bones und Dixie lautstark darüber stritten, wer verlieren würde.

»Hallo, Kleine. Viel Glück«, sagte Bear und hob sein kantiges Kinn. Er hatte ebenmäßige, markante Gesichtszüge und tief liegende, honigfarbene Augen, mit denen er bestimmt bei jeder Frau landen konnte.

»Okay, dann zeig uns mal, was du kannst, Schätzchen«, sagte Bullet zu Faith. »Kennst du die verschiedenen Spielvarianten? Shanghai? Killer? Fuchsjagd? Splitscore?«

»Ja, die kenne ich alle, aber auch Cricket oder Round the Clock.« Faith sah, wie Bear und Bones sich verstohlen ansahen, und dann Sam mit einem Blick bedachten, den sie nicht deuten konnte. Er drückte ihr einen Kuss aufs Haar. Um unmissverständlich deutlich zu machen, dass sie zu ihm gehörte? Ein leiser Schauder durchfuhr sie.

»Shanghai«, sagte Bones und starrte Faith unverhohlen an.

»Faith?« Dixie bedeutete ihr, dass sie als Erste an der Reihe war.

»Zeig's ihnen.« Sam gab ihr einen Klaps auf den Hintern.

Bones, der sie aufmerksam beobachtete, und Sam mit seinem Klaps sorgten dafür, dass Faiths Nerven in Flammen standen. Sie atmete tief durch und ging im Geiste noch einmal die Spielregeln für Shanghai durch. Das Ziel war es, die Zahlen eins, zwei, drei und so weiter nacheinander zu treffen. In jeder Runde ging es jedoch nur um eine Zahl, sie musste also mit allen drei Darts die Eins, die Zwei und so weiter treffen, um die höchste Punktzahl zu erreichen.

»Du schaffst das, Schätzchen«, ermutigte Bullet sie und machte sie nur noch nervöser.

Faith schloss für einen Moment die Augen, konzentrierte ihre Gedanken und lockerte die Schultern. *Ich kann das. Ich kann das. Ich kann das.*

Es gab zwei Möglichkeiten zu gewinnen: Entweder mit der höchsten Punktzahl am Ende des Spiels oder mit einem Shanghai – ein Single, ein Double und ein Triple der Zahl erzielen, die bei der entsprechenden Runde galt. Das schmale äußere Segment zählte doppelt, während das innere Feld die dreifache Punktzahl brachte. Das war ihre Spezialität. Normalerweise war sie wirklich gut, aber ein hell loderndes Nervenkostüm war nicht die ideale Voraussetzung. Wahrscheinlich konnte sie von Glück sagen, wenn sie die Scheibe überhaupt traf.

Eigentlich brauchte sie einen Drink. *Oder drei.*

Sie öffnete die Augen und konzentrierte sich nur auf die Scheibe, blendete die Musik, den Klaps auf den Hintern und die Gespräche um sie herum aus. Der schlanke Pfeil fühlte sich vertraut an, als sie die Hand zurückzog und losließ. Der Pfeil beschrieb in der Luft einen eleganten Bogen und landete direkt auf der Eins.

»Ja!«, schrie sie und sprang begeistert in die Höhe. Kaum hatte sie wieder festen Boden unter den Füßen, hätte sie sich am liebsten vor Verlegenheit in die hinterste Ecke verkrochen.

»Gut gemacht, super!« Sam zog sie in einen Kuss und entfachte das Feuer in ihren Nerven aufs Neue.

Bullet nickte anerkennend. »Verdammt, Schätzchen, du hast es geschafft.«

Sam presste seine raue Wange an ihre und sagte so leise, dass nur sie es hören konnte: »Du bist so hinreißend, dass ich mit dir in meinem Haus Darts spielen möchte. Und zwar nackt.«

Sie schnappte nach Luft, und ihr Körper reagierte sofort, von ihren harten Nippeln bis zu der Hitze, die zwischen ihren Beinen glomm.

»Ich versuche nur, dich ein bisschen abzulenken.«

»Warum?«, flüsterte sie. »Willst du, dass wir verlieren?«

Seine Augen glühten. »Nein. Ich möchte dich gewinnen.«

Er trat einen Schritt zurück, während sie alle Mühe hatte, so zu tun, als hätte er nicht gerade etwas ganz Wundervolles gesagt.

Dreizehn

Wenn es um Faith ging, konnte sich Sam nicht benehmen. Zumindest nicht ganz. Er war ihr mit Haut und Haaren verfallen. Sobald sich ein rosiger Schimmer auf ihren Wangen zeigte oder sie etwas tat, was so gar nicht zu der zurückhaltenden und besonnenen Frau passte, die sie normalerweise war, musste er einfach ihre spielerische Seite hervorkitzeln. Nach der ersten Dartrunde, als seine Bemerkung über ein Dartspiel im Adamskostüm sie derart aus der Fassung gebracht hatte, dass ihre Pfeile es kaum bis zur Scheibe schafften, hatte sie angefangen, seine Anzüglichkeiten zu erwidern. Jeder verstohlene Blick, jedes erhitzte Wort, jede sinnliche Berührung machten sie zur puren Versuchung und verlangten ihm alles an Selbstbeherrschung ab. Zum Glück war sein Hemd lang genug, um die Latte hinter seinem Reißverschluss zu verbergen.

Jetzt stand Faith neben ihm, ihre Hand tief in die Gesäßtasche seiner Jeans geschoben, und ihre Finger strichen langsam über seinen Hintern. Ihre andere Hand ruhte unter seinem Hemd auf seinem Bauch. Zwei Finger hatte sie direkt über dem Reißverschluss in seinen Hosenbund gehakt.

Sie spielten die letzte Runde. Die Jungs und Dixie hatten den ganzen Abend mit Faith geplaudert und Witze gerissen.

Bevor er beschlossen hatte, mit ihr ins Whiskey Bro's zu fahren, hatte er überlegt, wie es sein würde, wenn er Faith einen seiner geheimsten Rückzugsorte zeigte, aber er hatte nicht das Gefühl, seine Privatsphäre verloren zu haben. Dass Faith dabei war, machte alles so viel besser.

Sie sah ihn mit einem Blick an, der sagte: *Ich will dich*, und dieser Blick stand im Widerspruch zu einem anderen Blick, den er schon so gut kannte und der *Ich muss mich benehmen* sagte. Ob sie seine Blicke ebenso leicht lesen konnte? *Bleib bei mir. Ich werde gut zu dir sein.*

Die reinste Folter.

»Mir ist gerade eingefallen, woher ich dich kenne«, sagte Bones zu Faith.

Faith schluckte schwer und lächelte Bones vorsichtig an. Sam spürte, dass sie zu tief in die schwelende sexuelle Spannung zwischen ihnen verstrickt war, um Bones ihre volle Aufmerksamkeit zu schenken.

»Woher denn?«, fragte Sam an ihrer Stelle.

Bones sah absolut gepflegt und proper aus, und wenn er ein Hemd anhatte, das seine Tattoos bedeckte, wirkte er mit seinem akkuraten Haarschnitt und den ernsthaften Augen im Whiskey Bro's genauso exotisch wie Faith sich bei ihrer Ankunft gefühlt haben musste. Jetzt jedoch hatte er einen Bartschatten, trug ein verblichenes schwarzes Tanktop, Jeans und schwarze Bikerstiefel und passte mit seinen Tätowierungen und einem Bier in der Hand perfekt ins Bild.

»Vom Krankenhaus«, antwortete Bones. »Du arbeitest mit Jon Butterscotch zusammen, nicht wahr?«

»Ja.« Faith fuhr aus ihren Träumereien hoch und nahm ihre Hände von seinem Körper. Er wusste, dass sie sich Gedanken um ihr professionelles Image machte, und konnte sehen, wie diese Sorge ihre Augen füllte. »Woher kennst du Jon?«

»Ich bin Onkologe. ›Bones‹ klingt besser als ›Doc‹. Dort muss ich dich gesehen haben.«

»Ich assistiere ihm manchmal bei Operationen.« Ihr Blick ging zu Sam und dann wieder zu Bones.

Bones musste ihre Nervosität ebenfalls gespürt haben, denn er lächelte und sagte: »Keine Sorge. Es ist nichts Schlimmes daran, hier zu sein. Butterscotch wäre es egal, wenn er es wüsste.«

»Oh, das ist es nicht.« Ihre zitternde Stimme klang nicht sehr überzeugend.

Sam legte seinen Arm um sie, in der Hoffnung, ihre Nerven zu beruhigen.

Bones lachte. »Ich bin Arzt geworden, damit ich mir keine Gedanken machen muss, was meine Chefs über meinen Lebensstil denken. Ich verstehe, dass du nervös bist. Aber ehrlich, ich kenne Jon, und solange du keinen Ärger machst, schert er sich nicht darum, was du in deiner Freizeit treibst.«

Sie atmete erleichtert aus.

Zu Sam gewandt sagte Bones: »Aber ich wette, dein Bruder wird etwas dazu zu sagen haben, dass du Faith hierherbringst. Er ist ziemlich konservativ.«

»Um Cole kümmere ich mich schon«, versicherte Sam. Dabei richtete er sich eher an Faith als an Bones. Er spürte, wie sich ihr ganzer Körper versteifte, hob ihr Kinn mit dem Finger an, sah ihr in die Augen und wünschte sich, er könnte ihre Sorgen ein für alle Mal verschwinden lassen. »Ich kriege das hin. Das verspreche ich dir.« Er senkte seine Lippen auf ihre, als sich Bones abwandte, und küsste sie so lange, bis die Spannung in ihrem Körper nachließ und sie sich an ihn schmiegte.

»Okay, ihr Turteltauben«, sagte Dixie. »Faith, du bist dran.«

»Danke, Dixie.« Sams Blick war immer noch auf Faith gerichtet. »Mach dir keine Gedanken um Cole. Ich bin sicher, dass er keine Einwände haben wird. Okay?«

Sie nickte und trat zur Seite. Sam holte sein Handy hervor und schickte Cole eine weitere Nachricht, während Faith ihren ersten Pfeil warf. *Müssen reden. Bitte melde dich, sobald du wieder in der Stadt bist.* Er hasste die Vorstellung, dass sich Faith um irgendetwas Sorgen machte, vor allem um den Job, der ihr so am Herzen lag. Sam wusste in seinem tiefsten Innern, dass es Cole egal war, was sie in ihrer Freizeit machte. Er war zu professionell, um sich in das Privatleben seiner Angestellten einzumischen. Sam war stolz auf seinen Bruder, und er war überzeugt, dass Cole ihn ebenfalls respektierte, auch wenn er seinen bisherigen Lebensstil nicht gutheißen konnte. Ein Anruf würde Faiths Bedenken besänftigen, und er würde dafür sorgen, dass dieser Anruf kam, bevor sie ihm in der Praxis gegenübertreten musste.

»Dein Mädel hat ein Single und ein Double«, sagte Bear zu Sam.

Sam steckte sein Handy in die Tasche. Faiths Augen waren auf die Scheibe gerichtet. Ihr Atem ging ruhig, ihr Körper war leicht nach rechts geneigt, ihr rechter Fuß stand ein paar Zentimeter hinter ihrem linken und ihre Schultern waren parallel zum Boden. Aller Augen waren auf sie gerichtet, als sie die Hand zurückzog und ihre Augen noch schmaler wurden. Mit der Anmut einer Tänzerin streckte sie den Arm vor, ihr rechter Fuß glitt auf die Zehenspitzen und der Pfeil segelte durch die Luft und landete auf der Triple 20.

»Shanghai!«, jubelten alle.

Bullet riss Faith in die Arme und wirbelte sie lachend herum, während sich Dixie und Bear an sie drängten. Faiths

Blick suchte Sams, voller Stolz, und als Bullet sich aus der Menge befreite, Sam seine lächelnde Freundin brachte und sie in seine Arme legte, lösten sich alle Gedanken an Cole in nichts auf.

Faith sah so glücklich und sexy aus, als sie in Sams Augen starrte, ihre Hände an seine Wangen presste und ihren Mund auf seinen senkte. Es war kein Kuss voll ungezügelter Leidenschaft oder ein Kuss, der sagte: *Nimm mich, sofort.* Es war ein ungewohnter Kuss, den er für die Unendlichkeit erleben wollte. Es war der Kuss eines Paares, das einen Moment teilte und Minute für Minute, Stunde für Stunde an seiner gemeinsamen Geschichte wob.

Als sich ihre Lippen öffneten, lächelte sie immer noch. »Siehst du, was ich erreichen kann, wenn du mich nicht heiß machst?«

»Du steckst voller Überraschungen.« Er stellte sie auf den Boden und flüsterte ihr ins Ohr: »Ich würde gerne sehen, was du erreichen kannst, wenn du heiß bist.«

»Dann solltest du mir vielleicht einheizen, wenn wir alleine sind, *Braden.*«

Die Einladung nehme ich gerne an.

Sam bezahlte ihre Zeche und hielt Faith dabei fest im Arm. Sie verabschiedeten sich, und gleich darauf streifte die frische Luft seine warme Haut, trug aber absolut nichts dazu bei, ihn zu beruhigen. Noch bevor sich die Tür hinter ihnen geschlossen hatte, lag sie in seinen Armen. Sam drängte sie an die Außenmauer der Bar und ihre Münder verschmolzen in einem gierigen Kuss. Sie klammerte sich an seinen Rücken, als seine Hände über ihre Rippen fuhren und seine Daumen die Unterseite ihrer Brüste berührten. Sie stöhnte, und er verspürte das schmerzliche Verlangen, seine Hände und seinen Mund mit ihren Brustwarzen zu füllen und sie mit der Zunge zu umschmeicheln. Ihre Hüften schoben sich vor, und er wurde so hart, wie er es den ganzen Abend nicht gewesen war. Wenn er nicht sofort dafür sorgte, dass sie hier wegkamen, konnte er für nichts garantieren.

Widerstrebend löste er sich von ihr. »Komm, wir verschwinden.«

Sie legte den Arm um ihn, noch bevor sein Arm ihre Taille gefunden hatte. Oh Gott, wie sehr er das liebte! *Nimm mich, Baby. Mach mich dein.*

Am Motorrad angekommen nahm er ihr Gesicht in die Hände und sah ihr in die Augen. Ungezügelte Leidenschaft schlug ihm entgegen. Er nahm sie erneut in einen rauen Kuss. Seine Lippen waren hart, seine Zunge suchte, sein Körper war verzweifelt, und als sie ihre Hände in sein Haar schob und sich fest darin verkrallte, stöhnte er. Er küsste ihren Mund, ihr Kinn, vergrub sein Gesicht an ihrem Nacken, küsste, saugte, voller Begehren.

»Sam. *Oh Gott*, Sam.«

Eine kaum hörbare Stimme in seinem Hinterkopf ermahnte ihn, die Kontrolle wiederzuerlangen, doch als sie ihre Fingernägel in seinen Rücken bohrte, entzündeten sich Feuerströme in seinen Adern. Er küsste sich zurück zu ihrem Ohr, fuhr mit der Zunge um den Rand und knabberte dann an ihrem Ohrläppchen.

»*Ohmeingott.*«

Sie keuchte, als er an der empfindlichen Haut unter ihrem Ohr knabberte und leckte. Als sich ihre Hände heiß und eifrig unter sein Hemd schoben und über seinen Rücken fuhren, fiel ihm wieder ein, dass sie jederzeit ertappt werden konnten. Schließlich war dies ein öffentlicher Ort – und er hatte versprochen, sich zu benehmen. Dabei wollte er sich schon längst nicht mehr benehmen. Er ballte die Hände an ihren Hüften, damit er ihr nicht die Kleider vom Leib riss, und löste sich von seiner köstlichen Vorspeise.

»Faith.« Ein Blick in ihre hungrigen Augen und er hatte Mühe, die Worte hervorzubringen: »Nach Hause. Ich bringe dich nach Hause.« Seine Hände zitterten, als er sie auf das Motorrad hob.

Sie klammerte sich an seine Unterarme und ihre Augen bettelten um mehr. Es war unmöglich: Er konnte sich nicht von ihr fernhalten. Er setzte sich rittlings auf das Motorrad, sodass er ihr gegenübersaß, und nahm ihr Gesicht in die Hände.

Seine Gefühle sprudelten aus ihm hervor. »Wie oft habe ich dich in den letzten vierundzwanzig Stunden so gehalten?« Er wartete ihre Antwort nicht ab, außerdem glaubte er nicht, dass sie hätte antworten können, selbst, wenn sie gewollt hätte. Ihre Wangen waren gerötet und in ihren Augen glühte ein lustvoller, benommener Blick.

»Noch nie habe ich eine Frau so gehalten. Bei anderen war ein Kuss das Letzte, was ich im Sinn hatte. Deine Küsse verzehren mich, und dich so zu halten, dir in die Augen zu sehen, dein schönes Gesicht in meinen Händen zu fühlen, bringt uns so viel näher zusammen. Wenn wir nichts als diese Küsse hätten, wäre das reine Folter, aber ich könnte damit leben.«

»Lieber Gott, Sam«, sagte sie atemlos. »Küss mich.«

Er nahm ihren eifrigen Mund in einem harten Kuss nach dem anderen. Ein Motorrad, das plötzlich zum Leben erwachte, katapultierte sie zurück in die Wirklichkeit. Ihre Lippen lösten sich voneinander, aber keiner von beiden sah in die Richtung, aus der das Motorengeräusch kam. Schließlich lehnte Sam seine

Stirn an ihre, legte ihr die Hand um den Nacken und versuchte, den Adrenalinstrom einzudämmen, der ihn überschwemmte.

»Nach Hause, Baby. Ich muss dich nach Hause bringen.«

Auch die kühle Nachtluft, die ihr auf dem Weg zu ihrer Wohnung über die erhitzte Haut strich, konnte Faiths Kopf nicht leer fegen. An den Mann gepresst, den sie mit jeder Faser ihres Körpers begehrte, und von den Vibrationen des Motorrads umgeben, schaffte sie es nicht, einen einzigen klaren Gedanken zu fassen. Als sie ankamen, wusste sie nur, dass sie mehr von Sam wollte, und an der Art, wie er den Kiefer anspannte und verstummte, als sie die Treppe hochstiegen, erkannte sie, dass er in seinem Innern einen ähnlichen Kampf ausfocht.

Die Stille legte sich wie eine schwere Decke auf ihren Schultern, als sie die Schlüssel aus ihrer Tasche fischte. Sie wollte, dass *Sam* sich auf sie legte. Die Zurückhaltung in seinen Augen ließ ihr Herz anschwellen. Er hielt sich zurück, weil es das war, was sie gewollt hatte, aber jetzt, als sie beide ihre wortlosen Schlachten schlugen, wünschte sie, sie hätte nicht so hartnäckig darauf bestanden, dass sie sich nur küssten und sonst nichts.

Sie schob den Schlüssel ins Schloss und Sams Arme schlangen sich um ihre Taille. Mit geöffneten Lippen überschüttete sein heißer, köstlicher Mund ihren Hals mit Küssen und elektrisierte jede winzige Zelle ihres Körpers. Sie drückte die Tür auf, lehnte den Hinterkopf an seine feste Brust und bot ihm so einen besseren Zugang zu allem, was er wollte. Seine Hand glitt über ihr Top, tastete sich über ihren Busen und ließ sie erschaudern. Mit der anderen Hand drehte er ihr Kinn zu ihm und plünderte und nahm, küsste fordernd und labte sich mit einer Heftigkeit an ihr, die all ihre Sinne überschwemmte.

Mit seiner freien Hand umfasste er ihre Brust. Sein Daumen strich mit langsamen, kreisenden Bewegungen über ihren Nippel, und mit meisterlicher Präzision verstand er es, ihn gerade fest genug zu necken, dass er Lustgefühle direkt zwischen ihre Beine schickte. Sie versuchte, sich umzudrehen und ihm das Gesicht zuzuwenden, aber er hielt sie an Ort und Stelle. Seine harte Länge drängte an ihren Rücken, als er den Kuss vertiefte und sie verzehrte – Körper, Geist und Seele.

Als er sie schließlich in seinen Armen drehte, löste er sich nicht von ihr, sondern fuhr fort, sie langsam und verträumt zu küssen, als hätte er alle Zeit der Welt, um diese Nähe zu genießen. Das Geräusch einer zugeschlagenen Autotür riss Faith aus ihrem lustvollen Delirium und sie zog sich widerstrebend von ihm zurück. Sie krallte die Hand in sein Hemd und zerrte ihn in ihre Wohnung. Mit einem gezielten Fußtritt schloss er die Tür, wandte aber den Blick nicht von ihr. In seinen Augen lag etwas Wildes, Urtümliches, das ihr das Gefühl gab, sexy und ausgeliefert zu sein. Sein kraftvoller Körper bewegte sich mit stiller Überzeugungskraft und schloss die Distanz zwischen ihnen. Faith stand reglos da und leckte sich nervös die Lippen. Sie versuchte, nicht über ihn herzufallen, denn: *Junge, Junge, wie gerne wollte sie über ihn herfallen.* Seine sexuelle Anziehungskraft machte ihn für jede Frau, die ihm über den Weg lief, so attraktiv, und hier war sie, die vorerst letzte in einer langen Reihe von Frauen. Die Eifersucht grub ihre Krallen in ihr Herz und forderte Blut. Sie versuchte erfolglos, die hässlichen Gefühle wegzuschieben, doch ein Blick in seine Augen reichte und die Krallen verschwanden. Sam gehörte jetzt ihr, weil er es so wollte, und er hatte viel dafür getan, dass sie sich bereit erklärte, ihm zu gehören. Er trat näher und saugte den Sauerstoff aus dem Raum.

Seine Hand legte sich schwer um ihren Nacken und zog sie zu sich heran. Ein teuflisches, verlockendes Lächeln umspielte seine Lippen. Sie liebte alles, was er mit ihrem Nacken anstellte. Er konnte die Nase an der zarten Haut vergraben, daran saugen, sie küssen oder mit dem Daumen darüberstreichen, wie er es jetzt tat, während er sie anblickte, als sei sie eine Göttin: schön, sexy und unendlich verführerisch. Sie selbst sah sich nicht so, aber Sam verlieh ihr dieses Gefühl. Sein Verlangen war nicht zu leugnen, sein Gesicht und sein Körper und auch seine Hände sprachen davon, als sie wieder unter ihr Top glitten und ihren Rücken erkundeten. Seine Finger krümmten sich um ihre Schultern und er drückte sie an sich.

Die gespannte Erwartung war gnadenlos. Sie war nass und keuchte und krallte die Hände so fest in sein Hemd, dass es wahrscheinlich Spuren auf seiner Haut hinterließ. Sein Herz pochte so wild wie ihres, und er suchte so eindringlich in ihren Augen, dass sie sich fragte, wonach er suchte. *Bestätigung?* Sie stellte sich auf die Zehenspitzen und küsste ihn aufs Kinn. Es war rau und kratzig und sein berauschender, moschusartiger Duft überwältigte sie. So männlich, so *Sam.* Mit geöffneten Lippen küsste sie eine federleichte Spur an seinem Kiefer entlang. Ein kehliges Stöhnen rumpelte in seiner Brust und drang aus seinen Lungen, und sie wollte mehr davon hören. Sie biss sachte in seine Unterlippe und fuhr dann mit der Zunge darüber.

Seine Finger packten ihre Schultern fester, als er zischend die Luft ausstieß und sie in die Arme schloss. Er senkte seinen

Mund in einem qualvollen, langsamen Kuss auf ihren, trug sie ins Wohnzimmer und setzte sie auf die Couch. Er beugte sich über sie, küsste ihre Lippen, ihren Hals, ihren Mund. Seine Hüften rieben sich mit verführerischen Bewegungen an ihren, während seine Arme sie umfangen hielten.

»So schön«, flüsterte er an ihrer Wange. »So sexy. Wie soll ich mich da benehmen?« Seine Hand fuhr über ihre Rippen und drückte sanft ihre Brust.

Faith sog keuchend die Luft ein. Seine Finger tanzten über ihre Haut und seine Erregung rieb sich an ihrer geschwollenen Mitte, bis es ihr fast die Sinne raubte.

Sie wollte nicht, dass er sich benahm. »Wir benehmen uns nur ein bisschen«, brachte sie mühsam hervor.

Seine Mundwinkel zuckten, aber seine Augenbrauen zogen sich zusammen. »Ich bin nicht sicher, was das bedeutet.«

»Ich auch nicht«, gab sie zu. »Aber ich möchte nicht aufhören.«

Sie zog seinen Mund an ihren und gab sich der Leidenschaft hin, die in ihrem Inneren brannte. Sie schob ihre Hände durch sein Haar, über seine Schultern und seinen Rücken hinunter, um jeden Zentimeter von ihm zu spüren. Sie zerrte an seinem Hemd, um seine Haut zu fühlen. Er richtete sich auf und zog es aus. Sein nackter Oberkörper war eine Augenweide und Faith beugte sich vor und küsste seine Brust. Er stützte sich auf eine Hand, während die andere immer noch mit ihrem Nippel spielte. Unter ihrer Zunge spürte sie jede Bewegung seiner Brustmuskeln. Sie fuhr mit der Hand darüber, verharrte an seinen Brustwarzen und nahm sie schließlich in den Mund, um die harten Spitzen mit der Zunge zu umschmeicheln.

»Lieber Gott«, stieß er zwischen zusammengebissenen Zähnen hervor.

Seine Augen waren geschlossen, Kiefer und Nacken waren angespannt. Sie liebte es, dass er sich ihretwegen zurückhielt. Und wenn er losließ? Wie würde er dann sein? Sie küsste seinen Hals und zog ihre Zunge entlang der Länge. Ein weiteres Knurren entfuhr seiner Kehle. Er senkte den Kopf, und als er die dunklen Augen öffnete, schwamm blanke Freude darin. Mit einem räuberischen Blick richtete er sich auf. Sie war seine bereitwilligste Beute und keuchte auf, als sie die beeindruckende Erektion sah, die sich unter seiner Jeans abzeichnete. Er musterte sie ernst – alles an ihr. Einen Moment schloss er die Augen, als wollte er die Kontrolle zurückgewinnen, und sie setzte sich auf, legte ihm die Hände an die Seiten und küsste seinen Bauch. Sie fühlte jeden seiner Atemzüge an ihrer Zunge, spürte die Zurückhaltung in seinen Muskeln.

Ihre Blicke trafen sich. Sie streckte die Hand aus und spielte mit seinen Brustwarzen und reizte ihn weiterhin mit ihrem Mund.

»Faith.« Er spannte den Kiefer an.

Sie sah ihn unverwandt an, hörte aber nicht auf, ihn zu küssen, zu lecken und zu berühren. Er packte den Saum ihres Tops und schob es ein Stück hoch.

»Okay?«

Sie nickte stumm. Nicht eine Sekunde lang wollte sie aufhören, ihn zu schmecken. Er zog ihr das Hemd über den Kopf. Ihre Halskette fiel zwischen ihre Brüste in ihrem Spitzen-BH. Er nahm sie ihr behutsam ab und legte sie auf den Tisch neben der Couch. Er bewegte sich mit quälender Langsamkeit, das Selbstvertrauen, das ihn sonst nie im Stich ließ, war durch ihre selbst auferlegten Grenzen gebremst. Sie liebte es, dass er sie genug respektierte, um die Dinge langsam angehen zu lassen. Sie sehnte sich verzweifelt danach, ihn ungezähmt und wild zu erleben, aber nicht jetzt. Was sie jetzt hatten, war perfekt, und irgendwie musste er das gewusst haben.

Er schob einen Träger ihres BHs von ihrer Schulter. Er ließ sie nicht aus den Augen, als er erst die eine, dann die andere Schulter küsste, den anderen Träger herunterschob, den BH aufhakte und ihn auf den Boden warf. Ihre Brüste fielen schwer aus den Körbchen. Sie wartete darauf, dass sie unter seinem sinnlichen Blick verlegen erröten würde, doch für eine derartige Verschwendung von Gefühlen war kein Platz, während ihr Körper in schmerzlicher Sehnsucht nach diesem atemberaubenden Mann vor ihr pulsierte.

Vierzehn

Faith lag unter Sam, offen und vertrauensvoll und so schön, dass ihm der Atem stockte. Ihr dunkles Haar war wie ein Fächer ausgebreitet, ihre Lider schienen schwer von Verlangen. Ihre seidig schimmernden, vollendet geformten Brüste waren von der Sonne unberührt und bildeten einen bezaubernden Kontrast zu ihrer gebräunten Haut. Die dunklen Spitzen lockten ihn. Er legte sich behutsam auf sie und genoss ihren ersten Hautkontakt, als hätte er ein kostbares Geschenk bekommen.

»Spürst du das?«, flüsterte er. Ihr wild pochendes Herz und der entrückte Blick in ihren Augen reichten ihm als Antwort. »Das sind *wir*. So richtig. So perfekt.«

Die Dringlichkeit, mit der ihre Münder aufeinanderprallten, strafte seinen zärtlichen Tonfall Lügen. Ihre Zungen schlängelten sich umeinander, ihr Atem mischte sich, ihre Lippen brannten. Er würde nie genug davon bekommen, sie zu küssen, sie zu berühren. Seine Hände hasteten fieberhaft über ihre Rundungen, von der Hüfte bis zu den Brüsten und wieder zurück, und spürten, wie ihr Körper erbebte. Er streichelte ihre Brüste, während sich ihre Hüften in perfekter Harmonie bewegten und seine Erregung schmerzhaft nach Erlösung drängte. Er zog sich zurück, zupfte sanft an ihrer Unterlippe, was ihm ein sexy Stöhnen einbrachte. Eine Spur leiser, flüchtiger Küsse zog sich über ihren Hals, ihren Nacken und schließlich – endlich – ihre Brüste und ihren Körper unter ihm. Er saugte die feste Knospe an seinen Gaumen und sie krallte die Finger in sein Haar und hielt ihn fest. *Oh ja, Baby. Zeig mir, was dir gefällt.*

Sie wölbte sich gegen ihn und drängte ihn, den Mund weiter zu öffnen. Er nahm mehr von ihrer köstlichen Brust, hielt sie mit beiden Händen und liebkoste sie.

»Das fühlt sich so gut an.« Ihre Worte kamen schnell und hitzig.

Er widmete der anderen Brust die gleiche Aufmerksamkeit, und als er sie zusätzlich mit den Zähnen neckte, hoben sich ihre Hüften vor Wonne. Sam wollte jeden Zentimeter ihres wunderschönen Körpers kosten. Mit quälender Langsamkeit fuhr seine Zunge um ihre Brustwarze, ohne jedoch die Spitze zu berühren, obwohl sie versuchte, ihn dorthin zu lenken. »Gott«, zischte sie.

Er verschränkte ihre Hände mit seinen, hielt sie neben ihrem Kopf fest und ärgerte sie weiter. Ihre Augen schlossen sich und sie biss sich auf die Unterlippe, bis er sie erneut in einem harten Kuss nahm.

»Halt dich nicht zurück.« Das klang herrischer, als er beabsichtigt hatte. »Ich bin gierig«, sagte er in milderem Ton und begegnete ihrem berauschenden Blick. »Ich möchte jedes kleine Geräusch hören, das du für mich machst.«

Sie biss sich wieder auf die Lippe und er zupfte sie mit den Zähnen frei.

»Nur ich kann heute Abend auf diese Lippe beißen.«

Ihre Augen weiteten sich ein wenig angesichts seiner Forderung. Er küsste sie sanft und fuhr dann mit seiner Zunge über ihre Lippen.

»Okay?«, fragte er und gab ihr damit die Kontrolle zurück.

Wieder senkte er seinen Mund auf ihre Brust, ließ seine Zunge um ihre Brustwarze wirbeln und rieb seine Härte an ihrer Mitte. Als er kräftig an ihrer wundervollen Brust saugte, keuchte sie vor Wonne und warf ihm einen Blick zu, in dem ungezähmte Leidenschaft loderte. Er ließ ihre Hände los, schob sich an ihrem Körper herunter und leckte und küsste ihren Bauch, die Rundung ihrer Taille. Er rollte ihre Brustwarzen zwischen Finger und Daumen und drückte gerade so fest zu, um sie wieder genüsslich nach Luft schnappen zu hören. Er fuhr mit der Zunge erst um ihren Bauchnabel herum, um dann langsam und sinnlich hineinzugleiten. Jeder Stoß seiner Zunge ließ sie aufstöhnen und die Hüften aufbäumen. Noch einmal drückte er ihre Brustwarzen, während seine Zunge eintauchte und sie ihre Finger in sein Haar krallte. Der Schmerz, den er auf seiner Kopfhaut verspürte, war lustgetränkt. Als er sie ansah, um sich zu vergewissern, dass er keine Grenzen verletzte, schloss sie die Augen und warf keuchend den Kopf zurück.

Mit den Zähnen knöpfte er ihre Jeans auf. Ihr Körper wurde still und ihre Augen öffneten sich.

»Sag mir, wenn ich aufhören soll, Baby, und ich gehorche sofort.«

»Hör nicht auf«, sagte sie schnell.

Mist. Sie war so verdammt sexy. Er schob sich schnell auf sie, nahm ihr Gesicht in die Hände und küsste sie gierig.

Dann schob er ihre Jeans auf und zog sie vorsichtig aus. Sein Mund wurde trocken, als er sie nur mit einem schwarzen Spitzenhöschen bekleidet daliegen sah. Ihre Haut war gerötet, ihre Lippen glitzerten nach ihrem Kuss, und ihre Hände – diese zarten, weiblichen Hände – zerrten ihr Höschen herunter. Er half ihr, es abzustreifen, dann beugte er sich zwischen ihre Beine. Mit den Händen fuhr er über ihre Oberschenkel und strich mit den Daumen über ihre feuchten, dunklen Locken. Mit zarten Küssen verwöhnte er die Innenseite ihrer Schenkel und bemerkte, wie sie die Hände in die Sofakissen krallte, als sich ihre Hüften ihm entgegenwölbten. Gott, sie ahnte ja nicht, was ihr Begehren in ihm anrichtete.

Seine Daumen glitten zu den Falten zwischen ihren Beinen und ihrem Geschlecht und spreizten sie für ihn. Die zarte Haut glänzte und der Geruch ihrer Erregung war berauschend. Der erste Schlag seiner Zunge brachte ihre göttliche Süße zum Vorschein. Stöhnend öffnete sie die Schenkel noch weiter. Er liebkoste sie mit der Zunge, leckte und reizte sie und genoss ihre raschen Atemzüge und die hochgewölbten Hüften. Seine Zunge beschrieb sanfte Kreise um ihre geschwollenen Klit, und als er zwei Finger tief in ihre samtige Wärme schob, schwebte ein langes, kehliges Stöhnen von ihren Lippen. Er saugte an ihrer empfindlichsten Stelle, und seine Finger suchten unwillkürlich den Punkt, der sie auf den Gipfel der Leidenschaft treiben würde. Ihre Fersen drückten sich in die Sofakissen und sie spannte die Schenkel an. Er stieß sie mit den Ellbogen weiter auf, sodass Finger und Mund ihr Werk noch besser vollbringen konnten und er sie weiter und weiter necken konnte.

»Sam!«, rief sie, während ihr Körper zitterte und bebte.

Ihre Mitte pulsierte um seine Finger, während sie ihren Höhepunkt auskostete. Als die letzten Wogen verebbten, übernahm seine Zunge die Arbeit, die zuvor seine Finger gemacht hatten, fuhr über ihre Klit und jagte sie gleich zum nächsten Höhepunkt.

»Sam!«, rief sie wieder – und er liebte es verdammt noch mal, wenn sie seinen Namen so hemmungslos ausstieß, während sie an seinem Mund zerbarst, ihn mit ihrer Erregung überschwemmte und sich ihm ganz überließ.

Die Nachbeben ließen ihre Hüften zucken. Sam besänftigte ihre geschwollene Mitte mit seiner Zunge und küsste ihre empfindlichen Lippen, bevor er seine Finger wieder hineinschob, um ihr ein weiteres Feuerwerk zu bescheren. In dem Moment, in dem ihr Körper explodierte, senkte er seinen Mund wieder auf sie.

»Sam, Sam, Sam. Gott, Sam«, rief sie und packte seine Haare. Ihr Kopf schlug von einer Seite zur anderen, als sie den Höhepunkt erreichte. Er genoss das rhythmische Pulsieren, jeden sexy Laut, ihren süßen Geschmack, bis sie ermattet zurücksank und ihre Finger sich entspannten.

Er nahm sie in die Arme und küsste ihren Hals, ihre Brust, ihre Wange und schließlich ihren Mund. Sie erwiderte den Kuss mit der Energie einer satten Geliebten, müde und zärtlich.

»Ich möchte mich bei allen Frauen bedanken, an denen du vor mir geübt hast.«

Er lächelte, weil er verstand, dass sie es als Kompliment meinte, aber es schmerzte ihn trotzdem, denn er wusste, dass sie daran dachte, wie er mit anderen Frauen zusammen gewesen war. Aber eigentlich war es nur natürlich, dass sie daran dachte. War das nicht genau der Grund, warum sie die Dinge langsam angehen wollte?

Sie sah ihn voller Bedauern an. »Ich kann nicht glauben, dass ich das gesagt habe. Es tut mir leid. Ich hasse es, daran zu denken.« Ihre Lippen verzogen sich trotz der schmerzlichen Gedanken, die ihr durch den Kopf gehen mussten, zu einem verschlafenen Lächeln, und in diesem Moment wuchs sie ihm noch mehr ans Herz.

Er küsste sie sanft. »Ich weiß. Ich hasse es, mir dich mit

einem anderen Mann vorzustellen. Aber das ist jetzt vorbei. Ich gehöre dir und nur dir.«

Faith stieß einen erleichterten Seufzer aus. Sams geschlossene Augen machten sie jedoch nervös.

»Es tut mir leid, dass meine Vergangenheit dir Schmerzen bereitet.«

»Du hast mir doch gesagt, dass du dich nicht für deine Vergangenheit entschuldigst«, erinnerte sie ihn. Der Sinneswandel verwirrte sie.

»Nein. Ich sagte, ich schäme mich nicht für meine Vergangenheit, und das tue ich tatsächlich nicht. Schönheit in Unvollkommenheit und in der Entwicklung, weißt du noch? Ich entwickle mich weiter. Wir entwickeln uns weiter. Aber es tut mir leid, wenn dich das traurig oder wütend macht.« Er küsste sie sanft.

Sie sollte ihn in Zukunft Sam, den Ehrlichen, nennen, weil er unverblümt zugab, dass er wegen seiner Vergangenheit keine Scham empfand. Nicht, dass sie dachte, er müsse sich schämen. Auch wenn sie es ihm anfangs nicht geglaubt hatte: Er hatte noch nie eine Frau betrogen, weil er sich nie auf eine Beziehung eingelassen hatte. Und es konnte wohl keine Schande sein, seine Freiheit auszuleben.

»Ich bin nicht traurig oder wütend«, versicherte sie ihm. »Nur ein bisschen eifersüchtig und vielleicht eingeschüchtert.«

»Wenn es dich beruhigt, kann ich dir versichern, dass ich auf jeden Mann eifersüchtig bin, der dich vor mir berührt hat. Und dem Kerl, der dich verletzt hat, würde ich am liebsten an die Gurgel gehen. Aber eingeschüchtert solltest du dich auf keinen Fall fühlen. Dir kann niemand das Wasser reichen.«

Sie zog die Linie seines Kiefers mit dem Finger nach und fühlte sich in seinen Armen geborgen genug, um genauso ehrlich zu sein wie er.

»Ich bin nicht so erfahren, wie sie es sind. Ich möchte dich nicht enttäuschen.« Sie schnappte nach Luft. »Und, du lieber Gott, Sam. Du hast gerade all diese unglaublichen Dinge mit mir gemacht, und hier liege ich, nackt und glücklich nach meinem Orgasmus, und habe mich gar nicht revanchiert. Verstehst du? Ich bin nicht sehr gut darin.«

Sie verschränkte die Arme vor der Brust. Plötzlich machte ihre Nacktheit sie verlegen. Er schob ihre Arme beiseite und fuhr mit der Hand von der Mitte ihrer Brüste bis zu ihrem Bauchnabel.

»Du bist wunderschön.« Er küsste sie. »Und erfahren genug. Tu einfach das, was sich richtig anfühlt, und wenn einer von uns etwas mehr oder etwas anderes will, dann kriegen wir das auch hin.« Er küsste sie und sah sie mit einem zärtlichen Lächeln auf den Lippen an. »Außerdem benehmen wir uns heute Abend ein bisschen.«

Er griff über sie hinweg, nahm sein Hemd und half ihr, es anzuziehen. »Da. Fühlst du dich jetzt wohler?«

Sie tastete nach ihrer Unterhose und zog sie an. »Jetzt schon.«

Er grinste. »Es ist wunderbar, dich in meinem Hemd zu sehen, aber dich nackt unter mir zu sehen, war noch wunderbarer.«

Als sich ihre Lippen berührten, fühlte sie sich leichter und ruhiger. Alles, was er sagte, kam direkt von seinem Herzen. Sie war es nicht gewohnt, dass ein Mann ihr sagte, er wolle ihre sexy

Laute hören oder sie nackt unter sich liegen sehen, aber sie liebte es, diese Dinge von Sam zu hören.

Lange lagen sie da, machten Pläne für den morgigen Abend und zögerten das Ende ihres Dates hinaus. Als sie widerstrebend von der Couch zur Tür gingen, streckte Faith die Hand nach ihrem Top aus, doch Sam packte ihr Handgelenk.

»Am liebsten würde ich mir vorstellen, dass du heute Nacht in meinem Hemd schläfst.« Er nahm sie in die Arme. »Außerdem brauche ich die kalte Luft, um mich auf dem Heimweg abzukühlen.« Er presste seine Hüften an ihre, seine Erregung war noch immer hart. »Ich finde es schrecklich, dich zu verlassen.«

»Ich auch. Ich habe das Gefühl, als wären wir seit Monaten zusammen. Wie kann so viel in so kurzer Zeit passieren?«

»Meine Mutter sagte einmal, dass sich Seelenverwandte schon beim ersten Kuss so fühlen, als seien sie seit Ewigkeiten zusammen.«

Bei dem Wort *Seelenverwandte* schlug ihr Herz höher. Glaubte er das wirklich oder gab er nur die Weisheit seiner Mutter zum Besten? Bei der Art, wie er sie ansah, hatte sie das Gefühl, als würde er sich dieselbe Frage stellen.

»Bis morgen, Süße.« Sie küssten sich erneut, und Sam hielt ihre Hand, bis er aus der Tür war und ihre Fingerspitzen sich nicht mehr berührten.

Faith schaute ihm nach, als er die Treppe hinunterging, bevor sie in ihre Wohnung zurückkehrte. Sie stand am Fenster und sah zu, wie er mit nacktem Oberkörper auf sein Motorrad stieg und davonfuhr. Sie war viel zu aufgekratzt, um schlafen zu gehen, daher wusch sie sich, schnappte sich ihren Laptop und setzte sich auf die Couch, um bei den Mädels vom WAC vorbeizuschauen. Sie hatte ein schlechtes Gewissen, weil sie mit einem Mann zusammen war, dem sein zweifelhafter Ruf vorauseilte. Vor solchen Männern warnte sie ihre Mitglieder normalerweise.

Sie gab ihr Passwort ein und dachte an Sam. Er hatte keine Zeit darauf verschwendet, seinen Ruf zu leugnen. Stattdessen schien er all seine Energie darauf zu verwenden, ihr zu zeigen, wer er wirklich war. Oder zumindest, wer er *jetzt* war.

Einige der Threads enthielten Kommentare zu Sam. Er sei so heiß und so nett, hieß es da. Ein Mitglied sagte, sie würde sich gerne eine Nacht um die Ohren schlagen, wenn sie seine Gespielin sein könnte. Faith schluckte die Eifersucht und das Unbehagen herunter, die dieser Kommentar in ihr auslösten. Zumindest waren ihre Schuldgefühle nun nicht mehr so schlimm.

Sie suchte nach Liras Posts und fand einen vom Vormittag. Erst schrieb sie, wie sehr sie sich von ihrer Schwester betrogen fühlte und wie traurig sie sei, dass Emmie nicht nur ihren Vater, sondern auch ihre Tante verloren habe. Faith tat es in der Seele leid. Offenbar hatte Lira Mühe, einen Mittelweg zu finden: Einerseits wollte sie einen Schlussstrich ziehen, andererseits wollte sie das Richtige für ihre Tochter tun.

Sie las weiter und war überrascht, dass Lira bereits für Sam arbeitete.

Er ist ein unglaublicher Chef, ganz professionell, aber auch freundlich. Nachdem er mir mein Aufgabengebiet erklärt hat, auf das ich mich riesig freue, fragte er, wie Emmie die Trennung verkraftet. Faith, wenn du das liest: Wenn alles gut geht, bin ich beim Barbecue der Rough Riders dabei, um zu helfen! Ich hoffe, es klappt alles so, wie wir uns das vorstellen, und ich hoffe, dass wir uns dann sehen können.

Faith lehnte sich geschockt zurück. Sam hatte ihr nicht nur

beim WAC geholfen, er hatte auch sein Versprechen wahr gemacht, Lira zu unterstützen. Das zählte für Faith noch mehr als seine Hilfe, die er ihr mit dem WAC angeboten hatte. *Sam Braden, du bist doch immer für eine Überraschung gut.*

Am Donnerstagabend hatten sie einen Termin bei Brent. Sobald sie die rechtlichen Details geklärt hatte, würde sie Kontakt mit den Frauengruppen und Hilfsorganisationen aufnehmen, die sie herausgesucht hatte, und anfangen, ein Netzwerk für die Gruppe aufzubauen. Sie wollte gerade eine private Nachricht an Lira tippen, um sie wissen zu lassen, dass sie auf der Suche nach einem Therapeuten oder jemanden war, mit dem sie ihre Probleme besprechen konnte, als sie eine Nachricht von ihr bekam. Anscheinend hatte Sam ihr per E-Mail einen Namen und eine Telefonnummer geschickt, die er von seiner Schwester Tempest erhalten hatte, und sie hatte bereits einen Termin für eine kostenlose Beratung vereinbart.

Faith lehnte sich mit offenem Mund zurück. Noch vor einer Woche hätte sie sich nicht träumen lassen, dass Sam sich für eine Frau, die er nicht in sein Bett locken wollte, solche Mühe geben würde. Inzwischen kannte sie Sam besser, als sie es in so kurzer Zeit für möglich gehalten hätte, und war zwar erstaunt, fand es aber durchaus überzeugend.

Kurze Zeit später vibrierte ihr Handy. Sie holte es aus ihrer Handtasche und lächelte, als sie Sams Namen sah. Bei der Nachricht musste sie noch mehr lächeln. *Mit dir hätte meine kalte Dusche mehr Spaß gemacht.*

Sie schlang die Arme um den Oberkörper und spürte sein weiches Hemd auf ihrer Haut. Die Erinnerung an das, was sie getan hatten, kehrte zurück, und sofort wurde ihr ganz heiß. Der arme Kerl. Sie hatte ihn wirklich auf dem Trockenen sitzen lassen. Aber er hatte sie nicht gedrängt oder ihr ein schlechtes

Gewissen gemacht. Sie fragte sich, wie viele Männer so gut damit umgegangen wären, und dann kam ihr ein ganz anderer Gedanke: Sam war es gewohnt, mit Frauen bei ihrer ersten Begegnung zu schlafen, und für viele von ihnen blieb es bei dieser einen Begegnung.

Dadurch fühlte sie sich noch geborgener und noch mehr wertgeschätzt. Trotzdem konnte sie es sich nicht verkneifen, ihn zu ärgern. Sie schrieb ihm eine Nachricht: *Wenn ich gewusst hätte, dass Duschen auf dem Programm steht, hätte ich mir vielleicht überlegt, ob ich mit dir nach Hause fahre.*

Seine Antwort kam prompt. *Ich kann noch mal duschen. Komm vorbei.*

Sie lachte, als sie ihm zurückschrieb. *Geht nicht. Mein Freund hat mich total geschlaucht.*

Sie legte das Handy gar nicht erst aus der Hand, weil sie wusste, dass gleich die nächste Nachricht kommen würde. *Dann sieh zu, dass du ein bisschen fitter wirst, als Vorbereitung fürs nächste Mal. Dein Freund hat schließlich einen Ruf zu wahren.*

Sie dachte über diesen Ruf nach und fragte sich, ob die Leute – die Frauen – in der Stadt auf die Barrikaden gehen würden, wenn sie erfuhren, dass Sam nicht mehr auf dem Markt war. Sie antwortete: *Ich werde deinen Ruf nicht ruinieren und herumerzählen, dass du dich wie ein wahrer Gentleman benommen hast – vorausgesetzt, du ruinierst meinen Ruf nicht und behauptest, ich sei keine Dame.* Vor dem Absenden fügte sie hinzu: *Das ist deine Schuld. Dieser Monster-Vibrator, den du Motorrad nennst, ist das perfekte Vorspiel!*

Ihr Telefon klingelte und Sams Name blitzte auf dem Display auf. Ihr stockte der Atem.

»Hey«, sagte sie nervös.

»Wie geht es meinem Mädchen?« Seine Stimme war leise

und heiser und ihr lief das Wasser im Mund zusammen wie einem von Pawlows Hunden.

Ich wünschte, du wärst hier. Sie schluckte die Worte herunter, weil sie wusste, dass er auf der Stelle zu ihr kommen würde. Und dann wäre sie morgen bei der Arbeit zu nichts zu gebrauchen. Außerdem sollte sie wirklich abwarten, bevor sie mit ihm schlief, oder?

»Ich vermisse dich«, sagte sie stattdessen.

»Ich dich auch. Also gefällt dir mein Motorrad?«

Sie hörte das sexy Necken in seiner Stimme. »Darauf zu fahren ist herrlich. Aber der, an dem ich mich festgehalten habe, hat mir noch besser gefallen.«

»Ich mag deine Antworten. Der Abend heute war sehr schön. Ich war mir nicht sicher, ob du dich im Whiskey Bro's wohlfühlen würdest, aber ich wollte etwas Besonderes mit dir teilen und bin froh, dass du dich darauf eingelassen hast.«

Sie lehnte sich zurück, spielte mit dem Saum seines Hemdes und lächelte. Seine Aufmerksamkeit gefiel ihr. »Ich fand es wunderbar, mit dir dort zu sein.«

Er schwieg einen Augenblick, dann sagte er: »Faith, das ist nicht der einzige Grund, warum ich anrufe. Ich habe nachgedacht, seit ich bei dir war, und nach deiner Nachricht wollte ich mit dir über meinen Ruf sprechen. Ich wünschte, dieser verdammte Ruf würde einfach verschwinden. Ich hasse den Gedanken, dass meine Vergangenheit einen so großen Einfluss auf dich hat. Ich weiß es wirklich sehr zu schätzen, dass du mir eine Chance gibst.«

»Sam«, sagte sie zerknirscht. Sie wusste nicht, wie sie reagieren sollte. Er war der gefragteste Mann in der Stadt, und er war überhaupt nicht der, für den die anderen Frauen ihn hielten. Sie hatten vielleicht großartigen Sex – sie schluckte die

Galle herunter, die ihr in die Kehle stieg –, aber sie hatte das, was an ihm am besten war: seine Ehrlichkeit und seine Gefühle.

»Du brauchst nichts zu sagen«, versicherte er ihr. »Ich wollte nur, dass du es weißt. Eigentlich habe ich nie über das nachgedacht, was ich getan habe, und hätte mir nie vorstellen können, dass es mir wichtig ist, was jemand über meine Vergangenheit denkt. Aber es ist mir wichtig. Es ist mir wichtig, was es mit dir macht. Du bist mir wichtig, Faith.«

Ach du lieber Gott. Da war sie wieder, seine unverblümte Ehrlichkeit.

»Zieh dich nicht von mir zurück. Lass dich nicht abschrecken. Ich weiß, ich kann ziemlich direkt und fordernd sein …«

»Ich lasse mich nicht verschrecken. Es ist nur …«, sie kniff die Augen zusammen. »Ich hätte nie gedacht, dass ich dich so sehr und so schnell mögen würde.« *Ogottogott. Ehrlichkeit kann ganz schön beängstigend sein.* Wie zum Teufel schaffte er das?

»Faith?«

Selbst aus diesem einzigen Wort war seine Erleichterung herauszuhören. »Ja?«

»Ich wünschte, ich könnte jetzt sehen, wie du rot wirst. Schlaf gut, Süße.«

In dieser Nacht lag Faith lange wach und dachte über Sams Ruf nach. Wie würde sie sich fühlen, wenn sie eines Tages tatsächlich in ein Restaurant oder eine Bar in der Stadt gingen? Wie sich *Sam* wohl dabei fühlen würde? Er hatte gesagt, dass er sich nicht mit ihr zusammen in der Stadt zeigen wollte, bis er sicher war, dass ihr Bild von ihm nicht durch die Handlungen anderer beeinflusst wurde. Also rechnete er vermutlich damit, dass es ziemlich unangenehm werden würde. Sie schloss die Augen und versuchte sich vorzustellen, wie sie Hand in Hand mit Sam ins Whispers ging. Sofort begann ihr Herz, panisch zu pochen, und sie riss unwillkürlich die Augen auf. Allein der Gedanken daran war beängstigend. Würde sie jemals dafür bereit sein?

Sie rollte sich auf die Seite, griff nach ihrem Handy und überlegte, ob sie Vivian schreiben sollte. Sie hatte versprochen, sie anzurufen, und außerdem wollte sie ihr sagen, dass sie mit Sam zusammen war. Aber Vivian würde ihr sicher eine Standpauke halten oder sie an all die Dinge erinnern, die sie an ihrem gemeinsamen Abend im Whispers gesagt hatte.

Sie legte das Telefon auf den Nachttisch zurück und beschloss, den Anruf zu verschieben, bis sie sich ganz darauf konzentrieren konnte. Als sie die Augen zumachte, sah sie wieder die Bilder jenes Abends vor sich. Sie dachte an ihren Spaziergang am Strand und an den sehnsüchtigen Blick in Sams Augen, als ihre Freundinnen sie weggezerrt hatten. Sie dachte an ihn, als er sich mit nacktem Oberkörper über sie beugte und sie ansah, als sei sie einfach perfekt. Er gab ihr das Gefühl der Wertschätzung und Geborgenheit, trotz seines Rufs. Er gab ihr das Gefühl, wichtig zu sein.

Sie klammerte sich an diese Gefühle und zählte die Stunden, bis sie ihn wiedersah.

Fünfzehn

Am Donnerstagmorgen trat Sam auf die Veranda seines Hauses am Wasser und winkte Nate zu, der gerade aus seinem Truck stieg.

»Sieh mal, wer heute früh um zwei bei uns aufgetaucht ist.« Nate wies mit dem Daumen auf Ty, der im Schneckentempo vom Beifahrersitz kletterte.

»Jewel war bestimmt begeistert.« Sam schüttelte den Kopf. »Warum bist du nicht hierhergekommen?«

Ty reckte sich gähnend. »Ich dachte, du könntest vielleicht Besuch haben. Ich wohne bei Shannon, solange sie in Colorado ist, aber zu Nate war es näher.«

Wie gerne hätte Sam gestern Abend Besuch gehabt. Er und Faith hatten sich gegen neun Uhr treffen wollen, aber sie musste ins Krankenhaus, um bei einer Notoperation zu assistieren. Den Mittwoch nur mit Telefonaten und Handynachrichten zu überstehen und Faith nicht zu sehen, erwies sich als viel schwerer, als er sich vorgestellt hatte. Schon beim Aufwachen hatte er ernsthafte Entzugserscheinungen gehabt und konnte es kaum erwarten, sie heute Abend zu sehen.

»Wo warst du? In den Bergen?«, fragte Sam. Er und Nate wohnten am Fluss. Jeder von beiden besaß ein paar Hektar bewaldeten Grund und Boden, was ihnen nur recht war, weil sie auf diese Weise ihre Privatsphäre wahren konnten. Shannon dagegen lebte in der Stadt, und Sam konnte sich nicht vorstellen, wo Ty den Abend verbracht haben mochte, wenn Nates Haus näher gelegen war.

»Lagerfeuer auf dem Grat.« Ty zog sich die Kapuze seines Sweatshirts über den Kopf und ließ sich auf die Verandatreppe sinken. Der »Grat«, ein Felsenplateau mit Blick auf den Fluss, lag tatsächlich näher an Nates Haus als an Shannons.

Nate und Sam tauschten einen vielsagenden Blick. Für Sam und Ty war es nichts Ungewöhnliches, die ganze Nacht durch die Stadt zu ziehen, ein paar Stunden zu schlafen und dann den ganzen Tag bei Rough Riders zu arbeiten.«

»Ich hatte dir eine Nachricht geschickt.« Ty schaute ihn an.

»Ja, hab ich gesehen. Du hast gefragt, ob ich abends weggehen wollte.« Sam hatte ihm ein knappes *Nein danke* geantwortet. »Gehst du mit uns laufen?«

»Ja, er geht mit uns laufen.« Nates militärische Seite zeigte sich nicht nur in seinem kurz geschorenen blonden Haar. »Komm schon, beweg deinen Hintern. Du kannst meine Verlobte nicht um zwei Uhr morgens wecken und dann erwarten, dass ich dich Faulpelz so einfach davonkommen lasse.«

Ty schüttelte die Kapuze ab und fuhr sich mit einer Hand durch sein langes dunkles Haar. Er streckte eine Hand aus, damit Nate ihm beim Aufstehen half. Nate schüttelte den Kopf.

Sam ergriff seine Hand und zerrte ihn auf die Füße. »Von mir aus könntest du hier hocken bleiben, während wir laufen, aber wenn mein kleiner Bruder den Feldwebel herauskehrt, wird's ungemütlich. Ich müsste ihn schon umbringen, und dann käme keiner von uns zum Laufen.«

Seit Jahren drehten sie morgens ihre Runde durch die Berge, zumindest, wenn sie alle zu Hause waren. Nate war mehrere Jahre bei der Armee gewesen und Tys Termine waren kaum planbar. Daher war Sam froh über jede Gelegenheit, mit seinen Brüdern zusammen zu sein.

Nachdem Ty sein Sweatshirt ausgezogen hatte, liefen sie in gemäßigtem Tempo die Straße entlang, damit Ty Zeit hatte, aufzuwachen. Ein paar Minuten später hatten sie ihren Rhythmus gefunden und liefen auf einem der vier Meilen langen Wege nebeneinander her.

»Wann rückst du endlich damit heraus, was zwischen dir und Faith ist?«, fragte Nate. »Oder sollen wir so tun, als sei nichts passiert?«

Er musste nur ihren Namen hören und schon breitete sich ein seliges Grinsen auf seinem Gesicht ab. »Oh doch, da ist was passiert, keine Frage.«

»Meinst du das ernst?« Die Überraschung in Nates Stimme war nicht zu überhören. »Cole schärft dir ein, dass du die Finger von ihr lassen sollst, und kaum hat er der Stadt den Rücken gekehrt, machst du dich an sie heran? Warum musst du dich denn so auf sie versteifen?«

»Ich denke, wir wissen, was *das* bei ihm bedeutet«, scherzte Ty.

»Nein, so ist es nicht.« Sam duckte sich unter einem Ast. »Ich date sie nicht, weil Cole mir gesagt hat, dass ich sie in Ruhe lassen soll.«

Nate schnaubte. »Ach nein? Erzähl uns doch nichts. Du hast doch schon lange ein Auge auf sie geworfen. Verdammt, ich weiß noch, wie du vor ein paar Monaten im Tap It warst und sie mit einem Typen hereinkam. Ich dachte, du hättest den Kerl erwürgt, wenn er ihr zu nahegekommen wäre.«

Sam spannte den Kiefer an. An diesen Abend erinnerte er sich nur zu gut. In ihrem knappen schwarzen Kleid hatte Faith so heiß ausgesehen. Das Haar hatte sie im Nacken zusammengebunden wie eine sexy Lehrerin. Der Typ, mit dem sie im Tap It aufgetaucht war, war ein bebrillter Langweiler. *Das genaue Gegenteil von mir.* Er beschleunigte sein Tempo, um den Abend aus dem Kopf zu bekommen.

»Und Cole hat ihn schon genauso lange davor gewarnt, mit ihr anzubandeln«, fügte Ty hinzu.

Sie liefen ein paar Minuten schweigend hügelan, vorbei an Bäumen und Büschen, bis zu einer Lichtung, von der aus man den Fluss überblicken konnte. Dies war einer von Sams Lieblingsplätzen. Irgendwann wollte er ihn Faith zeigen, vielleicht um einen Sonnenaufgang oder Sonnenuntergang zu sehen.

»He, pass auf!« Ty packte Sam am Hemd und zerrte ihn zur Seite. Eine Schlange glitt unmittelbar vor ihnen über den Weg.

»Danke.« Sam schüttelte den Kopf, um aus seiner Verträumtheit aufzuwachen, aber seine Gedanken waren durchdrungen von Faith. Offenbar hatte sie sich in seinen Gehirnwindungen häuslich niedergelassen.

Nate schloss zu Sam auf und lief neben ihm, während sie von der Lichtung aus einen weiteren Pfad ansteuerten. »Du machst das wirklich, nicht wahr?«

»Jep.«

»Wie lange?« Nates Ton war nicht vorwurfsvoll, sondern besorgt.

Sam spannte den Kiefer an und fragte sich, ob sich sein Bruder um ihn oder um Faith sorgte. »Solange sie mich haben will. Oder so lange, wie es dauert, sie davon zu überzeugen, dass wir gut zusammenpassen.«

»Du Mistkerl.« Nate lachte. »Dass ich das noch erleben darf, dass es Sam Braden erwischt. Es geht schneller, als man denkt, nicht wahr?«

»Ich ermahne mich immer wieder, dass ich einen klaren Kopf behalten muss. Reiner Selbsterhaltungstrieb, schätze ich. Aber immer, wenn ich an sie denke – also praktisch ständig …« Er hielt inne und versuchte, seine Gedanken zu sammeln. »Wie war es bei dir und Jewel? Ich weiß, dass du sie schon ewig liebst, aber irgendwann verschwendest du keinen Gedanken mehr an andere Frauen. Kam das über Nacht? Wenn ich mir die letzten ein, zwei Jahre ansehe, habe ich das Gefühl, als sei Faith die ganze Zeit da gewesen. Irgendwie hatte ich sie wie eine Sehnsucht im Hintergrund, die ich nicht stillen konnte. Ich habe nach ihr gesucht, ohne es zu wissen. Wenn wir unterwegs waren, am Wochenende bei Rough Riders – ich habe immer gehofft, sie zu sehen.«

»Ja, so passiert es«, antwortete Nate. »Du lebst dein Leben und im nächsten Moment kannst du nicht mehr ohne sie sein.«

Ty überholte sie und drehte sich um. Rückwärts laufend sagte er: »Hoffentlich ist das nicht ansteckend. Ich freue mich für euch zwei, aber was auch immer es auch sein mag, ich will es nicht.« Lachend lief er neben ihnen her.

»Vor zwei Wochen hätte ich noch genauso geredet«, sagte Sam zu ihm. »Aber so ist es viel besser. Du hast ja keine Ahnung, was du verpasst.«

Ty schnaubte und wechselte das Thema. Er erzählte von seiner nächsten Bergtour, und Sam war eigentlich ganz froh, an etwas anderes zu denken. Er vermisste Faith so sehr, dass er am liebsten sofort zu ihrer Wohnung gerannt wäre, nur um sie lächeln zu sehen.

Das Gespräch wandte sich der Arbeit zu und Nate

berichtete von den Irrungen und Wirrungen im Leben eines Restaurantbesitzers. »Könnt ihr euch vorstellen, dass ich zwei meiner Aushilfskräfte dabei erwischt habe, wie sie im Vorratsraum rumgemacht haben?«

»Mich wundert nur, dass es erst jetzt passiert ist.« Sam lachte. »Komm schon, Nate. Du weißt doch selbst, wie du mit zwanzig warst.«

»Aber mal ehrlich«, sagte Nate. »Ich sollte wirklich nur Mädels oder nur Jungs einstellen. Wenn Jungs und Mädels zusammenarbeiten, kann man die Hormone mit Händen greifen.«

»Hast du vielleicht eine Bürokraft übrig?«, fragte Ty. »Sam braucht jemanden, der seinen Schreibtisch rettet, bevor der unter der Papierflut verschwindet.«

Sam erklärte ihnen, dass er es mit Lira versuchen wollte. »Bisher macht sie ihre Sache sehr gut. Sie hat an einem Tag mehr geschafft als ich an drei. Außerdem hat sie schon einen Online-Kalender eingerichtet, in dem alle unsere Touren bis zum nächsten Winter vermerkt sind. Ich hatte das alles in Tabellen eingetragen, aber so ist es viel einfacher.

Bei Gruppen von zehn oder mehr Leuten pro Tour brauche ich jemanden, der im Hintergrund alles organisiert, die Versicherungsdokumente sortiert und den Überblick über die Zahlungen behält. Und ich brauche jemanden, der sich traut, den Faulpelzen die Stirn zu bieten, die ihr Geld zurückwollen, weil sie freitags um sieben beschließen, dass der Wochenendausflug für zwölf Personen, den sie vor zwei Monaten gebucht haben, nicht so lustig klingt wie die Aussicht, im heimischen Wohnzimmer auf dem Sofa zu hocken und Bier zu trinken.«

»Sie braucht auf jeden Fall Nerven wie Drahtseile. Das kann

ich bestätigen«, sagte Ty. »Vor allem Betriebsausflüge können ein Albtraum sein.«

»Da hast du leider recht. Wie auch immer, ich werde euch berichten, wie es mit Lira läuft. Für den Fall, dass sie sich gegen uns entscheidet oder dass es aus irgendeinem anderen Grund nicht klappt, könnt ihr ja Augen und Ohren offen halten.«

»Ich kann dir da nicht helfen«, sagte Nate. »Ich habe nur hormongeschüttelte Gören, die außer Sex nichts in der Birne haben. Aber ich höre mich um.«

Nach ihrem Lauf warfen sie ihre Hemden auf die Veranda und gingen im Garten auf und ab, um sich abzukühlen.

»Wie wär's mit einem Bad?«, fragte Ty.

Nate warf Sam einen Blick zu. Seine Augen glitzerten gefährlich.

»Oh Mist. Ehrlich?« Tys Blick ging zwischen seinen Brüdern hin und her. Dann rannte er los in Richtung Wasser, Nate und Sam dicht auf den Fersen.

Ihr Gelächter erfüllte die Luft. Sam überholte die anderen beiden, doch Nates kräftige Hand hielt ihn zurück und riss ihn zu Boden. Ty raste an ihnen vorbei und sein triumphierendes Lachen brachte Sam und Nate auf die Beine. Wie oft waren sie zu Hause bei ihren Eltern zum Wasser gerannt? Manche Dinge änderten sich nie, und als Sam Ty von hinten auf den Rücken sprang und ihn umwarf und Nate sich auf sie stürzte, war er froh darüber. Darum ging es im Leben wirklich: um diese Balgereien, in denen sich bedingungslose Loyalität und ein brüderlicher Sinn für Unfug mischten. Sie wälzten sich auf dem Boden, kämpften und forderten sich gegenseitig heraus und ließen sich schließlich keuchend vor Lachen auf den Rücken fallen.

Ty stemmte sich hoch, fuhr sich mit einer Hand durchs

Haar und streckte Sam die andere Hand entgegen. »Komm schon, du Idiot. Lass uns schwimmen gehen.«

Sam wollte gerade nach seiner Hand greifen, als Ty wild lachend davonrannte.

Sam und Nate sahen sich an und verdrehten die Augen. Sekunden später waren sie aufgesprungen, zum Steg gelaufen und stießen sich gegenseitig ins Wasser. Einer nach dem anderen tauchten sie wieder auf. Sams Gedanken wandten sich in eine neue und überraschende Richtung. Er war jetzt fast einunddreißig Jahre alt, und zum ersten Mal dachte er nicht nur ans Hier und Jetzt, sondern darüber hinaus. Das war es, was er eines Tages wollte. Eine eigene Familie und Kinder, die füreinander durch dick und dünn gingen.

Nate und Ty verschwanden unter der Wasseroberfläche und Sam dachte wieder an Faith. Als seine Brüder ihn in die Tiefe zerrten, ergab er sich kampflos, so sehr war er mit seinen Gedanken bei ihr.

Faith war den ganzen Tag mit Nachuntersuchungen und den üblichen Erledigungen beschäftigt, die der Praxisalltag mit sich brachte. Es war hektisch, doch das konnte ihre Stimmung nicht beeinträchtigen. Als sie letzte Nacht nach einer langen Not-OP mit Jon endlich eingeschlafen war, hatte sie von Sam geträumt. Ein erotischer Traum nach dem anderen, in denen er sie erst wie gebannt ansah, um sie schließlich mit Händen und Mund von Kopf bis Fuß zu verwöhnen. Als sie schweißgebadet aus dem Schlaf hochfuhr, war sie kurz vor einem Orgasmus. Sie hatte keine Wahl, als die Augen zu schließen, sich Sam vorzustellen und selbst Hand anzulegen – und so zu tun, als sei es Sam.

Um Viertel vor sechs wartete Faith in ihrer Wohnung auf Sam, der sie zu ihrem Termin mit Brent abholen wollte. Sie hatte geduscht und sich umgezogen und saß auf dem Bett, das Handy schweigend ans Ohr gepresst. Am anderen Ende hörte sie Vivian atmen. Sie war verstummt, nachdem Faith ihr erzählt hatte, dass sie mit Sam zusammen war.

»Bist du noch da?«

»Ja«, sagte Vivian ernst. »Ich versuche gerade, das zu verarbeiten, was du gesagt hast.«

»Viv, ich weiß, was du sagen wirst. Er ist gefährlich für mich. Er verkörpert alles, wovon ich mich fernhalten sollte. Ich weiß, wie wir über ihn geredet haben, aber er ist überhaupt nicht so, wenn wir zusammen sind.«

»Natürlich nicht. Was soll er auch machen? Frauen aufreißen, während er mit dir zusammen ist? Faith«, sagte sie mit einem sanfteren Ton, »ich will nur nicht, dass er dir wehtut. Versprich mir, dass du nicht in die Falle tappst, in die wir immer wieder tappen, und sein schlechtes Verhalten wegdiskutierst, weil du dir *wünschst*, dass er anders sein möge, als er tatsächlich ist.«

Faith seufzte erleichtert. Sie hatte erwartet, dass Vivian ihr ordentlich den Kopf waschen würde, und war froh, dass ihre Reaktion nicht so heftig ausfiel, wie sie befürchtet hatte. »Versprochen. Nicht einmal *Sam* versucht, seinen Ruf schönzureden. Und er denkt in erster Linie an mich, Viv. Ich weiß, angesichts seiner Vergangenheit ist das schwer zu glauben, aber so ist es. Er meint sogar, wir sollten uns erst zusammen in der Stadt zeigen, wenn er sich sicher sein kann, dass ich ihn nicht wieder als *den* Typen betrachte, wenn sich ihm reihenweise Frauen an den Hals werfen.«

»Im Ernst? Vielleicht bin ich einfach nur zynisch, aber für mich hört es sich an, als würde er an sich denken, nicht an dich. Er möchte nicht in die Situation geraten, sie abweisen zu müssen, also tut er so, als ginge es um dich.«

Dieser Gedanke war Faith auch schon durch den Kopf gegangen, aber sie hatte ihn beiseitegeschoben. War sie gerade dabei, sich Sam schönzudenken?

»Hallo? Bist du noch da?«, fragte Vivian gereizt.

»Ähm. Ich denke nur nach.«

»Mir geht es nicht darum, Sand ins Getriebe zu bringen, aber vielleicht solltet ihr es mal ausprobieren und sehen, wie er sich verhält, wenn ihr in seinem angestammten Revier seid. Und dann schau dir genau an, was *du* in dieser Situation über *ihn* denkst. Das Letzte, was du brauchst, ist, dir etwas vorzumachen und dir einzureden, dass er immer so ist, wie du ihn erlebst, wenn er nicht herausgefordert wird.«

»Das ist ja das, was ihm Sorgen bereitet. Was *ich* von *ihm* halte.« In ihrem Magen breitete sich ein ungutes Gefühl aus. Hatte er sie womöglich mit seinem guten Aussehen und seinen süßen Worten um den Finger gewickelt? Mit seiner scheinbar unerschöpflichen Aufmerksamkeit und Rücksichtnahme? Mit seiner Ehrlichkeit? Auf keinen Fall. Das konnte sie nicht glauben.

Andererseits hatte Vivian vielleicht recht.

»In schwierigen Situationen zeigt sich, aus welchem Holz wir geschnitzt sind.« Faith kamen plötzlich die Worte ihrer Mutter in den Sinn. Sie war sich nicht einmal sicher, ob sie sie auf sich oder auf Vivian bezog.

»Stimmt. Danke, Mama Hayes.«

Sie unterhielten sich noch ein paar Minuten über Sam,

dann über den WAC, über die Hilfsangebote, die Faith zusammengestellt hatte, und schließlich über das bevorstehende Treffen mit dem Anwalt. Als Sam vor ihrer Tür stand, gingen Faiths Gedanken wild durcheinander. Sie vertraute ihm. Sie vertraute ihm *wirklich*. Aber sie war schon einmal verletzt worden und hatte Signale übersehen, die sie wahrscheinlich hätte erkennen müssen.

»Hey.« Seine Mundwinkel verzogen sich zu einem Lächeln, als sich sein Arm um ihre Taille legte, und sein Blick schien zu sagen: *Endlich halte ich dich wieder in meinen Armen. Ich habe dich vermisst.* Und: *Küss mich*, bevor ihre Münder einander fanden.

Für den Bruchteil einer Sekunde erstarrte sie und dachte an das, was Vivian gesagt hatte, aber gegen seine süßen Küsse und sein Herz, das ruhig und kräftig an ihrem pochte, kam sie nicht an. Bis auf einen winzigen Rest verschwanden alle Zweifel, die Vivian in ihr geweckt hatte. Dieser Rest ließ sie jedoch den ganzen Weg zu Brents Kanzlei nicht los.

Sam öffnete die Tür seines Trucks, und als sie aussteigen wollte, stand er da und verstellte ihr den Weg. Ein unüberwindliches Hindernis, das sie fragend ansah und ihre Sorgen aufspürte, als stünden sie ihr auf die Stirn geschrieben.

»Was ist?«

»Was meinst du?« Ihre Stimme klang dünn und zaghaft.

Er trat näher an sie heran und eine Hitzewalze rollte auf sie zu und verzehrte sie. Angesichts der Besorgnis in seinen Augen kehrte das Gefühl zurück, geborgen und wichtig zu sein. Und dieses Gefühl der Geborgenheit kämpfte mit dem Teufel, der ihr unablässig ins Ohr flüsterte.

»Du bist in Gedanken ganz woanders. Ist es der Termin mit Brent? Bist du nervös?«

Ja, wollte sie sagen. Die kleine Lüge wäre so einfach, sie musste sie nur von der Zungenspitze schnippen. Aber Sam anlügen, wenn er ihr gegenüber so brutal ehrlich war? Auf keinen Fall. Sie kniff die Lippen zusammen und schüttelte den Kopf.

»Faith, was ist es? Ist in der Praxis etwas passiert?«

Wieder schüttelte sie den Kopf. Sie war ein wenig benommen und hatte ein schlechtes Gewissen, weil sie an ihm gezweifelt hatte. Aber Vivians Einwände waren auch nicht ganz von der Hand zu weisen und sie musste vorsichtig sein. Vielleicht hatte sie sich alles eingeredet und sah nur das, was sie sehen wollte.

»Nur ein bisschen überwältigt.« Wenigstens das war keine Lüge.

Er schlang die Arme um sie und hielt sie fest. »Wir können ein andermal hingehen, Brent hat bestimmt nichts dagegen. War viel zu tun in der Praxis? Möchtest du lieber einfach chillen?«

»Lieber Himmel, du bist so gut zu mir.« Sie schüttelte insgeheim den Kopf, weil sie sich Sorgen gemacht hatte, weil sie ihm nicht gesagt hatte, was sie wirklich bewegte. Und nicht zuletzt auch, weil sie sich nicht sicher war, ob sie sich die Situation nicht vielleicht doch schöndachte.

»Ich hoffe, das ist gut. Oder meinst du damit eher: ›Lieber Himmel, du bist so gut zu mir und jetzt muss ich mit dir Schluss machen‹?« Sein Lächeln sagte ihr, dass er die zweite Variante nicht wirklich in Betracht zog.

»Nein, keine Sorge. Es ist alles okay. Lass uns reingehen.«

»Wenn du dir ganz sicher bist.« Er hielt ihre Hand, als sie den Parkplatz überquerten und mit dem Aufzug zu Brents Büro fuhren.

Sie rang mit ihren Gedanken, als sie die leere Kanzlei betraten. Bei einem Anwalt hatte sie eigentlich eine teure, protzige Einrichtung erwartet, Brents Räume sahen jedoch modern und minimalistisch aus. In der Lobby standen vier einfache schwarze Stühle und ein niedriger Glastisch. In einem Regal neben dem mit einer Glasplatte versehenen Empfangstresen lagen ordentlich aufgestapelte Zeitschriften. Offenbar kamen sie außerhalb der regulären Bürostunden, denn außer ihnen war niemand da und alles war still.

»Ich schicke Brent eben eine Nachricht und sage ihm, dass wir hier sind.« Sam griff in seine Tasche und holte sein Handy hervor.

Faith konnte nicht anders, sie musste einfach einen Blick darauf werfen. Es war dasselbe Handy, das er ihr gezeigt hatte. Kein Wegwerfhandy. *Siehst du, Viv?* Gleich darauf hatte sie ein schlechtes Gewissen. Sie hätte nicht zulassen sollen, dass Vivian Zweifel in ihr säte. An ihm zu zweifeln war einfach dumm.

Eine Tür öffnete sich und ein breitschultriger blonder Mann mit einem strahlend weißen Lächeln und weit ausgebreiteten Armen kam in die Lobby. »Sammy, wie geht's dir?« Er umarmte Sam und klopfte ihm auf den Rücken.

»Super. Danke, dass du dir Zeit für uns nimmst.« Sams Arm legte sich wieder um Faiths Taille. »Das ist meine Freundin, Faith Hayes. Faith, Brent Holloway, der beste Anwalt weit und breit.«

»Das ist kein Scherz. Ich bin wirklich der Beste«, sagte Brent mit einem schelmischen Funkeln in seinen blauen Augen. »Kommt mit.« Er führte sie in sein Büro.

Bevor Faith neben Sam Platz nahm, erhaschte sie einen Blick auf das Meer in der Ferne. Sie liebte das Wasser und der Anblick half, ihre Nerven zu beruhigen. Sam griff nach ihrer

Hand und verschränkte seine Finger mit ihren. Er lächelte sie nachdenklich an, als wüsste er, dass sie das auch brauchte. Sie war so eine Idiotin, dass sie sich Sorgen machte. Ohne ihn wäre sie nicht einmal hier bei Brent, der sich um die rechtlichen Fragen im Zusammenhang mit ihrer Website kümmern würde.

»Also, Faith.« Brent legte seine Hände flach auf den Schreibtisch. »Women Against Cheaters? Frauen gegen Fremdgänger? Ich denke, der Name spricht für sich. Erzähl mal, was ihr macht, was eure Ziele sind, und dann sehen wir, wie wir möglichst unkompliziert alles so hinkriegen, dass ihr auf der sicheren Seite seid.«

Sie erklärte, wie die Website entstanden und dass die Mitgliederzahl im letzten Jahr enorm gestiegen war. »Ich hätte nie damit gerechnet, dass mehr daraus werden würde, aber inzwischen fallen mir jede Menge Möglichkeiten ein, wie wir den Mitgliedern weitere Hilfsangebote zugänglich machen können. Ich bin mir nicht sicher, wie man das am besten macht, aber ich versuche zumindest, ein Netzwerk aufzubauen, das Empfehlungen für Therapien, Karriereberatung oder möglicherweise reduzierte Anwaltskosten bietet.« Der neugierige Blick, mit dem Brent Sam und sie abwechselnd betrachtete, entging ihr nicht.

Dann erläuterte sie, wie die Spendensituation aussah. Den Betrag, den Sam überwiesen hatte, hatte sie noch gar nicht angerührt, und sie gestand Brent, dass sie nie um Spenden gebeten und auch nicht erwartet hatte, viele zu bekommen.

»Ich denke, wir können das Spendennetzwerk enorm ausbauen«, sagte Sam.

Faiths Kopf fuhr herum. Seit sie den Termin mit Brent vereinbart hatten, hatte Sam das Thema WAC nicht mehr angeschnitten.

»Brent«, fuhr Sam fort, »erinnerst du dich noch, als wir Geld für den Mannschaftssport in der Schule gebraucht haben?«

»Als wir von Haus zu Haus gegangen sind und Spenden gesammelt haben?« Brent hob eine Augenbraue.

»Ja, das habe ich ein, zwei Tage gemacht, aber danach habe ich einen Brief verfasst, in dem ich die Geschäftsleute um Spenden gebeten habe. Und dann habe ich alles meiner Mutter gegeben, die den Brief und die Sammelbüchse zu ihren Meetings der Wirtschaftsvereinigung mitgenommen hat, in der sich die kleinen und mittleren Unternehmen in Peaceful Harbor organisieren. Kaum eine Woche später hagelte es Spenden!«

Brent lachte und zeigte auf Sam. »Du hast geschummelt. Ich wusste es! Du hast immer die meisten Spenden eingesammelt.«

»Hey, das war nicht geschummelt. Es war einfach nur gut durchdacht.« Zu Faith gewandt sagte Sam: »Die Leute in der Stadt würden definitiv hinter euren Bemühungen stehen. Ihr helft Frauen, alleinerziehenden Müttern. Nachdem ich mich einen Nachmittag lang mit einigen Mitgliedern unterhalten habe, interessiert es mich sehr, wie es ihnen geht.«

Bei diesem Eingeständnis ging Faith das Herz auf und die Zweifel, die Vivian in ihr ausgelöst hatte, traten weit in den Hintergrund. Ihre Gefühle mussten sich auf ihrem Gesicht gespiegelt haben, denn Sam bedachte sie mit einem warmen Blick.

»Wirklich. Ich denke immer wieder an Brittany und wie sie sich wohl gefühlt haben muss, als sie ihren Freund bei Fremdgehen ertappt hat, und an Lira«, sagte er leise. »Was hat ihre Schwester bloß mit ihr angerichtet? Am liebsten würde man Lira packen und sie in eine bessere Familie pflanzen, nicht wahr?«

»Ja«, sagte sie atemlos und setzte in Gedanken hinzu: *Wenn du so etwas sagst, wünsche ich mir, ein Teil deiner Familie zu sein.*

Sechzehn

Anderthalb Stunden später verließen Sam und Faith die Kanzlei mit einem soliden Geschäftsplan in der Tasche. Die Regeln und Vorschriften für gemeinnützige Organisationen waren zu kompliziert, doch Brent wollte alle Unterlagen vorbereiten, die sie brauchten, um den WAC als GmbH eintragen zu lassen, mit Phil D'Amato über die Versicherung sprechen und Faith schließlich alles zur Unterschrift vorlegen. Faith schien mit dieser Lösung zufrieden zu sein. Sie war viel entspannter als bei ihrer Ankunft, was Sam beruhigte. Obwohl sie einander näherkamen, wusste er, dass ihr scharfer Verstand ihr noch manchen Stolperstein in den Weg legen würde. Bisweilen trübten Zweifel ihren Blick, und er freute sich auf den Tag, an dem das nicht mehr passierte.

Er schloss die Tür des Trucks auf und zog sie in einen Kuss. Sie stellte sich auf die Zehenspitzen, und mit dieser kleinen Bewegung, mit der sie versuchte, näher an ihn heranzukommen, streichelte sie jeden sehnsüchtigen Zentimeter seines Körpers.

»Danke, dass du das vorbereitet und mich begleitet hast. Brent ist wirklich großartig.«

»Für dich würde ich doch alles tun.« Er stahl sich gierig einen weiteren Kuss.

Sie klammerte sich an sein Hemd und stöhnte an seinen Lippen und alles an ihm wurde lebendig. Er hob sie in die Arme, und ihre Beine schlangen sich wie von selbst um seine Taille, als er sie gegen den Wagen stützte und den Kuss tiefer werden ließ.

»Den ganzen Tag hab ich an dich gedacht«, sagte er und setzte kleine Küsse auf ihre Mundwinkel. »Du warst so sexy da oben in der Kanzlei, so geschäftsmäßig und professionell.«

Sie drehte den Kopf und fing einen Kuss, der für ihre Wange gedacht war, mit den Lippen auf. Er war heiß und feucht, drängend und fordernd. Sams Hände umfassten ihren Hintern und brachten ihm ein weiteres herzzerreißendes Stöhnen ein.

»So sexy. Ich liebe das.« Sein Mund tastete sich zu ihrem Hals.

»Sam ...« Den Kopf nach hinten gebeugt, bot sie ihm diese empfindliche Stelle dar.

Seine Zunge fuhr über den heftigen Pulsschlag an ihrem Hals. Ihre Fingernägel hinterließen Spuren auf seiner Haut und machten ihn hart wie Stahl. Ein Auto in der Nähe piepte, als hätte jemand den entsprechenden Knopf auf einer Fernbedienung gedrückt. Sam fuhr zurück und spähte in die Dunkelheit. Ein paar Meter entfernt stand Brent und schüttelte den Kopf.

»Lieber Himmel«, murmelte Sam. »Unsere Küsse lassen mich alles ringsum vergessen. Dabei stehen wir mitten auf einem Parkplatz.«

»Und das ist schlecht?« Ihre Stimme klang verspielt, verlockend.

Er drückte sie fester gegen den Wagen, gegen seine Erregung, und ihre Augen weiteten sich.

»Ich dachte, wir benehmen uns.« *Bitte sag mir, dass wir uns nicht mehr benehmen müssen.*

Schweigen glitt zwischen sie wie eine Schlange und er sehnte sich nach der verbotenen Frucht.

»Das war vorgestern.« Sie küsste eine federleichte Spur über seine Lippen und jeder kleine Kuss war erregender als der nächste.

Das war vorgestern. Drei Worte, die reichten, um sein Gehirn in Flammen aufgehen zu lassen. Er konnte sich nicht einmal erinnern, was sie für den restlichen Abend geplant hatten. Sam war sich vage bewusst, dass Brents Auto vom Parkplatz fuhr. Ohne Faith loszulassen, öffnete er die Wagentür und setzte sie auf den Sitz, sodass sie ihre unerbittliche Kussfolter auf seinem Mund ohne Unterbrechung fortsetzen konnte. Jeder Kuss, jeder warme Atemhauch auf seiner Haut verstärkte sein Verlangen. Als sie sich zurückzog, die Augen halb geschlossen, pulsierte sein ganzer Körper vor Begehren. Er schloss die Beifahrertür, ging zur Fahrerseite, startete den Motor und versuchte verzweifelt, die Kontrolle wiederzuerlangen. Der Wunsch, sie gleich auf dem Vordersitz des Trucks zu nehmen, war überwältigend, aber er respektierte sie viel zu sehr, als dass er riskiert hätte, dass sie jemand ertappte.

Er zog sie an sich und nahm sie erneut in einem glühenden Kuss, der ihm fast die Sinne raubte. Er befestigte ihren Sicherheitsgurt neben sich und wollte, dass sie in der Nähe war, als er den Parkplatz verließ. Ihre Hand ruhte auf seinem Oberschenkel und drückte ihn leicht. Ihre andere Hand glitt auf die ihr abgewandte Seite seines Gesichts. Sam hielt die Augen angestrengt auf die Straße gerichtet, als sie zum Angriff überging, sich an seinem Kinn entlang zum Hals küsste, an seinem Ohrläppchen zupfte und mit der Zunge darüberfuhr.

»Faith«, sagte er atemlos. »Ich halte es bald nicht mehr aus.«

»Ich weiß«, flüsterte sie ihm ins Ohr. »Aber ich kann einfach nicht anders.«

Er bog in eine Seitenstraße ein. Er war kurz davor, die Fassung zu verlieren. Jeder Muskel in seinem Körper war angespannt, und wenn ihr Daumen nur noch ein kleines Stückchen näher an seine Mitte geriet, konnte er für nichts garantieren.

Er bog um eine Kurve, fuhr ein, zwei Kilometer eine weitere Seitenstraße entlang und steuerte dann an den Straßenrand, gerade als Faiths Zunge in sein Ohr glitt und er kaum noch an sich halten konnte. Hastig hielt er an, stellte den Motor ab, und drei Sekunden später hatte er die Sicherheitsgurte gelöst und Faith lag verführerisch lächelnd unter ihm.

»Du kannst es nicht lassen, was?« Er zupfte mit den Zähnen an ihrem Kinn. »Willst du mich in den Wahnsinn treiben?« Mit der Zunge zeichnete er ihre Lippen nach. Sie wollte sich aufsetzen und seinen Mund einfangen, aber er zog sich zurück. »Oh nein, meine Süße. Du bist nicht die Einzige, die dieses Spielchen spielen kann.«

»Sam.« Sie drängt ihre Hüften an seine Erregung.

»Sag mir, was du willst, Baby. Du sagst mir, ich soll mich beherrschen, und dann machst du mich wild. Ich bin nicht sicher, wo wir stehen.«

Sie lachte leise und zog sein Gesicht näher heran. Er stemmte sich gegen den Kuss und ließ seinen Mund einen Hauch über ihrem schweben, während sie verzweifelt versuchte, an ihn heranzukommen. Er fuhr mit seiner Hand über ihre Flanke und wölbte sie um ihre Brust. Sein Daumen spielte mit ihrer Brustwarze, so wie sie es liebte.

»Sam«, bettelte sie.

»Willst du, dass ich mich benehme, oder soll ich dich gleich hier nehmen, hart und heftig? Langsam und sinnlich? Oder beides, Baby? Willst du das?« Er schob ihr Hemd hoch, nahm dabei den BH mit, befreite eine schöne Brust und leckte ihren hoch aufgerichteten Nippel.

»Lieber Gott. Sam.«

»Ich habe meinen Namen oft genug gehört, um zu wissen, wie ich heiße. Sag mir, was du dir wünschst.« Sein Mund senkte sich auf ihre Brust und saugte kräftig. Ihr ganzer Körper bog sich auf dem Sitz. Eine Hand streichelte ihren Bauch, bevor sie sich in ihre Jeans schob. Seine Fingerspitzen streiften ihre Nässe. Er brannte innerlich, als er einen Finger in sie tauchte. »Gott, Baby, du bist so bereit für mich.«

Sie biss sich auf die Unterlippe.

»Oh nein. Schluss damit.« Er zupfte die Lippe mit den Zähnen frei. »Sprich mit mir, Baby. Ich werde dir nicht geben, was du brauchst, wenn du nicht mit mir redest.«

Wortlos wölbte sie ihm die Hüften entgegen, und er zog seine Finger aus ihrer Jeans, steckte sie sich in den Mund und saugte daran. Ihre Augen weiteten sich und ihre Münder prallen in einem gierigen, nassen Kuss zusammen. Der Schmerz zwischen seinen Beinen breitete sich über seinen ganzen Körper aus, als er jede ihrer köstlichen, weichen Rundungen ertastete. Ihre Nägel ergriffen Besitz von seinem Rücken, und als sich ihre Lippen voneinander lösten, waren beide atemlos, und die wilde Leidenschaft in ihren Augen machte fast kurzen Prozess mit ihm.

»Du bist die beste Art von Folter«, flüsterte er zwischen zwei Küssen. »Aber du bist mir zu wichtig und ich will nicht, dass wir uns in Verlangen verstricken und du es hinterher bereust. Du musst mir sagen, was du willst, Faith.«

Zweifel trübten ihren Blick. *Mist.*

»Faith?«

Sie wandte den Blick ab und sein Herz brach entzwei.

Mit dem Fuß stieß er gegen die Windschutzscheibe des Trucks. Wie konnte er sie nur so falsch verstehen? Er hatte fest damit gerechnet, dass sie ihm sagen würde, sie begehre ihn so sehr, wie er sie begehrte. Und er begehrte sie mehr als seinen nächsten Atemzug, aber nicht so. Nicht, wenn sie ihm nicht in die Augen sehen und es ihm nicht sagen konnte. Und – *Wie konnte ich bloß so ein Idiot sein?* – nicht im Truck.

Er schloss für einen Moment die Augen und rang um Fassung.

»Es ist okay, Baby.« Er küsste sie leicht, schob seine Enttäuschung beiseite und gab ihr zu verstehen, dass er ihre Unentschlossenheit akzeptierte. Er schob sich aus dem Wagen, bevor er der Hitze, die durch ihn loderte, oder der Gier, die in seiner Hose pulsierte, nachgeben konnte. Stattdessen konzentrierte er sich auf die Emotionen, die in seinem wunden Herzen keimten.

»Sam?« Mit funkelnden Augen setzte sie sich auf. »Lässt du mich auf dem Trockenen sitzen?«

»Nein, Baby. Du bist nass und hungrig, keineswegs trocken.« Er zog sie an den Rand des Sitzes und drückte ihre Hand an seinen Reißverschluss, um ihr zu zeigen, welche Wirkung sie auf ihn hatte und dass er dasselbe schmerzliche Verlangen verspürte wie sie. »Und ich bin hart wie Stein.«

Sie stieg aus dem Wagen und er griff nach ihrer Hand. Ihre gekränkte Miene traf ihn bis ins Mark. Er beugte sich herunter, um sie zu küssen, und sie drehte sich weg.

»Wo ist der Mann, der von sich behauptet, dass er sich nimmt, was er braucht?«, fragte sie halb neckend, halb verärgert.

Bis jetzt hatte er seine Gefühle zurückgehalten, doch nun brach die Frustration aus ihm hervor. »Der Mann, mit dem du nichts zu tun haben wolltest? Das ist der Mann, den du jetzt begehrst!? Ich kann mich nämlich in den Mann verwandeln, den du dir vorstellst, solange du klar sagst, was du willst.«

Sie starrte ihn mit einem verblüfften Blick an, der ihn fast umbrachte, aber nun konnte er seinen Frust nicht länger herunterschlucken.

»Sag es mir, Faith. Willst du den Mann, der sich nimmt, was er will, wo immer er will, egal, was danach passiert?«

»Nein. Oder doch? Ich weiß es nicht.« Sie wandte den Blick ab.

»Baby.« Seine Stimme wurde weicher, als er sie in die Arme nahm. »Du bist genauso zerrissen wie ich. Deshalb sendest du widersprüchliche Signale. Ich sehe es in deinen Augen. Du willst mich und im nächsten Moment bist du dir nicht mehr sicher. Das ist der Grund, weshalb ich aufgehört habe.«

Wieder biss sie sich auf die Unterlippe.

»Es ist okay«, versicherte er ihr. »Ich bin hier und ich fahre auf dich ab. Und das nicht nur heute oder morgen. Aber, Faith, du hast meine Art zu denken verändert. Ich wollte dich im Truck lieben – mit meinen Händen, meinem Mund, meinem Körper. Mir ist klar, dass der Truck nicht der richtige Ort ist, aber das ist nicht der Punkt. Wenn wir uns lieben, muss ich sicher sein, dass du dich wirklich darauf einlässt. Vor ein paar Tagen hast du dich auf mich eingelassen. Ich habe es gefühlt, gesehen, geschmeckt. Als du auf der Fahrt an mir herumgespielt hast, warst du da, mit Haut und Haaren, aber als ich eben auf dir lag, schwelte in deinen Augen ein Zweifel unter der Leidenschaft.«

Die Enttäuschung in ihrem Blick gab ihm fast den Rest. Er versuchte, das Richtige zu tun. War es nicht das, was sie wollte und was sie verdiente? Für einen Mann, der glaubte, Frauen zu kennen, verhielt er sich plötzlich wie ein ungeschickter Anfänger.

»Bei dir ist alles anders, Baby. Es passiert leicht, dass man Blicke falsch deutet, aber Worte sind deutlich. Ich brauche eine klare Linie. Und du hast gesagt, dass du sie auch brauchst. *Vollständige Transparenz.* Wenn wir an diesen Punkt kommen, wenn ich weiß, dass du nicht an mir zweifelst, dann werde ich mich keine Sekunde zurückhalten, das verspreche ich dir, Baby.«

Faith war die Kehle wie zugeschnürt, als sie Sam beobachtete, wie er am Straßenrand auf und ab ging. Manche Männer brauchten Anzug und Krawatte, um so auszusehen, als könnten sie es mit der ganzen Welt aufnehmen. Bei Sam war es anders. Egal, was er anhatte, strahlte er ein Selbstvertrauen aus, das sie überwältigend fand. Bisher hatte sie dieses Selbstvertrauen nie schwanken sehen, außer wenn es um sie ging. Er war dafür bekannt, dass er sich nahm, was er wollte. *Außer bei mir.* Bei ihr war wirklich alles anders.

War es nicht das, was ich wollte? Was ich verlangt habe?

Ohne es zu merken, hatte sie diesen Keil zwischen sie getrieben. Was er heute Abend in ihren Augen gesehen hatte, waren die Dinge, die Vivian zu ihr gesagt hatte und die Faith versuchte, wegzuschieben. In ihrem Herzen wusste sie, dass ihre Freundin falschlag. Aber Sam war so auf sie eingestimmt, dass er ihre Gefühle aufspürte, bevor sie Zeit hatte, sie zu verarbeiten. Wo die meisten Männer den Moment des Zögerns gar nicht wahrgenommen oder ignoriert hätten, hatte Sam ihn sofort aufgegriffen. Er war so sehr darum bemüht, alles richtig zu machen, wenn es um sie ging, und das nahm sie noch mehr für ihn ein. Sie kam sich wie eine Idiotin vor, dass sie überhaupt an ihm gezweifelt hatte.

Sie streckte die Hand nach ihm aus. Seine Augen waren so voller Reue, dass die Schuldgefühle fast ihr Herz versengten.

»Es tut mir leid, dass ich überreagiert habe«, sagte er. »Ich hätte das alles nicht sagen sollen.«

»Nein, ich war diejenige, die überreagiert hat. Du hattest recht, und ich weiß es zu schätzen, dass du meinetwegen aufgehört hast, auch wenn ich nicht sicher war, ob ich es wollte.«

»Also war da tatsächlich ein Zögern? Gott sei Dank! Du hast mich so fassungslos angesehen, dass ich dachte, ich hätte mir das nur eingebildet.«

»Da war wirklich ein Zögern, Sam, aber nicht, weil ich aufhören wollte. Ich habe nur meine Gefühle unter die Lupe genommen. Vorhin habe ich mit Vivian telefoniert, und danach dachte ich, du wolltest dich vielleicht nicht mit mir in der Stadt zeigen, weil …« Sie hielt inne. Sie musste es nicht aussprechen. Er wusste, warum, und sie wusste es auch.

»Es ist egal, warum«, erklärte sie. »Die Wahrheit ist, ich wollte, dass du mich liebst, aber ich konnte nicht schnell genug denken, und es war mir peinlich, das laut zuzugeben. Ich will dich, Sam. Alles von dir. Aber manchmal muss eine Frau einfach *genommen* werden.«

»Lieber Himmel, Baby«, flüsterte er und lehnte seine Stirn an ihre. »Wenn es ums Nehmen geht, kenne ich mich aus, aber bei dir kann ich nicht ignorieren, was ich sehe. Mit allen anderen – vor dir – vielleicht. Aber nicht bei dir, Faith. Niemals. In den letzten Tagen musste ich all meine Disziplin aufwenden, um dich *nicht* zu nehmen, und ich warte so lange, wie du brauchst, um dir sicher zu sein.«

»Das weiß ich und ich weiß es zu schätzen.« Sie wusste, dass es für ihn die reinste Folter sein musste, zu hören, dass sie an ihm zweifelte und ihn gleichzeitig aufgeilte. Eigentlich war sie nicht so, dass sie einen Mann scharfmachte, um ihn dann im Regen stehen zu lassen – aber genau so musste es für ihn aussehen.

»Sag mir, was dir durch den Kopf gegangen ist oder was Vivian meinte. Dass ich an anderen Frauen interessiert bin? Dass ich mich nicht beherrschen kann, wenn wir in die Bars oder Lokale gehen, in denen ich normalerweise abhänge?« Der Schmerz in seiner Stimme traf sie wie ein Keulenschlag. »Und trotzdem wolltest du mit mir schlafen? Kein Wunder, dass du durcheinander warst.«

»Nein. Ich glaube nicht, dass du an anderen Frauen interessiert bist. Ich glaube dir das, was du mir sagst. Aber nach dem Gespräch mit Vivian habe ich mich gefragt, ob ich nur sehe, was ich sehen will.« Das Geständnis lag ihr wie ein Bleiklumpen im Magen. »Aber als wir bei Brent waren, wurde mir klar, dass meine Sicht auf dich ganz anders ist als die anderer Leute, weil ich dich wirklich kenne. Alle anderen kennen den Mann, der du warst, oder den Mann, von dem sie gehört haben. Daher ergibt es einen Sinn, dass Vivian eine verzerrte Sicht auf dich hat.«

»Aber wenn du das glaubst, woher kam dann das Zögern, das ich in deinen Augen gesehen habe?«

»Einerseits habe ich versucht, Vivians Worte aus dem Kopf zu kriegen, weil ich weiß, dass sie nicht wahr sind. Andererseits ist es leicht, selbstbewusst und sexy zu sein, wenn du abgelenkt bist.«

»Wenn ich am Steuer sitze«, sagte er.

»Ja. Oder wenn ich dir eine Nachricht schreibe«, räumte sie ein.

Sein Blick wurde sanft. »Deine Nachrichten sind sexy.«

»Bei dir traue ich mich mehr als bei jedem anderen. Manchmal muss ich mir wirklich Mühe geben, deinem Blick standzuhalten und nicht die Hände vors Gesicht zu schlagen. Du sagst Dinge, bei denen ich rot werde, aber ich liebe es, sie zu hören.«

»Baby, bei mir muss dir nichts peinlich sein. Ich möchte deine Gefühle respektieren, auch wenn das bedeutet, dass ich abwarten muss, bis ich dir näherkommen kann. Ich möchte, dass du an *mich* glaubst, egal, was andere Leute sagen. Und die Leute sagen immer etwas, verhalten sich auf eine bestimmte Weise. Ich habe das nicht vor dir versteckt. *Das* war der Grund, warum ich warten wollte, bevor wir uns zusammen in der Stadt zeigen. Meine Güte, selbst deine beste Freundin traut mir nicht über den Weg.«

»Das ist mir egal«, sagte sie entschlossen, und obwohl es sich wie ein Verrat an ihrer besten Freundin anfühlte, war sie überzeugt davon. Sie hatte einen Fehler gemacht, als sie sich von Vivians Bedenken hatte beeinflussen lassen, auch wenn sie wusste, dass Vivian nur ihr Bestes wollte.

»Sie ist deine beste Freundin. Es kann dir nicht egal sein«, sagte er. »Baby, beim Rough-Riders-Barbecue wirst du es live und in Farbe erleben, und ich werde wissen, wie ich damit umgehe. Andere Frauen bedeuten mir nichts. Du bedeutest mir alles, und ich werde weiterhin alles tun, damit dir niemand wehtut. Und dazu gehört auch, dass ich mich zurückhalte, wenn ich etwas in deinen Augen sehe, das mich beunruhigt.«

Sie hatte einen Kloß im Hals, als sie die Zärtlichkeit in

seiner Stimme hörte.

»Aber von jetzt an«, sagte er, »brauchen wir ein Signal. Etwas, das mir sagt, dass es wirklich in Ordnung ist, wenn es in Ordnung ist.«

»Wie wäre es, wenn ich Nein oder Stopp sage, wenn es nicht in Ordnung ist? Nein sagen kann ich.«

»Ja«, sagte er mit einem hitzigen Funkeln in den Augen. »Das kannst du wirklich gut.«

»Ich habe dich ja gewarnt, dass ich nicht einfach bin.«

»Aufrichtig ist mir wichtiger als einfach, glaub's mir. Das ist gut, Faith. Es ist viel besser, offen über alles zu sprechen, als die Signale des anderen falsch zu interpretieren und sich unnötig Sorgen zu machen.«

»Danke für dein Verständnis. Ich kann es kaum glauben, dass wir uns deswegen nicht ernsthaft gestritten haben. Es tut mir leid, Sam. Ich hätte nicht an dir zweifeln sollen, aber es ist lange her, seit ich mich sicher genug gefühlt habe, um mich aufs Eis zu wagen.«

»Baby, bei mir bist du immer in Sicherheit.«

Faith war nach dem Gespräch erleichtert, als sie jedoch vor dem Tap It aus dem Truck stieg, war sie das reinste Nervenbündel. Sam sagte, er wolle auf keinen Fall, dass sie sich um etwas Sorgen machte, was möglicherweise eines Tages eintreten könnte. Und sie solle auch nicht glauben, dass er nicht mit ihr gesehen werden wolle, weil er nicht mit dem umgehen könne, was da auf sie zukam. Daher hatte er darauf bestanden, dass sie sich ein Lokal in der Stadt suchten. Zumindest hatte sie ihn davon abhalten können, ins Whispers zu gehen. Das wäre ihr doch eine Nummer zu groß gewesen.

»Wir müssen wirklich nicht hierher gehen«, sagte sie sicher zum hundertsten Mal in der vergangenen Viertelstunde.

Er schloss sie in die Arme und lächelte sie an.

»Hey, wir sind nur ein Typ und seine Freundin bei einem Dinner-Date. Ich hätte nicht so viel Theater darum machen sollen, dass wir noch abwarten sollten, bevor wir uns zu zweit in der Stadt sehen lassen. Das war egoistisch. Ich habe mir so sehr gewünscht, dass du mich magst und nichts deine Meinung von mir jemals ändert, egal, was andere Leute sagen oder tun.« Er strich ihr eine Haarsträhne hinters Ohr, so ruhig wie eine leichte Brise.

»Aber ich *mag* dich, so, wie du es dir wünschst. Ich musste Vivian und die Zweifel hinter mir lassen, die sie mir in den Kopf gesetzt hat. Und ich habe es geschafft. Mir musst du nichts beweisen.«

»Das ist gut, Baby. Dann sollten wir jetzt gemütlich essen gehen.«

Sie stiegen die Treppe hinauf, und Faith fragte sich, was sie erwartet hatte, wenn sie das Tap It betraten. Es war ja nicht so, als würden Frauen in aller Öffentlichkeit über ihn herfallen. Vielleicht machte sie auch zu viel aus seiner Vergangenheit. Möglicherweise hatte Sam sich geirrt und niemand, der sie zusammen sah, würde sich komisch aufführen.

Bevor er die Tür öffnete, sagte Sam: »Da drinnen geht es nur um dich und mich. Nur um uns. Niemand sonst zählt.«

Sie gingen hinein, der Lärm der überfüllten Bar zu ihrer Rechten vermischte sich mit dem einladenden Geplauder aus dem Restaurant zu ihrer Linken. Der verlockende Duft von Gewürzen und Gegrilltem hing in der Luft.

Die zierliche Tischdame lächelte Sam zu. »Hey, Sam.« Sie sah seinen Arm um Faiths Taille und schenkte Faith das gleiche gewinnende Lächeln. »Hallo. Zwei zum Abendessen?«

»Ja bitte. Natasha, das ist meine Freundin, Faith.« Sam sah Faith unverwandt an. »Natasha ist mit Shannon zur Schule gegangen.«

»Ja, das stimmt«, sagte Natasha und schenkte nun Faith ihre volle Aufmerksamkeit. »Shannon ist eine Nummer für sich. Kommt mit, wir suchen euch einen Tisch.«

Faith war sich der Augenpaare bewusst, die Sam folgten, als sie in den hinteren Teil des Restaurants gingen. Ihre Gedanken wurden düsterer, als sie es wollte, aber einige der Frauen versuchten gar nicht, ihre Neugier zu verstecken. Es machte sie verlegen und, was noch schlimmer war, sie fragte sich, ob Sam mit einer von ihnen etwas gehabt hatte.

Nachdem er Faith den Stuhl an den Tisch gerückt hatte, setzte er sich ihr gegenüber und nahm ihre Hand. Sie bemerkte, dass ein Paar am Nachbartisch sie verstohlen beäugte. Wahrscheinlich war Sam für sie gar nicht der Verführer und Eroberer, als der er in der Stadt galt, aber sie konnte nicht anders: Sie musste jeden Blick analysieren.

»Du siehst heute Abend wunderschön aus.« Seine Stimme riss sie aus ihren Gedanken. »Hallo. Hier geht es nur um dich und um mich. Machen wir uns das nicht kaputt. Hast du Lust auf einen Drink?«

»Oder drei?«, antwortete sie und hasste sich dafür, dass sie so unsicher war. Das war dumm. Es bestand kein Anlass, so nervös zu sein. *Wir sind nur zwei Leute, die zusammen zu Abend essen.*

Ihre Kellnerin trat an den Tisch. Sie sah Scarlett Johansson zum Verwechseln ähnlich und warf Faith einen flüchtigen Blick zu. Dann richtete sie ihre dick geschminkten Augen auf Sam und Faith schien vergessen. »Sam, wie geht's? Seit der Strandparty habe ich gar nichts mehr von dir gehört.«

Er sah sie mit einem kühlen Ausdruck an, den Faith noch nie bei ihm gesehen hatte. »Hallo. Danke, mir geht's gut.« Er wandte sich wieder an Faith und sagte: »Können wir bitte eine Flasche Arietta Cabernet Sauvignon bekommen?«

Die Blondine kniff die Augen zusammen. »Sicher«, sagte sie knapp und ging davon.

»Hast du ...?« Sie hielt den Atem an. Eigentlich wollte sie die Antwort nicht hören.

»Mit ihr geschlafen? Nein.«

»Warum benimmt sie sich dann so?«

Ein langsames Lächeln kräuselte seine Mundwinkel. »*Weil*

ich nicht mit ihr geschlafen habe.«

Sie beugte sich vor und flüsterte: »Aber ich dachte, du hättest nie Nein gesagt.«

Sam stand auf, und Faith bekam plötzlich Angst, dass sie einen Schritt zu weit gegangen war. Bestimmt würden sie das Lokal auf der Stelle verlassen. Er stellte jedoch nur seinen Stuhl neben ihren, setzte sich und nahm ihre Hand wieder in seine. Seine Augen sahen sie unverwandt an. »Ich habe Frauen zurückgewiesen. Frauen haben mich zurückgewiesen. Nicht oft, aber es ist passiert. Was möchtest du sonst noch wissen?«

Verlegenheit überschwemmte sie, und sie spürte, dass sie rot wurde. Sie fragte sich, ob Haut allein durch Gedanken Feuer fangen konnte. Wie hatte sie ihm nur eine solche Frage stellen können? Und er hatte sie auch noch beantwortet. *Also wirklich!* Was war los mit ihr? Aber okay, jetzt waren sie so weit gekommen, da konnte sie auch weitermachen. Viel schlimmer konnte es kaum werden.

Sie holte tief Luft und betete, dass er nicht hinausstürmen und sie wie eine Idiotin allein sitzen lassen würde. Und eine Idiotin musste sie wohl sein, denn sonst würde sie sich nicht so benehmen. Sie sagte: »Könntest du dich einmal umsehen und mir sagen, ob du eine Frau siehst, mit der du geschlafen hast? Dann brauche ich nicht zu versuchen, es herauszufinden.«

Er drehte sich um und schaute sich im Restaurant um. Dann begegnete er ihrem Blick so ruhig wie eh und je. »Bist du sicher, dass du es wissen willst? Oder ist das so ein Mädelstrick? Du tust so, als wolltest du es wissen, aber wenn du es herausfindest, machst du Theater?«

Sie lachte, aber insgeheim krümmte sie sich vor Verlegenheit. Das musste bedeuten, dass er mindestens eine Frau erkannt hatte, mit der er geschlafen hatte. »Sag es mir nicht. Wahrscheinlich will ich es eigentlich doch nicht wissen.«

Er ließ seine Hand in ihren Nacken gleiten und drückte seine Wange an ihre. Wie schaffte er es, mit einer einzigen Berührung ihre Spannung verschwinden zu lassen?

»Es gibt nur eine Frau, mit der ich schlafen möchte, und sie ist so sehr damit beschäftigt, herauszufinden, wer ihre Konkurrenz ist, dass sie gar nicht mitbekommt, dass sie keine hat.«

Er fuhr leicht mit den Lippen über ihre, als die Kellnerin den Wein brachte.

Sie stellte die Flasche auf den Tisch, die Augen auf Sams Hinterkopf gerichtet, und mit einer Hand auf der Hüfte sagte sie: »Sieht aus, als wäre dein Appetit so unersättlich wie eh und je. Was darf ich euch zu essen bringen?«

Ohne sich von Faith zu lösen, sagte Sam: »Wir haben uns noch nicht entschieden.«

Faith tat die Kellnerin leid, trotz der spitzen Bemerkung, die sie losgelassen hatte. Von Sam zurückgewiesen zu werden, fühlte sich wahrscheinlich hundertmal schlimmer an als die Eifersucht, die die junge Frau in ihr geweckt hatte.

Sam küsste Faith sanft, dann setzte er sich auf seinen Stuhl, ohne ihre Hand loszulassen. »Darf ich dich etwas fragen?«

»Sicher.«

»Sieh dich einmal um. Hast du hier mit jemandem geschlafen?«

»Ich?« Sie lachte, als sie sich im Restaurant umschaute. Beim Anblick von Roger Waylin, einem Typen, mit dem sie vor ein paar Monaten ausgegangen war, blieb ihr fast das Herz stehen. Rasch drehte sie den Kopf weg. Zum Glück hatte sie sich nicht auf Rogers Annäherungsversuche eingelassen. »Nein. Niemand.«

Sam drehte sich um und starrte Roger an. Dann sah er sie an und sein Mund verzog sich zu einem zufriedenen Lächeln. »Gut zu wissen.«

Er schenkte den Wein ein und reichte Faith ein Glas. »Auf uns.«

»Die einzigen Leute, um die es hier geht.« Ihr Glas berührte seins mit leisem Klirren.

Während des Essens blieb Sam neben ihr sitzen und schenkte Faith seine volle Aufmerksamkeit, berührte ihren Oberschenkel, ihre Hand, ihre Wange. Sie fütterten sich gegenseitig, und als sie mit dem Essen fertig waren, hatte Faith längst vergessen, warum sie anfangs so nervös gewesen war. Sie tranken und flirteten, und Sam küsste sie so oft, dass sich all ihre Verlegenheit in Luft auflöste.

Sie beugte sich vor und streifte seine Lippen mit ihren. »Sollen wir uns die Rechnung geben lassen und noch zu mir gehen, um meine *Kommunikationsfähigkeiten* zu trainieren?«

Hitze loderte in seinen wunderschönen Augen auf.

Zehn Minuten später fanden sie küssend zu Sams Truck zurück. Ihre Körper klebten praktisch aneinander, als Sam seine Schlüssel herausfischte.

»Sammy!«, rief eine Frau quer über den Parkplatz.

Sam erstarrte, seine Lippen noch immer auf Faiths, seine Augen ernst.

»Sam! Hey, Sam! Komm, lass uns etwas trinken!«, rief eine andere Frau.

Sam und Faith sahen beide auf und erblickten eine Gruppe von Frauen, die kichernd und schwatzend auf sie zukam.

»Sollen wir sie einfach stehen lassen?«, fragte er mit einem anzüglichen Lächeln.

Ja! »Meinst du?«

»Es sei denn, du willst zusehen, wie ich ihnen sage, dass sie abhauen sollen.«

Sie klemmte ihre Unterlippe zwischen die Zähne und ließ sie sofort wieder los. »Beeil dich!«

Achtzehn

Sam und Faith stolperten in einem Gewirr aus Gliedern und Mündern, Gelächter und Betteln in ihre dunkle Wohnung. Faith ging rückwärts den kurzen Flur hinunter zu ihrem Schlafzimmer, schob Sams Hemd hoch und ließ seine Lippen gerade lange genug los, dass er es über den Kopf ziehen und auf den Boden fallen lassen konnte. Sie zog ihr Top aus und warf es achtlos beiseite. Er liebte diese selbstbewusste Seite an ihr. Ohne Sam aus den Augen zu lassen, löste sie den Verschluss vorne an ihrem BH und streifte den Hauch von Spitze ab. Ihre Brüste waren wie glühende Monde an ihrer gebräunten Haut. Sie senkte das Kinn und sah durch ihre unglaublich verführerischen Wimpern hindurch zu ihm auf.

Sam zog sie in die Arme. Seine Stimme war heiser vor Verlangen. »Allein dein Anblick raubt mir den Atem.«

Er presste seinen Mund in einem erbarmungslosen Kuss auf ihren, und seine Länge wurde noch härter, als ihre Brustwarzen seine nackte Brust berührten. Die Gefühle, die ihn durchströmten, waren berauschend. Lust pulsierte in seinen Adern, erfasste seinen ganzen Körper, brannte in seiner Brust und machte den letzten Rest an Beherrschung zunichte.

»Baby«, sagte er drängend an ihren Lippen, bevor er sie

erneut in einen wilden Kuss verwickelte, viel wilder, als er beabsichtigt hatte. Er wusste nicht einmal, was er hatte sagen wollen. Er konnte einfach nichts zurückhalten – keinen Laut, keinen Blick, kein lustvolles Stöhnen, das sich aus seinen Lungen in ihre ergoss.

Er vergrub die Hände in ihrem Haar und vertiefte den Kuss noch mehr, um sich endlich an ihr sattzutrinken. Ihre Hüften stießen an seine, die Bewegung riss ihn in die Wirklichkeit zurück. Sie standen in der Tür zu ihrem Schlafzimmer, und als er in ihre vor Verlangen schwelenden Augen sah, hoffte er, dass sie beide immer noch dasselbe wollten.

»Ja, Sam«, sagte sie klar und deutlich.

Verdammt, Gott sei Dank. Ihre Lippen prallten in einem weiteren brutalen Kuss aufeinander, der sich wie eine Explosion entlud. Sie streichelten und tasteten und plünderten ihre Münder und kämpften gleichzeitig jeweils mit dem Hosenknopf des anderen. Sam zog seine Brieftasche aus der Gesäßtasche, während sie ihre Kleider auf dem Weg zum Bett auf den Boden fallen ließen. Er nahm ein paar Kondome heraus und warf sie auf den Nachttisch, ohne den Kuss zu unterbrechen. Schließlich lösten sich ihre Münder lange genug voneinander, dass Sam jede ihrer wundervollen Rundungen mit Blicken verzehren konnte. Als er sie ansah, waren ihre Augen auf seine bereitwillige Länge gerichtet, und ihre Zunge glitt über ihre Unterlippe.

»Grundgütiger, du bist wunderschön«, sagte er.

»Du … du aber auch«, sagte sie und sah ihm direkt in die Augen.

»Faith, du hast ja keine Ahnung, was du mit mir anstellst. Jedes Wort.« Er fuhr mit dem Daumen über ihre Lippen. »Jeder Blick.« Als er sie in einen trägen Kuss nahm, wurde sein Inneres weich von zärtlichen Gefühlen, während alles andere an ihm noch härter wurde. Dieser Zusammenprall der Emotionen entfachte eine ungeahnte Sehnsucht.

Er hob sie in die Arme und legte sie aufs Bett. »Die Antwort war Nein«, sagte er. Verwirrt runzelte sie die Stirn, während er sich zwischen ihre einladend gespreizten Schenkel schob. »Im Restaurant. Ich habe keine Frau gesehen, mit der ich geschlafen habe. Ich wollte, dass du es weißt, aber danke, dass du mich genug magst, um nicht weiter auf einer Antwort zu pochen.«

Sie streckte die Hände nach ihm aus. »Das ist Schnee von gestern. Und selbst wenn, wäre ich jetzt trotzdem hier.«

Am liebsten wäre er sofort tief in sie eingetaucht, wollte fühlen, wie ihre Wärme jeden Zentimeter von ihm aufnahm, wollte sie sich endlich zu eigen machen. Er küsste ihre Mundwinkel und ihr Kinn, sog an ihrer köstlichen Unterlippe und genoss die wohligen Laute, die aus ihrer Kehle drangen, während sie sich unter ihm wand.

Sie hob den Kopf und ihre Augen – Gott, ihre Augen sagten alles: *Ich will dich. Ich brauche dich. Liebe mich.*

»Sag es mir«, bat er.

»Ich will dich, Sam. Liebe mich.«

Er wusste, wie schwer es ihr fiel, die Worte auszusprechen, und musste ihr einfach einen weiteren umwerfenden Kuss geben. Sonst wäre er mit einem *Danke, dass du mir vertraust* herausgeplatzt, und das hätte sie nur noch mehr in Verlegenheit gebracht. Stattdessen nahm er ihr Gesicht in beide Hände und sagte: »Die ganze Nacht, Süße.«

Mit beiden Händen packte sie seine Taille und hob ihre Hüften gegen seine Härte. Ihre feuchte Mitte lag lockend an seinen Hoden und jagte ihm Hitzewellen über den Rücken. Er küsste sich hinab zu ihren Brüsten, liebkoste sie mit den Lippen, streifte die empfindlichen Brustwarzen mit den Zähnen und saugte daran, so wie sie es mochte. Während seine Hände über ihre Hüften strichen, küsste er jede Rippe, jeden Zentimeter ihres Bauches, bis sie sich keuchend unter ihm bog. Ein Stückchen tiefer noch, und dann war er bei ihren nassen Locken angekommen, die er mit seiner Zunge umspielte. Der Duft ihrer Erregung raubte ihm fast die Sinne. Er spreizte die Hände auf den Innenseiten ihrer Oberschenkel, senkte den Mund auf ihre zarte Spalte und verschlang ihre nasse Haut. Die Dringlichkeit und Sehnsucht, die er so lange unter Verschluss gehalten hatte, brachen sich unerbittlich Bahn. Er streichelte und saugte und schob seine Zunge tief in sie hinein. Ihre Finger krallten sich in das Laken, sie wölbte sich gegen seinen Mund und stöhnte durch zusammengebissene Zähne, und er wusste, dass sie sich zurückhielt.

»Komm für mich, Baby. Lass los«, drängte er, während er mit gekrümmten Fingern den Punkt reizte, der ihr das meiste Vergnügen bereitete. »Du schmeckst so gut, siehst so schön aus. Zeig mir, wie sehr du mich willst.«

Sein Mund strich über diese empfindlichen Nerven, bis ihre Mitte anschwoll. Ihr ganzer Körper krümmte sich, als sie dem Höhepunkt entgegenjagte. Er spürte, wie sich ihr Innerstes anspannte und um ihn pulsierte. Immer wieder flog sein Name wie ein Gebet über ihre Lippen und mit einem lustvollen Stöhnen zerbarst sie schließlich an seinem Mund.

Die Lust überrollte Faiths Körper wie eine Hitzewalze, als Sam noch einmal über ihre überempfindlichen Stellen herfiel und sie streichelte und leckte, bis sie alles um sich herum vergaß. Solche

Orgasmen, die mit jedem sanften Zungenschlag und jedem Reiben seiner Finger neu angefacht wurden, hatte sie noch nie erlebt. Ihre Haut war schweißnass, sie glühte, als sei sie elektrisch aufgeladen, und bebte der Erlösung entgegen.

Sie keuchte auf, als Sam sich von ihr löste und die kalte Luft zwischen ihren Beinen sie erschrocken den Kopf heben ließ. Seine Finger fuhren fort mit ihrem Zauberwerk, und er sah sie mit einem Ausdruck in den Augen an, der pure Leidenschaft verriet. Guter Gott, der Mann war fleischgewordener Sex. Er musste gewusst haben, dass der Hunger in seinem Blick, die glitzernde Nässe an seinem Mund, die ihre Säfte hinterlassen hatten, und seine Finger, die den geheimen Punkt in ihrem Innern streichelten, sie wieder bis kurz vor den Höhepunkt treiben würden. Seine große, heiße Hand glitt über ihren Bauch und bekam ihren Nippel zu fassen. Jeder Druck mit Daumen und Zeigefinger schoss wie ein heißer Blitz genau zwischen ihre Beine. Seine Lippen kräuselten sich zu einem Lächeln, bevor sie sich wieder auf ihr Geschlecht senkten und seine Zunge das betörende Spiel seiner Finger unterstützte. Genussvolle Wogen strömten über ihre Arme und Beine bis in die Zehenspitzen. Seine Zähne streiften ihre zarte Haut nur, die Berührung war jedoch rau und hart genug, um den Funken ihres Orgasmus zu zünden. Eine mächtige Woge der Wonne durchflutete sie, versengte sie und riss sie mit sich. Dann sank sie wieder herunter, tiefer und tiefer, während Sam sie leckte und küsste, bis die letzten Ausläufer der Flut verebbt waren.

Sam überstürzte nichts, stieß seine begierige Härte nicht in sie. Er setzte sich auf die Knie, streichelte seine eindrucksvolle Erektion und legte die Finger um die Basis, während sich an der Spitze eine schimmernde Perle bildete. Sie liebte es zu sehen, wie er sich berührte, und wusste, dass er versuchte, nicht zu kommen. Dass er sie ansah, als sei sie das wundervollste Wesen der Welt, machte sie mutig und gierig. Mit zitternden Armen richtete sie sich auf. Sie zögerte einen Moment, als die Realität sie einholte.

»Sam, hast du …?« Sie musste diese Frage stellen. Zu ihrer eigenen Sicherheit.

Er legte ihr die Hand an die Wange, sein Blick war warm und liebevoll. »Ich habe keinen ungeschützten Sex, Baby, und ich lasse mich zweimal im Jahr testen. Ich hatte keine festen Beziehungen, aber ich habe auch keine Dummheiten gemacht.«

Sie atmete erleichtert auf, ließ ihre Zunge über seine geschwollene Eichel gleiten und genoss es, ihn zum ersten Mal zu schmecken. Seine Hand blieb an der Basis, als sie mit seinen Hoden spielte, sie leckte und spürte, wie sie anspannten. Seine Augen brannten, als sie mit der Zunge eine glitzernde Spur auf seinen Handrücken zeichnete, um sich dann an seinem harten Schaft emporzutasten. Er hielt ihr seine Erektion entgegen und sie nahm sie Stück für Stück auf. Ein mitreißendes Stöhnen entfuhr ihm. Sie schob seine Hand beiseite, legte ihre eigene an ihre Stelle und streichelte seine Härte, während sie sie tief in ihren Mund aufnahm. Ihre Wangen wurden hohl, wenn sie sich zurückzog, um ihn gleich darauf wieder weit in sich aufzunehmen. Sie wollte nicht, dass er kam, noch nicht. Aber sie wollte ihm dieselben Wonnen bereiten, die er ihr geschenkt hatte. Sie wollte diese Intimität für sie beide.

Mit der Hand an seinem Schaft ließ sie sich wieder auf das Bett sinken und sah Sam dabei unverwandt an.

»Kondom«, sagte er.

Sie strich mit seiner Länge über ihre Schamgegend und zog ihn herunter. »Ich will dich zuerst an mir fühlen.«

»Himmel, Baby«, flüsterte er, als er seine kräftigen Arme

unter ihre Schultern schob und ihr Gesicht in beide Hände nahm. »Du stellst meine Selbstbeherrschung auf eine harte Probe.«

Sein Mund stahl sich auf ihren, ihr Atem floss ineinander, während seine Zunge zwischen ihre Lippen drang. Ihre Hände fuhren über seinen Rücken zu seinem nackten Hintern. Sie packte die festen Kuppeln und ließ seine Hüften auf- und niederwippen. An ihren Lippen stieß er einen knurrenden Laut aus, der all ihre Entschlossenheit dahinfegte.

»Kondom«, sagte sie und streckte die Hand aus.

Auf seinen Lippen spielte ein Lächeln, als er ihre tastenden Finger mit seinen verschränkte und sie mit einem atemberaubenden Kuss festhielt.

»Sam!«, keuchte sie zwischen zwei Küssen. »Ich halte es nicht mehr aus.«

Er ließ den Kuss tiefer werden, riss sich dann los, und ihr ganzer Körper erschauderte. Sein durchdringender Blick hatte etwas von einem Raubtier, doch hinter diesem Hunger entdeckte sie das, was er wirklich suchte, und sie schloss ihn umso mehr in ihr Herz.

»Liebe mich, Sam. *Jetzt.*«

Er schnappte sich ein Kondom, riss es mit seinen Zähnen auf, hatte es in Sekundenschnelle übergestreift und beugte sich nun über sie. Ihre Knie öffneten sich weiter, als er sich langsam auf sie senkte und sein Oberkörper ihre Brust berührte. Er fühlte sich so gut, so warm und so stark an. Sie dachte, er würde in sie hineinstoßen, unfähig, sich noch einen Augenblick länger zurückzuhalten, doch Sam war immer für eine Überraschung gut.

Er gab ihr bedächtige, schillernde Küsse und zündete ein Feuerwerk in ihren Kniekehlen, in den Armbeugen und an anderen Stellen, von denen sie nie geahnt hätte, dass sie Funken sprühen konnten. Er drang langsam in sie ein und küsste sie, während sich ihr Körper dehnte, um seine Härte aufnehmen zu können, bis er ganz in ihr begraben war. Ihre Blicke trafen sich, ihre Gier war zu einem hemmungslosen, sinnlichen Raunen geworden, als sie sich zu bewegen begannen und ihren Rhythmus fanden. Sam bewegte sich kraftvoll und gebieterisch, packte ihre Hüften und wölbte ihren Körper ein wenig, bevor er in Tiefen vorstieß und Lustpunkte zum Glühen brachte, von denen sie nicht gewusst hatte, dass sie existierten. Sie spürte seine geballte Kraft unter ihren Händen, und als er sie erneut auf den Gipfel der Leidenschaft trieb, hielt er sie dort, keuchend und verzweifelt, bis sie es kaum noch aushielt. Gerade als sie dachte, sie würde explodieren, wurden seine Stöße schneller und Spiralen der Ekstase zerbarsten in ihr.

»Sam«, rief sie.

Er blickte auf, sein Gesicht eine Maske aus Spannung und Männlichkeit. »Noch einmal«, sagte er mit zusammengebissenen Zähnen.

Er packte ihre Beine unter den Knien und schlang sie sich um die Taille, als er wieder und wieder diese geheime Stelle fand. Aus ihrer Kehle strömten Laute, die sie nicht zurückhalten konnte, als die Hitze sie durchdrang und sie sich bei jedem atemberaubenden Stoß aufbäumte. Sam richtete sich auf, den Körper fest und angespannt, und mit dem nächsten Stoß gab er sich der erlösenden Explosion hin. Sein heißer Atem strich über ihre glatte Haut, als er sie in die Arme schloss.

»Ich bin dir verfallen«, murmelte er mit rauer, satter Stimme. »Du besitzt mich.«

»Du bist kein Mann, den man besitzt«, erwiderte sie, obwohl ihr seine Worte, wie alles, was er sagte und tat, ein

Gefühl der Geborgenheit gaben. »Du bist ein Mann, den man erleben muss.«

»Nenne es, wie du willst, aber in deinem Herzen solltest du wissen, dass du mich besitzt.« Er küsste sie auf die Stirn. »Ich bin gebrandmarkt und glücklich darüber.«

Faith stockte der Atem. Sollte sie es wagen, ihm zu glauben?

Lange lagen sie eng umschlungen da. Irgendwann stand Sam auf und ging in seiner ganzen nackten Pracht ins Badezimmer, um das Kondom abzustreifen. Faith schoss der Gedanke durch den Kopf, dass er in den Spiegel sehen und sich an den Sam erinnern könnte, als den ihn alle kannten – und in den er sich vielleicht zurückverwandeln wollte. Ihr Herz zog sich bei dieser Vorstellung schmerzhaft zusammen. Sie dachte an seine zärtlichen Worte, an seine Aufrichtigkeit, aber sie musste auch realistisch sein. Sie setzte sich auf, das Laken über der Brust zusammengerafft, und wartete auf den vernichtenden Schlag.

Sam kam aus dem Badezimmer, und mit einem Blick auf sein zufriedenes Lächeln und die Emotionen in seinen Augen wusste sie, dass sie nichts zu befürchten hatte. Nun galt es nur noch herauszufinden, wie es sich *wirklich* anfühlte, *Bradens Braut* zu sein.

Sam hatte es letzte Nacht nur mit Mühe geschafft, sich von Faith zu verabschieden. Nichts hatte ihn auf die Gefühle vorbereitet, die ihn beim Liebesspiel überwältigt hatten. Er wollte nicht nur bei ihr bleiben, er wollte auch eine Schublade in ihrer Kommode belegen und seine Zahnbürste zu ihrer auf den Waschbeckenrand im Badezimmer legen. Für einen Mann, der sich früher kaum jemals die Telefonnummer der Frauen notiert hatte, mit denen er schlief, und schon gar nicht die Nacht bei ihnen verbrachte, waren solche Wünsche geradezu lächerlich. Es war verrückt. *Wahnsinnig.* Und was noch schlimmer war: Er hatte es so sehr gewollt, dass er Angst bekam, er würde sie erdrücken, sie einengen, zu viel von ihrer Zeit beanspruchen. Mittlerweile konnte er darüber nur noch den Kopf schütteln. Frauen liebten Aufmerksamkeit, oder? Aber sie hatte ihn nicht gebeten zu bleiben, also hatte er vielleicht Grund, sich Sorgen zu machen. Noch nie hatte er so intensiv über eine Frau nachgedacht. Wer immer auch behauptet hatte, die Liebe wachse mit der Entfernung, lag vollkommen richtig damit. Inzwischen waren mehr als fünfzehn Stunden vergangen, er hatte einen langen Arbeitstag hinter sich und war nun zu Faiths Wohnung gefahren, um sie zu ihrer Verabredung abzuholen, und hätte sich doch wahrhaftig immer noch selbst in den Hintern treten können, weil er nicht über Nacht geblieben war.

Anstatt mit ihr in den Armen einzuschlafen, war er nach Hause gegangen und hatte Cole eine weitere Nachricht geschrieben und ihn gebeten, ihn auf der Stelle anzurufen, sobald er am nächsten Samstagmorgen in Peaceful Harbor ankam. Sam wollte auf keinen Fall riskieren, dass sein Bruder von irgendjemand anderem erfuhr, dass er mit Faith zusammen war. Er wusste, dass Cole sein Handy ausgeschaltet hatte. Für den Notfall hatte er seiner Familie die Nummer des Hotels gegeben, in dem er mit seiner Frau die Flitterwochen verbrachte. Sam überlegte hin und her, ob er versuchen sollte, ihn dort zu erreichen, aber um einen Notfall ging es ja streng genommen nicht. Nur um Faiths Seelenruhe.

Sam nahm zwei Stufen auf einmal, bis er voller Vorfreude vor ihrer Wohnungstür stand. Sie hatten sich tagsüber geschrieben, aber das war nichts im Vergleich zu dem Gefühl, Faith in den Armen zu halten. Wie konnte es bloß sein, dass sich ein paar Stunden wie ein ganzes Leben anfühlten?

Er hatte kaum geklopft, da ging die Tür schon auf und Faith stand in Shorts und einem Bikinioberteil da, das jede ihrer köstlichen Rundungen unter der offenen Rough-Riders-Jacke hervorblitzen ließ. Ihr Anblick war unwiderstehlich, von ihrem schönen Gesicht bis hin zu ihren langen Beinen, die sich so verführerisch um seine Taille geschlungen hatten, als sie kam.

In ihrem Lächeln lag mehr als ein Hauch von Versuchung. »Vermutlich ist es okay so?«

»Du siehst geradezu sündig aus.« Er hatte sie gebeten, sich Badezeug anzuziehen, aber jetzt überlegte er, ob das geplante Date wirklich eine gute Idee war. Wie sollte er den Abend überstehen, ohne über sie herzufallen? Er trat ein, schob ihre Jacke auseinander und legte ihr seine Hände um die Taille. Ihre Haut war warm und weich. Hinter ihm fiel die Tür ins Schloss.

Faith schlang ihm die Arme um den Hals und stellte sich auf die Zehenspitzen. »Ich denke, du musst mich jetzt küssen.«

»Ich mag es, wenn du kommunizierst.«

Hungrig fand sein Mund ihre Lippen. Der Kuss erregte ihn an all den richtigen Stellen. Sie presste ihre sanften Kurven an ihn und er konnte nicht widerstehen: Er musste einfach die Hände um ihren perfekten Hintern wölben und sich an dem Stöhnen weiden, das ihr entfuhr.

»Ich habe dich vermisst, Baby.« Er küsste sie erneut. Ihr Körper verschmolz mit seinem, als er einen Kuss an den anderen reihte, vom Hals bis hin zu der zarten Stelle direkt unter ihrem Ohr.

»Ich habe den ganzen Tag an dich gedacht.« Wieder stellte sie sich auf die Zehenspitzen, ihre Hände umklammerten seinen Nacken. »Du weißt doch, dass mich das wahnsinnig macht, oder?«

»Ja, das weiß ich.«

Sie bog den Kopf zurück, sodass er ihre zarte Haut noch besser liebkosen konnte, und wand sich in seinen Armen. Die süßen, verführerischen Laute, die sie dabei von sich gab, waren wie eine Einladung, der er kaum widerstehen konnte. Seine Hand fuhr unter der Shorts am Rand ihres Bikinihöschens entlang, dann schob sich ein Finger unter den seidigen Stoff und tauchte in ihre Nässe ein.

»Mm. Zu wissen, dass du nass bist, macht mich verrückt.«

»Gott, Sam«, hauchte sie kaum hörbar.

Er zog seinen Finger zurück und küsste sie. Ihre Augen waren halb geschlossen, und er hätte schwören können, dass in ihr dieselbe Leidenschaft brannte wie in ihm, aber er brauchte Bestätigung. »Können wir spielen, Baby?«

»Von jetzt an brauchst du nicht mehr um Erlaubnis zu fragen, um mich zu berühren, es sei denn, ich sage ausdrücklich Nein.« Sie presste ihre Lippen auf seine, erkundete, suchte, *nahm* seinen Mund mit ihrer Zunge.

Sam hakte seine Finger in den Bund ihrer Shorts, riss sie mitsamt der Bikinihose herunter und schob Faith an die Wand hinter ihr. Auf ihren Wangen flammte erregte Röte auf, als er ihre Beine weit spreizte, bevor er sie erneut küsste.

»Mach die Augen zu«, sagte er und ließ seine Hände an ihren Schenkeln auf und ab gleiten. Als sie mit geschlossenen Augen dastand, wanderte seine flache Hand über ihren Bauch. Er liebte den rosigen Schimmer auf ihrer Haut und ihre erwartungsvollen Atemzüge, während er leise Küsse auf ihren Hals hauchte und mit den Fingern ihren Bauchnabel umrundete.

»Mmmh, wenn ich dich berühre, atmest du anders.« Seine Hand tastete sich weiter nach unten, bis sie die feuchte Spalte zwischen ihren Beinen erreicht hatte. Mit einem Finger strich er langsam von hinten nach vorn über ihre Klit, immer wieder. Ihr Atem ging stoßweise, sie schob die Hüften vor, doch er nahm die Einladung nicht an. Den Mund an ihren Hals gelegt, zog er ihr Bikinioberteil an einer Seite herunter, sodass ihre schöne Brust zum Vorschein kam. Derweil trieb sein Finger weiterhin sein Spiel mit ihrem geschwollenen Geschlecht.

»Wenn ich deine Brustwarze reize, spürst du es hier« – er drückte seine Finger zwischen ihre Beine – »nicht wahr, Baby?«

»Ja«, flüsterte sie mit zittriger Stimme.

»Mal sehen, ob ich dich zum Höhepunkt bringen kann, ohne in deinen süßen Körper einzudringen.«

Ihr gepresstes Stöhnen feuerte ihn an.

Gestern Abend hatte sie gesagt, dass sie genommen werden wollte, und diese Worte spielten in seinem Kopf wie eine Melodie. Er leckte an ihrer Brustwarze, bis sie sich ihm steif und gierig entgegenstreckte, und drückte den Daumen auf die empfindliche Stelle zwischen ihren Beinen. Sie packte seinen Arm und drückte seine Hand, aber er weigerte sich, in sie einzutauchen.

»Nein, Baby. Vertrau mir. Lass dich gehen.«

Ihr Kopf fiel zurück und sie atmete schwer. Er zwirbelte ihre Brustwarze zwischen zwei Fingern, bis sie sich auf die Zehenspitzen stellte und seine Finger wieder zwischen ihre nassen Falten rutschte. Er rieb und sog und drückte und streichelte sie immer weiter auf den Gipfel der Leidenschaft. Ihre Hände krallten sich in seinen Arm, und er verschloss ihren Mund mit einem betörenden Kuss, der einen Wirbelsturm des Verlangens durch seinen Körper jagte. Seine Lust steigerte sich, drängte nach Erlösung, als sie seinen Namen rief. Ihr Geschlecht pulsierte an seiner Hand und bettelte darum, dass er in sie eindrang, aber er setzte sein unerbittliches Spiel fort.

»Das ist es, Baby.« Er sank auf die Knie, presste ihre zitternden Hüften gegen die Wand und bedeckte ihre tosende Mitte mit seinem Mund.

Sie ballte die Hände in seinen Haaren, bäumte sich auf und kam laut und hart. Kaum hatte sie den Höhepunkt überschritten, stieß sie keuchend seinen Namen aus.

»Sam. Ich brauche dich in mir«, bettelte sie und versuchte mit zitternden Händen, seine Boardshorts herunterzuschieben.

Er verschränkte seine Finger mit ihren und küsste sie. Dass sie sich an seiner Zunge, seinen Lippen, seinem Atem schmecken konnte, hätte ihn fast die Beherrschung gekostet. Er musste seine ganze Willenskraft aufbieten, um sie nicht an Ort und Stelle zu nehmen, aber er wollte so viel mehr mit Faith. Sie sollte wissen, dass das, was er für sie empfand, so weit über die körperliche Lust hinausging, dass sie es nie wieder in Frage stellte.

»Wir haben ein Date.«

Sie senkte ihre Lippen auf seine und küsste ihn, doch plötzlich riss sie sich los. »Moment mal, was war das?«

Der Klang ihrer Stimme ließ seine Entschlossenheit brüchig werden. »Unser Date?«

Mit Entschlossenheit in den Augen sah sie ihn an. »So lässt du mich nicht stehen. Nimm mich, Sam. Sofort.«

Die Welt um ihn herum verschwand in einem Wirbel der Begierde, als er ein Kondom aus seiner Brieftasche zog, seine Shorts herunterzerrte und die Latexhülle überstreifte. Mit einer einzigen Bewegung drang er tief in sie ein. Sie verharrten beide in der Hitze ihrer Vereinigung. Sie fühlte sich so gut, so eng, so willig an. Mit jedem Stoß und jedem animalischen Laut aus ihren Kehlen loderte die Leidenschaft noch heller auf, die sie verzehrte. Sie leckten und bissen, Mund, Schultern, Arme, Brust, alles, was sie zu packen bekamen. Die Geräusche ihres hektischen Liebesspiels erfüllten die kleine Wohnung. Seine Gedanken zersplitterten, bis nur noch ein einziger übrig war: *Faith. Faith. Faith.* Eine heiße Woge kündigte seine Erlösung an, und er hob sie in seine Arme und drückte sie noch tiefer auf seinen Schaft.

Ihr Kopf fiel nach hinten. »Oh Gott. Gleich … Ich komme.«

Er packte ihren Hinterkopf in einer ungestümen, besitzergreifenden Geste und presste seinen Mund auf ihren, wollte die Woge der Gefühle spüren, wenn sie den Höhepunkt erreichte. Ihr Innerstes zog sich um ihn zusammen und molk seine Ladung direkt aus ihm heraus. Jeder heiße Schwall trieb ihn höher und brachte sie näher zusammen.

Als die Lustwellen allmählich verebbten, war er in ihr verloren. Faith starrte in seine Augen und fuhr ihm mit dem Finger über die Wange. »Du bist all das, was ich nie für möglich gehalten hätte.«

Verstrickt in sie und seine alles verzehrenden Emotionen erwiderte er: »Und du bist genau so, wie ich immer wusste, dass du bist.«

Nachdem sie sich küssend und neckend geduscht und angezogen hatten, saßen sie endlich in Sams Truck und machen sich auf den Weg zu ihrem geheimen Ziel. Während sie die von Bäumen gesäumten Straßen entlangfuhren, hatte Sam den Arm um Faiths Schulter gelegt. Sie schmiegte sich an ihn und fühlte sie sich so entspannt wie lange nicht mehr. Vielleicht war Sex vor einem Date eine gute Idee. *Vielleicht sollte ich vor jedem Date kommen.* Bei dem Gedanken musste sie leise lachen.

»Was gibt's zu lachen?«, fragte er.

»Nichts. Ich denke nur nach.«

Er gab ihr einen Kuss auf die Schläfe und seine Augen wurden ernst. »Über uns?«

Entspannte sich sein Gehirn eigentlich jemals? Im Moment hatte es nicht den Anschein, aber in Zukunft vielleicht? Oder würde er immer bei ihr sein, mit Leib und Seele, mit all seinen Gedanken? Das, so stellte sie fest, wäre wohl die wunderbarste Sorge von allen.

»Ganz schön neugierig heute Abend, wie?« Sie konnte ihm unmöglich sagen, woran sie dachte. Es war schlimm genug, dass sie ihm befohlen hatte, sie zu *nehmen*. Sie hatte sich in einen Vamp verwandelt. Eine Femme fatale. *Eine monogame Schlampe.* Wieder lachte sie. *Oh, Mist!*

Er sah sie aus den Augenwinkeln an. »He, du feierst eine Party und ich bin nicht eingeladen?«

»Glaub mir, du willst nicht wissen, was mir durch den Kopf geht.« Natürlich war ihr klar, dass das nicht stimmte. Aber wenn sie ihm sagte, wie sehr sie ihr Liebesspiel genossen hatte, würde eins zum anderen kommen, und dann würden sie ihr Ziel nie erreichen, und sie war so gespannt darauf, was er sich für den Abend ausgedacht hatte.

Er bog auf einen Feldweg ein. Die tief stehende Sonne tauchte den Fluss in romantisch schimmerndes Licht. Sam parkte zwischen zwei hohen Bäumen und drehte sich zu Faith um. Seine Augen waren so warm, so liebevoll, dass ihre Gedanken Purzelbäume schlugen. Er fuhr ihr mit dem Daumen über die Lippen.

»Da liegst du absolut falsch. Wenn du lächelst, wird meine ganze Welt heller. Ich möchte wissen, was dich zum Lachen bringt. Und ich möchte wissen, was das Luder in dir hervorkitzelt«, sagte er und drückte ihr einen sinnlichen Kuss auf die Lippen.

»Wie schaffst du das?« Gedankenverloren zupfte sie mit den Zähnen an ihrer Unterlippe, nur um es gleich wieder sein zu lassen. *Lieber Himmel.* Er hatte sie voll im Griff, im besten Sinne des Wortes.

»Was meinst du?«

»Du gibst mir das Gefühl, als könnte ich dir alles sagen. Als wollte ich dir alles sagen.«

Er hielt ihren Blick gefangen, und die Anziehungskraft zwischen ihnen, die ihr mittlerweile so vertraut war, schien stärker als je zuvor.

»So wie du in mir den Wunsch weckst, ein besserer Mann zu werden.«

»Sam.« Es war ihr egal, wie verträumt ihre Stimme klang. Sie fühlte sich wie in einem Traum. Er war ein Traum. »Bist du Frauen gegenüber immer schon so aufrichtig gewesen? Deine Offenheit ist entwaffnend.«

»Ich habe dir ja gesagt, dass ich immer ehrlich bin. Komm mit.« Er führte sie um den Truck herum und holte zwei Schlauchreifen von der Ladefläche.

Wie konnte ich die übersehen? Eigentlich wusste sie die Antwort: All ihre Aufmerksamkeit war auf einen großen, dunklen, verführerisch ehrlichen und heißen Mann gerichtet. Er reichte ihr eine Kühlbox, warf sich eine Decke über die Schulter und klemmte sich zwei Handtücher unter den Arm.

»Machen wir Tubing?«, fragte sie aufgeregt lächelnd. Sie hatte diese Sportart kennengelernt, als sie gerade nach Peaceful Harbor gezogen war.

»Ist das okay?«

»Mehr als okay. Aber wo sind wir hier? Diesen Teil des Flusses habe ich noch nie gesehen.«

»Weil er in meinem Privatbesitz ist.« Er wies mit dem Kopf auf ein Wäldchen am Ufer. Über den Baumkronen war ein Dachfirst zu sehen.

»Du lebst hier? Am Wasser? Das wusste ich nicht.« Ein Haus in den Wäldern, mit einem Zugang zum Fluss. Das passte zu ihm und seiner Vorliebe für alles, was mit Wasser zu tun hatte, eine Umgebung, wie für ihn gemacht.

»Ich besitze ein paar Hektar Land. Nate und Jewel wohnen

um die nächste Kurve, nicht weit von meinem Haus. Aber von Paradise Cove darfst du niemandem erzählen.« Er führte sie zwischen den Bäumen hindurch zum Ufer.

Sie lächelte. »Paradise Cove? Die Paradiesbucht?«

»Mach dich bloß nicht lustig darüber. Es ist meine Bucht, also suche ich den Namen aus.«

Am Saum des Wassers ließ er die Gummischläuche und die Handtücher fallen, breitete die Decke am sandigen Ufer aus und nahm ihr die Kühltasche ab. Dann stemmte er die Hände in die Hüften und musterte Faith genüsslich von Kopf bis Fuß. Sein Blick hinterließ eine Flammenspur auf ihrem Körper. »Okay, ziehen wir uns aus«, meinte er und zwackte vielsagend mit den Augenbrauen.

»Typisch Mann.« Mit gespielter Verzweiflung verdrehte sie die Augen. »Das hatten wir doch gerade erst.«

»Ich meinte nicht, dass wir rummachen sollen, obwohl …« Er streifte sein Hemd ab und warf es auf die Decke. »Baby, das eben in deiner Wohnung war nur die Vorspeise. Schnell und schmutzig.« Seine Augen wurden sündig, als er die Lücke zwischen ihnen schloss und sie in die Arme nahm. »Du bist heute noch nicht richtig geliebt worden und wir haben so viele Jahre nachzuholen.« Er küsste ihren Nacken, ihr Ohr, ihre Wangen, ihre Nase.

Seine verspielte Munterkeit brachte sie zum Lachen. »So viele Jahre?«

»So viele, dass man sie gar nicht mehr zählen kann«, sagte er und nahm ihren Mund in Besitz.

Guter Gott, er konnte wirklich küssen. Sein Mund hypnotisierte sie, er war hart und schnell, dann wieder weich und sinnlich, ohne sich von ihren Lippen zu lösen. Wenn er sie in den Armen hielt, als wollte er sie nie wieder gehen lassen, durchfuhr sie ein sengender Blitz. Sie stellte sich auf die Zehenspitzen und merkte jetzt erst, dass sie ihn förmlich ansprang, ihre Hüften an seinen rieb und die Finger in seinen Rücken krallte. Grundgütiger, sie wurde schon wieder feucht zwischen den Beinen. Er war ohne Zweifel die beste Art von Sucht, die sie sich vorstellen konnte. Ein Zwölf-Schritte-Anti-Sam-Programm? Nein danke.

Sie wand sich aus seinen Armen und lächelte über ihre intensive Verbundenheit. »Ich werde noch ganz verrückt nach Sex.«

»Es ist doch nichts dagegen einzuwenden, wenn du den Mann an deiner Seite begehrst.« Er packte sie und knabberte an ihrem Hals.

»Ach du lieber Gott. Sam!« Lachend und keuchend riss sie sich los. »Irgendwann bin ich so weit, dass ich bei jedem Kuss lauter schmutzige Sachen machen möchte, egal wo wir gerade sind.« Sie schnappte sich einen Gummischlauch und stolzierte zum Wasser.

Plötzlich baumelten ihre Beine in der Luft. Sie kreischte und trat um sich, als er sie unter einem Arm ins Wasser trug, während er seinen Schlauchreifen unter den anderen Arm geklemmt hatte.

»Sam!« Sie hatte Mühe, ihren Reifen festzuhalten. Mit einem Arm klammerte sie sich an seinen Hals, die Beine hatte sie um seine Taille geschlungen. »Das war dein Plan, oder? Dass ich ganz wild nach dir werde und mich wie ein Äffchen an dich kralle?«

»Ich wünschte, ich wäre so kreativ, aber die Wahrheit ist, dass du von hinten so sexy ausgesehen hast und ich nicht widerstehen konnte. Ich musste dich einfach packen.«

Wow, sie liebte es, das zu hören.

Ein rascher Kuss, dann ließ sie ihren Reifen los. Sam packte sie unter den Armen und setzte sie darauf. »Jetzt lass die Finger von meiner Badehose, und lass uns das Wasser genießen, bevor es dunkel wird.«

»Du bist echt nervig.«

Er sprang auf seinen Reifen und griff nach ihrer Hand. »Ich habe nie gesagt, du würdest es leicht mit mir haben.«

Sie legte den Kopf zurück und ließ sich mit geschlossenen Augen durch die Bucht treiben. »Aber jeder weiß, dass Sam Braden leicht zu haben ist.« Sie öffnete ein Auge, sah, dass er plötzlich die Kiefermuskeln anspannte, und bekam sofort ein schlechtes Gewissen. »Aber ich kenne den *echten* Sam und der ist komplizierter als ein Zauberwürfel.«

Zwanzig

In der Abendsonne ließen sich Sam und Faith durch die Bucht treiben. Außer ihren Stimmen war nur das friedliche Rascheln der Blätter und das Plätschern der Wellen zu hören, die an ihre Gummireifen schlugen. Sam hatte die Augen geschlossen. Auf dem Wasser schien er eher zu Hause zu sein als an Land.

Als Faith seine Hand drückte, schlug er die Augen auf. »Wie bist du zu Rough Riders gekommen? Wusstest du immer schon, dass es das ist, was du mit deinem Leben anfangen willst?«

»Wasser, Klettern, Fallschirmspringen, das war immer mein Ding. Ich habe so gut wie keinen Abenteuersport ausgelassen. Auf dem College habe ich Geologie und Umweltingenieurwesen studiert und gleichzeitig versucht, herauszufinden, was ich später einmal machen wollte. Und natürlich war es mir wichtig, mit dem Abschluss meine Eltern zu beruhigen.«

»Deine Eltern scheinen sehr nett zu sein, obwohl ich sie nicht so gut kenne.«

»Das wird sich bald ändern«, sagte er leichthin und ihr wurde bei diesen Worten ganz warm ums Herz. »Mein Vater ist ein typischer Ex-Militär, und meine Mutter, tja, sie ist eigentlich das genaue Gegenteil von ihm. Dad bestand darauf, dass wir alle einen Abschluss machen, und am liebsten hätte er es gesehen, dass wir in seine Fußstapfen treten und zur Armee gehen. Aber ich wusste schon bald, dass das nichts für mich ist. Ich bin zu rebellisch, zu unruhig. Nate« – seine Miene wurde nachdenklich und ein leichter Schmerz schwang in seiner Stimme – »ist der Einzige von uns, für den diese Art zu leben wie geschaffen war.«

Faith hatte gehört, dass Jewels Bruder bei einem Auslandseinsatz ums Leben gekommen war und dass Nate sich selbst die Schuld dafür gab. Näheres wusste sie jedoch nicht.

»Jedenfalls habe ich Praktika in Geologie und Ingenieurswesen gemacht, aber ich wollte mehr. So kindisch es auch klingen mag, ich wollte nicht, dass jemand anders meinen Tagesablauf bestimmt.«

»Das ist nicht kindisch. Es klingt eher so, als hättest du dich selbst gut genug gekannt, um zu wissen, womit du glücklich werden würdest.«

»Ich war nicht so zielstrebig, wie ich hätte sein sollen. Nach dem College bin ich ein Jahr lang herumgereist, bin gewandert, mit dem Rucksack auf dem Rücken, und habe in Hostels übernachtet oder gezeltet. Einmal war ich mit meinem Cousin Wes, der dort draußen lebt, in den Colorado Mountains unterwegs, und er schlug vor, dass ich mir Anbieter von Abenteuertouren ansehen sollte. Damals war Rough Riders nur ein Bootsverleih mit fünf Kajaks. Kaum der Rede wert.«

Er zog ihren Reifen näher an seinen. »Du hast dich zu weit weg angefühlt.« Er lächelte, während er die Reifen zusammenhielt, und sagte: »Ich habe mich mit dem Mann getroffen, dem die Firma gehörte, und er wollte sich zur Ruhe setzen. Er verlangte nicht viel dafür, weil der Laden kaum etwas abgeworfen hat.«

»Hattest du keine Angst, dass es schiefgeht und du dein ganzes Geld verlierst?«

Er schüttelte den Kopf. »Angst hatte ich nie. Ich war

begeistert und konnte es kaum erwarten, mich mitten ins Getümmel zu stürzen und dem Ganzen meinen Stempel aufzudrücken. Ty war zu diesem Zeitpunkt etwa neunzehn, aber er kletterte schon seit Jahren, und wir sind im Sommer zusammen losgezogen, seit er ein Teenager war. In der Anfangszeit von Rough Riders hat er mir sehr geholfen. Er wusste, welche Art von Abenteuertouren ich anbieten sollte, welche Ziele ich ansteuern, was ich akzeptieren und wo ich meine Grenzen ziehen sollte. Schon damals war er wie ein wandelndes Lexikon. Er ist so verdammt schlau, dass es mich manchmal echt umhaut.«

Sie wusste, dass er und Ty sich nahestanden, aber sie hatte keine Ahnung, dass ihre Freundschaft so tief ging. »Du bist also einfach eingestiegen? Und deine Eltern haben nicht versucht, dich davon abzubringen?«

»Ja, eigentlich schon. Ich glaube nicht, dass mein Vater von meiner Idee begeistert war, aber er kannte mich gut genug und wusste, dass er mich nicht würde umstimmen können. Im Gegenteil, wenn er versucht hätte, mir die ganze Sache auszureden, hätte ich mich erst recht in den Gedanken verbissen. Er erklärte mir, worauf ich mich als Unternehmer gefasst machen müsste. Wer weiß? Vielleicht war das seine Art, mich davon abzubringen? Aber ich glaube, er wollte mich nur auf die raue Wirklichkeit vorbereiten. Er hat mir alle möglichen Anlaufstellen und Netzwerke genannt, wo ich Erkundigungen über Saisonbetriebe und die Auswirkungen von Rezessionen auf Unternehmen wie meines einholen konnte. Das waren sehr wertvolle Informationen, sie haben mir geholfen, viele der üblichen Fallstricke zu umgehen.«

»Und deine Mutter?« Maisy Braden hatte Faiths Herz erobert, als sie ihr die Sorge um ihren Sohn offenbart hatte. *Bitte brechen Sie meinem Jungen nicht das Herz. Er kann hart wie*

Stein sein, aber er hat einen weichen Kern.

Seufzend sah Sam in den Abendhimmel. »Meine Mutter hat uns immer gesagt, wir müssten das lieben, was wir tun, was immer es auch sein mag. Mein Vater ist für berufliche Sicherheit und Stabilität zuständig und meine Mutter kümmert sich ums Seelenheil. Sie ergänzen sich gut.«

Als er Faith ansah, war sein Blick warm und gefühlvoll, und sie wusste, dass sie keinen Tag mehr ohne diesen Ausdruck in seinen Augen verbringen wollte.

»Erzähl mir etwas über die Abenteuertouren«, sagte sie. Allmählich dämmerte ihr, dass sie kaum etwas über sein Unternehmen wusste, außer dass er Bootsfahrten anbot.

»Ich organisiere alle möglichen Expeditionen, meistens in der Nebensaison. Bergtouren, Klettertouren, Campingausflüge, Raftingtouren.«

»Du reist also viel?«

»In manchen Monaten mehr als in anderen.«

Sie nickte und spürte, wie sich ein Riss in ihrem Herzen auftat. Sie würde ihn schrecklich vermissen, wenn er unterwegs war.

»Hey.« Seine Stimme wurde nachdenklich. »Das kriegen wir hin. Es ist ja nicht so, dass ich die ganze Zeit weg bin. Manchmal nur zwei oder drei Nächte. Ich habe einen Kumpel, Cal, der mir bei den Reisen in den Westen hilft, und jetzt, wo Tex mit an Bord ist, muss ich nicht mehr jede Tour selbst leiten.«

»Ich will nicht in dein Unternehmen hineinfunken, Sam. Wenn du wegmusst, packe ich mir die Kühltruhe mit Eis voll und versuche, nicht daran zu denken, wie du auf einem Berg oder einem Fluss unterwegs bist und holde Jungfern in Not um deine Aufmerksamkeit streiten.« Sie wandte den Blick ab. Bei dem bloßen Gedanken krampfte sich ihr der Magen zusammen.

»Hey, Süße«, sagte er mit einem so liebevollen Tonfall, dass sie aufsah.

Der Ausdruck in seinen Augen kittete den Riss in ihrem Herzen. Jedes Mal, wenn sie an ihm zweifelte, sagte ihr ein Blick in seine ehrlichen Augen, dass dieses Gefühl reine Verschwendung war.

»Das sollte kein Dealbreaker sein, Faith. Ich möchte, dass das funktioniert, was wir zusammen haben, und ich werde alles dafür tun. Und was Frauen angeht: Ich trenne strikt zwischen Arbeit und Vergnügen. Bei meinen Touren habe ich mich nie auf irgendwelche Techtelmechtel eingelassen, Cole sei Dank. Er hat es mir wieder und wieder eingebläut, als ich Rough Riders gekauft habe.«

Sie stellte sich ihren Chef vor – den klugen, professionellen, fürsorglichen Dr. Braden –, wie er Sam eine Standpauke über Geschäft und Sex hielt. Der Gedanke allein war befremdlich, noch abwegiger erschien ihr jedoch die Vorstellung, dass sich Sam solche Belehrungen über sein sehr aktives Sexleben angehört haben sollte. Daran erkannte sie, dass Sam seinen Bruder respektierte und dass er sein Geschäft nie aufs Spiel gesetzt hätte. Und sie würde ihn nicht bitten, es ihretwegen zu tun.

Er setzte sich auf und balancierte so gekonnt auf dem Reifen, dass sie ihn hätte küssen können, wenn sie es versucht hätte. Der eindringliche Blick in seinen Augen hielt sie jedoch davon ab, es zu versuchen.

»Ich hatte bisher keinen Anlass, meine ursprünglichen Geschäftspläne zu überdenken, aber das bedeutet nicht, dass ich es nicht tun kann oder tun werde. Ich habe dir gesagt, dass ich dich nicht im Stich lasse, und ich meinte es ernst. In der Nebensaison hat mich nichts an diese Gegend gebunden.« Er ergriff ihre Hand. »Bis jetzt.«

Einundzwanzig

Die Sonne versank am Horizont, als sie es sich auf ihrer Picknickdecke gemütlich machten. Sam schenkte ihnen ein Glas Wein ein und begann, das Abendessen auszupacken, das er zubereitet hatte. Die Abenteuertouren in der Nebensaison gingen ihm nicht aus dem Kopf, und er überlegte hin und her, wie er es so hinbekam, dass er mit Faith zusammen sein konnte. Die Vorstellung, länger von ihr getrennt zu sein, gefiel ihm überhaupt nicht, aber bis jetzt war ihm noch keine Lösung eingefallen.

»Also, wir haben einen griechischen Orzo-Salat mit Shrimps und Gemüse. Gutes Essen braucht ein paar Farbkleckse, sonst schmeckt es nicht, finde ich.« Er zwinkerte ihr zu. »Dann hätte ich noch Wassermelonen-Gurken-Salat, Zuckererbsen, Salat mit Radieschen aus Tempests Garten und Baguette im Angebot. Viel ist es nicht, aber es ist leicht und lecker. Und zum Nachtisch …« Er warf eine Packung Skittles auf die Decke.

»Du magst sie also wirklich?«

»Ich bin immer ehrlich, wie ich schon sagte«, erwiderte er nicht ohne Stolz.

»Sam, das sieht köstlich aus. Hast du das alles zubereitet? Wann denn bloß?«

»Ich bin zwar ehrlich, aber alle meine Geheimnisse kann ich dir trotzdem nicht verraten. Außerdem werde ich mir immer Zeit für uns nehmen.«

Sie sah ihn an, als sähe sie ihn zum ersten Mal, mit großen staunenden Augen. »Oje. Mein Abendessen besteht normalerweise aus einem Müsliriegel und Eiscreme.«

»Hey, ein Mann muss beizeiten lernen, für sich selbst zu sorgen. Und wenn du nächtelang in den Wäldern schläfst, bereiten dir die kleinen Dinge umso mehr Freude, die du für selbstverständlich hältst, wenn du ein Dach über dem Kopf hast.«

»Ich wette, das Jahr, in dem du umhergezogen bist, hat bei deinen Überlebensfähigkeiten Wunder gewirkt. Vielen Dank für all die Mühe, die du dir gemacht hast.« Sie spießte einen Shrimp auf und steckte ihn in den Mund. »Mm. Köstlich.«

Sie aßen und plauderten über Sams Jahr nach dem College und dann wandte sich das Gespräch wieder Rough Riders zu. Sam erzählte ihr, dass Lira jetzt für ihn arbeitete, und sie erwiderte, dass sie es auf der Website des WAC gesehen habe.

»Lira erwähnte auch, dass du eine Therapeutin gefunden hast, an die sie sich wenden kann«, sagte Faith.

»Eigentlich hat Tempe sie gefunden. Sie hat ein paar Therapeuten aufgetrieben, die bereit sind, über die Unterstützung eurer Mitglieder zu verhandeln. Ich bin mir nicht sicher, ob sie kostenlose Sitzungen oder Rabatte anbieten, aber ich habe ihre Info im Truck.«

»Du hast mit Tempe über meine Website gesprochen?«

»Am Morgen nach der Autowaschaktion habe ich mit meiner Familie zu Mittag gegessen. Tempe ist Musiktherapeutin und kennt so viele Leute. Ich habe sie einfach gefragt, ob sie von irgendjemand wüsste. Keine große Sache.«

»Sam, das ist eine riesige Sache. Danke.« Sie umarmte ihn. »Du hast so viel für uns getan: die Stelle für Lira, deine Spende, der Kontakt zu Brent und jetzt das. Vielen Dank.«

»Ich habe dir ja schon bei der Autowaschaktion gesagt, dass ich helfen will.«

Sie knabberte an ihrer Lippe. »Es tut mir leid, dass ich dir nicht geglaubt habe.«

»Ist schon okay. Ich hätte mir vielleicht auch nicht geglaubt.« Das strahlende Lächeln, mit dem Faith diese Bemerkung quittierte, wärmte ihn durch und durch. Sam räumte ihre Teller zusammen, stand auf und reichte ihr seine Hand. »Gehen wir ein Stück?«

»Ich finde es wunderbar, dass du so gerne spazieren gehst.«

»Umso mehr, wenn du bei mir bist.« Er nahm ihr Sweatshirt und half ihr, es anzuziehen. »Nicht, dass dir kalt wird. Schließlich ist dein Badezeug noch nass.«

Sie gingen am Ufer entlang und lauschten dem sanften Plätschern des Wassers.

»Wie bist du in Peaceful Harbor und in Coles Praxis gelandet? Wolltest du schon immer im medizinischen Bereich arbeiten?«

Sie nickte. »Ich helfe gerne anderen Menschen und interessiere mich sehr für Medizin.«

»Aber warum Peaceful Harbor? Es ist ja nicht gerade der Nabel der Welt.«

»Ich bin nicht weit von zu Hause aufs College gegangen und habe immer gedacht, ich würde meinen Abschluss machen, in meiner Heimatstadt arbeiten, heiraten ...« Nachdenklich blickte sie über das Wasser. »Dann kam alles anders, und es war zu schwierig, in Oak Falls zu bleiben, also habe ich online nach einem Job gesucht. Dabei fiel mir Coles Anzeige ins Auge. Nach

Oak Falls ist es nicht so weit, also kann ich nach Hause fahren, wann immer ich will, und Cole und Jon sind wirklich nett.«

»Also hast du dich ein paarmal mit ihnen unterhalten und warst hin und weg?«

»Ja, kann man so sagen.«

Es war nicht zu übersehen, dass noch mehr hinter dieser Geschichte steckte, und Sam wünschte, sie würde ihm genug vertrauen, um sie mit ihm zu teilen. Aber er wollte sie nicht drängen. Sie war hier, und das war ihm genug, bis sie bereit war, darüber zu reden.

Sie gingen zur anderen Seite der Bucht, kletterten auf einen großen Felsblock, ließen die Beine über den Rand baumeln und betrachteten den Mond, der sich auf der tintenschwarzen Wasseroberfläche spiegelte. Als Faith ihren Kopf an seine Schulter lehnte, hob er ihre Hand und drückte einen Kuss darauf. Seine Zuneigung für sie wurde jedes Mal ein bisschen größer, wenn sie zusammen waren. Die Worte seines Vaters kamen ihm in den Sinn: *Wenn du erst einmal davon gekostet hast und zum ersten Mal echte Liebe unter Erwachsenen erlebst, die jeden deiner Gedanken gefangen hält, wirst du alles dafür tun, um mehr davon zu bekommen. Du willst ganz darin eintauchen.*

»Ich habe Oak Falls verlassen, weil mein Freund mich betrogen hat.«

Faiths Stimme riss ihn aus seinen Träumereien und seine zärtliche Begeisterung sackte angesichts ihres Geständnisses in sich zusammen. Sein erster Gedanke war, dass er den Kerl umbringen wollte, der sie verletzt hatte, doch dann richtete er seine Aufmerksamkeit auf das Vertrauen, das sie ihm schenkte. Er nahm sie in die Arme.

»Das tut mir leid. Das muss sehr schmerzhaft gewesen sein.«

»Es war nicht lustig, so viel ist sicher. Er meinte, ich hätte ihn nicht genug beachtet, und sagte, ich wollte ihn eigentlich gar nicht. In meinem Leben sei kein Platz für ihn und ich könne ihn nicht glücklich machen. Es kam aus heiterem Himmel, um es gelinde auszudrücken. In meiner Heimatstadt zu bleiben, war danach keine Option. Wir waren schon so lange zusammen. Ich dachte, ich würde meinen Abschluss machen und JJ heiraten.« Sie zuckte die Achseln, aber der Schmerz in ihren Augen, in ihrer Stimme, war mit Händen zu greifen.

»Es war demütigend und es tat lange weh. Ich war immer davon ausgegangen, dass wir beide dasselbe wollten, und dann stellte sich plötzlich heraus, dass ich mich geirrt hatte.« Sie hielt inne und holte tief Luft. »Ich habe Monate gebraucht, um den Gedanken abzuschütteln, dass er mich betrogen hat, weil ich etwas falsch gemacht habe oder ihm irgendwie nicht genug war. Jetzt weiß ich, dass er mir tatsächlich einen Gefallen getan hat, dass es das Beste war, was mir passieren konnte. Aber damals? Ich glaube, ich war so beschäftigt mit Ausbildung und Arbeit, dass ich nicht groß darüber nachgedacht habe. Oder vielleicht habe ich nicht groß über ihn nachgedacht, was eigentlich noch schlimmer ist.«

»Baby, fremdgehen, jemanden betrügen, das ist keine Lösung.« Er musste sich zusammenreißen, um die Wut, die er auf diesen Mistkerl hatte, unter Kontrolle zu halten. »Selbst wenn ihr beide Probleme hattet, ist das nicht der Weg, damit umzugehen. Der Typ hatte dich nicht verdient.«

Sie sah ihn an. »Seltsam, dass ausgerechnet du das verstehst. Du sagtest doch, du hättest noch nie eine Freundin gehabt.«

»Ich habe gesagt, dass ich seit der Highschool keine Freundin mehr hatte. Seit ich sechzehn war, um genau zu sein.«

»Erste Liebe?«, fragte sie mit einem neugierigen Lächeln.

»Ich weiß es nicht. Das erste Mal für alles, denke ich«,

räumte er ein. »Aber ich war fast noch ein Kind. Ich wusste überhaupt nicht, was Liebe ist. *Die erste Verliebtheit* trifft es wahrscheinlich besser.«

»Und der erste Herzschmerz?«

»Der erste und letzte.« Er sah ihr in die Augen und verspürte das Bedürfnis, ihr zu erzählen, was er noch niemandem erzählt hatte. »Wir waren nur zwei Monate zusammen, aber mit sechzehn brannten unsere Hormone lichterloh, und jede Minute fühlte sich an wie ein ganzes Leben. Sie hieß Keira Jacobson und lebte zwanzig Minuten von Peaceful Harbor entfernt. Lieber Himmel, ich habe seit Ewigkeiten nicht mehr an sie gedacht. Aber damals konnte ich nur an sie denken. Wir haben uns bei einem Footballspiel kennengelernt, und danach haben wir uns ein paarmal in der Woche gesehen. Eines Tages war ich ein bisschen früher dran als sonst, ich weiß nicht mehr, warum. Vielleicht habe ich meine letzte Stunde geschwänzt oder so. Ich fuhr zu ihrer Schule und sah, wie sie einen anderen Kerl küsste.« Er zuckte die Achseln.

»Also hast du Schluss gemacht?«

Er schüttelte den Kopf. »Nicht sofort. Das war später am gleichen Abend, nachdem sie mir gesagt hatte, dass er ihr nichts bedeutete, er sei nur ein Freund und sie hätten sich hinreißen lassen – ein paar Mal.«

»Oh, Sam.« Sie kletterte auf seinen Schoß und schlang die Arme um seinen Hals. »Es tut mir leid. Ich finde es schrecklich, dass du am eigenen Leib erlebt hast, wie sich das anfühlt.«

Das Mitgefühl in ihren Augen war echt, und es berührte ihn umso tiefer, als sie wusste, dass er sich danach auf keine feste Beziehung eingelassen hatte. »Ich war jung und unerfahren. Ich habe sie einfach aus meinen Gedanken verdrängt und weitergemacht.«

»Und hast beschlossen, dass nichts für immer bleibt«, sagte sie. Sie wusste noch genau, was er über Wabi-Sabi gesagt hatte. »Dann war das der Anfang deines unverbindlichen Lebensstils.«

»Das weißt du noch?«

»Ich erinnere mich an alles, was du sagst. Es grenzt schon an Obsession.« Sie nahm sein Gesicht in beide Hände und küsste ihn. »Denk nicht schlecht von mir.«

Als er das neckische Glitzern in ihren Augen sah, hätte er am liebsten erwidert, wie wunderbar er es fand, dass sie sich an seine Worte erinnerte. Dass er ihre Obsession sein wollte. Und das würde er nicht nur zum Spaß sagen, sondern es war ihm ganz ernst damit.

»Warum sollte ich schlecht von dir denken? Ich finde, du bist unglaublich mutig. Du bist von deiner Familie, deinen Freunden, der Zukunft, die du geplant hattest, weggezogen und hast in einer fremden Stadt ganz von vorn angefangen.«

»Musst du gerade sagen. Du stürzt dich in alle möglichen Abenteuer, die mir im Leben nicht in den Sinn kämen. Fallschirmspringen?« Sie verdrehte die Augen. »Hört sich schrecklich an.«

»Du wirst es mit mir zusammen probieren.« Er schlang ihr die Arme um die Taille. »Wir probieren alles zusammen. Aber es ist ein himmelweiter Unterschied, ob du dich traust, eine physische Herausforderung anzunehmen, oder den Mut aufbringst, alles hinter dir zu lassen, was du dein Leben lang kanntest. Ich lebe immer noch in meiner Heimatstadt, umgeben von Menschen, die mich bedingungslos lieben, und werde wahrscheinlich nie hier wegziehen.«

Sie sah ihn ernst und fragend an. »Das ist etwas anderes. Ich hätte meine Familie und Freunde nie verlassen, wenn ich mir sicher gewesen wäre, dass ich es aushalte, ständig meinem Ex über den Weg zu laufen. Aber es ging einfach nicht. Und du? Du warst mutig genug, hierzubleiben und das große Herz wegzusperren, das ich so lie– … so mag.«

Sam konnte das gierige Grinsen nicht zurückhalten, das sich auf seinem Gesicht ausbreitete. »Du liebst mein großes Herz.«

»Ich mag dein großes Herz.« Sie lehnte die Stirn an seine Brust. »Mag, mag, mag.«

Er brauchte es nicht zu hören. Er hatte die Gefühle in ihren Augen gesehen, und das würde ihm reichen, bis sie beide bereit waren zuzugeben, dass das, was zwischen ihnen geschah, alles übertraf, was sie je gefühlt hatten. Aber er konnte nicht widerstehen, er musste sie einfach aufziehen. »Und welche anderen großen Dinge liebst du sonst noch an mir?«

»Sam!« Flammende Röte überzog ihre Wangen.

Er zog sie in einen keuschen Kuss. »Ich liebe deine riesigen Brüste – ups, ich meine, dein riesiges Herz.«

Sie versetzte ihm einen spielerischen Schlag und beide lachten.

»Hör auf, an meine Brüste zu denken. Sag mir lieber, was mit Keira passiert ist.«

»Sie hatte keine großen Brüste.«

Wieder stupste sie ihn. »Typisch Mann! Ich meinte natürlich, wie es mit Keira weiterging. Hast du sie in den sozialen Medien oder so verfolgt?«

»Du kennst mich doch inzwischen gut genug. Jemanden zu verfolgen ist gar nicht meine Art. Obwohl ich es mir bei dir durchaus überlegen würde.« Er beugte sich vor und stahl sich einen weiteren Kuss. Er bewunderte Faith dafür, dass sie nicht eifersüchtig auf das war, was er für Keira empfunden hatte, und dass sie ihn nicht für seinen Lebensstil verurteilte.

»Soweit ich gehört habe, hat ihr Vater eine neue Stelle

angenommen, und kurz darauf sind sie weggezogen. Was ist mit dir? Hast du das große Herz dieses Kerls genauso geliebt wie meins?«

»Ich dachte, ich hätte ihn geliebt, aber …«

Sie biss sich auf die Lippe und er strich mit seinem Daumen darüber.

»Ich mag es, wenn du mich so berührst«, gestand sie leise.

»Und ich höre gerne, was du magst.«

»Sam, was ich jetzt sage, hört sich ziemlich abgedroschen an. Aber in diesen zwei Jahren habe ich für ihn nie das empfunden, was ich für dich empfinde, und wir sind erst seit ein paar Tagen zusammen.«

»Dito«, flüsterte er und küsste sie erneut. »Aber ich habe mich schon lange in dich verguckt. Schon als ich dich zum ersten Mal gesehen habe.«

»Dito.«

Sam hatte gewusst, dass er ihr nicht gleichgültig war. Warum sonst hätte sie so verlegen und nervös werden sollen, wenn er Cole in der Praxis besucht hatte? Es bereitete ihm jedoch ein ungeahntes Vergnügen, diese Worte aus ihrem Mund zu hören. »Du warst meine verbotene Frucht.«

»Verboten?«

»Cole hat mich gleich beim ersten Mal gewarnt.«

Ihre Augen weiteten sich.

»Du darfst ihm nicht böse sein. Er ist ein schlauer Bursche. Er will nicht, dass ich dein Leben ruiniere. Er schätzt und respektiert dich als Mitarbeiterin und dein Wohlergehen ist ihm wichtig. Und wie alle anderen in der Stadt weiß er leider nur zu gut, wie ich war. Zu gefährlich für jemanden wie dich.«

Er erinnerte sich an den Nachmittag in der Praxis, als sie das zu ihm gesagt hatte und wie zerrissen sie trotz ihres selbstbewussten und ernsthaften Auftretens ausgesehen hatte.

Faith wurde rot. Sie wusste noch genau, was sie da gesagt hatte, doch es dauerte nur einen Wimpernschlag, bis sie ihre Verlegenheit in den Griff bekam und zum Gegenangriff überging. »Ohne deinen Bucheinband bist du auch nicht übel.«

»Nicht übel, wie? Ich muss mir wohl mehr Mühe geben.«

Sie lehnte wieder den Kopf an seine Schulter. »Bleib einfach so, wie du bist. Ich mag meine Version von Sam wirklich.«

Er wusste, er würde nie aufhören, der beste Mann zu sein, der er für sie sein konnte. Nicht in einer Woche, einem Monat … vielleicht ein Leben lang?

Zweiundzwanzig

Sam und Faith blieben noch lange am Wasser, redeten und küssten und streichelten sich und taten alles, um das Ende ihres Dates hinauszuzögern. Faith sah zu, wie Sam die Handtücher und die Decke hinter den Sitzen im Truck verstaute, und in ihrer Brust ballte sich ein beklemmendes Gefühl zusammen. Sie überlegte sich einen Vorwand nach dem anderen, um noch nicht nach Hause zu fahren. *Wir könnten Eis essen gehen. Einen Spaziergang am Strand machen. Tanzen gehen.* Aber dazu müsste sie sich erst umziehen, und eigentlich wollte sie weder Eis essen noch spazieren oder tanzen gehen. Sie wollte einfach Zeit mit Sam. Um mehr über ihn zu erfahren, um in seinen Armen zu liegen. Die Wucht, mit der sie diese Sehnsucht traf, brachte sie aus dem Gleichgewicht.

Sie gingen um den Wagen herum zur Beifahrertür, und als er die Hand nach dem Türgriff ausstreckte, sagte sie: »Sam –«, genau in dem Moment, als er »Faith –« sagte.

Seine Lippen kräuselten sich zu einem Lächeln. »Du zuerst.«

Sie kämpfte gegen den Drang an, sich auf die Lippe zu beißen, kämpfte gegen die ängstliche Enge in ihrer Brust. Der liebevolle Blick in seinen Augen machte ihr Mut.

»Ich möchte nicht, dass der Abend endet.«

»Und ich überlege die ganze Zeit krampfhaft, wie ich dich in mein Haus kriege, ohne dass ich wie ein Lustmolch dastehe.«

»Okay.« Kaum war ihr das Wort über die Lippen geglitten, ließ das Gefühl nach, das ihr die Kehle zugeschnürt hatte. Mit Sam zusammen zu sein, war richtig. Seit dem Tag, an dem sie ihre Ausbildung zur Arztassistentin begonnen hatte, verspürte sie zum ersten Mal wieder diese Klarheit, die Gewissheit, dass sie die richtige Wahl getroffen hatte. Und als sie Sam ansah, der vor Glück nur so strahlte, wusste sie, dass sie auf den richtigen Weg zurückgefunden hatte.

Sams Haus lag am Ende einer Straße, die sich kilometerweit durch den Wald schlängelte. In Faiths Bauch flog ein ganzer Schmetterlingsschwarm auf, als sie die kiesbestreute Zufahrt hinunterfuhren und neben seinem Motorrad, einem Quad und einem Jeep zum Stehen kamen.

»Hast du Besuch? Du kannst mich ruhig nach Hause bringen, wenn es dir besser passt.«

Sein wortloser Kuss war ihr Antwort genug. »Willst du immer noch nach Hause?«

»Nur, wenn du auch kommst.« Ihre Augen weiteten sich. »Ich meine …«

»Du hast es genauso gemeint, wie du es gesagt hast, hoffe ich.« Er küsste sie erneut.

Dieser Kuss war anders, nicht so drängend und hungrig wie ihre Küsse früher am Abend, bevor sie zu ihrem Date aufgebrochen waren. Alles fühlte sich anders an, weniger hektisch, irgendwie realer. Im Laufe der letzten Stunden hatte sich ihre Beziehung geändert, etwas hatte sich verschoben. Oder vielleicht hatte diese Veränderung schon viel früher begonnen.

Sam stieg aus und half ihr aus dem Truck. »Ich habe keinen Besuch. Das sind meine Spielsachen.«

»Ah, das hätte ich mir ja denken können.«

Sams Holzhaus stand auf einem grasbewachsenen Hügel. Große Fenster, die fast alle offen standen, schauten auf das Wasser hinaus. Kein sorgsam gestalteter Garten, kein gepflegter Rasen, sondern scheinbar wild wuchernde Sträucher und Bäume umgaben das Anwesen wie willkürlich aufgestellte Wachposten. Faith musste an das denken, was er ihr über seine Suche nach Schönheit in Unvollkommenheit erzählt hatte. Zwei bunte Kajaks lagen halb im Gras verborgen am Waldrand und um eine Feuerstelle waren Stühle aufgebaut. Ein Holzsteg ragte auf das dunkle Wasser hinaus. Hier war es so friedlich, so anders als auf den Betonstraßen unter ihrem Balkon. Es war, als stünden sie in einer ganz anderen Welt und nicht nur ein paar Autominuten von der Stadt entfernt.

»Es ist wirklich schön hier draußen«, sagte sie, als sie die Stufen zur Veranda hinaufstiegen.

Er küsste sie. »Du bist wirklich schön hier draußen.«

Er zeigte seine Zuneigung so offen und küsste sie so oft und so zärtlich, dass sie seine Bekundungen mit Genuss erwartete. Es war ihr ein Rätsel, wie solch ein liebevoller Mann jahrelang ohne eine feste Beziehung leben konnte, aber sie schätzte sich glücklich. Wahrscheinlich mangelte es nicht an Frauen, die versucht hatten, sich Sam zu angeln, und wenn es ihnen gelungen wäre, hätte sie nie das Vergnügen gehabt, mit ihm zusammen zu sein.

Er öffnete die Eingangstür, die in einen Wohnbereich mit offener Küche führte. Mit seinen dunklen Möbeln, einem Holzofen und dunklen, breiten Holzdielen strahlte der Raum eine maskuline Behaglichkeit aus. An den Wänden hingen Bilder von Sam und seiner Familie und, so vermutete sie, seinen Freunden.

Er schaltete die Stereoanlage ein und eine sanfte Melodie schwebte durch den Raum. »Mach es dir gemütlich. Ich bin gleich wieder da«, sagte er und verschwand durch eine Tür links von der Küche.

Faith sah sich die Fotos an. Eines zeigte Sam an einem Seil hängend an einer Felsklippe. Seine Augen strahlten vor Freude. Auf einem anderen Bild saß er mit Ty und ein paar anderen Männern inmitten von Wasserstrudeln auf einem riesigen Floß. Sie ging von einem Bild zum nächsten und weidete sich am Anblick des hinreißenden Naturburschen, der sich immer mehr in ihr Herz stahl. Schließlich stand sie vor einem Foto, auf dem Sam und Cole mit Watstiefeln im kniehohen Wasser standen und angelten. Sams Haar war windzerzaust, die Wangen gerötet. Sie stellte sich einen jüngeren Sam vor, der gerade seine Firma gegründet hatte und Coles Ratschläge befolgte. Sie betete, dass ihre Beziehung zu Sam keinen Keil zwischen ihn und seinen Bruder treiben würde. Es beunruhigte sie ein wenig, dass Cole ihm geraten hatte, die Finger von ihr zu lassen, aber sie würde sich dadurch nicht die Laune verderben lassen. Eigentlich war das auch gar nicht möglich: Alles, was Sam tat, tat ihr gut.

Sie ging durch den gemütlichen Raum und kam zu einem Foto von Sam und seinen Eltern. Er sah aus wie ein mürrischer Teenager, mit schlaksigen Armen und Beinen, der dringend zum Friseur gemusst hätte. Wie es wohl gewesen sein musste, die Freundin dieses Sechzehnjährigen zu sein? Sie wünschte, sie hätte ihn damals gekannt. War er als Jugendlicher schon so liebevoll gewesen? Hatte er Keira auch das Gefühl gegeben, etwas Besonderes zu sein, so wie er es bei ihr tat?

»Das war auf der Ranch meines Onkels Hal in Weston in Colorado. Siehst du die Pferde im Hintergrund?« Sam schlang von hinten seine Arme um sie. Sein Atem roch nach Pfefferminze.

»Ich wünschte, ich hätte dich damals schon gekannt«, sagte er und drehte sie in seinen Armen. »Ich hätte aufgepasst, dass du dich nicht mit dem Kerl einlässt, der dir wehgetan hat.«

Ihr wurde warm ums Herz. »Und vielleicht hätte ich verhindern können, dass Keira dir wehtut.«

»Wenn ich doch bloß nicht so viel Zeit und Energie darauf verschwendet hätte, meine Gefühle für dich zu bekämpfen. Ich wünschte, ich hätte dich gleich gefragt, als ich dich zum ersten Mal gesehen habe.«

»Ich hätte mich nicht darauf eingelassen«, sagte sie ehrlich. »Ich war damals zu sehr verletzt. Ich war nicht bereit und wahrscheinlich warst du auch nicht bereit für mich.«

»Dann hoffe ich, dass wir diese Zeit nachholen können. Ich bin mir nämlich nicht sicher, dass mir die Zeit mit dir jemals reichen wird. Selbst wenn wir für den Rest unseres Lebens jeden Tag miteinander verbringen, werde ich wahrscheinlich immer noch das Gefühl haben, dass es nicht genug ist.«

War das möglich? Dass sie so schnell eine Welt voller Wünsche und Hoffnungen aufbauten? War es das, was mit Liebe gemeint war? Traf es einen aus heiterem Himmel, wenn man gar nicht auf der Suche war? Und dann auch noch mit jemandem, bei dem man es am wenigsten erwartet hätte?

Er rieb seine Nase an ihrer und wiegte sich im Takt der Musik. »Was sagt dieser Blick? Was denkst du?«

Ihre Körper waren so perfekt aufeinander abgestimmt, als würden sie seit Jahren zusammen tanzen, genau wie an jenem Abend auf dem Dach des Mr. B. Konnte es sein, dass ihre Herzen ebenso im Takt waren?

»Ich denke daran, dass dieses neue Wir so gigantisch ist«,

gestand sie. »Da sind so viele Gefühle.«

»So geht es mir auch. Lass uns nicht dagegen ankämpfen.«

Seine Lippen fuhren federleicht über ihre und sie atmete ihn tief in sich ein. Selbst sein Duft war ihr inzwischen vertraut. Ein einziger Hauch löste in ihr ein Gefühl von Geborgenheit und Verlangen aus. Sie tanzten langsam im Kreis, ihre Füße bewegten sich kaum und ihre Herzen stolperten übereinander. Sie drückte ihm einen Kuss auf die Brust, spürte jeden Punkt, an dem sich ihre Körper berührten, und genoss es, dass seine Hände besitzergreifend auf ihrem Rücken lagen. Wenn sie für immer so in seinen Armen bleiben könnte, würde sie als glückliche Frau sterben.

Sein Mund senkte sich lockend auf ihre Lippen. Sein Kuss war leidenschaftlich, ohne rau zu sein, und gab ihr das Gefühl, auf einer unsichtbaren Wolke höher und höher zu steigen. Kaum hatten sie sich voneinander gelöst, vermisste sie seinen Geschmack. Sie vermisste ihn, doch dahinter steckte kein gieriges Verlangen. Was sie empfand, war größer, eine deutliche Sehnsucht, die sich aus geheimen Quellen tief in ihrem Innern speiste. Versteckte Winkel, von denen sie gar nicht gewusst hatte, dass sie sich in Sehnsucht verzehren konnten, und die ihr das Gefühl gaben, an einem Abgrund zu stehen. Sam starrte sie an, und die unverfälschten Emotionen, die sie in seinen Augen sah, verzauberten sie. Sie hatte sich ganz und gar in ihm, in ihrem Wir verloren.

»Bleib heute Nacht bei mir«, flüsterte er an ihrer Wange und dann fand sein samtweicher, dunkler Blick ihre Augen. »Lass mich dich lieben, bis die Sterne verblassen, und dich halten, bis die Sonne aufgeht.«

Die Gefühle schnürten ihr die Kehle zu. Ihre Stimme klang wie ein Hauch. »Liebe mich, Sam.«

Sam verschränkte seine Finger mit ihren, und als er sie ins Schlafzimmer führte, wusste sie, dass sie sich an diesen Moment erinnern würde, an den Blick in seinen Augen und die zitternde, schmerzende Liebe, die für immer in ihr blühte.

Als er an seinem Bett stand, dem Bett, das er noch nie mit einer Frau geteilt hatte, in dem Holzhaus, das bisher sein Heiligtum gewesen war, erkannte Sam, dass sein Leben sich in zwei unterschiedliche Phasen aufgeteilt hatte. *Vor Faith* und *mit Faith.* Mit ihr in seine Lieblingsbucht zu fahren oder sie in sein Haus zu lassen, war ihm ganz selbstverständlich vorgekommen. Er streifte ihr ein Kleidungsstück nach dem anderen ab und küsste jedes Fleckchen Haut, das sich ihm offenbarte, bevor er sich nackt auszog. Er spürte die Hitze in Faiths hungrigem, liebevollem Blick, den sie über seinen Körper wandern ließ, und er wurde von Emotionen erfasst, die größer waren als alles, was er bisher erlebt hatte.

Er hielt ihren Blick gefangen, als er das Kondom über seine harte Länge zog und sie auf das Bett legte. »Ich möchte alles mit dir teilen«, flüsterte er.

»Ja, Sam. Alles«, sagte sie und streckte die Arme nach ihm aus.

Er nahm ihr Gesicht in beide Hände und gab all seine Gefühle in diesen Moment, diese Umarmung, diesen Kuss, als er in ihre enge Hitze sank. Sie hob die Hüften und zog ihn tiefer hinein. In seinem Kopf drehte sich alles von den gewaltigen Emotionen, die ihn verzehrten. Er verschränkte seine Hände mit ihren, bewegte seine Hüften und umschmeichelte ihre Lustpunkte. Ihr Körper bebte und wand sich unter ihm, als sie ihren Rhythmus fanden.

»Ich bin dir verfallen, Baby. Mit Haut und Haaren.«

Er nahm sich ihren Mund, und stieß nun schneller und härter zu. Ihre Finger krümmten sich um seine und ihre Augen schlossen sich.

»Mach die Augen auf, Baby. Lass mich sehen, was du fühlst.«

Flatternd öffneten sich ihre Augenlider und offenbarten Feuer, Lust und Hunger. Er hob sich ihre Beine um die Taille und verlangsamte seine Bewegungen. Er wollte, dass dieser Blick und diese Empfindungen, die sich steigerten, sich aufbauten und in ihm pulsten, nie vorbeigingen. Als sich ihre Fingernägel in seine Haut gruben, war der Schmerz so exquisit und so intensiv, dass er keinen einzigen Gedanken mehr festhalten konnte.

Ihre Schenkel spannten sich um ihn und wieder eroberte er ihren Mund.

Keuchend und flehend klammerte sie sich an ihn. »Sam. Sam –«

Ihr Körper wölbte sich, sie vergrub das Gesicht in seinem Nacken und ergab sich dem mitreißenden Höhepunkt. Lustvolle Schreie erfüllten den Raum, hallten in seinen Gedanken wider und zogen ihn weiter in sie hinein. Ihre feuchte Hitze ließ den Sog aus Verlangen immer schneller wirbeln, und als sie sich an seinem Rücken festkrallte und ihn in die Schulter biss, schwand der letzte Rest an Zurückhaltung dahin. Er hielt sie so fest, dass er Angst haben musste, sie zu verletzen, aber er war machtlos, konnte seinen Griff nicht lockern und kam und kam und kam.

Danach lagen sie lange da, ihre schweißglänzenden Glieder

ineinander verwoben. Sams Gedanken surrten und taumelten und trotzten jeder Anstrengung, sie festzuhalten. Als er von ihrem Körper glitt, rollte er zur Seite, und sie bewegte sich mit ihm, sodass sich ihre Nasen berührten.

Mit einem letzten Rest an Energie suchten ihre Lippen einander und stahlen sich matte, satte Küsse. Irgendwann, als er schon längst jedes Zeitgefühl verloren hatte, stand er auf und entsorgte das Kondom. Schwebend fanden sie in den Schlaf, wachten auf, liebten sich und schliefen wieder ein. Jedes Mal war es intensiver und intimer als zuvor, und als die ersten Sonnenstrahlen durchs Fenster schienen, war Sam so voll von Faith, dass er kaum an etwas anderes denken konnte.

Während sie schlief, strich er ihr die Haare aus der Stirn, drückte einen Kuss auf ihre weiche Haut und flüsterte: »Ich ertrinke in dir, Süße.«

Dreiundzwanzig

Für Faith gab wohl kaum etwas Schöneres, als in Sams Armen aufzuwachen. Ihre Zimmerpflanzen kümmerte es jedoch herzlich wenig, dass sie viel besser schlief, wenn sie sich an seinen wunderbaren Körper schmiegte, oder dass der atemberaubende Sex den Schlafmangel lohnte. Sie musste unbedingt daran denken, sie zu gießen, wenn sie das nächste Mal nach Hause kam. Seit einer unfassbaren, seligen Woche verbrachte sie die Nächte mit Sam in seinem Haus, und wenn sie kurz in ihrer Wohnung vorbeischaute, hatte sie es immer furchtbar eilig. Sie checkte die WAC-Website, packte hastig ein paar Sachen für den nächsten Tag zusammen oder gab sich Sams Küssen hin. So wie Joghurt und Gemüse in ihrem Kühlschrank vermutlich längst Schimmel ansetzten, drohte ihren Grünpflanzen ein schrecklicher Tod durch Verdursten.

Sam stand unter der Dusche und spülte Shampoo aus seinen Haaren. Sie liebte es, das seifige Wasser über seinen festen Körper tropfen zu sehen. Ach was, die Pflanzen konnten warten. Mit Sam zusammen zu sein, war viel besser. Er zog sie unter die Dusche und küsste ihren Hals. Sie hatten sich gerade geliebt und schon flammte neues Verlangen in ihr auf.

»Woran denkst du?«, fragte er zwischen zwei Küssen.

»An dich. An Sex. Und an meine Pflanzen, aber meistens an Sex. Mit dir.« Warum plapperte sie so albernes Zeug? Sie waren seit zwei Wochen zusammen und immer noch wirbelte er ihre Gedanken hoffnungslos durcheinander.

Er drehte das Wasser ab und trat aus der Dusche, um ein Handtuch zu holen.

»Hab ich ein Glück«, sagte er, als er es sich umwickelte und sie an seinen nass glänzenden Körper zog.

»Bist du nervös wegen Cole?«, fragte er und pflanzte träge, feuchte Küsse auf ihre Schulter.

Beiden standen heute schwierige Gespräche bevor. Sam bestand darauf, an Coles Haus zu warten, wenn er und Leesa von ihren Flitterwochen zurückkehrten, damit Cole aus seinem Mund erfuhr, dass er und Faith fest zusammen waren. Nach der Telefonkonferenz, die Faith mit einer Frauengruppe geplant hatte, stand endlich eine Aussprache mit Vivian auf dem Plan. Seit ihrem letzten Telefonat war Faith nicht drangegangen, wenn sie angerufen hatte. Ihr war klar, dass Vivian versuchte, sie zu schützen, aber ihre Zweifel an Sam ließen Faith ihre eigenen Überzeugungen in Frage stellen. Sie wollte ihre Beziehung nicht untergraben, vor allem, weil Sam sich solche Mühe gab. Sie glaubte an ihn und irgendwie musste sie es Vivian beibringen. Von nun an würde sie sich in ihrer Haltung zu Sam nicht mehr durch die Meinung andere Leute beeinflussen lassen. Vermutlich kannte sie ihn besser als jede andere Frau auf der Welt.

Sie schloss die Augen, schob die Gedanken beiseite und genoss das Gefühl seiner Lippen auf ihrer Haut.

»Faith?«

Ohne die Augen zu öffnen, sagte sie: »Ja?«

Als die Küsse aufhörten, sah sie ihn an. »Cole. Dein Boss.

Du erinnerst dich, oder? Großer, ernster Typ? Der mir gesagt hat, dass ich mich von dir fernhalten soll?«

»Was ist mit ihm? Oh! Tut mir leid.« Sie war so in ihren eigenen Gedanken versunken gewesen, dass sie seine Frage ganz vergessen hatte. »Nein, ich mache mir keine Sorgen, ob er unsere Beziehung akzeptiert.« Anfangs hatte sie der Gedanke nervös gemacht, dass Cole von ihrer Beziehung erfahren könnte, doch nun war sie viel ruhiger. Nein, es war eine andere Sorge, die sie beschäftigte. Keine große und drückende Sorge, aber eine, die nicht aufhörte, an ihr zu nagen. Sie wollte jedoch nicht darüber sprechen.

»Aber?« Sam sah sie ernst und erwartungsvoll an. Er verdiente die Wahrheit, auch wenn sie ihr nicht viel Gewicht beimaß.

»Aber da ist etwas anderes. Wirklich nur der Hauch einer Sorge. Wahrscheinlich kaum der Rede wert.«

»Das gibt es bei uns nicht, das weißt du doch. Jede Sorge ist es wert, dass man darüber redet.«

Er schaffte es immer wieder, sie zum Erzählen zu bringen. Es war eines der Dinge, die sie am meisten an ihm liebte, doch das bedeutete nicht, dass es ihr leichtfiel, darüber zu sprechen.

»Aber es ist wirklich nur eine winzigkleine Sorge.«

Er hob eine Braue und legte die Arme um sie. »Baby, du bringst mich noch um den Verstand.«

»Weißt du …« Sie fuhr ihm mit dem Finger über die Brust und hoffte insgeheim, sie könnte ihn damit ablenken. »Weißt du, was ich besonders an dir mag? Du bist immer bereit, dich allem zu stellen, sei es nun gut oder schlecht.«

»Weil es nichts gibt, mit dem wir nicht umgehen können.«

Das brachte sie zum Lächeln, und sie hatte das Gefühl, dass er recht hatte.

»Und?«, drängte er.

Verdammt. Selbst wenn sie damit umgehen konnten, fühlte es sich wie ein Verrat an, es auszusprechen, aber er hatte die Wahrheit verdient. »Also gut. Aber ich mache mir nicht wirklich Sorgen deswegen, okay? Ich habe über meinen Job nachgedacht. Was ist, wenn zwischen uns etwas passiert?«

»Falls wir uns trennen, meinst du?«

Sie zuckte mit der Schulter. Eigentlich wollte sie nicht einmal daran denken, dass sie sich trennen könnten, aber sie war nicht naiv. Schließlich hatte sie am eigenen Leib erfahren, dass Beziehungen in die Brüche gehen konnten, und sie versuchte, realistisch zu sein, auch wenn ihr eine Trennung sehr unwahrscheinlich vorkam.

Er küsste sie sanft. Das selbstbewusste Lächeln, das sie so sehr liebte, reichte bis zu seinen Augen. »Dann hast du wirklich nichts zu befürchten.«

Dass er ihre Beziehung mit solcher Arroganz betrachtete, fand sie wunderbar. Und wie immer glaubte sie ihm. »Dein Bruder wird glauben, dass ich dir Drogen ins Essen gemischt habe.«

Wortlos trocknete er sich ab, und als sie ihm ins Schlafzimmer folgte, hatte sie das Gefühl, dass er dasselbe dachte wie sie.

Als sie in ihr Höschen schlüpfte, war sie sich bewusst, dass er sie beobachtete. Sie hätte schwören können, dass er eine Fernbedienung hatte, die jedes Mal, wenn dieses lüsterne Schwelen in seinem Blick erschien, elektrische Ströme durch ihren Körper jagte. Dass er splitterfasernackt und offensichtlich erregt war, half nicht gerade.

Er kam zu ihr, die Augen so dunkel, dass ihr Herz dahinschmolz.

»Sam.« Sie schüttelte den Kopf und machte einen Schritt zurück.

Er trat näher. »Was ist?«

Sie legte ihm die Handflächen an die Brust und hielt Abstand zwischen ihnen, obwohl ihr hungriger Körper darum bettelte, von ihm berührt zu werden.

»Du sagtest doch, du wolltest bei Coles Haus auf ihn warten. Und ich habe in einer halben Stunde eine Telefonkonferenz mit einer Frauengruppe.« Außerdem hatte sie vorgehabt, die Hilfsangebote für die Mitglieder auf der Website des WAC zu veröffentlichen. Einige der Unternehmen, die sie per E-Mail angeschrieben hatte, hatten Links zu ihren Kontaktformularen gesendet, und die wollte sie den Mitgliedern so schnell wie möglich zur Verfügung stellen. Wenn sie sich jetzt mit Sam vergnügte, würde sie die Telefonkonferenz verpassen und Vivian einen weiteren Tag aus dem Weg gehen. Und danach wäre sie zu nichts zu gebrauchen. Sam liebte sie so, wie er alles tat: Er gab alles, was bedeutete, dass er auch die letzte Unze Energie aus ihr herauspresste. Sie genoss es. Sie verzehrte sich danach. Aber heute brauchte sie ihre Energie. Und ja, vielleicht war sie doch ein bisschen besorgt wegen seiner Unterhaltung mit Cole.

Er nahm ihre Hand und drückte einen Kuss auf die Handfläche. »Und das ist ein Problem, weil …?«

Grundgütiger, er stahl ihr den Atem, den Verstand, und wenn er noch näher kam, würde sie sich verflüssigen und dann in den Ritzen zwischen den Bodendielen verschwinden. Er senkte den Blick auf ihren Mund, verweilte dort und ließ ihre Lippen vor Erwartung kribbeln.

»Sam«, flüsterte sie.

Er hielt ergeben die Hände hoch. »Keine Hände.«

»Als würde das helfen.« Ihre Brustwarzen sehnten sich nach seiner Berührung. Sie war kurz davor, nachzugeben. »Damit erreichst du nur, dass ich dich noch mehr begehre.«

»Ein Kuss.« Er trat näher und drückte seinen harten Schaft an ihr Höschen, als er seinen Mund auf ihren senkte.

»Du bist unersättlich.«

»Nur nach dir.« Er liebkoste mit den Zähnen ihre Unterlippe. »Woran denkst du gerade?«

»Hm?« Ihre Gedanken hatten sich in nichts aufgelöst.

Er gluckste. »Was geht dir durch den Kopf?«

»Was meinst du wohl?«

»Ich liebe es, wenn du an mich denkst, aber du warst mit deinen Gedanken ganz woanders. Geht es um die Arbeit an der Website?« Ein Kuss auf ihren Hals, dann presste er seinen Körper fest an ihren.

Guter Gott, er fühlte sich so gut an. »Mm-hm.«

»Und macht die Aussicht auf dein Gespräch mit Vivian dich nervös?«

»Ein bisschen.« *Aber das ist nicht der Grund, weshalb ich am ganzen Körper zittere.*

»Lädst du sie zum Barbecue ein? Bis dahin sind es nur noch zwei Wochen.«

Der Gedanke an das Barbecue riss sie aus ihrer hormongetränkten Trance.

Sam runzelte die Stirn. »Bist du nervös wegen des Barbecues?«

»Nein.« Unter seinem eindringlichen Blick verdrehte sie die Augen. »Vielleicht ein bisschen, was wirklich albern ist.« Sie drehte sich um, um ihre Shorts zu greifen, und Sam zog sie an sich.

»Es ist nicht albern. Wir respektieren deine Gefühle,

erinnerst du dich?«

»Du machst es mir wirklich schwer, meine Gefühle zu respektieren, weil sie überhaupt keinen Sinn ergeben. Ich habe nicht den geringsten Grund, nervös zu sein. Du bist der wunderbarste Freund der Welt. Aber deine ganze Familie und praktisch die ganze Stadt wird da sein, also bin ich ein bisschen nervös. Wie gesagt, es ist albern, aber so ist es nun mal.«

»Du hast recht. Es wird der reinste Menschenauflauf. Die meisten Gruppen, die ich bei ihren Touren begleitet habe, werden auch dabei sein. Es ist ein Marketing-Event, aber es soll auch das Gemeinschaftsgefühl fördern und mich bei meinen Sponsoren als Anbieter etablieren. Aber das ist es nicht, was dir Sorgen bereitet, nicht wahr?«

Sie senkte den Blick. Es war ihr peinlich, ihm einzugestehen, dass sie eifersüchtig war. Er hob ihr Kinn. So machte er es immer und las dann in ihrem Gesicht wie in einem offenen Buch. Da war kein Urteilen in seinen Augen, keine Anspannung, nur Bewunderung. Umso irrwitziger kam ihr das grünäugige Monster vor, das seine Krallen in ihr Herz schlug. Mittlerweile waren sie an einem Punkt in ihrer Beziehung angekommen, an dem sie einander wortlos verstanden. Das Verstehen, das nur aus gegenseitigem Respekt und ihrer intensiven Verbundenheit erwachsen konnte, bedurfte keiner Worte.

»Du musst hier wissen«– er legte seine Hand auf ihr Herz – »dass ich das im Griff habe. Ich werde dich nicht enttäuschen.«

Sie holte tief Luft und nickte. »Ich weiß. Auch wenn ich mich anhöre wie ein totaler Loser: Es hat gar nichts mit dir zu tun. Es ist meine eigene dumme Eifersucht.«

Wieder breitete sich dieses freche Grinsen auf seinem Gesicht aus. »Mein Mädchen ist eifersüchtig?«

Sie verdrehte die Augen. »Nur ein ganz kleines bisschen. Nicht, weil ich mir Sorgen um dein Verhalten mache. Fast würde ich mir wünschen, dass es das wäre, aber diese Ausrede hast du mir gründlich ausgetrieben. Nein, ich bin mir selbst im Weg.«

»Du weißt genau, dass ich das liebe, nicht wahr?«, sagte er lachend und küsste sie auf die Wangen, bis sie ihn wegstieß und ebenfalls in Lachen ausbrach. »Du solltest Vivian einladen.«

»Warum?«

»Weil ich nicht nur dir beweisen werde, dass du dir keine Gedanken machen musst, sondern sie auch mit eigenen Augen sehen kann, dass kein Grund zur Sorge besteht. Wenn du weißt, dass sie auf deiner Seite steht, wirst du dich besser fühlen. Und vielleicht drückst du dann auch ihre Anrufe nicht mehr weg.« Er küsste sie erneut und nahm eine Unterhose aus seiner Schublade.

Du weißt, dass ich nicht drangegangen bin, wenn sie angerufen hat? Natürlich weißt du es. Du hast meinen Verstand infiltriert. »Mir musst du nichts beweisen, aber ich bin nicht sicher, ob es eine gute Idee ist, sie einzuladen.«

Er hatte seinen Slip noch nicht ganz angezogen, hielt in der Bewegung inne und sein Blick wurde sündig. »Willst du Nacktspiele spielen?«

Mit dir? Immer. Pfui! Wie schaffte er es nur, sie so vom Thema abzulenken? »Nein. Ich meine Vivian einladen. Sie ist noch pessimistischer, als ich es war, als wir beide uns kennengelernt haben. Und sie kennt dich nicht so gut wie ich. Sie wird alles genau unter die Lupe nehmen.«

»Das heißt, du hast kein Vertrauen in mich. Keine Nacktspiele für dich, meine Süße.« Er zog seine Slips hoch und tätschelte ihren Hintern. »Wenigstens einer von uns hat Vertrauen in mich.«

Vierundzwanzig

Faith goss ihre kränkelnden Pflanzen und flehte sie an, durchzuhalten. Sie sprach mit den Organisatorinnen des Frauenzentrums und las und beantwortete neue Beiträge auf der WAC-Website. Hilary sollte befördert werden und Brittany hatte einen neuen Mann kennengelernt. Beide klangen gespannt und neugierig, aber auch misstrauisch. Das große Thema in den Foren war Liras Stelle bei Rough Riders. Sie hatte zwar noch kein Angebot für einen Vollzeitjob, überlegte aber schon mit den anderen Frauen zusammen, ob es ratsam sei, aus ihrer Heimatstadt nach Peaceful Harbor zu ziehen. An ihren Lebenshaltungskosten würde sich kaum etwas ändern und sie müsste einen neuen Babysitter und einen Kinderarzt für Emmie suchen. Ihr Ex würde offenbar keine Einwände erheben, wenn sie tatsächlich wegziehen wollte, was viel über sein Verhältnis zu seiner kleinen Tochter aussagte. Der mit Abstand größte Pluspunkt eines Umzugs war gleichzeitig das größte Problem: die Loslösung von ihrer Familie.

Faith hielt sich mit ihren Diskussionsbeiträgen zurück, auch wenn es bei Liras Überlegungen, nach Peaceful Harbor zu ziehen, nicht allein um die Stelle bei Sam ging. Zum einen, weil sie Sam gegenüber voreingenommen war, und zum anderen, weil sie keine Ahnung hatte, wie sich eine Trennung von ihrem nichtsnutzigen Vater auf lange Sicht auf Emmie auswirken würde. Vermutlich wäre es das Beste für die Kleine, da er sowieso kein Interesse zeigte, sie zu sehen. Aber in solchen Sachen hatte sie keine Erfahrung. Lira brauchte wirklich professionelle Unterstützung.

Sie schrieb einen Kommentar, in dem sie Lira alles Gute wünschte, und machte sich dann an die Gestaltung der Seite mit den Hilfsangeboten. Es dauerte jedoch nicht lange, da schweiften ihre Gedanken zu Sam und dem bevorstehenden Rough-Riders-Barbecue. Eigentlich hatte sie gedacht, das Gespräch zwischen Sam und Cole würde ihr mehr im Magen liegen, doch es machte ihr nicht halb so viele Sorgen wie das Barbecue. Auch Sams Bemerkung, sie habe kein Vertrauen in ihn, ging ihr nicht aus dem Kopf.

Sie hatte vollstes Vertrauen in ihn. Sie selbst war diejenige, der sie nicht traute. Eifersucht war ein böser und hinterhältiger Begleiter, mit dem sie nicht allzu viel Erfahrung hatte. An jenem Abend im Tap It hatte es sie schlimm erwischt, aber Sam hatte das grünäugige Monster mit seiner selbstbewussten, ehrlichen Art zum Teufel gejagt.

»Hab Vertrauen«, flüsterte sie sich selbst zu, als sie nach dem Telefon griff und Vivians Nummer wählte.

»Hallo. Sie sprechen mit der früheren besten Freundin von Faith«, näselte Vivian. »Ich bin auf der Suche nach einer neuen besten Freundin. Bitte hinterlassen Sie eine Nachricht nach dem Signalton.«

Faith zuckte zusammen und fühlte sich mehr nur als ein bisschen schuldig. »Tut mir leid, dass ich dich nicht zurückgerufen habe.«

»Sag mir nur eins. Hast du eine neue beste Freundin oder

bist du von Sam in Beschlag genommen?«

»Niemand könnte dich jemals ersetzen, also ist es Letzteres.« Sie schloss die Augen und wartete auf Vivians mahnende Worte.

»Aha, von Sam in Beschlag genommen. Hm. Wie geht es dem Playboy?«

»Vivian.«

»Tut mir leid. Wie geht es Sam, dem Schwerenöter?« Ihre Stimme troff vor Sarkasmus.

»Er ist absolut wunderbar, aber ich möchte, dass du das selbst siehst. Hast du am übernächsten Wochenende schon etwas vor?«

»Könnte sein. Ist er wirklich wunderbar?« Ihr Ton wurde weicher. »Er behandelt dich gut? So gut, wie du es verdienst?«

»Er ist tatsächlich wunderbar, und ja, er behandelt mich gut. Aber ich möchte, dass du dich höchstpersönlich davon überzeugst, um deines eigenen Seelenfriedens willen. Er veranstaltet einen Grillabend bei Rough Riders und ich könnte deine Unterstützung gebrauchen.« Faith hatte gar nicht gemerkt, wie nervös sie war, bis sie die Worte ausgesprochen hatte.

»Du machst dir Sorgen. Ich höre es an deiner Stimme.«

»Ich mache mir keine Sorgen wegen Sam. Ich weiß nur nicht, wie eifersüchtig ich sein werde, wenn ein paar Frauen von früher auftauchen. Ich könnte eine Freundin an meiner Seite gebrauchen.« Sie ging in ihrem Wohnzimmer auf und ab.

»Woher weißt du, mit wem er sich vergnügt hat?«

»Ich weiß es nicht. Und ehrlich gesagt spielt es keine Rolle. Ich weiß, es klingt unglaublich, wenn man bedenkt, was du über Sam weißt, aber ich habe das Gefühl, als könnten wir es mit der ganzen Welt aufnehmen. Als könnte uns nichts auseinanderbringen.« Sie erzählte Vivian von dem Abendessen im Tap It und von den wenigen Gelegenheiten, bei denen sie in der vergangenen Woche auf andere Frauen gestoßen waren, mit denen er entweder gefeiert oder anderweitig seinen Spaß gehabt hatte – sie wusste es nicht und wollte es auch nicht wissen. Bei all diesen Begegnungen hatte sich Sam gleichermaßen selbstbewusst, höflich und korrekt verhalten.

»Wow«, sagte Vivian. »Im Ernst, Faith. Für dich hat er sich wirklich um hundertachtzig Grad gedreht.«

»Ja, das hat er. Und ich schwöre, Viv, dass ich nicht nur sehe, was ich sehen will. Er ist es, er ist der richtige Mann für mich. Er ist romantisch und rücksichtsvoll. Und es ist idiotisch und peinlich, dass ich so nervös bin. Und so eifersüchtig. Aber das ist normal, oder? Nervös zu sein? Seine Familie wird auch da sein, was auch ganz schön nervenaufreibend ist und mir wahrscheinlich mehr Sorgen macht als nötig.«

»Es ist völlig normal, und selbstverständlich komme ich zum Barbecue.«

Faith stieß einen Seufzer der Erleichterung aus. »Vielen Dank.«

»Ich muss gleich los. Mom und ich gönnen uns eine Wellnessbehandlung und dann gehen wir shoppen.«

»Hat sie sich von ihrem Freund getrennt?« Immer, wenn sie mit einem Mann Schluss gemacht hatte, lud Vivians Mutter ihre Tochter zu einer kombinierten Wellness-Shopping-Tour ein.

»Jep, aber es ist okay. Der Typ war langweilig und außerdem gefallen mir unsere gemeinsamen Ausflüge. Apropos Trennung, in unserem Forum habe ich gelesen, dass Lira jetzt bei Sam arbeitet. Stimmt das?«

Faith erklärte ihr, dass Sams Firma immer größer geworden war, und berichtete von dem Termin bei Brent und dem rechtlichen Rahmen, den er für den WAC schuf. Als sie schilderte, welchen Anteil Sam an dieser Entwicklung hatte, war Vivian beeindruckt.

»Faith, dann war seine Spende tatsächlich nicht nur ein Versuch, dich in sein Bett zu locken.«

»Hab ich ja immer gesagt. Er möchte, dass ich mich mit den kleinen Firmen hier vor Ort in Verbindung setze, um Spenden zu sammeln. Ich weiß noch nicht, was ich davon alles umsetzen werde, aber er hat gute Ideen. Ich habe es dir doch gesagt, Viv. Er ist wunderbar. Es ist so seltsam, dass wir so weit gekommen sind. Es ist …«

»Schicksal«, sagte Vivian. »Du hast endlich einen Mann gefunden, der dich verdient. Noch bin ich nicht hundertprozentig überzeugt, aber in zwei Wochen werde ich ja mit eigenen Augen sehen, was von der ganzen Sache zu halten ist. Schließlich wissen wir alle, dass die Orgasmusbrille mindestens ebenso verzerren kann wie die Bierbrille.«

»Du spinnst! Zuerst lässt du mich an ihm zweifeln, dann bist du ganz begeistert von ihm und jetzt ruderst du zurück?«

»Nein, das abschließende Urteil steht noch aus. Dass er Lira hilft und dich bei all den rechtlichen Fragen unterstützt, lässt mich fast schwach werden. Jetzt bist du ganz offiziell die Inhaberin eines Unternehmens. Damit kann ich später mal angeben, dass ich dich kannte, als …«

»Was auch immer.« Faith lachte. »Vielleicht triffst du beim Barbecue einen netten Mann und ziehst irgendwann auch hierher. Das wäre doch lustig, oder?«

»Ach, geh mir doch weg mit deinen netten Männern! Sorry, aber um Männer mache ich immer noch einen großen Bogen.«

Sie unterhielten sich noch ein paar Minuten, und als sie auflegten, hatte sich das aufgeregte Flattern in Faiths Magen beruhigt. Vivian würde nie zulassen, dass sie sich beim Barbecue als die eifersüchtige Freundin aufführte. Im Gegenteil: Sie würde ihr helfen, alles mit einem Lachen abzutun.

Während sie weiter an der Seite mit den Hilfsangeboten arbeitete, gingen ihre Gedanken zu Lira. Sie überlegte, ihre vertraute Umgebung hinter sich zu lassen und an einem neuen Ort ganz neu anzufangen. Und das mit einem kleinen Kind. Sie floh, vor der Demütigung und vor ihrem gebrochenen Herzen, so wie Faith es damals getan hatte. Faith hatte sich damals jedoch nur um sich selbst kümmern müssen, und außerdem hatte sie Vivian und ihre eigene Familie, die ihr jederzeit geholfen hätten. Und jetzt war ihre größte Sorge, dass sie auf ein paar Frauen eifersüchtig sein könnte, die überhaupt keine Rolle mehr spielten?

Ihre Probleme waren überhaupt keine. Es waren Ärgernisse, mehr nicht. Lira hatte echte Probleme: eine Familie, die sie nicht nur nicht unterstützte, sondern ihr das Leben schwerer machte, und ein kleines Kind, das sie allein großziehen musste und das später hoffentlich mehr Verantwortungsbewusstsein an den Tag legen würde als ihre eigene Schwester und Mutter. Diesen Teufelskreis zu durchbrechen, würde nicht leicht werden.

Aber alles war möglich, wenn man es nur wollte. Teufelskreise ließen sich ebenso durchbrechen wie Gewohnheiten und Eindrücke.

War Sam nicht der beste Beweis?

Was Lira zu erreichen versuchte, erforderte ungeheure Anstrengungen, und dabei brauchte sie Hilfe. Zur Hölle mit ihrer verrückten Familie. Lira hatte Faith, Vivian und alle anderen Mitglieder des WAC, die sie Tag und Nacht emotional unterstützten.

Sie klickte sich zu den WAC-Foren durch und fand den neuesten Beitrag von Lira, mit siebenundfünfzig Antworten von einunddreißig Benutzern. Einunddreißig Freundinnen, die für sie da waren, ihr Ratschläge gaben und sie aufbauten.

Und außerdem, so wurde Faith nun klar, hatte Lira Sam, der ihr die Möglichkeit zu einem neuen Job und vielleicht sogar zu einem neuen Leben eröffnete.

Ihr Sam. *Vertraue mir.* Und ob sie ihm vertraute!

Sie überlegte, welch ein Glück es für sie beide war, dass Sam ein Teil ihres Lebens war, und dann fiel ihr Vivians Bemerkung über das Schicksal ein. Sie postete einen Kommentar.

Lira, in schwierigen Situationen zeigt sich, aus welchem Holz wir geschnitzt sind. Ich bin so stolz auf dich, dass du dich von deinem Ex nicht unterkriegen lässt. Ich denke, das Schicksal ist auf deiner Seite, und ich denke, alle in unserer Gruppe würden mir beipflichten, dass die Familien, die wir durch Freundschaft schaffen, oft stärker und hilfreicher sind als die, in die wir hineingeboren wurden. Ich habe Vertrauen in dich, Lira. Wenn du Dinge wirklich ändern willst, wirst du es auch schaffen. Viel Glück bei Rough Riders. Falls ich dir irgendwie helfen kann, sag mir bitte Bescheid.

Es war ein Überfall aus dem Hinterhalt und eigentlich ziemlich egoistisch, Cole auf seiner Veranda abzufangen, kaum dass er mit Leesa von seiner Hochzeitsreise zurückkehrte. Andererseits sprachen sich bei den Bradens auch die unwichtigsten Kleinigkeiten in Windeseile herum, und Cole hatte es verdient, von Sam selbst zu erfahren, dass er sein Wort gebrochen hatte.

Er ging ungeduldig auf Coles Veranda auf und ab, und sein Magen verknotete sich, als eine schwarze Limousine in die Zufahrt einbog. Sam und Ty hatten beide angeboten, sie vom Flughafen abzuholen, aber Cole wollte den Luxus ihrer Flitterwochen bis zur letzten Sekunde auskosten und Leesa die beste Reise ihres Lebens schenken. Noch vor zwei Wochen hatte Sam nicht nachvollziehen können, warum sich Cole solche Mühe machte, wenn die Flitterwochen doch vorbei waren. Jetzt, wo er mit Faith zusammen war, waren ihm die Motive vollkommen klar. Sam liebte Faiths Lächeln so sehr, dass er alles tun würde, nur um es aufblitzen zu sehen. Sie hatte verschiedene Arten zu lächeln und er liebte sie alle. Ihr verlegenes Berühr-mich-Lächeln, ihr keckes Ich-weiß-du-willst-mich-Lächeln und ihr selbstbewusstes Ich-bin-eine-Karrierefrau-Lächeln. Aber am meisten liebte er das Lächeln, das beim Aufwachen um ihre Lippen spielte. Das Lächeln, das ihm sagte, dass sie nirgendwo lieber sein wollte, dass sie neben niemand anderem aufwachen wollte. Das Lächeln, das ihm sagte, dass sie ihm gehörte.

Cole half Leesa aus dem Auto. Beide lächelten, waren sonnengebräunt und sahen hinreißend aus. Sam hatte Cole noch nie so entspannt gesehen. Er legte Leesa einen Arm um die Schultern und sah sie an, als sei sie der Mittelpunkt seiner Welt. Leesa steckte ihr blondes Haar hinter das Ohr und erwiderte sein Lächeln mit einem Strahlen in den Augen. Auch das verstand Sam nun. Es war das, was er jedes Mal fühlte, wenn er mit Faith zusammen war. Im Moment kam er sich jedoch wie ein Voyeur vor und fragte sich, ob sein Auftauchen eine gute Idee gewesen war.

»Hey, Sam.« Coles Stimme riss ihn aus seinen Gedanken.

»Ich dachte, ich würde euch zu Hause willkommen heißen.« Den Stier bei den Hörnern zu packen« war das beste Mittel gegen flatterige Nerven, also eilte Sam mit großen Schritten zum Wagen und nahm dem Chauffeur die Reisetaschen ab.

»Lass doch, das kann ich machen«, sagte Cole.

»Du hast alle Hände voll zu tun.« Sam beugte sich vor und küsste Leesa auf die Wange. »Ihr seht toll aus.«

Leesa seufzte. »Es war unglaublich schön. Euer Cousin weiß wirklich, wie man Gästen das Gefühl gibt, etwas Besonderes zu sein.«

»Treat hat Champagner und Massagen für uns arrangiert und an unserem letzten Abend hatten wir ein Strandrestaurant ganz für uns allein.« Cole schloss die Tür auf und Sam folgte ihnen ins Haus. »Er hat alle Register gezogen.«

»Das ist typisch für ihn«, sagte Sam. Treat machte keine halben Sachen. Für ihren entfernten Cousin Blake Carter hatte er eine Doppelhochzeit auf einer Insel organisiert, und als ein Sturm nicht nur die Hochzeit, sondern auch die Kleidung aller Gäste ruiniert hatte, schaffte er innerhalb von vierundzwanzig Stunden neue Festkleider heran. Die Hochzeit wurde genauso schön, wie es sich alle erhofft hatten, in einem von Treats exklusiven Resorts.

»Ich habe Tempe versprochen, dass ich sie gleich anrufe, wenn wir angekommen sind, also lasse ich euch zwei alleine.« Leesa küsste Cole und Cole drückte sie zärtlich an sich.

Sam wandte sich ab, aber Leesas Kichern war nicht zu überhören. Er freute sich für die beiden.

»Ich liebe dich«, sagte Cole im sanften Ton eines zufriedenen Liebhabers. Dann landete seine Hand auf Sams Schulter und sein Ton wurde ernst. »Begrüßungskomitee?«

»Das nimmst du mir nicht ab, oder?«

»Kaum. Komm mit.« Cole führte ihn auf die hintere Veranda.

Vom Ozean wehte eine kühle Brise und brachte Erinnerungen an ihre Jugend mit sich. Unzählige Abende hatten sie am Wasser gesessen und über Gott und die Welt geredet.

»Bist du froh, wieder zu Hause zu sein?«, fragte Sam und versuchte, seine Nerven zu beruhigen.

Cole wies auf die Stühle und sie ließen sich darauf nieder. »Mir ist es egal, wo ich bin, solange Leesa bei mir ist.« Er beugte sich vor, die Ellbogen auf die Knie gestützt. »Ich habe deine Nachrichten bekommen und überlegt, ob ich anrufen sollte. Aber wenn etwas mit Mom oder Dad gewesen wäre, hättest du es gesagt. Was ist los, Sam?«

Seit Tagen hatte sich Sam die Worte zurechtgelegt, doch nun war sein Kopf wie leer gefegt.

»Ich wollte es dir persönlich sagen, bevor du es von irgendjemand anderem hörst.« Er sah Cole unverwandt an. In dessen Augen lag so viel von der Ruhe und Gleichmut ihres Vaters, der so anders war als er. Es war seltsam beruhigend. »Ich bin mit Faith zusammen.«

Coles Augen verengten sich. »Mit Faith? Meiner Angestellten? Der einzigen Frau in Peaceful Harbor, von der du bitteschön die Finger lassen solltest? Ich hatte dich ausdrücklich gebeten, nicht mit ihr zu spielen.«

»Ja, und ich spiele nicht mit ihr.«

Cole lachte leise. »Sam, das ist alles, was du tust. Du nimmst, du spielst und ziehst weiter.« Er stand auf und ging auf und ab. »Du hattest mir versprochen, dass du sie in Ruhe lässt.«

»Nein. Ich habe dir versprochen, dass ich ihr Leben nicht vermasseln werde, und das tue ich nicht.«

Cole starrte ihn so lange schweigend an, dass Sam Bauchschmerzen bekam. Als er schließlich sprach, war sein Ton gleichmäßig, ruhig, nicht anklagend. »Warum ausgerechnet Faith, Sam? Sie ist ein nettes, kluges Mädchen, und sie hat hier keine Familie, die sie auffangen könnte, wenn du sie fallen lässt. Und« – sein Blick wurde ernst – »sie ist meine Angestellte.«

Sam verkniff sich die Antwort, die ihm auf der Zunge lag, und versuchte, ruhig zu antworten. Damit konnte Cole normalerweise am besten umgehen. »Weil ich mit ihr ausgehen wollte, seit ich sie zum ersten Mal gesehen habe. Das weißt du, Cole. Und du weißt auch, dass ich nur so oft in deiner Praxis war, weil ich sie sehen wollte.«

»Klar, es war eine Herausforderung. Das vergesse ich immer wieder, dass du nicht die Finger davon lassen kannst.«

Sam stellte sich ihm in den Weg. Wut brodelte in ihm, als er Coles feindseligem Blick begegnete. Er respektierte seinen Bruder, und dieser Respekt hinderte ihn daran, in die Luft zu gehen.

»Du hast mir bisher immer gute Ratschläge gegeben«, sagte Sam hitzig. »Sowohl für mein Unternehmen als auch für andere Bereiche meines Lebens. Und ja, ich war immer der Typ, der genommen und gespielt hat und dann weitergezogen ist. Das kann ich nicht abstreiten. Und du hast recht, wenn du sagst, dass Faith nett und klug ist. Sie ist auch süß und sexy und witzig, und all diese Dinge haben mich zu ihr hingezogen.«

»Ihr Aussehen ist es, was dich zu ihr hingezogen hat. Wenn du in der Nähe bist, wird sie so nervös, dass sie kaum einen klaren Gedanken fassen kann.«

Sam nickte. Innerlich rauchte er vor Zorn. »Ist das Aussehen nicht das, was einem als Erstes ins Auge fällt? War es bei dir mit Leesa nicht auch so?« Ohne Coles Antwort abzuwarten, fuhr er fort: »Und ja, sie wurde nervös, wenn ich in der Nähe war. Manchmal passiert es immer noch, und jedes Mal vergucke ich mich mehr in sie. Und vielleicht hast du recht mit der Herausforderung.«

Er wandte sich ab, zu unruhig, um stillzustehen, als er das aussprach, was er die ganze Zeit gewusst hatte. »Vielleicht hat es damit angefangen, dass ich ihre Aufmerksamkeit auf mich lenken wollte.« Er straffte die Schultern und sah seinen Bruder an. »Aber dabei ist es nicht geblieben. Der Abend eures Hochzeitstages hat alles verändert.«

»Im Ernst, Sam? Du hast in der Nacht nach unserer Hochzeit mit ihr geschlafen?«

Sam schnaubte. »Ist es das, was du von mir denkst?«

Mit einem schweren Seufzer ließ sich Cole auf seinem Stuhl nieder. »Ist es nicht das, was alle von dir erwarten?«

Sam verschränkte die Arme vor der Brust. Die Wahrheit versetzte ihm einen schmerzhaften Stich. Er setzte sich Cole gegenüber und fragte sich, warum er angenommen hatte, dass dieses Gespräch anders verlaufen würde.

»Ja. Das ist, was alle von mir erwarten.« Sam fuhr sich mit der Hand übers Gesicht. »Aber so bin ich nicht mehr. Nicht mit Faith. Und ich dachte, gerade du würdest das verstehen.«

Cole musterte Sam eindringlich, und Sam fragte sich, was er sah. Einen enttäuschten Bruder? Einen Mann, der sich einer derart gewaltigen Lawine aus Emotionen gegenübersah, dass er keine Ahnung hatte, was da auf ihn zukam?

»Sam, ich möchte dir glauben. Du bist mein Bruder und bist mir lieb und teuer. Und du bist ein Braden, was bedeutet, dass irgendwo unter dem rauen Playboy ein Mann steckt, der weiß, was Loyalität heißt. Und diese Loyalität geht über die Familie hinaus. Verdammt, ich möchte, dass du dich verliebst und so glücklich bist wie Leesa und ich, und du weißt, dass ich große Stücke auf Faith gebe. Ich bin nur skeptisch. Was passiert, wenn es dir langweilig wird?«

»Lieber Gott, Cole. Kennst du sie überhaupt? Sie ist unglaublich. Mir wird bestimmt nicht langweilig.«

»Das weißt du nicht«, sagte Cole freundlicher.

»Ich weiß es, Cole.« Er klopfte sich mit der Hand aufs Herz. »Hier, wo es wichtig ist. Ich hätte nie gedacht, dass ich es ausgerechnet dir beweisen müsste.«

Sam stand auf und Cole folgte ihm. Als er einen Schritt zur Seite machte, packte Cole ihn am Arm und wirbelte ihn herum.

»Sam —«

»Was?« Er konnte seinen Ärger nicht mehr verhehlen, obwohl er nicht sicher war, ob er wütend auf Cole war, weil der ihm nicht glaubte, oder auf sich selbst, weil er sich unentrinnbar an seinen Ruf gekettet sah. Er schüttelte Coles Hand ab. »Ich weiß deine Ehrlichkeit zu schätzen und freue mich, dass ihr schöne Flitterwochen hattet. Ich wollte dir eure Heimkehr nicht versalzen. Ich wollte nur, dass du es von mir erfährst, bevor du es von Jon oder Ty oder von irgendjemand anderem hörst.« Er wandte sich zum Gehen, blickte über die Schulter zurück und sah Coles gequälten Blick. »Tu mir nur einen Gefallen. Lass nicht zu, dass sich all das auf Faiths Stellung in der Praxis auswirkt.«

»Komm schon, Sam. Dafür kennst du mich doch gut genug.«

Mit einem knappen Nicken ging Sam davon. Die Erkenntnis, dass er sich jedem gottverdammten Menschen in der Stadt würde beweisen müssen, schnürte ihm die Kehle zu. Und er war selbst schuld daran.

Fünfundzwanzig

Am Montagmorgen brach Sam zu seiner Laufrunde auf, noch bevor die Sonne aufgegangen war. Er ließ Faith nicht gerne allein zurück, aber seine unrühmliche Vergangenheit ging ihm seit seinem Gespräch mit Cole nicht aus dem Kopf, und wenn er ehrlich war, war er von Coles Reaktion enttäuscht. Er musste sich all das emotionale Durcheinander vom Leib rennen, sonst würde er explodieren.

Er strengte sich noch mehr an und lief noch weiter als sonst. Der vertraute Laufrhythmus auf dem Waldboden half ihm für gewöhnlich, seine Gedanken zu entwirren. Er überquerte die Straße und bog in einen Weg ein, der an Nates Haus vorbeiführte. Als er aufblickte, sah er seine Brüder auf sich zukommen. Er hielt sein Tempo aufrecht, weil er wusste, dass Nate und Ty ihn einholen würden. Und richtig: Kurze Zeit später liefen sie neben ihm her.

»Ich dachte nicht, dass du heute laufen gehst«, sagte Nate.

»Ich hab es gebraucht.«

»Probleme mit Faith?«, fragte Ty.

Sam warf ihm einen vernichtenden Blick zu. »Wenn es Probleme gäbe, wäre ich bei ihr und würde nicht versuchen, mir die verdammte Frustration aus dem Körper zu rennen.« Sollten sie tatsächlich nicht gehört haben, was passiert war? Er war sich sicher, dass Cole sich einem von ihnen anvertraut hätte.

»Was ist los?«, fragte Nate.

»Nichts, was ich nicht in den Griff kriegen könnte.«

»Daran habe ich keinen Zweifel«, sagte Nate. »Aber warum solltest du es alleine versuchen?«

Sam dachte über diese Frage nach, während sie einen Hügel hinaufliefen. In einem Fichtenwäldchen wurde der Pfad so schmal, dass sie hintereinander laufen mussten. Sie hatten sich immer gegenseitig unterstützt, aber für seinen Ruf war er selbst verantwortlich. Er hatte ihn sich verdient, das Bild, das andere von ihm hatten, sogar bewusst aufgebaut. Und zwar allein. Mit seinem Ruf konnte er umgehen, das Problem war jedoch, dass er nicht nur ihn selbst betraf. Er berührte auch Faith, und sie war bereit, hocherhobenen Hauptes allen gegenüberzutreten, die um seine Vergangenheit wussten, auch wenn es unangenehm war. Verdammter Cole. Er hatte Sams felsenfestes Selbstvertrauen erschüttert. Wenn sein eigener Brucer nicht sofort glaubte, dass er es mit Faith ernst meinte, was würden dann die Leute denken, mit denen er gefeiert hatte? Und was erwartete ihn beim Barbecue?

Der Weg wurde breiter und ebener, und nun liefen sie wieder nebeneinander.

»Ich versuche es nicht alleine«, sagte Sam schließlich. »Ich habe ja Faith an meiner Seite. Und ich hasse den Gedanken, dass die Leute mir vielleicht nicht glauben, dass ich es ernst mit ihr meine. Ich hasse den Gedanken, dass sie mit all dem Mist konfrontiert wird, den meine Vergangenheit mit sich bringt.«

»Ah«, sagte Ty. »Jetzt hab ich es kapiert. Hör zu, das ist einfach: Du nimmst dir jeden vor, der dir dumm kommt, und ich lenke die Frauen ab.« Er grinste verschmitzt. »Nicht, dass ich was dagegen hätte.«

»Mir macht das alles nichts aus, aber ich mache mir Sorgen wegen Faith. Ich habe Cole gesagt, dass wir zusammen sind, und er hat mich zusammengestaucht. War nicht gerade hilfreich.«

»Natürlich hat er das«, erwiderte Ty gereizt. »Typisch Cole. Ruhig, korrekt und tugendhaft wie eh und je. Aber wenn's holprig wird, kommt er nicht mehr klar. Das können wir besser. Er macht sich Sorgen um seine Angestellte. Dass dich so leicht nichts umhaut, weiß er, aber Faith? Verdammt, Sam. Sie arbeitet schon lange für ihn. Er sorgt sich um sie wie um seine Schwester.«

»Vielleicht ist das das Problem. Ich dachte, er würde sehen, wie ernst es mir mit ihr ist, und akzeptieren, dass ich mich verändert habe, egal wie schnell es passiert ist. Stattdessen hat er mir das Gefühl gegeben, als würde ich mit ihrem Leben russisches Roulette spielen.«

Zunächst hatte er Faith nicht erzählt, was Cole gesagt hatte, weil er nicht wollte, dass sie sich Sorgen machte, und auch, weil er seinem Bruder schon bald beweisen würde, dass er sich irrte. Dann wäre die ganze Sache sowieso vergessen. Er hatte ihr einfach gesagt, Cole wolle sicher sein, dass er sie nicht verletzen würde. Er hatte sie nicht angelogen, sondern hatte ihr nur etwas verschwiegen, und das hatte an ihm genagt. Gestern Abend war er schließlich mit der Wahrheit herausgerückt, und danach schien Faith genauso sauer auf Cole zu sein wie er, Sam, auf sich selbst sauer war, dass er sich überhaupt einen solchen Ruf erworben hatte.

»Du weißt doch, dass Cole die Dinge von allen Seiten betrachten muss, um dann die Einzelteile zusammenzusetzen«, sagte Nate.

»An Leesa ist er aber anders herangegangen.«

»Mach dir nichts vor«, sagte Nate. »Meinst du wirklich, dass er es mit seiner Beziehung nicht genauso gemacht hat wie mit allem anderen? Er hat vielleicht nicht mit uns darüber gesprochen, aber ich wette mit dir, dass er seine Gefühle fein säuberlich seziert hat.«

»Trotzdem hat er mir die Augen geöffnet. Jeder gottverdammte Mensch in dieser Stadt sieht mich als den Typen, der jede Nacht eine andere vernascht. Mir ist es egal, wenn ich ihnen beweisen muss, dass ich eben nicht dieser Typ bin. Aber es ist mir nicht egal, was es mit Faith macht.«

»Und was hast du jetzt vor?«, fragte Ty.

Sam zuckte mit den Schultern und steuerte auf einen weiteren Pfad zu. Er konnte noch nicht aufhören, sich zu quälen. »Ich selbst sein. Dass dieses Ich nicht der ist, den alle zu kennen glauben, ist mir schnurzegal. Alles, was zählt, ist, dass Faith unbeschadet aus der ganzen Sache herauskommt.«

»Nein, so siehst du das falsch«, sagte Nate. »Was zählt, ist, dass sie sich am Ende noch sicherer ist, was eure Beziehung angeht. Und das wird sie. Wenn du dir etwas in den Kopf setzt, dann ziehst du es auch durch.«

Sie liefen noch ein paar Kilometer und verbrachten die letzten zwanzig Minuten damit, sich gegenseitig hochzunehmen, was Sam half, sein Gedankenwirrwarr aufzulösen. Als die Sonne über den Horizont kroch, verabschiedete er sich von seinen Brüdern und lief nach Hause.

Er schaute über das Wasser und dachte daran, wie sehr er es immer geliebt hatte, hier zu leben, am Wasser und in Peaceful Harbor. Sam wusste, dass er genauso unvollkommen war wie das steinige Flussbett, aber in seinem Herzen war ihm eines klar: Egal, wie oft er schon gefallen und wieder aufgestanden war, trotz aller Wunden und Narben, die er davongetragen hatte, war er perfekt für Faith. Sie brauchte einen Mann, der ihr treu war, einen Mann, der sie anbetete, einen Mann, der sich für die Dinge interessierte, die ihr wichtig waren. Er war dieser Mann.

Er dachte an seine Brüder. Ty war sein Begleiter bei Abenteuern aller Art, immer bereit, sich kopfüber in riskante Situationen zu stürzen. Nate war ernst und hatte keine Angst, ihn herauszufordern. Er hatte ein Herz für die Schwachen und Benachteiligten und ließ sich nichts gefallen. Während Sam und Ty zu spontanen Entschlüssen neigten, hatte Nate mehr Ähnlichkeit mit Cole, als er jemals zugeben würde. Oft musste er etwas von allen Seiten betrachten, bevor er eine Entscheidung traf. Und Cole? Cole war schon immer der Gute gewesen. Der brave Junge, der nie in Schwierigkeiten geriet oder rebellierte. Er hatte immer auf sie alle aufgepasst und manchmal sogar den Kopf für Dinge hingehalten, die er gar nicht verbrochen hatte.

Das war es, woran Sam sich jetzt zu erinnern versuchte, während er in Gedanken ihr Gespräch noch einmal durchspielte. Cole war vorsichtig und genau, vor allem aber war er fürsorglich. Wahrscheinlich war er deshalb ein so guter Arzt und – wie Sam zugeben musste – ein so einfühlsamer Bruder. Je länger er über das nachdachte, was Cole ihm ohne Rücksicht auf seine Gefühle gesagt hatte, desto mehr wusste er die Haltung seines Bruders zu schätzen – und desto klarer wurde ihm, dass sie gar nicht so weit voneinander entfernt waren.

Auch wenn Cole es nicht glaubte: Seine Sorge um Faiths Wohlergehen spiegelte die von Sam wider. Und das bedeutete, dass sie immer noch im selben Team waren.

Normalerweise sehnte Faith die Tage nicht herbei, an denen sie zu beschäftigt war und keine Zeit für eine Mittagspause hatte. Cole war von seiner Hochzeitsreise zurück, gebräunt und entspannter, als sie ihn je gesehen hatte, was allerdings nicht viel sagte. Cole entspannte sich bei der Arbeit nicht. Niemals. Er war immer aufmerksam und konzentriert, was man an seiner gerunzelten Stirn und dem eindringlichen Blick seiner dunklen Augen unschwer erkennen konnte. Sie konnte praktisch sehen, wie sich die Zahnräder in seinem Kopf drehten und Informationen ausspuckten, die er wahrscheinlich vor zehn Jahren gelernt hatte und noch bis ins kleinste Detail abrufen konnte. Er war unglaublich klug, aber nicht arrogant. Das wollte etwas heißen, denn schließlich gehörte er zu den Besten seiner Zunft.

Heute war seine Stirn fast glatt, sein Blick war locker und nicht angestrengt, ein untrügliches Zeichen, dass ihm seine Flitterwochen gut bekommen waren. Sie freute sich für ihn, trotzdem mied sie alle Gelegenheiten wie Pausen, in denen das Gespräch auf private Dinge kommen könnte. Sam hatte ihr widerstrebend erzählt, wie Cole auf seine Nachricht reagiert hatte, und es ärgerte sie. Auf keinen Fall wollte sie etwas sagen, was sie bereuen würde.

Sie stellte sich vor, wie eine Unterhaltung zwischen ihr und Cole verlaufen könnte. Er würde so etwas sagen wie: *So, du bist also mit meinem Bruder zusammen?* Und sie würde dabei heraushören: *Du schläfst also mit Sam, dem Frauenheld?* Bei dem bloßen Gedanken ballte sie unwillkürlich die Fäuste.

Noch eine Patientin, dann war sie fertig für den Tag. Vielleicht hatte sie Glück und Cole wollte dieses Gespräch noch weniger als sie.

Nachdem sie die Beweglichkeit überprüft hatte, stellte sie

den Fuß der Patientin auf den Untersuchungstisch. Jackie Geiger war achtzehn Jahre alt, hatte gerade erst mit Joggen angefangen und hatte Schmerzen an den Außenseiten der Knie.

»Sie sagten, Sie hätten vor zwei Wochen angefangen zu laufen?«

»Ja. Drei Meilen pro Tag.« Jackie war zudem eine begeisterte Schwimmerin und Radfahrerin und war während der Highschool in der Basketballmannschaft ihrer Schule gewesen.

»Und machen Sie davor und danach Dehnübungen?«

»Hm, nein, nicht wirklich. Im Grunde stehe ich morgens auf, ziehe meine Laufsachen an und los geht's.« Sie zuckte die Achseln, aber der entschuldigende Blick in ihren blauen Augen sagte Faith, dass sie genau wusste, wie schlecht das für ihre Gelenke war.

»Nach der Untersuchung und aufgrund der Tatsache, dass die Schmerzen beidseitig auftreten, würde ich von einer Überlastung ausgehen. Geben Sie den Knien zwei Wochen lang Ruhe, nicht laufen, Fahrrad fahren, schwimmen oder andere Sportarten betreiben, die den Schmerz verstärken könnten.«

Jackie seufzte. »Nicht einmal schwimmen?«

Faith lächelte. »Nein, es sei denn, Sie haben gerne Schmerzen.«

»Okay«, gab sie nach.

»Großartig. Gegen die Schmerzen schreibe ich Ihnen Tabletten auf. Wenn Sie Ihre Gelenke zwei Wochen lang schonen, müsste das Problem von allein verschwinden. Aber machen Sie vorsichtshalber einen Termin für in zwei Wochen, dann sehen wir weiter und machen eventuell weitere Untersuchungen.«

»Und dann kann ich wieder laufen?«, fragte Jackie hoffnungsvoll.

»Ja, wenn Ihre Schmerzen verschwunden sind, aber Sie sollten es langsam angehen lassen und sich vor und nach dem Laufen dehnen. Sie haben nur einen Satz Knie. Achten Sie also darauf, dass sie gesund bleiben.« Faith ging zur Tür. »Sie können sich wieder anziehen und dann machen Sie vorne am Empfang den nächsten Termin aus, okay?«

Vor dem Untersuchungsraum füllte sie Jackies Karte aus und zog ihr Handy aus der Tasche, um nachzusehen, ob sie neue Nachrichten hatte, als Cole um die Ecke kam.

Der entspannte Blick in seinen Augen wurde ein wenig ernster. »War das deine letzte Patientin?«

Ihre Nerven waren sofort hellwach. »Ja.« Früher war es so einfach gewesen, mit ihm zu reden, aber jetzt war die Spannung zwischen ihnen mit Händen zu greifen. Vielleicht waren es auch nur ihre Nerven, die verrücktspielten.

»Großartig. Hast du einen Moment Zeit? In meinem Büro?«

Nein, definitiv nicht. Ich möchte nicht darüber sprechen, dass ich mit deinem unglaublich heißen Bruder schlafe. »Klar.«

Seine Mundwinkel bogen sich leicht nach oben, aber vor lauter Nervosität konnte sie nicht genau sagen, ob es ein lockeres Lächeln war oder etwas anderes. Sie folgte ihm in sein Büro. Als er die Tür hinter ihr schloss, krampfte sich ihr Magen zusammen.

Das ist nicht gut. Benimm dich normal. Setz dich. Gut. Lächle. Das Lächeln wollte ihr nicht recht gelingen, daher beschloss sie, sich dumm zu stellen und so zu tun, als könnte es hier auf gar keinen Fall um Sam gehen.

Cole setzte sich auf den Stuhl neben ihrem. Das hatte er noch nie gemacht und prompt wurde sie noch nervöser. Normalerweise saß er hinter seinem Schreibtisch. Er drehte sich so, dass er ihr direkt ins Gesicht sehen konnte, schlug die Beine übereinander und holte tief Luft.

»Also«, sagte er und nun war das Lächeln eindeutig. »Bist du genauso nervös wie ich?«

»Äh? Nervös? Wieso?«

Er hob eine Augenbraue.

Du kaufst mir das nicht ab, wie? »Ja. Ein bisschen ängstlich. Bitte glaub mir, dass ich meinen Job liebe. Ich hoffe, dass meine Beziehung zu Sam kein Problem für meine Stellung in der Praxis ist, weil ich die Patienten liebe und du und Jon so wunderbar seid. Ich verspreche, ich werde nicht zulassen, dass sich mein Privatleben auf meine Arbeit auswirkt.« *Außer wenn dein Bruder unangemeldet auftaucht und sich bis auf die Unterhose auszieht. Oh Gott, jetzt denke ich an Sam in seiner Unterwäsche!*

»Ich glaube nicht, dass deine privaten Angelegenheiten jemals die Qualität deiner Arbeit beeinträchtigen. Dafür bist du viel zu professionell.«

»Ja. Genau. Das bin ich.« *Puh.*

Seine Augenbrauen zogen sich zusammen und der kurze Moment der Erleichterung war dahin.

»Ich dachte mir, dass wir offen darüber sprechen sollten. Sam hat dir wahrscheinlich gesagt, dass ich ihn gebeten hatte, sich nicht mit dir zu verabreden.« Er sprach ruhig und fest, wie der Fachmann, der er war.

»Ja, und darüber wollte ich mit dir reden.« *Heiliger Mist, halt die Klappe!* Sie hatte keine Ahnung, woher ihr Selbstbewusstsein plötzlich kam, aber sie hatte das Gefühl, ihre Beziehung zu Sam und ihre Eigenständigkeit schützen zu müssen. »Ich weiß es zu schätzen, dass du dir Sorgen um mich machst, aber ich kann solche Entscheidungen selbst treffen.«

Er nickte stumm und musterte sie aufmerksam.

Ich bin gefeuert. Das war's.

Er holte erneut tief Luft und schien die gesamte Luft im Raum einzusaugen. »Es tut mir leid, dass ich meine Grenzen überschritten habe.« Er hielt inne, und irgendwann gelang es ihr, weiterzuatmen. »Du arbeitest hart, Faith, und bist eine hervorragende Arztassistentin, und Sam ist nicht gerade für feste Beziehungen bekannt. Ich wollte nur nicht riskieren, dass ihr beide …« Er wandte den Blick ab, und als er sie wieder ansah, ließ er diesen Gedanken noch einen Moment in der Schwebe. »Dass ihr zwei zusammenkommt und, nun, dass du verletzt wirst. Du bist eine nette junge Frau, Faith, und die Vorstellung, dass Sam dir wehtut, macht mir Sorgen.«

Sie schluckte die Wut herunter, die in ihr brodelte, umklammerte die Stuhlkante und zwang sich, professionell zu bleiben.

»Ich verstehe zwar, woher deine Sorge stammt, schließlich weiß ich, welchen Ruf Sam in der Stadt hat. Aber er ist wirklich der rücksichtsvollste, fürsorglichste und einfühlsamste Mann, den ich je kennengelernt habe.« Als sich ihr Herz öffnete, wurde ihr Ton sanfter. »Alles an ihm war unerwartet, und ich habe mir die Entscheidung, mich auf ihn einzulassen, nicht leicht gemacht.« Sie musste lächeln, weil sie daran dachte, wie er bei der Autowaschaktion sein Hemd ausgezogen hatte, nachdem sie ihm unmissverständlich die Meinung gesagt hatte. »Der arme Kerl hat sich wirklich alle Mühe gegeben, um mein Vertrauen zu gewinnen.«

»Sam?« Cole starrte sie überrascht an.

»Jawohl, Sam. Dein Bruder, der Mann, von dem jeder weiß, dass er einen Bogen um feste Beziehungen macht, hat sich mit mir eingelassen. Und ich vertraue ihm, Cole. Das ist wirklich alles, was du wissen musst.« Junge, Junge, das fühlte sich verdammt gut an. Und beängstigend. Auf jeden Fall unheimlich.

Cole nickte und ein Lächeln zeigte sich auf seinen Lippen. »Das kam überraschend.«

Sie lachte leise. »Ja. Für mich auch. Es tut mir leid. Ich hätte nicht so heftig werden sollen, aber … ich –« Sie unterbrach sich. *Ich bin dabei, mich in Sam zu verlieben*, hatte sie sagen wollen, aber das ging Cole nichts an.

»Und du glaubst wirklich, dass Sam sich ändern kann?«

»Nein. Ich glaube, er hat sich bereits geändert«, sagte sie. Und dann platzte es aus ihr heraus: »Aber leider glaubst du offenbar nicht daran.«

»Nein, es ist nicht so, als würde ich ihm nicht zutrauen, dass er sich ändert. Sam ist unglaublich intensiv, fokussiert und intelligent. Wenn er sich etwas vornimmt, bringt er es auch zu Ende.« Nachdenklich rieb er sich das Kinn. »Aber das ist eine Seite von Sam, von der ich dachte, dass es sie längst nicht mehr gibt.«

Seine Schultern entspannten sich und sein Ton wurde weicher. »Ich dachte, ich müsste euch zusammen sehen, um zu glauben, dass es echt ist. Aber das zeigt nur, dass ich ein Idiot bin, oder?«

Ihr Lachen löste sich, bevor sie sich in Erinnerung rufen konnte, dass Cole ihr Chef war. Ihm beizupflichten, dass er tatsächlich ein Idiot sei, war vielleicht keine gute Idee.

»Ja«, sagte er und lachte ebenfalls. »Ich bin ein Idiot. Es tut mir leid, dass ich mich in deine Angelegenheiten eingemischt habe.«

»Ist schon okay«, log sie. Er war immer noch ihr Chef.

»Nein, ist es nicht. Du bist meine Angestellte, nicht meine Schwester. Es stand mir nicht zu, ihn von vornherein von dir fernzuhalten.«

»Du hast es gut gemeint und das weiß ich zu schätzen. Aber ich habe Vertrauen in Sam.« Und dann musste sie trotzdem die bange Frage stellen: »Du wirst mich doch nicht feuern, wenn zwischen uns etwas schiefgeht, oder?«

Er starrte sie so lange wortlos an, dass ihr ganz mulmig wurde. Was war, wenn er sagte, er hätte dann keine andere Wahl?

Als er aufstand, erhob sie sich ebenfalls, straffte die Schultern und wappnete sich gegen das, was sie am meisten fürchtete.

»Dieser Sam. Der rücksichtsvolle, fürsorgliche und einfühlsame Mann, den du beschrieben hast, das ist der echte Sam. Das ist der Bruder, von dem ich dachte, er sei inzwischen viel zu tief begraben, um jemals wieder aufzutauchen. Ich glaube nicht, dass wir uns über dieses Szenario Gedanken machen müssen. Es sei denn, du beschließt, Sam zum Teufel zu jagen. In diesem Fall …« Er zuckte mit den Achseln, doch das schelmische Blinzeln in seinen Augen war eindeutig.

»Ist das dein Ernst? Plötzlich schiebst du mir die Schuld in die Schuhe, wie?«, sagte sie scherzhaft, während sie in den Flur traten.

Sie war so erleichtert, dass sie ihn am liebsten umarmt hätte. Aber er war immer noch ihr Chef. Gott sei Dank.

Sechsundzwanzig

Als Sam am Montagabend an seinem Haus ankam, war er überrascht, Tempes Auto in seiner Einfahrt und unten am Wasser ein Lagerfeuer zu sehen. Im Büro war es später geworden als geplant, weil er mit Tex die nächsten Touren durchgesprochen und mit ihm abgeklärt hatte, wer welche Aufgaben übernehmen würde. Tex hatte sich als zuverlässig und tatkräftig erwiesen, und Sam war froh, dass er offenbar vorhatte, länger bei Rough Riders zu bleiben. Anschließend hatte er sich bei Lira erkundigt, wie sie zurechtkam, und hatte sich dann eine Stunde lang das neue Buchungssystem angesehen, das sie eingerichtet hatte. Sie machte einen hervorragenden Job und schien die Arbeit zu genießen. Bei Rough Riders lief alles bestens, und aus einer Nachricht, die Faith ihm geschickt hatte, schloss er, dass ihr Gespräch mit Cole gut verlaufen war, was seinem Tag das Sahnehäubchen aufsetzte.

Wahrscheinlich sollte er sich bei Cole dafür entschuldigen, dass er am Samstag einfach so davongestürmt war, doch er brauchte noch ein, zwei Tage, um sein gekränktes Ego zu hätscheln. Dass er so empfindlich reagierte, überraschte ihn selbst, aber anscheinend war es ihm wichtiger, als er zugeben wollte, was sein Bruder von ihm hielt.

Er verdrängte diesen Gedanken und stieg aus dem Truck. Der Klang von Tempes Gitarre begrüßte ihn, als er zur Feuerstelle hinunterging. Er konnte den Blick nicht von Faiths schönem Gesicht wenden, das im Schein der Flammen leuchtete. Gerade lachte sie über etwas, das Tempe gesagt haben musste. Sie zusammen mit seiner Schwester zu sehen, berührte ihn tiefer, als er je erwartet hätte.

»Hi«, sagte sie, als er sich zu ihr hinunterbeugte und ihr einen Kuss gab.

»Hey, Baby. Ich habe dich vermisst.« Er umarmte seine Schwester. »Mit dir habe ich gar nicht gerechnet, Schwesterherz. Schön, dich zu sehen.«

»Tut mir leid, ich hätte vorher anrufen sollen, aber ich habe mein Lied fertig geschrieben und wollte es dir unbedingt vorspielen.« Tempe hatte ihr blondes Haar zu einem Pferdeschwanz gebunden. Sie strich ihren leichten Sommerrock glatt und legte ihre Gitarre auf den Knien ab.

Sam setzte sich neben Faith auf einen Stuhl und griff nach ihrer Hand. »Großartig. Ich kann es kaum erwarten, es zu hören.«

»Ich habe mich gerade bei ihr bedankt, für die Empfehlungen für Lira und die anderen Mitglieder«, sagte Faith.

»Hey, wenn es um die emotionale Gesundheit geht, helfe ich gerne«, sagte Tempe. »Außerdem kann man nie wissen. Eines Tages brauche ich eure Website vielleicht.«

»Nur über meine Leiche«, sagte Sam. »Ich bringe jeden um, der dich betrügt.«

Faith drückte seine Hand. »Bruderliebe vom Feinsten.«

»Und er meint es wirklich ernst«, sagte Tempe. »Aber so, wie es im Moment mit Dates aussieht, besteht wohl keine

Gefahr, dass er jemanden umbringen muss.«

Reifengeräusche auf dem Kies ließen alle herumfahren.

»Habe ich die Einladung zur Party verpasst?«, sagte Sam und fragte sich, warum Nate plötzlich auftauchte. Mit Jewel. Sie stiegen aus und winkten.

»Ich habe ihm gesagt, dass ich zu dir fahre«, sagte Tempe. »Ich habe ihn nicht eingeladen, aber wann braucht Nate schon eine Einladung?«

Seine Geschwister waren natürlich jederzeit willkommen, aber nachdem er Faith in den letzten Wochen immer für sich allein gehabt hatte, war Sam verwöhnt. Er war selbst erstaunt, wie enttäuscht er war, dass er sie für ein paar Stunden mit anderen teilen musste.

»Nate? Nie.« Zu Faith gewandt sagte Sam: »Tut mir leid, Baby. War wohl nichts mit unserem Abend zu zweit.«

»Der läuft uns ja nicht davon. Ich freue mich, dass sie hier sind.«

An ihrer Stimme erkannte er, dass sie sich tatsächlich freute, auch wenn sie etwas nervös wirkte. Sam stand auf, um Nate und Jewel zu begrüßen.

»Sieht aus, als hättest du Glück gehabt.« Jewel zog die Augenbrauen hoch.

Sam umarmte sie. »Ich bin der glücklichste Mann der Welt.«

»Quatsch«, sagte Nate und zog Sam von Jewel weg. »Der glücklichste Mann der Welt bin bitteschön ich.« Er drückte Tempes Schulter. »Hallo, Schwesterchen. Schön dich zu sehen.«

Dann stand Nate vor Faith und breitete die Arme aus. »Komm mal her.«

Faith wurde rot, als sie aufstand, und Nate nahm sie in die Arme.

»Die Frau, die Sammy gezähmt hat, muss ich einfach umarmen.«

»Sam kann man nicht zähmen«, sagte sie, als Sam sie auf seinen Schoß zog. »Und ich möchte es auch gar nicht. Monogam reicht mir schon.«

Nate lachte. »Und darum bist du genau die richtige Frau für Sam.«

»Daran musst du dich gewöhnen«, sagte Jewel zu Faith. »Bei den Bradens sagen alle das, was sie gerade denken.« Sie küsste Nate. »Vor allem mein Braden.«

Ein weiteres Auto kam die Einfahrt hinunter und alle drehten sich um. Beim Anblick von Coles Wagen ballten sich Sams Muskeln zusammen. Gleich dahinter kam der seiner Eltern, gefolgt von Shannons Auto, das sie Ty überlassen hatte.

»Hm, kann sein, dass ich allen erzählt habe, dass wir zu dir fahren.« Nates Lächeln stand dem der Grinsekatze in nichts nach. »So kann sich Faith ganz allmählich mit den restlichen Bradens anfreunden.«

Sam schüttelte den Kopf, als seine Familie den Rasen in Besitz nahm. Sie rösteten Marshmallows und überboten sich gegenseitig mit Weißt-du-noch-Geschichten über Sam.

Faith lauschte diesen Geschichten gespannt und zog ihn immer wieder damit auf. Während Sam beobachtete, wie seine Familie Faith in ihren Kreis aufnahm, hatte er plötzlich das Gefühl, als würde sich eine Leere füllen, deren Existenz er noch nicht einmal erahnt hatte. Der einzige Wermutstropfen war die Art, wie er und Cole sich gegenseitig beäugten. Offenbar warteten sie beide auf den richtigen Zeitpunkt für ein Gespräch.

»Wisst ihr noch, wie Sam bei Onkel Hal reiten gelernt hat?«, fragte seine Mutter mit einem amüsierten Funkeln in den blauen Augen. Sie konnte es kaum erwarten, einen seiner peinlichsten Momente haarklein zu schildern. »Er war damals acht und ein richtiger kleiner Angeber …«

Cole ergriff die Gelegenheit beim Schopf und trat zu Sam. »Können wir reden?«, fragte er leise.

Sam spürte Faiths Blick auf sich und hielt einen Finger hoch, um anzuzeigen, dass er gleich wieder da sei. »Sicher.« Sie gingen ein Stück vom Lagerfeuer weg, und Sam versuchte nicht einmal, so zu tun, als würde nicht die ganze Familie ebenso den Atem anhalten wie er selbst.

»Hör zu, Cole. Ich schulde dir eine Entschuldigung.«

»Was?« Cole schüttelte den Kopf. »Sam, *ich* schulde *dir* eine Entschuldigung dafür, dass ich so reagiert habe. Es war ungerecht und unangemessen. Du bist ein ehrlicher Bursche, und ich hatte kein Recht, an dir zu zweifeln. Es tut mir leid.«

Sam hatte einen Kloß im Hals, und Coles Miene deutete an, dass es ihm ähnlich ging.

»Danke«, sagte Sam. »Aber deine Sorge war berechtigt, und du wolltest auf mein Mädchen aufpassen, also kann ich dir kaum böse sein. Ich hätte nicht einfach wegrennen sollen. Die Wahrheit zu hören ist nicht einfach, aber hey, das gehört dazu, wenn man etwas ändern will, oder? Ist das nicht der erste Schritt? Zugeben, dass man ein Problem hat?«

»Du hattest kein Problem, Sam. Als junger Kerl bist du tief verletzt worden und hast dir nie selbst die Chance gegeben, damit fertigzuwerden. Du hast es in dir vergraben.«

Sam überlegte einen Moment. Er wusste, dass das zumindest teilweise stimmte.

»Du hattest einfach einen anderen Lebensstil als ich«, sagte Cole. »Aber nicht vollkommen anders. Du warst aktiver, aber verdammt, auch ich wollte mich jahrelang nicht binden. Ich war ein Idiot, Sammy, und es war nicht fair von mir, dir nicht zu glauben. Es tut mir leid.«

»Das nächste Mal, wenn du mir etwas so Wichtiges nicht glaubst, kriegst du einen Tritt in den Hintern«, scherzte Sam.

»Das hat deine Freundin schon erledigt. Ich hatte mich geirrt. Ihr passt perfekt zueinander. Ich hatte keine Ahnung, dass sie so zäh ist.«

Cole legte ihm einen Arm um die Schulter und in Sams Welt rückte ein weiteres Teilchen an die richtige Stelle.

»Zäh ist überhaupt kein Ausdruck. Weißt du, ich glaube nicht daran, die Vergangenheit wieder aufleben zu lassen, und zum Glück« – sein Blick schweifte zu Faith – »Faith auch nicht. Wir konzentrieren uns beide auf das Jetzt und die Zukunft. Und aus meiner Sicht sieht meine Zukunft verdammt perfekt aus.«

Siebenundzwanzig

Wenn Glückseligkeit ein Ort wäre, dann hätte Faith ihn in Sams Armen gefunden. Umrahmt von seinem festen, heißen Körper aufzuwachen, war das Schönste, was sie sich vorstellen konnte. Der Samstagmorgen war inzwischen zu ihrem Lieblingstag geworden. Während Sam weiterschlief, sah sich Faith in dem Schlafzimmer um, das sie seit drei Wochen mit dem Mann an ihrer Seite teilte. Mittlerweile hatte sie sich daran gewöhnt, dort zu schlafen, doch die Nächte waren immer so voll von Sam gewesen, dass sie sich gar nicht richtig darin umgesehen hatte.

Es fühlte sich kraftvoll und männlich an, wie Sam. Bettwäsche, Decken und Teppiche waren in Gold-, Braun- und dunklen Orangetönen gehalten. In die dunklen Holzwände waren drei große Fenster und eine verglaste Tür eingelassen, von der aus man auf die Terrasse trat. Sie hatten sich angewöhnt, dort zu frühstücken und auf das Wasser hinauszusehen. Ihr WAC-Ordner lag neben ihrem Laptop auf einem kunstvoll gestalteten Tisch aus Treibholz, der zwischen zwei abgeschabten Ledersesseln vor den Fenstern stand, wo sie gestern Abend stundenlang gesessen und geredet hatten.

Über dem Fußende des Bettes hing ein eiserner Kronleuchter mit überzeugend wirkenden Kerzenimitationen von der gewölbten Zimmerdecke. Alles in diesem Raum sah robust und durchdacht aus, kein Vergleich zu den schlichten weißen Wänden in ihrer Wohnung. Aber das war eine der Seiten, die sie an Sam liebte. Durch ihn wurde sie ruhiger, weniger hektisch und bekam eine andere Sicht auf die Dinge. Für sie war ihr Wohnzimmer immer eher ein Arbeitsplatz gewesen, an dem sie ihre To-do-Listen abhakte. In Sams Haus dagegen war jeder Raum ein Ort zum Genießen. Und wie alles an Sam waren sie einzigartig und interessant.

Ihre Topfpflanzen waren inzwischen in sein Wohnzimmer umgezogen und ein wenig Liebe und Wasser hatte sie zu neuem Leben erweckt. Ihre Haarbürste, Lotionen und Parfümflasche standen auf seiner Kommode neben seinem Herrenduft. Ihre Zahnbürste hing neben seiner im Badezimmer. *So schnell kann sich alles ändern. An einem Tag bin ich Single, und am nächsten Tag wache ich in Sams Armen auf und mein Herz ist so voll, dass der bloße Gedanke daran mir den Atem raubt. Ich bin ganz sicher die glücklichste Frau der Welt.*

Sie drehte sich in Sams Armen und sein Griff um ihre Taille wurde fester.

»Steh nicht auf«, sagte er schläfrig und sexy.

»Ich habe keine Eile.«

»Mm.« Er küsste sie auf die Schulter.

»Ich bewundere gerade dein Schlafzimmer. Mir fällt jetzt erst auf, wie persönlich es sich anfühlt. So wie dein ganzes Haus.«

»Mir gefällt es so.« Er öffnete die Augen und streckte die Beine. Seine harte Länge drückte gegen ihren Oberschenkel und sofort war sie an allen richtigen Stellen hellwach.

Als sie ihm mit den Fingern durchs Haar fuhr, schloss er die

Augen wieder. »Mm. Ich liebe es, wenn du mich so berührst.«

Normalerweise wäre gleich danach eine seiner typischen eindeutig-zweideutigen Bemerkungen gekommen, doch als er sagte: »Du bist die erste Frau, die ich hierher mitgenommen habe«, war sie geschockt. Dass er keine der anderen Frauen in sein Haus gelassen hatte, bestätigte das, was sie empfand. Er gab ihr immer wieder das Gefühl, etwas Besonderes zu sein.

Er öffnete die Augen und drückte seine Lippen auf ihre. »Du siehst überrascht aus. Ich habe dir doch gesagt, dass mit dir alles anders ist.«

»Alles, was du tust, überrascht mich, Sam. Wie sollte es auch anders sein? Die ganze Zeit über hast du nichts davon gesagt, aber jetzt begreife ich es allmählich. Ich habe gerade darüber nachgedacht, dass du mir ebenso privat, so eigen vorkommst wie dein Haus. Du schleichst dich zu Whiskey Bro's, wenn du chillen willst, ohne ständig unter Druck zu stehen. Du lebst hier, fernab von Nachbarn.«

»Nate ist mein Nachbar.«

»Ja, aber so nah ist sein Haus auch wieder nicht. Und du tauschst keine Telefonnummern mit den Frauen aus, die du kennengelernt hast, und bist auch nicht in den sozialen Medien, außer als Inhaber von Rough Riders.«

Seine Augen zwinkerten belustigt. »Hast du mich gegoogelt?«

»Nein.« Sie lachte. »Ich war neugierig, als ich am Tag der Autowaschaktion die Bilder für den WAC ins Netz gestellt habe. Von dir fehlte jede Spur, nur Rough Riders tauchte auf. Das finde ich sehr aufschlussreich.«

Er setzte sich auf und stopfte sich das Kissen in den Rücken. Sie lehnte sich an seine Brust. »Wieso ist das aufschlussreich?«

»Bevor wir uns verabredet haben, bist du mir ein paarmal

im Whispers und in der Stadt aufgefallen, und da warst du immer von Menschen umgeben – von Männern und Frauen. Ich dachte, du bist der Typ, der jede Minute in einem Pulk von Leuten unterwegs ist und dem das so gefällt. Ich habe dich nur dann allein gesehen, wenn du zu Cole in die Praxis gekommen bist.«

»Eigentlich bin ich zu dir gekommen, um dich zu sehen«, korrigierte er.

»Okay.« Sie verdrehte die Augen. Sie genoss den Gedanken, dass er gekommen war, um einen Blick auf sie zu erhaschen, obwohl er ihr so lange widerstanden hatte. »Jetzt, wo ich dich besser kenne, verstehe ich, dass dein Haus ein weiterer Zufluchtsort ist, auf dem du so sein kannst, wie du wirklich bist, wie im Whiskey Bro's.«

»Du meinst also, du wüsstest alles über mich.« Er presste seine Lippen auf ihre und fuhr mit seiner Hand über ihren Arm. Ein wohliger Schauder durchlief sie.

»Nicht annähernd, aber ich liebe es, so viele verschiedene Seiten an dir kennenzulernen. Du bist noch viel komplexer, als ich dachte.«

»Dann hoffe ich, dass du mich nie ganz durchschaust, sodass ich dich immer wieder aufs Neue fasziniere. Ich habe über unser Gespräch neulich nachgedacht und über die Touren, die ich begleite. Warst du schon mal beim Camping oder Rafting? Oder Klettern?«

»Meine Schwester und ich waren früher schon mal mit Rafts unterwegs, allerdings nicht im Wildwasser, so wie du es bei Rough Riders anbietest. Und JJ, mein fremdgehender Ex, hat sich für all das interessiert, aber ich bin bisher bestenfalls eine Felswand hochgeklettert.«

Seine Augen blitzten kalt auf. »Ich hasse es, dass er auch nur die geringste Ähnlichkeit mit mir hatte.«

»Er hatte nicht die geringste Ähnlichkeit mit dir, jedenfalls nicht in den Bereichen, auf die es ankommt. Er hatte nur zufällig die gleichen Hobbys.« Sie berührte seine Wange und sein Blick wurde wieder warm.

»Danke, Baby.« Er küsste sie erneut. »Zurück zu uns. Du hast also keine Angst vor Abenteuersportarten. Das ist ein Plus.«

»Selbst wenn ich Angst hätte, würde ich sie mit dir probieren, weil sie dir Spaß machen. Ich möchte diese Dinge mit dir teilen, wenn es das ist, was du wissen willst.«

»Ja, es geht in diese Richtung. Du bekommst doch Urlaub in der Praxis, oder?«

»Sicher, zwei Wochen. Drei ab dem nächsten Jahr, glaube ich.«

»Vielleicht müssen wir daran ein bisschen drehen«, sagte er mit diesem unnachahmlichen Selbstbewusstsein, das so typisch für ihn war. Was ging wohl in seinem attraktiven Kopf vor? Faith wartete gespannt. »Denn dann sehe ich keinen Grund, weshalb du nicht einige Touren mit mir zusammen machen könntest.«

Ihr Herz setzte einen Schlag aus. »Das klingt, als wäre es selbstverständlich, das alles gemeinsam zu erleben.«

»Ist es das denn nicht?« Er hob ihr Kinn und sah ihr in die Augen. »Wenn ich an morgen denke, sehe ich dich an meiner Seite. Ich möchte über uns nachdenken und herausfinden, wie es weitergeht.«

Er wurde ihr von Tag zu Tag wichtiger und ihm ging es offenbar ähnlich. Dass er das aussprach, was sie empfand, berührte sie so, dass sie kein Wort herausbrachte.

»Lass uns irgendwo hinfahren und es ausprobieren«, sagte er aufgeregt. »Dann sehen wir, wie es uns gefällt, wenn wir zusammen unterwegs sind. Wir könnten wandern, angeln und unter den Sternen schlafen oder mit dem Raft den Fluss hinunterfahren und uns für die Nacht eine schöne Stelle suchen.«

»Ich habe noch nie unter den Sternen geschlafen. Das hört sich wundervoll an, aber das Barbecue steht bevor. Wie kannst du es dir leisten, dich auszuklinken?«

»Ich finde es hinreißend, dass du dir Sorgen um mich machst, aber die Veranstaltung ist unter Kontrolle. Jetzt, wo Lira die Koordination übernommen hat und Kunden kontaktiert, ist alles im grünen Bereich. Sie ist übrigens erstaunlich. Wenn sie zum Barbecue kommt, werde ich mit ihr reden, ob sie sich eine feste Stelle bei uns vorstellen kann.«

»Du glaubst ja nicht, wie glücklich mich das macht. Sie braucht das so dringend, Sam. Das wird ihr ganzes Leben verändern.« Sie berührte seine Wange und fügte hinzu: »So, wie du meins verändert hast.«

Er gab ihr einen verlockenden Kuss in die zarte Kuhle an ihrem Hals. »Dito, Baby. Ich muss noch ein paar Dinge im Büro erledigen, aber dann können wir los. Du musst nur ein paar Sachen zusammenpacken und dir überlegen, was du machen willst. Eine Flussfahrt mit unbekanntem Ziel, einen Nachmittag mit Fallschirmspringen, eine Wanderung oder was auch immer dein kleines Herz begehrt.«

»Als hättest du das nicht alles schon bis ins Kleinste geplant«, zog sie ihn auf. Er hatte ja keine Ahnung, dass das, was ihr Herz begehrte, gar nicht weit entfernt war.

Nachdem Sam zur Arbeit aufgebrochen war, fuhr Faith nach

Hause, um zu packen. Auf ihre Frage, was sie denn mitnehmen sollte, hatte er ihr eine typisch männliche Antwort gegeben: bequeme Kleidung, ein zusätzliches Paar Schuhe und ansonsten nur das Notwendigste. Was zum Teufel war das Notwendigste? Sie konsultierte ihren guten Freund Google und wurde mit nicht enden wollenden Listen bombardiert. Demnach umfasste das Notwendigste Ausrüstungsgegenstände aller Art, spezielle Schuhe, Hosen und Jacken, Sonnencreme, Spray gegen Mücken und andere Naturphänomene. Bei dem peinlichen Punkt »im Freien auf die Toilette gehen« hielt sie entsetzt inne. Heiliger Strohsack! Wieso hatte sie nicht daran gedacht? Das wäre wirklich ein bisschen zu viel des Guten. Für ihn natürlich nicht, schließlich redeten Männer nur zu gerne über solche Dinge, während Frauen immer so taten, als müssten sie nie.

Nun brauchte sie entweder eine gute Ausrede, um sich aus der Affäre zu ziehen, oder sie holte sich fachkundige Hilfe. Sie schnappte sich ihr Handy und rief Charley an, die einzige Frau, die sie kannte, die genug Erfahrung mit dem Leben in der Natur hatte, um ihr sagen zu können, ob sie die ganze Sache einfach abblasen sollte. Eigentlich wollte sie sie gar nicht abblasen. Sie liebte es, Zeit in Sams Welt zu verbringen und ihn in einer Umgebung zu sehen, die schon so lange ein Teil seines Lebens war.

»Hey.« Charley war außer Atem.

»Hallo. Hast du einen Moment Zeit für mich?«

»Oh mein Gott!«, rief Charley. »Wie groß? Wow!«

Faith hörte zu, wie Charley am anderen Ende schrie und brüllte. Wahrscheinlich hatte sie gar nicht mitbekommen, dass Faith in der Leitung war. Ihre Stimme schien mal näher, mal weiter entfernt vom Telefon zu sein, als würde sie mit den Armen rudern. Faith lehnte sich lächelnd zurück und wartete, bis sich ihre Schwester wieder meldete.

»Tut mir leid«, keuchte sie. »Dane hat einen Hai gefangen. Ein Riesenvieh, vielleicht acht Fuß lang. Das werden wir bald genauer wissen. Sie waren schon seit Stunden hinter ihm her und markieren ihn jetzt. Du solltest ihn sehen. Er ist wunderschön.«

Bei der Vorstellung, in die Nähe eines Hais zu geraten, zuckte Faith zusammen. Viel lieber wollte sie erfahren, wer Dane war. Charley ging fast nie aus, mit ihrer Ausbildung, dem Praktikum und ihrem Nebenjob in der Bar hatte sie genug zu tun. Vermutlich gab es keinen Mann auf der ganzen Welt, der mit ihrem Tempo mithalten konnte.

»Wer ist Dane?«

»Ihm gehört die Brave Foundation. Hab ich dir doch schon mal erzählt, oder? Dane Braden? Der Typ, bei dem ich mein Praktikum mache?«

»Nein, alles was du gesagt hast, war … Moment mal. Dane *Braden*?«

»Ja. Ich bin sicher, dass du von ihm gehört hast. Er ist nur der beste Hai-Tagger weit und breit.«

»Mit dem Markieren von Haien kenne ich mich nicht so aus. Ist er mit Sam Braden verwandt?«

Sie hörte Charley schreien: »Hey, Lacy! Ist Dane mit einem Sam Braden verwandt?«

»Wenn er in Maryland ist, hat seine Frau gerade gesagt, dann ist er mit ihm verwandt. Warum? Kennst du ihn?«

»Das ist mein Sam.« Sie musste lächeln. Der Gedanke, dass der Mann, für den Charley arbeitete, mit Sam verwandt war, gefiel ihr. So fühlte sie sich Charley ein wenig näher.

»He, warte mal. Ist er der Typ, der mit allen Frauen schläft, die ihm über den Weg laufen?«

Faith verdrehte die Augen. »Von wem hast du das denn?«

»Von Vivian natürlich.«

Ich bringe sie um! »Das darf doch nicht wahr sein, wann hat sie dir das gesagt?«

»Ich weiß es nicht. Vor ein paar Wochen? Nach dem Wochenende, an dem sie bei dir war, denke ich.«

»Vielleicht war er mal so ein Typ, aber jetzt ist er es nicht mehr, vielen Dank.«

»Hm.«

Sie stellte sich vor, wie Charley sich mit dem Zeigefinger auf ihre Wange klopfte, wie sie es immer tat, wenn sie über irgendwelche komplizierten biologischen Sachen nachdachte, mit denen Faith nichts anfangen konnte.

»Bevor du meinen Freund unter die Lupe nimmst, brauche ich deine Hilfe.«

»Wegen Sam Braden? Tja, Beziehungen sind nicht wirklich mein Fachgebiet.«

»Nein, ich meine es ernst. Wir machen eine Raftingtour über Nacht, und ich habe online nach Ideen gesucht, was ich packen soll. Dass ich im Wald auf die Toilette gehen muss, ist mir gar nicht in den Sinn gekommen. Char, was soll ich bloß tun?«

»Im Wald zu kacken ist normal, Faith.«

»Aber was ist mit Toilettenpapier? Wird es Bären anlocken? Und was ist mit …«

»Moment mal«, sagte Charley in ihrem Halt-die-Klappe-Ton. »Bevor du in Panik gerätst: Es ist bei Weitem nicht so schlimm, wie du es hinstellst.«

»Also sollte ich den Ausflug nicht absagen?«

»Ich bitte dich! Meinst du das ernst? Weil du vielleicht im Wald pinkeln musst?« Charley lachte. »Ich liebe dich,

Schwesterherz, aber du bist wirklich die Einzige, die daraus ein Problem macht.«

Charley erklärte ihr, dass es biologisch abbaubares Toilettenpapier gab und dass man Müll und andere Unappetitlichkeiten in Löchern vergrub.

»Aber ich dachte, Sam gehört eine Firma, die Abenteuertouren anbietet.«

»Ja, das stimmt.«

»Dann kennt er sich mit dem ganzen Scheiß aus. Ha! Das war jetzt keine Absicht. Du musst dir keine Sorgen machen. Nimm bequeme Kleidung, Schuhe und Sonnencreme mit, mehr nicht.«

»Bist du sicher, dass du nicht doch eigentlich ein Mann bist? Das ist so ziemlich genau das, was Sam mir gesagt hat.«

»Ich mag ihn jetzt schon.« Im Hintergrund brüllte jemand und Charley sagte: »Ich muss Schluss machen. Viel Glück und lass dich nicht stressen. Du kannst dich verstecken, er wird dich nicht sehen und Bären werden dich auch nicht fressen. Hab dich lieb.«

Faith starrte auf ihr Handy und schüttelte den Kopf. Sie liebte ihre chaotische Schwester, aber »Lass dich nicht stressen«? Sie würde an nichts anderes denken können. Vielleicht konnte sie zwei Tage einhalten.

In der ersten halben Stunde auf dem Wasser glitt das Raft glatt und leicht wie eine Schlange im Gras den Fluss hinunter. Je weiter sie sich jedoch von der Zivilisation entfernten, desto reißender wurde die Strömung. Sam saß im hinteren Teil des

Rafts und paddelte, während er Faith im Auge behielt, die mit dem Paddel hantierte wie ein Profi. Bevor sie von Rough Riders aufgebrochen waren, hatte Sam ihr eine kurze Einweisung über Techniken und Sicherheitsvorkehrungen gegeben. Allerdings war er überzeugt, dass sie davon nicht viel mitbekommen hatte, weil sie es kaum abwarten konnte, endlich aufs Wasser zu gehen. Inzwischen waren sie schon seit über einer Stunde unterwegs, nach dem Stand der Sonne zu urteilen vielleicht schon fast zwei Stunden.

Faith sah über ihre Schulter zurück und ihr strahlendes Lächeln reichte bis hinauf zu ihren Augen. Er konnte sich nicht erinnern, sie jemals so schön oder so glücklich gesehen zu haben. Sie neigte kurz das Gesicht zur Sonne, dann wandte sie sich wieder dem Fluss zu.

»Bist du mit einem Mann namens Dane Braden verwandt?«, fragte sie.

»Er ist mein Cousin. Kennst du ihn?«

Erneut warf sie einen Blick zurück und er beugte sich vor und küsste sie. Ihre Lippen berührten sich kaum, der Kuss schien wie ein Hauch in der Luft zu schweben. Sam spürte diese Beinahe-Küsse am ganzen Körper, sie waren mindestens so verlockend wie ein tiefer, leidenschaftlicher Zungenkuss.

»Mm«, sagte sie und wandte ihm wieder den Rücken zu. »Charley macht ein Praktikum bei seiner Stiftung.«

»Cool. Ich hatte ganz vergessen, dass Dane draußen in Harbourside ist. Ich glaube, er und seine Frau bekommen bald ein Baby.«

»Tja, das scheint ihn nicht davon abzuhalten, hinter Haien herzujagen. Jedenfalls haben sie heute Morgen einen Hai markiert.«

»Typisch Dane. Er ist einer von denen, die eine Vision

haben und sie umsetzen. Er ist unerbittlich.«

»Von der Sorte kenne ich noch einen.« Sie warf einen Blick über die Schulter. »Es ist so schön hier. Ich bin froh, dass du es vorgeschlagen hast.«

»Es gibt kaum etwas, das so lebensbejahend ist wie ein Fluss. Ist es nicht unglaublich, dass ein kleines Rinnsal zu einem Bach und schließlich zu einem Fluss werden kann?« Er ließ den Blick über die felsigen Flussufer, die dichten Wälder und die Pflanzen schweifen, die aus dem Wasser ragten. »Denk nur, wie viele Pflanzen und Tiere dieser Fluss ernährt. Der Fluss gibt und gibt und gibt – Nahrung, Wasser, Transportmöglichkeiten.«

»Das klingt, als sei der Fluss für dich ein Lebewesen.«

»Ja, das ist er. Wie ein Liebhaber küsst er das Ufer, fesselt deine Aufmerksamkeit und verlangt dir Respekt ab.«

»Als deine Geliebte hoffe ich, dass ich nie nach Fluss riechen werde.«

»Ah, aber das tust du. Erdig, verführerisch und rein, mit einem Hauch von ›Ich will Sam‹.«

Sie lachte. »Wie schaffst du es, dass sich alles so wundervoll anhört?«

»Ich sage einfach, wie es ist.«

»Dann sag mir, was das Weiße da vor uns ist.« Sie sah ihn mit großen Augen an.

Sie näherten sich einer Ansammlung kleiner Stromschnellen, kaum der Rede wert.

»Kleine Walzen. Sie spritzen ein bisschen, sind aber ungefährlich.«

»Sagt der Mann, der vor nichts Angst hat.«

Er hörte die Sorge in ihrem Ton und beruhigte sie. »Weißt du noch, was ich dir zum Paddeln in Stromschnellen gesagt habe?«

»Jep.«

»Gut. Das Raft kippt ein bisschen und du wirst nass, aber wir paddeln einfach weiter flussabwärts. Es ist ein breites Fahrwasser, ohne Hindernisse, Baby. Glaub mir, alles wird gut.«

Als die Strömung schneller wurde, hob und senkte sich das Raft, spritzte nicht nur ihre Ausrüstung, die vorne befestigt war, sondern auch Faith von oben bis unten nass.

Erst schrie sie erschrocken auf, dann lachte sie. »Ich bin pitschnass!«

»Das war mein hinterhältiger Plan. Damit du dich ausziehen musst.«

Lachend manövrierten sie durch die rauere Strömung. Faith kreischte, als ihr Wasser ins Gesicht spritzte, aber es war ein Freudenschrei, der Sam noch glücklicher machte. Faith war ihm so vorsichtig und besonnen erschienen, dass ihn die selbstbewusste Art, wie sie an das Rafting und Camping heranging, überraschte. Er hatte angenommen, dass sie sich erst langsam an die neue Erfahrung herantasten müsste. Der Unterschied, das begriff er nun, lag darin, dass sie ihm inzwischen vollkommen vertraute.

Faith wandte ihm ihr nasses, glückliches Gesicht zu. »Das hat so viel Spaß gemacht! Ich möchte es noch mal machen.«

Er beugte sich vor und drückte ihr einen harten Kuss auf die Wange. »Zweifle nie wieder daran, dass wir füreinander geschaffen sind. Du warst so cool, Baby.«

Mit Faith eine der größten Freuden seines Lebens zu teilen, ihre Aufregung zu spüren, zuzusehen, wie sie paddelte, ohne einen einzigen Schlag auszulassen, und das Wissen, dass sie diese Abenteuer künftig gemeinsam bestehen würden, ließ Sams Herz anschwellen.

Achtundzwanzig

Zuzusehen, wie Sam sich bewegte, und nicht vor Wollust zu sabbern, war etwas, das Faith trotz aller Anstrengung noch nicht im Griff hatte. Als Sam jedoch die Ausrüstung vom Raft holte, ein geeignetes Areal für das Zelt aussuchte, Kochtöpfe an der Stelle aufstapelte, wo er später Feuer machen wollte, und schließlich seine Gitarre hervorzog, wurde nicht nur ihr Mund feucht. Ihr rauer Naturbursche hatte ein romantisches Herz, und das ließ *ihr* Herz höherschlagen.

»Du hast deine Gitarre mitgebracht?« Sie nahm sie ihm ab, als er eine kleine Tasche aus dem Gepäckstapel am steinigen Ufer hervorzog.

Ein leichtes Lächeln hob seine Lippen. »Ich dachte, ich könnte meinem Lieblingsmädchen etwas vorspielen. Aber das, was ich hier in dieser Tasche habe, dürfte dir noch besser gefallen.«

Sie verdrehte die Augen. »Kondome?«

»Die auch.« Er hielt eine Packung Kondome hoch. »Aber darüber freust du dich bestimmt noch mehr.« Er hielt die Tasche auf und sie spähte hinein. »Biologisch abbaubares Toilettenpapier, biologisch abbaubare Babytücher und …« Er zog eine Flasche Handdesinfektionsmittel heraus.

Sie legte die Gitarre auf die Zeltrolle und umarmte ihn. »Du bist wahrscheinlich der beste Freund in der Geschichte des Universums.«

»Wer hätte gedacht, dass Toilettenpapier so eine Wirkung haben kann?« Er ließ die Tasche fallen und küsste sie sehnsüchtig.

Die Sonne versank langsam am Horizont, die letzten Sonnenstrahlen tauchten den Ort, an dem sie die Nacht verbringen wollten, in ein überirdisches Licht und eine sanfte Brise ließ die Bäume rascheln. Nach ein paar weiteren Küssen, bei denen es ihr bis in die Fußspitzen kribbelte, lösten sie sich widerwillig voneinander und begannen, ihr Nachtlager aufzubauen. Faith kam kaum dazu, mitanzupacken, weil Sam geschickt und mit geübten Handgriffen das Zelt aufbaute und eine Grube für das Lagerfeuer aushob. Gemeinsam machten sie sich auf den Weg, um Brennholz zu sammeln, und Faiths Gedanken begannen zu wandern.

»Um Bären müssen wir uns keine Sorgen machen, oder?«

»Ach was. Ich bin mir ziemlich sicher, dass Bären auf sich selbst aufpassen können.« Er tätschelte ihren Hintern, als sie sich bückte, um einen Zweig aufzuheben.

»Im Ernst: Gibt es hier Bären?«

»Sicher, im Wald leben Bären, aber die Chance, einen zu Gesicht zu bekommen, ist gering.« Er stieg über einen Stein und hob einen dicken Ast auf. »Wahrscheinlich wirst du eher Schlangen, Spinnen —«

Sie wirbelte herum. »Sam!«

Mit seiner freien Hand zog er sie an sich. »Hör auf, dir den Kopf zu zerbrechen. Ich pass auf, dass dir nichts zustößt.« Er besiegelte sein Versprechen mit einem Kuss.

Als sie beide nicht mehr tragen konnten, brachten sie das Holz zu ihrem Lager und legten es an der Feuerstelle ab.

Sam fegte Holz- und Rindensplitter von ihrem Hemd. »Du musst unbedingt aus deinen nassen Sachen.«

»Bist du einfach nur fürsorglich, oder ist das wieder ein Trick, damit ich mich nackt ausziehe?«

Ein teuflisches Grinsen war die einzige Antwort. Dann bückte er sich und begann, das Holz in der Mitte der Feuerstelle aufzuschichten. Faith konnte sich schon gar nicht mehr erinnern, warum sie sich den Kopf zermartert hatte, was sie packen und wo sie zur Toilette gehen sollte. Wie immer hatte Sam alles unter Kontrolle. Und alles unter Kontrolle zu haben bedeutete für ihn, zuallererst auf das zu achten, was sie brauchte. Sie lächelte, als ihre Gedanken zu ihrem Gespräch am Morgen wanderten. *Wenn ich an morgen denke, sehe ich dich an meiner Seite. Ich möchte über uns nachdenken und herausfinden, wie es weitergeht.* Sam verkörperte alles, was sie sich bei einem Mann je erhofft hatte, auch wenn sie sich nie hätte vorstellen können, sich ausgerechnet in ihn zu verlieben. *Der Sam, mit dem ich nie gerechnet hätte*, dachte sie. *Die Zukunft, mit der ich nie gerechnet hätte?* Ihr Herz schwoll an bei diesem Gedanken.

Als er sie ansah, klebten sein nasses Hemd und die Shorts an Brust und Beinen und seine Augen klebten an ihr. Er warf ihr einen Kuss zu und sie fing ihn mit der Hand auf und legte dann ihre Hand an ihre Wange. Bevor ihr Herz überquoll, ging sie schnell ins Zelt, um sich umzuziehen. Sam hatte ihre Sachen neben die Schlafsäcke gestellt. Sie nahm ein sauberes, flauschiges Handtuch, das er für sie zurechtgelegt hatte, drückte es an die Brust und sonnte sich in seiner Fürsorglichkeit.

Als sie aus dem Zelt kam, hatte sie die Sachen an, die Sam ihr in Chelsea's Boutique gekauft hatte. Das Feuer knisterte und funkelte im schwachen Abendlicht und sein Widerschein tanzte in Sams dunklen Augen. Er drehte sich um und weidete sich an ihrem Anblick. Dann stand er auf und zog sein Hemd aus, bevor er sie in die Arme schloss.

»Da ist ja mein sexy Mädchen.«

»Danke für das Handtuch.«

»Ich werde immer für dich sorgen.« Er küsste sie zärtlich. »Ich liebe dieses Outfit an dir. Es erinnert mich an den Abend, als du dich für mich entschieden hast.«

»Wie hätte ich dir widerstehen können? Du hättest sowieso nicht aufgegeben, also dachte ich, ich könnte mich genauso gut treiben lassen.«

»Ist es das, was du tust? Dich treiben lassen?«

»Schon lange nicht mehr.« *Nein, ich falle eine Klippe hinunter.* Die Worte lagen ihr auf der Zunge, und bevor sie herauspurzelten, wechselte sie rasch das Thema. »Ich hatte fast damit gerechnet, dass du über mich herfällst, als ich mich umgezogen habe.«

»Also, ich habe es in Erwägung gezogen. Oder besser gesagt: Ich habe davon geträumt. Aber weil dir die großen bösen Bären solche Angst einjagen, dachte ich, ich lasse dich besser in Ruhe.« Sein zarter Kuss auf ihren Hals jagte einen Schauder über ihren Rücken. »Das einzige wilde Tier, vor dem du dich fürchten musst, ist die Bestie in mir, die so gerne herauskommen und spielen möchte.«

»Dieses Tier macht mir überhaupt keine Angst.«

Er lehnte sich zurück und sah sie fragend an. Sie kannte diesen Blick. Er suchte nach der Klarheit, von der sie zu Beginn ihrer Beziehung gesprochen hatten. Vom ersten Moment an hatte er ihr vollständige Transparenz geboten, und endlich war sie in der Lage, ihm mit der gleichen Offenheit zu begegnen. Sie vertraute ihm voll und ganz. Er musste es einfach sehen.

Sie schlang ihm die Arme um den Hals und küsste sein kratziges Kinn. »Absolute Klarheit?«

»Du hast ja keine Ahnung, wie viel mir das bedeutet.«

Gegen den Kloß in ihrem Hals sagte sie: »Oh doch. Für mich ist es auch eine große Sache.«

»Ich werde dich nie enttäuschen, Baby.«

»Ich weiß.« Sie drückte ihm einen Kuss auf die Brust. »Deine Haut ist kalt.«

»Ich habe mein Hemd ausgezogen, damit ich dich nicht nass mache. Setz dich ans Feuer und wärm dich auf. Ich ziehe mich schnell um und kümmere mich dann ums Abendessen. Oh, und siehst du die Büsche da drüben?« Er zeigte nach rechts zum Waldrand. »Die ganzen Toilettensachen habe ich da hinten hingestellt. Und ein paar Löcher hab ich auch schon gegraben, damit du nicht buddeln musst, wenn du musst.« Er sagte es so, wie wohl nur Männer es sagen, so, als sei es das Normalste der Welt.

Sie verbarg ihr Gesicht in den Händen. »Ich werde rot, oder?«

»Wie eine Tomate.« Er schob ihre Hände weg und küsste sie auf die Nasenspitze. »Von nun an ist das Thema Toilette tabu. Wir tun einfach so, als müsstest du nie.«

Sie schubste ihn spielerisch in Richtung Zelt, weil sie vorhatte, hinter den Büschen zu verschwinden, während er sich umzog – und dankte den Mächten des Universums, die fürs Camping zuständig waren, dafür, dass er so umsichtig war.

Sam grillte Würstchen und Gemüse, dazu gab es Reis. Seine Kochkünste am Lagerfeuer brachten ihm ein paar weitere Bonuspunkte bei Faith ein. Während sie aßen, ging die Sonne unter und ließ den Himmel zum Abschied blau und purpurn leuchten. Sam hatte immer gerne gezeltet, aber dieser Abend allein mit Faith, weit weg von Arbeit, Alltag und seiner wuseligen Familie, war etwas ganz Besonderes.

Der Fluss plätscherte leise, und als Sam zur Gitarre griff, begleitete ihn ein Chor aus Baumfröschen, Grillen und anderen Geräuschen des Waldes. Zuerst spielte er James Ottos »Groovy Little Summer Song«. Neben ihm auf der Decke am Feuer wiegte sich Faith im Takt der Melodie, während er von einem Lied sang, zu dem sie tanzen, zu dem sie träumen und zu dem sie sich verlieben konnten. Die Gefühle in seinem Herzen strömten in seine tiefe Stimme, und er erkannte, dass er nicht nur einen seiner liebsten Countrysongs sang. Er sang für Faith. Auch ihr Blick war voller Emotionen – und Klarheit. Die klare Entscheidung, sich auf ihn einzulassen, nach der er sich gesehnt hatte, war jetzt da. Er sprang auf, hatte das Bedürfnis, sich zu bewegen, aber nicht mit derselben Rastlosigkeit, die ihn sonst immer umtrieb. Das war anders. Es war ein tiefer, unaufhaltsamer Drang, sich gemeinsam mit Faith zu bewegen, um sie noch weiter in seine Welt zu holen. Er griff nach ihrer Hand und zog sie hoch. Seine Finger fanden die Saiten, als würden sie nach Hause zurückkehren, er machte da weiter, wo er aufgehört hatte, und tanzte mit Faith, während er die Worte sang, die für sie bestimmt waren.

Sie bewegte sich anmutig, nur mit einem leisen Hauch von Verlegenheit in ihren schönen Augen. Er gab ihr einen Kuss, ihre Schultern berührten sich für einen Moment und ihre Zurückhaltung verschwand. Ihre süße Stimme verwob sich mit seiner, zusammen sangen sie den Refrain, und Sam wäre am liebsten in diese leise, weiche Stimme hineingekrochen, um sich für die Nacht zur Ruhe zu legen. Als das Lied zu Ende war, spielte er weiter, nur um ihr zuzusehen, wie sie sich im Mondlicht drehte.

»Dieses Lied habe ich noch nie gehört.«

»Nein?« Er legte die Gitarre auf die Decke, nahm sie in seine Arme und tanzte langsam weiter zu der Melodie, die in ihm nachklang.

Sie sah ihn lächelnd an. »Ich könnte dir die ganze Nacht zuhören. Deine Stimme ist so beruhigend.«

Er legte seine Wange an ihre, schloss die Augen und genoss das Gefühl ihrer Körper, die zu einem einzigen verschmolzen zu sein schienen. »Deine Gefühle für mich lassen sie in deinen Ohren so klingen.«

»Was du nicht sagst, weiser Mann.«

Schweigend tanzten sie weiter, eingehüllt in das Gefühl, zusammen zu sein. Mehr brauchten sie nicht.

»Du zähmst meine Rastlosigkeit.« Seine Worte kamen, ohne dass er darüber nachgedacht hätte, und nun strömten sie nur so aus ihm heraus. »Du erdest mich auf eine Weise, die ich noch nicht ganz verstehe. Wenn ich nicht bei dir bin, denke ich an dich.« Er nahm ihre Hand und sie setzten sich wieder auf die Decke. Die Wärme des Feuers erleuchtete ihr schönes Gesicht. Er strich ihr die Haare von der Schulter, unfähig, einen einzigen Gedanken festzuhalten, während die Worte sprudelten. »Wenn wir zusammen sind, möchte ich nicht, dass die Zeit jemals vorbeigeht, was ziemlich abgedroschen klingt. Aber so etwas habe ich noch nie empfunden.«

»Natürlich hast du das«, sagte sie mit einem kecken Lächeln. »Als du sechzehn warst.«

Er lachte leise. »Nicht einmal annähernd.« Nach einer Weile fügte er nachdenklich hinzu: »Das hier ist größer, realer. Was ich für dich empfinde, hat nicht nur mit Hormonen zu tun. Am Anfang war es vielleicht so. Mit sechzehn fühlte ich mich unbesiegbar. Ich hätte nie gedacht, dass mich jemand zurückweisen und sich für einen anderen entscheiden würde.

Jetzt bin ich fast einunddreißig und weiß, dass es ein Irrtum war. Du bist den ganzen Tag von Leuten umgeben. Ärzte, Rechtsanwälte. Menschen, die mehr zu deiner Welt gehören als ich.«

»Ich will aber keinen Arzt oder Anwalt …«

Er drückte einen Kuss auf ihre Lippen. »Das weiß ich. Ich will damit nur sagen, dass ich nicht mehr unbesiegbar bin. Ich habe Fehler und Schwächen, und unsere Beziehung hat mir die Augen dafür geöffnet. Faith, ich liebe dich.«

Mit tränenfeuchten Augen ließ Faith seine Worte einsinken. Nicht nur sie brauchte einen Moment, um sie zu begreifen, ihm ging es genauso. Er hatte sein Geständnis nicht geplant, nicht damit gerechnet, aber er hätte es auch nicht zurückgehalten.

»Sam«, flüsterte sie atemlos.

»Du musst jetzt nichts sagen, aber ich konnte es nicht für mich behalten. Du bist meine Schwäche, meine verborgene Bruchlinie. Ich bin noch lange nicht perfekt und weiß, dass ich Fehler machen werde.«

Ihre Augenbrauen zogen sich zusammen, und er wusste, dass sie an die Fehler dachte, die sie so verletzt hatten und die sie nie wieder erleben wollte.

»Ich meine nicht, dass ich dich betrüge. Du weißt ja, dass das Fremdgehen in meinen Augen gar kein Fehler ist, sondern eine bewusste Entscheidung, jemanden zu verletzen, und das werde ich dir nie antun. Nie und nimmer. Mit Fehlern meine ich das, was uns täglich passiert. Ich verspreche dir, dass ich zu einer bestimmten Zeit zu Hause sein werde, und dann kommt mir bei der Arbeit etwas dazwischen. Oder ich schlage jemanden zusammen, der sich dir gegenüber respektlos verhält.«

Eigentlich hatte er nur Spaß machen wollen, um sie weiter lächeln zu sehen, aber gleichzeitig wusste er, dass es stimmte. Er würde alles für sie tun.

»Als du mich bei der Hochzeit hast abblitzen lassen und mich gefragt hast, ob mir schon die Mädels ausgegangen seien, hat etwas in mir klick gemacht. Ich wollte keine dieser Frauen, Faith. Ich wollte dich, und du hast mich dazu gebracht, alles zu hinterfragen, was ich über mich wusste, um dein Vertrauen zu gewinnen.«

Sie senkte die Augen und er hob ihr Kinn und küsste sie erneut.

»Ich bin froh darüber. Du hattest recht. Ich war deiner nicht wert, so wie ich war. Ich wusste es damals nicht, aber ich brauchte deine Zurückweisung, denn hier drinnen –« er legte die Hand aufs Herz – »wusste ich, dass du einen besseren Mann verdient hast, als ich bis jetzt war. Du verdienst es, dich ohne den Hauch eines Zweifels auf deinen Partner verlassen zu können, und zwar immer. Wenn du eine Schulter zum Ausweinen brauchst, jemanden, der deine Hand hält. Einen Freund, mit dem du über deinen Beruf und deine Hobbys sprechen kannst, mit dem du lachen und albern sein und den du unter den Sternen lieben kannst. Ein Mann, der dich lieben wird, auch wenn du zwanzig Kilo zunimmst oder einer schrecklichen Krankheit zum Opfer fällst. Ein Mann, bei dem du nie befürchten musst, dass er dich belügt, dich betrügt oder dir das Herz bricht.«

Er nahm ihr Gesicht in die Hände und sah ihr in die Augen. »Ich bin dieser Mann, Faith. Ich bin dein Mann.«

Zu den Klängen der Natur und dem sicheren, steten Schlag ihrer Herzen streckte sie die Arme nach ihm aus. Liebe spielte in ihren seelenvollen Augen, in ihrer zärtlichen Berührung, als ihre Münder und Körper zusammenkamen und sie sein Gelübde mit ihrer Leidenschaft besiegelten.

Neunundzwanzig

Faith erwachte, als die Matratze neben ihr einsank. *Sam.* Eine Woche war vergangen seit dem Abend im Wald, als Sam ihr sein ganzes Herz anvertraut hatte. Seitdem schwebte sie wie auf einer Wolke. Damals war sie so überwältigt gewesen, dass sie kaum ein Wort herausbringen konnte, und nun wartete sie auf den richtigen Moment, um ihm zu sagen, dass sie ihn auch liebte. Sie wollte ihm eine ebenso wundervoll romantische Erinnerung mitgeben, wie er sie ihr geschaffen hatte. Und in der vergangenen Woche voller Glückseligkeit, als sie abends spazieren gegangen waren, Filme angeschaut – und immer das Ende verpasst hatten, weil sie viel zu sehr mit sich beschäftigt waren – und über ihre Hoffnungen und Träume geredet hatten, war es passiert. Es war nur ein winziger Schritt gewesen, der sie noch vom Abgrund getrennt hatte, doch nun war ihr klar, dass sie Sam liebte, ganz und gar, mit Haut und Haaren. Heute Abend wollte sie es ihm endlich sagen, wenn das Barbecue vorbei war und er noch auf einer Welle der Euphorie ritt. Sie hatte jede romantische Sekunde genau geplant.

Sie griff nach ihm, ohne die Augen zu öffnen.

»Guten Morgen, meine Schöne.« Er drückte seine warmen Lippen auf ihre, als sich ihre Augen öffneten.

Er roch nach Seife und Sonnenschein und Sam. Sie blinzelte den Schlaf aus den Augen und sein attraktives Gesicht wurde deutlicher.

»Hallo. Du hast ohne mich geduscht?«

»Ich bin laufen gegangen und dachte, ich erspare dir den Schweiß von sechs Meilen.«

»Ich liebe es, wenn wir zusammen schweißtreibende Sachen machen«, provozierte sie ihn. Als sie sich aufsetzte, sah sie ihren Namen über dem Rough-Riders-Logo auf seinem schwarzen Tanktop. Ihr Herz pochte wie wild. Sie zog den Stoff glatt, um besser lesen zu können.

»Faiths Kerl?«

»Für dich hab ich auch eins.« Er hielt ein anderes schwarzes Tanktop hoch, auf dem stand: *Sams Braut.*

»Oh mein Gott, Sam.« Sie riss es ihm aus den Händen und grinste so breit, dass ihre Wangen wehtaten. »Ich dachte, ich bin Bradens Braut.«

Er zog sie an sich. »Beim Barbecue wird es vor Bradens nur so wimmeln. Ich möchte, dass es vollkommen klar ist, wer von uns das Glück hat, dein Kerl zu sein.«

Das Herz war ihr so voll von Sam, dass sie wahrscheinlich lächelte wie ein verliebter Teenager. Dass Vivian sie mit der Aufschrift auf ihren Tops gnadenlos aufziehen würde, war ihr egal. Vermutlich würden alle Frauen beim Barbecue denken, sie hätte Sam gezwungen, dieses Top zu tragen, aber auch das war ihr egal. Sie fand es einfach hinreißend, dass Sam nicht nur an solche Details dachte, sondern die Shirts mit offensichtlichem Stolz zur Schau stellte.

»Wird es dir nicht peinlich sein, vor allen Kunden, Freunden und der gesamten Familie damit aufzutreten?«

»Baby, ich würde dich am Leib tragen, wenn ich könnte.«

Er küsste sie erneut und sie krallte die Finger in sein Hemd und hielt ihn fest.

»Danke, dass du so viel Geduld mit mir gehabt hast, und danke, dass du so viel riskiert hast.«

»Wir haben beide viel riskiert.«

»Du mehr als ich.«

»Nein, mein Mädchen, du solltest dein Licht nicht unter den Scheffel stellen. Du hast es gewagt, dich auf den riskantesten Mann in der Stadt einzulassen. Ich musste nur der Mann sein, der ich immer schon war – nur hast du mir erst gezeigt, wer dieser Mann ist.« Er zog sie hoch und drückte sie an sich. »Ich muss zu Rough Riders, und du musst nach Hause, um dich mit Vivian zu treffen, sonst reißt sie mir den Kopf ab, weil ich dich nicht mit ihr teile. Das Barbecue beginnt um sechs. Das vergesst ihr zwei doch hoffentlich nicht, wenn ihr in der Stadt herumlauft und euch amüsiert?«

»Ganz bestimmt nicht, Mr. Braden.« Sie nahm das Tanktop vom Bett. »Und schon gar nicht, wenn ich so ein schickes neues Top habe.« Sie stellte sich auf die Zehenspitzen und gab ihm einen Kuss. Prompt legte sich sein Arm um ihre Taille und der Kuss wurde intensiver.

»Ich werde dich vermissen«, sagte er.

»Ich werde dich auch vermissen. Bist du sicher, dass ich nicht früher kommen soll? Ich könnte mich mit Vivian beim Barbecue treffen.«

»Tagsüber wird auf dem Gelände das reinste Chaos herrschen. Lauter Jugendliche und junge Familien, sodass man keinen Fuß vor den anderen setzen kann. Am Nachmittag haben sich acht Freunde von Patrick zum Helfen angesagt. Außerdem sind Lira, Tex und ich dabei, also sind wir gut aufgestellt. Vor allem müssen wir aufpassen, dass die Kinder keinen Unfug machen, für etwas anderes werden wir kaum Zeit haben. Genieß deine Zeit mit Vivian. Aber ich hätte dich gerne an meiner Seite, wenn es richtig losgeht.« Er blickte auf sein Hemd. »Du lässt deinen Kerl doch nicht hängen, oder?«

Mein Kerl. »Ich möchte bei niemandem so gerne sein wie bei dir.«

»Hier tummeln sich bestimmt an die zweihundert Leute.« Vivian strich sich die blonden Haare aus dem Gesicht und sah sich am überfüllten Strand um. Bis zum offiziellen Beginn des Barbecues war es noch eine halbe Stunde, doch alles war schon voll von Menschen.

Faith blickte suchend um sich. Auf dem Parkplatz hatte sie ein paar Motorräder entdeckt, daher überraschte es sie nicht, Bullet und Dixie mit einer Gruppe von Leuten am Bootshaus stehen zu sehen. Als sie sich mit Vivian durch die Menge schob, erkannte sie Bones, der sich mit Cole und Leesa unterhielt. Bones Tätowierungen waren unter einem Polohemd versteckt. Ohne die wilden Tattoos und die zerschlissenen Jeans und Lederstiefel sah er eher aus wie ein Arzt und nicht so sehr wie ein Typ, der in einer Biker-Bar herumhing – die ihm auch noch gehörte. Sie freute sich, dass sich diese Seite von Sam mit der eher öffentlichen Seite vermischte.

»Wie willst du Sam in diesem Durcheinander finden?«, fragte Vivian. »Vielleicht hätte er blinkende Lichter in diese Tops nähen lassen sollen.«

»Halt die Klappe.« Vivian zog sie schon den ganzen Nachmittag mit ihrem »Sams Braut«-Top auf. »Ich werde ihn schon finden. Komm mit.«

Sie schlängelten sich durch die Menge, umgeben vom Duft gegrillter Hotdogs und Hamburger, von Gelächter und Stimmengewirr. Faith lauschte. War da irgendwo Sams Stimme? Wenn sie doch nur größer wäre! Dann könnte sie die Menge überblicken, so aber war ihr Blickfeld auf Brüste, Rücken und Kinderköpfe beschränkt.

»Faith! Vivian!«

Faith fuhr herum. Lira in einem Rough-Riders-T-Shirt winkte und drängte sich zu ihnen durch. Ihr strahlendes Lächeln machte sie zu einem ganz anderen Menschen als noch vor ein paar Wochen bei der Autowaschaktion. Sie war wie aufgeblüht und die Resignation in ihrem Blick war verschwunden. Mit Tränen in den Augen umarmte Faith sie. Sam hatte Lira wirklich ein neues Leben gegeben.

»Ist das nicht herrlich?«, sagte Lira. »Unglaublich, wie viele Leute gekommen sind. Sam meinte, es seien mindestens achtzig mehr als in den vergangenen Jahren. Und er sagte, dass sie das mir zu verdanken hätten.« Sie kreischte begeistert und umarmte Faith und Vivian noch einmal. »Vielen Dank für die Autowaschaktion! Dieser Tag hat mein ganzes Leben verändert. Sam hat mir heute Morgen einen Vollzeitjob angeboten.«

»Glückwunsch!« Faith drückte sie erneut. »Ich freue mich so für dich. Also ziehst du wirklich hierher?«

»Nun, wir wissen es noch nicht genau. Ich muss so viel organisieren: eine Wohnung, einen Babysitter und solche Sachen. Es gibt viel zu bedenken. Aber im Moment kann ich von zu Hause aus arbeiten, bis ich weiß, wie es weitergeht. Oh, und Sam hat mich seinem Freund Brent vorgestellt. Er will mit seinem Partner sprechen, der für die Scheidungssachen zuständig ist.« Mit gedämpfter Stimme fuhr sie fort: »Er hat gesagt, sein Partner würde mir kostenlos helfen. Ich konnte es gar nicht glauben.«

Brent drängte sich durch die Menschenmenge zu ihnen durch. »Hey, Faith. Schön, dich wiederzusehen.« Er umarmte sie. »Schickes Top.«

Sie sah an sich herunter. Das Shirt mit der Aufschrift hatte sie ganz vergessen. Sie lachte. »Das war Sams Idee. Brent, das ist meine Freundin Vivian.«

»Hallo, wie geht's?« Brent umarmte sie ebenfalls.

»Jetzt geht's schon viel besser«, erwiderte Vivian kokett.

Faith verdrehte die Augen. Ihr fiel auf, dass sich Brent zu Lira stellte. Anscheinend bemerkte Vivian es auch, denn sie stieß Faith vielsagend an.

»Dein Freund hat sich wirklich selbst übertroffen«, sage Brent und sah sich anerkennend um.

Faith folgte seinem Blick und sah Sam mit Ty und ein paar Frauen am Wasser stehen. Sie wappnete sich gegen einen eifersüchtigen Stich, aber er blieb aus. Für so abscheuliche Gefühle war in ihrer Beziehung kein Platz mehr. In diesem Moment hob Sam den Blick und sah sich suchend um. Sie liebte ihn so sehr, dass es wehtat. Er hatte sie entdeckt und ihr Herz schwoll an. Er warf ihr einen Luftkuss zu, dann sagte er etwas zu der Gruppe, mit der er zusammen war, ohne Faith aus den Augen zu lassen, und kam auf sie zu.

Vivians Hand auf ihrem Arm riss sie aus ihren Gedanken. Brent und Lira standen ein wenig abseits und redeten.

»Weißt du noch, wie sehr ich dagegen war, dass du mit ihm spazieren gehst?«, sagte Vivian schnell.

»Wie könnte ich das vergessen?«

»Offenbar tut er dir richtig gut. Du siehst so glücklich aus wie lange nicht mehr, und dass du deinem Chef die Meinung gesagt hast, weil er nicht an Sam geglaubt hat? Das ist neu, Faith. Du hast dich auch verändert.«

Ja, sie hatte sich tatsächlich verändert. Zum Besseren. Nichts an ihrer Beziehung machte sie nervös oder misstrauisch. Sam gab ihr das Gefühl, geliebt und geschätzt zu sein, und machte sie mutig und zuversichtlich.

Sie waren ein gutes Team, in jeder Hinsicht. Gewandt und selbstsicher kam er nun auf sie zu. Obwohl zahlreiche Frauen jede seiner Bewegungen verfolgten, betrachtete er sie mit unverhohlener Zärtlichkeit.

Sie konnte den Blick nicht von dem Mann abwenden, der ihr ihren Glauben an Beziehungen zurückgegeben hatte. Und vielleicht sogar ihren Glauben an sich selbst.

Sein Arm legte sich um ihre Taille, als er seine Wange an ihre legte. »Gott, ich habe dich vermisst, Baby«, sagte er und gab ihr einen Kuss, der ihr Herz tanzen ließ.

»Ich freue mich, dass du kommen konntest«, sagte er zu Vivian, bevor er sie in die Arme schloss.

Mit verträumtem Gesichtsausdruck sank Vivian in seine Arme. »Ich nehme alles Schlechte zurück, das ich je über dich gesagt habe«, meinte sie.

Sam streckte die Hand nach Faith aus und zog sie an seine Seite, dorthin, wo sie am liebsten war. »Will ich das überhaupt wissen?«

»Nein«, sagten Vivian und Faith wie aus einem Mund.

»Ich hole mir etwas zu trinken«, sagte Vivian. »Und außerdem steht dort drüben ein supersexy Typ, den ich mir genauer ansehen will.«

Faith und Sam folgten ihrem Blick – zu Tex.

»Ich habe eine Schwäche für Tattoos«, sagte Vivian und drängte sich zielstrebig durch die Menge.

»Sie macht eine Pause von Männern, also droht Tex keine Gefahr.«

»Tex kann auf sich aufpassen. Um den mache ich mir keine Sorgen.«

Faith schlang ihre Arme um Sams Hals. »Diese Menschenmengen sind unglaublich. Bist du zufrieden mit der Beteiligung?«

Mit einem teuflischen Blick presste er seine Handfläche auf ihren Rücken und hielt sie ganz fest. »Doch, mit der Beteiligung bin ich zufrieden, aber noch glücklicher bin ich, weil du jetzt hier bist.«

»Wir waren schon um halb fünf hier und da war schon alles voll.«

»Die meisten Leute sind früher gekommen. Kein Problem. Hattet ihr einen netten Nachmittag, Vivian und du?«

»Ja, und weißt du, was das Beste ist?« Bevor er antworten konnte, sagte sie: »Ich hatte Angst, ich könnte eifersüchtig sein, aber ich bin es nicht. Nicht mal ein bisschen.«

»Das ist gut, denn du hast überhaupt keinen Grund, eifersüchtig zu sein.« Sein Blick ging zu Cole, der auf sie zusteuerte. Sam legte seinen Arm wieder um ihre Taille, und ein Lächeln breitete sich auf seinem Gesicht aus, als sein Bruder zu ihnen trat.

»Hi«, sagte Cole und nahm erst Faith und dann Sam in den Arm.

Seit ihrer Aussprache begegneten sich Faith und Cole in der Praxis wieder mit der gewohnten Lockerheit, und auch die Spannungen zwischen den Brüdern war verschwunden, nachdem sie sich bei ihrer spontanen Familienzusammenkunft entschuldigt hatten.

»Hallo. Wo ist Leesa?«, fragte Faith.

»Sie ist bei unserer Mom. Tempe und Jewel sind auch da. Wahrscheinlich werden sie bis in alle Ewigkeiten über unsere Flitterwochen reden.« Coles belustigter Blick ging zwischen Faiths und Sams Tops hin und her.

»Wolltest du etwas sagen?«, sagte Sam herausfordernd.

»Wer hätte das gedacht«, erwiderte Cole schmunzelnd.

»Das war Sams Idee«, sagte Faith schnell, als sei sie ihm eine Erklärung schuldig.

Cole hob abwehrend die Hände. »Ich sag ja gar nichts. Ich werde mich hüten, irgendwelche dummen Bemerkungen zu machen.«

»Das bekomme ich wohl in Zukunft immer wieder aufs Butterbrot geschmiert, was?« Er hatte sie ein paarmal damit aufgezogen, dass Sam ihr Selbstbewusstsein zu ungeahnten Höhen getrieben habe, aber sie wusste, dass er nur Spaß machte. Diesen Ton schlug er nur bei Leuten an, die ihm besonders nahestanden.

»Lass nur, ich kümmere mich darum«, sagte Sam und tat so, als wollte er auf Cole losgehen. Der wich ihm gekonnt aus und konterte mit einem vorgetäuschten Fausthieb.

Es war ihr nicht leichtgefallen, Cole die Stirn zu bieten, aber sie war froh, dass sie es getan hatte. Als sie die beiden nun so herumalbern sah, wie es nur in einer Familie möglich war, wusste sie, dass das Band zwischen den Brüdern alles aushalten konnte.

So wie bei uns.

Dreißig

Sam drehte seine Runde durch die Menge, begrüßte die Gäste und plauderte mit jedem ein wenig. Lira hatte Unglaubliches geleistet, es war ihr tatsächlich gelungen, viele ehemalige Sponsoren und Kunden zusammenzubringen. Gruppen, die er seit mehr als vier Jahren nicht mehr gesehen hatte, waren gekommen, und einige meldeten sich bereits für künftige Kletter- oder Raftingtouren an. Sam festigte den Kontakt zu einer Handvoll neuer Sponsoren und Lira nahm ihre Daten auf. Sie hatte Online-Formulare für Sponsoren eingerichtet und auf einem Tisch vier Laptops aufgebaut, an denen man sich anmelden konnte. Außerdem achtete sie darauf, dass jeder der Gäste eine Visitenkarte mit der Internetadresse von Rough Riders bekam. Sam war überzeugt, dass eine Vollzeitstelle für Lira genau die richtige Entscheidung gewesen war, und war erleichtert, dass sie und ihre Tochter von nun an nicht nur ein festes Einkommen hatten, sondern auch krankenversichert waren.

Als sich der Abend dem Ende zuneigte und die Gäste allmählich aufbrachen, folgte Sam dem Klang von Faiths Lachen und fand sie mit Vivian, Jewel, Tempe und Leesa am Wasser auf einer Decke sitzend. Kaum hatte er sich neben sie gesetzt, breitete sich Schweigen aus.

»Störe ich?«, fragte er. Insgeheim musste er grinsen. Die Blicke, die sie sich zuwarfen, waren vielsagend genug.

»Wir haben uns über dich unterhalten«, sagte Tempe.

Jewel gab ihr einen Klapps auf die Hand. »Also ehrlich, Tempe. Du solltest es ihm doch nicht sagen.«

Faith presste die Lippen zusammen, als müsste sie mühsam ein Lachen unterdrücken. »Was hast du ihnen erzählt?«, fragte Sam.

»Nichts. Also, jedenfalls nicht viel«, räumte sie ein.

»Sie musste uns gar nichts erzählen. Diese Tanktops sagen doch alles. Shannon lacht sich kaputt, wenn sie das sieht.« Tempe zückte ihr Handy und schoss ein paar Fotos.

Sam schüttelte lachend den Kopf. Heute konnte ihm nichts die Laune verderben. Er hatte die Frau seines Lebens an seiner Seite, eine neue Angestellte, und die Veranstaltung war ein Riesenerfolg.

»Du hast sie sogar in deine Bucht mitgenommen!«, sagte Tempe, als sie ihr Handy weglegte. »Das ist gigantisch!«

»Lieber Himmel«, murmelte er. Nicht, dass er versucht hätte, es geheim zu halten, aber Tempes Enthusiasmus kam ihm ein wenig übertrieben vor. Wahrscheinlich würde seine Familie wochenlang immer wieder davon anfangen.

»Ich finde das süß«, sagte Jewel.

»Und so bedeutsam«, fügte Leesa hinzu.

»Und romantisch«, sagte Vivian und stieß Faith in die Rippen.

Er war seltsam stolz auf all diese Dinge, mit denen er Nate und Cole aufgezogen hatte, als sie sich in Jewel und Leesa verliebt hatten.

»Wenn es euch nichts ausmacht, lasse ich euch jetzt allein,

damit ihr ungestört schwärmen könnt, was für ein toller Freund ich bin.« Er zog Faith auf die Füße, um sie zu umarmen, und ihr Drink ergoss sich über sein Top.

»Oh nein! Tut mir leid!«, jammerte sie und versuchte, die Flüssigkeit abzuwischen.

Ein Griff, und Sam hatte das Hemd über den Kopf gezogen. »Ist nicht schlimm, ich hole mir ein anderes Hemd aus dem Büro.«

Faith starrte hungrig auf seine nackte Brust.

»Warum kommst du nicht mit?« Über die Schulter gewandt sagte er: »Ich bringe sie gleich zurück.«

»Wer's glaubt, wird selig«, rief Tempe ihnen nach.

»Es tut mir so leid.« Ihre Hand fuhr über seine feuchte Brust und seine Bauchmuskeln, und als sie zu ihm aufblickte, konnte er nicht anders, als sie zu küssen.

»Nein, tut es nicht.«

Sie rannten fast zum Büro, blieben aber alle paar Schritte stehen und küssten sich. Sobald sie die Tür hinter sich geschlossen hatten, fanden sich ihre Münder in einem gierigen Kuss. Faiths Hände fuhren über seinen Rücken, er schob seine unter ihr Top und entlockte ihr damit ein sexy Stöhnen.

»Das können wir nicht machen«, sagte sie, als er sich an ihrem Hals entlangküsste. »Oh Gott, das fühlt sich so gut an.« Ihr Atem ging stoßweise. »Wir können nicht ...« Er rieb seine Erregung an ihrer Hüfte. »Vielleicht doch.«

Er lehnte sich zurück und sah in ihre lustvollen Augen. Sie war zu seiner Welt geworden. Sie war die Luft, die er atmete. Sie so zerrissen zu sehen, zwischen dem Feuer der Begierde und dem Bemühen, das Richtige zu tun, erinnerte ihn an die Millionen Gründe, warum er sich in sie verliebt hatte. Sie war ebenso vorsichtig wie frech und sie gehörte ihm.

»Du hast recht.«

»Meinst du?« Sie runzelte die Stirn. Sie hakte die Finger in den Hosenbund seiner Jeans. »Bist du sicher?«

»Überhaupt nicht. Aber du hast wahrscheinlich recht.«

Plötzlich ging die Bürotür auf und Nate steckte den Kopf herein. »Hey –« Er schloss die Augen. »Tut mir leid, Mann. Ich hätte klopfen sollen.«

Faith lief feuerrot an. Sam stöhnte, gab ihr einen kurzen Kuss und holte sich ein Hemd aus einem Regal in der Kammer, in der er Extras aufbewahrte. »Alles okay. Wir haben ja nichts gemacht.«

Nate öffnete die Augen. »Es tut mir wirklich leid.«

»Ich sehe mal, was Vivian macht.« Faith verließ hastig das Büro.

»Ich wollte sie nicht in Verlegenheit bringen.« Nate räusperte sich. »Oder dir die Tour vermasseln. Zieh dein Hemd runter, ja?«

Sam sah auf seine Erektion hinunter und zupfte an seinem Hemdsaum. »Neidisch?«

»Auf diesen Wurm?«, spottete Nate.

»Nennt man Pythons heutzutage so?«

Nate lachte. »Da sind ein paar Typen draußen. Einer von ihnen fragt nach dir.«

Sam folgte Nate aus dem Büro, sah sich nach Faith um und entdeckte sie zusammen mit Vivian bei den Erfrischungen. Seine Stimmung hellte sich auf, wie jedes Mal, wenn er sie erblickte.

»Sammy!« Jacob Warner, ein untersetzter blonder Mann, der vor ein paar Jahren ein paar Touren mit Sam unternommen hatte, schüttelte ihm die Hand und schlug ihm kräftig auf den Rücken.

»Warner, wie geht's dir? Gehst du immer noch klettern?«

»Aber ja. Als ich die Einladung zum Barbecue bekam, musste ich einfach kommen. Mann, du hast mein Leben verändert.« Sein Lächeln ließ seine dunklen Augen leuchten. »Was du nach der Klettertour zu mir gesagt hast, hat mich befreit.«

»Ach du liebes Lottchen, Faith, sieh nur.« Vivian stieß Faith mit dem Ellbogen an, die sich gerade mit Lira unterhielt. Sie zeigte zum Strand.

Faiths Augen richteten sich auf Sam. »Ich weiß. Sam ist heiß, nicht wahr ...« Sie umklammerte Vivians Arm, als sie den Mann, mit dem Sam sich unterhielt, erkannte. Eine Woge aus Wut und Schmerz drohte, sie in die Knie zu zwingen. JJ.

»Was macht dieses Arschloch hier?«, zischte Vivian. Sie stürmte davon und zog Faith mit sich.

Faith hatte JJ nicht mehr gesehen, seit sie aus Oak Falls weggezogen war. Natürlich wusste sie, dass er es war – der Mann, der ihr Herz gebrochen und sie aus dem Leben verdrängt hatte, das sie sich über Jahre aufgebaut hatte. Trotzdem ergab es keinen Sinn, ihn dort mit Sam stehen zu sehen.

JJ lachte über etwas, das Sam sagte.

Sie erstarrte innerlich und wäre fast hingefallen. *Oh Mist.* Er kannte Sam? Wie konnte das sein? Was zum Teufel war los?

»Ich schaff das schon«, sagte Faith zu Vivian. Sie war sich sicher, dass ihr Rauch aus den Ohren quoll, und es war ihr egal. Er hatte es nicht verdient, mit ihrem Freund hier zu sein, an ihrem glücklichen Ort. Zorn drängte den Schmerz beiseite, ließ sie ihren Schritt beschleunigen, entschlossen, ihren Platz an Sams Seite zurückzuerobern.

»Mann, Sam, diese Reise hat mein Leben verändert«, sagte JJ.

»Ja, es war ein toller Aufstieg«, erwiderte Sam.

»Nein, Mann. Das war es nicht.« JJ verstummte abrupt, als Vivian Faith nach vorne zerrte. Verwirrt sah er sie an. »Faith?« JJ schüttelte den Kopf, als hätte er ebenso große Mühe zu begreifen, was hier vor sich ging.

»Hey, Baby.« Sam legte seinen Arm um ihre Taille. Er spürte, dass ihr ganzer Körper wie erstarrt war. Er sah sie besorgt an. »Alles okay?«

JJs Blick fiel auf Faiths Top. »Moment mal. Sams Braut? Ihr zwei?« Er zwinkerte ihnen zu. »Ihr seid zusammen?«

»Warner, das ist meine Freundin, Faith«, sagte Sam so stolz und selbstbewusst wie immer.

»Du kennst JJ?« Die Verwunderung in ihrer Stimme war unüberhörbar.

Er packte sie fester. »JJ? Wie bei deinem Ex?«

»Ja.« Beide drehten sich zu JJ um, der breit grinsend vor ihnen stand.

Wut durchzuckte Sam, ließ ihn den Kiefer anspannen und seine Augen zu Schlitzen verengen. »Verdammt«, murmelte er. Er verschränkte die Arme vor der Brust, senkte das Kinn und trat auf JJ zu. Die Beine wie massive Säulen aufgepflanzt, schob er sich als schützende Wand zwischen ihn und Faith.

»Das ist ja wirklich zu komisch«, spottete JJ. Er rieb sich mit der Hand über das Gesicht. »Das gibt's doch nicht.«

In Faiths Kopf drehte sich alles. Warum war er hier? Woher kannte er Sam? Warum wusste *sie* nicht, dass er Sam kannte?

JJ sah Faith amüsiert an. »Du bist mit diesem Kerl

zusammen? Mit dem Typen, der mir *gesagt* hat, ich soll dich betrügen?«

Faith stockte der Atem. Sie stolperte einen Schritt zurück und klammerte sich an Vivian, um nicht zu fallen.

»Ich habe damals viel Mist geredet«, sagte Sam mit eisiger Stimme. »Aber ich hätte weder dir noch sonst jemandem je gesagt, er solle seine Freundin betrügen.«

»Nun tu nicht so, als wüsstest du nicht mehr, wie du in dieser Bar herumgehangen hast, mit einem Mädel unter jedem Arm«, fauchte JJ. »Wie du dich darüber ausgelassen hast, dass Monogamie nicht natürlich sei und …«

Faith hörte kaum noch zu. Sam hatte ihm gesagt, dass er sie betrügen solle? Monogamie sei nicht natürlich? Als sie sich abwandte, spürte sie, wie ein Riss durch ihr Herz ging. Vivian nahm ihre Hand und zog sie weg.

»Faith, warte.«

Vivian drehte sich um, um etwas zu sagen, aber sie musste etwas in Sams Blick gesehen haben, das sie innehalten ließ. Mit einem Schritt war Sam bei ihnen und schloss Faith in die Arme. *Gott. In deinen Armen. Mein Lieblingsplatz. Ich habe so viele Lieblingsplätze. Mit dir zusammen.* Faith sah ihm in die Augen und entdeckte Liebe und Zärtlichkeit darin. Und zum ersten Mal auch Angst.

Sams Angst zu sehen, erschreckte sie. Hatte sie einen Fehler gemacht, als sie sich auf ihn einließ?

»Hast du diese Dinge gesagt?« In ihren Ohren klang ihre Stimme zerbrechlich und fremd.

»Baby, ich habe damals alle möglichen Dinge gesagt, aber ich hätte ihm nie gesagt, dass er fremdgehen soll. Fremdgehen, Betrügen, das war noch nie ein Teil von mir. Das weißt du. Ob ich gesagt habe, dass Monogamie nicht natürlich ist oder dass es dumm ist, sich zu binden?« Er sah ihr in die tränenglänzenden Augen und der Schmerz in seinem Blick ließ sie fast zusammenbrechen. »Ja, könnte sein, dass ich das gesagt habe. Wahrscheinlich habe ich es gesagt. Aber so bin ich jetzt nicht mehr.«

Sam, der Ehrliche. Ihr Sam. Sie schloss die Augen und drückte ihm die Lippen auf die Brust. »Ich brauche Zeit, um das zu verarbeiten. Du solltest wieder zu deinen Gästen gehen. Das ist ein wichtiges Ereignis und es sind immer noch viele Menschen hier.«

Einunddreißig

Faith ging ruhelos am Ufer auf und ab. Sie hatte Sam schließlich überredet, zu seinen Gästen zurückzukehren, weil sie nicht zulassen wollte, dass JJ »das Arschloch« Warner Sams großen Tag kaputtmachte, selbst wenn sie selbst das Gefühl hatte, als hätte ihr jemand den Boden unter den Füßen weggezogen. Wenigstens hatte sie sich zurückgehalten und JJ nicht an den Kopf geworfen, was sie am liebsten mit dem höhnischen Grinsen auf seinem Gesicht angestellt hätte.

»Sag mir, was ich tun kann«, sagte Vivian bestimmt zum zehnten Mal in der letzten halben Stunde.

Faith setzte sich in den Sand und starrte auf das Wasser. »Nichts.«

»Du klingst so ruhig. Ich würde diesen selbstgefälligen Mistkerl von JJ mit dem größten Vergnügen zusammenschlagen.«

»Das ist der Grund, weshalb ich dich so liebe.« Faith zog sie zu sich herunter. »Ich bin nicht ruhig. Ich bin total panisch. Und ich versuche herauszufinden, was zum Teufel gerade passiert ist.«

Sie sah ihre beste Freundin an, die bei ihr gewesen war, als JJ ihr versehentlich eine Einladung geschickt hatte, die für jemand anderen gedacht war. Vivian hatte ihr geholfen, sich für ihr geheimes Date fertig zu machen, das sie so beflügelt hatte. Welche Frau wäre nicht begeistert, sich heimlich mit ihrem Freund in einem Hotelzimmer zu treffen? Dass er ihr erzählt hatte, er würde mit seinen Kumpels übers Wochenende wegfahren, hätte ihr eigentlich die Augen öffnen müssen. Wie aufgeregt sie gewesen war, als sie an die Tür des Hotelzimmers geklopft hatte! Insgeheim hatte sie sich gefragt, ob dies die Nacht der Nächte werden würde. Der Abend, an dem er um ihre Hand anhielt. Auf die Frau, die in Spitzendessous aus dem Badezimmer kam, als er, nur mit einer Boxershorts bekleidet, die Tür öffnete, war sie nicht gefasst gewesen. Ebenso wenig wie auf das bodenlose Gefühl der Demütigung und Verzweiflung, mit dem sie weinend aus dem Hotel gelaufen war. Es war, als sei sie durch ein Wurmloch gefallen und an einem Ort gelandet, an dem nichts einen Sinn ergab.

Vivian hatte sie damals gerettet. Sie hatte ihr zugehört, mit ihr gemeinsam überlegt, wie es weitergehen sollte, und sie schließlich bestimmt, aber herzlich aufgefordert, sich zusammenzureißen und nach vorn zu schauen.

»Viv, du hast Sam und mich erlebt. Sehe ich ihn durch eine Orgasmusbrille?« Noch während sie die Frage mühsam hervorstieß, brannte ihr der bittere Geschmack ihrer Worte auf der Zunge und sie wusste die Antwort. Was immer gerade passiert war, es hatte nichts mit dem zu tun, was sie damals mit JJ durchgemacht hatte. Und so sehr sie Vivian in jener schrecklichen Zeit gebraucht hatte: Das hier war anders. Vivian musste ihr nicht mehr helfen, das durchzustehen. Sie würde es schaffen. Sie und Sam. »Warte, sag lieber nichts.«

»Oh doch, dazu werde ich etwas sagen. Natürlich siehst du ihn nicht durch eine Orgasmusbrille. Ich glaube, mit diesem

Mann hast du einen ungeschliffenen Diamanten gefunden. Obwohl« – hier stieß Vivian sie mit der Schulter an und wies auf Sam, der über den Strand auf sie zukam – »ich nicht glaube, dass es irgendeinen Unterschied macht, durch welche Brille du ihn betrachtest. Du kannst ihn nur als den sehen, der er ist. Er war von Anfang an brutal ehrlich zu dir, seit er dich zum ersten Mal gefragt hat, ob du mit ihm ausgehst. Du hast ihn gefragt, ob ihm schon die Mädels ausgegangen seien, und er hat geantwortet, es seien noch ein paar übrig.«

Bei Sams Anblick wirbelten Faiths Gedanken wild durcheinander. Zum Glück musste sie nicht nachdenken. Sie erinnerte sich an jedes Wort, das sie an jenem Abend gesagt hatten.

»Er sagte, er wollte mich.«

Sam hockte sich neben sie. »Hey, Baby.«

»Was ist mit deinen Gästen?«

»Ty und Tex kümmern sich um alles. Du bist schon lange hier unten.« Jedes seiner Worte war von Sorge getränkt. »Ich halte es keine Sekunde länger aus, nicht bei dir zu sein. Ich möchte hier sein, bei dir, und mich mit dem ganzen Mist auseinandersetzen, der passiert ist. Bitte schick mich nicht weg.«

Faith stiegen Tränen in die Augen. »Dich wegzuschicken ist das Letzte, was ich will.«

Vivian berührte Faiths Arm, eine stumme Botschaft, die Hilfsangebot und Frage zugleich war. *Ich lasse euch allein, okay?*

»Ich helfe Ty und Tex beim Aufräumen und dann kann Tex mich zu meinem Auto zurückbringen.« Vivian umarmte Faith und flüsterte: »Sag jetzt nichts. Seine Tattoos sind heiß und ich hatte eine lange Männerpause.«

Faith brauchte das Lächeln, das Vivians Worte ihr entlockten, doch als sie sich wieder Sam zuwandte, griff er nach ihrer Hand, und ihr Herz wurde bleischwer.

»Sollen wir ein Stück gehen und reden oder sitzen bleiben?«, fragte er.

Sie zog ihn wortlos in den Sand und holte tief Luft. Der Blick über den Fluss ließ die Erinnerung an ihre Raftingtour und den Abend aufsteigen, an dem Sam ihr gestanden hatte, dass er sie liebte. Für den heutigen Abend hatte sie so romantische Pläne gehabt. Dass er in diese herzzerreißende Spannung münden würde, hatte sie überhaupt nicht auf dem Radar gehabt.

»Es tut mir leid, Sam. Ich hoffe, ich habe da oben keine Szene gemacht und dich in Verlegenheit gebracht.«

»Du hast keine Szene gemacht, aber um mich in Verlegenheit zu bringen, würde es noch viel mehr brauchen als eine Szene.« Er griff nach ihrer Hand und sie war froh darüber. Offenbar brauchte er die Verbindung zwischen ihnen ebenso wie sie. »Baby, was immer ich zu Warner – JJ – gesagt haben mag: Es tut mir leid, wenn ihn das dazu gebracht hat, dich zu verletzen.«

»Das weiß ich. Ich habe über alles nachgedacht, was wir durchgemacht haben. Über alles, was ich seit der Trennung von ihm durchgemacht habe. Damals dachte ich, er hätte mich gebrochen. Dass er mich vernichtet, mein sicheres kleines Leben in abertausend Stücke geschlagen hatte, aber er hat mich nicht gebrochen. Er hat mir einen Schlag in die Magengrube versetzt und mich aufgeweckt. Heute glaube ich, dass ich das gebraucht habe. Ohne Grund ist kein Mann in einer Beziehung so unglücklich. Ich war dieser Grund. In diesem Punkt hatte er recht.«

»Faith –«

»Hör mich an, bitte. Ich sage nicht, dass er hätte

fremdgehen sollen. Er ist ein absolutes Arschloch, weil er das getan hat. Das ändert aber nichts an der Tatsache, dass die Dinge, die er damals gesagt hat, stimmten. Ich ging ganz in meiner Arbeit, meiner Ausbildung auf, war mit meinen Freundinnen und meiner Familie beschäftigt. Aber für ihn hatte ich keine Zeit. Sein Fremdgehen hat mich gezwungen, mich selbst anzusehen und herauszufinden, wer ich war. Und es war ein langer, harter Weg, Sam. Ich habe viel geweint, habe an mir gezweifelt und an meiner Fähigkeit zu lieben und geliebt zu werden. Aber ich habe auch meinen Stolz gefunden und festgestellt, dass ich jemand bin, der seine Arbeit liebt und eine Website aufzieht, weil er verletzt ist. Das bin ich. Das wird sich nie ändern.«

Sam war die Kehle wie zugeschnürt, seit dem Moment, als er begriffen hatte, wie Warner, Faith und er selbst zusammenhingen. Er hasste es, dass der heutige Tag so viel Schmerz aus Faiths Vergangenheit hochgespült hatte. Schmerz, den er so gerne ausgelöscht hätte.

»Faith, du musst mir nicht sagen, wer du bist. Ich weiß, wer du bist. Ich liebe die, die du bist. Ich liebe es, dass du hart arbeitest und du alles unternimmst, um anderen zu helfen. Ich liebe es, dass du mir nichts durchgehen lässt und rot wirst, wenn ich dich anmache. Ich bin nicht Warner. Ich respektiere dich und möchte, dass du ein erfülltes Leben hast – mit mir und allein.«

»Ich glaube dir«, sagte sie mit gesenktem Blick. »Aber zwischen das Wissen, wer ich bin, und dem, was da oben passiert ist, haben sich Selbstzweifel geschoben, und ich habe mich gefragt, ob ich wieder in die alten Muster zurückgefallen bin. Dass ich mich so sehr bei meiner Arbeit und meiner Website engagiere, dass ich gar nicht sehe, was vor meiner Nase liegt. Bin ich von einem Fremdgeher zum nächsten gelangt?«

Das Gewicht ihres Geständnisses legte sich schwer auf seine Brust. War seine Vergangenheit endlich zurückgekommen, um ihn zu vernichten?

»Ich kann nicht leugnen, dass diese Stimme in meinem Kopf aufgetaucht ist. Das zu leugnen würde bedeuten, dass ich tatsächlich wieder die bin, die ich früher war, und die bin ich nicht mehr. Also erzähle ich dir, was mir sonst noch in den Sinn gekommen ist, denn das sind wir, nicht wahr? Du und ich, wir respektieren unsere verrückten Gefühle, stimmt's?«

Wir. Es gab also noch ein Wir. Dem Himmel sei Dank! »Absolut. Das Gute, das Schlechte, das Verrückte und alles, was dazwischenliegt. Wenn du es fühlst, möchte ich es auch fühlen.«

»Gut.« Sie sah ihm in die Augen und sagte mit zitternder Stimme: »Es war wirklich schwer zu ertragen, als er meinte, du hättest ihm gesagt, dass er mich betrügen sollte.«

Er unterdrückte den Drang, noch einmal genau darzulegen, was er damals gesagt oder nicht gesagt hatte. Das wusste sie schon alles. Was sie jetzt brauchte, war, dass er ihr zuhörte.

»Und dann dachte ich an das, was du gesagt hast, bevor wir zusammengekommen sind.« Mit sanfterer Stimme fuhr sie fort: »Beim Fremdgehen bedarf es einer kognitiven, bewussten Entscheidung, die jemand in dem Wissen trifft, dass er seinem Partner wehtut. Sam, es ist egal, was du damals zu ihm gesagt hast. Wenn er vorhatte, mich zu betrügen, dann hätte er es sowieso getan. Er hat das, was du gesagt hast, so verstanden, wie er es verstehen wollte: als würdest du damit etwas absegnen, was er so oder so tun würde.«

Sam atmete tief aus. Er hatte gar nicht bemerkt, dass er die Luft angehalten hatte. »Gott sei Dank, dass du das verstehst.«

Ihr Lächeln war wie eine weitere Rettungsleine, an die er sich klammern konnte. »Und dann habe ich bei meiner angstvollen Nabelschau noch etwas herausgefunden. Was JJ war oder ist, ändert nichts daran, dass ich so bin, wie ich bin. Und es ändert nichts daran, dass du der bist, der du bist. Ich bin stärker als früher, ich weiß besser, wer ich bin und was ich will. Und was noch wichtiger ist: Ich bin nicht mit verbundenen Augen in diese Beziehung – in unsere Beziehung – gestolpert. Ich weiß, wer du bist, und ich vertraue dir, Sam. Ganz und gar.«

Sie setzte sich auf Sams Schoß und schlang die Arme um seinen Hals. Sein Herz war so voll, dass es zu bersten drohte.

»Als ich mich darauf eingelassen habe, mit dir auszugehen«, sagte sie in dem süßen Ton, in dem sie normalerweise mit ihm sprach und der sein Herz aus einem ganz neuen, wunderbaren Grund noch höherschlagen ließ, »habe ich deine Vergangenheit als Teil des Gesamtpakets angenommen. Was mit diesem Idioten passiert ist, war Teil dieses Pakets, genauso wie er ein Teil des Gepäcks ist, das ich mit mir herumschleppe und das du so freundlich angenommen hast.«

»Baby, weißt du eigentlich, wie unglaublich du bist? Oder wie stolz ich bin, dein Freund zu sein?«

»Meinst du mich?« Sie lachte. »Die Verrückte, die immer dasselbe redet?«

»Nein. Ich meine die intelligente, eigensinnige Frau, die ihren Prinzipien treu ist. Ich könnte dich nicht mehr lieben.« Er presste seine Lippen auf ihre. »Verdammt. Sieh dir das an. Ich liebe dich noch mehr als vor einer Sekunde.« Er küsste sie erneut. »Okay, ich habe mich geirrt. Ich könnte und werde dich jeden Tag mehr und mehr lieben.«

Sie lachte. »Willst du das Verrückteste von allem hören?«

»Geht es noch verrückter?«

»Oh ja, das kommt davon, wenn du dich mit mir einlässt.« Sie lachte. »Seit dem Moment, als du mir gesagt hast, dass du mich liebst, will ich dir dasselbe sagen. Ich wollte den perfekten Zeitpunkt abwarten, weil ich es ebenso romantisch und wunderbar machen wollte wie du. Ich hatte gedacht, der heutige Abend wäre ideal. Nur wir zwei hier unten am Wasser, am Ende deines großen Tages. Ich hatte es so akribisch geplant wie du unser erstes Date. Ich wollte Hinweise verteilen, die dich zum Wasser führen sollten. Und da würde ich in einem Kreis warten, den ich in den Sand malen wollte.«

Lieber Gott, ich bin der glücklichste Mann der Welt. »In einem Kreis?«

»Schönheit in Unvollkommenheit und in der Entwicklung.« Sie kletterte von seinem Schoß und zeichnete einen Kreis in den Sand. Das Herz schlug ihm bis zum Hals, als sie seine Hand nahm und ihn zu sich in den Kreis zog.

»Laut Google ist der Kreis das Symbol für Unvollkommenheit.« Sie legte ihm die Arme um die Taille. »Und wir sind das Symbol für Entwicklung.«

Er starrte in ihre liebevollen Augen und ertrank darin.

»Sam?«

»Ja?«, brachte er mühsam hervor. Ihm war der Hals vor lauter Gefühlen wie zugeschnürt.

»Ich glaube, du hast tatsächlich aufgehört zu atmen.« Sie presste ihm die Hand auf die Brust und lächelte ihn an. »Du wartest, stimmt's?«

Sie kannte ihn so gut, dass er nicht einmal versuchte zu

antworten.

»Ich liebe dich, Sam, mit allen Unvollkommenheiten.« Sie stellte sich auf die Zehenspitzen und schwebte einen Atemzug von seinen Lippen entfernt. »Sam?« Sie legte ihm die Hand an die Wange.

Er war so voller Emotionen, dass »Hm?« alles war, was er sagen konnte.

»Du musst mich jetzt küssen.«

Epilog

Drei Wochen später

»Kaum zu glauben, dass hier für dich und Faith alles angefangen hat.« Sams Mutter hakte sich bei ihm unter. Das Mr. B. war für ein festliches Abendessen mit den Fishers geschlossen. Hier sollte nach Krissys Tanzabend gefeiert werden. Krissys Auftritt war spektakulär gewesen, sie schien das Tanzen im Blut zu haben.

Den ganzen Abend hatte er Faith kaum aus den Augen lassen können. Sie stand am anderen Ende des Raumes, unterhielt sich mit Leesa, Jewel und Tempe und wiegte sich in ihrem knappen schwarzen Kleid zur Musik. Immer wieder hatte sie ihm verstohlene Blicke zugeworfen, die ihn wie ein Hitzestrahl trafen.

»Es hat lange vor jenem Abend angefangen, Mom. Ich wusste es nur nicht.« Faith war vor zwei Wochen in sein Haus gezogen und Lira hatte den Mietvertrag für ihre Wohnung übernommen. Sam hatte Lira angeboten, von zu Hause aus zu arbeiten, falls sie lieber in ihrer Heimatstadt bleiben wollte, aber sie hatte entschieden, dass ein sauberer Schnitt besser war, als ständig im Schatten ihrer schmerzvollen Vergangenheit zu leben. Sam konnte es nur zu gut nachvollziehen. Immerhin hatte Faith es ebenso gemacht, und er war heilfroh, dass es so gekommen war, sonst hätte er sie wahrscheinlich nie kennengelernt. Er hoffte, dass auch Lira in Peaceful Harbor ihr Glück finden würde.

Seine Mutter lächelte ihn an, ihre dichten blonden Locken umrahmten ihr glückliches Gesicht.

»Ich habe mich nie groß in dein Privatleben eingemischt, aber du sollst wissen, dass ich dich nie nach deiner Lebensweise beurteilt habe. Wir alle gehen unterschiedliche Wege, Sammy. Deiner hat dich zu Faith geführt.«

»Danke, Mom. Das bedeutet mir viel.«

Sie blickte zu der Gruppe hinüber, bei der Faith stand. »Sie ist wunderbar, weißt du?«

»Oh ja, ich weiß.« In diesem Moment sah Faith ihn an und er schickte ihr einen Luftkuss quer durch den Raum. Sie legte die Finger auf die Lippen, als sei sein Kuss tatsächlich dort gelandet.

»Du bist auch wunderbar, Schatz.« Sie küsste ihn auf die Wange.

»Meinst du nicht, dass du ein bisschen voreingenommen bist?«, neckte er. Sein Vater und Nate gesellten sich zu ihnen.

Ace legte seiner Frau einen Arm um die Schulter und sagte: »Drei sind vergeben, jetzt bleiben noch drei.«

»Noch zwei«, sagte Ty. »Ich warte auf eine flotte Bergsteigerin mit einem wachen Auge und einem Körper für …«

»Ty!« Ihre Mutter schüttelte den Kopf. »Das Ende dieses Satzes will ich gar nicht hören.«

»Warum?«, fragte Ty unschuldig. »Nächste Woche breche ich nach Spanien auf zu einem Fotoauftrag und habe vor, die spanische Kultur mit all ihren Facetten bis in alle Einzelheiten kennenzulernen.«

Natürlich ließ Nate es sich nicht nehmen, ihn aufzuziehen, und Sam nutzte die Gelegenheit, um den Raum zu durchqueren und etwas Zeit mit seinem Lieblingsmenschen zu verbringen.

Unterwegs sprach Cole ihn an. »Ich habe mit Jon geredet.«

Sam blieb stehen. »Und?«, fragte er gespannt.

»Er ist einverstanden, dass Faith vier Wochen Urlaub bekommt, sodass sie mit dir reisen kann. Aber wenn sie länger als vier Tage am Stück weg ist, brauchen wir mindestens zwei Wochen Vorlaufzeit, damit wir jemanden anfordern können, der für sie einspringt.«

»Das ist super. Vielen Dank.«

»Gerne, aber ich habe das Gefühl, dass deine Freundin es nicht mag, wenn du hinter ihrem Rücken planst.«

Cole hatte recht, aber bald würde sie reichlich zu planen haben, und da hatte er diese eine Sorge aus dem Weg räumen wollen. »Es war ja für einen guten Zweck. Ich glaube, sie wird mir verzeihen.«

Faiths Puls beschleunigte sich, je näher Sam kam. Ihre Welt hatte sich in den letzten Wochen so sehr verändert und Sam hatte jeden einzelnen Schritt begleitet. Die Seite mit den Hilfsangeboten, die sie für Women Against Cheaters erstellt hatte, wurde pro Tag fast zweitausendmal aufgerufen, und morgen wollten Sam und sie zu einer Versammlung von Kleinunternehmern gehen, um herauszufinden, ob es noch andere Möglichkeiten gab, ihre Gruppe zu unterstützen. In der Praxis ging es wie immer zu wie im Taubenschlag und ihr

Verhältnis zu Cole hatte nicht gelitten. Im Gegenteil: Es schien sogar noch tragfähiger geworden zu sein.

»Sammy ist auf der Pirsch«, flüsterte Tempest ihr zu. »Wie hältst du es nur aus, wenn er dich so ansieht?«

Faith hoffte, dass es keinen Tag geben würde, an dem er sie nicht so ansah.

»Meine Damen.« Sam trat zwischen Tempest und Leesa und zog Faith in seine Arme. »Ich habe dich vermisst.« Er küsste sie zärtlich.

Tempest seufzte. »Ich weiß nicht, welchen Liebestrank du ihm gegeben hast, aber wenn ich einen Mann finde, kannst du es ihm bitte spritzen, was auch immer es ist?«

Faith lachte. Sie nahm kaum wahr, dass sich die anderen Frauen zurückzogen. Umso deutlicher nahm sie jedoch Sams muskulösen Körper an ihrem wahr.

»Du hast alle verschreckt.« Sie schlang ihm die Arme um den Nacken. Dass er alle anderen verschreckte, machte sie nicht unglücklich, wohl aber ein wenig verlegen. Aber sie hatte gelernt, dass auch das zu einem Leben mit Sam dazugehörte. Dieser Hauch von Verlegenheit kam von seiner überwältigenden Liebe zu ihr und die wollte sie um nichts in der Welt aufgeben.

Sam ging nicht auf ihren scherzhaften Vorwurf ein. Ihr war klar, dass es ihm nichts ausgemacht hätte, wenn er eine ganze Armee verscheucht hätte, ein weiterer Punkt auf der langen Liste der Dinge, die sie an ihm liebte.

Sie bewegten sich zur Musik und sahen einander dabei in die Augen, und Faith war sich sicher, dass ihre Körper für alle sichtbare Funken sprühten. Auch das gemeinsame Tanzen war ihr inzwischen so vertraut. Mindestens einmal am Tag tanzten sie, egal ob zu tatsächlicher oder zu eingebildeter Musik, und für gewöhnlich führte das dazu, dass sie gierig über einander herfielen. Am liebsten mochte sie es, wenn Sam sie beim Kochen oder bei einem Spaziergang in die Arme nahm und sang, während sie tanzten. Sie liebte die Art, wie seine gesungenen Gefühle direkt von seinem Herz in ihres drangen.

»Weißt du noch, als du nicht mit mir tanzen wolltest?«, fragte er.

»Ich glaube nicht, dass ich das jemals vergessen werde. Dich zurückzuweisen war so unglaublich schwer.« Im Raum war es ganz still, nur die Musik und das leise Rascheln war zu hören, wenn ihre Körper einander streiften. Faith fragte sich, ob alle sie beobachteten, aber Sam versperrte ihr die Sicht. *Mein leidenschaftlicher Sam.*

»Ich bin froh, dass ich nicht mehr fragen muss.«

»Ich auch.«

»Es gibt vieles, bei dem ich nicht mehr fragen muss.« Er presste seine Lippen auf ihre. »Dabei zum Beispiel.« Er vergrub die Nase an ihrem Hals. »Und dabei.«

»Sam«, sagte sie kichernd. »Das macht mich verrückt.«

Er legte seine Wange an ihre und sagte: »Ich weiß.«

Seine tiefe Stimme jagte ihr einen Schauder nach dem anderen über den Rücken. Er lehnte sich weit genug zurück, um ihr in die Augen zu sehen, und die Tiefe der Gefühle in seinem Blick ließ ihr Herz ruhiger werden.

»Eins gibt es aber noch, was ich dich fragen muss.«

»Tatsächlich? Ich dachte, ich hätte dir eine Pauschalerlaubnis erteilt.«

»Ich möchte eine Pauschalerlaubnis für deine gesamte Zukunft. Touren, Babys, tanzen unter den Sternen. Ich möchte alt und grau mit dir werden, und wenn wir zu viele Falten haben, um sie zu zählen, dann sind es doch immerhin *unsere*

Falten, Baby. Unsere Unvollkommenheiten, jede aus einem Leben geboren, in dem wir einander geliebt haben.«

Faith brachte kein einziges Wort zustande, während ihr die Tränen über die Wangen liefen.

»Heirate mich, Faith. Lass mich dich lieben, dich in Verlegenheit bringen und mit dir tanzen, bis zu dem Tag, an dem du mich zu Grabe trägst. Dann warte ich auf der anderen Seite auf dich und weiß, dass wir auch das gemeinsam erleben, was immer es auch sein mag.«

Sie schluckte ein paarmal und versuchte, Worte aus ihrer Kehle zu pressen, aber ihr Herz war geschwollen und ihre Brust hatte sich zusammengezogen und sie konnte kaum stehen. Aber nicken konnte sie.

»Baby, ich —«

»Du musst es hören, nicht wahr?«, brach es halb lachend, halb weinend aus ihr hervor. »Als würdest du zulassen, dass ich Nein sage! Ja, Sam. Ich möchte deine Frau sein. Ich möchte unsere Babys bekommen, Touren machen und mit dir alt werden. Aber vor allem möchte ich, dass du mich für den Rest meines Lebens so ansiehst wie jetzt.«

Sams Mund nahm von ihrem Besitz, während er sie hochhob und herumwirbelte.

»Ich liebe dich, Baby«, sagte er. Als Faith endlich den Blick von ihm wandte, sah sie die Frauen, die weinten und lächelten, und die Männer, die strahlten und jubelten.

»Eins noch.« Sam stellte sie wieder auf die Füße, griff in seine Tasche, zog einen funkelnden Verlobungsring hervor und schob ihn ihr auf den zitternden Finger.

Sie konnte kaum den Blick von dem rundgeschliffenen Diamanten wenden, der in einem Kreis aus kleineren Diamanten ruhte. Eine Reihe winziger Diamanten schmückte die breite

Ringschiene, die mit verschlungenen Mustern aus Weißgold verziert war. Das Strahlen der Edelsteine verschwamm in einem neuen Tränenschwall.

»Sam, der Ring ist wunderschön. Er hat so viel von uns.«

»Unser Kreis für die Ewigkeit, Baby.« Er küsste sie lange und genüsslich, während die Umstehenden Beifall klatschten und johlten.

»Du musst lächeln, Schatz. Deine Familie kann dich sehen.« Er zeigte auf den Bildschirm über der Bar, wo ihre Eltern, Vivian, Charley, Mack und Sams Schwester Shannon winkten und ihnen via Skype gratulierten.

Zum Glück hielt Sam sie fest, sonst hätten die Beine unter ihr versagt.

»Wie hast du das hinbekommen? Du hast meine Familie doch noch gar nicht kennengelernt.« Sie winkte ihren Eltern zu. Die Augen ihrer Mutter waren feucht, ihre Nase vom Weinen gerötet, und ihr Vater lächelte stolz auf sie herunter. »Ich hab euch lieb, Mom und Dad.«

»Wir dich auch, Schätzchen«, sagte ihr Vater.

»Ich konnte dich nicht bitten, meine Frau zu werden, ohne zuerst mit deinen Eltern zu sprechen«, erklärte Sam. »Vivian, die alles für dich tun würde, hat das für mich eingefädelt.«

Faith presste die Hand auf den Mund, um nicht laut aufzuschluchzen, als sie zu ihrer besten Freundin aufschaute. Vivians Tränen spiegelten ihre eigenen wider und beide sagten gleichzeitig: »Ich hab dich lieb.«

Sams Mutter war die Erste, die Faith umarmte. »Herzlichen Glückwunsch, Schatz. Wir sind so froh, dich in unserem Leben zu haben.«

Einer nach dem anderen hieß sie unter Tränen und Umarmungen im Kreis der Familie willkommen. Faith fing sich schließlich so weit, dass sie mit ihrer Familie und Vivian über Skype sprechen konnte. Bevor sie sich verabschiedeten, vereinbarten sie, dass sie und Sam bald nach Oak Falls fahren und ihre Eltern besuchen würden, und Vivian versprach, bald wieder nach Peaceful Harbor zu kommen. Faith ahnte, dass sie Vivian bei dieser Gelegenheit nicht allzu oft sehen würde, denn ihre Freundin hatte ihr gebeichtet, dass sie weiterhin Kontakt zu Tex hatte. Offenbar war die Männerpause kein Thema mehr.

Als der Abend sich dem Ende zuneigte, zog Sam sie in einen letzten Tanz im Mr. B. »Nun müssen wir uns nur noch auf ein Datum einigen.«

»Warum habe ich das Gefühl, als hättest du schon längst einen Termin im Sinn?«

Danksagung

Ein Buch schreibt man nie allein, und ich bin meinen Fans, meinen Freunden und meiner Familie zu Dank verpflichtet. Sie inspirieren und unterstützen mich jeden Tag aufs Neue. Ich würde mich freuen, weiterhin in Kontakt mit Ihnen, meinen Leserinnen, zu bleiben. Sie können ja nie wissen, ob Sie sich nicht eines Tages in einem meiner Bücher wiederfinden, wie einige Mitglieder meines Facebook-Fanclubs bereits feststellen konnten.

Wenn Sie mir noch nicht auf Facebook folgen, kann ich es Ihnen nur wärmstens empfehlen! Wir haben jede Menge Spaß, wenn wir über unsere liebenswerten Helden und selbstbewussten Heldinnen diskutieren. Außerdem versuche ich immer, meine Fans mit den neuesten Nachrichten aus der Welt unserer fiktiven Freunde zu versorgen. Sie finden uns unter: www.facebook.com/MelissaFosterAuthor

Und vergessen Sie nicht, sich für meinen Newsletter einzutragen, in dem Sie über Neuerscheinungen, Werbeaktionen und Events informiert werden (in deutscher Sprache): www.MelissaFoster.com/Newsletter_German

Wie immer gilt mein besonderer Dank meinem hervorragenden Lektoratsteam: Kristen Weber, Penina Lopez, Jenna Bagnini, Juliette Hill, Marlene Engel und Lynn Mullan sowie meinem deutschen Team: Rita Kloosterziel, Cathérine Fischer, Rabea Güttler und Judith Zimmer. Und natürlich meinem wunderbaren Mann Les.

Vereinte Herzen

Die Bradens (Peaceful Harbor)

LOVE IN BLOOM – HERZEN IM AUFBRUCH

Eins

Steve Johnson zog sich das durchgeschwitzte T-Shirt aus und griff nach seiner Wasserflasche. Es ging doch nichts über einen Lauf vor dem Morgengrauen, erst recht nach einer Nacht, in der man schlecht geschlafen hatte. Er ließ die leere Flasche und das T-Shirt auf den Stufen seines rustikalen Holzhauses zurück und überquerte den Hof, um am Hackklotz noch die restliche Anspannung loszuwerden. Normalerweise reichte ein Sechsmeilenlauf durch das unwegsame Gelände in den Bergen von Colorado, um ihn auf andere Gedanken zu bringen, aber nicht an diesem Morgen.

Die Sonne schien ihm auf die Schultern, als er ein Stück Holz mitten auf dem Baumstumpf legte, der ihm als Hackklotz diente, und versuchte, nicht an den Grund dafür zu denken, dass er letzte Nacht nicht hatte schlafen können. Tief atmete er den Duft der Natur und die Ruhe ein. Er kannte jedes Geräusch und jeden Geruch der Gegend, konnte jedes Tier und jede Pflanze im Wald bestimmen und das Wetter präzise vorhersagen. Sein Körper war so gut an die Berge angepasst, als wäre er ein Teil von ihnen.

Er hob die Axt hoch über die Schulter, während sich die Gedanken, die er zu verdrängen suchte, wie hartnäckige Diebe erneut einen Weg in seinen Kopf bahnten, und zerteilte das Holzstück. Das laute Knacken, das durch den Wald – und seinen Kopf – hallte, ließ den Grund für sein Unbehagen jedoch wieder deutlich in den Vordergrund treten. Shannon Braden war zurück – und sie war letzte Nacht an Cal Hayden geschmiegt auf dessen Pferd nach Hause gekommen.

Steve knirschte mit den Zähnen und griff nach dem nächsten Holzblock.

Die kluge, heiße Shannon, die redete wie ein Wasserfall. Er kannte sie seit Jahren. Seine Schwester Jade war mit Shannons Cousin zweiten Grades Rex verheiratet. Shannon hatte vor einiger Zeit wegen eines Forschungsprojekts über Rotfüchse mehrere Wochen in den Bergen verbracht und auf der Ranch ihres Onkels in Weston gewohnt, aber Steve wusste, dass die Firma, für die sie arbeitete, nun die leer stehende Hütte gleich um die Ecke gemietet hatte. Dort sollte sie während der restlichen Laufzeit des Projekts wohnen. Er schwang die Axt und dachte an die Wochen, in denen sie sein friedliches Leben durcheinandergebracht hatte mit ihrer Lebensfreude und nicht enden wollenden Gesprächen – die größtenteils einseitig verlaufen waren, was sie nicht zu stören schien. Ihn auch nicht, wie er sich eingestehen musste. Es war immer heiß, Shannon reden zu hören, um welches Thema es auch ging. Sie hatte seine Gedanken gefesselt wie keine Frau vor ihr, was mal wieder typisch war. Denn Steve stand nicht auf bedeutungslose Affären, und Shannon lebte in Peaceful Harbor in Maryland, er jedoch in den Bergen Colorados, womit Shannon Braden eindeutig in die Tabu-Kategorie fiel.

Die letzten Wochen, in denen sie für die Hochzeit ihres Bruders nach Hause zurückgekehrt war, ließen sich nur als ruhig bezeichnen, und die Tatsache, dass Steve das nicht nur aufgefallen war, sondern es ihm auch missfallen hatte, warf ihn ein bisschen aus der Bahn.

Er dachte erneut an den vergangenen Abend zurück. Etwa zwei Stunden nach seiner Ankunft war Cal den Berg wieder heruntergeritten. Während Steve die Axt schwang, fragte er sich, ob Shannon wohl letzte Nacht ein privates Forschungsprojekt mit dem Cowboy Cal begonnen hatte.

Er legte das nächste Holzstück auf den Block, sagte sich, dass ihn das verdammt noch mal nichts anging, was diese Frau so trieb, und schlug so fest zu, dass die Scheite nach beiden Seiten wegflogen. Das nächste Stück Holz, der nächste Schlag. So arbeitete er sich die Anspannung aus dem Leib, während die Sonne gen Zenit wanderte und der kühle Frühlingsmorgen angenehmer wurde.

Ein Vogelschwarm stieg aus den Baumwipfeln auf. Steve hielt mitten im Schlag inne, und ein Lächeln umspielte seine Lippen. *Shannon.* Er zerteilte das nächste Holzstück und versuchte, seinen beschleunigten Herzschlag bei dem Gedanken daran, dass sie in sein Leben zurückkehrte, zu ignorieren.

Der süße Klang ihres Summens drang an seine Ohren und ihm lief ein wohliger Schauder den Rücken herunter. Er hörte das Rascheln von Blättern und grinste noch breiter. Himmel, er musste sich wirklich zusammenreißen.

»Hallo, Mann aus den Bergen.«

Nur mit Mühe und Not konnte er sich das alberne Lächeln verkneifen und es durch ein hoffentlich weniger lüsternes ersetzen, als er sich zu der viel zu fröhlichen und unglaublich scharfen Brünetten umdrehte. Shannon hatte sich das Haar zu einem lässigen Knoten hochgesteckt, aber einige dunkle Locken fielen ihr über die Schultern. Sie hielt in jeder Hand eine dampfende Kaffeetasse. Ihr pinkfarbenes T-Shirt schmiegte sich an ihre Brüste, und er musste auch das auf die Liste der Dinge schreiben, auf die er trotz aller gegenteiliger Bemühungen reagierte. Sein Körper hatte dummerweise nicht begriffen, dass diese Frau tabu für ihn war. Es war ihm sehr viel leichter gefallen, ihre Gegenwart zu ertragen, als sie noch im Haus ihres Onkels gewohnt hatte. Immerhin hatte sie da bei jeder Begegnung wenigstens einen BH getragen.

Er senkte den Blick, um sie nicht anzustarren, aber ihre flanellene Pyjamahose saß tief auf ihren Hüften und ließ einen schmalen Streifen glatter Haut direkt unterhalb ihres Bauchnabels erkennen. Großer Gott, diese Frau war einfach umwerfend. Sicherheitshalber starrte er ihre Lederstiefel an. Damit konnte er nichts falsch machen, Stiefel waren nun mal nicht sexy. Leuchtend pinkfarbene Schnürsenkel baumelten locker auf dem dunklen Leder, und ihre Hose bauschte sich auf den Stiefeln, sodass auch hier Haut aufblitzte. Steve stellte sich vor, wie sie die nackten Füße in die Stiefel gesteckt hatte, um mit ihrem umwerfenden Lächeln im Gesicht aus der Tür zu stürmen. Irgendetwas stimmte offenbar nicht mit ihm, denn er fand selbst dieses Bild sexy.

»Die solltest du lieber zubinden.« Er fuhr sich mit einer Hand durchs Haar und knirschte mit den Zähnen, denn sein ganzer Körper stand komplett unter Strom.

»Alles klar, *Mr. Sicherheitsbeauftragter*. Du hast mir auch gefehlt.« Sie drückte ihm mit einem scheuen Lächeln eine Tasse in die Hand. »So, wie du ihn magst: schwarz wie die Nacht.«

Sie war viel zu süß, viel zu freundlich und viel zu kurze Zeit hier für jemanden wie ihn.

Er nahm die Tasse entgegen. »Danke, Butterfly.« Der Spitzname kam ihm ohne Nachdenken über die Lippen, genau wie damals, als sie das erste Mal in seinen Hof geflattert kam wie ein Schmetterling, seinen Körper in Aufruhr versetzt hatte und wieder davongeschwirrt war. Überrascht stellte er fest, dass er es vermisst hatte, das Kosewort auszusprechen, während sie fort gewesen war.

»Gern geschehen, Grizz.«

Grizz. Mann, selbst das hatte ihm gefehlt. Ihr Blick ruhte auf seiner nackten Brust und verweilte dort lange genug, dass er ihn noch etwas tiefer spürte. *Viel tiefer.* Sie bekam rote Wangen und richtete ihre wunderschönen haselnussbraunen Augen auf seine Axt – die in seiner Hand, nicht die in seiner Hose.

»Bereitest du dich auf kalte Nächte vor oder willst du zum Serienmörder werden?«

Mit dir in meinem Bett hätte ich nichts gegen kalte Nächte. Wie aufs Stichwort reagierte sein Körper und erinnerte ihn daran, dass er schon viel zu lange nicht mehr mit einer Frau zusammen gewesen war.

»So interessant das Leben eines Serienmörders auch sein mag, ist es vermutlich nichts für mich.«

»Das denke ich auch. Da müsstest mit Menschen in Kontakt treten.«

»Dein freches Mundwerk hat mir gefehlt«, spottete er. Ihr Mundwerk, oder vielmehr ihre vollen Lippen, beschäftigten ihn schon, seitdem sie sich auf Rex’ und Jades Hochzeit vor einigen Monaten wiedergetroffen hatten. Aber da sie nur so lange bleiben würde, bis ihr Projekt abgeschlossen war, würde es auch beim Spott bleiben.

»Ich hab dich gestern mit Cal ankommen gehört. Wie lange bleibst du?« Dabei hatte er sie nicht nur gehört, sondern war hinausgegangen, um herauszufinden, wer angeritten kam. So hatte er sie hinter Cal sitzen sehen, die Arme um ihn geschlungen, als sie am Aussichtspunkt vorbeigekommen waren. Die beiden hatten im Mondlicht ausgesehen wie das Motiv einer kitschigen Ansichtskarte.

»Ein paar Wochen. Viereinhalb, vermute ich. So ungefähr jedenfalls.« Sie streckte sich und reckte einen Arm, wobei sie noch mehr Haut in der Bauchgegend entblößte.

Folter. Reine, wundervolle Folter.

»Du hättest mich anrufen können, damit ich dich abhole.« Er wandte den Blick ab und staunte über sich selbst. *Du hättest mich anrufen können?* Er hatte doch gar nichts gegen Cal. Der war ein netter Kerl und einer der angesehensten Pferdetrainer der Gegend. Außerdem konnte es ihm ganz egal sein, mit wem Shannon ihre Zeit verbrachte. Zugegeben, sie war heiß und clever und er mochte ihre freche Art, aber er mochte sein Leben genau so, wie es jetzt war. Das Letzte, was er brauchte, war ein geselliger Mensch wie sie, der Lärm und Chaos mit sich brachte und ihm vorschreiben wollte, was er zu tun oder wie er zu leben hatte.

»Ich weiß.« Sie scharrte mit einem Fuß über den Boden. »Treat und Max kamen nachmittags vorbei und haben mich mit zu Onkel Hal und meinen Cousins genommen. Cal war auch dort und bot an, mich zurückzufahren. Er wohnt ja in Preston. Erst als wir bei ihm zu Hause angekommen waren, schlug er vor, dass wir reiten. Außerdem weiß ich doch, dass du nur ungern in die Stadt kommst.«

Na super, jetzt musste er sie sich auch noch auf Cals großer Pferderanch vorstellen.

Er trank seinen Kaffee aus und gab ihr die Tasse zurück. »Danke. Der war genau richtig.« Dann legte er das nächste Holzstück auf den Hackklotz. »Du solltest dir gut überlegen, wen du mit in deine Hütte nimmst«, sagte er, während er ihr den Rücken zugewandt hatte.

»Und ich dachte, ich hätte meine überfürsorglichen Brüder zu Hause gelassen.« Sie seufzte. »Cal stellt wohl kaum eine

Gefahr da. Er kennt Rex schon ewig.«

Steve legte sich die Axt auf die Schulter und überlegte, was er darauf erwidern sollte. Schließlich sollte sie ihn nicht als einen großen Bruder ansehen, außerdem kannte er Cal auch schon seit einer Ewigkeit. Cal war kein Mann, der eine Frau ausnutzen würde, was Steves Magen jedoch nicht daran hinderte, sich beim Gedanken an die beiden zusammenzuziehen.

»Er ist ein *Freund*, Steve.« Sie kniff die Augen zusammen, als er die Axt herunternahm. »Jetzt tu nicht so, als hättest du noch nie eine Frau mit in deine Hütte genommen.«

Er warf ihr einen vielsagenden Blick zu, der ihr zu verstehen gab, dass er das *auf gar keinen Fall* tun würde. Dafür war ihm seine Privatsphäre viel zu wichtig.

Ihr fiel die Kinnlade herunter. »Was? Ist dir denn nie langweilig? Bist du nie einsam?«

»Eigentlich nicht«, antwortete er und schwang die Axt. Das war eine gottverdammte Lüge, jedenfalls seitdem Shannon in sein Leben geflattert war und dafür gesorgt hatte, dass Gefühle in ihm aufstiegen, die er bis dato erfolgreich hatte ignorieren können.

»Warum nicht? Das ist doch nicht normal.« Sie leerte ihre Tasse und stellte sie neben seine auf den Boden, während er das Holz spaltete und zum nächsten griff. »Was machst du, wenn du Lust bekommst?«

Er lachte leise auf. »Fragst du mich das im Ernst, Stadtmädchen?«

»Ich würde Peaceful Harbor nicht gerade als Stadt bezeichnen. Es ist eher ein Städtchen am Meer, und du hast meine Frage nicht beantwortet.«

»Das könnte daran liegen, dass du Fragen stellst, die du

lieber nicht stellen solltest.« Bei diesen Worten spaltete er das nächste Holzstück.

Sie grinste. »Schau mal einer an: So ein großer, starker Mann hat Angst, über Sex zu reden.«

»Was ist denn los mit dir?« Er stellte die Axt ab und stützte sich auf den Griff. Bevor Shannon nach Hause gefahren war, hatte er immer mit einem strategisch platzierten *Hmm-mmm* durchkommen können. »Ich meine, mich zu erinnern, dass du bei deinem letzten Aufenthalt auf dem Berg nicht so an meinem Sexleben interessiert gewesen wärst.«

Ihr Blick wanderte über ihn hinweg, und er war sich nicht sicher, ob sie seinen Körper abschätzte oder bewunderte.

»Keine Ahnung«, erwiderte sie mit schelmischem Grinsen. »Du stehst da wie ein Holzfäller mit deinen eins ... siebenundachtzig?«

»Eins neunzig«, korrigierte er sie und seufzte.

»Genau. Eins neunzig, nackter Oberkörper, verschwitzt, muskulös, zerzaustes Haar.« Sie gestikulierte mit erhobenen Händen, wobei ihr T-Shirt hochrutschte. »Du hast dich vermutlich seit einer Ewigkeit nicht rasiert und könntest einer der Kerle auf dem Pinterest-Board ›Richtig heiße Kerle‹ sein. Ein Mann, der so aussieht, *kann* einfach nicht ohne Sex leben.« Sie zuckte mit den Achseln und bekam gerötete Wangen. »Und da habe ich mich gefragt ...«

»Wie wäre es, wenn du das bleiben lässt?« *Denn wenn du noch länger über mein Sexleben redest, will ich dich daran teilhaben lassen, in allen nur denkbaren Varianten.* »Pinterest? Was zum Geier ist Pinterest?«

Sie riss fassungslos die Augen auf. »Ich hatte ganz vergessen, dass du rein gar nichts über die *wirkliche* Welt weißt. Pinterest ist diese großartige Social-Media-Seite ...«

»Vergiss es. Das ist so weit von der wirklichen Welt entfernt wie nur möglich. Heutzutage geben sich die Menschen damit zufrieden, in einem Zimmer zu sitzen, auf Bildschirme zu starren und sich mit Leuten zu unterhalten, die sie gar nicht kennen, anstatt einfach ihr Leben zu genießen. Körper sollen sich *bewegen*, Butterfly. Das Wetter muss man *erleben*. Würden sich die Menschen eher wie Tiere benehmen, dann wäre die Welt ein besserer Ort.«

Als er Verletztheit in ihren Augen aufflackern sah, bereute er seine Worte sofort wieder. Manchmal vergaß er, dass er nicht der Einzige war, der seinen eigenen Lebensstil für den richtigen hielt. Schnell versuchte er, das Thema zu wechseln.

»Warum bist du eigentlich so früh schon hier?«, erkundigte er sich.

»Die Firma hat mir ein neues Projekt angeboten und mein Boss bei meinem richtigen Job hat mich dafür beurlaubt. Dafür bin ich ihm sehr dankbar. Ich werde das Verhalten der Grau- und Rotfüchse vergleichen und bin jetzt erstmal hier, um die Graufüchse zu suchen. Du weißt doch, dass Rotfüchse Randhabitate bevorzugen, während Graufüchse lieber in bewaldetem Bergland leben?« Randhabitate lagen auf der Grenze zwischen zwei Lebensräumen wie Feld und Wald. Sie wartete nicht auf seine Antwort, sondern fuhr mit ihrer Erklärung fort. »In so gut wie jeder Hinsicht ähneln sich ihre Lebensart und ihre Entwicklungsgeschichte, nur dass die Grauen scheuer und etwas kleiner sind und an anderen Stellen ihren Bau errichten. Ich werde sie studieren, um herauszufinden, ob ihre Verhaltensmuster Gründe für ihre Habitatpräferenz erkennen lassen, und ich hatte gehofft, du hättest vielleicht Zeit, mir zu zeigen, wo ich sie finden kann.«

Diese Bitte überraschte ihn. Die Rotfüchse hatte sie

wochenlang studiert und ihn nicht ein Mal um Hilfe gebeten.

»Heute klappt das aber nicht, Butterfly.« Sein Tag war bereits verplant. In der vergangenen Woche hatte er einige Mittzwanziger beim Feiern an einem der Felsvorsprünge erwischt und einige von ihnen waren ihm am Vortag erneut aufgefallen. Also musste er eine Runde drehen, um sicherzustellen, dass sie nicht zurück waren und erneut Ärger machten, und er wollte auch weiter bergab und seine alten Kumpel Mack und Will Cumberland besuchen. Erst gestern hatte er erfahren, dass die Cumberland-Ranch zum Verkauf stand: gut zweihundert Morgen Land in Weston, angrenzend an den Nationalpark, in dem Steve ein Jahrzehnt lang als Ranger und Naturschutzexperte gearbeitet hatte. Er war in Weston aufgewachsen und lebte nun zwar zwei Städte weiter, aber seine Kleinstadtwurzeln waren noch immer vorhanden. Er wollte versuchen, seine Freunde davon zu überzeugen, das Land dem Nationalpark zuzuschlagen, anstatt es zu verkaufen.

»Wie schade. Ich hatte mich schon so darauf gefreut, von all den verrückten Sachen zu hören, die du während meiner Abwesenheit erlebt hast.« Sie wackelte mit den Augenbrauen, während sie ihn neckte.

Er schüttelte grinsend den Kopf. »Pass da draußen auf dich auf. Ich habe vor Kurzem ein paar feiernde Kids erwischt. Sie sind vermutlich harmlos, aber Männer und Alkohol … Sei einfach vorsichtig. Hast du das Pfefferspray gefunden, das ich in deiner Hütte deponiert habe?«

»Das warst du?« Sie kniff die Augen zusammen. »Dir ist schon klar, dass ich eine erwachsene Frau bin?«

Heiliger Strohsack, und wie ihm das klar war.

Shannon beobachtete, wie Steve die Axt schwang. Er war genauso gebaut wie die Berge, die er so liebte: stark und robust, mit beachtlichen Muskeln, die er ehrlicher, harter Arbeit verdankte. *Reinste Perfektion.* Und diese Haare? *Großer Gott.* Wie es wohl sein musste, hindurchzufahren und ihn zu küssen? All diese harten Muskeln unter seiner Haut zu spüren? Den Mann zu entdecken, der sich hinter der rauen Schale verbarg? Sie sagte sich, dass dies *Wünsche* und keine *Bedürfnisse* waren, auch wenn es sich anders anfühlte. *Die Art von hartnäckigen Wünschen, die eine Frau dazu bringen, ihre Fantasien mit eigener Hand zu befriedigen.*

Komm wieder runter, Mädel.

Shannon war selbst überrascht gewesen, wie sehr sie Steve vermisst hatte, als sie für die Hochzeit ihres ältesten Bruders Cole nach Hause zurückgekehrt war. In den Wochen während ihres ersten Aufenthalts hier hatten sie schließlich nur wenige gestohlene Augenblicke miteinander verbracht. Meist hatte sie ihn bei der Arbeit an seiner Ausrüstung oder auf seinem Hof unterbrochen, bevor sie abends zur Ranch ihres Onkels nach Weston zurückgekehrt war. Doch er hatte sie mit seiner Leidenschaft für alles, was die Wildnis zu bieten hatte, sowie seinem endlosen Wissen darüber fasziniert. Und er unterschied sich stark von all den anderen Männern, die sie kannte. Sein Aussehen oder materielle Dinge waren ihm völlig egal. Er war ein echter Kerl mit unerschütterlichen Ansichten und Vorstellungen. Irgendwie hatte sie bei ihren beinahe täglichen Unterhaltungen und in den Wochen, in denen sie darauf gehofft hatte, ihn zu sehen, eine starke Zuneigung zu ihm entwickelt.

Als man ihr diesen Auftrag *und* die Hütte anbot, hatte sie daher ohne zu zögern zugesagt. Steve hatte ihr so sehr gefehlt, dass sie die Anziehungskraft, die er auf sie ausübte, nicht mehr leugnen konnte, und sie wollte herausfinden, ob sich daraus etwas entwickeln würde.

Nun, wo sie hier war, spürte sie bei seinem bloßen Anblick ein Prickeln am ganzen Körper. Dass sie ihn tatsächlich nach seinem Sexleben gefragt hatte – und am liebsten im Boden versunken wäre, sobald ihr diese Frage über die Lippen gekommen war –, ließ eindeutig erkennen, dass sie sich ein wenig am Riemen reißen musste.

Er wischte sich den Schweiß von der Stirn und seine gebräunte Haut schimmerte in der Morgensonne. »Brauchst du etwas aus der Stadt?«, wollte er wissen und legte das nächste Holzstück auf den Hackklotz.

Sie konnte den Blick nicht von seinen bemerkenswerten Bauchmuskeln und der Rundung seines Bizeps abwenden, der sich bei jeder Bewegung wölbte. »Aus der Stadt?«

Er grinste sie schief an und holte ein weiteres Mal mit der Axt zum Schlag aus. »Ja, aus der Stadt. Du weißt schon, von diesem Ort, an dem Leute, die *Pinterest* mögen, leben.«

Sie zwang sich, den Blick abzuwenden und zu den Bäumen hinüberzuschauen, die im Wind schwankten, die Steine zu ihren Füßen zu betrachten, alles, außer ihn anzusehen.

»Ich weiß, was eine Stadt ist. Ich bin nur überrascht, dass du dorthin fahren willst.« Jeder wusste doch, wie ungern Steve seine geliebten Berge verließ.

»Ich hab was zu erledigen.«

In die Stadt zu fahren war schon etwas Besonderes. Anders als ein schneller Abstecher zum nächsten Supermarkt von ihrem

Apartment in Peaceful Harbor dauerte die Fahrt in die Stadt hier dreißig bis fünfundvierzig Minuten, je nachdem, in welche Stadt man wollte. Das hatte sie letzte Nacht gemerkt, als ihr aufgefallen war, dass sie zwei sehr wichtige Dinge vergessen hatte: Pop-Tarts und Toilettenpapier. Die einsame Rolle Toilettenpapier, die sie in der Hütte vorgefunden hatte, würde zwar noch ein paar Tage ausreichen, aber ohne Pop-Tarts würde sie nicht lange überleben. Außerdem konnte sie Steve ja unterwegs vielleicht dazu überreden, in der Abenddämmerung mit ihr nach Graufüchsen Ausschau zu halten. *Perfekt!*

»Kann ich dich begleiten?«, fragte sie hoffnungsvoll. »Ich muss noch ein paar Dinge besorgen.«

»Ich kann sie dir auch mitbringen. Was brauchst du denn?«

Sie biss sich auf die Unterlippe und wollte ihn eigentlich nicht anlügen. Aber wenn sie ihn bat, ihr das mitzubringen, was sie wirklich haben wollte, würde er alleine losfahren, und sie musste auf eigene Faust nach den Habitaten suchen. Jetzt, wo sie sich ausmalte, das später zusammen mit ihrem knackigen Mann aus den Bergen zu tun, hatte sich dieser Gedanke jedoch bereits in ihr festgesetzt.

»Frauenkram. Das möchtest du bestimmt nicht kaufen.« Da war sie raus, die Notlüge. »Darf ich bitte mitfahren?« Sie schenkte ihm ihren besten flehenden Blick. »Ich verspreche auch, dir nicht das Ohr abzukauen.« *Noch eine Lüge!* Offenbar hatte sie keine Kontrolle über das, was aus ihrem Mund kam, erst recht nicht in seiner Nähe.

Er murmelte sich leise etwas in den Bart und lehnte die Axt an den Baumstumpf. »Ich muss aber unzählige Zwischenstopps einlegen.«

Sie machte vor Freude einen Satz und rannte los, um ihn zu umarmen. Dabei rutschte ihr Fuß aus dem Stiefel, sie geriet ins

Stolpern und warf sich ihm förmlich an den Hals. Seine Haut war heiß, sein Körper hart, *und er schien von Sekunde zu Sekunde härter zu werden.* Außerdem roch er nach Mann und Moschus und … sie klammerte sich noch immer an ihn.

Shannon räusperte sich und brachte ein leises »Danke« über die Lippen. Sie stützte sich an seiner Brust ab – *wow!* –, fand ihr Gleichgewicht wieder und schob den Fuß zurück in den Stiefel. »Nur ein weiterer Zwischenstopp. Mehr nicht. Versprochen.«

»Du scheinst es ja kaum erwarten zu können, einkaufen zu gehen.« Er hob die Holzscheite auf, die er gehackt hatte, und stapelte sie auf einem Unterarm, als wären es Zahnstocher.

»Ich freue mich nur, wieder hier zu sein. Vielleicht kannst du mir ja heute Abend helfen, die Habitate ausfindig zu machen? Es ist bestimmt amüsanter, wenn wir sie gemeinsam suchen gehen.«

Er schenkte ihr einen irritierten Blick. »Es ist ziemlich lange her, dass jemand meine Gesellschaft als amüsant bezeichnet hat.«

»Dann gibst du dich mit den falschen Leuten ab. Und ich werte das als Ja.« Sie schnappte sich die Kaffeetassen und konnte nicht aufhören zu grinsen.

»Ich fahre in zwanzig Minuten los.«

»Ich bin ruckzuck wieder da.« Als sie mit federnden Schritten zu ihrer Hütte eilte, hörte sie noch, wie er »blitzschnell« murmelte und leise lachte.

Ende des Auszugs

Wenn Ihnen die Vorschau gefallen hat, können Sie *Vereinte Herzen* bei Ihrem Online-Buchhändler erwerben und weiterlesen!

Truman keine Hilfe gebraucht, und als die schöne Gemma Wright versucht, ihm unter die Arme zu greifen, reagiert er nicht gerade charmant. Aber Gemma hat ihre ganz eigene Art und schafft es schließlich, den Panzer um sein Herz zu durchdringen. Als Trumans dunkle Vergangenheit seine Zukunft in Gefahr bringt, steht seine Loyalität auf dem Prüfstand und er muss die schwerste aller Entscheidungen treffen.

Love in Bloom – Herzen im Aufbruch

Für noch mehr Vergnügen lesen Sie die Bücher der Reihe nach.
Sie werden in jedem Band bekannte Figuren wiederfinden!

Bisher erschienen in deutscher Sprache:

Die Snow-Schwestern

Schwestern im Aufbruch
Schwestern im Glück
Schwestern in Weiß

Die Bradens (Weston, Colorado)

Im Herzen eins
Für die Liebe bestimmt
Freundschaft in Flammen
Wogen der Liebe
Liebe voller Abenteuer
Verspielte Herzen
Ein Fest für die Liebe (Hochzeits-Kurzgeschichte)
Nachwuchs für die Liebe (Savannahs & Jacks Baby)
Happy End für die Liebe (Hochzeits-Kurzgeschichte)

Die Bradens (Trusty, Colorado)

Bei Heimkehr Liebe
Bei Ankunft Liebe
Im Zweifel Liebe
Bei Rückkehr Liebe
Trotz allem Liebe
Bei Aufprall Liebe

Die Bradens (Peaceful Harbor)

Geheilte Herzen
Voller Einsatz für die Liebe
Liebe gegen den Strom
Vereinte Herzen
Melodie der Liebe
Sieg für die Liebe

Bisher erschienen in englischer Sprache/bald auf Deutsch:

The Remingtons

Spiel der Herzen
Im Dschungel der Liebe
Herzen in Flammen
Herzen im Schnee
Liebe zwischen den Zeilen

The Bradens & Montgomerys (Pleasant Hill and Oak Falls)

Embracing her Heart
Anything for Love
Trails of Love

…

Entdecken Sie Melissa Fosters Bücher auch auf:
www.melissafoster.com/herzen-im-aufbruch

www.ingramcontent.com/pod-product-compliance
Lightning Source LLC
Chambersburg PA
CBHW031615180726
48284CB00005B/1550